FRAGMENTS OF THE HEART

THE SPECTRUM OF MAGIC - BOOK 3

BETH HODGSON

FRAGMENTS OF THE HEART

Interior map and character illustrations by Beth Hodgson

www.thespectrumofmagic.com

First Edition: September 2024
ISBN: 978-1-7327130-3-1
Printed in the United States of America

To my children, whom I love with all my heart.

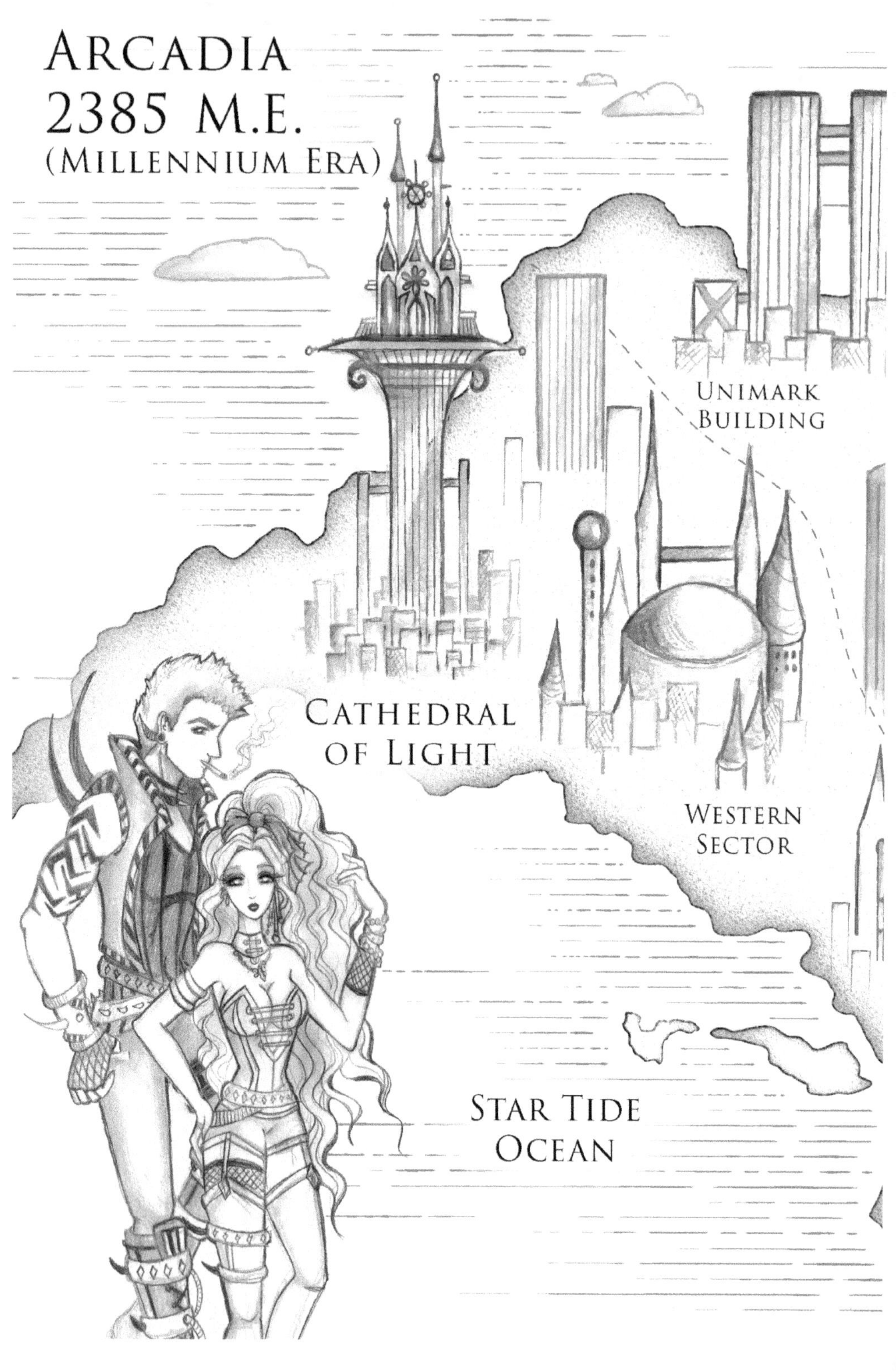

Arcadia
2385 M.E.
(Millennium Era)
Unimark Building
Cathedral of Light
Western Sector
Star Tide Ocean

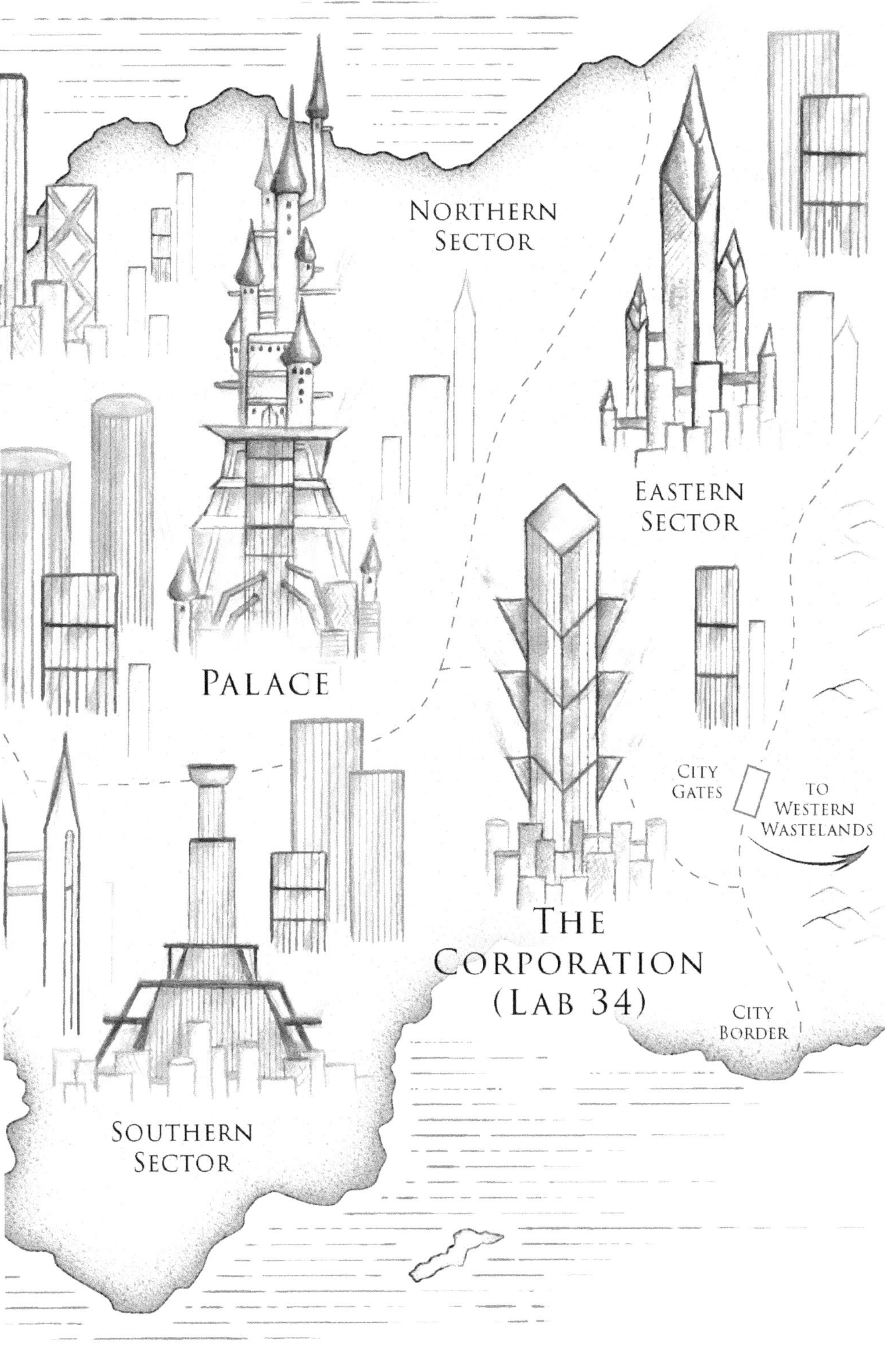

Northern
Sector
Eastern
Sector
Palace
City
Gates
To
Western
Wastelands
The
Corporation
(Lab 34)
City
Border
Southern
Sector

THE TWIN
KINGDOMS

OLYMPIA

THE
UNITED
KINGDOMS
2385 M.E.
(MILLENNIUM ERA)

ILLUMINA

WESTERN
WASTELÄNDS

STAR TIDE
OCEAN

ARCADIA

ICELANDIC
SEA
KINGDOM
OF YORK
THE
GREAT
LAKE
THE SECOND
KINGDOM
EASTERN
WASTELANDS
THE SOUTHERN
KINGDOMS

THE PINNACLES CAMP
VICTOR'S CAMP
WAYSIDE CAMP
OLD WOMAN'S CAMP
ARCADIA

OLYMPIA
NORTHERN CAMPS
ILLUMINA
CROSSROADS CAMP
INDIGO CAMP
THE REFUGE
FOOL'S HOPE CAMP
WESTERN WASTELANDS
2385 M.E.

World Sectors 1-6
4403 P.A.
(Post Apocalypse)
Ruins of W.S. 1
Lands of Desolation
Toxic Currents
Safeland Hideouts
W.S. 2
Mines of W.S. 2

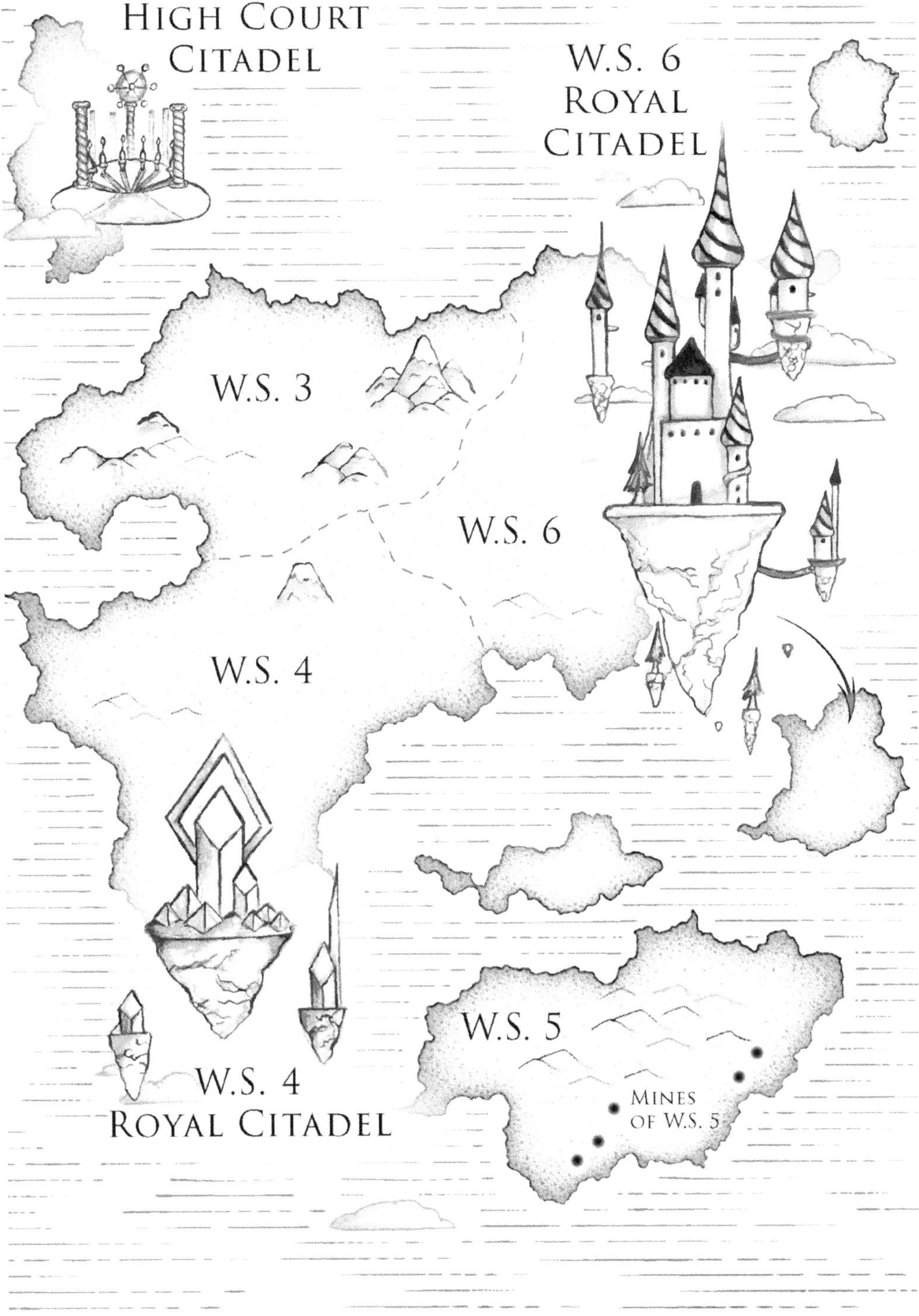

High Court
Citadel
W.S. 6
Royal
Citadel
W.S. 3
W.S. 6
W.S. 4
W.S. 4
Royal Citadel
W.S. 5
Mines
of W.S. 5

PROLOGUE

◆

Light streamed in from the palace hall's tall windows, casting a gleam of gold across the white marbled floors, reflecting onto the palace's high ceilings. Soft clacks of shoes scuffed against the floors as advisors, councilors, and other members of the court made their way to their beloved spot for noontime prayer.

The princess of the court smiled at one of her beloved advisors as they crossed paths. He flashed her a quick smile in return, bowed, then walked off, apparently having no time for any sort of conversation. It didn't bother her, as she was on her way to the kingdom's high cathedral for prayer, just as he was. The princess smoothed her long, deep-crimson hair over her shoulders and adjusted the golden circlet that framed her forehead, as it had shifted out of place. She fluffed her garnet-red dress, then continued.

As she headed to the cathedral, she passed by her courtiers and subjects. All had stopped to revere the sight of her, for she was the world's greatest beauty, and everyone held her in the highest regard. There was no jealousy in the court, for the world had been turned and made anew. She had read of the old world's pain, hurts, and sorrow, but had never experienced such a feeling. Supposedly there had been a time when the world experienced great pain, but that was washed away. This world was filled with light, love, devoutness, joy, songs, and prayer. All the emotions that make the heart whole. The magics of the world had been restored, and only one of each color of magic had remained on the new earth. The princess once had red magic in the old world of pain, but she couldn't remember any of it. It didn't matter. She was happy and content with the life she was living.

Down the kingdom's main street, the princess saw the grand crystal cathedral in the distance. The bell towers of the church rose to the heavens in prayer, resplendent in their glory. The bells chimed in harmony as the crowds gathered. The streets gleamed of gold, as the sun shone brightly this day, just as it did every day. The air smelled of fresh blooms, and the air was crisp and cool.

The princess neared the cathedral, the crowds parting for her to enter. Standing in the front was the princess's fiancé, the prince. He beamed a smile as he watched her approach. His eyes burned of orange fire; his hair shone like copper. He was one of the seven gifted on earth who remained from the old earth. Blessed with the gift of the orange.

"Princess," he said, bowing as she approached.

"My prince," she said. The princess blushed, noticing the immediate desire in his eyes.

"I've been waiting to see you all day," he said. He took her hand, kissed it gently.

"I must admit, I couldn't wait to see you either," the princess said as she took his arm.

He leaned in, then kissed her lips. Desire flooded her body as she drank deeply from their connection. How she wanted to keep kissing, like a sweet addiction to her favorite summer wine.

Suddenly, she pulled away, then composed herself. "We aren't yet married in the God of Light's eyes," she said, playfully slapping his tunic.

"I know," he whispered in her ear. "We need to remedy that."

The princess glanced out of the corner of her eye at the crowds cheering at their kiss. It was all very public.

"Yes, we do," she whispered back with a bright smile.

"Marry me now."

The princess chuckled. "It's impossible."

"Why not? We are at the cathedral," the prince said.

"You know why not," the princess said playfully. "It's noontime prayer."

"I can wish, can't I?" He stared deep in her eyes, then glided his hand softly across her cheek. "Your eyes are like the color of clear skies, so very crystal blue. I can see your soul through them every time I look at you." He leaned in once again, brushing his lips on her cheeks. "So beautiful you are."

The prince held out his arm to escort her, and the princess accepted. The crowd cheered louder while the couple walked inside the double doors.

Melodious chants from *Songs of the Heart* echoed throughout the cathedral as the prince led her inside to their royal pew. Her mother was already praying on the kneeling board at their pew. Her mother was revered by everyone on earth and considered the holiest of holy persons on earth, for she was the one who made the earth anew. A white-gifted.

Her mother gave them a warm smile as the couple seated themselves, then turned back to her prayers.

The church bells rang out in a familiar tone, and the congregation went silent, including the chants from the choir. The congregation turned their bodies toward the entrance where the High Priest would appear—the one and only yellow-gifted on the planet. The High Priest appeared at the back of the church, then walked in a procession down the church aisle as the priest chanted and sang, gently swaying their incense balls. The High Priest got to the altar, and then the congregation faced forward and got seated.

The priest said a few prayers in the heavenly language, then raised his hands.

It was time for noon prayer.

The entire congregation knelt on their respective kneeling boards in their pews. The princess did likewise, then closed her hands in prayer. Whispers filled the cathedral as everyone began to pray. The entire kingdom would be in prayer—on the streets, in their homes, in the palace—for it was the perfect world, and all gave thanks for perfection.

Most every time, the princess didn't know what to pray about. She lived in the new world made in the God of Light's image, and all was perfect. She knew it was the right thing to do, to still pray for light and love in the world, and that after, one's heart would be filled to the brim with eternal joy. Sometimes she wondered: The world was at peace, so why pray now? It was what she was supposed to do, and she did very much believe in the God of Light.

More whispers echoed around her. Many were deep in prayer. Her fiancé, the prince, had always prayed in silence. The princess flushed thinking about him; he was model perfection. Handsome, desirable, and devoted to the God of Light. She couldn't wait to be wed to him.

As her thoughts unloaded within her mind, a picture entered in its place: white light. Pure white light.

The white light felt warm, and very beautiful to look at. Prismatic in its form, the light glimmered with the different colors of the spectrum. It was pure air, as if the God of Light himself breathed upon the earth and surrounded it within his exhale.

Suddenly, a loud crack rang out, echoing across the white expanse.

Whipping toward the direction of the sound, the princess gasped at a monstrous black tear in the middle of the white atmosphere.

Shrieks rang from the tear in the dimension fabric, with evil leaking its foulness and permeating her world. Through the strange and terrifying tear warbled a starry night sky, rippling like translucent water.

The princess was paralyzed with fear, the terror tremoring within the deep depths of her heart. Never had she felt like this. Never.

Within the rippled dimension, a vision appeared from the other side of the tear. A young woman about her age stood before her. Green eyes, long wavy emerald-green hair, with porcelain skin and soft pink lips. Green magic radiated from this woman, dancing around her like balls of sparkly light. But something else too: deep hurt.

The woman looked past the princess's eyes and straight into her soul. The woman's eyes burned with vibrant green energy, and suddenly, her pain became the princess's pain.

This pain, it cut deep into the princess's bones. She ached from the destitution, despair, and devastation of this woman's soul. It was beyond repair; her soul had been fragmented into thousands of little pieces, unable to be restored ever again.

Her soul hurt deep.

How was she to survive this pain? These emotions?

Was this what sadness felt like?

Overwhelmed with emotions, the princess shed a tear.

She had just shed a *tear*.

Startled, the princess jolted her eyes open from prayer. Her breathing was irregular, her forehead beaded with sweat. Her long crimson tresses fell back into her face, so she pushed them over her shoulder once more.

Everyone was still silent in prayer. The bells of prayer rang out while the High Priest continued to whisper his prayer.

What is happening?

Her heart beat hard as she thought about the strange vision in her prayer. She felt defiled from the hurt and sadness she had just experienced. Why had she felt this? This was a perfect world, void of such things.

Her eyes stung, causing her to rub them. Wetness coated her fingertips.

She had, in fact, shed a tear, and not just in her vision.

The princess turned to her fiancé, the prince, whispering low in his ear, "I will meet you back at the palace."

His eyes opened with alarm, meeting hers. "You must finish your prayers; you will be noticed if you leave," he whispered with urgency.

The image of the green-gifted woman flooded her mind.

"I must go," the princess said with finality.

The prince nodded, then turned back to his prayers.

Quietly, the princess moved with such grace that no one seemed to notice. As she slipped outside the church and into the golden streets, she saw the crowds were still in the midst of their own prayers. A few subjects took private peeks at her quickly walking by, but they remained as they were, not daring to meet her gaze.

The princess finally made her way back to the palace. All the servants in the kingdom were still on the floor in prayer. She passed by, slipping inside her chambers.

Shaken, she sat down on a sofa, her heart still pumping with the terror from what she had seen. The light in her room seemed dim and dull, lacking its normal beauty.

Hoping that the light was beautiful and bright outside, she stepped out onto her balcony, into the noon light of the sun, which always made her feel at peace. The sky, the light, the clouds, the palace, the kingdom…it was all so beautiful. But somehow, the colors were not the same as they once were. They, too, were dim, just as her chambers had been.

Perhaps the vision had disturbed her so much that it interfered with her joy.

She sat, trying to calm herself with prayer. This time she prayed with urgency. And it was private, in her chambers—not for her subjects to witness, and what she actually felt deep in her soul.

Why had the God of Light given her that horrible experience? That feeling? This world was supposed to be perfect. Why was this happening?

Minutes became hours. Knocks came from her chamber, but she didn't want to answer. The princess didn't have the heart.

In the corner of her eye, she saw the prince from across the way, outside on his balcony. He was far off and didn't notice her, as there were many other palace balconies among the many towers and turrets. It had been hours since she had seen him, when she'd left the chapel with no explanation. Though they had plans to see each other at dinner, the princess figured she should pay him a visit to apologize for leaving so quickly.

Just as she was about to step inside, a woman came up from behind the prince, rubbing his back.

The princess froze.

The woman leaned against his back, then kissed the nape of his neck.

The princess took a step back as she watched in horror.

The prince laughed as he twirled the woman to face him, then kissed her passionately.

The woman…was the spitting image of her.

She took another step back. Did the prince know that wasn't her? It had to be someone else…

The prince and the woman were still locked in their kiss.

It has to be a dream, she told herself. *Just like the white light.*

Then the woman and the prince began to undress each other in the throes of desire as the woman burned with white light.

This was no dream at all…

She began to tremble. A queasy feeling churned within her stomach, as if she had the urge to vomit. Yet another feeling that she knew nothing about. But it was all happening.

Her stomach twisted as the prince and the identical woman became more intimate. White light enveloped them as they explored each other's body in a way that the princess had never known.

Jealousy entered her heart for the first time.

In disbelief, she shuffled backward.

Water collected in her eyes, then released down her cheeks. The princess wiped the moisture, then looked at her fingertips.

Tears.

She had cried a new set of tears.

Vigorously, she shook her head. "No…" she whispered.

She glanced up at her fiancé, the prince…

The gleaming half-naked body of the prince shone while the imposter kissed his neck. A hand went lower and lower…

The princess shrieked. Then *ran.*

She didn't know where she was running to, she just ran. Far, far away from that horrid, wretched scene.

As she ran, a flood of memories came rushing into her mind all at once. Memories of her past hurts, pain, sorrows. All those who had betrayed her in the old world—memories that were supposed to be no more. Lovers, family, friends. Everyone. And now, she had witnessed more betrayal in this new perfect world, a world that was supposed to have *no* pain.

She screamed as she ran past all the servants and courtiers; all stopped in wonder and confusion as she ran by.

Her tears streamed down her cheeks until her vision was nothing but a blur.

It didn't matter.

She just kept running.

"A broken heart cannot be wholly restored. The wound will remain, eventually healing to a scab. But that scab can be torn off, fragmenting the heart once more."

—Poetic verse from Songs of the Heart Volume I

"What have you done, oh my soul? You wandered aimlessly through darkness, embracing its kiss. Though you are tempted by its sweetness, its poison will seep into your soul, destroying you from the inside out. For the path of darkness leads to transgression. Who will lead you out of despair and into the light? For the depths of sorrow can be a pit of eternal damnation."

—Poetic verse from Songs of the Heart Volume V

CHAPTER 1

◆

VIOLET

Ikaria's shimmering violet portal flowed around her, then dispersed as she set her dainty feet upon the steps of the High Court. Behind her, swooshes from Vala's magic, followed by the priest's grunt.

Proudly holding her head high, Ikaria was crowned with her sorceress horns, which rose to the heavens, her violet hair trailing behind her, nearly touching the floor. She wore the most revealing black-and-chrome-plated chest armor that one could ever obtain, and her shimmering midnight-ebony skirts detailed with waist-high slits. She wanted the world to know who they were dealing with. Because after all, they all labeled her an evil sorceress. Witch. Heretic. A *beautiful* one at that.

I very well will play the part I am given. And I will relish doing so, she thought as she glanced at the citadel with a smug expression.

"I don't know why you insisted on porting out here," Auron said. "It would have been easier to be inside."

Ikaria's eyes narrowed. "My dear priest, if I did that, I couldn't be destructive in doing so."

"Do you think anyone has seen us yet?"

"I do not know, priest," Ikaria answered, then smiled darkly. "I personally find it rude that no one has. Let us announce ourselves, shall we?"

Vala suddenly stood in front of her. "I still think we should remain discreet until we find your sister."

Ikaria walked past her, then turned her head. "Absolutely not. It's high time I shake this citadel to its *core*."

"But…" Auron was about to argue, but Ikaria headed toward the citadel's main gates, leaving him in the dust.

As she moved, her flowing hair and skirts trailed behind her, and she raised her hands, palms up.

Violet magic poured out of her hands, causing hard friction between her magic and the pillars to her sides. The stairs began to wobble and shake. Each step she took was more violent than before, the stones beneath her feet crumbling. A golden translucent barrier covered her—the same barrier that protected Auron and Vala from behind.

Voices in the distance called out.

"Who's there?" yelled a guard.

"BELINDA!" Ikaria shouted, ignoring the guard. She funneled more force under her feet. With a jolting movement, the hillside that the stairs were built upon began to rock violently. Ikaria laughed as she snapped her fingers, sending the pillars crumbling upon themselves as she passed.

A battalion of guards ran toward Ikaria, but then stopped when they realized who it was. Some looked mortified. Others were paralyzed with fear. A few brave fools ignored the fact that she was far superior to them in every way.

"IT'S THE SORCERESS!" shouted another guard.

Ikaria whipped her hand out in front of her, shooting a large bolt of violet force mixed with her adjacent power of lightning.

The guard screamed, and the others stopped dead in their tracks.

"I want my sister!" Ikaria demanded.

"Well, you can't have her," snarled one of the guards. The guards drew their enchanted swords and shields, while others who were gifted summoned their red gift.

"This is what the High Court is made of? Little boys who play pretend soldier?" Ikaria eyed them, unimpressed. "Come, little boys, show me what you got." She motioned with her finger, taunting them.

"You won't be laughing when you're dead," said one of the guards.

"I'll get any that show up from behind us," Vala said.

"Good."

The guard who'd just spoken charged Ikaria, his body behind his shield, his sword high above his head. From behind, a screeching sound as Vala's magic halted a weapon from behind. Ikaria could only assume Vala was making the guard fling his weapon backward.

Ikaria whirled her hands together, then blasted the guard with a malevolent thundering shock. The violet lightning cracked the enchanted shield, with the imbued power dissipating.

The guard's eyes went wide with disbelief. Without hesitation, Ikaria flicked her hands again, sending a sweeping shock to the entire group of soldiers, funneling more and more force and electricity behind her spell. The ground underneath her shook violently, the surrounding area crumbling upon itself.

It's a good thing the priest has excellent barriers, she thought as massive chunks of stone and wood fell on their barrier, diminishing into nothing as they hit.

The men screamed in agony as she continued her spell. Fried flesh, smoke from their clothes, screams… Blood.

"I am the Sorceress Ikaria! Take that to your grave!" she spat.

The men all dropped dead, with stones from the pillars falling on top of their corpses.

"We must hurry inside before they move Ayera," Vala warned.

"The sorceress!" called out a gifted to other gifted men and women.

"Oh, this will be fun," Ikaria said, smirking.

"You will pay for your crimes," another said as they started shimmering orange around them.

"You all look pitiful. Come on, arrest me. I beg of you." Ikaria laughed.

The world started morphing around Ikaria. The pillars were rebuilding themselves, and the guards that lay dead on the ground rose, as if they had never died.

"It's an illusion," Auron called out.

"Thank you for that information, priest," Ikaria said sarcastically. As if she couldn't have figured it out on her own. "Just keep us shielded. I have something in mind."

Closing her eyes, Ikaria drew upon the energy deep within her life force. Her veins coursed with magic so strong, it could hardly be contained.

Seep into those gifted minds like poison! she commanded her magic.

Suddenly opening her eyes, her violet energy sprang directly into the other gifted's minds. With a whoosh of her hands, her magic was released from her veins and into the minds of the gifted. The gifted screamed as their heads exploded with her energy. Chunks of flesh, blood, and bone flung everywhere. All except Ikaria's trio. Auron's barrier shimmered a bright gold as the cadavers flicked onto the barrier, then melted away.

"I'm glad your barrier protected my clothes too. I mustn't look like a slob." Auron sighed.

Get ready, priest… Ikaria called out inside Auron's mind. *That white-gifted whore will be showing up any minute to get my magic.*

I'm already thinking about it.

Good.

The trio ran up the stairs, with everything around them destroying itself. Fires broke out in the gardens, and water fountains flew upward, pouring onto the courtyard. Blasts of violet magic knocked over stonework, walls, stairs, anything that got in their way. Ikaria had promised scorched earth, and she always made good on her promises.

They came to the entrance of the High Court. The marbled statues that once looked like beautiful holy priests and clerics were shattered, scattered upon the ground. The doors were half open—the guards weren't there.

"BELINDA!" Ikaria screamed again, her voice echoing inside the hall as she entered.

There were screams from the citizens and lords—all non-gifted—as they ran in the complete opposite direction.

"BELINDA! ELYATHI!" Floors underneath her rumbled, causing the walls to crack.

Ikaria felt a surge of her power as she narrowed her eyes. Shooting her hands out directly to her sides, violet magic that flowed from her manicured fingertips shook the walls of the citadel, which rumbled and groaned in response.

Sister…where are you?

Ikaria scanned the citadel with her mind, trying to find her sister.

More screams from the citizens, all scattering like rats.

"Such pests you all are," Ikaria commented at the scrambling crowd, then saw a cleric of the court robed in yellow. Reaching out with her magic, Ikaria clutched the cleric tightly with her power, dragging them to her. "You hear that?" Ikaria snarled in his face.

The cleric tried to cast a protection spell as he made a small whimper. Auron countered this, creating a dark barrier that ate away the cleric's feeble attempt.

Ikaria clutched him tighter, causing the cleric to cry out in pain.

"I don't think you realize the severity of the situation," Ikaria spat in his face. "I want my *sister*, and I want her NOW!"

Ikaria whipped the cleric away hard, her violet magic still enveloping him. The force of the hurl was so great, upon impact against the wall, she heard bones snap.

"I think they get the point," Auron commented, seeing a scampering citizen run by their barrier.

"No, they don't," Ikaria persisted.

"We have indeed heard your request. But it is denied," called out a feminine voice. A deep red magic shimmered before their eyes, revealing High Justice Belinda. Dressed in the finest red velvet robes that fitted her figure to perfection. Her long, flowing ruby hair trailed down her backside, adorned with a golden circlet encrusted with garnets and rubies. Her body glimmered with gold jewelry and red gemstones.

Just seeing that redheaded bitch made Ikaria's skin crawl.

"Your sister has much to account for," Belinda stated. "She is in violation of several laws of the High Court. Therefore, she is our prisoner."

Ikaria tsked. "Unfortunately for you, our sector doesn't adhere to your laws. Now, kindly give me my sister."

"No." Belinda remained frozen, then gave a cold smile. "She isn't going anywhere. And neither are you."

With a flood of fury, Ikaria shot out a pure wave of force so great that everything shattered around Belinda. But as for Belinda, she proudly stood unscathed in the same spot, everything around her destroyed.

"You cannot defeat me, Ikaria."

Ikaria laughed. "If I didn't hate you so much, perhaps I'd consider your little statement precious." Auron's magic began to flood inside her body. "But I don't!"

Ikaria! Be careful! warned Auron inside her mind.

Ikaria shot a giant blast of force straight to Belinda's heart. Just as her spell was about to land, Belinda gently made a circular motion, then spun the blast around back toward Ikaria.

It hit Ikaria so hard that she pummeled into Auron, who was knocked back into Vala and into the walls. Dust and sand particles sprinkled on them from the splitting walls above.

Where was your shield, priest? Ikaria murmured in his mind.

The blast was too great... he answered.

Suddenly, a deep-red ice shard hurtled straight toward them, but it sank straight into Auron's refreshed protection barrier, melting away.

She has other magics, priest, Ikaria warned Auron. *Just funnel your magic into me, and let's be done with it!*

Ikaria felt Auron's magic flow into her, and she started gathering all of her colors—her main magic along with her adjacents...

With another soft motion of her hands, Belinda parted the air in front of her, ripping open a red dimension in front of them. Everything in the world was tinged red, and instantly, Auron's power was severed from Ikaria's body.

And so was her violet magic.

Auron looked around quickly. "Vala!"

But Vala was gone.

Auron tried to cast a spell, but it fizzled.

Belinda remained stone-faced. "You are in my dimension now."

"Hypocrite," Ikaria called out. She summoned her adjacent red magic, but it wouldn't work.

Frustrated, Ikaria tried again, then glanced at Belinda, narrowing her eyes.

Belinda raised her chin, then eyed her, sending a wave of red magic surrounding the pair of them. The earth reached up and clutched them.

"I am the ultimate red-gifted, and have complete control. All red magic submits to me in this dimension," Belinda stated, nearing them. Her appearance shifted into the most beautiful, holy, and angelic being. Her eyes were like burning fires, with long glossy red hair flowing in the wind. Her lips were the color of blood, which contrasted with her icy pale skin. The sun, moon, and stars radiated around her, causing her robes to shimmer in their light.

"I cannot wait until you eat your own words," Belinda said, her hands glowing with deep-red magic. "You know nothing of your future, but I know every outcome."

Stars fell from the red heavens above, and Belinda hurled them at them with her magic, one by one. Each one turned into starfire as it hit the ground, morphing into a wildfire wall. The fire got closer and closer—and hotter.

"Vala!" Auron called out.

"It's no use, priest…"

Ikaria's body was paralyzed, burning with deep-red magic. The air in her lungs became like stone, and she could no longer breathe. The fires were just about to wash over them like a fiery tidal wave.

Looking down, Ikaria saw her skin age within seconds, then melt off her body. The combination of magics that Belinda possessed were too great. The red bitch was using her own gift, the dark side of her gift, along with almost every other color of the spectrum combined—except green and violet. And somehow, her power had been boosted.

Never had Ikaria felt this helpless. It infuriated her. She should have had Auron funnel his magic into her sooner, but she also knew that they only had a short amount of time to combine their magics before they exhausted their life force.

Fire enveloped Ikaria, and she could no longer take it. She screamed as a sharp object cut her arm.

They are going to get my blood.

As Ikaria cried out, she saw Elyathi through the flames, tinged in red on the other side of the fiery dimension. She was heading toward them, clutching the necklaces hanging around her neck…

"You see her?" Belinda said. "All I have to do is lift this red dimension, and your gift is mine. You hear that, Ikaria? You will lose in the end. You always have and always will."

Ikaria saw a familiar face behind the red dimension, then reassessed the situation.

"It's too bad that you haven't considered this entrapment," Ikaria said, bored.

"Such a talker, but never a true testament to your lying, honeyed words." Belinda raised an eyebrow, then lifted her hands filled with fire magic. Within the depths of her eyes burned the fires of purity…or hell itself.

The red dimension flickered.

Suddenly, the world paused in the very moment that the red dimension flickered into the full dimension of all colors—the normal world. Belinda was in her normal form, the fires were gone…even Ikaria's skin was beautiful. But her arm…there was a cut.

Ikaria gasped for breath. Auron fell to his knees.

"I have it paused, but not for long!" Vala screamed. "Go!"

Auron's magic, which had been flowing to her, resumed. Ikaria felt all his magics within her life force. Yellow…orange…green… Ikaria fused their magics together.

Ikaria raised her hands high, and with a giant burst, blasted the entire High Court Citadel with powerful white light.

Walls shattered, crumbling. People screamed, debris everywhere.

"Get in the portal!" screamed Vala. "She is coming!"

"I will get you, you sinful, vile woman!" screamed Elyathi.

Auron's barrier surrounded the trio, and this time they were encased with the pure white light of the Spectrum of Magic. "We don't have long!"

"IKARIA! I WILL GET YOU!" Derek's voice called out.

"Hello, Derek. It's a shame you showed up so late in the hour, as I am leaving. Lucky for you, I will see you again. You can count on that."

"GET HER!"

Ikaria saw another white light, this time foreign to her and Auron's combined magic of the Spectrum.

"I can only counter his spells for so long! NOW GO!" Vala screamed.

"Get to your feet, you dogs!" shouted Ikaria. With another blast of white force, Ikaria destroyed the room they were in. White dust was everywhere; only Vala's portal could be seen.

"Just because I leave now doesn't mean you have one-upped me or that you can celebrate. On the contrary, I will return and finish you all!" Ikaria called out, seeing the silhouettes of Elyathi, Belinda, and Derek—and other members too. "Every day that my sister is in captivity, I will *take* one life. And if you hurt her in any sort of way, even a mere scratch on her delicate skin, and I find out about it, I will remove a limb from each one of you, one limb per one scratch of my sister's" She whipped around to Elyathi. "And that goes for you too, you white *witch bitch*! I'm coming for you! I'm coming for you *all*!"

Magics were cast, but Auron's white light of protection melted their spells like butter.

I will come for you, sister! Ikaria called out in her mind. Wherever you are, I will find you!

Ikaria and Auron ran inside the portal together, and Vala followed, then sealed the portal behind them.

Blue magic washed away from her body, and Ikaria lay aimlessly on golden floors, somewhere in the World Sector Six citadel.

Her mind was spent, her body weak, her clothes torn and tattered. She flopped over, catching her breath.

They'd almost had her blood. Almost.

Ikaria smiled, then laughed manically.

But they didn't…

CHAPTER 2

◆

RED

She was beautiful. So fucking beautiful.

Kyle watched as Emerald lay next to him, inhaling and exhaling soft breaths as she slept. Her long lashes remained closed, and her pink heart-shaped lips had a slight purse. He couldn't take his eyes off her beauty; it was as if he were seeing her for the first time.

Being next to Emerald felt right. Like being home. In fact, he was home. He just wanted to live in this perfect moment forever.

"I love you, Em," he whispered. Kyle lightly brushed his hand softly against her cheek. "So much."

Though Emerald was still asleep, his gemstone necklace shimmered a soft glow in response. It contained a piece of Emerald's life force, but to hell if he knew how. None of it mattered anymore. He had been finally reunited with Emerald after years of being apart. Well, to him it was years. For her it was just a few months. The necklace was one of the only things he had left from his life as Rubius.

Rubius. Just thinking of that life pissed him off. Twenty-seven years of living an entirely different life, in a completely different time, not knowing who he had been in the past. It was all bullshit. He had searched for Emerald his entire damn adult life to find her, only to discover she was living in a different time. It was fucked up. After all, what god would be so cruel, to destine him to live a life without his complement—his true soul mate? One that was made for him, and him for her? What kind of god did *that*? He'd had to strike a bargain with the devil himself to make his way back to his love.

Kyle shuddered. *Thank god I'm here now.* And that was for damn sure. This life, this was where he was meant to be. Not some harp-playing fool who kissed the High Court's pompous asses. It just felt right being in this time era, with Emerald.

He began to sing softly. The song that had led her to him in the labyrinth of his mind. As he sang, he gently brushed aside her cascading wavy locks of green hair, revealing more of her delicate pale face, then kissed the top of her head.

She stirred, though Kyle couldn't say whether it was from his touch or his song. Emerald lazily opened her eyes, then suddenly realized that he was there next to her. Her bright green eyes widened with joy, instantly giving him life and energy. He couldn't help but flash her a huge grin of his own.

"You're awake? I expected you to sleep in," Emerald said, giving him a glowing smile in return.

"Couldn't sleep," Kyle answered.

"How come?" she asked softly.

Kyle chuckled. "Oh, you know. Taking a nap after coming from the depths of Hell isn't my idea of rest."

"I just came from there too, you know, and I was able to get sleep," she said playfully. As she spoke, she reached for the gemstone that hung around his neck. It burned brightly at her touch, and she smiled in wonder.

"It's so strange," she said curiously as she turned over the gemstone. "I wonder why my future self created this?"

"I dunno." Kyle glanced down at Emerald, then placed his hand on hers. "I'm just glad your future self did. Otherwise, I would've been screwed. And maybe I never would have found you."

Emerald sucked in a breath in awe at the gemstone one last time, then glanced up at him, smiling. With clumsy movements, Emerald inched her body toward his, taking the bedsheets with her. It was comical to him, watching her struggle to get close to him. She was too damn cute.

Kyle chuckled as he put his arm around her as she rested her head on his chest.

"What's so funny?" Emerald giggled as her vibrant eyes met his.

"You look like a burrito all wrapped up like that."

"Hey! I do not!" she protested. She freed her hands from the sheets, then grabbed a pillow and whacked him in the face.

"Burritos are meant for eating," he joked.

Whacked again.

"The hell was that for?"

Zaphod squawked in the corner as if the damn bird were laughing.

Kyle turned to the bird. "You think that's funny too, birdbrain?"

Zaphod whistled, and Emerald laughed.

"Damn bird." Kyle turned back to Emerald, reaching for her. "You think this is funny?"

"Yes, I do!"

"Oh yeah? I'll show you funny! Get over here!" Kyle reached for her retreating burritoed body as she laughed hysterically. Kyle caught ahold of the sheet, dragging her back to him.

"That's not fair!"

"Not fair? What's not fair is you beating me up with that pillow!" He tickled her as she continued laughing.

"You're a tough guy. I thought you can handle stuff like that," Emerald said with a smirk.

"Not when I'm not paying attention!"

Their eyes met as they paused. Then Emerald burst out laughing. "I suppose I kind of do resemble a burrito," she said.

"I'll say. And you know how I feel about burritos."

"Do tell," she whispered smoothly.

Kyle leaned over, then locked his lips onto hers, not letting go. The taste of her was water to his dry soul. He needed more—more of her. She responded in need, slipping her tongue against his as she climbed on top of him. He could feel her longing, her desire, for his body.

"Em…"

"Hm?" She nibbled on his ear, then kissed his neck.

"I fucking want you…"

Emerald lightly pressed her hands against his chest, then glided downward to his lower abs. "We should meet with Geeta soon," she teased.

"Can we just pretend that she doesn't need to see us and stay here longer?"

"Kyle!" Emerald giggled as she slipped off his body. "She has been waiting for us."

He adjusted himself, then cleared his throat. "I just want to spend one day of enjoying you, and *only* you. Hell, I spent a lifetime trying to find you, and well, here we are. Besides, dealing with Geeta's attitude is not my idea of the best way to spend my first day back in Arcadia."

Emerald chuckled. "Geeta can be abrasive at times."

"Abrasive? That's an understatement." Kyle snorted. He sighed as he stretched out in the bed. Zaphod squawked. "See! The birdbrain thinks so too."

Emerald gave him a sweet smile. "Kyle, believe me. I would rather spend the entire day with you without any cares, but I am queen of Arcadia. I have responsibilities." She smiled. "Besides, you do get to spend the day with me."

Just not the type of day I was hoping for. He cleared his throat. "I suppose you're right," Kyle muttered. "Let's get this over and done with. That way we can spend less time with bullshit and more time together."

"Kyle? Really? Bullshit?" Emerald raised her eyebrow.

"You know I'm kidding, right? I just like to give Geeta shit, even if she's not in the same room as me." Kyle chuckled, thinking of Geeta. He missed her too, though he didn't want to admit it. Geeta probably missed him as well, not that she would ever admit it either.

Kyle stretched out one last time, then got out of bed. *I'd give anything for a smoke right now*, he thought as he yanked on his black leather pants then zipped up his fly. He leaned over and grabbed his ragged shirt, one that was from his future. It was shredded to ribbons from the battle in Hell. Kyle stared at it, then shuddered. Another damn reminder of the future. And Elyathi. The last he saw of that psychotic woman had been in the future citadel, with Derek.

How the hell am I going to tell Emerald about her crazy-ass mother? Kyle sighed, thinking about the worst of it—that Derek wasn't in control of Emerald during her compromise; Ikaria was. *I'll tell her when the time is right,* he decided.

"Hey? Are you okay?" Emerald asked, suddenly in his view.

Kyle met her eyes, then gave her a smirk. "Yeah, everything is all good."

"Good."

She was already out of bed and stretching. Through her sheer nightdress, Kyle saw her belly had already developed a slight bump. Inside that bump was his child. He was going to be a father. The thought was somewhat nerve-wracking, but also exciting.

At her vanity, Emerald swept her hair to one side, brushing it. The back of her neck was exposed, begging to be kissed.

He came up from behind, placing a soft kiss in that very spot.

She giggled, then turned her head to face him. "Sorry that you have to wear your old clothes."

"You mean I can't dress up in one of your nighties?"

Emerald playfully whacked him with her brush.

"Owww, that hurt," Kyle joked, rubbing his arm.

"I'm sure it did." Emerald laughed. "If you want, I can ask one of my handmaidens to get you a set of palace clothes."

"It's cool. I'll just hold off and get some from my place," Kyle said, shrugging.

He froze the moment the words left his mouth.

Emerald knew exactly what he was thinking. "Don't worry. You still have your apartment. Rosie has been taking care of it while you've been away. I didn't want to forget you…" Emerald whispered with a jittery voice.

"I love you, Em," he whispered, holding her as he stroked her hair through his ringed fingers. "Somehow, I never managed to forget you completely. My soul had held on to some of my memories of us. Guess my life force didn't want to ever let you go."

Emerald blinked away a small happy tear, then nudged her forehead next to him, embracing his hands. "It was all my fault."

"Hey," Kyle said strongly. "Don't be doing that. It wasn't your fault. None of it."

Should he mention the situation with the sorceress? What she had confessed during the future battle?

Zaphod squawked from the corner of the room. Both of them broke their embrace, glancing at the bird.

Guess not.

"See? Zaphod says so too," Kyle joked, while Emerald chuckled with him.

He brushed her cheek gently, staring into her gleaming bright-green eyes. Full of life.

Emerald smiled back at him and leaned in to kiss him.

Suddenly, Zaphod let out a loud squawk.

"Really, bird?" Kyle said. "You really need to be fed at *this* moment?"

Zaphod whistled in protest, then flew across the room and landed on Kyle's shoulder. He gave him a soft pat on the head as the bird cooed, with Emerald joining in.

Kyle turned to look at Emerald. "Listen, if it's all right with you, let's to go to my place after we meet Geeta. It would be kinda nice to see it again."

Emerald smiled. "Sure. It's always fun to visit Rosie."

Right then, his stomach made a loud, rumbling growl.

Emerald raised her eyebrows, then gave him the brightest smile, giggling. "I think someone needs something to eat."

He smiled at her. "Damn straight."

Emerald stood up from her vanity, holding out her hand for him to take as she gave him a bright smile. "Let's go quiet that rumbling, shall we?" she said.

Kyle went over to her, then did the best he could to formally take her hand, kiss it, then hold it. "Anything to be with you."

On cue, his stomach made another loud noise. Embarrassed, Kyle rubbed the back of his neck.

Emerald glanced down at his stomach, arching one of her brows. "Guess we'd better hurry," she said with a smile as she yanked his hand toward the door.

CHAPTER 3

✦

ORANGE

The day was warm, too warm for Drew's liking. The air was humid, and his skin was sticky. Telly seemed to be enjoying the weather, however.

"Drew," Telly called from the lakeshore. "What are you waiting for?" She was in a bright orange one-piece bathing suit. The wind rustled her short hair, giving a slight wave to it.

"Coming," Drew answered. He yanked off his T-shirt, then tossed it on top of their beach blanket and headed toward the shore. In the distance, Drew could faintly see the spires of the twin palaces rising up from the treetops surrounding the lake.

This place, Telly's home of the Twin Kingdoms, seem to make Telly livelier. He didn't care for the Twin Kingdoms, though. Too cold in the winter and too muggy and humid in the summer. But the forests on the outskirts of the kingdom had lush trees unlike any he had ever experienced. And within the two combined megacities, lakes glistened throughout, the city having been built around many of them. It was one of the things he did enjoy about Telly's homeland: the people respected nature. All he'd known was Arcadia prior to visiting the Twin Kingdoms.

Telly was already ankle deep in the water. The sand here was different from the beaches where he grew up. Drew technically wouldn't even call this place a beach. More like a sandbar surrounding the lake. Beaches were near the ocean. At least, that's what he considered a beach.

"Are you still thinking about work?" Telly teased.

"No, not this time."

"Drew, I'm shocked." Telly mimicked a surprised gesture. "I think you set a new record for 'not thinking about work.'"

"I don't always think of work," Drew muttered. He scooped up some lake water with his hands, then poured it on his forehead. "It's so humid."

"They say it's the most humid in twenty-five years." She held out her hand, showing one side of an empty clamshell. "Look what I found." The sunlight hit the white iridescent enamel shell just right, causing it to gleam flecks of violet, blue, green, and a hint of yellow.

"I like it," Drew said, giving her a smile. Then he grabbed her waist, pulling her to him. "But I like you more."

"Oh, Drew," Telly said, playfully pushing him. "Give me a sec. I want to go put this with our stuff before we take a swim."

"Sure."

Drew waded around in the warm lake water as Telly ran to their things. A few water vehicles were going about in the lake, creating waves. He turned around to watch Telly fumble around with her beach bag. The moment she put the shell inside her purse, her apartment keys fell out. She put her keys in, then her sunscreen fell out. One item after another, this happened. Drew could swear he heard her grumbling all the way from where he stood.

Drew smiled. Telly was a klutz, there was no denying that. She had been trying to curb her carelessness over the years they had worked together, but every so often, she had moments like these.

She was so perfect. His perfect dream woman.

It would be a perfect time to ask her…

He didn't have a ring, but he had been planning on getting one. Work was so busy. But even without a ring, he could ask her.

Telly saw that he was watching her, then called out, "What are you looking at?"

"You."

"And? You think this is funny?"

Affirmative.

Static.

"I do."

Telly whipped her chin-length wavy blonde hair out of her face, then marched right up to him into the water. "You're going to pay for that!" She kicked at a wave of water, sending it splashing up into his face. Streaks of water ran across his glasses.

Telly giggled, then did it again.

Malfunction.

Drew laughed, then latched on to her, dragging her farther into the water as Telly laughed.

White noise.

The farther they swam, the more Drew noticed long seaweed floating up from the lake bottom. The radius of the seaweed fronds had to be at least a half a foot long. Many of them gently brushed their stems across his legs. Their slimy tentacles clung to his leg. He braved them, but deep down, he couldn't deny that the seaweed was gross.

"I don't know how you people in the Twin Kingdoms swim in these lakes," Drew called out.

"You get used to it," she answered.

The water got colder the longer they swam. The more he expended energy, the more chilled to the bone he was.

Drew glanced over at Telly. She was happily floating in the water on her backside, relaxing.

"Aren't you freezing?" he said as his teeth chattered.

Telly lazily rolled her head toward him. "This water is cold to you? Really?"

"Yes, it is. Maybe we should swim back."

"Let's swim to that other shore. I want to check out that side of the lake," Telly said. "I've always wanted to see what's behind that big tree."

Malfunction.

"Okay." Drew sighed with a shiver.

As they swam, weeds glided across his legs. Drew tried not to think of them. In the back of his mind, he kept thinking about all the leeches and chiggers that made their home in the weeds, making him anxious.

One weed latched on to his leg. Drew tried to kick it away, but another did the same. Then another.

Frantically, Drew glanced at Telly. She was still swimming ahead of him, unaware of the situation.

Cannot compute.

Drew yanked his leg, but more weeds wrapped around him.

Static.

"Drew! Come on!" Telly yelled out.

The entire lake became orange, with the weeds holding him tight.

Blip. Blip. Static.

Five percent capacity.

"Drew!"

Suddenly the weeds were like tubes with knives darting into his legs. Burning pain shot through him.

"Help!"

"Drew? Why aren't you swimming?"

Four percent capacity.

The tubes pulled him under the water. He couldn't breathe. Frantically, Drew tried to swim to the surface, splashing every which way.

Malfunction.

Three percent capacity.

"TELLY!" he screamed.

Blood filled his mouth.

Static.

"DREW!"

Two percent capacity.

White noise.

Malfunction.

"YOU CAN'T DIE!"

Blip.

Blip.

Blip.

Blip.

Blip.

Blip.

Blip.

…

CHAPTER 4

Ayera sat in the farthest corner of her cell, listening to the murmurs of the other prisoners. There were cries of torture, hunger pains, and the insane rambling of nonsense to themselves—and answering themselves in return. She was tired to the point of exhaustion. The air was chilling to the bone, and her cell, comprised of dirt and stone, had no warmth to give. The air was musty and damp, making it hard to breathe. Her nimble shoes had holes, her robes were torn, and her hair was matted, though she did the best she could to knot it at the top of her head.

What hope was there now? The gifted in World Sector Six had lost their power, and she was now a prisoner of the High Court. What had become of her sector? What was the fate of her sister? Had the High Inquisitor gotten the best of her? Had Ikaria lost her power, like the others, to the white-gifted woman?

There were a few times Ayera could have sworn she heard her sister's voice—either in the prisons or in her mind. But she knew very well it wasn't so. The mind played awful tricks when left alone too long. Whatever her sister's fate was, Ayera prayed that she would destroy the white-gifted woman once and for all.

A sudden flood of fury and a sense of injustice washed over her. How could it be that someone like her, who strove to do right in the world, had ended up imprisoned? Angry tears flooded her eyes until her vision became blurry. She told herself she wouldn't cry. But these tears of fury couldn't be held back, wetting her cheeks.

There was a sudden flurry of loud voices coming from outside her cell, becoming progressively louder. Ayera turned, wiping at her dirty, tear-stained face with the hem of her kimono, listening to the commotion. With the noise, faint orange light grew outside her cell, burning brighter by the minute, then stopped right outside.

Ayera sat up as she saw silhouettes of men moving outside her cell door. There was an iron clanking sound and a loud creak as her door opened. A man cast a red fireball in the palm of his hand, lighting up the area surrounding him, allowing Ayera to see his face. At first, she assumed it was the High Inquisitor—the man was the same height and had similar features to him. But as she looked more closely, there was no mistaking that this man was a prominent High Court captain, with a distinguishing captain's helmet and elaborate armor. His face was smooth and handsome, eyes like glowing red coals, and his long red hair was swept back, fastened securely. There were a couple of other guards that accompanied him, but the High Inquisitor was nowhere to be found.

"Lady Suzuki, I have come to verify your identity," he announced.

"I am Empress of World Sector Six, lest you have forgotten," Ayera said as she stood, holding her head high. "And why do you keep me imprisoned? I've had no trial, no sentence. Is this what you do? Imprison an empress without any information other than a disagreement over written matters?"

"High Inquisitor Rubius had stripped you of your title back in World Sector Six. Lest *you* have forgotten?" the captain shot back with snark, glancing at her. "And don't worry, you will soon have the trial you so desperately desire."

"You. All of *you*," Ayera said as she narrowed her eyes at him. She shook her head in disgust. "I don't know why it took me so many years to see it." The statement wasn't intended for the captain, but directed at the mere thought all who followed the High Court.

There was almost a sense of cruelty in the way the man raised an eyebrow at her. "Might be best to save all of your banter for the High Court."

"High Court? Surely you mean the pack of hypocrites. Anyone working with that *woman* is damning themselves. She is the most disgusting human being, taking away the gifted's power." Ayera gave the captain a once-over, then dared to say, "And *you* are no better."

"They didn't tell me that you had so much *spunk*." The captain snorted, then waved his hand. "I have seen enough to identify the prisoner," he said to the guards around him.

Instead of moving out, the captain moved farther into her cell as the guards behind him snickered. When the iron doors slammed shut, she knew they had locked her in with the captain. Alarm rang through Ayera's body, and every inch of her wanted to scream.

"What are you doing?" Ayera said nervously as she backed up until she was flat against the cell wall. If she could retreat further, she would have, but there was nowhere to go.

Instead of answering her, the captain crouched down to her level, eyeing her. His red glimmering eyes flared with magic, and a sharp, insincere smile spread across his face.

"Never had a taste of royalty before," he said low under his breath. The guards behind the bars laughed, pressing their faces against the bars to see inside.

"If you are insinuating what I think you are," Ayera said, leaning back in disgust, "I do hope you know that the Lord of Darkness has a special lake of fire for your kind." As much as she wanted to burst into tears, she was paralyzed with a fear she had never known until this very moment.

"You think I care for the afterlife?" The captain leaned in, grabbing her robe.

"I should think so, being with the High Court!" Ayera fought back, slapping his hand away.

The captain grabbed her wrists, forcing her to the ground.

Ayera cried out as he pinned her down, leaning on top of her. The guards behind the bars cheered, mixed with sexual grunts.

"Don't do this!" Ayera screamed as she struggled against the captain.

"Oh, but I do want to," the captain said. He grabbed her obi, yanking it to untie it. More loud noises came from the guards outside the iron gate. Ayera kicked, cried out, pushed, whatever she could do to get away. Instead, her kimono loosened, and with it, a feeling of defeat settled over her.

Ayera screamed, so the captain pushed his thick hand across her mouth. Through her muffled screams, Ayera fought, trying to kick him. It was no use—the captain far outweighed her, and his strength couldn't be matched.

"What's going on in here?" called out a low voice.

The guards outside the iron gate went silent. The captain jumped to his feet, straightening out his tabard, his armor, and smoothing back his hair.

"Nothing, sir!" chimed the guards.

The captain pushed his lips against her ear. "If you speak of this, when I come back and *finish* the job, I won't be as nice," he whispered sharply. With that, the captain hopped to his feet.

Another shadow appeared outside the gate, with the captain at full stance. Ayera clutched her robe, wiping at her tear-stained face, still shaking.

"Captain? Is that you in there?" a man said, peering inside the cell. Ayera noticed this man was far more decorated than the red-gifted captain, and had the gift of the orange.

"Indeed, Commander. I was ordered to confirm the identity of the former empress," the red-gifted captain said. "It's her, all right."

Though shaken, she would not stand for the captain's threats. If she was going to die, she'd take the captain down with her in shame.

"The man tried to have his way with me!" Ayera cried.

He glared at her. "She lies!"

The commander looked at the captain sternly, then shifted his eyes to Ayera. She was shaking uncontrollably.

"You don't need to go into the cells to confirm identities, Captain," the commander said. "Next time I catch you inside a cell, I will dock your wages for two months and have you doing latrine duty."

"Yes, Commander, sir."

The commander gestured for the guards to open the door, and the captain walked out. The guards closed and locked the cell again, then followed their captain. The orange-gifted commander glanced at Ayera, his face lit up with his magical torch.

Did he want to say something else? Ayera wanted to tell him what exactly had transpired until he showed up, but her mouth couldn't form the words, and she remained silent, still shaking.

Damn that bastard... I'll kill him with my bare hands if I find him messing with her!

Ayera paused in shock. Had she...heard the commander's mind? The two of them exchanged glances in continued silence until the commander walked off.

She watched until the light of his torch faded, and darkness settled back around her. She remained against the dirt wall in her cell, then slumped down, still shaken. Her body trembled, relief that the captain didn't get to follow through with his evil intentions flooding through her. With the heat of the fiery magic gone, Ayera shivered, rubbing her upper arms inside her kimono while listening to the echoes of the other prisoners. Cries of prisoners being tortured, others just moving throughout their cell.

Tears stained her face as her stomach sank into her gut and despair settled into her being.

But she also knew something far worse…

Death awaited.

If she was going to be a martyr, then so be it. But she wasn't going to go down without a fight.

I am going to die, she told herself, fighting back her tears. *Is this truly the end for me? To die by the injustice of the court?*

There was a sudden sensation, like fingertips softly brushing her skin. It was a touch of peace, serenity…giving her a sense of calm and relief.

Ayera jerked her body, looking to her left and right. She sensed someone was *with* her.

"Hello?" she called out.

There was no answer.

"I know someone is here with me," she pressed.

Then the feeling was gone, leaving her feeling empty.

Ayera stood, peering into the darkness, rubbing her forearms, but only the mutterings of the prison answered her. Was she going mad? She hadn't been there nearly as long as the insane prisoners. More tears came, this time trickling down her cheeks.

I must have imagined it, she told herself as she crouched into a ball, trying to sleep off the nightmare she was living.

CHAPTER 5

◆

BLUE

Derek stormed into Elyathi's quarters, fuming. The former queen of Arcadia was nowhere in her sitting chambers. She had told him to meet him there; Derek could only assume that she was checking on that green-gifted.

He paced evenly around the room, replaying the recent chain of events as he waited. He clutched his hand in rage, thinking about Ikaria. Once again, she'd one-upped him.

Dammit!

Derek turned, then summoned a wineglass. It floated toward him, then filled itself to the brim with its dark contents. Derek took a long drink, then ran his ringed fingers through his sweaty curls. He was furious with himself. He and Elyathi arrived just as Ikaria escaped the citadel.

If only I had been more in tune with the flow of time! Derek took another drink, furrowing his brow. *If only the damn High Court messengers had been quicker about it! If only I had been quick about it!*

He had felt rumblings of the citadel structure—everybody had to some degree. Derek had only been at the citadel a very short time; at times the citadel did rumble from certain magics or even the weather. He'd assumed that was the case then too. But in reality, the majority of the damage had been done on the complete opposite side of where Derek had been when Ikaria arrived, making it seem not so significant. And on top of that, it took longer to be informed what was happening, since the gifted were on Ikaria's side of the citadel at the time. The only silver lining that came out of it was that Elyathi's chambers hadn't been touched by the damage.

What he needed to do was become the most powerful gifted so Ikaria could finally be six feet in the ground, and Elyathi could bring forth the new world. After all was said and done, Derek could finally live his life in peace with Emerald—without the shadow of Ikaria in the back of his mind, mucking things up again.

I must travel back in time and end this once and for all.

"Derek, is that you?" Elyathi called out from the next room.

Derek wiped the edge of his mouth, then cleared his throat. "It is. Sorry I didn't announce that I was here. I've thought of nothing but Ikaria and forgot my manners."

"It's quite all right." Elyathi faded slowly into view with orange magic, her eyes glistening like the setting sun. "I had to check on Suresh."

"We are fortunate that Ikaria didn't find him," Derek said.

"Indeed. Though she is strong with her magics, you are most powerful with yours. Rest assured, Suresh is secure in your dimensional time spell."

Derek noticed that Elyathi had a new dress on, this time in pale lavender fabrics. He couldn't help but notice her neck lay bare, with moonstones dangling from her earrings, complementing her pale skin, which looked soft and smooth, and warm…

Derek swallowed hard, then turned away. What he needed to do was see Emerald, and soon. This had already gone on for far too long.

"Lady Elyathi, I must return to Arcadia. Do what was initially asked of me. I'll bring that damn cyborg scientist here so what's-his-face can activate the cyborgs on this side of time. Besides, I want to see Emerald. I miss her."

Derek paused, then thought of Emerald. The last time he'd seen her, they were hardly on speaking terms. She wouldn't travel to the future, not with him anyway. But for her mother? That she would.

"Yes," Elyathi murmured. "I miss my daughter very much. I want her to be with me as we enter the new world."

He sighed, thinking about the entirety of the situation. "I'm not sure if I can convince Emerald to return with me."

"Do not worry about Emerald. I will convince her. Focus on that cyborg." A flicker of emotion came over her face, then she gestured to him as she sat on a sofa. "Derek, let us speak of important matters before you leave. Because ultimately, you have a great hand in the making of the new world."

He flicked his hand with his adjacent magic of violet, the goblet refilling itself with more wine, then sat down next to her. "What is it?"

Derek watched as Elyathi's fingertips lingered on her gem and vial necklaces. His blood began to burn, then he looked down at his wine. What in damnation was he feeling? It was like she had her own spell or aura about her.

"I had to be sure before I told you about the spell."

Derek took a drink, perplexed. "What spell?"

"The final spell," she breathed. "I know now after our little skirmish in World Sector Six that what I had felt deep within my soul is true." Elyathi leaned in, her long wavy hair tousled over her shoulders. As her body edged toward his, Derek felt a strong pull of desire. "I need my *complement* to cast the other half of the spell," she said.

Derek could smell the light scent of lavender perfume. The same fragrant scent as Emerald's. Desire, wanting, lust…it was bottled in that perfume. His blood pumped through his body. He resisted every temptation that came across in his mind, shoving it aside.

"Derek…do you feel what I feel?"

Her words startled him. Had she heard what he was thinking?

Derek nervously ran his fingers through his dark blue curls. What he had felt was a *pull*. A *draw*. It was like two magnets that wanted to be joined together, and he was one of the magnets.

"My lady…I do not know how to answer," Derek said, choosing his words carefully as his eyes nervously met hers. Never had he felt so confused until this moment.

Elyathi laughed softly. "You are my complement, Derek. You and I are meant to be opposites of each other within our own wheel. It is in our very nature to work together. That is why you feel a connection, the magnetic bond."

"How is that possible? I am blue-gifted…" Derek paused at his words, then he shot up and met her gaze. "I…I am to become a black-gifted, aren't I?" Derek said slowly.

"You are, and you must. The draw is strong, and it will only get stronger now that we have found each other. With every hour that you don't reach your full potential, it will get worse for you, as it does for me. You must unlock the gift of the black and become my complement, and quickly. With you *taking* all six colors of the gift, and with me *receiving* all six colors of the gift…together we can channel the final spell and create the new earth."

They exchanged glances, and suddenly, Derek felt a hint of shame. He *had* stolen Emerald's magic—by drinking her blood when she had been asleep in his time spell.

Does she need Emerald's magic? Just as I needed some of hers? Derek thought. He sincerely hoped not. The guilt over everything that had happened to Emerald was torture enough.

"What is it, Derek?"

He pushed away his shame, then asked, "I still don't understand why you haven't collected Suresh's magic. You aren't thinking about taking Emerald's magic from her, are you? If that is the case, then I don't think I could wholeheartedly continue with this."

"That is not my intention," Elyathi cooed. "You must understand, in order to activate the ultimate spell, I need each color of the gift, then I must activate them simultaneously." Elyathi held up the gems with her neck held high. "But the magic has to be from a willing gifted. They must believe in the new world."

Derek lit up. "Suresh…"

"Yes, I must convince him. These gems—all from willing gifted. You can see their souls: Belinda, Perserine, Tyllos, and Borgen. They believe in the new world, for I promised them that they can rule in their own part of the new world I create. With that promise, they willingly gave a part of their life force. As for Suresh…" Elyathi paused, holding out the vial of his pulsating green blood. "I am waiting for him to be willing. Once he is, I can transmute his blood into a gem. I must capture that moment of his willingness. The willingness of the life force of the blood will be activated by their link, making it so that I can lock his decision within the gem."

"What of Ikaria?" Derek pointed out. "She will never give her blood willingly. You can bet on that."

"Indeed, she wouldn't," she agreed. "But with the strength in your adjacent violet magic, you must overcome her mind and change her perspective. Through your power in control of her will, she will freely offer her magic to me."

Derek paused. "There is also a violet-gifted back in Arcadia that I confronted. An enemy of mine—she was working with Kyle Trancer. Since I am going back, I will pay her a visit."

Elyathi's eyes sparkled. "The violet-gifted. The High Court knows of her but had her lost."

"I will find her, and overcome her mind if I am able to," Derek said. "That way, you have your violet magic one way or another." He paused, thinking about his own adjacent violet magic. "What of Suresh? I could convince him by force as well."

Elyathi shook her head. "It won't work. Violet magic falls under force of the mind and body; because of this law of magic, the final spell will accept a *compromised* violet-gifted. As for a green-gifted, it simply will not work."

At her words, Derek felt a small tinge of worry about Emerald. She wasn't going to be used by her mother for the final spell—Suresh was enough. But why wasn't Emerald planned as a part of the spell?

Emerald will be okay. Elyathi knows what she is doing, he assured himself.

Derek rose from his seat, taking one last drink. "I will seek out other gifted blood," he said. "For you and for myself."

She smiled. "Good. There is one last thing you must know about this spell. The dark side of the blue: use it when funneling in your black magic." Her eyes glimmered like pearls in the light. "If you do this, the new world will only have one timeline, as I have mentioned before. *You* are the only one that can do this, as your main color is blue, and you can tap into the dark side of the blue."

He nodded. "I understand. It would certainly make things easier for us. There would be no possible alternate timeline, or something or someone in the future or past that could interfere." Derek smiled, then bowed to her. "I will do this for the both of us. It guarantees our safety if something were to go wrong."

"Precisely." Elyathi rose to her feet, then looked over her shoulder. "Before you go, I have a gift for you."

"Gift?"

"Come and see."

Derek followed Elyathi down a hall, one that he had never noticed prior. She made another turn, which led them to a far more narrow hallway. She presented a key from her pockets, then unlocked the door with a click, and they both slipped inside.

As Derek entered, he immediately noticed three gifted heavily bound together in a group, gagged and fearful. They all noticed him too, making loud moans and fearful muffles. Through their bindings, Derek saw what color gifted they were: red, orange, and yellow.

Derek shot Elyathi an alarmed look. "This…is my *gift*?"

"I discussed this with the other high justices in advance, and we are all in agreement. These gifted will be serving a great cause."

It was Ikaria all over again, but this time, it was from someone he trusted. Completely.

"How long have they been here?" Derek said, still in shock.

"Since coming back from World Sector Six. I knew then you needed to complete your role in unlocking the black gift. Belinda sent guards to collect them in secret."

"I…" Derek turned back to look at them as the gifted made more muffled cries.

"There is no reason to be alarmed, Derek," Elyathi began. "Their blood will be a part of your blood—one to bring the new world." Elyathi walked gracefully up to the bound gifted; all were wide-eyed with alarm. "You all will be rewarded for your deeds, for you are a part of something far greater than you can imagine. You are doing the God of Light's work." Elyathi presented an enchanted dagger, handing it to him.

Derek slowly took it from her, his hands beginning to shake.

This can't be happening.

"You must be the one, Derek. You must steal their gift," she stated. "You already took of my daughter's blood, did you not?"

"Yes…" Derek lowered his eyes.

"Do not feel guilty, Derek. You aren't taking their lives, only a few drops of their blood," her voice echoed.

Hearing Elyathi say the words instantly calmed him. She was right. Why was he so worried?

It's just a scrape and a few drops…

Derek slowly met her eyes. It was as if her soul pierced his own with her glance. His soul stirred wildly, as if in need. Pushing the thought aside, Derek turned toward the three bound gifted. The orange-gifted who faced him breathed heavily through his gag, grunting furiously.

"I am taking what is mine," he whispered to the orange-gifted man. "No more than that."

The orange-gifted's words were muffled loudly behind the gag. Then Derek raised the dagger and swiftly sliced the man's exposed arm with a clean swipe.

The man cried out behind his gag. The other two gifted did the same as they eyed the transaction with alarm.

Ignoring the man's muffled cries, Derek slowly licked the man's glimmering blood. It had a soft glow to it, pulsating to let him know that the man was indeed gifted. The taste of the blood was delightful, almost too good to be true. The taste, his senses… Derek just wanted to keep tasting the powerful life force, prolong this ecstasy, to keep his mind exploding with delight. It felt so good.

"Derek," Elyathi interrupted. "You must move quickly to the next gifted before the new powers consume you."

Still in his magical haze, Derek tried to focus as he glanced at the next gifted. A yellow-gifted woman. She was weeping, but somehow her sadness was insignificant to Derek.

The newfound orange power still hammered in his life force, all the way up to his ears as he crawled toward her. The yellow-gifted woman made noises, but it was nothing compared to the rhythm in his heart. Derek gripped his dagger, then sliced her arm. The gifted woman cried out from behind her gag. The cut was sloppy. He didn't care; the sparkling blood streaming down her arm looked delicious.

Derek latched on to her arm viciously. She made a noise against her gag as he mashed his lips against her cut. Her blood flowed onto his lips and against his face as he consumed her yellow gift. The life force behind her yellow gift was strong. He wanted more of this power…more of this gift. Somewhere, rattling in the back of his mind, he knew he had to move on. There was another gift waiting.

The world was already spinning with ecstasy, which made it difficult for Derek to understand what was happening. Through his euphoria, he heard the call of the red-gifted magic on the other side of the bound group. It was calling to him, begging to be taken from that woman's red-gifted body.

Derek crawled over to the next gifted. He hadn't notice until now that this was the attractive red-gifted woman he had seen earlier in the citadel. She had been trying to give him wanting eyes ever since he had appeared at the High Court Citadel, trying to make herself known.

The woman made a muffled squeal, her eyes wide and pleading at Derek.

Confused and drunken with power, Derek said, "I thought you said that you had them captured right when we returned."

"I personally swapped her with another due to the nature of her desires," Elyathi answered. "She must pay for her sins."

Everything was a blur except skin—that was in clear focus. He didn't know what body part was the woman, nor did it matter. He raised his dagger, then sliced. There were screams within his mind. Was he linked to her mind? Had he accidentally wandered into her thoughts with his adjacent magic?

Derek saw the bloody, glowing skin. Radiant and beautiful. That blood called out to him. Then, Derek's lips found their way to the blood. He drank. And drank. His senses went wild, his body wanting to experience all power, all lusts, all desires all at once. It raged in his being, then turned into anger—*wicked* anger—and rage.

He needed the power. He desired the power.

He wanted to rule all of time.

He wanted it *all.*

Derek kept drinking the woman's red gift, blood running down his lips, his chin, and his face as he rubbed his cheeks against her body. Her gift felt soft, like Emerald's well-endowed bosom, which gave him much pleasure…

Emerald, I long for you…

"Derek," Elyathi called out.

Elyathi's face entered his mind. Her shining face. Her beautiful, delicate face…

Everything was spinning as all the power pounded through his veins.

"Power," he whispered hoarsely. "I need more power…"

"And you will have it," Elyathi whispered in assurance. She eyed the bound gifted in disgust as she walked over to them, holding the hem of her dress up to ensure no blood soaked into the white cloth. "Your purpose has now been served. May the God of Light shine upon you."

Derek's heart raged and pounded throughout his entire being as Elyathi held out her hand, soaking in all three of their life forces, fully consuming them with her magic. Her magic consumption ended, and they slumped over like deadweight.

A wave of nausea that came and went for a second, then yet a stronger stir of his life force. A pounding sexual rage flooded his body. He broke out in a sweat, and the room went blurry. Every sense in his flesh desired sexual gratification, as if he had been deprived for many years. His mind raged with urge. He clutched the floor, holding back the flood of sexual desire that coursed through his body.

There were manic mutterings and cries filling the air, then he was overcome with a deep blue magic that washed over him.

"I look forward to your return…" Elyathi's voice echoed.

CHAPTER 6

✦

GREEN

The two of them walked through the palace on their way to breakfast. Emerald snuggled her head against Kyle's arm with her hands clasping his biceps as he hummed a happy tune. Zaphod was perched on his other shoulder, cooing to his song. Kyle's scent lingered in the air, invigorating her every sense.

Life had returned to her. Kyle had been alive all this time—*truly alive.* She'd walked in darkness for so long—all those months she had felt so alone. Now that they had been reunited, and with Kyle by her side, everything in her soul had healed, and the joy in her heart had returned. She couldn't help but smile.

Kyle gave her a curious look, pausing his tune. "What is it?"

"It's just, I am so happy," Emerald said, feeling her cheeks flush. *Happy to be living in this moment with you.*

He chuckled, then startled her as he swooped her up into his arms with Zaphod flying off his shoulder squawking. He then whispered in her ear, "I heard that."

"Kyle!" Emerald giggled. "You heard my mind?"

He leaned in, then whispered in her ear, "I've never been happier either, Em. Happy to be living in this moment with you too."

His warm voice made her heart pound with excitement.

A guard passing by happened to notice, resulting with them busting up with laughter when the guard turned down another corridor.

"Do you think he saw us?" Her body slid against his as he lowered her.

"Most definitely."

"Good." He chuckled. "Probably the biggest thrill he got all day on guard duty."

Emerald gazed at Kyle, then grabbed the hem of his borrowed green jerkin. He looked cute in the royal getup—with black leggings and boots, and his green gemstone hanging around his neck. The green brought out the contrast of his fiery, spiked red hair. Though she did like his bleached hair, his true gifted-hair color was very attractive. In a way, she almost preferred it.

"God, they make these things tight," he said, yanking at the neckline. "Don't mind me if I turn blue at breakfast."

"You'll be fine."

"Says the woman not wearing the outfit."

"You wear chokers. What's the difference?"

Kyle snorted. "There's a big difference. I adjust the collar to fit my neck. I wouldn't be surprised if the previous owner died of suffocation."

Zaphod cawed in agreement.

"See? Even Zaphod agrees," Kyle said, pointing to his pet.

"If you must know, the previous owner is still alive and well; he just so happens to be a sector lord that left his travel wardrobe in his chambers from his last visit."

"It's good to know that I just might survive wearing this outfit, then."

Emerald stopped mid-tracks and directed him to face her. She glided her hands up his chest, then undid the top button of his collar." His eyes met hers, and they both smiled at each other. "Better?"

"Yeah. Thank fucking God I can breathe again," he said. He glanced at her, his red eyes glowing in the shadows. "But you know, you can do that thing with your hands again."

"You mean this?" Emerald ran her hands down his chest, this time in the opposite direction, landing on his lowers, then gave it a soft squeeze.

Kyle's eyes brightened like lit coals, giving her a sexy smirk. "Okay, that made wearing this shitty outfit all worth it," he said. "If you want, we can find an abandoned hallway…"

"We should get going," she teased as she pretended to walk away.

"Why you gotta tease me like that, Em? That's just fucking terrible of you, leaving me all wound up like that," he called out from behind her.

Emerald giggled. "If you recall, we already had some fun earlier."

"Yeah, but I can go again…"

"Again, he says…"

"It's your loss. Just sayin'." Just then, his stomach growled.

"Your stomach says otherwise," Emerald pointed out.

"Rain check?"

"Oh, you!" Emerald slapped his chest playfully, then turned away from him.

"Hey!"

Suddenly, he touched her hand gently, and the mood was very different.

Emerald stopped, glancing at him curiously. "Are you okay, Kyle?"

Kyle studied her, then took her hand, placing it on his chest, his hand against hers. "Everything's perfect."

Emerald blushed, then hugged him. His strong arms were so warm and inviting.

"I missed you, Em," he whispered.

"I missed you terribly, Kyle. I can't live without you." Her eyes stung with tears, but these were the good kind.

He tightened his grip on her, agreeing with a silent response. Then he kissed the top of her head, running his fingers through her hair. "You won't ever have to," he reassured her with a whisper.

His stomach let out a big-ass growl.

"Again?" he scolded his stomach. "Way to fucking ruin the moment!"

"Come on, let's feed you," Emerald said, yanking his hand.

They entered her private dining chambers. The black marbled floors reflected the daylight sun, giving a golden shine to the blackened floors. The mirrors picked up their reflections as they were escorted by a palace servant.

"Looks like you'll have to perch on one of the chairs, old friend," Kyle told the bird.

Zaphod flew over to one of the dining chairs, then sat on the top of it, cooing.

A servant that was holding out a seat for Emerald eyed Zaphod carefully.

"Let me get this," Kyle told the servant. The servant moved out of Kyle's way, confused. Kyle then slid out the seat for her.

"Kyle, you don't have to do that. That's their job."

"Nonsense," he said. "I kind of always wanted to do that anyway. Never got the chance."

"Well, then, in that case, thank you, kind sir," Emerald said, playing along. She sat down in her chair, and he slid her closer to the table, then she placed her napkin on her lap. Zaphod whistled in approval. She glanced up and watched Kyle take a seat near her. She reached out her hand, and he took it, kissing it again.

In the corner of her eye, the servant gave them another confused look. Emerald felt a pang of awkwardness. Between the servant and the guard earlier, soon everyone would be talking.

I just need to figure out how to address this with the court. She paused. Was that even necessary? How many kings and queens had had consorts ever since time began? Why should she have to address it? Kyle was now a part of her life, and everyone would just have to get used to it.

"Can I get Her Majesty anything?" the servant asked.

"My usual, please," Emerald said.

The servant turned to Kyle. "And for you, sir?"

"This is Master Kyle," Emerald announced. "He will be staying in the palace indefinitely."

"Master Kyle?" Kyle repeated. Emerald playfully kicked him under the table. "Oh yeah, Master Kyle. Damn straight."

The servant bowed to Kyle, not responding to her announcement, then said, "Can I get you anything, Master Kyle?"

"Do you have any breakfast burritos?"

"Indeed we do, Master Kyle."

Kyle beamed. "A breakfast burrito, please. And some coffee. Black. Also, can you get a piece of bread or some crackers for the bird over there?"

"Yes, Master Kyle." The servant bowed, then took off.

"I'm not sure how I feel about this Master Kyle business."

"You'll get used to it."

Emerald watched as Kyle studied his surroundings, almost as if he were going to be attacked at any moment. She found it cute, and her mind wandered to his formal appearance once again; his polished royal appearance made her want him even more. Kyle looked like a handsome prince with his own sort of flair. She imagined being on top of him in his royal garb...

Emerald bit her lip. He was tempting to say the least.

Kyle noticed her glance. "What?"

"What do you mean?" Emerald asked, suddenly turning flushed.

"There you go again, Em. Giving me a weird look and acting strange. Is that common up here?"

"Perhaps you might think I'm giving a weird look, but I assure you, I'm not."

"Then what do you call it?"

"I think your term would be called 'checking you out.'"

Kyle leaned back in his chair, then puffed out his chest. "How's this: Do I look lordish enough for you?"

"Oh, *my lord.*" Emerald pretended to fan herself breathlessly.

They both laughed.

Just then, the servant came back with Kyle's coffee, bowed, then left again. Emerald watched as he slurped his coffee, then gave a relieved smile. "God, this coffee is good."

"I'm glad you like it."

"Hell yeah, I do."

"I wonder where Geeta is? She said that she had to talk to us about a few things."

"Who cares?"

Emerald raised her eyebrow. "You don't care for Geeta?"

"Well, of course I care for Geeta. I just don't wanna see her right now. She'll probably bring some impending doom news." He yanked on his collar again, undoing another button.

Emerald smiled at him. "We'll see about that."

"I'm willing to bet everything I got." He paused. "Which isn't much."

"We can head to your apartment after my council meetings. If you want, I can have several guards come with us to help pack. After all, if you are to live here with me in the palace, you will need your belongings."

Kyle froze for a moment, and his eyes flared a bright red. After a second, he took a gulp of his coffee.

The servant came in, placing each of their meals in front of them, bowing.

"Excuse me, could you please find the Protector of the Realm and send her here? She's somewhere in the palace, or at least, last I heard," Emerald stated.

"If needed, call for Councilor Emerys, and he can locate her."

"Right away, Your Majesty," the servant said, bowing and taking off.

Emerald looked back at Kyle and noticed he was visibly frustrated.

"Kyle, we do need to speak to Geeta at some point. She has been waiting to speak to us, so we best do it now."

He sighed, leaning back in his chair. "It's not about Geeta. When we go to my apartment, there's no need for all the guards, that's all. I'll just grab a few things."

"Why just a few?" Emerald gave him a confused look. "You don't want all of your things?"

"Well, I dunno. Derek might come back, and he's king and all. And I'm just… You know, I got an idea. Why don't we stay at my apartment for a while? I know it's small and everything, but at least we would be down in the heart of the city. You know, where all the action is at." He gave her an endearing smile. "Like old times, yeah?" He took another gulp of his coffee, avoiding her gaze.

"Kyle, are you serious? You know that's not possible. I am queen. Queens live in the palace," Emerald started. "And don't worry about Derek for now."

"But you can still 'queen' at my apartment, can't you?"

"I have many matters to attend to here at the palace. It's where the Inner Council meets. Emerys and the others need me. Arcadia needs me…"

Kyle coughed nervously, then rubbed the back of his neck. "Yeah, forget it. It was a silly idea anyway," he said. "But I would still like to keep my apartment. I've grown fond of that hellhole." His eyes flickered with a hint of frustration, but it left almost as fast as it came. He took a ravenous bite of his food, then drank more of his coffee.

Emerald felt bad. Was she being unreasonable?

There was an uneasy silence for a moment, then Emerald said, "Kyle. I wasn't trying to…"

"Forget it, Em," he said, his fiery eyes glimmering. He placed his hand on top of hers and smiled. "Let's just eat our breakfast, yeah?"

Emerald returned his smile as a voice rang out from the other side of the room.

"There you are."

They both turned to see Geeta standing in the doorway. She had on a black-lace suit coat with puffed sleeves and tight formal black pants. Her hair was styled in her usual purple mohawk, but she wore more lavish silver earrings in her fully pierced ear, with a simple diamond stud in the other ear. Even her bindi was more elaborate than usual. In her hand she held the precious staff, which glowed with the intensity of her violet magic.

"Geeta!" Emerald said, getting up from her seat. The two woman gave each other hugs, then Geeta gave her a formal bow.

Geeta then turned around, giving Kyle a cool smile. "I'm glad you're back. I *kind of* missed you, big guy." She gave him a side hug, with him returning to his breakfast.

Kyle snorted through a smile. "Well, I'm *kind of* touched, Geeta." He finished his burrito, then pushed his plate aside.

"Who's this fellow?" Geeta asked as she bent over to pet Zaphod. The bird whistled with delight.

"That's Zaphod. He's a loyal friend."

Geeta face melted from her usual stiff expression to a hint of joy. "I remember seeing him in another form. A rat in the odd dimensional world we were in."

"Yeah, he's been through thick and thin with me." Kyle took another sip of his coffee.

Could Zaphod be…Rosie's rat? She would definitely have to see what Kyle thought about it.

"Let's just start this meeting or whatever," Kyle continued. "I've got things to do."

"An attention span of a two-year-old," Geeta said.

"Can't a guy just eat his breakfast in peace? Or did I really come here to listen to you give me shit constantly?"

"It seems the gods willed it so," Geeta said. "Moving on to more important matters." She cleared her throat, then began. "I got a transmission from the wastelands while I was at the palace waiting for our meeting. You will be happy to know that Olympia is no longer a threat. At least, out in the wastelands. The camps drove the Olympian army back to their lands."

Emerald breathed a sigh of relief. "The war is over?"

"Not necessarily. The army has retreated back to Olympia—for the time being. Communications out in the wastelands have been restored. The source of the disruption of the communications was a gifted boy. A red-gifted boy that only can access the dark side of the red."

There was another gifted outside of Arcadia?

"How is this bad news, then? So what if there is another gifted running around?" Kyle asked.

"The issue is that Olympia took Gwen when they retreated, leaving Drew mangled and in critical condition in the process." Geeta sighed. "Drew almost didn't make it, but Telly managed to get him stabilized, and he's now on life support. Every second is critical."

Emerald's heart fluttered. Her hands began to shake. "Can they repair him?"

Geeta took a deep breath. "They are compiling a list of parts they need in hopes that Your Majesty will get them from the Corporation."

"Done," Emerald stated. "Have them send it to the palace right away once completed." She paused. "Geeta, who is Gwen? Why did they take an Arcadian citizen?"

Geeta met her eyes. "Gwen is Drew and Telly's daughter."

Emerald's and Kyle's mouths both dropped.

"Wait. You are telling me that that cyborg has a *daughter*?" Kyle said incredulously.

"I never knew that either," Emerald chimed in. "Geeta, we need to get that girl back. She is my responsibility. She's an Arcadian citizen."

"Agreed," Geeta said. "I had planned on staying here in Arcadia for a while, but I must make a visit with the wasteland camp. I need to see if Victor has awakened, see if there is anything I can do to help Drew, and get Gwen back safely."

"Victor?" Kyle chimed in. "Oh God, don't tell me that he's hurt too."

Geeta raised her eyebrow. "Victor has gray magic."

Emerald's eyes went wide as she set down her coffee cup gently. "*Gray magic?*"

"Gray magic?" Kyle repeated with his eyes wide.

"Gray magic!" Zaphod whistled. "Gray magic!"

"You talked?" Kyle whipped his head toward Zaphod. "He really talked!"

"Gray magic! Caw!"

"Holy hell, he talked!" Kyle said in surprise. "The bird has never talked before...ever!"

"Fascinating," Geeta said, eyeing the bird steadily.

Kyle turned to Geeta, leaning in. "But for real, is Victor okay?"

"He hasn't awakened from his newly gifted state yet," Geeta stated.

"Oh, that," Kyle reminisced. "All I remember is that I woke up butt-ass naked with everyone staring at me after I turned."

"I didn't need to hear that," Geeta muttered. "One thing that I should tell you is this: before I left to assist Your Majesty, it was discovered that Olympia also has cyborgs infused with aspects of the gift."

Emerald shot her an immediate look. "What gift do they possess?"

"The yellow gift. Mostly shield magic."

"Great," Kyle stated, then leaned into her. "Doom and gloom."

Emerald sighed. "Geeta? What does gray magic do?"

"I don't know much since I had to leave the battle, but it seems that it nullifies all other magics that are in close vicinity."

A gifted boy outside of Arcadia. How did he get his magic? Was he born with it just like her? And now Victor, having gray magic? What did it do? Nothing in *The Spectrum* mentioned a gray gift of magic that Emerald knew of. Similar to white magic… Her mother had white, Victor now had gray…the sorceress at one point had black.

Geeta and Kyle gave her a look, almost as if they felt Emerald's thoughts.

"There is much concern surrounding this gifted boy, and these new magics," Geeta said.

Kyle looked down at his empty plate, then shifted in his seat. "Em, I dunno how to word this…there is something you should know about your mother."

Emerald furrowed her brow. "My mother?"

"Yeah, your mother."

"If you are referring to her white magic, then I already know." Emerald continued. "When we were hiding out in Victor's camp a few months back, he told me about my mother having white magic. She had hid her power from almost everyone while she lived, including me and my father."

There was more uncomfortable silence.

Emerald blinked. "What? What are you not telling me?"

"That's just the thing though, Em. Your mother is still living—in the future."

Her mother was alive? Living in the *future*? Emerald shook her head in disbelief. "I…I don't understand. That's not possible. She died many years ago. I was at her funeral…"

Kyle shifted his eyes downward.

"I saw them bury her with my own eyes!"

Kyle frowned. "I dunno what to even say, Em. But what I can say is that I personally talked with your mom."

"*You*...talked with my *mother*?"

"Yeah, in the future. While I was Rubius."

"Rubius?"

Kyle sighed. "My future self that was reborn." Zaphod let out a loud caw. "Yeah, I didn't want to mention that name anymore, but I had to!" Kyle scolded the bird. He then turned to her. "Em, there is more to this than your mother living in the future." His fiery eyes gazed at her. "She is seeking out other colors of magic for the High Court."

"*What?*"

"I know this is hard..."

"*Impossible.*"

Kyle sighed. "It's not impossible. I know this for certain."

"I...I just don't understand." Emerald turned away in her seat, tearing up again. "First you tell me my mother is alive. Now that she is seeking out colors of magic? *Why* would she do this? My mother was a devout believer in the God of Light and followed *The Spectrum*'s scriptures religiously. It has been written that the gifted should remain pure, even in their given magic. What purpose would it serve for her to gather all the colors of magic? Why would she do so?"

"Your mother wants to eradicate magic from the world," Kyle said with a stony face. "Right now, many people from the future are getting their magic taken from them by your mother. The High Court's goal is to only have people with magic that they deem worthy. But not only that, it is said that she wants to reshape the world because she is some so-called chosen gifted." His eyes met hers. "Personally, I think she will end up consuming everyone's magic. But who knows."

"What you are saying sounds nothing like my mother. Are you sure this woman was my mother? What if you have the wrong person?" Emerald pressed.

"He's right," Geeta said. "You were being pursued by other blue-gifted from the future while you were under that spell." She pulled out a note from her pocket, then presented to her. "You should take a look at this."

Emerald took the note from her, then opened it.

"A blue-gifted woman had this with her when she traveled here while you were in your comatose state," Geeta added. "If you recall, High Priest Auron is from the future—she is his niece. The High Court threatened to eradicate the people from her world sector—and her—if she didn't bring you to the future. This note"—Geeta gestured to it—"was written to convince you to return with her to the future."

Emerald opened the small scroll with a broken seal of wax on it. It was her mother's handwriting. Quickly, she read it as tears formed in her eyes.

My dearest daughter,

You will be most happy to hear that I have been alive and well these many years. I know you probably thought me dead, for when I escaped your time era, it was staged to look as if I had passed on to the heavenly realm. But alas, I have been in the future, and have thought and prayed about you in every spare moment. I know this is much to take in, but I ask desperately for you to return with the blue-gifted, to the future where I am. I have a place for you, waiting for your arrival. When you return to me, we will finally be reunited, and we can live in peace. How much I miss you, my sweet love. Please return to me! I will be waiting.

Your forever loving mother,

Elyathi, former Queen of Arcadia

Emerald's hands shook as she held the letter close to her heart. "My mother…she's alive," she whispered. She took a deep breath, then leaned back in her seat, stunned. The dining hall was silent, and Emerald watched as Geeta and Kyle exchanged worried glances at each other, then looked to her.

All of these years, her mother had been living elsewhere. Her mother was *alive*. Another thought came to her. What if she *could* see her mother again? After all, her mother wanted to see her as well.

A surge of emotions ripped wildly through her life force. It was confusing. Her mother. All this time she was alive. Just as Kyle had been alive. But yet, according to Kyle and Geeta, her mother was dangerous.

Tears started to fall down her cheeks.

"Em…I'm really sorry to be the one to tell you, " Kyle said.

"It's just hard for me to hear this news." Emerald took a deep breath, then wiped at her tears.

He remained silent, giving her a soft kiss on her hand. "I know. That's why

I didn't want to." He took a deep breath.

As Emerald lowered the note, Kyle leaned over, taking a peek at the note over her shoulder. Emerald glanced up at him, watching his eyes as they scanned the note. His face turned dark, and his lips curled into a snarl.

"My mother sounds sincere about wanting to see me," Emerald said defensively, holding the note as if guarding it with her life.

"Don't get me wrong—she is sincere in wanting to see you. Told me so herself at dinner once. I don't question that." Kyle paused as he walked around the room in thought, then turned to her. "You got to look past all that and see her motives. I know all about it, Em. I saw her with my own eyes take a *room full* of gifted's life forces. Believe me, she is *very* serious about it, and warned me to stay the fuck out of her way."

"She said those exact words?"

"Well, not those exact words. They were more in fancy queen terms, but it is what she really meant. She also stated strongly that if I got in her way, or found you, she'd take my magic away too."

"Out of everything that you all have told me, what I find hard to believe the most is that my mother has the power to take away one's magic," Emerald said.

"What? Are you saying you don't believe me?"

"It's hard to stomach all of this, Kyle."

"Em. *Look* at me." Kyle's face was red, almost the color of his hair and eyes. "I lived twenty-seven fucking years as Rubius. I have seen magics that one would only see in their wildest dreams. A world that is so different that it's hard to believe that it is real. But it's the future." His eyes flickered like wildfire. "Believe me when I say this: Your mother stole magic, leaving helpless gifted without their gifts. I don't doubt that she will do the same to you too, regardless of how much she loves and cares for you. She wants a new world, and she will do anything to get her way."

Deep in her heart, she felt the passion and depth in his words. Sighing, she said, "Kyle…I do believe you. It's just, everything that I knew of my mother is being turned upside down."

"I know it's a hard pill to swallow." Kyle gave her a sympathetic glance, frowning.

"My mother…didn't want you to find me? How did she know about us?"

"When I was regaining my memories of Arcadia, I made a connection between her and you. I had asked her if she has a green-gifted daughter. That was when she snapped at me and threatened to take away my magic…and my cock, if I got anywhere near you." He paused. "I forgot to mention that Derek is with her too. At least, last I saw."

"So that's where he went," Geeta stated. She rose from her seat, then walked toward the viewing window, glancing out at the city in thought. "This is worse than I thought."

"You think?" Kyle said.

"If Derek is with Emerald's mother," Geeta said, "he would have the power to send her back here to take your power. Or bring you to the future."

Hearing them talk about Derek made Emerald sick. Her mother too. How was it possible that life had sunk to a new low? She had finally gotten the love of her life back, but it came with a price.

Kyle came over to her, holding her in his arms.

"Hey…it'll be all right," he said softly.

"Just hold me, Kyle. I don't want to be anywhere but here," she whispered through her tears.

His lips touched brushed her ear, then he whispered, "I will do anything and everything to protect you. Even if it means from your own mother."

"He's right," Geeta called out softly. "Kyle must stay close and protect you. We cannot let your mother nor Derek get to you or your magic." She paused. "There is one thing that we do have in our favor."

Emerald glanced at her, and Kyle asked, "And what's that?"

"The children," Geeta stated.

Emerald let out a breath, while Kyle glanced over at her with a dead-serious expression.

"When Elyathi wrote this letter begging you to come to the future, I am betting she did not know that you were pregnant. But now that Derek has gone to her, perhaps she might be aware of the children. If this is the case, I do not think she would jeopardize the babies' lives. Only the magic." Geeta eyed them. "Which is why you must be protected, My Queen."

Her heart and stomach felt sick. Really sick. Everything was out of her control, and she couldn't stop it all from happening. She didn't have that kind of power. But she needed to do *something*.

Emerald released her grip, and Kyle looked down at her.

"What is it?" Kyle asked.

"I don't want to hear any more of this. It's something that is out of my control for the time being," Emerald said. "But what I can do is be in contact with the Corporation. Be prepared for the list of parts for Drew. Quite possibly plan on retrieving the girl."

Geeta nodded. "Let me speak to Victor and the camp about the girl. I will let you know if the palace needs to intervene or if the wastelanders already have a decent plan."

"With Garrett, it's fifty-fifty. Half the time he's got a good plan, the other half it's pretty lousy," Kyle stated.

Geeta shot him a look. "I will send word soon, My Queen."

"You leaving now?" Kyle asked.

"Does that make you happy?" Geeta asked.

"Yes and no. Now I don't have anyone to give shit to."

Geeta ignored his statement and instead handed him the staff. "I took care of it while you were gone."

He waved his hand at it. "I can't take it. You should have it."

"It's yours. It's not right of me to hold on to it forever." She nudged it toward him. "Take it."

Kyle hesitated, then slowly reached out and accepted it. The orb on the staff glowed an intense red, vibrating brighter and brighter. As it did so, red lightning and fire swirled around it in motion, then slowly faded away.

"I forgot how badass this staff is."

Geeta smiled at him. "Take care. Both of you." She paused. "By the way. I left you something in the Queen's chambers."

"A present? Geeta, I don't know what to say." Kyle smiled at her.

"Don't say anything." She smirked. "You'll ruin the moment."

Emerald stood, then nodded. "Please let me know about the girl."

"I will," Geeta said. She bowed, then closed her eyes and bathed herself in a violet light.

In a flash, Geeta was gone, leaving her and Kyle alone in the dining hall once more.

CHAPTER 7

◆

VIOLET

"Sorceress Ikaria, the lords are ready to meet," Lord Jiao said, taking a bow as he averted his eyes.

"Excellent," Ikaria called out from her hot tub. She leaned back in the water, giving her body one last moment of pleasure. A handsome blond servant was in the water with her, giving her charming smile. Ikaria flashed her own devious smile, then neared him in the pool. "It's been fun," she said as she ran her hand down his chest, then playfully slapped his cheek.

Lord Jiao coughed and turned his body the other way, embarrassed.

Ikaria rose from the steamy pool, with her long violet hair streaming down her naked flesh, accentuating her curves and heavy breasts. It was frigid on her balcony patio, and the icy winds were relentless. It matched her heart—icy, cold, and calculating. "There's nothing like a good romp with a strapping blond man and a hot soak," Ikaria called out to Jiao. "Don't you agree?" Before Jiao could answer, Ikaria continued. "You do not need to answer. We all know you prefer a woman's touch."

Lord Jiao cleared his throat.

"By the way, Lord Jiao, what time is it?"

"It's high noon."

"I believe it's that time of day to once again fulfill my vow. I can't disappoint the High Court now, can I?"

"It would be a disgrace, Sorceress."

Ikaria sneered. "Yes, I quite agree." That damned Belinda and the High Court. She was *so close* to rescuing Ayera.

If you think I ruined your life before, just you wait, Derek. You and that white-gifted whore of yours. Belinda too. There will be nothing left of the lot of you the next time I return.

Ikaria stood proudly in the nude, facing the cold winds. Then she summoned her violet magic deep within her life force. The power thrummed in her veins, vibrating throughout her body. Then with a giant release, she snapped open her hands and eyes.

The violet magic shocked out across the sky. In the distance, thunder rumbled.

"What did you do?" asked the blond lord, still in the hot tub.

"I murdered another gifted in the High Court Citadel." Ikaria turned to face Lord Jiao, who was trying to not make eye contact. "This one was a cleric of the court, I do believe."

With another gesture, Ikaria wafted a gentle wave of her violet-red magic from her fingertip. Warm winds brushed against her naked flesh, drying her and her hair completely. With another wave of her fingertip, this time with her violet magic, she summoned her kimono off the bench, then flew it over to herself and put it on. The violet power continued to flow around her as it perfected the folds and retied her obi. Makeup suddenly appeared out of nowhere, reapplying where it had smudged, while the violet magic fixed her hair combs, ornaments, and jewelry.

A hand mirror floated to her, and Ikaria grasped it, inspecting her image. "There," she said approvingly as she glanced at her reflection one last time. She eyed Lord Jiao, who was still fully turned away from her. "I am ready, Lord Jiao."

Lord Jiao turned toward her with his cheeks red, bowing. He offered his arm to escort her, and she took it, just as any empress would. Taking his hand reminded her how much she missed her servant Suri.

She's probably in the bowels of the High Court Citadel, unlocking my sister's cell at this very moment.

As the two of them walked in silence toward the audience hall, Ikaria heard Lord Jiao's thoughts. He missed his gift. A strange twang of emotion stirred in her. She felt sorry for the lord. After all, he was one of the true loyalists who'd supported her in the shadows. The last time she had felt a bit of sympathy was Derek not getting his dream girl. It had now became a full-scale production, with him being a thorn in her side. He was as bad as the High Court.

"By the way, have you seen the High Priest or Lady Vala since we returned?" Ikaria asked. "They were supposed to have met me by now."

"I was given word that they were taking care of something but would be prepared to meet you at the council meeting," Lord Jiao said.

"I see." Ikaria eyed newly golden halls, thinking of the priest. Sunlight poured into the windows, reflecting the pearls, prisms, and golds everywhere. Why couldn't Auron put his prophetic words to good use when it mattered? Make the ancient machines come alive? Perhaps give her a youthful appearance? Anything but a citadel made of solid gold with precious metals. The only thing that satisfied her was that she herself resided in a golden citadel, whereas the High Court and that white bitch sat in a dilapidated one.

They came to the audience hall, with the all the members of World Sector Six's court standing, awaiting her arrival. Ikaria basked in all her glory as she strutted down the main aisle. As she passed the lords of the court, Duke Wellington gave a slight sneer. She would file away that for later.

Auron and Vala were already present, standing right next to the throne. They made eye contact, then nodded in respect as she walked up.

"Where have you been, priest?" Ikaria whispered.

"Vala and I were checking up on Oriel," he whispered back. "Can you hear my thoughts?"

"Allow me to."

Ikaria summoned her violet gift, flooding her mind. At once, their connection was completely open and established in her mind. A wave of his thoughts came through to her.

Oriel is awake, Auron's voice murmured in her mind.

Ikaria shot him a look. *And?*

He spoke of another green-gifted to Katrina. I don't know anything more than that.

Wonderful. Just what we need. We will converse about this later.

Another pause, then the two of them glanced at each other one last time, then Ikaria turned away. She then seated herself in the royal throne, waving the royal scepter. Court was now in session.

Duke Wellington rose from his seat. "Who does the sorceress think she is, taking the Empress's seat? She has her own place in court! I don't recall voting on who is the temporary regent of this sector!"

Ikaria began her address to the court, ignoring him. "Lord Jiao's sources have informed him that my sister was whisked away to a new cell after the destruction."

"Did you hear what I said, Sorceress?" the duke challenged.

Ikaria looked over at Lord Jiao. "Lord Jiao, who is this man that addresses me without any sort of priority?"

"Duke Wellington, Enchantress."

"Ah, Duke Wellington." Ikaria darted her eyes directly into the duke's. "You question my authority? I am sister to the Empress, and next in line to the throne, am I not? Unless, of course, you forgot my lineage? If you would like, I can have the historians pull the records," Ikaria stated nonchalantly.

"You were imprisoned!" he countered.

"A minor detail."

"I oppose this!"

Ikaria belted out a laugh, sending it echoing through the hall. "Who is to rule in her stead, Duke Wellington? You? One of the other lords? I think not. I am the only one who has the man parts to go after the High Court. Lest you forget, I have opposed them from the very beginning. If everyone in this sector had listened to my advice from the start, including my *sister*, we wouldn't be in this mess, would we now? In fact, we would have been developing technology if it had been up to me, and just one more step ahead of them."

"I say we have a vote," the duke challenged. "Lineage or not, the Empress still lives, which means only a temporary regent is needed right now. Besides, I heard that you just got back from the High Court—without the Empress. It seems that your plan has failed. Who knows what else might fail in the near future under your leadership."

Without another thought, Ikaria shot an invisible slap at the duke, hitting him across the face with her violet magic. Through her magic, she felt the satisfaction of the blow.

"You want to vote for a regent?" Ikaria called out. "Go ahead. *Do it.*" She glanced at the court. "Let me declare to the court that I can and will crush the High Court and get back my sister, *at all costs*. Though I was interrupted during my last attempt, it does not deter me from retrieving her another way. There are many ways to get to one goal. And have you forgotten how I slaughtered half of their gifted in the citadel? Or the fact that their very structure lies half in ruins? They are still mopping the blood off their floors and trying to make repairs. I just crushed another bug before I came to this meeting. But if you think I am not fit to be regent of this section, let's have that vote, shall we?"

Ikaria eyed the duke in a mental mind game, narrowing her eyes. She leaned back into the throne with a smug look on her face.

"Might I say something?" Auron said, addressing her and the lords.

"Ah, High Priest Auron," Ikaria said. "Always a pleasure. You may speak."

Auron sighed at her, then stood before them, skimming the crowd. "For many years, I have opposed the sorceress at every turn. She is wicked, vile, twisted, and has delusions of grandeur."

Ikaria snorted, while the lords murmured. Auron always had a sense for drama. All men did.

"That being said, she has fervor and love for our lands, and opposes the evil that permeates our land—the High Court. They have stolen what the God of Light gave us—our power. She is here to fight that, and has the power to do it. Not only that, but you all know, just as I do, that she has the most methodical mind within this sector, with ten times the knowledge of anyone else here. With her power, her willful spirit, and a mind more cunning than any other person I have ever known—who else would be fit to lead us to victory?" Auron stared them down. "Just think: Sorceress Ikaria went only with myself and Lady Vala into the lions' den. And sure, she didn't achieve rescuing her sister." His golden eyes swept across the room. "But I assure you, she *will*. And if others support her, imagine with a whole sector behind her what she can do."

The lords started talking amongst themselves, mumbling. Some nodded, some opposed.

Auron called out over the crowd. "I fully support the enchantress Ikaria being temporary regent to this sector until we get our empress back."

The court broke out into a loud noise. Lords and ladies talking over each other, each reasoning with either Auron or the duke.

Auron's speech made her heart stir. Just a little. Through the corner of her eye, Ikaria glanced at him. He turned to face her, then bowed to her in respect. Though she was surprised at his gesture, there was no chance that she would show it. Instead, she nodded back to him, holding her head high.

Lord Nyko stood, with the court hushing down. "High Priest Auron is right.

Ikaria has a love for our sector that is equal to the Empress, though she shows it much differently. I, too, support her fully."

"I have always supported her," said Lord Jiao standing. "And I continue to support her with my life."

There were more murmurs throughout the audience hall.

"I oppose the sorceress," called out another lord.

"As do I!" called out one of the ladies.

"If we choose the technology, the High Court will disown us!" called out another lord.

Ikaria stood, awaiting for everyone to quiet down. Then she spoke. "Yes, it is true. The High Court will come at this sector in any possible way and form as long as I sit on this throne," Ikaria said pointedly at the last lord's statement. "But have you forgotten what has transpired in our sector? The High Court sent Rubius to our sector to terrorize me and steal my gift, while the white-gifted stole yours! And you all seemed to follow my sister's lead in being against the High Inquisitor at that time. I plan to follow her lead by opposing the High Court—just as my sister did prior to her arrest. Just look around you." Ikaria gestured at the halls. "These golden halls are the result of my power combined with High Priest Auron's. We have the *power* to defeat the High Court." Ikaria clacked her heels as she swept down from her throne, eyeing all the lords and ladies. "One little hiccup, and you all want to run sniveling under your mothers' skirts. Well, I am not your mother. I am the enemy's worst nightmare. The High Court will get what's coming for them, you can be assured of that. And just like us, their gifted death toll will rise to record highs if they don't give me back my sister—your empress. So, what will it be? Go ahead, make your choice. Because you will only have me this once. After that, I will get my own support and go after them my own way, and I'll take my gifts with me elsewhere."

The room all peered at her. Some had eyes of disdain—some for her, others for the High Court. In most of them, Ikaria could sense their sadness, confusion over what had transpired. Some wanted revenge. She couldn't blame them.

"All those in favor of Enchantress Ikaria being regent of the sector, say aye," Auron called out.

"Aye," called out the majority of the room.

Ikaria smirked, still towering over the room as she stood proudly.

"All those who oppose," Auron called out.

There were a few "nays."

Auron looked to Ikaria. "Enchantress Ikaria will remain regent of our sector until our empress returns."

"I'm glad you all got your priorities sorted," Ikaria commented as she smoothed her tresses. "Me being royal blood and all, this was completely unnecessary. However, it is quite refreshing to hear declarations of allegiance. Now, since this whole thing became an issue—which was a complete waste of time, especially since we don't have a lot of time for what we need to do— let us waste more time by having each of you coming up and swearing your loyalty to me."

She didn't need each noble to swear to her; she heard their allegiance within their non-gifted minds loud and clear. It was much more fun proving a point to teach everyone a lesson.

Auron swiftly came up to her, then whispered, "You had to go and do this?"

"Of course. Why wouldn't I? I'm tired of the duke's games, and he needs to learn a lesson. All who opposed me do. In fact, this is a great way to show all of World Sector Six who's in charge, and that I don't put up with temper tantrums."

Auron sighed, then straightened up and headed to his spot in court.

One by one, each noble approached her, pledging their allegiance, bowing to her, then going back to their seat in court, with the next lord or lady following suit. Finally, when the line dwindled down to nothing, only Duke Wellington was left.

The duke approached her slowly, then cleared his throat. "Well, it seems others put their faith in you…"

"Speak up. I cannot hear you, duke," Ikaria said nonchalantly. "I am getting on in age, as you are well aware."

"Others put their faith in you," he said loudly. "I do not. But for the good of our sector, I will pledge my service to you."

"How thoughtful of you. At least you are honest. I don't like you either, so we are even." Ikaria then eyed the court. "Now, as first order of business, let us discuss the Empress."

A lord stood up from the crowd, and Ikaria nodded in approval for him to speak. "Sorceress, how do you plan to go about getting the Empress back?" the lord asked. "Since your first attempt didn't work out as planned, what is your new strategy?"

"Enchantress," Auron corrected him, and Ikaria darted a surprised smile at him.

"Enchantress," the lord corrected.

"Prior all that had transpired, I sent my servant Suri after High Inquisitor Rubius and his airship. My hope is that she has already retrieved the Empress after my charade with the court. My informants haven't received word of Suri yet, but that doesn't mean Suri hasn't rescued the Empress. The High Court wouldn't release that information, in order to keep up false reports within the sectors."

"Suri? She is a mere waif. What can she possibly do?" Duke Wellington called out from the audience.

Ikaria was about to strangle the man with her violet magic when Auron stepped forward. "Suri is very much capable. I was with her when she boarded the Empress's prison airship. She might appear just a meek servant, but rest assured Suri is much more than meets the eye. She has precision far sharper than anyone that I have ever seen. She moves like a skilled assassin and is well-equipped with her gift."

"Suri? She's gifted?" the duke repeated.

"Are you hard of hearing, duke? You are quite exhausting today," Ikaria said.

There were murmurs and even a few smiles.

"I just…I didn't know…"

"Of course you didn't know. Do you think a skilled servant like my Suri would just make herself known to fools such as yourself? I think not." She clutched the edge of the armrest.

The duke remained stunned as others in the chamber nodded.

Ikaria raised her chin up high, then glanced at the entire hall. "My sister will be on trial soon, and you know how fair that will be. We can count on an execution sentence. In the meantime, we must prepare."

Auron shot her a look. "Prepare for what?"

The room was silent as she narrowed her eyes. "*War.*"

Shouts erupted wildly throughout the hall, invigorating not only the nobles and all of World Sector Six. It invigorated her soul. And her revenge. There was approval, some disapproval. It didn't matter. After all, she had the ultimate say.

And war it was going to be.

Ikaria waved her scepter, and the room became silent.

"I will be sending out ambassadors to each world sector in order to gain their support—and artifacts," Ikaria announced. "I will activate all artifacts brought to me and then assign them to those who choose to join me for the storming of the High Court. We will be like the very plague that they drained us with for these many years, taking away our gifts. This time, we will be their plague. I have already started by offing one gifted per day, just as they have done to us. But it will grow into something they will be unable to manage. We will be armed with the very technology they fear most. They will weep tears of blood in their fear."

This time, Jiao stood forward, then bowed.

"Yes?" Ikaria eyed him.

"Enchantress, most of us hardly know anything about these ancient artifacts. And those who do don't know how to activate them," he pointed out.

"Excellent point. So glad you asked." Ikaria smirked proudly. "Let it be known to the court that I was given the power to understand the ancient technology when I was blessed with the gift of the black. Though I no longer possess that gift, I have retained the knowledge from that time. All artifacts found will be presented to me immediately, and I will personally activate them—if I am able to. I will not sleep until all of them are activated, as we will need them for the war."

Ikaria glanced at Auron. *Is that good enough for you, priest?*

Auron gave a hopeful look, then smiled. *It is. I am hopeful that we will get Ayera back. I'm worried they'll kill her before we get to her.*

The High Court won't do anything until she is given a proper trial.

I hope not.

Ikaria turned to the audience hall members. "Lady Vala. Arise."

Vala made her way to the front, then stood before Ikaria. She was dressed in an elaborate blue robe and adorned with gold jewelry on her neck and ears. Vala bowed, meeting her eyes. "Yes, Enchantress?"

"I need you to go to each world sector, starting with your old homeland— Sector Four. Tell Khari Ramla what all that has happened. Convince your old court to join us against the High Court. If they accept, have them start sending the artifacts to us with the help of their blue-gifted. Also, have the Khari select four other blue-gifted that he trusts to send out to the other sectors to retrieve artifacts from the other willing sectors. We must start united if we want to go against the High Court and Elyathi."

"Four? Why not five ambassadors?"

Ikaria smiled. "You don't miss a beat, do you? Yes, four. I don't want anyone going to World Sector Three. There are too many spies in the High Court's sector."

"And what of World Sector One?" Vala echoed. "There is no court, only abandoned towers scattered throughout the skies. There are no noteworthy gifted, magics, or artifacts in that sector."

Ikaria gave a half smile. "Don't go judging places that you haven't been to. Can you tell me for a fact they don't have any gifted? No magic? Nothing of importance?"

Vala looked confused. "Well, no."

"Precisely. Now stop believing everything you've been told by the High Court. Go there yourself and see if that's all true. I, for one, don't believe it for a second, and neither should you."

Vala bowed, then fervently placed her hand on her heart. "With all my passion, all my might, all my persuasion, I will do my utmost best."

"Good." Ikaria glanced at the rest of the court. "I hereby declare all technology reinstated in our sector. I want any and all artifacts that we have in our sector to be brought to me to be activated. In the meantime, I will have list drawn up for those in the assault, the leaders that will be assigned to them, and how the weapons will be designated."

The audience hall whispered loudly with excited whispers.

"You are all dismissed." Ikaria waved the scepter.

The entire court bowed to her, then parted the aisle for her as she walked toward the doors. She could hear Auron and Vala behind her.

"High Priest Auron."

He came over to her, bowing. "What is it?"

I need more information about that green-gifted.

I will update you once I know more.

Thank you. Always the dutiful one, you are.

He hinted at a smile, then left with Vala.

There was one detail left she needed to work out and plan, but it was no matter for the court. No, it was a personal and private matter.

Cyrus.

✦ ✦ ✦

After the council meeting, Vala walked out onto one of the citadel platforms. Never had she felt the weight of the world depending on her as she did now. Convince the other sectors to join a war? She was known for her silver tongue, but this? Joining the world-renowned evil sorceress to go against the High Court? It was certainly a bit of a stretch. The one thing she had been counting on was news of Ikaria's destruction of the High Court Citadel reaching the other sectors—perhaps that would sway other sectors to join them. But it also might work against them.

Vala glanced at one of the giant golden-chain bridges in the distance. The one that linked the royal citadel with a smaller island seemed so insignificant.

Taking a deep breath and closing her eyes, Vala felt her blue gift, her dimensional space magic, flowing through her body from head to toe. Opening her eyes, Vala stood on the island that she'd viewed from afar mere seconds ago. Her favorite little island.

There was a sudden gust of cool wind, blowing her dress freely in the air as if it were dancing. As the wind died down, Vala headed toward the entrance and walked through the crumbling stone structure, coming to her favorite spot where she drank her afternoon tea. Instead of her usual table and pillows, there was a small cot with her servant Katrina next to her father, former High Justice Oriel.

Vala paused in the doorway, smiling sadly. Just prior to the meeting, Oriel had awakened from his temporary insanity and spoke of a green-gifted to Katrina.

Vala recalled seeing a glimpse of a green-gifted right as she had reappeared back in the citadel, trying to save it from utter calamity. There had been so much going on at the time, so many magics, so many gifted—all fighting. Vala assumed she had imagined a blip of greenish-blue portal magic. But now? She was now convinced that it was not her imagination.

Oriel was resting, taking light and slow breaths. With the trauma of losing his gift, along with the intense battle with the white-gifted woman, it had sapped not only his mind but his energy and strength. All these years, she'd never known of her father until now. And he happened to be a high justice. Former high justice. There were so many mixed emotions within her that she couldn't even grasp them fully.

Vala clenched her teeth. *Elyathi will pay*, she thought bitterly.

Katrina neared her, bowing. "My lady."

"How is he?" Vala asked.

"He's been sleeping mostly," Katrina answered. "I offered him food, but he wouldn't take any." Her dark eyes met Vala's. "He's been adamantly asking for you when he's awake."

"Has he mentioned the green-gifted?"

Katrina frowned. "It is a man that can travel through time. He was last at the High Court Citadel."

That has to be the same man I saw.

"Vala? Is that you?" Oriel called out.

Vala and Katrina turned to him, with Vala answering, "Yes, it is."

She neared Oriel, then knelt down next to him. His eyes were weak—no longer did he have his blue-gifted eyes. He now had a natural, non-gifted appearance with deep brown eyes and black hair.

Sad and taken aback, Vala sucked in her breath. "I…I'm sorry that I couldn't save your gift."

Oriel shifted his head, studying her. "It wasn't yours to save. It was all my fault."

"But if I'd had my head on straight all these years and studied my gift instead of daydreaming of the red gift, maybe you wouldn't be where you are today, and the Empress would be back in her throne," she said bitterly.

"Oh?" Oriel raised an eyebrow in surprise. "Is that what you think? That you aren't strong in your gift?"

"Yes."

Oriel let out a weak chuckle.

"What is so funny? I'm being serious."

Vala and Katrina shifted glances at each other, with Oriel's laughter dying down. Finally, he gestured for her to take his hand. Vala reached out her hand, and he took it firmly.

"These hands…they have more power than you will admit to." He shook her hand firmly again. "In these veins is the same blood as mine—the blue gift from our ancestors. This blood, your blood, was the only blood that had the power to trump mine."

"What are you talking about?" Vala asked incredulously.

Oriel gestured for her to come closer, so Vala leaned in. "For years, I hid the portals to Arcadia in the hope that no one would find them. But you, *you* were curious. You scried time as you grew up, did you not?"

"Um, yes…"

His dark eyes shot her a look. "Scrying time is hard in itself for any blue-gifted—not to mention visiting the past."

Vala blinked. She had no words. "Scrying time is *hard*?"

Oriel laughed again, this time louder. "My dear, it takes years of practice for a blue-gifted to achieve it."

"If it's so difficult to achieve, then why outlaw it?"

"To stave off a few that could," he said. "I also didn't want the portal to be seen—even by the High Court." He paused. "But as you visited other times, you unknowingly 'reset' the space-time continuum with your power. This allowed the sorceress to find the portal to Arcadia—and ultimately you and the other gifted to battle Ikaria. I had been hiding that portal for years. Unfortunately it's now known to the others, so my attempt was all in vain."

Vala met his eyes, sucking in her breath. "You were *countering* them?"

"I hadn't always; I truly believed in their cause for a long time. But over the years, my heart…it changed." He paused, then frowned.

Vala grabbed his hand, then the two of them exchanged soft smiles. "Please, I do not hold anything against you. I do know a thing or two of people dealing with their past. For isn't it my gift?"

Oriel looked surprised, then chuckled lightly. "You definitely didn't get your humor from me."

She giggled in return, then leaned in. "Father…what really happened to you back at the citadel?"

Oriel sighed, then met her eyes. "The green-gifted…" He paused. "I knew he was going to be at the High Court Citadel at a certain point in time. But I also knew if I didn't interfere with the event, his life force would be acquired by the High Court. The High Court had poisoned me, but I sent myself through the space-time continuum, freezing myself and casting the spell for me to unfreeze at that very moment in time where the green-gifted would show up."

Vala's eyes went wide. "To have him heal you…"

Oriel nodded. "…and to stop the High Court from capturing him."

"Then you must have succeeded," Vala said. "I know of this man. I saw him leave this time through a portal after you were injured."

Oriel sighed with relief. "Good. It is imperative that he stays far away from this time—that blue-gifted and Elyathi. That green-gifted is linked to many outcomes that could lead to much destruction if the High Court has his gift."

Vala nodded, then gripped his hand in reassurance. "I'm sure he's long gone."

"Let us continue to pray for his safety."

"I will." Vala smiled. "Get lots of rest while I'm away."

"Oh?" Oriel's head shifted. "Where are you off to?"

"To the other sectors to gather the ancient technology," Vala stated. "Ikaria has outright declared war on the High Court."

"That is not surprising."

"I'll say."

"Katrina will take good care of you while I'm away. I don't know when I'll return. It could take time convincing the other sectors to hand over their artifacts."

His face turned grave, then he nodded. "Vala…" he whispered softly, waving his hand, gesturing for her to come closer. "There is something that only you can do with your gift. You and *only* you. Listen to what I am about to say, for it is the most important thing you need to know above all else."

"What is it?"

"If time were to collapse…"

"If time were to *collapse*?" she interrupted.

His eyes met hers, continuing. "If you see time fall upon itself, it is imperative that you find a man in the time rift and *get* to him. You will only have moments to get to him before all is lost. This man's magic will save you," he said. "If you don't find him during this possible calamity, then the entire world is doomed to Elyathi's final outcome. *Forever.*"

"I don't understand. Time collapsing?" Vala said.

"I saw it for myself within the flow of time—before I lost my gift." Oriel's eyes glimmered with tears. "It is the only hopeful future left if the High Court were to collect the remaining powers. It is what I saw in *one* outcome. *Only one* that can save us from Elyathi's new world."

"Who is this man? What's his name? What does he look like?" Vala pressed.

"He is gifted." Oriel sighed. "I haven't much else to tell you, but I do know this: You will know him the moment you see a *lack* of magic."

"Lack of magic? What does that mean?"

"I am sorry I cannot be of more help. That is all I know," Oriel whispered. "You must go now. Time is short, as you know, and Ikaria is impatient. She might decide to change her plans once more and leave World Sector Six if you don't get her what she asks."

Vala nodded. "That's the truth," she said, placing a hand on her heart. She leaned over, then rested a hand on his forehead. "Goodbye, Father."

"Until we meet again, child," he whispered. His eyes were weary, slowly closing.

Vala took a step back, then took one final glance at Oriel. Her father.

The entire world will be doomed? Vala sighed. More weight upon her shoulders. As if she didn't have enough. Get all the sectors to join a war? Time falling upon itself? And now only she could get to some gifted man who had a lack of power to save the world from one outcome?

The impossible was being asked of her.

Vala glanced one last time at her father, then turned away.

How was she ever going to convince other sectors to join a war?

CHAPTER 8

◆

ORANGE

Suri watched in silence as she studied one of the nearby islands, its silhouette eclipsing the sunset. Jude stood next to her, squinting his eyes, doing the same. She placed her hand gently over her tunic where the vial containing the enchantress's blood rested. It was safe. It was the only thing she had left of Ikaria.

The two had been fortunate to land on an island after their fall from the High Court airship. It wasn't a long fall, but definitely a lucky fall considering where they had landed. But what aggravated Suri the most was that she'd failed the enchantress by not saving the Empress. She was determined to remedy that.

Jude sighed. "I know I shouldn't complain, but it's hard not to. I'm tired, Mistress Suri." He glanced out into the vast horizon of scattered floating islands that dotted the skies, then slumped down to the ground. "I've prayed for a way off this island, and have no answers."

"I am still thinking how to best proceed, Master Jude," Suri said. "It seems that island over there is getting closer to us as time passes."

"I noticed," he said, his golden eyes focused on the nearby island. "I wonder if there is something on it that could be useful? An old airship? Maybe even an old established portal to port us elsewhere?"

"I hope so." Suri held out her hand. Slowly, with the use of her orange magic combined with some violet, Suri drew the moisture toward her hands, then transmuted it to water, taking a precious drink. Then she did it again, crouching down and offering it to Jude.

Jude carefully took a drink from her cupped hand, then breathed a sigh of relief. "Thank you. I needed that."

"I'll get some food for us," she said.

Suri headed toward a grassy clearing. How were they to get off the island? Suri had pondered it ever since they had fallen upon it. Even with Jude's protection magic, they were too far up to make any sort of daring jump to the earth below. Though the priest was strong in his gift, it wouldn't protect them from their ultimate doom. Just as Jude had pointed out, she had hoped there was something on the next island that could aid them.

Suri came upon the glen, kneeling and plucking as many strands of grass as she could until her hand was full. When she was satisfied, Suri summoned a swift jolt of orange magic, infusing it into the grass blades. Suddenly, they shifted, then assimilated together like dough. Then, with another burst of her magic, the dough rose, forming itself into hot bread, as if it had come out of the oven. Suri then grabbed the hem of her yukata and pulled it up to her waist, exposing her legs. After placing the hot bread in the folds of her robe, she walked back to Jude.

As she approached, Jude smiled. This wasn't the first time she had transmuted grass into bread, and he knew exactly what she had in the folds of her robe.

"You read my mind. I'm starving!" he said with a smile.

"I did, in fact, Master Jude. You were in need of substance," she said, revealing the bread. Suri pulled a chunk from the bread, handing it to Jude.

He devoured the hot bread, opening his mouth to cool it down as he ate. "Umgph…if's haht."

Suri eyed him, not breaking a smile. "You will burn your tongue."

"Iffs aw wight," he continued as he choked down the food.

The pair of them ate and drank conjured water as they stared off at the nearby island. It seemed like the island had been nudging itself nearer to them since she went to the clearing. The sun was dropping fast, and the air was getting frigid. Jude shivered.

"We should get some sleep," Suri said. "Let's head to the grove."

Jude nodded as he stuck his hands under the armpits of his robes. Suri was grateful that at least they both were clothed with decent robes. Otherwise they'd be frozen by now. There was only so much she could transmute with what little was on the island.

The grove wasn't exactly a grove that one would imagine. Both referred to it as a grove, but in reality, it was just three small trees arranged in a triangle. The pair of them were able to fit between the trees, finding a little shelter against the wind. She had transmuted a few coverings for them to keep warm. The problem was there just wasn't enough substance to transmute for them to have proper shelter.

Night had already fallen, and the first stars of twilight were visible. Jude randomly cast his golden light, trying to clear any last-minute annoyances such as rocks and twigs before he made himself comfortable within the blankets before extinguishing his light.

"Good night, Mistress Suri," Jude said.

"Good night, Master Jude."

Suri wrapped herself in her own set of blankets, shivering in silence. As she was nodding off, she heard the murmur of Jude's prayers, with a shimmer of golden light coming from his folded hands.

✦ ✦ ✦

Dawn's early light came piercing through their tiny grove, waking Suri. Her face was numb from the windchill, her bones ached from the cold, and her fingers were frozen. They needed fire.

With her blankets still wrapped around her, Suri got up, fixing them to allow her to walk. Glancing down at Jude, she decided to let him sleep through the early morning. They needed all their strength in order to survive.

Suri headed back to the glen. The thought of picking more grass made her ache on the inside, but the thought of dying on the island with the enchantress's blood renewed her strength. She traveled farther than she had previously, coming upon an untouched patch of grass. After collecting what she needed, Suri transmuted two small loaves of bread, then headed back to Jude. The young man was awake and huddled in a ball of light, praying.

Suri turned her head upon seeing the golden light. It was known that if one stared into a priest's golden light from prayers, they would lose their eyesight permanently. Suri had seen it firsthand. And the deeper a yellow-gifted priest was in prayer, the more holy damage it would inflict on the spectator. It wasn't at random; it was because the holy power searched any witness for any unholy thing in their heart. And if the magic found an impurity of the heart, damage would be inflicted.

Jude must have heard her approaching, because she no longer heard his voice, and the glimmer of gold that was in the corner of her eye faded away.

"Thank the God of Light!" he said through his chattering teeth as Suri approached. "I need some sort of warmth."

Suri handed him the warm bread, and he smiled. "I would have been dead by now if it weren't for you," he said as he took a bite. His face melted into satisfaction as the warm bread hit his lips.

"I would have been too, if it weren't for your protection. I would have been flattened like a breakfast pastry," Suri said. She took a bite of her bread. It was uplifting to her spirits.

"Do you ever have weird dreams?" Jude asked as he shoved another chunk of bread in his mouth.

"No. I can't recall the last time I had a dream."

Jude's eyes went wide, then he shrugged. "I get them a lot. But it comes with the territory of being a yellow-gifted, I suppose."

It seemed that Jude wanted to talk about his dream, but Suri didn't want to delve into it. She gave no hint of emotion. "I suppose you are correct. It is probably part of the yellow gift's power."

It was true. She hardly ever dreamed. It had been years since she'd had a dream. The idea of dreams, fantasies…it was too abstract for her. She didn't like the idea of being led by emotions and dreams. Those who acted on such fantasies ended up making terrible choices.

"Have you checked on the nearby island?" Jude asked.

"I have not. I went straight to the clearing when I awoke."

They both exchanged glances, then Jude cracked a smile. "Shall we?" he asked.

Suri nodded, rising to her feet. As they walked toward the edge of the island, both were munching on their warm bread. Occasionally Suri would hold out her hand, transmute the air into water, both of them drinking from her cupped hand. Jude drinking out of her hand secretly disgusted her—any person that wasn't the enchantress gave her the shivers. But she very well couldn't let Jude die of thirst.

As they neared the edge of the island, Jude gasped, and Suri paused in her tracks. The other island had definitely gotten closer during the night, but it wasn't what they were in awe about.

"Mistress Suri!" Jude exclaimed, pointing to a black shape against the shining sun.

It was an airship.

Jude started dancing with excitement, spinning in circles. "Finally! An airship! Praise the God of Light!"

"Finish your bread and get ready," Suri said. "We are getting on that airship."

Jude shoved the remainder of his bread in his mouth, still laughing with excitement. "What you phamming on doing?" he asked with his mouth full.

"I will use my violet magic and fling us to the ship," Suri said. "You must be ready to grab on to the ship in case the magic drops us short of the deck."

Jude swallowed. "Okay." He focused his eyes. "I'll cast a shield around us."

The pair waited as the airship got closer. Occasionally, Suri would funnel some violet magic toward the ship, forcing it to come toward their direction. Though it was possible that the ship was on a course to fly over them, Suri didn't want to take any chances. But she couldn't waste all her energy on nudging the ship toward them. They needed the ship's attention.

Suddenly forming an idea, Suri funneled her illusion magic around and into her body. The orange magic glimmered around her, shimmering with orange flecks of light until the sparks died down.

"You look…not as pretty," Jude said, wide-eyed. "And without the gift."

"That is the plan."

Jude flushed, then made a sign of the Spectrum with his hand over his chest. "God of Light, forgive me for being unpriestly…"

"It is fine, Master Jude. You only speak the truth." Suri glanced at the airship nearing them. "It's best to mask my gifted appearance, for both our sakes. Do not reveal me being gifted at all costs."

"I won't."

"All right, I want you to build the largest shield of protection you can. It is the only way to get their attention."

Jude nodded, meeting her eyes.

"A word of caution, Master Jude. We must be prepared if this ship is aligned with the High Court."

Jude smiled. "I'm always on my guard."

"Very well."

They waited in silence, with Jude's stomach intermittently giving loud rumblings. He looked embarrassed, but Suri didn't say anything. That bread couldn't fill the void of a growing young man's stomach, but hopefully they'd resolve that soon.

As the ship neared, Suri gave him the signal.

"Now," Suri hissed.

The boy closed his eyes, then began to pray in the priest language. Suri closed her eyes. There was a burst of hot air around her skin, followed by a cold wind.

There was a long silence as Suri waited for Jude to give her clearance to open her eyes.

"I think it worked! The ship is veering toward us!" Jude exclaimed.

Suri opened one eyelid, noticing that Jude's light was gone. She opened both her eyes to see the airship. Indeed, it was approaching.

They waited, watching the airship inch its way to their island. Finally, it was close enough for her and Jude to move to the island's edge. There was a whole ship's crew at the edge of the airship deck, with a man at the center wearing a grand fashionable hat.

"You there! Are you stranded?" the man spoke with a booming voice.

Suri stepped forward, still masked in her orange magic as an unattractive woman. "Indeed, sir. We have been on this island for many days now," she called out. "We would be most obliged if you could give us a ride to whatever destination you have charted. We can make do from there."

The man took his hat off, then bowed properly. "Of course, m'lady."

A rope ladder dropped from their ship down to the isle. Jude grasped onto the ladder, then smiled at her. "I'm glad that worked out," he said under his breath.

"Speak no more of this. And do not let your guard down, Master Jude. We don't know these people."

"I'll protect you if needed," he said. Then he started climbing the rope.

Suri took a deep breath, then headed up the ladder. Though the boy was in the prime of his youth at seventeen, he seemed slow to get up the ladder—from the lack of nourishment if Suri were to guess. Every few steps, Suri paused, waiting for him to climb, until finally they made it to the deck.

As Suri climbed onto the deck, she immediately eyed her surroundings for any possible traps. The crew on board were mostly men, with a few muscled women scattered about.

The man with the fancy hat handed them a waterskin. "You must be thirsty."

"Thank you so much, kind sir," Jude said. He took it and drank as much as he could, then handed it to her.

Suri finished the waterskin, then handed it back to the captain. "Thank you, sir. We had little water while stranded. We are most obliged."

"You're welcome, m'lady." As he accepted the empty skin, Suri noticed that he had sparkling red eyes. For a gifted man to be sailing the skies meant that he was working for someone of importance.

"So, a priest and a woman, out on an isle in the middle of no-man's sky," he continued. "Not sure I want to know your story," he joked.

The crewmates howled with laughter.

Jude blushed. Suri didn't flinch. "We were passengers on another ship, sir," she said. "I had been leaning over the railing. I misjudged and slipped overboard. If it hadn't been for this priest here"—Suri eyed Jude—"I would have fallen to my death. His protection magic saved my life."

The captain smiled, then nudged Jude. "See, mates? Priests can be of use," he jested. More laughter. "Now quit your gawking and get to work!" he roared at them.

The crew dispersed, and the captain motioned for them to follow. "You're hungry, I suppose?"

"Very much," Jude said.

The captain smiled. "Well, let's remedy that. I'll get the cook to whip you up something to eat."

They both followed the captain inside the ship, then down the stairs. The halls were cramped, and they squeezed shoulders with the crew as they passed by.

"What sector are you from, sir?" Suri asked.

"Sector Two. This ship goes to and from the prison mines," he stated.

Far off from World Sector Two, Suri thought. Considering they had fallen shortly after they took off from their own Sector Six, the ship wasn't even in the path toward World Sector Two.

They reached the galley, and the captain stopped. "Two meals," the captain yelled into the kitchen.

"Captain, don't you want to eat?" the cook called out.

"Ah, you're right. Three, then," the captain said, knocking twice against the frame of the door. "Get me an ale while you're at it."

Suri side-eyed the cook, who smiled at her. She turned away as the three of them headed down the hall until they came into a spacious room with a few wooden tables and chairs.

"Have a seat," the captain said.

Suri took her seat in silence while Jude happily accepted. As Jude and the captain started making small talk, Suri gulped down another waterskin as she glanced at her surroundings. There wasn't anyone else in the room, but occasionally she saw crewmates pass by the door. She was beyond the point of exhaustion and looked forward to any substance in her body. She could smell the food coming from the kitchens, which was toying with her stomach and senses.

"Ah, here are our meals now!" the captain boomed.

Jude's eyes went wide with delight as his stomach rumbled loudly. "Meat!"

The captain laughed. "Nothing like a good slab of roasted salt meat smothered in garlic and rosemary," the captain said proudly, gulping at his mug of ale, sending it spilling down his beard. He wiped his beard, and Suri noted the rings on his fingers. All ten had rings. All were marked with different insignias.

I knew it.

The cook and two men placed the trays before them, then saluted to the captain.

"Dismissed." He gestured at them to leave.

"Yes, Captain." As the cook left, he knocked on the door frame twice.

"Let's eat!" he stated. The captain grabbed his fork and knife, starting to dig into his meal, with Jude doing the same.

Suri grasped her fork and shot a wave of violet magic in it, then flung it across Jude's tray so fast that it startled them both.

"What's the matter?" Jude asked.

"Do not eat this food. It is tainted," Suri hissed.

The captain jumped out of his seat, narrowing his eyes. "Tainted? Now why would you say that?" the captain snarled.

Suri swiftly swept one of her legs under the captain's legs, relying on an old fighting technique she had been trained in at an early age. It worked, and the big man was knocked to the ground. Relying on him being befuddled, she then sent a giant wave of force magic to the captain, locking him magically in place.

Suddenly, her illusion magic was dispelled from her body, her true appearance returning.

The captain struggled against her orange magic, though it was the violet force magic inside of her that she used. The rugged man tried to speak, but Suri searched his coat, finding an enchanted dagger.

"What is going on, Mistress Suri?" Jude asked, still confused.

"We were about to be drugged," she said.

Jude looked dumbfounded; the poor young man was too innocent at times.

"The two knocks. It was a sign for the cook to poison us," she explained, then loosely grabbed the captain's hand, pointing to a ring. "Recognize this?"

Jude sucked in a breath. "The High Court's insignia."

"We are nowhere near World Sector Two. I am sure they were on their way to the High Court. I wouldn't be surprised if word had already gone out for a bounty on our heads when they discovered what happened while the Empress was en route to her prison."

The captain continued to struggle. Suri sensed he was trying to use his magic.

"Captain," a crewmate called out. The door jiggled. "Captain?"

The captain grunted, and Jude and Suri glanced at each other.

"What are we going to do?" Jude asked.

"I will handle this," Suri answered. She channeled the dark side of her orange magic. Her throat twisted in pain, but she remained still. Jude watched with concern, then the pain in her throat subsided.

"Captain?" someone called out from behind the door.

"We're fine," Suri answered in the voice of the captain. The man shot her an angry look, and Jude smiled with satisfaction.

"Is everything okay in there?"

"I said we're fine!" Suri boomed.

"Why is the door locked?" the voice persisted.

"Just wanted some privacy," Suri grumbled in the captain's voice.

There was a brief moment of silence, then the door jiggled again. "I'm coming in." This time, it was the cook's voice.

A burst of hard red-magic winds pushed at the door, busting it from its hinges. There stood the cook, his hands full of fire.

Jude immediately cast a golden shield of protection around them as fire blasts smashed against their shields. It was just in time, as the fire fizzled out as it made contact.

The captain made loud grunting noises as the cook sent another wave of fiery blasts toward them. Jude's shield protected them once again, with the fire blasting by them. But behind them, a cloth banner caught fire. And it lit up quick.

The cook suddenly realized what he had done, then blasted water at it, but the fire spread too quickly.

Jude jerked his head to her. "The whole ship will burn!"

The captain, still being held down with her force magic, grunted loudly.

The cook panicked, sending more water toward the flames.

"Follow me, quickly," Suri hissed.

The cook sent another wave of water, but Suri opened the mess hall window, creating a wave of wind that fed the flames. They roared higher, and the captain screamed through the force magic.

Suri climbed out the window, with Jude doing the same. The flames were visible on the outside of the ship. There were screams and shouts of panic.

"We should put out the fire," Jude said.

"No. They are our enemies. Let them burn with their ship," Suri said.

Jude frowned but didn't protest. "This will just like last time," he said with defeat. "But now there will be no isle to save us…"

Suri eyed below. The boy was right. Just empty skies and the earth's surface far below. She wasn't sure his shield could save them from that fall…

She had an idea. One that she had considered before getting off the island. It was extremely risky, but it was the only option they had.

"Cast a bubble of protection around us."

"But…I don't think it will protect us from that fall!"

There was a blast from the other side of the ship, and huge flames rose, rocking the ship hard.

"Quickly!" she hissed.

A golden light enveloped them; this time it wasn't so bright that she had to shield her eyes. Behind them, the fire raged on. There were crackles of flames, with chunks of the ship falling to the earth.

Suri channeled her orange magic into the shield, pouring it all around it. Her orange magic embraced Jude's magic, seeping into the bubble, turning it completely orange.

"When I say, hold your breath as long as you can."

Jude clutched the airship tightly, then Suri said, "Now!"

Jude took a breath.

Then she sent a shockwave of transformation magic over Jude's bubble. It turned dark, and the ship disappeared. It felt like gravity shot through Suri's stomach and into her throat.

Concentrating on her life force, Suri sent out another wave of orange magic. Suddenly the dark bubble turned to a hollow iron ball. Her stomach dropped again as their iron ball of protection fell to the earth with even greater speed.

"I can't breathe in here!" Jude panicked.

Neither could she.

"Cast…another…wave of protection upon us," she uttered in the darkness of the iron ball. "When we hit the ground, it will be hard, and we might be smashed on the inside…"

Golden light appeared, and Suri's head began to feel weightless.

She was going to vomit or pass out of lack of air. The boy looked about to do the same.

Suddenly her body was thrown against the iron wall hard, and she heard a crack as she released her magic.

CHAPTER 9

♦

GRAY

*T*ime is running out! You must get up, Victor!

Victor gazed at the gray skies rumbling violently above him. The voice came from the heavens, but there was no one there. Just violent gray storms in this gray world that he was in. His body felt heavy, like rocks, leaving him unable to move.

Get up!

The urgency of the voice gave him reason to try. Victor struggled as he rolled over onto his back, then pushed with his arms with all of his might, attempting to get to his knees.

In response, the earth quaked violently with loud groans, knocking him completely on his back. To the side, the ground made a loud crack, then began to split apart.

The sin of the world must be eradicated...the sadness, the pain, and the suffering... Elyathi's voice echoed across the skies. *The Spectrum of Magic will sweep over the world in a way that none will have ever known, for no one is like me.*

There was a scream that echoed the heavens. Emerald.

Scrambling to his feet, Victor pushed his muscles with all his might just to stand. The earth was sapping him of his energy. Or had gravity changed its own laws? He couldn't get his bearings.

"Emerald?" Victor shouted.

The sky turned upside down and started melding with the earth. The earth began funneling up to the sky like a flowing river, slowly draining away, making the upside-down sky larger than before. Loud thundering and crackling noises sounded as the sky swelled across the face of the earth…or what was left of it.

The upside-down sky liquefied, melting into a stream that flowed into oblivion, where there was no earth left. The liquid gray sky shifted into a color—*blue*. A deep, dark blue. So blue that it appeared the color of midnight. As the midnight blue flowed into the nothingness, the color deepened to the purest black Victor had ever seen. The blackened stream poured its wrath upon the earth, flooding the space with evil.

Use your magic! called out the heavenly powerful voice.

Victor shook with fear. "I don't know how…"

It's been dwelling inside of you all this time. You must face what you fear most.

"I don't know if I am strong enough," Victor confessed.

I made you as I made iron. Strong to stand against the evil that permeates the Spectrum of Magic. Balance is lost, and now another one has strayed and will cause even more suffering. You must put a stop to this before all is destroyed.

"But how? How am I to stop this from happening?" Victor called out.

As quick as the words left his lips, darkness took hold of him, and his body was immobile.

You are the only one…

Victor cried out, but no one heard him. The light was gone. All he could do was watch as the liquefied earth, sky, time, and space melted away. There were strange wisps of magic in the nothingness that began to form from the liquefied black magic. This time it was white magic.

It is done, declared a voice. But this voice didn't come from the natural heavens.

It is time, said another voice. That was Elyathi's voice.

Victor cried out in horror. It was too late. The white void swept across the earth…

✦ ✦ ✦

He was awoken by a hard slap.

Victor gasped loudly. "Where am I?"

"Outside the refuge."

The air felt cold, making him shiver. Sweat ran down his forehead.

"Cold?" a familiar feminine voice called out.

"Very cold." His teeth began to chatter, and he felt goose bumps forming.

"Strange. The wind is pretty warm." It was Reila's voice. He could smell cigarette smoke, followed by the wind against his skin. It wasn't warm at all, at least not to him. Victor tried to focus his eyes. A blur of golds, oranges, and browns filled his eyes, though he couldn't see any details. But he could see *color*. He knew he was seeing the evening sky, with wisps of hot pink clouds soaking in the last of the sun's rays. But it all looked like a watercolor painting, one that a child would messily paint. Even though he couldn't see any of the details, he was thankful to be out of that hellish gray nightmare. Color never looked so beautiful until now.

Victor ran his hand against the side of his face, flinching. It stung where Reila had smacked him.

"You could have shook me until I woke up," he said.

Another puff of smoke. "Tried that, but it didn't work, and I had to get you to shut up."

"Shut up?"

Reila snorted. "You were yelling like a banshee. You could wake the dead with volume like that. I couldn't take it anymore. That's when I dragged your butt out here, hoping some sunlight would do you good."

Victor shivered again. "How long was I out?"

"Too long if you ask me."

His strange gray vision kept echoing in his head. The Spectrum of Magic was about to be completed once again, but in a way that had never been done before. A way that would change all of time and earth. And of all people, it had to be her. The one he had thought and cared about all these years.

Was it true? Could it be? Was his dream warning him of the future? Elyathi was alive in his dream. *It can't be. It's not possible.* And what of Queen Emerald? Was she in danger once more?

Victor gazed at the hot pinks and oranges, all swirling around him. Still, the details had not materialized before him. He had *magic*. True magic. He was a gifted. A gifted that didn't know what his magic did, nor how to even use his power.

"Reila, what happened while I was out? How did we end up here? Last I knew, we were deep out in the wastelands. Where's the Olympian army?"

"You used your fairy magic, allowing us to push Olympia back to the hellhole they crawled out of."

"I don't remember using any magic."

"Well, you did. When you were in your gray berserker mode, no one with magical abilities could cast magic around you. It was pretty damn cool."

Victor paused at her words. Why couldn't he remember any of that? Was that when he'd been locked in his gray nightmare?

Another shiver ran down his spine.

"Let's get you inside."

"Please."

Victor made it to his feet with his knees shaking, his legs like jelly.

"Whoa, big guy. Let me help you."

Then Reila's chiseled arms were around him, helping him sit up. More colors blurred in front of him. He turned to where he felt Reila next to him, still supporting his weight. She looked like a big splotch of paint against the muddled sky, her brown hair and brown eyes set against tanned skin mixed with her body tattoos, all one big mess.

"Thank you, Reila," he said.

"Don't get soft on me, Victor. I'll help you get inside. Looks like you need it."

He smirked, feeling refreshed by her hard sense of humor. "Is everyone still at the refuge?"

"If you mean everyone in the camp, then yes, they are. Honestly, we're all tired of being here. There's only so much we can take of that damn cave."

Elyathi...

Victor rubbed his head, trying to focus on Reila's face, but it seemed it was a lost cause. "Since I've been...out, have you heard anything about the former queen?" He suddenly lost his balance, leaning into her body as she held him firmly upright.

"*Former* queen? You mean the 'harlot of Illumina'?"

"Not that one. The queen of Arcadia."

Reila raised an eyebrow, taking another drag of her cigarette through her pursed lips. "Queen Elyathi? Didn't she die many years ago?"

"Yes..."

Reila eyed him suspiciously. "Are you okay? She's been in the grave for how many years now? I'm not some sort of medium. I thought you knew me better than that."

"Never mind," Victor breathed. "Just a strange dream, that's all." Victor tried to stand up straighter but stumbled a bit. Reila's support tightened. "I want to see the others. I need to know everything that's happened."

Reila sucked in her breath. "There's so much to say. No use blabbing out here. Let's save it for inside."

His eyes immediately darted to hers, but it was no use. His eyes still were out of focus, her face orangish in the light of dusk.

Victor motioned to Reila, indicating that he was ready. She took a final drag of her smoke, then dropped the butt, smashing it into the ground with her boot. His feet were heavy like weights and his mind lethargic as she guided him. If he could, he would go back to sleep, but there was no chance of that now. With every step, it heightened his anxiety over what had transpired while he was out cold. Had many of the wastelanders perished during the battle?

As they went through the caverns, many of the camp members passed by. Some said words of relief to him, thankful he was awake. Others gasped in astonishment. Faces were still a blur, and the darkness of the caverns didn't help.

They came to his tent, and there was a woman right outside it. She perked up when she noticed them.

"Victor. You're awake," Geeta said.

"Geeta," he breathed. The two exchanged smiles, then patted each other on the back.

"When I arrived, I was told you were still out cold," she continued.

"I was tired of watching him yell, so I woke him up," Reila said indifferently. "Guess it worked."

"Reila has a way of doing things," Victor said. "Always ends up physical."

"I have to admit, I was a bit worried you wouldn't wake from your trance," Geeta said. "Sorry I had to tie you to that vehicle."

"You did *what*?" Victor eyed her, then turned toward Reila. "You didn't tell me that."

Reila smirked. "At least it's all over with, eh?"

Victor shook his head, then wobbled, with Reila yanking him upright.

"Let's get you in your tent," she said.

The three of them entered the tent, and Victor settled down on his favorite sitting pillow. When everyone was situated, Reila explained everything that happened while he was out, with Geeta chiming in occasionally. The red-gifted boy. Queen Emerald in her trance. His magical gray state allowed the wastelanders to push Olympia back to their city. As news about Drew and Gwen was relayed to him, Victor's heart sank. Telly, Garrett, and Scion were compiling a list for the Arcadian Corporation.

"I need to see Drew," Victor said.

"That is one of the reasons why I came," Geeta said. "I was hoping that my healing could help him. I also wanted to know if you were okay."

Victor sighed. "Physically, I'll live. But otherwise?" He eyed Geeta. "Can I talk to you for a moment?"

Reila sat back on her pillow casually.

Victor raised an eyebrow at her. "*Privately.*"

"Whatever. I was leaving anyway," Reila said indifferently, getting to her feet and leaving the tent.

When the two of them were finally alone, Victor sucked in his breath, then met Geeta's intense violet eyes. "Geeta, I witnessed events while in my trance. Ones that I believe to be true."

Geeta's face remained serious. "Go on."

"In my vision, Queen Elyathi was *alive*. She sought to complete the Spectrum of Magic. I saw Queen Emerald being led away by her mother, wanting to be reunited with her. But it led to the utter destruction of our earth and time as we know it." Flashes of the vision came and went in his mind. "I can't shake this vision," Victor said, meeting Geeta's gaze. "None of it makes sense. Elyathi died many years ago."

Geeta remained silent for a moment, then spoke. "Queen Elyathi is alive. She is living in the future, working with the High Court."

Victor's heart sank into the pit of his stomach. "She is in the *future*?"

Geeta's head beaded with sweat as she wiped it, careful not to remove her bindi in the process. "I don't know exactly how she came to be in the future. During the battle in the wastelands, and while you were in your trance, there was a blue-gifted from the future that tried to kidnap Queen Emerald. They delivered a note—from Elyathi to Emerald." Geeta looked at him. "She wanted

Emerald to go to the future."

His nightmare was on the verge of coming true. "Emerald can't. If she does, it is the start of the entire calamity."

"We must ensure that she does not." Geeta glanced at him. "I do not think she would want to leave anyway, now that Kyle is with her."

Victor's head jolted, and his eyes went wide. "Kyle is *back*?"

Geeta gave a small smile. "He had been living in the future as a different person. His memories were restored, then he managed to show up back in Arcadia. Unfortunately for me, I have to listen to all his belly-aching. It seems that even death couldn't hold him in place."

"Son of a gun," Victor breathed.

"Perhaps this is the very reason that the Gods of the Spectrum brought him back to life," Geeta continued. "To keep Emerald safe."

"I hope so." He crossed his arms in distress, then flicked back his long gray dreads.

"I believe so. There is always a reason for everything," she said. Geeta was about to stand up, but she paused, then turned back to him. "What is it?"

Everything.

Victor looked away. "In my vision, it was apparent that I'm supposed to stop Elyathi from completing the Spectrum of Magic." His face toughened. "I don't even know how to use my magic, let alone stop her. And to find out she is in the future? The worst of it is that I have a strong feeling that events are going to fall into place quickly. If that's the case, our world will be gone forever because I cannot wield my magic."

Geeta crouched down, placing a hand on Victor. "I will do my best to teach you what I know. There are no guarantees that you will learn anything from me since I myself know nothing about gray magic, but I will do my best."

"Thank you, Geeta. I mean it."

"Let's find Telly. See how she's doing—and Drew. I know that the Queen is anxious about getting him repaired and finding Gwen."

Victor stumbled slightly as he rose to his feet. "Let's go."

CHAPTER 10

◆

ORANGE

Her soul was broken beyond repair. Drew was hanging on by a mere thread at two percent capacity. Gwen had been taken. Everything Telly loved and cared for had been ripped from her. All that remained of her was an empty shell.

Before, Telly had a sliver of hope of rescuing Gwen, but that was when Drew's awareness was intact and his readings were steady. Telly hoped that once he was repaired, they would go and get their daughter. With him now incapacitated, her hope had abandoned her. She was a walking corpse, doing what she could do to help Drew between her steady stream of tears.

Earlier in the day, Scion reported to her that Drew's readings had improved with his new adjustments. And with Queen Emerald backing new parts for Drew, it gave her strength, but at the same time, it gave her a hard dose of reality regarding the long road ahead of her.

I will murder every single one of those Olympians. Tears streamed down her cheeks at the thought. This was all their fault.

Telly wiped her watery eyes behind her glasses with the cowl from her turtleneck sweater as she emptied the remainder of the vial into the machine. Slowly the vial's contents infused with the other compounds. The machine began spinning the concoction as Telly watched. On the faceplate of the machine, the reading appeared. Satisfied with the numbers displayed, she turned away.

Her stomach churned, making her cry all over again. All she wanted to do was scream. Scream and cry. Maybe if she did it enough, Gwen would just reappear before her eyes and Drew would be fixed. The two loves of her life; she would lose them both if something didn't change. Already, her soul felt void. There was nothing but emptiness, fury, and sorrow. Her life was meaningless without them.

She glanced back at the machine as it spun her concoction. She would do anything to get her daughter back.

I swear on my life and soul that I will bring down all of Olympia to get you back, Gwen. I will tear that city-kingdom apart, inch by inch. I will destroy everything in my path!

She would get stronger. Physically. Mentally. And *magically*. Whatever it took to bring home her daughter safely.

From the corner of her eye, a vibrant yellow light glowed. Turning toward it, she saw Scion standing over Drew. The cyborg was focusing his magical yellow energy around Drew, creating a barrier around him. With a jerk of his hand, the barrier instantly melded to the shape of Drew's body, then soaked into his inner parts.

Scion opened his eyes, relaxing his cybernetic hands, which mechanically clicked with his movements. He clicked again as he cocked his head toward her. "His readings were at dangerous levels," he reported. "I infused more of my protection barrier power into his body, targeting the critical parts. It should sustain him while I install the next set of equipment."

"Thank you, Scion," Telly whispered. Just hearing about Drew's status made her want to beat the living shit out of someone. Every report and every update reminded her that Drew was lingering near death's door.

As Scion started the process of installing another part, Telly walked back over to the machine, checking on the new concoction she had been working on. The machine was done spinning the vials; the magical liquid inside the vials was crystal clear, despite the glowing aura of their magic.

Telly snatched at one of them, inspecting it. It was ready for the trial phase. Pocketing the vial, she rotated the vial holder, coming across one she was most curious about. It softly glowed red, pulsating as if it were a human heartbeat. Perhaps, in a way, it was a heartbeat. She had used Drew's blood, separating his main color into his adjacent colors. It was this red-powered vial that she wanted. One that could wreak destruction.

She narrowed her eyes as she grabbed the vial, pocketing that one as well.

She then walked toward a section of her workspace. Telly slid open a hidden compartment, looking at her new project in the drawer. A new magitech weapon. A prototype, one that would blast Olympia straight to hell. She had taken one of Gwen's designs and modified it so that it could use her new experimental vials. Her daughter had had the right idea with the design of the magitech weapon but didn't understand much of the engineering behind it. Her daughter was always so brilliant at ideas, especially when it came to technology.

Suddenly, Telly felt guilty and ashamed. She always was correcting Gwen on what was wrong instead of what was right.

Your design will be put to good use, my daughter, she thought. It would be poetic justice, using a weapon based on her daughter's original idea.

"Miss Hearly?"

Telly jumped, turning around. Scion was right behind her. "You startled me, Scion!" she scolded as she backhandedly slammed the drawer shut.

"I know this is a tense and difficult time. You're still processing much of what has happened."

"You think?"

"I do think," Scion confirmed. "As a matter of fact, I have processed this situation thoroughly. I have gone through our inventory of cybernetic parts. We only have fifteen percent of what is required to replace his damaged parts."

"I *know*," Telly snapped.

His eyes flickered, making a strange expression.

She paused, realizing that she was being too harsh with him. Clearing her throat, Telly continued, "At least we are getting help from the Corporation," she said in a softer tone. "Have you ran the updated diagnostics?"

"I have. Due to Drew being one of the first cybernetic models, there are some parts that he is in need of that the Corporation has stopped making. We must send someone out to scavenge those parts. It is possible there are some in the wastelands, or possibly on the black market."

"I could send a message to the Queen. She could convince the Corporation to make the parts." Telly sighed, then lowered her eyes.

He flashed his yellow eyes at her, giving her an unnatural expression. He seemed concerned. She suddenly felt terrible for her outburst.

"I'm sorry, Scion," she said softly.

"Sorry?"

Taking a deep breath, she said, "I shouldn't have yelled at you. It's just..."

His eyes flashed a vibrant yellow for a second, then he nodded. "You are facing much distress right now, Miss Hearly. It is a normal human expression."

"But it's still wrong of me," Telly said, her voice shaking. "I'm taking my anger out on the wrong person."

"There is no need to apologize." His mechanical clicks echoed as he neared her. "Do not worry. I will do my utmost best to get Drew fully operational." He clicked his hands, resting them on hers. "I promise on my circuits."

"On your circuits?" Telly repeated.

"Do humans not promise on things of this earth?"

"Yes...?"

"I am doing the same. After all, I am part human, am I not? I am as serious as any other humanoid would be in this situation."

"You are very much a human, Scion," Telly breathed. "Though I think everyone forgets it at times—including me."

Scion nodded. "It is easy to forget when you see the machinery inside of us. I feel sometimes, Miss Hearly. I feel the need to do everything I can to help. I share a bond with Andrew DiNapoli. Maybe it is due to the connection we had internally when he visited my brain waves. Maybe not. I do not know. But what I do know is that I must help him. He must live."

"Thank you." Telly smiled through her tears, giving him a hug. "You are a true friend." Just as she was about to pull away, she glanced over Scion's shoulder in the direction of her newly crafted weapon in the closed drawer. "I don't know what I'd do without you right now."

"You would be doing the same thing as you would be doing now, as my probability scans show."

She snorted. "That's not what I meant." Telly turned back to her machine, glancing at the concoction mixing in the vials as they spun in a circle. Grabbing the tablet, Telly scrolled through Drew's latest readings, then heaved a heavy sigh.

Noise came from outside their chamber.

"Gods of the Spectrum..." a woman's voice cursed.

Telly turned, seeing Victor, Geeta, Reila, and Garrett standing in the doorway.

Somehow, Telly was indifferent to that fact, and the fact that Geeta had returned from Arcadia. Nothing else mattered except Gwen and Drew. She didn't feel like chitchat; all she wanted to do was focus on what she needed to do.

"Miss Geeta," Scion greeted her. "Victor. I see you have finally awakened."

"I have," Victor said, nodding.

"Scion." Geeta nodded as she neared Drew's body. Victor hobbled over to the body with Reila's help, seating himself next to him.

"How is he?" Victor whispered.

"I transferred some of my yellow energy into his body, hoping that my shield would sustain him in a transfixed state until we can get him to a good status," Scion said.

"It seems that bought him some time," Geeta said softly.

Telly didn't know why, but Geeta's words suddenly made her extremely angry.

"Time? You think that bought him some *time*?" Telly snapped as she stepped out of the shadows, startling everyone. "Do you know that Olympia has *my* daughter?" Storming through the chamber, Telly sat down sharply, then hovered over Drew, adjusting some of the machinery hooked into him. "Scion is putting it politely, but as you can see, Drew is in critical condition. Do you know that he might not make it? Do *you*?"

"Telly…" Geeta started.

"Don't 'Telly' me, *Geeta*!" Telly snapped as tears began to stream down her cheeks. Telly whirled in her stool toward Geeta, then rose to her feet, getting in Geeta's face. "Where were you in the battle? Huh? Oh, that's right. You had to leave. If it weren't for that, perhaps Drew would've been okay. And if it weren't for him"—Telly pointed to Garrett—"then my daughter wouldn't have had to 'prove herself' to him. And most of all, if I had real magic, like the full power of my orange magic, I'd be able to blow Olympia all to hell!"

"Telly," Victor started.

"You stay out of this, Victor. You weren't even coherent while this all happened!" Telly snarled.

Geeta inched into Telly's face, their two noses almost touching. "I don't appreciate you blaming me for what happened," she warned. "Especially since you know what was happening to the Queen at the time. I *had* to leave!"

Unmoved, Telly didn't flinch. "That doesn't change *anything*," she said in a low voice.

"Perhaps if you weren't consuming yourself with these false truths and blaming those who love you most, then maybe—just maybe—the magic would grant you full access to its power!" Geeta said sharply.

She didn't know what came over her, but Geeta's words made her lose her shit. Telly shoved Geeta hard, and Geeta grabbed on to her wrists in defiance. Telly whipped her wrists, trying to break free of Geeta's grip, making her even angrier.

She just wanted to hurt someone, anyone, because everything hurt inside. She continued to push harder, with a new flood of tears streaming down her face. It was no use. Geeta was strong and she was…weak. Like always.

"Let *go*!"

"Telly, you cannot blame me! You know that the Queen was under attack," Geeta grunted.

"Screw you!"

"Telly! Stop this! We will get your daughter back!"

Everything hurt. Her heart hurt. Her body ached, longing for her family. Telly looked into Geeta's glowing purple eyes. Her own reflection stared back at her.

Have I become a monster?

A wide range of mixed emotions filled her soul. Suddenly, Telly went limp. Tears streamed down her face. Her lips quivered and her body trembled.

In defeat, Telly fell to the ground, sobbing.

All was silent except her sobs echoing in the cavern. "I…I…I'm sorry Geeta," she whispered. "I'm so sorry. I hate not being in control. If I had the ability to access my magic in its full form, then perhaps I would have been able to do more back at the palace, stopping that blue-gifted. And if I'd stopped that gifted from trying to take the Queen, then there would have been no need for you to leave the wastelands…"

In the corner of her eye, there was a glowing purple light gently flowing around her. It gently rested on her skin, then began seeping into her body.

"Breathe," Geeta called out softly. The violet magic entered her body, calming her mind. For a moment, Telly felt an overwhelming peace. It didn't replace her loss or her pain, but it did give her some assurance. "Telly, I have come to see what I can do for Drew. Maybe my magic can help sustain him until we get the parts we need."

Telly suddenly jolted her head up, meeting Geeta's gaze. "You came here for Drew?"

Geeta nodded. "And to see what I can do about Gwen."

Victor hobbled over to Telly, then knelt before her, whispering, "We will do whatever it takes to find Gwen and return her safely, and restore Drew. We all will."

Geeta walked toward Drew, then sat down on the stool next to his bed. The hums and beeps of his life-support machine were the only noises that could be heard. Telly stood aside, watching Geeta gently lay her hands on Drew's chest, directly on top of his heart. The others in the room remained silent, all waiting in anticipation to see Geeta work her magic.

Suddenly, a deep vivid glow of purple-violet magic filled the room. Telly couldn't see anything except Geeta's shadow within her violet magic, burning the entire room. Swirls of hot winds with glimmers of white sparkles flowed through the violet energy, channeling through the entire room with such force, but there was also a softness behind it. The magic funneled right into Drew's chest. Loud vibrating noises and fast beeps came from the life-support machine.

Telly wanted to run right into the violet healing light, but she knew to wait.

Seconds seemed like an eternity, but finally, the violet magic died down.

With her eyes glued to Drew's hand, Telly saw a slight movement before it went limp.

Hurrying up to Drew, Telly laid her hand on his heart—it was beating normally. Her eyes darted to his face. It remained like ice, frozen in time. His cybernetic eye wasn't powered on while his other eye remained shut. His skin felt cold too. Glancing at the machine readings, his numbers *had* improved, but there was no physical evidence that proved otherwise.

"He is now functioning at twenty percent capacity," Scion reported from behind them. His words went in one ear and out the other.

Telly felt Geeta's hand on hers as she whispered, "I'm sorry I couldn't do more."

Telly couldn't say anything. Her mouth felt dry, and her mind and body were too numb. After a long pause, Telly got to her feet and walked back into her corner, typing into her tablet, hovering over her workstation. She just didn't know what else to do.

A long, awkward silence went by, and eventually Telly realized that everyone had left the room except Scion. Though Telly could understand why, it bothered her that no one had offered any sort of solution to their current situation. It was very unlike Geeta or Victor.

Very unlike them, in fact, she thought. "I'll be back shortly," Telly called out to Scion.

Scion glanced over at her as Telly called forth her magic. A wave of pale orange burned around her, then she disappeared.

"Don't say anything to anyone," she ordered Scion.

"I won't, Miss Hearly."

Invisible now, Telly crept down the refuge cavern halls. If the group went anywhere, it would be either Victor's tent, Garrett's makeshift lab, or outside somewhere. She was betting they'd gone to Garrett's.

As she neared Garrett's chamber, she heard Victor's voice. Slowly, Telly inched her way to the entrance, watching. No one could see her, not even Geeta, since she lacked the orange gift. It was one thing she was grateful for.

"What information do we have at this point about Gwen's whereabouts? Is she even in Olympia at this point?"

Telly clenched her teeth. *They are discussing rescuing my daughter without me!*

"Let me show you what I have found out so far," Garrett said, typing into his main computer. Lots of monitors suddenly flashed maps and information.

Telly walked quietly into the room. On the screens appeared a map of Olympia with faint dots scattered throughout. Some of the dots were larger than others.

"Since the incident, I have been working non-stop to crack Olympia's mainframe, in hopes of finding any information on Gwen's location," Garrett started. "Last night, I was finally able to break into Olympia's mainframe map that pinpoints *energies* around the city." He paused, glancing at the screen. "That gifted boy emitted vast amounts of magical energy out in the wastelands. His power disrupts communications, electricity at times, even the sun. My thinking was that if this boy somehow accidentally emitted a huge burst of energy, it would be logged in the city's energy or communication logs."

There were a few dots that were larger than the others.

"This dot," Geeta said, pointing to one of the big dots. "Is that a release point from the gifted boy?"

Garrett entered commands on his keyboard, then looked at the map. "I looked into these larger points last night when I first broke into the program. My guess would be it's an effect from the Olympian cyborg's energy." He paused. "But they are so different than some of the smaller ones."

"So you think it could be the boy?" Victor asked.

"It's possible. I've been trying to log more of these types of larger energies to see if they have a pattern. It's strange that some of these bursts of power happen at the same time."

"Meaning?"

"Meaning that maybe the boy isn't the only one with magic," Garrett said.

"So you are saying that this map will log any magical energy, whether it be from the boy, cyborgs, or any other possible gifted?" Victor asked.

"Precisely."

"Why does it matter if the boy uses his magic?" Reila said casually. "We are looking for Gwen. Last I checked, Gwen doesn't have magic."

Telly couldn't believe that she was being left out of this conversation. A pit formed in her stomach, making her sick and sad at the same time.

Garrett cleared his throat. "Because I think it's possible that the Olympians would house Gwen with that dangerous kid. You have to think like them. To guard Gwen, Olympia would use their most powerful solider—that boy—to guard her."

Reila eyed him. "I'm not so sure…"

"Look, it's not a guarantee, but it's better than nothing," Garrett said.

Victor spoke up. "I think Garrett is onto something."

Geeta nodded.

Garrett sucked in a breath, continuing. "But…there is a downside to all of this. We need the kid to go haywire to get a good location on him. If he causally uses his magic, then the energy point will look like the others. And it could be days. Weeks. Months. There's just no telling."

"We don't have time to wait around," Geeta said. "I'm going to accelerate the process."

"You going to speed up time?" Reila snorted as she puffed her cigarette.

"No. But I can locate the boy with my mind and control his thoughts," Geeta answered. "I'll make him implode."

"That's what I'm talking about," Garrett said, nudging her. "Once he releases his energy, we can locate Gwen and go get her."

Victor nodded in approval. "Geeta, we need you with us."

"Of course I'm going," Geeta said. "You will need a port."

"I'm going with you too, whether you want me there or not," Garrett added.

"Count me in," Reila said.

Victor looked up to her. "Not this time. I need you to be in charge while I'm gone."

Reila huffed. "Really, Victor," she said, flicking an ash. "You know I can kick ass and take names."

"There is no one that can keep a tight ship like you. Can you imagine if I put Ryan in charge?" Victor pointed out.

Reila snorted through her smoke. "Why do you have to be so right?"

"Take the camp back to our lands. They need to go back to their home. The war is over, and they need to find peace once again. At least for the time being."

"Why can't you join everyone too? Why stay here?" Reila asked.

Victor and Geeta exchanged looks. "They will need my help," Victor said. "Drew will need looking after."

"Drew isn't stable enough to move," Garrett said. "Best to keep him here."

"He's right," Geeta said. "I will be staying here, doing what I can for Drew and Gwen, possibly staving off any Olympian attacks. Olympia might come searching for us again. Just like Garrett's device, what if the boy can somehow pinpoint us?" She paused. "Best to get the camp folks out of harm's way. It's a fight that they cannot be a part of. It's different this time."

Victor nodded. "I agree." He turned to them. "It's settled. Geeta, Garrett, and I will go."

Garrett suddenly cleared his throat. "Um, what about Telly?"

Yes, what about me? Telly thought bitterly.

"Telly should stay with Drew," Victor answered.

"But this is her daughter," Garrett pressed.

At least someone is thinking of me, she thought, fighting back tears.

"That is precisely why she needs to stay behind. She's going through a lot," Victor said.

"Victor's right," Geeta said. "She is completely irrational right now, for good reason. But irrational emotions can become huge mistakes that could cost us everything."

Garrett frowned but said no more.

Geeta got to her feet, and Victor as well. "All right. Let's get everyone to start packing…"

Geeta's voice faded as overwhelming emotions came over Telly. She inched her way out of the room and out into the cavern halls, then leaned back, sucking her breath in. They were planning on rescuing her daughter *without* her. Planning everything behind her back. *Irrational* was Geeta's reasoning. She might make *huge mistakes* the group said, not knowing that she was listening to every word.

I don't need them, she thought bitterly. *I'll rescue Gwen on my own.*

Telly turned away, heading down the halls into the heart of the refuge.

CHAPTER 11

◆

RED

The bright lights of Arcadia gleamed throughout the city as Kyle and Emerald trekked through the mid-levels. Flashing advertisements, neon signs, and holographic images painted the city in bright colors of light—even the grime soaked in its colors.

God, he missed the city. Kyle preferred the city lights at night, but it didn't matter. He was home. The emptiness he had felt as Rubius had now been filled living as "Kyle" back in Arcadia. This was his original and true life. His life force had been fractured, a piece of him splintered away to create Rubius. Now he was put back together again, fully restored, with the help of his true complement. As Rubius, Emerald had visited him in his dreams, and when he'd finally remembered who he was, it was as if all the fodder that filled Rubius's life force had shed away. Every time he thought about it, it was a clusterfuck. Why were some souls reincarnated, while others passed into the afterlife forever? After all, he had stood before the Almighty and the Dead Dude, so he knew the afterlife was no joke. But his soul had been recycled back into the lifestream… So what determined who got a new life?

Kyle took a long drag of his smoke. He never knew hurting his lungs with nicotine could feel so fucking good. It wasn't as good as sex, but pretty damn close.

"What's on your mind?" Emerald said playfully as she held his hand.

Kyle glanced over at her. Emerald gave him a goofy-cute-in-love smile. He couldn't help but smile back. Damn, she was so adorable. She was dressed in her street attire, swinging their interlocked hands and staring at all the shops as they walked by. He loved that Emerald had an adventurous heart. She still had yet a lot to see and explore—including her own kingdom.

"It's nothing, really," he answered.

"Nothing?" Emerald raised an eyebrow. "I know that look, and it's not nothing."

"Oh yeah?"

"Yeah," Emerald said. "Your eyebrows are pursed."

"Pursed?"

"Tense."

"Damn."

Emerald chuckled, then held his hand, guiding it to her cheek. "Tell me. What were you thinking?"

"How damn good this smoke is."

"Perhaps now you were thinking that. But before that?" Emerald said.

Kyle sighed. "It's just, why is it that some souls get reincarnated, while others go to the afterlife?"

Emerald paused, glancing at him curiously. "I assume it's the green magic that allows one to live a new life, but that's just my guess."

"Wait, green magic has that power?" Kyle's eyes searched hers. "Did I live…because of your magic?"

"Well, yes," Emerald said. Her eyes began to glow her eerie green, as if she was scared to tell him. "I did everything to bring you back with my magic. *Everything*. I used magic that I have never used before," Emerald breathed. "I…I didn't even know I had it in me. I believe it was a revival magic."

They met each other's gaze, her eyes watery, glazing over the glow.

"Hey, hey, hey," Kyle said quickly. "None of that. We are here now, together. Your magic kept me alive."

"Yes, though it was my fault to begin with…"

"Not true at all. You were under the influence of the sorceress. Unless you had a personal vendetta against me and wanted to kill me off," Kyle joked.

"No, Kyle!" Emerald protested, suppressing a chuckle.

"Then don't blame yourself," he said. He turned to the city, pointing to a busy area. "Look, I'm here now. I have lots to do to make up for lost time."

"Yes, you do." She leaned in, her chest on his, her hands playfully running through his necklaces. "Lots of lost time to make up for…"

Kyle leaned into her, then kissed her soft lips. So warm and inviting. Pure ecstasy in those lips.

A flash of Elyathi, and thoughts of her lunatic mother entered his mind. How in the hell was it possible that Elyathi was her mother? Emerald was so kind, sweet, and innocent. Elyathi was such a…

I don't wanna think about it! he told himself.

Pulling away, Kyle pretended they needed to get going. "While we are out one of these days, I wanna look at bikes."

Emerald blinked, almost in surprise. "Sure." She paused. "Are you okay? You pulled away quickly."

"Yeah, I'm fine," Kyle said. "I'm more worried about you."

"Me?" Emerald glanced away, looking at a string of shops nearby. She wasn't really looking at them, more lost in worry.

"Hey," he whispered, then kissed her gently. "I know that you are worried. About everything that is going on. I mean, you have good reason to be. But I'm with you, and I won't let anything happen to you. Try not to let it get to you. There is nothing you can do at this point, so you might as well not let yourself get all worked up about it. Soon the Corporation will be getting a list of parts to deliver to Drew. Geeta's doing what she can to help find that girl."

Emerald looked at him. "I am worried about everything, but mostly I am worried about you."

Kyle snorted. "Me?"

"Yes, you." She broke into a soft smile, nudging him sideways. "You lived an entirely different life."

"So?"

"So, you lived many years as a different person."

"I'm still the same soul."

Emerald leaned into him. "Doesn't mean that I can't worry about you, does it? It might be difficult for you to adjust back to your old life. And add to that, we will be parents soon."

Kyle smiled. He was going to be a father. Then he sighed inwardly. He really wasn't ready. But was any parent ready to have kids?

"Let's just live in this moment, yeah?" Kyle said. "You'll go nuts if you sit there and think about all your worries. Can you change anything by worrying?"

"Well, no…"

"Then come on," Kyle said, grabbing her hand. "Let's go have some fun!"

Emerald laughed. "I suppose."

"That's more like it."

"More like what?"

"Smiling. I like to see you smile."

She clutched his waist, then playfully yanked on one of his belt chains. "I'll try and remember that."

"Please do."

Kyle led her down a familiar set of escalators, then across several platforms. With each step, they got closer to his old stomping grounds.

As they turned a corner, Kyle stopped when he saw a tax booth. A flood of rage and fury came over him. It brought back old memories of their first arguments. Upper levels verses lower levels. Mid-levels getting fucked both ways... But as much as he wanted to go ballistic, he gritted his teeth and swallowed back fighting words. "Looks like the King didn't change the laws. Still need money, huh?"

Emerald looked just as stunned as he did. "I didn't know," she said defensively, stepping in front of him. "I asked *him* to change it."

Him. Just thinking about him made his boil with anger. *Fuck that guy! Fuck the tax!*

Kyle remained silent. It was obvious Emerald had noticed too. She paid the tax, and they both went through. There was awkward silence, then she yanked his hand, bringing them both to a stop.

"You don't believe me, do you?" she asked.

Kyle sighed, knowing that the conversation could turn into an argument at any fucking moment. Emerald tended to rely on others when it came to matters of the kingdom. Understandably, she couldn't do everything in Arcadia single-handedly.

Don't fuck this up, he told himself. Kyle softened his expression. "I do believe you Em. I just thought it would have been sooner rather than later, you know?"

She eyed him, then nodded. "I'll make sure to do something about it. I swear, Kyle, I didn't know."

"I believe you."

"Good."

His face softened as she returned a buttery smile. The two of them made their way down into the lower levels and into the streets. Familiar smells and sights overwhelmed his senses, causing him to forget their little tax spat. Being in the city was euphoric, even if the place reeked of vomit and piss.

They turned a corner, and there was a sight he never thought to be so happy to see: his shitty apartment building. The rundown bricks, the broken monitors, the roadway into the under-garage. The trash outside. He wanted to kiss the very foundation, that's how much it made his heart soar.

"We're here," she said.

Kyle sucked in a breath. "Yeah. It feels so good. Too good," he said proudly. He shifted his hands into his jacket pockets as if on autopilot, reaching in to grab his key card.

His key card.

"Shit!" Kyle kicked a trashcan.

"What's wrong?"

"I don't have my fucking key card," he grumbled.

"You mean *this* key card?" Emerald presented a key in her hand.

Kyle's mouth dropped open. "How…?"

Emerald grinned. "Let's just say I paid your rent while you were gone and got a key card out of the deal. I told Rosie that I lost it every time I came to visit, but it was kind of…not true."

"Em!"

"I wanted an excuse to see her too," she admitted.

"I never thought you to be the type."

"I thought…" Her voice wavered as she buried her head into his chest, holding him.

Kyle held her, brushing her vibrant green hair out of her face. "It's okay, Em. I would have done the same thing too," Kyle said softly.

They both looked at each other, and she smiled. Emerald tapped the key card, and the door clicked open. They walked to the elevator, taking it from the first level to Kyle's level. The elevator dinged, then opened to his level. It was all so strange to him, like he was doing this all for the very first time, but he wasn't.

As they approached his apartment door, Emerald gave him the metal door key. Kyle smiled devilishly, then inserted the key into the doorknob, jiggling and finagling with it. Just like old times. Rosie hadn't fixed the lock. He didn't mind. It kind of was a fun game to him.

Finally, the lock clicked, the door opened, and the two of them entered.

As soon as they were inside, Kyle paused. A wave of nostalgia hit him hard. Clothes thrown about. Empty whiskey bottles used to house cigarette butts. The crappy table he had and his piece-of-shit bed. And the smells. Stale cigarettes, rank clothing, and the musty floorboards. He'd missed this piece of shit. Hard.

Kyle slowly began to walk through his apartment, recalling the memories. His crappy bed, the little bathroom, the small table with the chair…he was amazed that it was exactly how he'd left it. There was even dirty underwear in a corner.

"I made sure nothing was moved," Emerald said softly as she stood off to the side of him.

"Really?" Kyle glanced at her, surprised.

She shyly looked down, shuffling her feet. "I…I just couldn't bear the thought of anyone touching anything after you…"

Kyle put his arm around her, then guided her body near his and hugged her. "I fucking love you, Em."

Emerald blushed.

"I mean it. No one has a heart like you. No one."

"I love you too."

Kyle leaned into her, kissing her sweet lips. It was like wine and honey, or a drink of water after a long ride on his bike. Her touch was cool and soft to his burning skin, water to quench his fiery soul.

As their lips parted, they exchanged smiles, Emerald brushing her fingertips through his necklaces one last time. He then turned his attention to his pile of clothes, sifting through them and sniffing each piece, determining if they were clean or dirty, tossing aside the dirty ones. Some were pretty rank, but he did manage to find one that smelled decent. He yanked it on, then noticed a pack of cigarettes.

"Gonna need these," Kyle said casually as he grabbed the box and shoved them into his pockets. From the corner of his eye, he saw Emerald rummaging through his pile, setting some clothes aside.

"What are you doing?"

"You are going to need more than just one outfit," she said. She was already packing a duffel bag for him.

His stomach knotted up from her statement. "Good point," he said.

Kyle looked around, realizing that his guitar was gone. "You don't happen to see my guitar lying around anywhere, do you?" he asked.

"No. I was going to ask you the same thing," she said.

Must've left it at Geeta's…before my death. "I'll have to pick up a new one for the time being."

"I can have the palace staff get you what you need," she said.

Palace staff? Oh, hell no. "It's okay. I'll get it."

"All right. Just know it's an option."

As Kyle combed through his apartment, he came across his sunglasses, slipping them on. *These will come in handy.* He then grabbed his stack of clothes, plopped down next to Emerald, and began packing.

Emerald eyed him curiously. "Why did you put on your sunglasses?"

"Gotta hide my eyes."

"Why? You look silly wearing them indoors."

"Says the girl who has been hiding her magic her entire life," Kyle said casually, grabbing another shirt, throwing it in his duffel. "You don't want me to scare everyone at the palace, do you? I already have enough to worry about fitting in there. Having red eyes will make it nearly impossible. Who has red eyes anyway? Um, let me think. No one. You, on the other hand, at least have an eye color that is normal."

"I think your red eyes are cute," she said. "Just like your red hair."

"You really like my red hair?"

"Yes, most definitely." She leaned against his shoulders, then plopped her head down in his lap. "Kiss me, you vampire." She giggled.

"Most obliged," Kyle said formally, playing along. He kissed her again, and she eagerly kissed him back. Her deep kiss was exhilarating, causing his hands to slide down her back to her butt. He then shifted his body on top of hers, still locked in their kiss, as he gently guided her to the floor. She moaned, kissing him deeper, her hand running wildly around his neck.

Just then, the door handle jiggled, startling them both, breaking up their kiss.

"Get back," Kyle whispered as his torso shot up.

Emerald slid out from under him as he rose to his feet.

The door handle clicked, slowly opening.

A fireball was forming within his mind. In his palm, he felt the heat from his life force.

Emerald pushed his hand aside. "Kyle! Don't!"

His fire spell wafted out.

Suddenly the door was fully open, and Rosie stood in the doorway. Before he could stop and explain, Rosie shrieked.

Kyle shot his hands up. "Oh my God! Rosie! It's me! Kyle!"

Rosie backed up, clearly shaken.

Emerald ran over to Rosie, patting her shoulder. "Rosie, it's okay. It's really him."

Rosie stared at him, her hands trembling. "It can't be…" her voice wobbled. Kyle remained as he was as Rosie slowly approached him. Her eyes took him in, studying him. "Are you a ghost?" she whispered.

Kyle laughed. "That's all you got to say after this entire time?"

Rosie stared at him wide-eyed. "You can't be real."

"Touch my arm, Rosie," Kyle stated.

Rosie hesitated, then nervously shuffled over to him. She reached out, her cold fingertips touching his forearm. "Kyle…" she whispered, then sucked in her breath.

"The one and only," Kyle said, smiling at her. "It's really me."

"I don't believe it…"

"It's really him, Rosie," Emerald said again.

Rosie ran her hands against his cheeks, then moved his face this way and that. It was amusing, so he stayed still while she inspected him.

Rosie frowned. "They told me you were dead…"

Kyle gently moved her hands off her face, then gave the old woman a big hug. Rosie cried happily in his arms, returning his hug, clutching him firmly. "Seems like they were wrong," he whispered.

She released herself from his embrace, then yanked his cheek like he was a ten-year-old kid, finally acting like her old self. "I just can't believe it," she said in typical Rosie fashion.

"Yeah, you wouldn't even if I told you." Kyle smiled at her, suddenly noticing that her shoulder was empty. "Where's that rat of yours?"

Rosie's eyes began to water as she pursed her lips.

Shit… "I'm sorry. I didn't mean to upset you," Kyle said quickly.

"It's…it's fine. Zaphod died the other night. I haven't had the heart to clean up his cage or his things," she said sadly. "I didn't think it was his time yet. He still had a few more years on him, and he was in good health." She shook her head, then teared up again. "I don't understand why."

Zaphod. His parrot… Both he and his parrot had appeared back in Arcadia the other night.

Could it be? Was Zaphod's spirit reincarnated in the future like me?

At that moment, it was like a bolt of lightning had struck his insides. That was the *same time* he had returned to Arcadia—with Zaphod. The parrot *had* to be Rosie's rat. He had been guarding him in the future. That's why the rat liked his future self, because it knew Kyle in his former life, then met him again in the future… Somehow, he just knew it to be true. But then, how did green magic factor in this scenario?

His head hurt thinking about it. Death. Afterlife. Even magic.

I need to get Zaphod here before Rosie dies of heartbreak.

Kyle grabbed his duffel. "Listen, Rosie, we gotta run. There's a few things we gotta do today," Kyle said. "But I'll be back later in the week."

Emerald turned to him. It was as if she had heard his thoughts. She gave him a nod of approval and a private smile.

Rosie smiled at him, wiping tears away bravely. "What are you doing wearing those silly things in here? Too famous for us down here?" she scolded. "Take those things off."

"Naw, it's not like that, Rosie. I'm tired, and I look like shit. You don't wanna…"

"You've always been so stubborn," Rosie huffed.

"Can't argue with that."

Rosie made a tut-tut sound, sighing. "You know you have pretty-boy eyes. Don't hide them."

"You're starting to sound like Jaxx."

"Who's that?"

"Forget it," Kyle muttered.

"What day do you think you'll be visiting? I want to make you my special banana bread."

Kyle rubbed the back of his neck. "I dunno. Em is busy being queen, you know?"

Rosie smiled at Emerald. "And a fine queen she is. I don't know why she chose to get involved with a guy like you."

"Hey!"

Rosie chuckled this time, playfully grabbing his cheek again. "You are too cute, even in your silly sunglasses." They smiled at each other, then she shuffled to the door. "If you happen to know, please give me a dial."

"Sure thing."

"I'll see you this week."

"See ya."

When Rosie left and the door closed, Emerald turned to him. "I felt your thoughts and agree with you. Your parrot is her rat. I got that feeling when Geeta met with us for breakfast."

"Yes." Kyle leaned in. "That's why he liked me as my future self—he knew me from my past life. The guy who sold Zaphod to me told me that he didn't like anyone, but somehow Zaphod instantly liked me. It's gotta be the same soul."

Emerald bit her lip. "I agree. The God of Light at work."

The God of Light. He was still pissed off about that whole thing. He wouldn't even be here if it weren't for his unholy bargain…

"Yeah, well, you were the one to cast the life spell on me," he said, taking another drag.

Emerald looked at him, curious but slightly disappointed. "What's wrong?"

"Nothing's wrong. Just wondering how Zaphod got involved."

"Wasn't he in our dreams?"

"You have a point," he said, sucking in his smoke. "My head hurts just thinking about all this. Let's get going."

Emerald smiled. "Sure."

Kyle threw the duffel bag strap over his shoulder, then took one last look at his apartment, feeling a little sad. As much as he wanted to live with Em, he couldn't envision living at that grand-ass palace. He would rather be at his shitty apartment. In his whole damn life prior, he'd complained about the shitty lower levels. Now that he had a chance to leave, all he wanted to do was live in the hellhole.

He sighed, then took one last look, then turned away, with Emerald leaning into his arm.

CHAPTER 12

◆

BLUE

The azure light faded from Derek's spell as his power washed away, revealing the space-time continuum. His heart still raced from his newfound colors added to his life force. Sweat poured from his brow, and his curls were sopping wet. Bloodstains were dried on his arms and parts of his clothing. Even his polished jewelry lacked luster, and his ruff fell flat.

Sitting up, Derek took in the beauty of the space-time continuum as he caught his breath. The mirror-like portals were whirlpools of energy, burning bright blue. Space itself was black as night, dressed with the stars like gems glittering. And the *power*. It radiated from every aspect of this place as it flowed through his veins. The flow of time seeped into his mind from that power. Time, events, knowledge…it played through his mind in a mere second, but yet the amount that flowed in his mind was thousands of years' worth of events. All he had to do was stop at whatever interested him and view what lay before him. Did the other blue-gifted feel this powerful with their time magic? Or was it as Ikaria once said, that some gifted are just more naturally talented? It was as if the flow of time answered him, and he liked his answer. No one matched him, for he was godlike with his power. Who was going to stop him? Certainly not Kyle Trancer.

Derek got to his feet, heading down the starry path toward the portal to Arcadia. With each step, portals bent toward him, as if bowing to him. Timelines, dimensions, portals, all of the space-time continuum. Derek felt their call for their master to command them.

King of Time, a dark voice whispered.

Derek paused at the closest portal. In its mirror-like magic, it twisted and morphed, then washed away, revealing alternate times.

Champion of Darkness, one to rule all of time. Come see what fate lies before you.

The portal in front of him suddenly swirled erratically in a different motion, glowing brighter than before. Its dance mesmerized Derek, seducing him. The strong feeling linked to his life force, and that time portal's energy was like another life-form, tantalizing his physical body, plunging deep into his heart.

His eyes were locked on the strange portal when it suddenly burst into a stream of flowing water, raging around him with an intense, bright flickering blue magic.

Show me! he commanded the magic.

Suddenly, the portal flickered with frosty black sparkles. Around the portal burned strong energy, like black water swirling into the void.

Within the black frosted dimension, he saw Elyathi's image. She glowed with pure white magic, gently sitting on a shore, as if she were a siren of the sea. She looked more beautiful in that moment than he had ever seen her before. No. She had always looked like that, but he had never taken the time to entertain such a thought.

She is made for you, whispered a voice in his feverish mind.

I know. I have a strange and fascinating desire for her, Derek admitted. *I am ashamed that I have these confusing thoughts. It sickens me!*

Your love for Emerald rings true, that is certain. But Elyathi's soul was created to be yours. You will be her darkness, and she will be your light, continued the whisper. *Does light not work in harmony with darkness?*

Are you saying I have these thoughts because Elyathi is my complement?

Yes, oh King of Time. Every color has its complement, colors that yearn to be with each other. Even the light needs darkness, the voice stated. *Your destinies have been intertwined since her existence. You must seize the light, work together to create your new world. For that is what the God of Light wanted…magic restored to the heavens in its rightful place.*

Once this is over with, I don't want to have this…this pull toward my complement. I love Emerald, and this feeling is creating too much conflict, Derek told the voice. *I am doing this all for her! With or without a complement, I need Emerald.*

A small laugh came, and then the voice answered, *Emerald will be yours. Completely yours, without a doubt. You will have your heart's desire. You will be with her, and she will love you fully. You won't have to worry about your inner turmoil with Elyathi. All will be well in the new world.*

Good, Derek said.

A dark stream of energy washed over him. Pain wracked his body, crippling his movements. The power continued to flow through his veins uncontrollably. Then, as if in ecstasy, the energy hummed in her life force, as if he was finally in tune with his true energy. He felt *strong.*

The portal in front of him flickered, with Elyathi's image melting away, replaced by Emerald. She sat by her window, heavily pregnant and in tears. Her handmaiden approached her, bowing.

Derek suddenly sobered up from his magical ecstasy the moment he laid eyes on her image. Guilt panged through him. Guilt over what he had done—no, what the sorceress had *made* him do.

I swear I will make this right, he promised the image. Emerald. She was even more beautiful, more radiant than he remembered. Her belly looked a bit more swollen due to the pregnancy. Desire swept over Derek. He wanted her. He needed her.

But a feeling lingered in his mind, one that had constantly plagued him. Was the child truly his? Or was it that good-for-nothing rocker's child?

Time funneled through his mind, flashing images, then pausing. *A boy…*

Derek studied the image that stood before him within his mind: a boy with the same features as him. It was as he had hoped. The boy was *his* child.

Another image swept over him. This time, it was another boy—one that didn't look like him. But strangely, this boy and the boy that looked like Derek were playing together.

Suddenly, realization hit Derek, and he knew. Emerald was pregnant with twins.

Yes, King Derek—king of all time. One is yours, the other is not, whispered the darkness.

The image changed to Emerald with the boys. Derek was there too. They were traveling together in a blue wave of magic. As the blue magic came over them, the boys screamed and melted away.

I cannot bring Emerald to the future while she is with child, Derek suddenly realized. It made sense—all the others who'd time traveled needed to have the green gift within their life force.

I must wait until the children are born. There is still plenty to do in the meantime.

His heart dropped, realizing how much he missed her. *I would give anything to see Emerald's desire for me once again. Anything.*

And so you will, answered the darkness.

Derek tried to move, but the magic flowing around him wouldn't allow him to.

Watch, King of Arcadia. See what is happening to your kingdom.

Remaining in place, Derek watched Emerald's image walk through the palace. More images flashed—to a point later in time. A party. Kyle was there, mingling with *his* people, the sector lords of Arcadia.

A flood of jealous rage came over Derek. He wanted to cast every single terrible spell he could think of to disintegrate that image: Kyle's image. But instead, the magic flowed around him, keeping him still. Derek watched as Emerald giggled with Kyle in her arms, behind a pillar of the palace. They were locked in a passionate kiss, Kyle's hands sliding down Emerald's body as the two embraced. Derek's stomach burned with anger and jealousy, sickened at the sight. He clenched his jaw in anger and disgust.

"I don't want to see this!" Derek shouted.

Just watch…

The image fast-forwarded again. Kyle hovered over Emerald, intimately touching her body in ways that Derek never had.

Derek screamed as the images fast-forwarded again. This time, it was only Emerald. She was sitting on a palace chair, facing Arcadia, the city spread out before her. The sun was setting, the deep orange golden rays shining on her pale face. In her eyes, tears formed, then ran down her cheeks. Her hand was on her belly; she was almost ready to give birth.

One of her handmaidens entered the room, bowing.

"Has he sent a transmission?" Emerald asked.

The handmaiden looked to the floor, shaking her head. "No, My Queen."

Emerald burst into tears, holding her pregnant belly.

"I'm so sorry…" her handmaiden whispered.

Emerald looked up, then clenched her jaw. The handmaiden left, and

Emerald sobbed. And sobbed.

Fast-forward again. Another image of Emerald and Kyle, this time together at the palace. Tears stung both their eyes, with rage brewing amongst them.

"Then *why*, Kyle? Why did you do this to me? To our children!" Emerald said viciously.

"You know what's sad, Em? You think you're right in all of this," he snapped. "But just remember this: You chose Arcadia over our love…"

The image distorted, then flickered away. The portal returned to its original state.

Derek stood in silence. Fury filled Derek's life force, but he swallowed his pride. The silver lining in the whole situation was that Kyle Trancer was going to hurt Emerald in a way that would tear them apart though heartbreak. From what time had showed him, Kyle left her alone in the palace, just as her father had. And the best part? The fool was going to do it all on his own. Derek didn't need to interfere. Kyle was going to ruin it *for* him. All he had to do was be patient. Be there for her when she needed someone most.

That was how Emerald would fall back in love with him. He wouldn't have to convince her, beg her. She would come on her own accord, love him with her own choice.

I'll take good care of you, Emerald. For I am the one who truly loves you. I always have and always will.

Everything was perfect. Their past would be erased, while her real love for him would remain in the new world.

Time was on his side. Everything was on his side.

Derek swiped his hand across the portal, and it wafted away completely. In its place were the star paths and glowing portals in the space-time continuum— all leading to Arcadia.

I must let Kyle's little charade play out, he decided. Derek glanced at the portal far across the space-time continuum, where Arcadia's portal for the Millennium Era was. If he let Emerald be for a while, then he would have time to do another task on his agenda.

The cyborg scientist.

But first, he needed a way to control him.

CHAPTER 13

♦

Gwen sighed as she lay in bed staring up at the ceiling. Within the speckled texture, she saw patterns and shapes of silly things like circles, hearts, and stars. Others looked like clouds, planets, and random objects like a transmitter or an escalator lift. One particular shape formed into the likeness of her mom.

Gwen burst into tears as the pattern of her mother stared back at her from the ceiling. *I never really meant what I said, Mom. I'm sorry I said those things...*

It seemed like an eternity since she'd been taken, though she knew it had only been a few days. She missed her mom so much. Her dad too. The thought of being away from her parents frightened her, but she tried to put on a brave face. It wasn't helping.

I wish I wasn't so stupid. I wouldn't be here right now if I had just stayed behind at the refuge!

Gwen pounded the bed with the back of her fist, fighting back her tears. She just wanted to cry all over again. About her stupidity. About her mom. About her dad. About getting captured. Even about Garrett. Would she ever see them again? That was what she was most scared about. What if the last thing she saw of her mom was Gwen yelling at her and her dad being mangled in the battle? As she wiped away her angry tears, she glanced at a certain corner of the wall. Anyone else would think it was just a corner. But being as tech savvy as she was, she knew better.

Freaking camera.

What she really wanted to do was to flip the finger at the camera. It took every ounce in her body to pretend she had no idea it was there. It was better that way. She didn't want the Olympians knowing that she knew they were spying on her. At times, she could have sworn that someone was in the room with her, watching her every move. Whenever she felt like that, she would yell out loud, telling *whoever* or *whatever* that she wasn't scared. Of course, there was never anyone there. That she knew of anyway.

There was a click at the door.

Gwen jerked her head up suddenly, wiping away her tears as fast as she could, then positioned herself casually on the bed.

An older maidservant entered. The same maid who had checked on her before. Probably midfifties or early sixties if Gwen had to guess. Her graying hair was pulled back tightly in a bun, making her big, sharp nose seem more prominent. "Hello, Lady Gwen," she greeted warmly as she bowed.

Gwen didn't say anything, just stared at her.

"The master would like your company," she stated warmly.

"The master?" Gwen repeated.

"Master Jihyun, Lady Gwen," the woman said. That was when Gwen noticed the maidservant held a stack of clothes. The woman walked over to the bed, then proceeded to lay them out for her.

Gwen turned away, starting to cry again. Through her muffled tears, she heard footsteps approach, then a hand rested on her shoulder.

"I am sorry, Lady Gwen," she whispered. "I…" The maidservant paused, then sucked in a breath. "I…I'll do my best to cheer you up while under my care."

Gwen eyed the camera, noticing the woman was doing her best to pretend not to notice it either. She obviously wanted to say more, but Gwen knew why she couldn't.

"Don't call me lady. I'm anything but," Gwen grumbled.

"Oh, but you are." She smiled. "I am sure that you will see your parents again." She brushed her cheek, then wiped away the tears. "Time will pass quickly, you will see. In the meantime, why don't you play with Master Jihyun?"

"I don't feel like it," Gwen mumbled. "He's just a kid anyways."

"That might be, but I am sure that playing his video games will help you feel better…for the moment at least." The woman smiled, giving her a pat on the back, indicating she should get ready.

Gwen eyed the clothing pile. "You expect me to wear that…Mrs.…?"

"You can call me Mae. And yes, I thought you would like a fresh change of clothes. I'll be taking you to Master Jihyun as soon as you're ready. He's been asking for you all morning."

Maybe Mae was right. Maybe it would make her feel better. After all, Gwen did like to play video games. Anything would be better than being pent up in a room day in and day out.

Gwen shrugged. "Fine, I'll go."

Mae smiled. "Master Jihyun is a sweet kid."

"Didn't seem so sweet out in the wastelands," Gwen muttered. "The last time I saw my father, he was in critical condition because of that kid, perhaps even worse…" Gwen gritted her teeth. "When he came into my room the other night, it was as if he was a completely different person. Does he have a mental problem?"

Mae side-eyed where the camera was positioned, which didn't go unnoticed by Gwen. "You must get ready," Mae stated, almost in a rehearsed fashion, completely ignoring her last statement. "I'll give you some privacy to get changed. I'll be right outside the door." Mae left, leaving Gwen still seated on the bed with her new set of clothes.

I wonder if she is under surveillance too?

Gwen unfolded the clothes, noticing that they were all gowns. All of them were pretty, she had to admit, though she wasn't into fancy dresses or frilly things. When she was a kid, she liked silly things like dressing up and putting on her mom's only set of high heels. Now it seemed so childish.

Looking at one of the dresses in green, Gwen brushed the fabric slightly. The cloth was soft, and the design was intricate.

Getting up, Gwen slipped into it, then quickly ran her fingers through her hair. She glanced in the mirror and frowned. She hated looking in the mirror at herself, especially in such fancy clothes. She would never be a "pretty girl," and no dress could fix that. Her upper body was too broad, her chest was flat, and she didn't have curves in her hips like all the other girls her age.

It's probably why Garrett doesn't like me, Gwen thought to herself, eyeing her reflection. She sighed loudly, then headed for the door.

In the hall, Mae had been waiting patiently. "That dress looks pretty on you."

"I don't think so."

"Why do you say that?" Mae asked.

"It's just…never mind."

Mae shrugged, then gestured for Gwen to follow her. They walked through the palace halls; it was the most beautiful building she had ever been in. Gwen been in the upper levels of Arcadia a few times, but a palace? Never. And with her being in a whole new city? In Olympia? It was unreal.

With all the pretty things around her, and the view of the whole city from the windows as they crossed many sky bridges, it helped her mood slightly, though it made her stomach uneasy. She glanced at the city below, which stretched as far as the eye could see, except a few mountains far off in the distance. Her parents were out there beyond those mountains. Was her dad okay? What about her mom? Had her mom found out what happened to her? Gwen tried not to cry thinking about it.

As they exited the skyway, Mae turned a corner into a little nook. Gwen was about to bump into her, but Mae yanked her into a far corner until they were face-to-face.

"We only have a few seconds without any cameras here before we move on, so please listen," Mae warned. "These people are dangerous. Do not give them any information. If you have magic as Councilor Jason has been speculating, then you must hide it at all costs. They have been doing things to Master Jihyun. I can't say for certain exactly what, but the master is not himself half the time." Her eyes flared. "He has uncontrollable nightmares."

They think I have magic?

Gwen was about to say something when Mae walked away, acting if nothing had happened. Quickly, Gwen followed. As they walked, Gwen realized the severity of the situation. She thought back to the wastelands, when the kid was mangling her dad with the dark-red magic. She'd been scared before, knowing what Mae told her. Now she was terrified. And she was going to visit this dangerous kid?

Her heart raced. What were the Olympians going to do to her?

Please let me survive this.

Mae led her to a darker corridor of the palace, coming upon double doors with a slew of guards.

"Ah, Mae," said Councilor Jason, who stood at the door's entryway. "The master looks forward to the girl."

Mae bowed deeply to him. "Councilor Jason, it is an honor." She turned to Gwen. "This is where I leave you."

Gwen shot Mae a look, then eyed the councilor. "You aren't coming with me?"

"Unfortunately, Mae doesn't have permission to access the master's quarters for the day," Councilor Jason answered in her stead. Gwen turned to look at Mae again, but the woman was already down the hall. "I will escort you the rest of the way."

Gwen nodded as her eyes trailed to Mae. The more she thought about Mae, the more she realized that the woman was probably in the same trap as Gwen. It made her realize that maybe she would never see her parents again.

"I need to know what happened to my father," Gwen said boldly. "I'm not moving a foot to give that kid company until I know what happened to him!"

Councilor Jason turned around, narrowing his eyes, and Gwen felt a shiver run down her spine.

"I said that the master is *expecting* you."

"I don't care what the master is expecting, but *I* expect some sort of answer if you want me to 'hang out' with him. The last I saw of my father, he was mangled all to heck because of your master!"

Jason raised his chin, his soft brown hair framing his face. "First, answer me this, then I will tell you of your father: Do you have the gift or not?"

"What do you mean by the gift?" Gwen feigned innocence.

Councilor Jason made no move. "You are going to get hurt playing these games, *little girl*, and in the process, you will hurt others. I prefer to *not* be a causality."

That definitely wasn't the response Gwen expected, but she had to give the guy kudos. "Well, you don't have to worry about me. I don't have the gift like my father."

Jason eyed her, as if analyzing whether what she said was true or not. He gave an arrogant snort, then said, "There are confirmed reports that your father is alive. That I can tell you with confidence. But how alive he is? That is undetermined."

Gwen felt a big relief, though it still could mean her father was hurt.

Without another moment to waste, Jason snapped, "Now *move*, before you end up like your father."

Gwen felt a tightness in her throat, and her heart raced. Taking a deep breath, she followed Councilor Jason as he led her through the double doors. In her mind, she prepared for anything unexpected, even if the guy was going to put a bag over her head and torture her. Gwen decided if he was going to try anything funny, she would knee him in the balls and run like hell, even if the guy was stronger than her.

But her imagination proved false. Instead, he walked in front of her, leading her into a room with blinding blue light.

Gwen blinked, realizing what was before her. It was a *magical* portal, just like the ones Geeta would summon back at camp.

Someone has portal magic? Gwen thought. The councilor didn't seem gifted, as he was concerned whether she was gifted. *So who, then?*

There were whispers, as if someone was saying something to Jason. He nodded, then motioned for Gwen to follow.

Gwen hesitated, but then Jason gave her a forced smile. "It won't hurt," he said. "I'll be traveling too."

"All right."

Gwen sucked in a breath as she and Jason stepped through the portal.

Suddenly, the world around them washed away, and she felt like she was falling in an endless sky. Just falling and falling as the pressure increased against her chest, as if cement were in her lungs.

Just when she was about to pass out, Gwen felt her feet planted firmly on flooring. The strange space-like sky washed away, revealing a dark room. It was nearly pitch black, with only a giant screen lit up in neon colors. Brightly colored holograms were scattered about, all pertaining to what was being played on the monitor: a video game. The boy had goggles strapped to him, with special electronic gloves, moving around wildly, completely into the game he was playing.

"Master Jihyun, Your father granted your request. Gwen is here to give you company," Councilor Jason called out.

Immediately, the boy ripped off his gaming headset and goggles. His eyes scanned the room, then he noticed her.

"Hi!" Jihyun exclaimed as he ran over to Gwen. "Do you want to play my new game? I just got it! You fight all these bad guys with these gloves!"

Without waiting for Gwen answer, he ran back to where he was playing then grabbed a pair of power gloves, then sprinted back, presented them to her.

"Whoa, you have these?" Gwen looked at the gloves. She had only seen pictures of the new gaming gloves; They were all the rage, and only the rich gamer kids had them. No one else could afford them. She only had played games on her computer keyboard and input device.

"I don't know how to play any games with those," Gwen said.

"I'll show you!" Jihyun said, putting on the gloves excitedly.

"I'll leave you both to it," Councilor Jason called out.

Jihyun didn't say anything to Jason, but continued to put on the gloves, then his goggles. Gwen turned to look over her shoulder, her eyes meeting Councilor Jason's. He gave her a hard stare, then closed the door behind him.

At least I don't have to see Councilor Creeps for the time being.

Turning back, Gwen watched as Jihyun made sweeping motions with his hands. A giant holographic menu screen appeared to them in neon pink, and Gwen saw him select a new game.

The menu screen disappeared after that, then the game started on the giant monitor before them.

On the screen, Jihyun's character appeared to be in a building, and he started running through it.

"Does the screen look 3D to you?" Gwen asked.

"I can't see the screen—that is for you to watch me," he said. "The entire world is all around me! It's real in these goggles!"

Suddenly, other game avatars started punching Jihyun's character. Jihyun countered with a punching motion of his physical body. The gloves picked up his motion, and his game avatar punched the villains in the game back, knocking them out.

Whoa, Gwen thought. *That's sick.*

"See that guy? I got him!" Jihyun said excitedly. "Watch this!"

His game avatar ran through the video game world, and more men came after him. This time, however, Jihyun did some sort of sweeping hand move. In the game, chain lightning shocked all the avatars in the game, killing them.

"Did you see that? Did you see?" he shouted excitedly again, jumping up and down, proud of himself.

"I did," Gwen said. "That's so cool, Jihyun."

"You should see what it looks like in the goggles. It's way cooler!" He ripped off his gloves in the middle of the game. Avatars were still coming at them. "You should try, Gwen!"

"Now?"

"Yes!" the boy urged.

"Okay, I guess," Gwen said, putting on the gloves quickly. Jihyun handed her the goggles. "You need these too."

Gwen put on the goggles. She was in the 3D world! It looked so real…

"Hurry! They're coming after you!" Jihyun said. "You gotta get those bad guys!"

"But what do I do?" Gwen said in a panic.

"Just punch them!"

The 3D game avatars were heading for her, and she started punching aimlessly. It was frightening how real the game appeared. Her heart pumped hard, though her brain was telling her it was all fake. The avatars came right up to her, so she tried to punch them. She could see her virtual hand punching the avatars, but she wasn't knocking them out.

"Harder!" Jihyun cried.

Gwen punched harder and swung around. In the game world, she knocked one out.

Suddenly she felt dizzy and sick. Really sick.

Ripping off the goggles, she looked around, but that made her feel worse. "Do you have a trash can?" she asked.

"Why?"

"I gotta throw up."

"There's one in the bathroom." He pointed to a small door.

Gwen ran into the bathroom, which was more like a water closet. She slid onto the floor toward the toilet, hovering her head over it, then hurled. Hard. Seeing her vomit in the toilet made her throw up all over again. She kept doing it until there was nothing left.

After getting everything out of her system, she raised her head from the porcelain bowl. Jihyun stood over her, making a disgusted face.

"Ewww! Throw-up!" he exclaimed.

Gwen wiped her mouth, irritated. "Why are you watching me throw up, *kid*?"

"I just wanted to see if you were okay. You know what? I did that my first time playing this game too.”

“Do you have any regular computer games? Ones that you play with a keyboard? Maybe I should stick with those,” Gwen said, flushing the toilet. She washed her mouth out in the sink with hot water, then washed her hands.

“I got lots of those. They’re in the next room. We can play them if you want. I got like a thousand games.” Jihyun waved excitedly, pointing to another room.

What’s with this kid?

“Come on, Gwen. Let me show you. We can play together! I have five computers!” He ran excitedly through another door, waving and jumping.

Five computers? Gwen sighed, then followed.

“What kind of games do you like?” Jihyun asked.

“I prefer role-playing games, but I’ll play just about anything.”

“I like those too. What’s your favorite food?”

“Noodles in a cup.”

“Never had those, but I have always wanted to try them,” he said.

Gwen’s mouth dropped open. “You have never had noodles in a cup?”

The boy shook his head. “Nuh-uh. What’s your favorite dessert?”

“What is this? Twenty questions?” Gwen retorted.

“I wanna know everything about you,” he said happily.

She sighed, giving in. “Triple-layer chocolate cake,” she admitted.

“I love that too!”

Jihyun excitedly jumped up and down, then ran into the next room, with Gwen following. This room had several computers—the most high-tech computers Gwen had ever seen—with many other cool gadgets.

Whoa.

“See? I told you I have five computers.”

“Don’t you have any friends?” Gwen said randomly, eyeing the new room.

“I only talk to my dad—the King, Vihaan, and sometimes Vihaan’s friend.”

Gwen held her breath. “*Your* dad is the king of Olympia?” she asked, totally in denial.

“He isn’t my real dad. I’m adopted,” Jihyun said, shrugging. “My real dad died when I was a baby. They don’t know what happened to my mother.”

“Hmm,” Gwen said, studying him. “Did your birth parents have magic too?”

"No. Just me. The King said I was special. They give me medicine to help me because I'm special."

"Medicine? What kind of medicine?"

It was the first time that Jihyun looked serious, and scared. "I have lots of nightmares," he said, his voice lowered. "Sometimes, I get so many, I become scary. So they give me medicine."

Gwen suddenly thought back to how crazy he acted out in the wastelands, then recalled Mae's warning. Her dad came to mind.

"I witnessed it myself," Gwen said in a low voice as her eyes stung with new tears. "My father was hurt badly."

Jihyun's eyes got wide again, then he frowned. "I don't remember anything that happened. I'm...I'm sorry if I hurt your dad, Gwen."

A tear fell, and Gwen wiped it away. She could tell that this kid was sincere.

Just when she was about to say something, Jihyun gave her a big hug.

"What's that for?"

"You are sad, and I'm trying to make you happy."

This whole thing was crazy. This boy who nearly killed her father didn't even realize it or remember anything about it, played video games, wanted to be friends, and gave hugs. Maybe Mae was right about the boy being sweet, and that the Olympians forced him to do cruel things.

Gwen sucked in her breath, "Thanks, Jihyun."

The boy smiled brightly at her. His smiles were contagious, given how big his round face and cheeks were. She couldn't help but chuckle, though she was trying to force it back.

"When you said you become scary, do you mean your magic is scary?" Gwen asked.

Jihyun nodded. "I can't control it. My magic comes to me, and I don't know what to do. So they give me medicine to make me better."

"You don't know how to work your magic?" Gwen asked, raising an eyebrow.

"Nuh-uh. It just comes to me, so people like Bryce give me medicine. If I become extra scary, Vihaan is the one who gives me my medicine. He can protect himself from me."

"Protect?"

"Yeah. He has magic too! Isn't that cool?" Jihyun nudged her. "Do you have magic Gwen?"

"No. I wish, though."

"It's okay. We can still be friends!" Jihyun turned away toward the row of computers. "Let's play the game. I'm so happy I have a friend! Do you know you are my first real friend ever?"

First real friend? The thought saddened her. All he had were a bunch of grownups around him, locked away with magic, having nightmares that were uncontrollable, with no friends…

What a terrible life. No wonder he has nightmares.

But what made her troubled was that they gave him medicine to control it. Was that how he used magic?

Suddenly, she realized that she had forgotten something. Gwen glanced at the ceiling, trying to be inconspicuous. The room was pretty dark, but she could still see the same shape of hidden cameras like in her room.

She sighed. Now they knew what they'd talked about. *Stupid me. I can't believe I was so dumb not to think about it before.*

Gwen turned back and smiled at him, then followed him to the set of computers. The boy gestured to the "best" setup, and she sat down, amazed. It was the most expensive gaming computer she had ever seen.

"Wow, this is insane," Gwen said, running her fingers across the keyboard. The keys were backlit with all the colors of the spectrum, flashing in different patterns. Her input device did the same, along with the speakers. She loved computers and technology. This piece of equipment was beautiful to her.

"Isn't it the best?" he said, sitting down to a nearby computer. He logged in, then scrolled through the list of games. "What game do you want to play?" he asked.

Gwen sighed. What was she? A kidnapped girl who was supposed to entertain the prince of Olympia? Some kidnapping…

She sat down. "You go ahead and pick."

"How about *Space Conqueror*? I like that one. You are on a planet shooting the bad aliens that are trying to conquer the galaxy," he said.

Gwen shrugged. "Sure, I'll try it."

Then he logged on, and they started their game. As they played, Gwen began formulating every possible way to get out of Olympia. She had little time before things would get bad for her, or worse, for her parents.

CHAPTER 14

◆

ORANGE

"One of the scavengers found this," Garrett called from the entryway, waving a cybernetic part in his hand. "I think we can use it. It's first gen."

"Bring it here," Telly said swiftly.

Garrett handed her a cybernetic chip. "I can't believe they found this. It's rare," Telly said, inspecting the piece. It was in decent condition for being out in the desert.

"Right? I was sure the Corporation would have to make a new one," Garrett said.

Turning to Drew, Telly started getting him ready for the implant switch.

Garrett stood beside her in silence. She could tell that he wanted to say something but was hesitating. Inwardly, Telly still felt intense bitterness toward him.

It's his fault for leading my daughter on, she thought. If he hadn't been so friendly toward Gwen, her daughter wouldn't have thought she needed to prove herself to him. And Drew wouldn't be in the state he was in if Gwen hadn't run off.

"Do you need help?" Garrett asked softly.

"Not this time."

Telly grabbed the alcohol and a rag, then started cleaning Drew's body, sterilizing the area for the chip transfer. His human eye was shut, but his cybernetic eye remained open, with many of the wires spilling out. She fought back tears.

Drew…I miss you…

Memories came over her as she continued to prep the area for transfer. There'd been a time when they'd visited the Twin Kingdoms. Several, in fact. But her favorite was when they had walked downtown in the blazing wintery winds of the kingdom. Drew had never experienced intense cold before, so she had decided to surprise him. She had led him down the mid-level skyways that took them directly to an outdoor platform. Telly would never forget his face that day.

Telly's eyes shifted to Drew's inanimate eyes. There was no expression behind them, just an empty shell, albeit a breathing one.

"Telly…" Garrett said as he stood on the other side of Drew.

Telly sighed as her memory faded, glancing up at Garrett.

He sat down on the stool, leaning in. "I know you don't want to talk to me. I can't even begin to know what you are going through. You're right, I feel responsible for what happened. We all do." He paused, his voice quieting. "I am doing everything that I possibly can to bring Gwen home to you."

"And *what* are you doing?" Telly said abruptly.

Garrett suddenly came into her line of sight. His face was like stone, his gaze unwavering. His facial circuit-board tattoos stood out all the more. "Do you really want to get into it? Do you, Telly? You better think about it before you ask me again." He smoothed his faux hawk back intensely, waiting for her to answer.

Telly's hands shook with anger as she fought back her tears. She wanted to stay angry. But she knew it wouldn't get her anywhere.

"I'm just so…lost. And *angry,*" she whispered.

There was a long pause between them, then Garrett gave her a sad but hopeful smile. "I promised you I would do everything to bring her home. You can count on me." He leaned in. "If you want to see what I am doing, I can show you."

Telly glanced up at him. "What is it?" She already knew what he spoke of, of course. Still, she pretended to be in the dark.

"I've been logging magical activity in Olympia. Through activity logs, I can pinpoint were the energy bursts are, and we can see if Gwen might be at these points," Garrett said.

"Are you thinking that Gwen is with that magical boy?"

"It would make the most sense. If Olympia knows that Drew has magic—

and that he's Gwen's father—they would likely place her with the boy to guard her." Garrett side-eyed Drew, then sighed. "They know the boy defeated Drew once. If they think he'll come to retrieve Gwen, they're probably counting on the boy defeating Drew again."

He is trying. "It is a good plan," Telly said softly. "Please let me know if you find anything unusual."

Garrett's face softened. "Of course. You'll be the first to know." His face shifted to Drew, then he frowned. "You sure you don't need any help?"

Telly glanced back at Drew. It was as if he was back in his cryogenic state, like he had been for years, and that he had never woken in the first place. She wiped the remaining tears from under her glasses, then shook her head. "This is an easy switch. You should work on finding Gwen through your program. It's the best hope we have," Telly said. "I'll have Scion fetch you if we need anything."

"Will do."

Will you really? Or will you and Geeta will keep it a secret...

Garrett turned away to leave as Scion entered. The cyborg was dressed in his usual black tank top, military combat pants, cybernetic parts glowing yellow throughout his skin, like the irises of his eyes. His hair was getting longer than the shaved cyborg haircut.

"Good day, Mr. Garrett," Scion said.

"Hey, Scion."

"Where were you?" Telly asked. "You snuck out when I wasn't paying attention."

"I was not trying to sneak out at all. I had to use the facility, Miss Hearly," Scion said. "You were focused on Drew."

"That's my cue," Garrett said, waving to them. "See you later, Scion." He darted out the door, leaving the two of them alone.

Telly and Scion worked in silence for a while as they removed parts that needed to be cleared for the installation of the scavenged chip. Drew's heart rate could be heard on the machine. Telly was completely focused on the exposed area.

Just as she removed the old parts, Scion broke the silence. "Miss Hearly."

"Hm?"

"I do not understand why are you keeping this secret from Garrett. He developed much of your camp's magitech weaponry. Why not allow him to help you?"

Telly whipped her head in his direction. "You…*know?*"

"I knew from the very start of your project," Scion said matter-of-factly. "What I do not understand is why you keep it hidden."

"I have my reasons. Let's just leave it at that."

"If you like."

"Yes, I do like."

"Hey, you two," a woman's voice rang out.

It was Reila. Telly went back to working on Drew.

"Any luck getting that list for Drew?" Reila said. "The sooner the better, Geeta says."

"There are a few more things that I require from the Corporation. It will take me precisely eighteen minutes to finish compiling the list," Scion said. "If you do not mind waiting here, that is. If not, you can always come back in eighteen minutes."

"What do I look like? An errand girl?" Reila retorted.

Scion cocked his head in confusion. "No. You look like Miss Reila to me."

"Fine." She trudged over to Drew, glancing over him. "Installing a new part?"

"Miss Hearly is installing a working brain implant," Scion answered. "The procedure will take approximately thirty-seven minutes and twenty-two seconds."

Reila sat down next to Drew, placing a hand on his human hand. Telly brushed wiring away, revealing the area where the new chip would be implanted. Grabbing her pair of lucky tweezers, she yanked out the fried chip with the wires still attached. One by one, she unplugged the wires connected to the old chip. Then, she carefully picked up the new chip with her tweezers, then plugged the chip into its spot on the circuit board and reconnected the wires. The sight made her heart hurt, but she managed the best she could to remain calm. She had to for Drew's sake.

Telly sighed with relief when she heard the heart machine beep.

"I'd never thought to say it, city girl, but I miss your man," Reila said in a quiet tone.

Telly's eyes welled up with tears.

"I also miss him," Scion added as he compiled his list.

Reila glanced back at him, unconvinced. "*You* miss him? I doubt that." Reila snorted.

"I do have humanity in me, despite what you think," Scion said, looking up from his tablet. "I consider myself one of your people now, as I have assimilated to your way of life at the camp. I will aid you in any way that I can."

Reila's eyes went wide, almost amused. "Well, ain't that something?"

Telly smiled to herself. She knew Reila's tough-girl exterior was just an act, especially around Scion lately.

Reila coughed. "How much longer?"

"Six minutes and eighteen seconds."

"Why do you gotta do that?"

"What are you referring to?"

"Speaking in robot language. Too many numbers hurt my brain."

"I prefer precise answers," Scion said.

"*This* one." Reila pointed at him, then huffed loudly. "I'll be out in the corridor. I don't think I can listen to any more of this cyborg jargon." She was about to leave, then said, "And about that tan. Keep it up." Then she ducked out of the cavern chamber.

"I only speak what I mean," Scion said, confused.

"Don't take anything she says seriously," Telly said. "She does it to me as well, and I'm not a cyborg. You and I—our minds are wired differently than hers."

"Hmm," Scion said, glancing at the empty corridor chamber entrance, where Reila had gone. "What did she mean by tan?"

"Now's not the time for explaining." Telly glanced over at Drew, then grabbed her tablet.

"According to my readings, Drew's body has successfully acclimated to the new part," Scion said. "It has increased his stability for the time being."

She breathed a sigh of relief, knowing that she could slip out for just a little while.

Getting up and stretching, Telly walked toward her temporary desk, opening the compartment. The new weapon glimmered even in the faintest light. There were improvements to be made, but she had to test a few things before doing so.

Scion's clicking movements rang across the cavern ground, as laser scans beeped. "List is complete," he said as he walked out to the corridor.

Telly heard Scion's and Reila's muffled voices in the cavern halls outside her chamber. From what Telly could make out, Reila was doing her best to flirt with Scion, while it all went over his head.

Telly turned away, slipping on a jacket, then grabbed the invisible magitech weapon, holstering it.

Scion reentered, looking confused. "It is a conundrum that I was once human. I do not think I will ever understand Miss Reila." His gaze then turned toward her. "Miss Hearly, where are you going?"

"To blow off some steam." She grabbed a few vials, stuffing them in her jacket. "If anyone comes looking for me, tell them that nature called."

Scion cocked his head. "Nature called? What does that entail?"

Telly sighed. Though she loved cyborgs, they were exhausting at times. It was the very reason Reila was so testy with the lot of them. "Relieving one's bodily waste. What you just did moments ago," she answered as she melded out of sight with her orange magic.

Scion's gaze was still locked on her, then he nodded, turning to Drew.

Telly exited the chamber, moving through the cavern tunnels as quiet as she could under her guise of orange magic. She evaded anyone who was left in the refuge, passing by anyone in the tight sections of the tunnels. Quickly, she made her way out of the entrance, passing Ryan and Chris, who were standing guard. She almost bumped Chris's side but caught herself just in time.

She exited the refuge and made her way north, into the vast wastelands. There was a small path, with numerous desert shrubs that hid it well, even to the air transports if they flew overhead. She took the path, walking her way around the mountain.

The jaunt was harder on her knees than she thought. *I'm too old for this. That, or I'm too out of shape.* She sighed, pulling out her canteen. She took a long drink, then slung it back around her chest again, hiking further north after being completely out of sight where the refuge and anyone standing guard would be.

After she deemed it safe, Telly released her magic, her body shimmering in orange with the sparkles softly blowing away in the wind. She took a long drink from her canteen, then placed it back at her side.

Reaching toward her thigh, Telly yanked the magitech weapon from her holster. She flipped the cartridge holder open, then fumbled in her jacket pocket, retrieving one of the vials. It was the red one. She slid it into the loading chamber, then slammed it shut.

Let's see what you got. Cocking the weapon, Telly aimed at a pile of rocks and fired.

The force of the weapon startled her, knocking her entire body back while the weapon discharged a foot higher than her initial aim. A split second later, there was giant explosion.

Telly fumbled with her glasses, straightening them on her face, then blinked. Miles of ice encapsulated the wastelands before her eyes. And not normal ice—it glowed a translucent red, shimmering with magic.

A deep chill was carried in the wind, causing her to involuntarily chatter her teeth.

Of course, she understood that red magic held the power of the elements. But how did the magic decide to choose to blast ice instead of fire? Or lightning? Was it at random? Staring at the magical iced area, Telly wondered if it would melt before anyone came across it. Then she sighed. Not like she could do anything about it.

She reached down into her jacket again, this time loading the yellow vial. Cocking the weapon, she fired.

This time, she was ready for the kickback, bracing the weapon on her shoulder. The vial wasn't visible as it shot out, but a few seconds later, a shimmer of gold flecks dusted the ground.

Was the magic protecting the ground itself? Did it need to be shot at a subject so it would protect that subject?

Curious, Telly walked toward the area where the golden flecks of magic shimmered on the ground. As she approached, the translucent shimmer grew brighter in the sunlight. She stopped at the edge of the magical barrier, then bent down. Telly swiped her finger across the area. It was the same sensation as when she swiped her computer tablet when she worked on Drew. The shimmer grew brighter as her finger slid across the area, leaving a gold path for a moment, then slowly fading away. The area seemed to have a magical barrier, like translucent glass but solid as iron.

Just like Scion's barriers.

Telly noticed that as the golden flecks died down, so did the glass-like sensation on her fingertip. She made a mental note that the barrier only lasted about five minutes, give or take. The red vial blast of ice magic still encapsulated the area. Why did the red magic last longer than the yellow? Was it because the red magic produced physical results, whereas the yellow magic didn't?

She needed to make more of the vials. Many, many more in order to get more answers. If she had the full power of her orange magic, she wouldn't need to rely so much on the randomness of the vial's choosing—such as the red vial choosing ice instead of fire magic. If she perfected her vials to the point where she could make the magic more specific, and if she had the power to make copies of her new concoction, just as Drew made copies of Princess Emerald's blood several months back, she would have a strong chance to take Olympia head on. She could thoroughly plan out rescuing Gwen once Garrett identified where they were holding her.

Could it be possible to become a full orange-gifted?

She thought back to what her turning vision had whispered. *It's because you don't believe*, it had told her.

Believe in what, exactly? Telly had thought about that moment over and over again, analyzing what the magic had meant. She had denied the magic's existence in the beginning. But over the course of seeing and using it, she now had no doubt magic was real. But there was something about the whole thing that she couldn't wrap her head around. Where did the magic come from? What was the explanation behind it all?

It was the very thing Telly was sure that was holding her back from embracing her gift.

Have you considered reading The Spectrum? Director Jonathan had asked her months ago.

I've never been a spiritual type. Telly sighed and pushed those thoughts aside.

Glancing one last time at where the magical blast had been, Telly summoned her orange magic, then faded away into the wasteland surroundings.

CHAPTER 15

✦

GREEN

As Emerald headed through the palace toward the Inner Council chamber, she noticed Emerys waiting for her in the main halls. He was standing poised in his long gray councilor robes, with his insignia ring, patiently waiting. The gray streak in his dark hair was more prominent than Emerald remembered.

"Emerys? Why are you out here?" Emerald asked as the councilor bowed to her. "Are you not attending the meeting?"

Emerys gave her a concerned glance. "I wouldn't miss it for anything, My Queen. I know you have been awake for some time now, and haven't really gotten a chance to speak with you alone. I thought this would be a good time before we join the meeting." He smiled at her.

Emerald nodded and beamed back. "By all means, let's walk together."

She took his elbow as they walked down the hall, passing through several of the palace skyways and into other chambers of the palace.

"You got my message? About the taxes?" Emerald asked.

"Indeed. I am ready to speak to the Inner Council."

"Good." She breathed a sigh of relief.

"By the way, I received word from the Protector of the Realm. She personally went to the Corporation and delivered the list of parts required for that cyborg."

Emerald felt a little weight off her shoulders. "Good. How long do you suppose it will take them to get all that is needed?"

"That I do not know, but I will ensure that I stay current and let Your Majesty know."

"Thank you, Councilor," Emerald said. "It means so much to me…" Emerald stopped, then smiled at Emerys.

"How are you feeling?" Emerys asked, glancing at her with concern.

"Tired, but fine, really." It was mostly true, though Emerald felt as if she were fighting extreme exhaustion every day. She tried to hide it.

"I'm glad you are better," Emerys said, then glanced at her. "My Queen, I'm not one to beat around the bush."

"You never were one to do so."

The two chuckled, then he grew serious again. "I learned about your pregnancy when you…were asleep," he said as his dark eyes met hers.

Emerald's cheeks flushed. If Emerys knew, then others must already know too. She turned to him. "It is true. I cannot deny it. Now that you know, I suppose there will be some formal announcement."

"I do want to make an announcement, though I think it wise to hold off," Emerys said as the two continued to walk. "With the squabble with Olympia, the King being gone…it would be safer to wait until you are closer to full term."

His reminder about Derek being gone suddenly made her nervous. What if Derek showed up soon? Emerald stopped, then put her hands on his arm.

Emerys glanced at her. "Your Majesty? Are you all right?"

"I am actually thankful that you are being so considerate of me, Councilor," Emerald said. "You truly are wise."

"I care for you, as I care for this kingdom. I always am humbled serving the kindest of rulers in all of the United Kingdoms." He smiled, then lowered his voice. "But I must ask you since we are on this subject. About your new guest."

Emerald's heart hammered hard, knowing the sound of his voice: confusion…or was it disappointment?

"Master Kyle? What about him?"

Emerys cleared his throat. "How long will he be a guest at the palace?"

"Indefinitely."

More silence, and Emerald could feel the tension rising.

"What of the King?"

Emerald turned red, then glanced at Emerys. "I will deal with the King once he returns. If he returns," she muttered under her breath. "I am happy, Emerys. For the first time, I am truly happy."

"My Queen, I have seen you grow from a young child into who you are now. I know what you say is true," Emerys said. "But I must advise you to be cautious."

Emerald turned to him. "Councilor…" She paused, thinking about how to say what she wanted to say. Her eyes met his. "What is the possibility of me divorcing the King?"

His eyes went wide as he sucked in a breath. "You don't mean it…do you?" Emerys said in disbelief.

"I do," Emerald said firmly.

Emerys grew serious. "The repercussions would be astronomical. You would lose everything—including your kingdom." He lowered his voice. "I know what laws have passed, and I can say without a doubt that you would be queen no more. You couldn't do that to your kingdom."

Emerald's heart dropped.

"Take this guest as a consort," Emerys urged. "But do so—"

He was interrupted with a few lords passing by. When they were no longer in earshot, Emerys leaned in. "Just be private with your personal life."

It looked like he wanted to say more, but they came upon the Inner Council doors, and the guards bowed to them.

"After Her Majesty," Emerys said, bowing.

Emerald nodded as the guards opened the doors, then walked inside. The glass-encased room was bright this time of day. Outside, the entire kingdom of Arcadia sprawled out as far as the eye could see, as the room was higher up than most in the palace. That is, besides hers, being in the tallest turret.

At the round table, all of the other councilors and advisors were already seated, except for Emerys, who took his spot.

"Thank you for coming on short notice, my lords," Emerald announced.

"It's not like we had much choice," the baroness stated. The lords chuckled, with Emerald smiling.

"I suppose you are correct in saying so, Baroness." Emerald nodded. She sat down, relieved. Her feet and ankles were swollen just from walking here from her chambers. It had been happening more often as of late. "I won't take too much of your time."

For a moment, Kyle slipped into her mind, and she couldn't suppress a smile. Pushing her thoughts aside, she took a drink of water, then addressed the advisors. "There are a few matters to be briefed about. First off, let us discuss Olympia."

Duke Uthgard motioned. "If I may, Your Majesty."

"Go ahead."

"Olympia has withdrawn from the wastelands. For the time being, there have not been any more front-line attacks. After we deemed it safe, I had the wastelanders return to their camps."

"I thank you for your assistance, Duke," Emerald said, nodding. "Though it seems that the war is over, there is something vexing that came out of it."

"What is it?" Lysander asked.

Emerald glanced at each advisor around the table. "Olympia has taken one of the wastelanders and is holding her prisoner."

"What does that matter?" asked one of the dukes.

"It matters because it is one of *our* wastelanders. She resides on our lands," Emerald said. "She is the daughter of two prominent scientists who created the cyborg technology for Arcadia."

"Surely Your Majesty won't let this slide?" Duke Uthgard suggested.

"Absolutely not," Emerald said. "I will not tolerate the abduction of any Arcadian citizen."

"What does Your Majesty suggest?" the duke continued.

"The Protector of the Realm is working with a small team of associates who hope to rescue the girl. They will be in contact with the palace if they need assistance or reinforcements."

"I will be glad to help lead another charge if necessary," the duke said.

"Thank you, Duke Uthgard."

"Are your powers needed to aid this rescue?" Lysander asked.

"Not at this moment, Councilor. Hopefully it won't come to it either, for my power must be guarded," Emerald said. Her mother and Derek popped into her mind, but she let it go. "I had to warn you so that if the situation does escalate, you are all prepared."

"Might I suggest that we contact the Olympian ambassador?" Lysander asked. "Perhaps we can sort this out through diplomacy."

"As much as I prefer a peaceful solution with both parties, I think we need to take a more unconventional approach, Councilor," Emerald said. "I am fed up with other kingdoms taking advantage of my good graces. I know that the

King had gone back and forth with the ambassador, and it was pointless." Emerald sighed. "If the team out in the wastelands runs out of options, then we can turn to talks as a last resort. But truly, it would be a *last resort,*" she stated firmly.

"Hear, hear," said the duke as the baroness nodded in agreement.

Emerald nodded, then continued. "Now that that's out of the way, let us move on to our next item on the agenda." She looked to Emerys. "Councilor?"

"Yes, Your Majesty," Emerys said. He walked over to one of the display platforms, then pressed a button on his communicator. A holographic screen appeared on the display, showing one of the laws.

"It has come to my attention that the tax still remains on citizens traveling between the city levels," Emerald continued.

"Was it to be changed, Your Majesty? His Majesty had no prior plans," said Councilor Diedrich.

"Yes. I had asked my husband to change this law prior to his absence. Whether it had been in the works or not, I want it done now," Emerald stated.

"It was never discussed, though His Majesty did have quite a list to fulfill. We never had access to his records." The baroness shrugged, then leaned in. "Begging your pardon for saying so, but is the rock star behind all of this?"

Her question took Emerald completely by surprise. She didn't know that others already were aware of Kyle.

"Rock star? You mean Master Kyle?" Emerald asked, not flinching.

"Well, yes," the baroness said. "The rumors are like wildfire in the palace. A *rock star* in the palace."

Emerys darted a look toward her.

"I didn't know everyone was aware that he was in here. It's only been a day since he…arrived."

The baroness grinned. "A day is all it takes, Your Majesty. It is my job to know who, what, where, and when. All of Arcadia is in love with the man. And when you get someone like that, how could someone like myself not find out? I, for one, am curious about this starlet that our city has suddenly become addicted to."

Emerald swallowed as if her throat had had a lump in it. "Master Kyle is not behind the tax. And just to reiterate, I want to fix the tax law permanently."

"I see," the baroness said, then raised an eyebrow.

The baroness's glance was like a dart into her mind, as if she knew she and Kyle were lovers without a single word. But was it really that bad? Everyone would eventually find out. After all, she'd had breakfast with him, and there were guards all over the halls who'd seen them kiss. She shouldn't be embarrassed about her true feelings.

It doesn't matter what they think, she decided. *Kyle is finally with me, and I won't let them spoil it.*

"It is nice to see all sorts of Arcadians addressing their concerns with the Queen," Councilor Diedrich said with a somewhat pointed tone. "As to the matter of the tax situation, there are still some debts that the kingdom has from your father. Hence, why the tax was imposed to begin with."

"I was under the impression that as wife to His Majesty, the King of York was to level out Arcadia's debts," Emerald said.

Emerys nodded. "That was in one of the initial proposals, My Queen. However, during the last days of your father's reign, that was not signed into the documents."

The sorceress had made a mess of everything, and now, their finances. Though she wanted to reach out to the kingdom of York for financial help, she bit her lip. Facing Derek's parents after everything that had happened would be uncomfortable for everyone. Especially if King Samir were to find out about Kyle…

"We will hold off on York for the time being," Emerald continued. "However, we will remove the tax. You all know very well that the lower-level citizens do not have the kind of money to pay the tax on a frequent basis. It is time to hold everyone accountable." Emerald looked to Emerys, and he nodded in approval. "That includes you, Councilor Diedrich."

"Your Majesty?"

Emerald eyed him evenly. "I've been told that some of you get kickbacks from this tax."

Councilor Diedrich suddenly looked pale. "I—I don't know what you mean by this…" he started.

"I had Emerys trace some accounts that tie to you, being lord of the mid-sectors. You get a kickback from the upper levels and some of the mid-level lords and corporation presidents to keep 'lower-level filth' out of their levels,"

Emerald said pointedly.

Several lords looked nervous, while the baroness smirked.

"Never."

Emerald brushed the display aside, bringing up some logged communications. "Does this mean anything to you?"

The councilors opened their mouths wide, and the baroness's smug look deepened.

"I know it is not you who started the tax, as you were not a part of this council at the time. However, after my father's death, you were persuaded to keep the tax, were you not?" Emerald said.

"Well, erm…yes…" the lord said.

Emerald stood up. "There are many other ways to tax our city. Drop the lower-level tax immediately. And find a better solution," Emerald said. "If you want to keep your position as a sector lord, I suggest you pay Arcadia's treasury back all that you have collected." She turned to Emerys. "Please hand the lord the bill, Councilor Emerys."

Emerys smiled secretly, then nodded. "This is Her Majesty's order, with the amount due." He slid the bill in front of the sector lord's place at the table.

"Please draw up the law and place it into the machine. I will wait," Emerald continued.

"Yes, Your Majesty."

As she waited, Emerald's stomach twisted again. It was the stress of it. Being pregnant, she couldn't deal with things like she could before. She placed her hand on her stomach. *Please stay strong, you two,* she told her womb silently.

It didn't take long for the Inner Council to write the amendment. They all agreed, then handed it to Emerald. She reviewed it, then nodded. "Seal it into law," she said.

Emerys took the sheet, then placed it into the law machine, scanning and uploading it. The machine beeped, and Emerald reviewed the law in the machine, satisfied.

"Thank you, everyone, for your time," Emerald announced. "I hope everyone knows that I am serious about *everything* that happens in this kingdom."

"Your Majesty," they said in unison as they bowed.

Emerald walked out of the room, thinking about talking to Derek's father. There was only so long she could avoid him.

She hoped that day would be a long way from now.

CHAPTER 16

✦

RED

Kyle sat outside on Emerald's private patio, playing his guitar as he puffed a cigarette. He deeply inhaled the smoke, savoring the moment. From time to time as he played, he glanced at the tops of the nearby skyscrapers. Above him, Zaphod was perched on the patio chair backing, cooing contently.

Thanks, Geeta, he thought as he played a tune. It was the "present" that she had referred to when he saw her. She had dropped it off with a note attached when he and Emerald were out. Though getting his guitar back was definitely a highlight of his new life, he found Geeta's note oddly satisfying too. *Don't be such an ass this time around,* the note had said. Kyle snorted. Geeta was something all right.

I wonder how Diego and the guys are doing?

Playing the guitar made him realize how much he missed the band and his buddies. He always had a good-ass time with the guys. Fucking around, having fun and all that. Kyle knew he had to protect Em in Arcadia; that part he swore. But what harm would it be to at least go visit the guys in the lower levels? It would take his mind off the current situation. He could bring Em with him.

He finished playing, then set the guitar between his lap, taking another puff of his cigarette. What was taking Em so long? It was midday. But he knew she had an important meeting this morning with a ton of things to sort through with the kingdom, from the Olympian war to the corporation providing cybernetic parts. Hopefully that damn tax too. Em had also mentioned something about York. He knew she was skirting the issue because it dealt with Derek's father. Just another damn thing to stress her out. As if she didn't have enough going on.

Glad I don't have to sit through those meetings, Kyle thought. He couldn't even imagine making it through one. Not that he would be invited. Just sitting with Geeta at breakfast a few days ago made his head hurt.

It was great getting out with Emerald and visiting his apartment. She was carefree when she was out of the palace. Playful, fun, cute, and lighthearted. Most importantly, she was herself—and had freedom. But at the palace, Kyle saw the transformation before his eyes—Em was more reserved, poised, and *stressed*. It was as if the weight of the world were on her shoulders and she was its prisoner. Even though she was free to do what she pleased now, it sure as shit didn't seem like it.

He couldn't imagine what she was dealing with. Being pregnant. Derek and her mother. God, what a mess. What he had told Em was true. He would raise both kids as his own. It wasn't her fucking fault that asshole fuck—and the sorceress—took advantage of her. Really, the sorceress was behind it all.

Kyle glanced at the skyline as he lit up another smoke. The hit of nicotine calmed him down. Slightly. What made him scared the most was that he didn't want to be like his father. That thought scared the shit out of him. His father was the biggest asshole, leaving his mother behind after she became pregnant. Kyle didn't want to fuck up his kids like his father fucked it up for him.

Not only that, he had no idea how to raise a kid. Hell, he had never even held a baby before.

I guess I will wing it, he told himself, though the thought didn't make him feel any better.

Zaphod cooed on his shoulder.

Kyle eyed Zaphod, knowing that his feathered friend felt his emotions.

"Yeah, I know. Can you believe I'm going to be a father?"

Zaphod cawed in response.

"First Geeta, now you? I know I'm not the most responsible human, but I have my moments."

Zaphod nudged him again, then cawed.

"You don't have to rub it in. Sorry that I've been depriving you of attention," Kyle said in a soothing voice. "Here you go, bud." He fed Zaphod a saltine.

Zaphod whistled, then snatched the cracker.

"Ya know, you'll never guess who I saw recently," Kyle said to him as he rubbed under Zaphod's chin. "I saw Rosie."

Zaphod looked up at him, then cocked his head curiously. "*Rosie!*" Zaphod cawed loudly.

Kyle blinked in surprise. That was the second time ever that the bird talked. "You remember Rosie?"

"*Rosie,*" the bird repeated. "Rosie," Zaphod cooed.

Kyle smiled at him, then rubbed under the bird's neck, feeling the softness of its down. "Well, I'll be damned," he said. "Looks like a visit is in order. Don't get too cozy. Maybe you'll wanna live with her, and I don't know how I feel about that."

"Rosie!" Zaphod whistled, then went back to eating his cracker. He had been thinking about Zaphod and Rosie. If Zaphod was happy to see Rosie, could he let the bird go? They had been through so much, getting back to Arcadia through the mental mind-maze fuck. But maybe, strangely, it was Zaphod's way to get back to Rosie through his second life, just like Kyle had. They both had a chance at a second life in Arcadia.

Kyle took a last drag, then smashed the cigarette butt, flicking it off the patio. Zaphod whistled in protest.

"I swear, you're just as bad as Geeta," he said as he stood and snapped up his guitar.

The two of them went inside. Emerald still wasn't back yet.

Hope she's okay.

He set his guitar within the velvety folds of its case, then went to the bathroom to get cleaned up. He splashed hot water on his face, making a huge mess across the counter. After towel-drying his face, he brushed his teeth. The odd taste combination of old smoke mixed with fresh mint lingered, causing his stomach to gurgle. He was hungry and hadn't eaten because he was waiting for Emerald. It was way past lunchtime. Well, his lunchtime anyway.

I could play the guitar some more, he thought. But then again, he had been playing for a while, and he was tired. *Maybe I'll just take a nap.*

Kyle plopped onto a sofa, making himself comfortable. Hopefully if he lay there long enough, he'd fall asleep and forget about his hunger. Hell, that was what Zaphod did twenty-four seven. His bird sat perched in his favorite corner in Em's bedroom, looking content.

Must be nice to have it easy, he thought as he glanced at Zaphod.

He lazily glanced at Emerald's artwork on the wall. There were drawings, paintings, sketches, all beautifully done in whatever medium she used.

Em really is fricking talented, Kyle thought as he studied her artwork. Her use of color was fantastic, and she had a knack for capturing a person's likeness.

As Kyle scanned the different pictures, he suddenly realized that a lot of them were of him—but when he was High Inquisitor Rubius. *How in the hell did she envision me as that...person?*

A shiver ran down his spine. It must be her gift, he thought as he remembered when he first met her. She had drawn a picture that resembled her, and a machine that sucked her magic from her body. She could see things in her mind's eye without realizing that it was a real person, event, or time era.

For some reason, a memory of Elder Moon—from his life as Rubius—came to mind.

Glancing down at his necklace, the one that Elder Moon gave him, Kyle clasped it. As he did, he felt Emerald's life force. What did it all mean? Why had Em put a fragment of her soul in this stone? And how did Elder Moon get this stone?

There was a click at the door, and it opened.

Kyle sat up, then beamed as Emerald stepped inside. "Hey," he called out.

She ran over to him and gave him a quick hug. "Sorry I'm so late. I had a lot of business to take care of," she said.

"It's okay, I know you gotta do that kind of thing," Kyle said. "Did you have fun?" he said in a parent-like voice.

"Not really." She giggled. "But you'll be happy to know that I put those lords in place about the tax laws."

Kyle inwardly smiled. "Good." *At least she's in a good mood. It'll make it easier on me.* Kyle cleared his throat. "Em. You know I will always protect you. From anyone and anything."

Emerald glanced at him curiously. "Yes, of course. I know that."

Kyle took a deep breath. "And of course, we are protected here at the palace."

"Mm-hmm."

Kyle rubbed the back of his neck while she looked at him curiously. "But, I also worry about you."

"Worry? Why?" Emerald asked. "I have you to protect me."

Let's try this again. Kyle glanced at her. "What I mean is: your stress. It's not good for you to be walled up here all day."

"What do you mean? We went to your apartment the other day." Emerald smiled. "I am a queen and have business to take care of."

"Of course. But in your spare time? Do you have to stay here?" Kyle sat up straighter, then held her hands. "I see the worry on your face. It's not good. You need to have fun once in a while. We can't just sit here day after day, afraid of your mother and Derek."

"I'm not afraid…"

"Yeah, but if you hide out here, you essentially are letting them win," he pointed out. "It's not healthy to sit in four walls all day."

They both gazed at each other, with her flushing. "I suppose you are right," she admitted. "I do feel happier when I'm out with you."

Kyle smiled, kissing her hand. "It's true. I see it too. Don't let anyone hold you prisoner from being you."

Emerald glanced at him. "What did you have in mind?"

"I dunno. I suppose it would be nice to go down and visit the lower levels." Kyle sighed. "The more I think of it, the more I miss it. Of course, I'd gladly give it up to be with you. But it's just that…I can't help but think of my old life. I kind of miss it. A lot."

Emerald took in a breath, then placed his hand on her cheek. "I want you to be happy, Kyle."

"I want you to be happy too. Didn't we have lots of fun, living below and doing God knows what?" He laughed. "You got to do your art, I got to play at shows. We had some wild nights."

She giggled. "We *did*…"

"I know, I know, you are queen," he muttered. "But being queen doesn't mean you have to have a death sentence for fun and happiness. Right? It felt good seeing Rosie, the old apartment, and just being in the lower levels. I felt at home. I know we aren't going to live there, but I had fun being with you there and just living. Besides, I would like to see the guys. They don't even know I'm here."

"*Rosie!*" Zaphod squawked.

Kyle chuckled. "See? He wants to get out too."

"He spoke again!"

"Guess that's how much he misses Rosie," Kyle joked.

Emerald smiled as she absentmindedly placed her hand on her tummy. His stomach did a flip as he was reminded of fatherhood on the horizon. "Okay. We can go to the lower levels and visit whenever you like. I know it means so much to you. Just know that I do have business to attend to, so I cannot always go with you. I know deep down that Derek or my mother will not try anything while I'm with child—but that's if they know about it. They wouldn't risk it, though they might try other methods," she said. "But as for Councilor Emerys, I don't know if he will like this arrangement."

"Don't worry about him. If he wants a demonstration of my abilities, I can show off for him to feel more safe about it." Kyle jumped up, smiling.

Emerald laughed. "I think that is unnecessary." She paused, placing a hand on his chest. "But I must take it easy. I'm tired a lot more than usual. The babies are draining my energy away, leaving me very little to none."

Kyle placed his hand on her belly, then kissed her. "I'll carry you, if that's what you wish."

"You're so cute."

"You know I will."

They kissed, this time much slower and much deeper. A warm desire came over him.

"Rosie!" Zaphod called out.

Startled, the two of them immediately pulled away. His heart thumped loudly in his chest.

Kyle turned to Zaphod, pointing at him. "You are the biggest cock-blocker!"

Emerald chuckled. "I don't think I would describe Zaphod using those choice of words. I think he really wants to see Rosie."

Zaphod cooed in agreement, with Kyle sighing. "Fine. We'll set you up on a date," he told Zaphod. "Happy now?" Kyle turned to Emerald, giving her his most handsome-devilish smile. "And while we are on that subject, can we see the guys soon?"

Emerald giggled, then playfully nudged him again. "All right. Only because you gave me that smile."

"I knew it would work," Kyle said.

Emerald smiled at him, then brushed his cheek gently. "We can go now if you'd like."

"Really?"

"Really."

"Well, hot damn."

"I'll take that as a yes." She laughed.

"It's a definite yes. I just need something to eat. Don't need much."

"Sure."

Emerald turned away, disappearing in her closet. He heard rummaging, and decided to put on some new clothes too. He went over to his duffel, pulled out a somewhat clean shirt, then threw it on. When he turned around, Emerald stood in black leggings and an oversized off-the-shoulder long black T-shirt. Something to hide her belly. But he could still see her extra curves. It was sexy as hell.

"You look great," he said, kissing her.

"I don't feel so great," she said, anxiously tugging on her sweater. "I'm starting to show."

"So?"

"So…I'm not the same shape as I used to."

"Who cares? You're pregnant."

Zaphod whistled.

"See? He agrees with me too."

Emerald shoved him playfully. "Kyle!"

"Em!" Kyle shoved her back, mocking her playfully.

"Let's get going. I'll have Glacia send for the transport," she said.

"Hey, can you have the driver drop us off somewhere incognito? I don't wanna cause a scene like last time," he said.

"Yes, absolutely." Emerald turned away, calling for Glacia.

Kyle smiled. He couldn't wait to see the guys.

It had been too long.

CHAPTER 17

✦

ORANGE

Pain shot through her entire body with each breath she took.

Suri was suddenly aware that she was *breathing*. She was *alive*.

Suri shot open her eyes and took another harsh breath, which caused her to wheeze. It hurt, like needles shooting into her airway. Jude was right next to her, also gasping for breath loudly. Around them was her transmuted metal, shattered like glass. Beyond them was a barren earth; the atmosphere was brownish, with dark-red bolts of lightning striking in the distance. The orangish-red soil was hard, like dried clay.

When they'd crashed into the earth, Suri released her magic, transmuting the metal into a brittle element, allowing it to break. It had saved their lives, but now they had a different road ahead of them: Surviving the planet's toxic air. She was tired, and her mouth felt dry and her lips cracked. It would be difficult to transmute other objects into water, as all her focus was on *surviving*.

Above, dark brown clouds formed in the brownish skies. Thunder rumbled in the distance. More red bolts of lightning flashed.

"I think a storm is coming," Jude pointed out, gasping for breath.

"Indeed," she replied. Seeing the rumbling thunderheads made her think of water once again. "We must try to find shelter. The rain will be contaminated."

"I can create a barrier to shield us," he offered. Jude cast a golden bubble around them, the sound of his prayers no more than a whisper. As his protective magic enveloped them, Suri cast her own magic, funneling it inside the barrier, faintly sparkling.

"Somehow, your magic…" Jude breathed, "it's helping."

Suri took a deep breath of clean air. "I'm cleaning our air trapped by your magical barrier. It gives us some way of surviving, though I don't know how much energy I will have to keep doing it. I'll do bursts when I can. Please keep your barrier intact as much as you can, but at the same time, conserve your energy. We must find some resource to keep us alive."

Jude took another deep breath, then coughed, hacking out the toxins. "I will do my best." He paused and skimmed their surroundings, then his eyes darted up toward the heavy clouds. "I don't know where we could go. The mines? People must be able to survive somehow if they send prisoners down there to work. Someone has to be in charge of them."

Suri knew of the mines. Everyone in the skies knew about them. The High Court and those who were in positions of power often threatened with the punishment of working the toxic mines of the earth.

"I think it's best to avoid the mines. They might think we are escapees if we happen across one."

"All right," he agreed.

The real issue was that she knew not where they were, not even what sector they were in. If she had to guess, it would be somewhere between World Sector Four and Six. And from the looks of it, there was hardly anything around them. Nothing but hard earth, cracked and dry, with patches of sand. In the distance were scattered mountains. Between them and those mountains were tangled and twisted metal structures, fractured and broken, scattered across the sands and dirt.

Suri took another quick survey of their surroundings, this time noticing a small metal beam rising from the desert ground.

"There," she said, pointing. "Head for that outcropping. It will get us out of the toxic rain for the time being."

Thunder cracked above them, the sky colored with flashes of lightning as they moved. Strangely, the lightning was the color of blood. They kept moving as the brownish clouds grew darker and the rumblings grew louder.

"Mistress Suri, do the clouds seem violent to you?" Jude asked.

"Very."

The boy glanced at the storm clouds curiously. Suri could tell he was struggling to maintain their protective bubble. She felt the same. Both of them were too weary and exhausted to purify the air, with very little energy between the constant use of their magic and the physical exertion of walking through the barren lands.

An hour passed as they traveled to the outcropping. Everything seemed to play tricks on their eyes. Things that appeared near were far, and things that were real ended up being a mirage.

At one point, Jude clumsily kicked a rock, then stumbled, weakly falling to his knees. The golden barrier that surrounded them flickered.

Suri bent over, yanking him up.

"I'm sorry," Jude wheezed. "I don't have much energy left…"

"You must keep moving."

Their barrier wavered again. He barely managed to stand on his feet. Harsh air seeped inside their barrier, his magic wavering.

Suri shook him. "You can't give up. If you do, we die. And that, I cannot allow. I have been given orders, and I mustn't fail, no matter what."

The protective bubble weakened again, allowing more of the toxic air to filter inside their barrier.

"Master Jude," Suri wheezed. "Please…"

"I…I won't give up," he managed to say. His face appeared brave, but his eyes were weak.

There was a sudden loud crack in the sky, then a flicker of red lightning. A deep red rain began falling. Hard rain.

Jude fell to the ground, wheezing harder as his barrier broke.

"Master Jude," Suri wheezed, crawling over and yanking his body.

Jude choked as his eyes fluttered.

Suri shook him. "Jude!" she coughed. The spores felt like knives in her throat.

The boy's eyes closed as he coughed and hacked. "I'm…so…tired…"

"Jude," Suri cried, shaking him again.

Suri quickly put her hand to his chest where his heart was. The boy was unresponsive.

The air was getting to Suri, choking her with every breath.

I'm sorry, Enchantress… Suri lay down, putting a hand on her chest, resting it over the vial. It felt warm and soft compared to the harsh world.

"Jude…" she managed to choke out.

Her eyes felt heavy, and she could no longer keep them open.

She didn't know how long she was out. It seemed like an eternity. But however long it was, a faint glimmer of golden-green light stirred her through the lids of her shut eyes. The next breath she took wasn't as sharp, nor her eyes as heavy.

This time she opened them to see bright green light. Her lungs didn't hurt as much, and she didn't feel so tired.

Another burst of light. Was it coming from Jude? It lit up his face and hands as he channeled green magic. Suri darted her eyes around, seeing trails of sparkly green light flowing around them, some of it seeping right into their lungs.

Suri took another breath. It didn't hurt. Jude's magic was restoring their damaged lungs.

Jude commanded the magic, speaking to it in the priests' holy language. The light was turning to a yellow-green, and Suri knew she should look away.

"It's okay to look, Mistress Suri," Jude called out. "I'm not praying in my heavenly language."

Suri glanced back at him, his face shining like a golden god. It made her see Jude in a new light. No more a teen, more like a youthful man.

She sucked in more of his green magic and felt her strength returning. "How?"

"A dream I had," he answered. "The green-gifted woman in my visions gave me strength." He blushed. "I don't have much in me, but I pray it is enough," Jude whispered. "I'm still figuring out this green magic stuff. Praise the God of Light for giving me the strength and power to heal us both."

Green-gifted woman? Was it the same woman that the enchantress stole magic from in the past?

Suri took a few more breaths. Though painful, it was not nearly as bad before. She rose to her feet.

Jude sucked in his breath loudly, then smiled. He stood too. "I'm ready to move, Mistress Suri. That is, if you are too."

"Yes." Suri nodded. "Before the storms get worse."

The two started walking quickly. If she had more energy, she would have run, but her limbs told her to take it slow. Jude's magic made her lungs feel better, but her limbs were still sore. The hard rain bounced off their barrier, setting off flashes of crimson magic as Jude's barrier dissolved the rains.

They made it to the outcropping, the thunder roaring above, and darted into the metallic structure. As they entered, Jude gave a loud sigh of relief. He cast a stronger barrier, and Suri purified the air with her transmutation, adding healing elements.

Jude plopped down against a wall, giving his feet a rest. Suri didn't sit, instead holding out her hand near the bubble. Both watched the toxic deep red rains fall outside the structure.

Curiously, Suri reached outside the barrier, making contact with the rain. It burned, her hand turning red and blistering. But Suri took a full hand of rainwater, then quickly brought it inside the barrier. With another quick spell, she transmuted it into clean water before it did any more damage. She took a drink, then closed her eyes, rolling her eyes back with delight. After a few more sips, she did the same for Jude.

Jude noticed her burns as he drank. After he finished, he motioned for her to hold out her hands.

Suri shook her head.

"Let me heal you," he said.

"It is not necessary. You must keep your strength."

"It is necessary. I insist." Jude smiled at her. "Besides, it will give me practice with this green magic."

Suri held out her hands, and Jude grasped them both, then closed his eyes. He remained still, without a prayer, even without a breath. Suri watched as the barrier around them faded, worried about whether this was a bad idea. The boy didn't flinch, just remained in deep focus. The barrier flashed brighter, then dimmed. Sweat beaded on his forehead and began to pour down his face.

Just as Suri was about to break Jude's concentration, a stream of green magic glowed brightly from his hands. Suri looked at it with wonder, almost in delight, as the magic wafted into the air around them. It floated, ribboning around her hands, then wrapped tightly around her palms and soaked into her skin, glowing an immense hot-green.

The flesh of her hands repaired themselves as the green magic soaked into her palms. Then, it faded away.

Jude opened his eyes, and Suri studied her palms. Her flesh wasn't fully restored, but all that remained were reddish scabs, as if Jude's magic had decreased the healing time by weeks.

Jude smiled in satisfaction, dripping with sweat. "I did it," he said in the most serious tone Suri ever had heard.

"Indeed," Suri said, inspecting her hands more, then turned to him. "You do realize that you will be hunted, Master Jude. For your green magic."

"I'm not really a green-gifted."

"That may be, but that doesn't mean that you won't be hunted," she stated smoothly. "The High Court yearns for this power you have. You must remember that."

Jude smiled in earnest. "I always will." His face turned serious. "You know, ever since I met the green-gifted princess back in time, my gift feels…right. I don't know how to explain it, but it just does."

Suri glanced at him. "Is the green-gifted woman the same princess in your dreams? The one that helps give you strength?"

He shook his head, turning serious. "No, it's a different woman. I know she exists, because she is always sent in a dream, a dream that is meant to be a vision." Jude's eyes glowed a bright yellow in the dark. "She lives in a fantastical world. I can't determine if it's in the past or future. It's hard to say." Even in the darkness, Suri knew he was blushing. "She's very pretty, but not with typical gifted features."

"What makes her different?"

Jude stared in wonder. "She has normal-color hair, like non-gifted. Blonde. But her eyes, they glow a vibrant green, full of life magic. She's my age too, or thereabouts. Though, in my vision, we are older when we meet. Ten years, maybe?" He paused. "She seems to know a lot about technology."

Suri sat in silence, thinking. *Perhaps we win the war against the High Court, and magic and technology is restored to our world.*

"Perhaps this woman is a good omen, and she is aiding your ability to further unlock your adjacent magics," Suri stated.

"I have heard of adjacent magics and other types, whispered by other priests. Never did I think that they were real," Jude said. "I'm glad they were wrong." His golden eyes lit up brightly as he grinned. "How else would you been able to survive without me?"

"Indeed." Suri gave him a cool smile. "I am forever grateful to you. Most wouldn't even bat an eye to help someone like me."

"It was the right thing to do," Jude pointed out.

"Most wouldn't, though."

"If I am to be a priest, I must set an example of what I believe." Jude looked straight into her eyes, and it was as if his golden eyes were piercing her soul. "Mistress Suri, I know you and the sorceress aren't religious. Religion aside, isn't it the right thing to do to be kind? To help others? What is life without a world of others to share it with? What is our world without kindness? Without empathy, our world isn't worth living in. That is, just being a good human."

Normally, these sort of words would go in one ear and out the other. None had ever shown her kindness or done things for her. Her parents were selfish and cared only for themselves—not even for each other. And growing up, everyone cared only for their personal gain at court. Love didn't exist, at least not in the circles she frequented, being a servant. Or perhaps she only witnessed the surface of others, and they wore their hardness like a shell, just as she had—a mask to cover her heart. But somehow, Jude's words hit a place in her heart that she had kept locked away.

There was only one person Suri felt cared for her, or at least showed some sort of favor with her, and that was the enchantress. Although she was cruel at times, Suri had chalked it up to her upbringing as well; no love was given toward her either. Or perhaps the enchantress rejected any sort of love.

There was a moment of silence between them as Suri reflected on her thoughts. Finally, she spoke. "You are wise, Master Jude. Wiser than most on the court," she said. "It is true, I am not one for any sort of religion. That being said, you will make a fine priest someday."

Jude's face melted into a smile, and she returned it. "I don't know if I will be able to be a full-fledged priest."

"Why is that?"

"Priests can't get married," he said. "If I happen to meet this woman in my visions…" His voice trailed off, embarrassed.

"You do realize that she's a vision, I hope."

"Don't worry, Mistress Suri. I will live in the here and now. If it's the God of Light's will that I become a priest, I will follow the path that is given to me."

The earth shook, startling them both. Deep crimson lightning flashed outside, followed by a crack of thunder. As the air settled, Suri heard a strange rumbling sound.

At first, she had thought it was more thunder. But the sound was constant, continuing with a low, rumbling hum.

Jude was about to speak, but Suri placed a hand on his arm lightly to get him to be quiet as she concentrated on the sound. Sounds of the hard rains were predominant, but the humming sound grew steadily, getting louder. The earth began to vibrate softly under their feet, so Suri curiously placed her hand on the ground. With each passing second, the vibrations became stronger. She darted her eyes outward, peering through the red rain and out into the harsh open desert, misty and muggy from the humidity.

"Did you hear that?" Jude asked.

"Quiet," she whispered.

The harsh red rain continued to pour down outside as they remained still. Under their feet, the ground rattled, the little pebbles around them shifting violently.

Then the roaring was so loud, they both jumped back in alarm.

Outside the outcropping was a machine. It was coming straight toward them.

"Do you see that?" Jude yelled. Their protective bubble flickered again, causing toxic air to seep in. "Sorry," he said quickly, realizing what he had done.

Suri funneled more of her orange magic through the bubble, purifying it once again, while Jude closed his eyes, saying a little prayer. More golden magic mixed with green magic flowed through their barrier.

"Get back," Suri warned.

Jude stopped, then the two of them shifted back into the farthest point in the shelter.

Suri cast her orange magic, then softly their bodies became invisible.

"Mistress…"

"Shh!"

The machine grounded to a halt with a loud metal clanking noise. Suri watched as a large plate opened on the side of the machine, and several men and a woman hopped out, their faces entirely covered by masks. In their hands was some sort of weapon that Suri had only seen once. A relic that she had bribed someone for, for Ikaria's collection.

"They were just here a moment ago," a distorted voice called out.

"My scans say that they are still here," said another masked person, their voice also distorted.

"There," said a deep mechanical voice as they pointed.

Directly at them.

They know we are here.

Without another moment to lose, Suri made a slight stealth movement with her hand. Suri hardly had any energy left in her life force, but she pulled what she could.

A sudden burst of dark orange power radiated from her body, making the two of them visible.

"A gifted!" yelled one of the masked people.

With another sweeping movement, Suri called forth her newly acquired violet magic that the enchantress had blessed her with.

A powerful, violent blast of her power in the shade of a deeper orange rocked the strange masked people backward. It was short-lived, as one of them held out a mechanical device that resembled a mirror, causing Suri's magic to be blasted straight back to her and Jude.

Jude's barrier instantly broke, and the two of them smacked into the metal structure.

"Mistress Suri…" Jude wheezed.

Involuntarily, she took a breath. She knew it was bad, but it was second nature to breathe. It was choking her…

In the corner of her eye, she caught a strange movement.

Hovering over her was a tall, imposing man. She couldn't see his face, as it was still entirely covered by a mask.

"Get these two on the vehicle and get back to the mines," he ordered.

Jude tried to fight the other men but was too weak.

"Sir…" Suri choked. "We must get back to the skies…"

The masked man laughed. "Trying to escape your punishment? I'll have you work the *pit*."

The others laughed with him as they grabbed her.

Suri tried to summon her magic, but her mind was too weak; her body was numb, and the air was overwhelming. Dizziness overcame her.

"We…must save…our empress…" Then Jude hacked and slumped over, barely conscious.

"You hear that? These are the ninnies we've been warned about." The bigger man laughed with the others. "You better make us rich." The masked man turned to the others. "Mask them both and get them loaded before they die on me."

Suri tried to speak, but the harsh air was too much. Her lungs locked up, and she coughed. She slumped to the ground, crawling next to Jude.

"Jude..." she whispered. If ever she felt protective of anyone besides the enchantress, it was this boy.

The next thing she knew, something extremely heavy was on her face. She blacked out just as Jude cried out her name.

CHAPTER 18

◆

WHITE

Elyathi had been seated at a small desk, eyeing a small carved-ivory box. She gently ran her hands over it before carefully opening the lid.

Elyathi paused for a moment, staring adoringly at what lay inside. Then she retrieved a white handkerchief from the box, lifting it to her lips. As she did so, she breathed in the scent that still lingered in the fabric, placing it against her heart and closing her eyes. The handkerchief was one of the most precious things she had ever owned—even more than her personal life force collection. It had once been Samir's. She had worn it in the pockets of her dresses each day, as if his spirit were with her, watching over her.

Samir, she thought as she took in the lingering scent of the cloth once again. Elyathi pictured him—his dark hair full of glossy curls, his dark eyes the color of coal, his thick eyebrows and strong jaw. Elyathi moved the handkerchief toward her cheek, caressing it. Being so close to Derek made her think of Samir all the more. Memories flooded her mind the more she lingered near Derek, as if her past permeated the very air that surrounded him.

How she had desired Samir the moment she laid eyes on him, and wanted no other. No other man made her feel so *alive.* Elyathi imagined that the handkerchief was his lips. She recalled the day it was given to her, though it was a terrible situation impressed upon them both.

How I wish to see you once again, she thought.

Did he ever desire her as she did him?

Elyathi flickered her eyes open with rage, thinking of Damaris, then held the handkerchief in her hand, admiring it one last time before she placed it back in the box. As she rose from her seat, she fixed her circlet back in place, then placed her hand on the orange gem around her neck. Filling herself with its power, orange energy surrounded her, then she went invisible and left her chambers.

As she walked thought the citadel, she couldn't help but eye the damage that had been done throughout certain halls. Large cracks in the infrastructure, dilapidated walls…many of the areas were surrounded by orange-gifted using their transmutation spells. There were non-gifted artisans and skilled workers trying to repair the more minor damaged-inflicted areas. The more damage that Elyathi witnessed, the more it incensed her. It was not right to think about another's demise, but with the wicked sorceress, Elyathi delighted in imagining all the ways Ikaria's final moments in this life could play out. The God of Light would approve of her thoughts because it was a thought and prayer of how to rid the world of unrighteousness.

Elyathi came upon the designated section for the yellow-gifted, making her way to the grand hall where Tyllos resided in his spare time. The bright plated gold in the halls, untouched by Ikaria's damage, were lined with thousands of tomes, books, and scrolls, all containing precious knowledge from the beginnings of the earth throughout history. There were a few study tables, lit either by candlelight or orange magic within lanterns. The mixture of orange and warm yellow candlelight illuminated the room. Accentuating the high ceilings were inlaid golden scroll designs encrusted with diamonds, adding to the glimmer of the halls.

There were sobs coming from one section of the study hall, with a group of High Court lords gathered.

Elyathi released her orange magic, then walked over to the gathering. The courtiers immediately noticed her.

"What is this?" Elyathi demanded.

"My lady?" said one of the higher lords. It was apparent that the lord didn't know her rank; many didn't who were lower in the court.

"I am the Lady Elyathi."

"I apologize," the lord said, recognizing her name. "I wasn't aware who you were or your status."

"Apology accepted," she said. "Now, what is meaning of this?"

The lord bowed, tears filling his eyes. "It's the sorceress."

Without a word, the group parted for Elyathi to peer upon the dead corpse, or what was left of it. It was like the other victims that Ikaria had murdered with her magic. From the examination of the body, it looked like Ikaria's violet magic force had entered the person's head, causing it to explode with such magnitude that they were unrecognizable. The whole scene was disgustingly grotesque. Only tatters of the robe remained.

Elyathi turned away. "Please get the guards to clean this up. I will inform the High Court."

"Yes, my lady," the lord said, with the others bowing. Many wiped away tears as they acknowledged her.

That vile creature will pay for her sins once and for all!

Elyathi stormed off down the hall. *I will get you for all that you have done to my daughter, my son-in-law, and now the High Court,* Elyathi thought with a sneer. *Your magic will be mine.*

She approached the personal audience chambers for High Justice Tyllos, his servants bowing.

"I am here to see High Justice Tyllos," she stated.

"Yes, my lady," one of the lead servants said, bowing. "The high justice is expecting you." The servant gestured for her to follow, leading Elyathi down the familiar hall of Tyllos's quarters.

They came to the grand solid-gold doors, then opened them. Tyllos was seated in one of the golden chairs, in the midst of a conversation with Perserine, who was also seated. Her short, shocking-orange hair had been brushed aside in a sweeping style, crowned with a golden jeweled headband. Borgen was at the end of the table, hunched over. His blue beard was nearly white from age, and his skin was nearly the same—so pale that it showed the blue veins in his face. Their eyes met Elyathi's, and they nodded.

"High Justice Tyllos. High Justice Perserine. High Justice Borgen," Elyathi said, nodding back.

"Lady Elyathi," he said. "Thank you for joining us. I am sorry for keeping you from World Sector Four. I know you were planning on leaving soon."

"I am. You caught me before I was to head out." She took a seat at the table, and the servant pushed in her seat. Another servant offered her wine, but she declined. "Where are Belinda and Nyrden?"

"I believe they are looking into the current status of the cyborgs' revival process. They should be here soon," he answered.

"You should know there is another one of the sorceress's victims right outside your halls, Tyllos," Elyathi stated, lifting her chin high.

Tyllos clenched his glass. "Will her list of crimes ever end?"

"She is wreaking terror upon our court, and I've had enough of it," Belinda's voice called out from across the hall. Elyathi and the others turned to see Belinda and Nyrden walking across the private hall, taking their usual seats. "Nyrden and I came across the spectacle on our way here as well."

"High Justices," Elyathi greeted them, while the others did the same.

"We should just execute her sister and be done with it," Nyrden continued.

"Hm," Belinda said, raising her eyebrow. "I wish that were the case. We must have patience and tread carefully. Continue our course as planned with the trial. All that matters in the end is that Elyathi gains Ikaria's power, but we must proceed with fortitude and patience. What good would it be if we were to execute her sister now? And without a trial? No, it would work against us."

"So are you saying that we won't execute that woman?" Nyrden demanded.

"Oh, we will. Patience, Nyrden. All in good time. We must be ready," Belinda said. She turned to Elyathi. "Speaking of patience. Lady Elyathi, you must deal with World Sector Four on our time before we deal with them on *their* time."

Elyathi nodded. "Now that Derek has gone to the past, I can focus on our goals in the present."

"Oh? King Derek of Arcadia has left us?" Nyrden asked.

"Indeed. Prior to the sorceress's fiasco in World Sector Six, we had talked about him capturing the cyborg scientists and retrieving my daughter. My son-in-law is determined to finish the task that he was given."

"I saw him leave within the blue dimension recently," Borgen confirmed. "I will be sure to aid him in any way I can with *our* gifted in his time era. I have been sending dreams through the lifestream to Vihaan, the yellow-gifted. He is working with a blue-gifted named Raghu. They have a trap set, and the perfect bait to lure the scientist."

"Perfect. Thank you, Borgen," Elyathi said.

"Lady Elyathi, tell me more of this King Derek," Perserine said, swishing her chalice around. "We know very little of him, and we are trusting him with so much."

Elyathi kept her posture, raising an eyebrow. "Such little faith you have in me, considering I am the God of Light's chosen."

"Don't mistake my trust in you, or the God of Light, Lady Elyathi. I only wanted to know if there is more to Derek than meets the eye." Perserine smiled daringly. "He is quite the man."

"It seems that Perserine is disappointed that she can no longer lay eyes on him," Belinda commented.

Nyrden snorted in disgust. "Please."

Perserine giggled. "I'm sure you are disappointed as well, Belinda."

"Perhaps," Belinda stated smoothly with a smile. "I daresay, he has the look of perfection. If I were born in a different lifetime, I would pursue him."

Their filthy, lustful talk about Derek was upsetting and out of line. Elyathi's cheeks flushed red with anger…and a little bit of envy? Elyathi swallowed back her fury. "As you are well aware, my son-in-law is already married. *To my daughter*," Elyathi stated pointedly to both the women.

"Yes, we are all quite aware of that, aren't we, Perserine?" Belinda said with her eyebrow raised.

"Of course." The orange justice smiled to herself, while Belinda changed her tune.

Elyathi gave the orange justice a cold, hard stare as Perserine gave her an "I don't care" happy smile in return.

How dare she.

Belinda took a drink of her wine. "Shall we move on?"

"Yes, please. I am tired of hearing anything pertaining to King Derek," Nyrden stated irritably. "It's quite annoying."

"I, too, am ready to proceed," Elyathi said coldly. She turned to look away, taking in the golden light of Tyllos's dining quarters.

"Lady Elyathi," Belinda said, "how confident are you that King Derek will bring the cyborg scientist to our time? We need to get these cyborgs in our time resurrected before we enter the new world."

"Very confident. I have no doubts whatsoever that my son-in-law will succeed."

"Good."

"Must we resurrect them? Perhaps there is another solution?" Perserine suggested.

Borgen raised his head. "We must. Though Oriel was the expert in viewing the flow of time, I have also seen what he saw. The cyborgs must be a part of our army in the new world to keep the peace and maintain society. Without them, there will be an uprising with the people in an alternate future. Chaos will break out, and our new world won't be as Lady Elyathi wills it to be."

"How is that possible?" Perserine asked. "Lady Elyathi has assured us that there will be no more pain in the new world. No more sadness."

"Admittedly, I do not know how the seed of chaos is planted," Borgen said. "But whatever it is, we need the cyborgs."

Elyathi sat quietly. Would the God of Light approve of such contraptions in the new world? It certainly wouldn't be a pure world, free of technology. She didn't like it, only because Damaris had contributed to their existence. But in the end, she wouldn't remember Damaris and all the terror he caused in her life, for everything would be made anew. All the horrific memories would be cleansed, and only the happy thoughts, dreams, and joy would remain. Some souls would not remember anything, given their current life circumstances. And if that was required for keeping a new world of peace, then so be it.

"You mustn't worry. Derek will bring the scientist here, along with my daughter," Elyathi said, poised.

"That's very well, but that cyborg needs to be able to survive the time travel," Nyrden pointed out.

"Her daughter is back in Arcadia," Tyllos said. "The cyborg lives in that time, remember?"

"Yes," Nyrden muttered.

"It is impossible for your daughter to travel at this moment in her time," Borgen said in a whisper voice, stroking his long, pale-blue beard. "She is pregnant."

Elyathi whipped her head in his direction, then rose from her seat. A sudden stroke of worry shot through her body. What if it was…that other man Derek had mentioned. It was said that the High Inquisitor was last seen jumping into a portal. A time portal. If she had to speculate, that filth of a man was with her daughter by now. What if her daughter had been ruined by the High Inquisitor?

Please let it be Derek's child. "Pray, tell me…" Elyathi said coolly as her feet gently clacked on the tiled floors. "Who is the father?"

Borgen frowned. "I do not know." He glanced up at her, his aged blue eyes speaking volumes. "But the *children* will not survive if she is brought to the future."

"Children?"

"Yes, children."

"Then I must warn her somehow," Elyathi said. "I must get a message to Derek."

Borgen nodded. "I will do what I can on my part in the space-time continuum. That is, if he is still there."

"Thank you, Borgen. If by chance, Derek has retrieved the cyborg scientist and brings him here, we can warn him. That is my prayer."

She was sickened by worry. But on the other hand, what if Derek had foreseen it in the flow of time? He was far more powerful than Borgen, and Borgen had seen the pregnancy. Perhaps Derek already knew.

I mustn't worry. Derek is more than capable. She shoved her thoughts aside.

"What ever happened to that green-gifted? Suresh?" Tyllos asked.

Perserine's face went stone-cold. "He escaped my magic," she snarled. "All with the help of Oriel, that old *fool*."

Elyathi remained emotionless. Suresh was her secret, for her and her alone. No one would know about him.

"I'm so disappointed with Oriel's lack of devotion," Elyathi said. "My daughter will have to make a sacrifice. I am sure she will have the will to do so. She is the ultimate picture of a pure heart."

Belinda smiled. "I daresay, if she is anything like you, then we are set. You are a shining example to us all, Lady Elyathi."

Elyathi returned her smile, though Belinda's smile seemed insincere.

"What are we going to do about that traitor whore of an Empress?" Nyrden asked.

There was a slap of wind across Nyrden's face as Belinda raised an eyebrow. "Do not use such language at this table."

Nyrden glared but said nothing, instead rubbing his cheek where Belinda's red wind had slapped him.

"As we know, Ikaria will show up to save her sister—either from her trial or her execution. We must continue our plans and set a date for Ayera Suzuki's trial. We will do exactly what Ikaria is doing. I will have Lady Elyathi visit the other sectors and move quickly between them. By doing this, we'll shake the other sectors into submission and let the world know the power this High Court has. No one will have the gift—only us. We will consume all the life forces we have stocked up. Only, instead of depending on these life forces to extend our lives, we will have a magnitude of power. Elyathi already has grown tremendously in her gift—she took out the entire room of gifted in World Sector Six. With everyone losing their gift, people will submit to us. Only the faithful will stand in the end, ready for the new earth. Let this be their final lesson from the God of Light."

"I will give Lady Elyathi time to drain the life forces, then have my clerks arrange the trial," Tyllos added. "This will reaffirm our position."

"What about Emperor Cyrus? What are we to do with him?" Perserine asked. "I grow tired of his banter."

Elyathi had a strong disdain for the Emperor. In her eyes, he was just as worldly as High Inquisitor Rubius.

"He says that he wants to take on the sorceress the next time she shows up," Nyrden said with a smirk. "I have been testing his newfound power; he is nearly complete as a full red, though not quite yet."

"I say let him do so," Belinda said. "If he succeeds in getting her blood—the chances of which are minuscule—then it is a win for us. And if he doesn't and perishes by her hand, it doesn't affect us either."

"Good. Then it is settled," Tyllos said, then turned to Elyathi. "I do hope you will be there for the trial, Lady."

Elyathi smiled, but it was empty. Her mind was still on her daughter's pregnancy. "I wouldn't miss this for anything. I will gladly show the world that I am the chosen one. It will give them hope and restore order for anyone who dares to stray from the light."

They all held their glasses high. "To the God of Light. To Elyathi."

"Yes, to the God of Light," Elyathi breathed.

They all downed their wine, and Elyathi rose from her seat. "I must be on my way." Elyathi glanced at Belinda, then nodded. "May the God of Light light your paths."

They nodded to her in reverence as she filled her life force with orange magic. The magic came over her, then slowly made her unseen once again.

As Elyathi headed out the double doors, she narrowed her eyes.

You are next. All of you.

And if any other man besides Derek had gotten her daughter pregnant, she would ensure that man never saw the dawn of the new world. His soul would burn in the eternal fire of damnation.

Forever and ever.

CHAPTER 19

GREEN

Soft magic of pale blues of shimmering light danced around him, creating a translucent, timeless prison. The magic was like little specks of dust, floating through the air, seen only in a streaming light. Through the barrier, Suresh saw a warped view of bright light streaming through the windows, while soft puffs of wind brushed against the pale curtains, causing them to sway in an eternal dance. That breeze seeped into the swirling blue magics, tingling against his hot skin. Everything past the window and its circumference was a magical blur, as if his eyes could no longer see afar.

Uncomfortable in his sitting position, Suresh tried to shift his body, but he couldn't move. His hands and body were bound. He struggled to lift his arms, involuntarily letting out a loud grunt. His body was working against him, the blue magics keeping him still. His tired eyes could barely lift his puffy eyelids from lack of sleep. Perhaps it wasn't the lack of sleep, but the lack of being stuck in a twilight sleep, in and out between day and night. In and out between time. Trapped in a time spell. Even though there was movement within this twilight time, time was kept tight around him. He was a prisoner, and there was nothing he could do but get lost in his own thoughts.

When was the last time he had seen Elyathi or the King of Arcadia—the ones who locked him in this place? It felt like years. Perhaps it had been years.

Suresh tried to focus on a spell, but his lips and mind felt clumsy. His mind scrambled, he couldn't think coherent thoughts. He could only feel a fraction of his life force within, which was more terrifying. Elyathi had the remainder of his life force.

His chest hurt just thinking about the partial loss of his gift. It was as if his body was torn, or a loved one was on the verge of passing away.

I feel so helpless. Gods help me.

There was a strange shift in the air, causing the hair on the back of his neck to rise. He looked into the flowing time dimension, like a rippling waterfall of time. Nothing else was different. The waterfall magic, the floating speckles, the endless time prison. All the same. But yet, he could sense that a presence was nearby.

Suresh waited in the silence. Nothing. But there was some sort of life force present.

Closing his eyes, he focused on the world around him—or lack thereof. Softness filled his soul with a sense of determination. A power brushed his mind, giving him peace.

It was that same foreign life force he had felt earlier. There was such power, strength, and vibrancy behind this life force. But there was also an overall serenity.

"Hello?" Suresh called out.

The strange life force vanished as quickly as it came.

Weakly, Suresh closed his weary eyes. *Gods of the Spectrum, help me*, he prayed in his mind. *What am I to do?*

Suresh felt a softness within, as if a beautiful mind had comforted him.

Slowly, he opened his eyes, glancing at the curtain of sparkling blue magics that kept him contained. That strange peace he felt was no more; it had been lost once again.

I shouldn't have intervened that day, Suresh thought as his mind flickered back to his encounter with the King of Arcadia. The first time he had seen the King was when the man was about to throw himself from the palace balcony, ashamed of his actions. There had been so much remorse oozing from that man's soul. It was the very reason Suresh felt the need to intervene. But now, when he briefly saw the King once again, there was a coldness within, a deep ravine of pride, arrogance, and power. The man had learned nothing from his past transgressions, it seemed. Suresh never liked the idea of anyone taking their own life, but seeing the outcome of his interference, there was a strange feeling of guilt that he should have let the man fling himself off the balcony that day.

The words of warning from the blue-gifted Oriel echoed in his mind. Elyathi was dangerous. All of time was going to be wiped away into a new earth. The High Court and Elyathi were searching for him because of his green gift.

It was too late. Elyathi had part of his life force. Suresh glanced around at his body, searching for cuts or scratches. Perhaps she even had his blood too. If she did, she'd probably made countless vials of his blood, distributing them to all the wrong people. Perhaps she had made a blood gem out of his blood, like the one he had seen in the storeroom deep within the citadel.

There was a strange flicker of the sparkling blue magical wall. The magical flow changed directions, then flitted to Suresh, seeping into his skin. It kept him stilled. Then, as if a magical sea parted, Elyathi entered his twilight world, the magic closing up behind her, locking them in this magical purgatory together.

A vial hung around Elyathi's neck, drawing his attention immediately. It called out to him as a lost child calls out to its mother.

His life force.

The vial radiated with green energy, mingling with the other colored gemstones. She had red, orange, yellow, and blue gemstones mixed in with his green vial of life force. The only color that was missing was violet. And there was one empty vial awaiting that color.

"Suresh," Elyathi cooed softly.

He lifted his eyes, heavy with sorrow. "Elyathi…"

Elyathi smiled warmly at him as she neared. It was strange, as if his mind was clearer the closer she was. It had to be his life force getting near his body that activated his mind. Or maybe it had been so long that he had seen anyone that his mind flipped a switch, understanding what was going on.

Elyathi seated herself on a simple throne across from him. Had that throne been there before? Strangely, everything around him seemed to be there…but not. As if these things existed between dimensions.

The dimensional magic surrounding them flickered again, the sparkles turning a deep, vibrant blue. Behind the magical blurry translucent wall of power, he saw a dark blur.

"He stands behind the magic. Why?" Suresh managed as his eyes trailed to Elyathi's.

"That?" Elyathi glanced over her shoulder, seeing the dark blur.

"Isn't that the blue-gifted that works with you?"

"Derek's long gone," Elyathi said indifferently. "That blob is one of the High Court members searching my chambers. They do that occasionally." She leaned in. "They'll never find you. Derek doesn't know, but he is the most powerful of any blue-gifted that lives. No one will detect this spell, and it only activates for Derek and me if we need to move between these dimensions."

She is hiding me from everyone else? It made Suresh wonder if Elyathi was working against the High Court. Wasn't she collecting souls for them?

"How long do you plan to keep me like this?" Suresh asked.

Elyathi smiled sadly. "I hope it won't be for too much longer."

Suresh's eyes locked onto the green vial that clung around her neck. "My life force…what do you plan to do with it? Steal it as you have other gifted?"

She reached out her hand, then caressed his cheek. "I wouldn't do that to you," she assured him.

"What of my blood? Do you have it like you have a fraction of my life force? Are you going to make copies of it, just as you have with the other gifted?"

"I do not have your blood; no one will have it. I only have this," she said in a whisper, raising the vial of his life force to meet his gaze. "I need to draw from its power, for I am the only one that requires it."

"The only one? For what? The new world?"

"I need it to complete my purpose."

"Why haven't you transmuted it?" Suresh asked, seeing the other gemstones around her neck. "You have other gemstones."

"I am giving you a choice."

Suresh paused, confused, as she repositioned herself on her throne.

As their eyes met once again, Elyathi asked, "Suresh, have you ever had regrets?"

He eyed her suspiciously. "Everyone has regrets."

"Indeed, we all do. With regrets, comes pain. Sadness. Loss of life. I'm not referring to dying, but losing the vibrancy of life. True joy, free to live in pure light." Elyathi sighed sadly. "Pain is hard to live with."

"There are many trials in this world, and life comes with waves of sadness and pain, Elyathi. That is the path of life," Suresh shot back. "Even with the trials we face, we also experience joyful times. These experiences counter the darkness—like dawn after a long night."

Her eyes flickered with anger for a second, then returned to their original state of warmth. "No one should have to live with certain types of pain. Ever."

"And you intend to change this?" Suresh countered. "To ensure no one experiences pain, sadness, and regret?"

"It's not a matter of intent. I will change this, for it was foreseen long ago," she said with certainty.

"If this *prophecy* is true, then the consequences that the entire earth will face will be monumental," he shot back. "You will destroy life, what is, and what is supposed to be. What the God of Light has designed."

"Suresh, what you know of the prophecy is from the perspective of former High Justice Oriel. Did you know that the former justice lived a life full of falsehood, sinful desires, and lust for power? Do you think for one moment that his lips would speak truth?" She gave a hard stare. "Actions and a life that one lives speak volumes of a person. Why put your trust in the words of a wolf, one who sought power—*my power*—for his own selfish desires?"

"People change over time," Suresh said. "Oriel included. He admitted to his life of sin, and he is paying the consequences of it now, with much guilt and regret."

Elyathi's eyes were like daggers as she clenched the armrests of her throne. "That may be true, but he has only seen a glimpse of a clear future; the rest has many possibilities, ones that he might think are evil. That man has no concept of *purity*, or a life of a pure heart. This, I have. *I* have walked the path full of light. I know what must be done."

"You twist your thoughts and words into a truth that is evil," Suresh said, sickened.

Elyathi frowned. "It's sad to see your perception of me warped. I genuinely had hoped for you to stand by my side as I complete my God-given purpose."

"Is everyone else to die? You are only keeping a select few?"

"Not at all. That would be cruel and sinful," she breathed. "Everyone will live. Past, present, future…we will all come together and live in the new world. I will ensure that there will be no more pain, hurt, and sorrow. Those memories will be wiped away, and no more tears will be shed in the new life."

"I don't understand," Suresh said. "If you are to bring all of time to a new plane of existence, to reshape the world all across time and compress them together…won't I already be there with you?"

Elyathi smiled, the whites in her eyes sparkling. "Yes, indeed. But there is more to it. I want willing people to be with me. To have purpose in their lives. To do great things with great purpose."

"Is it because I am green-gifted?"

"Yes. And no," she answered. "I want to gift you a throne in the new kingdom. Each color—ones who pledge their lives to me, will receive a high seat of honor in the new world. You are to be one of them—a ruler of their own kingdom, for I decide who reigns in the new world."

"Why me? Why not your daughter?" Suresh persisted.

"My daughter has another destiny." Elyathi leaned in. "Do you recall when we first met?"

Suresh nodded. "How could I not? I saw the most beautiful woman in all of time," he said, glancing at her as her face softened. "A soul so pure, but shrouded with fear and pain. I couldn't bear the thought of you passing away, life taken from you so suddenly." He paused. "I knew that would happen to you by feeling your life force with my green gift."

Her eyes started to water, and tears trickled down her cheeks. The whites of her eyes were startling against the redness. "You changed my life that day. For years, I suffered through mental and sexual evils. The servants came and went, acting like nothing ever happened when my husband tortured me. The evil was acceptable to them. I wrote letters to old friends for help. No one came. Not *one* soul stood up against the evil around me," Elyathi said with sharp bitterness. "Then, as I lay pregnant, wishing that I could return to my time or pass away, you appeared before me. It was the first ounce of kindness someone showed me. You not only saved my beautiful daughter, but you saved my life and my *soul.*

"When your healing magic restored me on that day, it renewed my spirit, giving me strength that I had never known. I still was weak facing my husband after that day, but inside, my life force had been awakened. I knew my power and my purpose. You *saved* me, Suresh. And by saving me, you contributed to the greatest prophecy ever spoken by a priest's tongue. You are a part of my life, Suresh. It is the greatest repayment for what you have done for me. I offer you a life free of pain, a life to rule over others because you have the strength within you. Because you gave me strength to fulfill my purpose here in this time on earth."

Suresh's heart dropped into the pit of his stomach. "This is pure madness," he whispered, shaking his head in disbelief.

"Madness? No. Everyone will be washed of their sins and reborn into a new life. No more evil, a heavenly realm on earth. Tell me, how is that madness? All magics will be sent back up to heaven, for the God of Light wants the earth restored to its true glory. No one should have the power any longer, except those who are pure—the ones who I deem fit in the next world." She smiled softly. "I will send all the magics back to the heavens, leaving one being to represent each color—just as it was in the birth of mankind—in your time."

Suresh paused at her words.

"Yes, Suresh. I know about you. You were the first of the gifted, back in ancient times. You and six others were blessed to be the very first gifted, each color fully represented."

Suresh blinked. "*How* do you know?"

Elyathi smiled warmly. "You have been studied by the court for many years. You, and the others in your time era…we know of you and the first gifted. To see how mankind corrupted the gift, using it as it wasn't intended… the God of Light had to restore order to the earth. He first sent a curse upon the ancient lands, allowing the gifted to die out. But after thousands of years of research, the gift was reactivated in the future through experimentation. The gift in the future was limited, only allowing the gifted to access one color of their life force—not their adjacents. To stop this false gift from spreading, that is how the prophecy of the chosen one came into being: me."

Suresh shook his head. "I don't believe it. Isn't Emerald the rebirth of magic? And through her, the experimentation?"

Elyathi looked serious. "She is now." She leaned in. "Because you altered the timeline of magic. If it weren't for you skipping through time, she wouldn't have had magic. I was created solely to stop this false gift from spreading like wildfire—from the experimentation through your people in the ancient times. Now, since you went through time, meeting me, who was also under a different timeline through a group of fanatics changing history, my role as the white-gifted changed. I was to send the false magics—and all of them are in this timeline—back to the heavens, and there was to be no more gifted, thus changing the world back to the God of Light's true intent.

"But now, my role is to wipe all magics off the face of the earth except one of each color, to restore the world to a new timeline, erase all that has been done, and reshape it into a new image—it is what the God of Light has called me to do." She breathed. "As for you, I want you, most of all, to join me. You, Suresh, are special to me. You changed everything to help me, and now, it is my turn to help you."

His insides twisted so hard that he wanted to vomit. He had changed time with his actions. All of this because of his compassion for this woman?

"It is vile, what you plan to do. You decide who is the one color to remain in the new world?" Suresh asked. "To choose me over your daughter is telling, making me doubt your intentions even further."

"As I said before, my daughter has a different destiny, one that the God of Light revealed only to me," Elyathi said with an edge. Her eyes suddenly flickered with hate, underlying with rage. She tried to hide it, but he saw right through her empty eyes.

This is why the gods forbid us to travel through time, he thought. No wonder. He'd created this time apocalypse. He was the one who activated her magic. He was responsible for the gift reawakening in the Millennium Era, with the experimentation starting at that point, and not the true point in the far future. His people's remains were the source of the experimentation, not Queen Emerald of Arcadia. That is, in the original timeline. If it weren't for him and his time traveling, or his interference, none of this would be happening. Time was going to be compressed into one timeline, and the world he knew would be remade in this wicked woman's image. All because of his compassion. Suresh couldn't help but shed a tear.

He glanced at his life force around her neck. "I cannot do it, Elyathi," Suresh said with finality. "Do you not feel the darkness behind this all? You will lead us down the path of emptiness."

Her empty eyes flickered with anger, but her words were soft as air. "You are completely innocent?" Elyathi countered, then eyed him. There was a pause between them. "I thought not," she said with finality.

Suresh was about to speak, but Elyathi gently held up her hand. "I will give you time to reflect upon what I have said." Elyathi got up, then turned to enter the time barrier curtain. She peered behind her shoulder, giving Suresh one last glance.

Suresh called out, "You are unleashing a great evil."

"According to who? Please reconsider what I have told you. You will find much truth in what I say." Elyathi passed through the watery time-dimensional wall. The magical sparkles fluttered like dust, then condensed into the watery curtain once more. Everything around him faded to a pale blue with bright sparkles of light.

Suresh sat in the eternal time barrier once more, alone.

The destruction of the world was imminent.

He needed to escape before it was too late. For all of time.

CHAPTER 20

◆

BLUE

Vala lifted her blue dimensional spell, revealing her citadel homeland in full color. There were guards off in the distance on the platform that led into the citadel, guarding the entrance. They immediately recognized her, as they were now accustomed to the comings and goings of her and the other blue-gifted. After all, they had the most blue-gifted of any sector. That was, until most were called into duty for the High Court.

"Lady Vala," said one of the guards as she approached. "You have returned from World Sector Six."

"I have." Vala nodded to them. "Is the Khari in session?"

"I do not know, but you can ask Lord Nnadi. He was here moments ago, running errands," the guard offered.

"Thank you."

Vala quickly moved into the citadel, then into the grand hall. Her long blue robes flowed behind her as she moved; it was her favorite garment, one that complemented the extremely short blue curls that framed her face. At this hour, the sun's rays shone bright inside the halls' upper windows, casting a warm orange glow over the bronzed halls. A few of the beams of light reflected on her large gold-plated earrings and necklace, making additional reflections of light. The magical lamps that decorated the halls were especially bright for this day, though Vala couldn't seem to understand why.

She made it through a few corridors, then caught a glimpse of Lord Nnadi at the end of the next hall.

"Lord Nnadi," she called out, raising her hand as she ran toward him.

The lord turned his head, then bowed. "Lady Vala?" he asked in surprise.

Vala ran up to him as she tried to catch her breath. Not very ladylike, but then again, she was quite unconventional at times. "I must speak to the Khari immediately. Do you know if court's in session?"

Lord Nnadi gestured for her to follow. "He is in a meeting, but I will interrupt for you to speak to him. The Khari has been worried and has been asking for you, as he heard a great deal of matters regarding World Sector Six. Us lords included."

Vala glanced at the lord, pressing her lips together with worry. "Quite frankly, I'm worried too. Much has transpired."

Lord Nnadi frowned. "I wasn't sure if what I had heard was true or just rumors."

"I'm sure whatever you heard, it's not rumors." Vala exchanged glances with him, then said, "I so wish to tell you more, but I have to save it for the Khari first."

"Indeed. Let's go." Lord Nnadi suppressed a chuckle as they began to walk. "I imagine that this is difficult for you."

"What's difficult?" Vala said as she fixed her circlet against her forehead.

"You holding back gossip."

Vala snorted, then eyed him. "The only thing that is difficult for me is that I was born a blue-gifted instead of red. The power of the wind looks exciting. As for you, I suppose that it is difficult for you too, to see Katrina every day and not say anything." She bit her lip with a smile.

The lord's cheeks turned red, not meeting her eyes as they walked. "What are you talking about?"

Vala hinted a smile. "I see you eyeing my servant. Don't think that I don't know." She lowered her voice. "Why don't you get it over with and ask her on an outing?"

Lord Nnadi suddenly looked flustered. "I…er…I…"

"Looks like we're here," Vala said, standing in front of the grand double doors. "Just in time too." She beamed.

"Yes…perfect timing," Lord Nnadi said, still flushed and flustered. "I will go speak to the Khari now."

"Thank you," Vala said, bowing.

Lord Nnadi returned shortly, signaling for her to enter.

As Vala followed Lord Nnadi inside, she saw Khari Ramla seated on his golden throne, cushioned with a plush red velvet seat. Well-dressed and decorated gifted lords—mostly in reds and oranges and a few blues—seated near the Khari on sitting pillows, were lined up all the way to the throne. Incense burned while the corner braziers roared with magical fires.

The lords on the pillows turned to face Vala as she walked with pride down the aisle. Her big golden disc earrings jangled, and her plated necklace clinked as she walked.

"Lady Vala," the Khari said, his headpiece feathers swaying as he spoke.

"Khari Ramla," Vala said, coming before him and bowing deeply. "I am very sorry to interrupt your meeting. I have urgent news from World Sector Six."

"It is quite all right. I have been anxiously awaiting any news from that sector, so your arrival brings me much relief." Khari Ramla gestured for a sitting pillow to be brought for Vala. She stood for a moment, allowing the servants to place the speaker pillow, then sat.

"We have heard the news of Sorceress Ikaria's destruction of the High Court Citadel, and that Empress Ayera is to be put on trial," the Khari said, then gestured. "Please speak and tell us what has transpired, Lady."

"You are correct, Khari Ramla. The sorceress made quite an impression on the High Court in an attempt to retrieve her sister. Unfortunately, she didn't succeed, and the Empress is still imprisoned by the High Court. It is said that she will be put on trial." Her eyes began to well up with tears, but she held her head proud and high. "High Justice Oriel has been stripped of his power by the white-gifted woman, led by the High Court. He remains at the World Sector Six citadel under the care of my uncle and the sorceress."

Khari Ramla's eyes went wide. "High Justice Oriel? He is *alive*?"

Talk erupted amongst the lords.

"Silence!" the Khari called out.

The hall went quiet, and Vala continued. "His death was staged by the High Court," she said. "They tried to murder him. But in a last ditch-effort, Oriel froze his body in the flow of time. It seemed to work, and he waited in limbo until he had met a green-gifted to heal him." She eyed the Khari. "He knew the exact moment this green-gifted would show up."

More wild whispers from the lords, then they died down. *Green-gifted,* they all whispered.

The Khari was stunned. "And where is this green-gifted now? At the World Sector Six citadel?"

Vala sighed. "We do not know. The last I saw of him was when a battle broke out at the World Sector Six citadel. The white-gifted woman was there."

"It is true," the Khari said softly. "The white-gifted is no myth."

"Very real indeed. She is the ultimate threat to our world," Vala said. "What I have learned from Oriel is that the High Court and the white-gifted woman are planning on destroying this world and everything in it—to be reborn to their liking."

At this, the entire room roared with anger and surprise. The Khari's face went grave. Though she was not invited to stand to address the room—it was the Khari's right to do so—Vala stood from her pillow, glancing into all the eyes of the room.

"I have pledged my service to World Sector Six on behalf of Sorceress Ikaria. Though I am a citizen of this sector, and the Khari is my true leader, current matters have led me to make a decision—and a stand. They need our help. The world needs our help. Empress Ayera will be put on trial. We all know it will not be a fair trial, and that she will be executed. Even more so, former High Justice Oriel has stressed that if we do nothing to stop this white-gifted woman and the High Court, we will not exist anymore, nor our lands—at least, not as we know them. We will be carbon copies of our souls, with certain memories erased, with no homeland. Instead, we will be under the High Court's rule in their new world for all eternity—or whenever we pass on to the heavens above, whenever they *choose* to let us do so in this new world."

"How is all of this possible?" asked a lord.

"Yes, Lady Vala has been known to spin a few tales in her time," said another lord.

Vala whipped her head to face the lord, her large gold-plated earrings jingling. "I assure you, this is no tall tale, my lord." She faced the court. "Let me tell you what you might consider a tall tale: I was summoned to the High Court months ago, as some of you might recall. You know that all the blue-gifted were summoned at one point or another. Though it was never disclosed why, the rumor was that the High Court needed to create permanent portals for easier travel." Vala snarled. "When I arrived, I was poisoned by the High Court and thrown into the flow of time—with specific orders to kidnap a green-gifted queen!"

The whole room erupted with noise.

"Quiet!" yelled the Khari.

Vala shot the lords a look. "I barely escaped death from poison and suffered time's effect on my body; if it weren't for this green-gifted queen, I would be dead." Vala stared down the lords. "I did this to protect my sector: because if I didn't do what the High Court asked, they would be coming after you. I did everything to protect *you*." There were loud mumbles from the lords as Vala continued. "You ask how this new chain of events is possible. The King of Arcadia has power over time. He sets the rules—and in the new world? It's up to him, the white-gifted woman, and the High Court!"

Wild shouting came from the lords once again. Vala looked right into the Khari's eyes. Her ruler always had been so confident, same as her people. But this time, she saw another side of him. Quiet and fearful.

The Khari stood from his pillow, then gestured.

The room fell silent.

"What does the sorceress want of us? To fight the High Court?" the Khari asked.

"Yes," Vala stated. "That's precisely what she wants us to do."

Another lord rose from his pillow. "So what are we to do? Storm the High Court Citadel? Even if we do agree to the sorceress's madness, the High Court has many gifted within the citadel, unlike our sector. They have taken many of our gifted away to work in their service. Not to mention that the plague has now come to our sector!"

"The true plague is the white-gifted woman!" Vala shot back. "Don't you see? If we don't defeat her and the court, this *plague* will continue. She is the sickness of our world!" Vala smoothed her short bangs to the side. "I fear that if and when this white-gifted woman returns to our sector, she will wipe out all of our power!"

The lords erupted into more talk, with the Khari raising his hand in silence.

The room quieted down, and Vala continued. "The sorceress Ikaria is requesting we send all technological relics to their sector." Vala turned to stare at the Khari. "She will activate them for us to use. Weapons."

"The sorceress has the power to activate artifacts?" the Khari said in disbelief.

Vala nodded. "She was given that power when she unlocked the gift of the black. Though her life force had been wiped clean and restored from the green princess in this past, the knowledge of that power still flows through her blood." Vala paused. "She also requests that I go to each sector and convince them to join. If they do, the sorceress asks that our sector send four blue-gifted emissaries to the other sectors to start collecting the artifacts."

Lord Nnadi spoke up. "How do we know if we can trust the sorceress? She was imprisoned only a short time ago!" he said. "She could be very well be collecting these artifacts for herself!"

"I cannot vouch for the sorceress on everything that she has done in the past." Vala gave the lords a cool stare. "Neither could I vouch for any of your past behavior. Tell me, who is born of perfection? Never made a mistake?" Vala stared down the room with her watery-blue eyes, and the lords glanced away. "Hm. That's what I thought." She walked down the aisle, still staring down the lords, then turned to the Khari. "If my uncle Auron does—who is the holiest priest I know—I put my trust in her as well."

"High Priest Auron trusts her?" the Khari asked.

"She is his complement."

The room went wild with whispers once again, and the Khari had to silence them once again.

"Sorceress Ikaria is High Priest Auron's complement? How strange the God of Light is," the Khari stated, pausing, then looking to the lords.

Vala could see that the Khari was swayed, but many of lords of the court were not.

"We will discuss matters and make a decision," the Khari said. "Meanwhile, please remain here."

Vala frowned. "No offense, my khari, but time is of the utmost importance. I must be on my way to the other sectors to speak with them." She glanced at the room. "Last time, it took several days of discussion to decide whether to stop the sorceress from succeeding."

"The very same sorceress that you now want us to help," pointed out a lord.

"Yes, the very same. How time has changed, hasn't it, Lord Monte?" Vala said. "Now, however, we don't have the luxury of having intellectual conversations on war. We only have moments before we lose everything. I cannot sit idly by while our world is on the brink of destruction."

The lords remained silent as the Khari studied her. "You are admirable, Lady Vala. You can be on your way while we discuss matters. We will make a decision within three days' time."

Vala nodded. "Very well. I'll be at World Sector Five, though I don't plan on staying there long either."

"I will send an envoy to locate you."

"Thank you, Khari." Vala bowed deeply, then turned to the lords, bowing. "Thank you, my lords."

Vala walked down the center aisle and out of the grand double doors. As they closed behind her, Vala breathed with disappointment. She'd seen the looks on those lords' faces. Help the sorceress? They weren't having it. What gave her some small hope was that the Khari was convinced. He, out of everyone else at court, respected her advice above most. He always had.

Vala turned away, sickened with worry. It wasn't starting off well. Hopefully she wouldn't have this same trouble with the other world sectors.

But somehow, she had a feeling she would.

CHAPTER 21

◆

RED

"Fucking finally," Kyle wheezed, stopping to catch his breath. "I wasn't sure if I was gonna make it."

"Hey, you were the one who wanted to avoid being seen," Emerald said, breathless herself. "This was the nearest point according to the transport pilot."

Kyle chuckled. "I'm not blaming you. Dude had to do what he had to do. It's just I now realize what shitty shape I'm in."

"Not as bad as me," she joked. "My feet are killing me."

"You have an excuse. I don't."

Emerald stopped in front of him. "You know, you could have used your orange magic to make the transport invisible. Maybe even morph us to look different so no one would notice us." She jabbed her pointer finger in his chest playfully.

Kyle paused in his tracks, dumbfounded. "Why the hell did I not think of that? That's fucking brilliant."

"Someone has to have the brains around here," Emerald said, touching his sunglasses. "Must you wear those? You're so handsome without them."

"You know I gotta," Kyle said.

"Do you?"

"Of course."

"Why?"

"Because my eyes are scary as hell."

Emerald darted her sparkling green eyes at him, sheepishly biting her lip. Then she quickly grabbed them, hiding them behind her back as she laughed.

"Hey!" Kyle darted for his glasses behind her back, but she kept evading him, laughing. He gave her a devilish grin, then grabbed her, kissing her, open mouth and all. He knew people were watching as they walked by; their minds were blaring loud, though it made it rather fun.

She kissed him in return, then whispered in his ear, "You win." She placed the glasses back on him, kissing him again. God, he wanted her. If this kept going, he was going to have a raging hard-on for the world to see.

Kyle quickly let go, then started walking.

"Why did you stop?" Emerald said, catching up with him.

"I didn't think you wanted to give Arcadia an X-rated show."

"Kyle!" She slapped him playfully, and he winced.

"It's true, though!"

They both chuckled, walking hand in hand as he led her down to the lower levels. Occasionally, he adjusted his shades. One of the arms on the frame was wiggly, making the sunglasses not exactly tight on his head, but he managed. It felt so damn good being in this lower-level shithole. The dirty streets, the piss, the drunks, the neon lights, even in the daytime…it was home.

He came to a familiar corner. So many memories on that corner back in the day. He had parked his bike there a few times. Other times, he hung out with the band or other guys who wanted to chill. Hell, he'd shared a couple of forties with the homeless there. That was, of course, when he didn't have his shit together before getting together with Sonja.

"We're almost there!" Kyle said with a grin.

They turned the corner, passing a few doped-up bums. Em edged near him as they walked down the street, pausing in front of the warehouse doors. Should he knock? Walk in? No…the guys probably had the doors locked so kleptos and tweakers wouldn't come wandering in. They'd been having issues getting broken into. Kyle paused. What would the guys say when he just suddenly showed his face? Everyone thought him dead.

This will be interesting…

"What are you waiting for?" Emerald asked, her green eyes sparkling at him.

"I dunno. It's so…strange," he answered.

Emerald placed her hand softly on his back in reassurance.

Kyle turned to the door, then pounded loudly, causing it to rattle. He snatched a smoke from his box, then lit up. There was a moment of silence, then Kyle pounded again.

"Open up, assholes!" Kyle yelled.

The passersby looked at him weird as they went to and fro. "You need a fix? I can get ya hooked up," said a strung-out dude.

"Thanks, man, not looking for that," Kyle answered him. *God, tweakers.* He remembered when he was that bad at one point. If he hadn't cleaned up his shit then, he very well could've been like homeboy talking to him.

Kyle pounded the door again. "Hell-o!"

Right as he was going to kick it, the door opened up, Diego standing in the doorway. His best friend's mouth dropped straight to the floor.

"HOLY SHIT!" Diego shouted.

"Hey, man," Kyle said.

"HO-LEE shit!"

"You already said that," Kyle said, blowing out smoke from his nostrils.

"Hi," Emerald added shyly from behind him.

"Holy shit! What in the flying fuck?" Diego blinked. "Aren't you supposed to be *dead*? How in the fuck?"

"Well, are you going to just stand there and yell profanities at me, or you gonna let my ass inside?" Kyle said.

Diego nearly toppled Kyle over, giving him a big man-hug. They pounded each other's backs with giant slaps as they let go. Kyle fixed his sunglasses, as people walking by were staring. "Dude, I fucking can't believe it, man!"

"Can we move this inside? I don't wanna give people a show," Kyle said, eyeballing the nearby street tweakers.

"Yeah, man, come on!" Diego waved them in.

Kyle and Emerald stepped inside, and Diego led them to the band. "You guys won't fucking believe it. Look who showed up!" Diego yelled.

"KYLE?" Kamren said with surprise that was completely out of character for him. He put down his drumsticks, running up to him. "Kyle!"

"Hey, man," Remy said in his usual fashion.

"What's up, assholes?" Kyle said.

"Queen Emerald!" Kamren continued, giving a strange bow.

"Would ya knock that shit off! It's just Em!" Kyle said.

Emerald giggled. "He's right. If you could, I prefer if you forget that I'm

Queen while I'm down here."

"I know, I know… It's just hard."

Remy eyed Kyle. "Glacia was telling me the truth, though I didn't believe her. You're *alive*," he said.

"You talked to Glacia already?" Emerald said.

"It's no secret I talk to her every day," Remy said. "She told me the first day Kyle made an appearance at the palace."

Figures. She can't hold a secret for more than five seconds.

Emerald's cheeks flushed red. "I…guess I forgot about you two."

"*What?*" Kyle turned an about face, then glanced at Remy, then back at Emerald.

"Glacia is seeing him," Emerald whispered in his ear. "I'll fill you in later."

Remy? With Glacia? *And here I thought I was polar opposites with Em.*

Kamren came close, inspecting them. "I can't believe it either…"

"So we gotta put up with this guy's shit all over again?" Diego laughed, taking a drink. "And what the hell is up with those shades. You look like a fucking douche."

"I fucking like them," Kyle said, plopping down on the old couch, taking a drag of his smoke.

"So?" Diego said. "Like, where have you been? What happened to you? Last time we saw you, some fucking weird robot dude fucked up our show. Then the authorities were grilling our ass. We had to spend a night in the slammer, thanks to your ass."

"Sorry, man."

Diego sat up, pointing his cigarette at Kyle. "See? That's the kind of shit that makes me pissed off. Just sorry? You know how I feel about jail! There are weird fucks in that joint." Diego flopped back down in his seat. "Anyways, Em's servant chick called me, heard that you were there to break up a wedding. Then…nada."

Kyle cleared his throat. What should he say? He didn't want a bunch of people knowing the truth, because who the hell would believe him about magic, resurrection, living a new life in the future?

"Listen, they arrested me because of Emerald," he said. "They said I kidnapped her. King Damaris was pissed off, and they put me in a special prison. One for high-profile people."

"No shit?"

"Dude, I'm telling you, my life has been a shit show the last few months," Kyle said. Emerald eyed him evenly, a glimmer of humor behind her expression. What he said wasn't necessarily wrong.

"Really? That's hardcore and shit. Well, what about the King now? He's all good with you out of jail?"

"Yeah. That's the entire reason I was able to get out."

"Well, we heard you were dead. That was the story that Glacia told us," Remy said.

"That's the thing. That's what they told everyone to make Em believe that was the truth," Kyle continued.

"Damn," Diego said. "That's some fucked-up shit right there. So we basically mourned your death and you were alive this entire time?"

"Yeah, sorry about that."

Kamren snickered while Diego took another drink. "Well, don't ask me to mourn your ass again."

"You didn't have to in the first place." Kyle sat down on the shitty couch, and Emerald joined him. He waved to Diego for a drink of his flask. Diego handed over the bottle.

"What are you up to now, man? You living at your old place?" Kamren asked.

"I'm living at the palace now," he said as he took a swig of whiskey from the flask.

"No shit. Really? Mr. All Important here," Diego joked.

Emerald glanced at him. "Yes, he's living with me now."

Kyle sighed inwardly. He knew exactly what they were thinking: he was upper-level fodder now. "Whatever," he said. "I'm staying with Em. That's all that matters." He turned to Emerald, whispering in her ear, "Should I tell them?"

"I don't mind," Emerald whispered back. "Just don't tell them about…"

"What are you two whispering about?" Diego called out.

"I won't," he said, then turned to the guys. "Anyway," he announced loudly, "I gotta be there for them." Kyle nodded to her tummy.

"Them?" Diego said, confused.

"Aw shit, really?" Kamren said. "Congrats, man!"

"What? What is going on?" Diego said, still confused.

"He's gonna be a fucking father, you dipshit," Remy said, smacking him on the back of the head.

"Hey, watch it, asshole," Diego said, then turned to Kyle. "Really? For real?"

"For real," Kyle confirmed.

"Well, shit. Congrats, my man. You're gonna be a dad. Better hope the kid ends up like Em and not you. I'd feel sorry if the kid has your sorry-ass features. Em is much better looking than you."

Kyle raised the flask. "That I agree with, man."

They both took a swig. That whiskey went down smooth. Too smooth with no bite, making it easy to drink more.

Diego grunted. "Well, I was gonna say that maybe you should start doing shows with us again. But since you're gonna be a father and shit, might not be a good thing."

"Shows," Kyle echoed. The word rolled off his tongue like the whiskey. Playing his guitar felt so fucking right…and playing at shows? It was a chance to have a regular excuse for freedom from the palace. A second chance at his old life doing what he loved.

"Well, duh. You're here, and we still need a lead vocalist. I know I have a badass voice and all, but Remy don't think so. After you supposedly died, we kind of got famous. Guess we needed your ass to die to make some money around here."

"That hurts," Kyle said.

"It should, but you know, if you show up, it would make us even bigger," Diego said.

"You think?"

"Yeah. For sure."

"Shows, huh?" Kyle said, taking a drag of his smoke. He looked over at Em, suddenly feeling kind of guilty. But why should he feel guilty? It was a love of his, something she knew about too. And playing his guitar made him realize how much he wanted to play in the band again. That was all he ever wanted. Play in a band and have her by his side. Now he had one of those things…

"I dunno. I gotta think about it," Kyle said, taking another swig, handing it back to Diego.

Emerald remained silent.

"Think hard on it," Remy said. "We got a show tomorrow night. Would be good of you to play with us."

"Can you imagine the crowd?" Diego laughed. "People all this time thinking you were dead…but you weren't. It'll be sick!"

"Well, I don't give a shit about that kind of thing."

"You will once you see the money roll into your bank account," Diego said.

"Why are you still down in the lower levels if you're famous?" Emerald asked, confused.

"It's the image," Diego said. "We can't be some punk band writing and practicing music in the upper levels. No one likes when you go corporate."

"They don't?"

Kyle nodded, turning to Emerald. "He's right. Fans want the real deal."

"Exactly," Diego said. "There's so many pussy bands that act all hardcore and shit, but then you find out they haven't even been down to the street levels. A bunch of fucking posers and shit."

The thought of playing at shows made his heart beat rapid-fire. The thrill of playing his music, singing his heart and ass off. It was exactly what he needed. He didn't give a shit about money. But then again, he was going to be a father. He didn't want to be a palace mooch either. This was a chance for him to step up and make some real dough to provide for his woman and children—while doing what he loved to do. He could actually afford shit for once in his damn life. Both lives, in fact. He could replace his motorcycle, pay Garrett back for ruining his, get more tats, and buy Emerald real gifts… His head was spinning with all the possibilities.

"I'll let you know," Kyle said as he got to his feet, Emerald doing the same. "Just send the details to Glacia, and she can tell me where if I decide to do it." Kyle glanced at Emerald. He could hear her thoughts, but they weren't clear to him. What was she thinking?

"I hope you'll do it. Would love to play with you again. Just like old times," Diego said.

"It's definitely not the same without you," Remy admitted.

"I'm touched, Remy, especially coming from your ass," Kyle said.

Remy snorted, then gave him a half smile.

Kyle turned to Emerald. "You ready?"

"Yes," she said, smiling at him. Emerald turned to the guys, waving. "Goodbye, hopefully I will see you soon."

"At the show tomorrow night," Kamren joked.

"Think about it, seriously, dude," Diego said.

Kyle turned away, lifting a hand up high in goodbye. He would think seriously. But Em…he couldn't tell what she was thinking. It was bothering him.

As they were leaving, Kyle turned to her. "You hungry?" he asked.

"A little, but I can wait until we get back at the palace," she answered.

"Why don't we eat while we're down here? I've got a place in mind," he said.

"Oh?" Emerald chuckled. "Where is it?"

"You'll see."

✦　✦　✦

Bustles of Arcadians flooded the skyways, escalators, and transport stops as Kyle and Emerald squeezed through the crowded mid-levels. Savory smells rose from the food carts, hitting his senses, making him even more hungry.

Kyle and Emerald unloaded at the end of the escalator, with Kyle leading the way. Emerald held his hand tightly, nervous about losing him in the crowd. He couldn't blame her; it was more packed than usual.

"Oh my god, it's the lead singer of Disorderly Conduct!" someone called out as they exited the platform. Kyle turned just as they snapped a photo.

Kyle froze, while Emerald shied behind him. "This is unexpected," he said to her under his breath.

"Kyle Trancer?" exclaimed a woman. She pulled out her communicator. "Oh my god, he has red hair!"

Oh shit.

"This could get bad," Emerald whispered.

"Yeah, I think you're right. Let's go," he whispered back to her. "Hurry." He grabbed her hand, then the two booked it.

Was it true what Diego said? That the band was famous? If it was going to be like this, he would have to be more cautious. That or do what Em suggested— use magic.

They managed to lose the gathered fans, and Kyle managed to find the specific diner he had in mind.

"Come on," he said, pulling her into the diner.

"Is the food good here?" Emerald asked.

"I dunno."

"If you have never had the food before, then how do you know about this place?"

"Let's just say that Geeta recommends it," Kyle said.

"She eats here?" Emerald asked, surprised.

Kyle smiled as they walked inside, the doorbell chiming. He glanced around at the diner. The booths, the countertops, the colors. Even down to the little details, it was the same as his dream.

"Hi," said a cashier. Kyle turned and saw a dude. He looked a bit scruffy, probably had a long night of drinking and was hungover.

"Hey, man. Table for two," Kyle said.

"Follow me," the man said, grabbing two menus.

He led them to a booth, then they both seated themselves. "Your server will be here in a jiff."

The man walked off, and Emerald picked up a menu. Kyle did the same. All-day breakfast. Breakfast food for lunch? Sounded good to him.

"Hiya. Do you need another moment?" a chipper woman's voice said.

Kyle looked up from his menu. Bubblegum pink lips, with short cropped hair to match. Sharp-cut bangs across her eyebrows, with heavy black eye makeup.

Yep. That's her.

"What d'ya recommend?" Kyle asked.

"First time here, I take it?" the pink-haired woman asked.

"Yeah. A good friend of mine recommended me this place."

"Aw, I'm so glad!"

"She comes here a lot," Kyle continued. Emerald put down her menu, eyeing him.

"Hey, don't I know you from somewhere?" the waitress asked, making a dramatic pout with her pink lips.

"I don't think so."

"Hm. You seem familiar." The waitress paused. "By the way, who told you about this place?"

"Her name's Geeta. You know her?" Kyle said.

"I know Geeta!"

"You're Nym, right? Geeta talks about you all the time," Kyle continued. From the corner of his eye, Emerald's mouth dropped open. God, Geeta was gonna kill him.

She'll thank me in the long run.

"What does she say about me?" Nym pressed as she batted her long eyelashes.

"All sorts of things. All good, of course," Kyle said.

Nym smiled brightly. "Good to know."

Kyle chuckled, then pretended to be clueless about the menu. He damn well knew what he wanted on the menu, but he had to play it up. "So, what's the best thing on the menu? You forgot to say."

"Oops," Nym said, flushing. She pointed to one of the specials. Breakfast burrito. Thank god. He wanted a damn burrito, but he needed to keep up the charade. "That one. It's the best."

"I'll have that and a cup of coffee. Black, please," Kyle said.

"Gotcha, Mr. Glasses."

"Sorry. Had a long night last night. My eyes look like hell."

"We've all had those nights." Nym smirked.

"No kidding. I'm regretting it now."

Nym giggled, then turned to Emerald. "And for you, doll?"

"Orange juice, please," Emerald said.

"Nothing else?"

Emerald hesitated, then said. "I'll have what he is having too."

"You got it." She wrote down the order, then walked off.

After she was out of earshot, Emerald leaned in. "Kyle! What are you doing?"

"Helping Geeta. She just doesn't know it yet."

"Helping *how*?"

"Geeta's not the type of person to put herself out there. So I'm doing it for her," Kyle said, shrugging.

Emerald looked at him for a moment, then suddenly understood. "Ah. I see. But are you sure you want to be doing this? What if Nym isn't...well, you know…"

"Don't know either, but doesn't hurt to at least try. Who knows? Maybe she's into both teams. Or a little bit of everything."

"How did you know she worked here?"

Kyle leaned back in the seat, sighing. "When I was regaining my old memories, I saw this place in Geeta's mind. Somehow I entered her mind by accident and stumbled upon this secret."

Emerald opened her mouth to say more, but Nym came back with the coffee, poured Kyle a cup, then placed a glass of orange juice in front of Emerald. "Your order should be up shortly."

"Thanks."

She winked, then moved in. "By the way, what has Geeta been up to? I haven't seen her in a while."

"She's been at the palace," Emerald cut in.

Nym's mouth dropped, and it looked like she was about to drop the coffee pot. "At the *palace*?"

"She was named Protector of the Realm," Emerald continued.

Kyle kicked her under the table. Emerald tried not to burst out laughing.

"Wow. For real? Protector of the Realm?"

"Yes," Emerald said, nodding.

"That's incredible! Good for her. She deserves it. I saw what she did…" Nym stopped herself, then cleared her throat. Kyle felt her thoughts slightly. Nym had witnessed Geeta's magic. "I wonder if I will ever see her again?"

"Probably. Might be a while, though," Kyle answered.

"You work at the palace too?" Nym asked quizzically.

"Something like that."

"I actually got Geeta the palace job," Emerald offered. Kyle tried hard not to chuckle.

Nym lowered her voice, leaning in. "They say that the King and Queen have special powers…like Geeta. Is that true?"

Emerald leaned in. "I have heard the same thing but haven't witnessed anything myself."

Nym smiled, then straightened her posture. "I have always kinda hoped that the rumors were true. It would be super cool to have a magical king and queen." She winked. "When you see Geeta, tell her I said hi, will ya?" Nym said.

"Sure thing." Kyle nodded.

There was yelling behind her, coming from the kitchen. "I think that's your order," Nym said, then quickly ran off.

Minutes later, she returned, serving them their food. It was the biggest fucking breakfast burrito he had ever seen. He was in burrito heaven.

"There you go. Two specials," Nym said, placing the hot sauce on the table with the ketchup. She pulled a piece of scrap paper out of her apron, then slid it to Kyle. It had a phone number on it.

"When you see Geeta, can you give that to her? In case she wants to get ahold of me? I'll be bummed if she can't stop by anymore."

"I'll give it to her when I see her," Kyle said. "I know she's gone on business, but she'll be back soon. Probably in a week or so."

Nym smiled again. "Thanks, doll." She looked at them both. "Enjoy. Just let me know if you need anything else." She was about to walk away, but then did a one-eighty, turning directly toward him. "I finally figured out how I know you," she said.

"Oh yeah?"

"You're the lead singer of Disorderly Conduct," Nym said in a low voice, then giggled.

"Well, shit. No hiding it, I guess," he said. How the hell did she know the band? *I guess the guys weren't kidding about our popularity.*

"Weren't you supposed to be dead?"

"Apparently. I'm here now, though."

Nym giggled while she shook her head. "Don't worry, *Kyle*, your secret is safe with me. I had no idea that Geeta knew you."

"Geeta doesn't like to say much of anything."

Nym laughed, then blushed. "She's a fun one. Make sure you give her my number, please."

"Don't worry. You have my word."

She winked, then walked away. Kyle's and Emerald's eyes met. They were both grinning.

"Kyle!"

He felt Emerald's kick under the table. "Ow!"

"I can't believe you did that!" Emerald whispered excitedly.

"I'll probably get my ass kicked by her when I show her the number," Kyle said, shrugging.

"Let's hope not." Emerald's face turned serious. "I can't believe that people know you. First it was those mid-level citizens, now her—*and* you have your glasses on." Emerald bit her lip. "I can't imagine what it would be like if you didn't have them on."

His stomach did a light flip. He couldn't believe it either. "I know. It's kind of weird. I'm surprised they didn't recognize *you*."

Emerald laughed, then waved him off. "It's hard for people to think that their queen would be eating in a diner on the mid-levels. Plus, I'm dressed like everyone else, and people dye their hair all sorts of colors down here."

"True."

Kyle dug into his food. Nym wasn't kidding—the breakfast burrito was the shit. The best damn thing he'd had in a long-ass time. From across the table, Emerald was digging in too, having no problem downing her food. He had never seen her eat that much. Well, she was pregnant after all. She needed to eat more. It was good for her and for the babies.

Her eyes met his with a strange look.

"What?" Kyle asked.

"I just thought of names," Emerald said slowly. "I want to see what you think."

He glanced at her curiously. "What did you pick?"

"Alexander and Nathan."

Kyle slowly touched her thoughts, and it was as if she knew what he was thinking. In a way, he gave her access without having to say it. Which name was going to be their child's?

"Nathan," she said with certainty.

Kyle put down the coffee cup. "How do you know they will both be boys? Why not pick out girl names just in case?"

"Because I know. It's as if my gift tells me everything about them," she said.

If she knew everything about them, then she had to know whether they were gifted or not. Dare he even ask? What if Derek's kid was gifted, and theirs wasn't? That would be his worst nightmare.

She glanced at him knowingly. "They both are gifted."

Kyle breathed a sigh, then leaned in. "Do you…know?" *The color of their magics,* he didn't say.

"I don't know," she said. "I can feel their magics, but it's hard to say who has what."

"Well, can you at least tell me what you can sort out?"

She shook her head. "It's not that easy. I can sense underlying colors, so what I'm feeling could be their analogous magics. I can't say for sure."

"I guess it will be a surprise when they are born," Kyle said. Would his son have his same magic? He hoped that his son would have some sort of time magic. It was already hard enough to beat that fuck Derek at his game without blue magic of his own. Maybe violet magic. That shit was OP, having mind powers, with red and blue as its adjacent magic.

Emerald took another bite of food. "We should probably get back to the transport soon. Emerys is probably worried sick up at the palace."

"Dude's gotta live a little." He took another bite. He wanted to ask her what she thought about him playing again. But did he really need permission from his girlfriend to do what he wanted? If she cared enough about his wants and desires, she would support him and his decisions. Wouldn't she?

His stomach jumbled.

Geeta told me to protect her. And of course, I am going to protect her with every ounce of muscle and magic in my body, he told himself. He loved Emerald like his own damn body and soul. They were one and the same. Their souls were meant to be together. But then, why was it so hard to bring up the band?

"Listen, Em. What did you think about what the guys said?" Kyle said vaguely.

"You mean about you playing at shows again?" she said, not missing a beat.

His heart fluttered. "Yeah. I was just thinking how much I miss it… What do you think about all of it? If I played at shows?"

Emerald didn't look at him for a moment, then shifted in her seat. Her vivid green eyes met his, making him feel guilty for asking. "Kyle, I want you to be happy. I want you to play."

"There is a 'but' in there," Kyle said.

"But I am pregnant. It's one thing to go out and visit the lower levels, like we talked about. But it's another thing to go to late-night shows. I'm always tired and don't have much energy. Especially at night." She paused and took another bite of food, making his stomach sink.

"So…?"

Emerald smiled as she swallowed her food. "I wasn't done, but I needed another bite of food." She leaned in. "What I'm trying to say is that I don't want the pregnancy to hold you back from your dreams. It isn't fair to you. I'll do what I must to make you happy. Because you make me happy. I'll attend the shows until my feet can't take it anymore." She smiled, her eyes sparkling a pale green.

Kyle's heart pounded with excitement. "You mean it? You're okay with it? I mean, I don't want you to just agree with me just because I want to."

"Yes, of course. I just don't like the idea of me being out late, as tired as I get. But I will do whatever I can to get a long nap in during the day," she said, smiling shyly at him.

"You're the best, Em." He grabbed her hand, kissed the top while she blushed. "Thank you."

"Anything," she said shyly. "I love you, Kyle."

Her face was innocent, sweet, and so beautiful. "I love you too," he whispered.

She gave him another smile. "Now, let's finish our food. I didn't realize how starved I was."

Kyle chuckled as they both dug in.

CHAPTER 22

◆

GRAY

"Victor!"

Victor glanced up from his pack as Elyathi opened the flap of his tent and hurriedly flopped down before him. Her pale eyes, full of life and love, glimmered with hope as she smiled brightly at him. Her colorless white hair flowed down the swell of her back, her lilac linen gown crusted with dirt.

"Victor," Elyathi repeated. "I heard that the camp is packing. We are moving again?"

He had heard it from his father. "Yes, my father is going to relocate the camp," Victor said, nodding.

"Do you know why, though?" Elyathi gave his tent a once-over, noticing that much of his stuff hadn't been packed. "Let me help you."

Victor's cheeks burned with embarrassment. "You don't have to. You should stay with the camp leaders."

"I want to stay with you," she breathed. "I feel safer when you are around."

Her innocent face was so sincere that Victor often felt guilty just having feelings for her. She was one of those perfect young women, the kind one would feel responsible for if their heart was crushed.

Sweat beaded on his forehead. "I'm glad that you feel safe around me, El, but consider the camp leaders," he said. "They are much more experienced in keeping people safe than me."

"That may be true, but I don't feel comfortable around them. I feel comfortable around you."

Victor bit his lip, unsure of what to say as he continued to pack.

Elyathi leaned in, her long white locks cascading down as she grabbed a few books to help him pack. "You didn't answer my question, though. Why are we leaving? Are the future people looking for me again?"

Victor grabbed another shirt in silence. Should he tell her? As he shyly glanced up, he was met with her impressionable glance. He couldn't hold back the truth. Her innocence demanded it.

"I heard that the newly seated King of Arcadia is searching for you," Victor began. "He is in a race with other suitors from neighboring kingdoms."

Elyathi looked serious. "But why me?"

He suppressed a laugh, raising his eyebrow. "Really?"

Elyathi blushed, her cheeks turning completely red. "They don't even know me. How can they want to marry me if they haven't even met me?"

"Elyathi…" Victor stumbled over his words. "The world is a very different place than what you see in this camp. Some men don't marry for love."

Elyathi furrowed her eyebrows. "Why not?"

How to explain it? "Because some men, including kings and princes, only care for a beautiful woman," he began. "It is the only thing they care about."

Elyathi looked like she had been hit in the face.

This is why you don't belong in the world.

"Here at the camp, we have been protecting you," Victor continued. "My father swore to the blue-gifted many years ago that we would do so with our lives. He warned us of people coming in search of you. Because of this warning, the camp takes it seriously. So if this King of Arcadia is pursuing you, then we must take that as a threat." He met her eyes. "It is the only way to keep you safe."

"But what if I want to meet him?" Elyathi whispered dreamily. "I cannot remain in hiding forever, Victor. What am I to do? Remain an unmarried woman, never finding love, for the rest of my days? Grow old without ever experiencing what true love feels like?"

It was the perfect moment to tell her how he felt. He had been in love with her for years. Why couldn't she see it? And why couldn't he find the courage to tell her?

"Elyathi, what if you were to find someone in the camp?" Victor asked. "Just because you remain here, doesn't mean you won't ever fall in love."

Elyathi glanced at him curiously, as if she had never considered it. "You think that's a possibility?"

"Of course."

Elyathi paused, then shrugged. "There aren't many options. Besides, a king—of age—pursuing me?" she said breathlessly with a secret smile. "He has only heard of me, and yet he wants to know me. It's like a fairy tale, Victor, like the romantic storybook you gave me."

Hearing her words made his heart sink. It hurt. She had never thought of him in that way. How could he ever compete with a *fairy tale* king, when he was just a wastelander caked with dirt and grime and had no standing?

She was young. Innocent, full of hope. Life. Love. Joy.

Victor...

Flashes of his gray vision came to him. Her face was full of despair, sadness, pain, hurt, depression...

The sin of the world must be eradicated...the sadness, the pain, and the suffering...The Spectrum of Magic will sweep over the world in a way that none will have ever known, for no one is like me...

Victor blinked, the memory fading away.

He was alone in his tent. In his lap sat one of his poetry books. Songs of the Heart, an old book comprised of ancient poetic writings from the scribes long ago. Of course, his copy had been reproduced for the United Kingdoms' masses. His recent thoughts of Elyathi had compelled him to read it. Especially the vision. Something about a broken heart.

Perhaps it was a way to tie in to his power. Or maybe there was an underlying message for him to stop the end of time from falling in upon itself...

He sighed, hoping that his exhaled breath would purge him of all his stress. It didn't work. He reached for his canteen, taking a drink of water.

Fairy tale king...

Victor shuddered, thinking about everything that would happen to Elyathi. She had sent letters to him after her wedding, pleas for help. Victor had tried to see her, but Damaris had her under lock and key. So many times, he had tried and failed. Then her letters stopped coming. Victor always wondered whether Damaris found out about her letters. Or had she given up hope since Victor hadn't been able to send any sort of message or even see her?

I wonder if she ever knew the truth of it.

Now, it seemed it was his destiny to see her once again. But it wouldn't be as it was, knowing that Elyathi would be ruined by Damaris. Somehow Victor had a strong feeling that Elyathi would blame him for not seeing her in the past. Elyathi didn't know how much he had tried. How his letters went unanswered, probably never reaching her. Then she had died. Or so he had thought. She had been alive all this time, and his gray vision was trying to warn him. Now, with her hate, Elyathi was going to destroy the world. Emerald was tied up in this mess too.

The Elyathi in his vision was full of light. But it was a warped light, and behind it lay a darkness so disturbing that he couldn't shake it no matter how hard he tried. Her eyes had shown him the cruelty possible behind the mask of purity.

He was suddenly hot. Extremely hot. Victor looked down and saw his hands jittering. His shirt was soaked.

I have to figure out how to use my magic before it's too late.

Victor glanced down at the most recent verse he had read:

What have you done, oh my soul? You wandered aimlessly through darkness, embracing its kiss. Though you are tempted by its sweetness, its poison will seep into your soul, destroying you from the inside out. For the path of darkness leads to transgression. Who will lead you out of despair and into the light? The depths of sorrow can be a pit of eternal damnation.

"Knock-knock."

Victor looked up from his book to see Reila poking her head inside the tent flap. "Come in," he said as he closed his book.

"You okay?"

"Yeah," he said, waving her inside.

Reila slipped between the flaps, then plopped herself on one of the sitting pillows. "Most of the vehicles are packed," she said. "Just a few stragglers here and there. Camp will probably be ready to go in two hours tops."

"I'll start making my rounds," Victor said as he threw on his shirt.

Reila was about to light a new cigarette, but Victor eyed her. "Good. Can't have the leader not say goodbye to his family," she said, putting the unlit cigarette away.

Victor smiled. "Thanks for taking my place for the time being."

She flipped her brown hair back into a ponytail. "Just doing my job. Not like I had a choice." She rifled through her pockets, holding up a note. "Also, I just wanted to let you know I got Scrap Yard's updated parts list."

"Scrap Yard?"

"That walking calculator that you call Scion." Reila straightened her posture. "Here," she said, waving the list in front of him.

Victor sighed as he took it. "Must you call him that?"

"Whatever. I'm leaving anyways. Not like it'll matter too much longer."

"How is Drew doing?"

"Same old, same old," she answered. "Scion replaced another part. Just waiting to see what happens, I suppose."

Victor sighed. "Hopefully you can get our camp back to some sort of normalcy."

Reila gave him a strange look, as if she knew his fears. "We will."

Victor thought about Gwen.

"It's the girl," Reila said slowly. "You're worried."

Victor glanced at her.

"We'll get the girl back, Victor," she said in a low voice.

"You're that confident?"

"Not really. I just pretend that I am. It seems to work out." Reila glanced over, noticing that Scion's shadow on the tent's canvas wall. For a brief moment, Reila shuffled her hair in a feminine sort of way, then posed herself in a certain manner. "What do you want, Scion?" she called. "I know you're out there."

Scion snapped his head inside the tent, his eyes trailing to her, then to Victor, then back to Reila.

"Miss Reila…"

"It's *Reila* to you."

"Scion, would you like to sit down with us for a minute?" Victor interrupted.

"That is not necessary, Victor. I will only be thirty-two seconds," he stated.

Reila sighed loudly.

Scion blinked. "Reila. I have come to say goodbye."

"Sure you have."

Victor smirked.

"I have," Scion continued. "It is uncertain when we will encounter each other again since I am to remain here, and you will travel back to the old camp. Due to this set of circumstances, my circuits urged me to see you once more."

Reila shot a glance at Victor, then shifted her gaze down to the tent floor. "Well, aren't you cute," she said. Victor caught her cheeks turning pink as she turned away and smoothed her ponytail. As she did so, her bicep muscles flexed, her heavily inked tattoos standing out. "I bet that is standard for you men cyborg types. Act all cute to any woman, regardless of how classy she is. Or should I say, how uncouth she is." She glanced over her shoulder back at Scion.

"Your assessment is incorrect," Scion pointed out. "You are the first. One out of three thousand and twenty-one women I have come in contact with in my cyborg life cycle."

"Don't I feel special?" Still glancing over her shoulder, Reila's eyes locked onto his. "I hate when you talk in numbers." She gave him a private smile, though Victor saw right through it. "Take care, Scion, you hunk of junk. Get that orange cyborg magician living again—for Telly's sake."

"Affirmative." Scion nodded with several clicking noises. "Goodbye, Reila."

"See you."

Scion lingered awkwardly for a moment, looking in her direction one last time, then closed the tent flap. His shadow rescinded into the cavern's darkness.

Victor raised an eyebrow at Reila. "Stop looking at me like that," Reila scolded him. "I said my goodbyes. What more do you want from me?"

"He's a cyborg," Victor said evenly.

"So?"

"He's not going to pick up on the hard-to-get type," Victor pointed out.

Her eyes jolted to his. "What? You think me and...*Scrap Yard*?" She shook her head. "No. Hell no. There is no way." She turned away, acting indifferent.

"Must you keep calling him Scrap Yard?"

"Fitting name," she said.

"I don't know what you have against him," he said, smiling.

"Whatever, Victor," she said smoothly. "Anyways, I'm going to finish packing my shit. See you outside."

She rose to her feet, then slipped out of his tent.

Victor glanced back down. His hand was shaking again.

CHAPTER 23

✦

YELLOW

Scion unscrewed his cybernetic finger from Drew's cable plug, glancing over at him and entering more code for stabilization. In the back of his partitioned mind, Reila's face kept appearing. It was odd that his thoughts were locked onto her. Maybe his programming had been hacked? Or perhaps a wire was faulty? He had thought to ask Miss Hearly about running a few diagnostic scans to see if everything was in order. But a feeling told him not to. In a strange way, he liked thinking about Reila and wanted to keep that information confidential.

Within his peripheral vision, Miss Hearly was engrossed with her project. She kept to herself mostly, except to get his input regarding Drew or about the prototype weapon, which was nearly every two hours. She had a mind like his, a photographic memory when it came to numbers and concepts. It was why their personalities were an eighty-three percent match.

They switched between monitoring Drew and working on the new magitech weapon. From his scans, Scion knew Telly emitted the signs of fear and had expressed extreme worry about Drew. But at the same time, she had also made clear that the weapon needed to be complete in order to rescue her offspring. At the moment, she was working on the weapon.

There was an alert on his scans. Someone was approaching their room.

"Miss Hearly," Scion called out. That was all he needed to say to warn her.

Quickly, the scientist waved her hand near her experimental table. The energy in 590-nanometers covered the entire diameter, then the project disappeared. Miss Hearly glanced over at him and nodded, walking over to

Drew and picking up her tablet.

Approximately eleven seconds later, Reila's face appeared in the doorway.

His heart rate went to 120 beats per minute.

"What are you doing here?" Miss Hearly called out. "Aren't you supposed to be gone already?"

"Sorry to disappoint you, city scientist, but we haven't left yet," Reila said casually. "Don't worry, we'll be out of your hair. We're leaving."

"Then what are you doing here?" Telly asked.

Reila's cheeks turned red, a strange human emotion for embarrassment.

What could Miss Reila be embarrassed about?

As she strutted inside, Reila glanced over at him, then her eyes quickly averted to Drew. "Yeah, well, I had to speak with this contraption before I took off."

She wants to talk to me? His heart skipped a beat. Why did his heart do this when Reila was near him?

Telly shrugged, then turned away.

Reila glanced at him leaning against the cavern wall. "Scion. Can I talk to you for a second?"

"That is a short time for a conversation, Miss Reila," Scion said.

Telly snorted from the other side of the room.

Reila sighed loudly. "Okay, more like five minutes?"

"Yes, Miss Reila."

She waved to him, a sign for him to follow her. He did as he was told and followed her. He suddenly had very little control over his nervous system as she led him out of the room and down the cavern hall.

"Where are you leading us?"

"You'll see," she answered.

His sensors were off the charts. Sweat poured down his face, but he couldn't understand why. Every step, he became more nervous. His hands were shaking outwardly, and his circuits shaking inwardly as Reila led him to a section of the refuge that he had never seen before. The section was dark, even for a human. She held no light but seemed to know where she was going.

It made no sense. It was irrational. So was his heart rate.

"Miss Reila, would you like a flashlight?" Scion asked.

"Shhh," Reila said.

He remained silent as she led him farther into the darkness. Then, without expecting it, she stopped, turning toward him. Before he could speak, she put her hand on him, peering at him in the darkness.

Heart rate one hundred and thirty beats per minute. His heart was in overload at this point.

"Miss Reila. I do not understand…"

"Shut up and kiss me, Scion."

Within a nanosecond, Reila's flesh was touching his, and her lips smashed against his, kissing him wildly. The softness of her lips was a stark contrast to her hard exterior. His wires hummed with excitement. His brain waves approved.

Her soft hands began to shift across his body, Reila whispering soft moans of delight.

His circuits wanted to explode. He took great pleasure in her touch and wanted to indulge in this sensory overload.

As her hands traveled upward from his chest to the back of the neck, she kissed him with such ferocity, like a wild animal. His circuits hummed in pleasure as a new wave of oxytocin flooded his body.

He wanted to give Reila the same pleasure that she had been giving him, so he mimicked her, blending their movements. His flesh had those memory movements stored in them, from the first time he had contact with his wife.

Scion stopped.

His wife.

Confusion entered his thoughts.

She was deceased.

That was in the past.

This feeling…he felt as he once had with his deceased wife…

He stopped kissing.

There was a silent pause between them. Though it was pitch black to the human eye, Scion could see her every movement with his infrared vision. Instead of her eyes giving him a hard stare, there was a glimmer of softness to them.

"Is this too much excitement for you?" Reila said quietly.

His heart rate escalated. He was confused. What he should say? Something in his circuits made him think it was unwise mentioning his deceased wife.

"No, Miss Reila. I…my programming and circuits approve of this action," he answered.

Never had Scion heard Reila giggle in the way she did just then. "Your programming approves? How about you? Do you approve?"

Did he approve? Yes, he did. Warmth flooded his body, and his circuits hummed again. He wanted to do everything he could for her. To make her happy.

"Miss Reila."

"I told you, my name is Reila." He saw a soft glimmer of light in her brown eyes. They were the color of bark, like a strong cedar tree. Just like her, so strong and beautiful.

"Scion?"

"Reila. I approve of this action," he answered quickly. He felt a wave of hot blood in his cheeks.

She smirked again, her body lingering next to his.

"Though I must point out that I am confused by your actions," he continued. "I thought you didn't care for me, with your odd name-calling, your grouchy manner, and the way you scold me when I inform you of current matters."

"Grouchy? Is that what you call it?" Reila giggled, then ran her hand down his chest and tucked it inside the tip of his belt. "You being a cyborg means you will have to try and pick up on my moods." She leaned in, then pressed her lips on his.

Her lips, her flesh, her touch, they made him so very irrational. The wetness of her lips, the taste of her tongue, her particular human smell that only she emitted…

It was all so different from his normal programming.

His heart rate went into the red range, but he did not care. Endorphins of his natural side flooded his mind, and all he could think about was her. His body was doing strange things.

Her lips released his, then she took a step back, slapping him playfully, glancing down at the part that identified him as a male specimen.

"*My*, my." Reila leaned in, then played with a wire that extended out of his mechanical back and into his neck. "Don't go and do anything stupid like get yourself killed. I kind of like you," she said, winking.

What did she mean by that? Of course that wasn't in his agenda.

She kissed two of her fingertips, then pressed it onto his cheek. "Goodbye for real this time, Scion."

Before he could respond, Reila ducked out of the cavern, leaving him alone. His scans had told him she was already heading in the direction of the refuge exit.

Reila *liked* him. His heart rate sped up exponentially after that thought.

As he walked back toward the cavern lab chamber, he kept smiling involuntarily. Stepping inside, he felt disjointed and confused. His mind was still on Reila.

"What was that all about?" Miss Hearly called out as she quickly hid a book behind her back.

He couldn't make up a lie. His programming wouldn't allow it. But he could not tell Miss Hearly the truth. He was *shy*.

"Hmm?" Scion said as he grabbed the tablet, acting as if he hadn't heard her. Another smile he couldn't help.

"I see," was all Telly said, with a strange expression on her face.

He turned back to look at Drew and heard Miss Hearly laugh quietly.

✦ ✦ ✦

The sun was setting as he exited the refuge. Victor walked down the path, and at the edge of the valley, he saw the wasteland vehicles grouped together. Some were already driving away, heading in the direction of the camp. Others were making last-minute preparations, loading their packs and scolding their children to get inside.

Several people passed by him, grabbing their belongings and strapping them to their dirt bikes.

"Any of you seen Reila?" Victor asked. They all shook their heads and shrugged.

He headed farther down the line of vehicles, saying his farewells to each group. It was disheartening, being left behind. He wanted to be with them; it was in his nature as a wastelander, being with his people.

Finally, he spotted Reila with her equipment, ammo, personal weapons, and her pack.

"There you are," Victor called out. "I was starting to wonder what happened to you."

"I had to take care of some last-minute business," Reila commented as she puffed her cigarette, tossing her equipment in the bed of the vehicle. She took a look around, scowling. "How long does it take to grab their crap and get it in a ground vehicle?"

Victor smiled. "Now you know how I felt all these years."

"Geez. I'll say."

She walked down the line, hollering at the camp members to hurry up and trudged back, climbing up in the bed of the vehicle. She smashed the cigarette butt on the side, then tossed it.

Victor walked over to her, hanging onto the vehicle bed's edge. "Be safe."

"I'm going to miss you. Not too much, though. I like being in charge." Reila smiled.

Victor smiled in return. "Don't burn the house down."

"We'll see." Reila got situated, then pounded on the cab. "Let's get a move on!" she ordered the driver.

The driver started the vehicle, and the others in the line did the same. Her eyes locked onto his, with a seriousness that Victor had never seen from her before.

"I hope you find that girl and figure out your fairy magic. Good luck, Victor," she called out over the roaring engines.

"I'll do my damnedest, Reila," Victor said.

"I know," she said as the vehicle started pulling away.

Victor watched as all the vehicles rode off into the desert dunes. From the rocky peaks of the wastelands, the orange sun had rested in its tips, slowly melting away. It was hard, watching his camp leave him behind. The worst part was that he didn't know when he would see them again.

If ever.

When the last vehicle was gone, a trail of dust brushed over the landscape, leaving him alone. The sounds of the vehicles got softer, until there was nothing but the silence. It was as if his soul were packed on those vehicles, leaving him just an empty shell.

Twilight hit the wastelands, the sky painted with hot pinks and deep purples. A few glimmering stars were scattered throughout, twinkling softly.

There were footsteps approaching. Victor turned around to see Geeta standing next to him.

"You aren't used to it, are you?" she said with a smile.

"I didn't realize you'd returned," he stated.

"A little while ago," she answered, then glanced in the direction of their old camp. "I wanted to give you space."

"You didn't want to say goodbye? I'm sure that some of them would have liked to see you again, being that you helped them out during the battle."

"No, I prefer not to," she said in a low voice. "There are times for saying goodbyes. This wasn't one of them."

Victor sighed, looking off into the distance. "You get the list to the Corporation?"

"I did. It will take some time," Geeta said, turning to him. "We must pray continuously that Drew stays alive. Thankfully, you have the best attendants to count on."

"Indeed."

The last of the vehicles disappeared from the horizon.

"I haven't been by myself, without a camp, my entire life," Victor said wistfully. "They are my lifeblood; it's as if someone's cut off my right arm."

"I know." Geeta turned to him. "But now we must move forward to the matter at hand."

Victor longingly gave one last look where the vehicles had disappeared, then turned to her. "Yes. There is much to do, and much for me to learn. I've already started trying to summon my magic."

Geeta raised an eyebrow. "And?"

He sighed. "No luck."

"You will eventually." Geeta sat down on a boulder, then gestured for him to sit. "There is something that I must speak to you of."

Now it was his turn to raise an eyebrow. "What is it?"

"I know the past that haunts you." Her vivid purple eyes were like darts, piercing his heart. "Of your affections."

Slowly, Victor brushed his dreadlocks out of his face, embarrassed. "I...I have tried to keep my thoughts guarded."

"I never purposely pry into one's mind. I only hear of things when they are loud in one's thoughts," Geeta admitted.

"Have you heard these thoughts just now?"

"Sort of," she confessed. "I heard much of it prior to you being gifted. But since you became gifted, it became like fragments, weaving in and out of my mind in waves. And as of now, they are crashing into the cliffs of your mind, spilling out for me to hear."

He looked away, unable to meet her eyes. It was the first time that anyone knew of his secret. His stomach twisted, making him feel sick to his core.

"It is nothing to be ashamed of," Geeta said. "Our feelings can't be helped. They are a part of us and who we are."

"Then you understand my dilemma."

Geeta remained silent, then nodded. "A difficult situation that puts you at a crossroads. No one ever said life was easy. Certainly not when it comes to love. We can have a deep love for one, be made specifically for that person, designed by the gods to work in harmony. But yet, sometimes it is our destiny that we cannot be together. Ever. For our paths have different endings."

So much truth in one statement.

Victor sighed. "A terrible thing."

"Indeed, very cruel of the gods. Many have died without ever having their love completed by their other half. Truly a sad situation. In these situations, you must be willing to let your love go. Leave these emotions in the past, where they belong."

Victor held his head high, staring once again out into the wastelands. "Believe me, I have been trying."

Geeta stared off in the distance. "It's hard to leave the past behind. We all battle our own demons. Even though you must leave these hurts and longings in the past, you also must realize that these are the emotions that sometimes feed our magic."

"Then why leave them in the past if they are essential to summoning our magic?" Victor pressed.

"The hurts that haunt you must leave," she said. "But the emotions? No. They must be stored away, available for you to control. They cannot and must not control you."

Victor knew that the gray magic was going to control him if he allowed it to. With gray magic, there was a dark side and a light side. If the gray magic "decided" what it wanted at that moment, everything would be out of balance…

He had to control it. And if he couldn't control the physical magic, at least he could control his mind and the balance of it.

Victor suddenly felt hope for himself. A small shred of hope. He sucked in a deep breath, then managed to turn back to her. "I think I understand what you are saying."

Geeta nodded. "I will show you what I have been struggling with," she whispered. "Perhaps you can learn from it."

Victor watched silently as Geeta closed her eyes and held out her hand. Slowly, in the palm of her hand, it gathered violet magic, growing in size like a balloon swelling. There was another violet light in the corner of his eye; he turned to see a very large boulder nearby, shaking out of place. It was the size of one of their ground terrain vehicles.

The violet magic banded around the boulder as it slid underneath it, shaking it loose until it floated several inches off the ground.

Victor watched the magic flow between Geeta's hand to the boulder, back and forth. Her face was focused…then he saw it.

Bitterness radiated from her face, a few tears gracing her cheeks.

Suddenly, Geeta screamed, startling Victor as she whipped her hand hard from left to right. The boulder flew across the wasteland like a toy ball in a slingshot. It was airborne for several yards, completely enveloped in violet magic. Keeping his eyes glued to the boulder, Victor watched as it crashed against another boulder on the ground, shattering. Many small rocks ricocheted as it crashed, the earth rumbling and making a godawful sound.

Geeta turned to him. Raw emotion stung her teary face. "*That* is what jealousy does to someone. Tears you apart from the inside out."

Victor looked at where the boulder crashed, then back at Geeta. Her eyes were clear of the sadness, and the energy that was there moments ago had fled.

"You must find your emotion and come to terms with yourself. You have to, otherwise we'll all end up like that boulder, for you will be the one to stop Elyathi."

Victor slowly nodded as he eyed the boulder.

It was now nothing more than dust particles flowing in the wasteland winds.

CHAPTER 24

◆

RED

Kyle lifted his shades as he looked at the address again, then looked at the venue building.

Holy hell, this place is huge.

"Is this the right place?" Emerald asked.

"It has to be. It's the address on the paper he gave me," Kyle said, flipping the paper in his hand in wonder. "Plus, this is the only venue in the area." Kyle lowered his shades over his eyes once again. "I guess it's no joke that the band has gotten big."

"Not as big as my tummy," Emerald said as she rubbed her stomach, glancing down. "I think they've gotten bigger."

Kyle put his hands on her tummy, smiling. "That's my boy!"

She smiled shyly, then glanced around. Palace security guards trailed behind them at a distance, keeping a close eye on them.

"Geez. Security guards too?" Kyle said. "Not sure about all this."

"Get used to it. There will be more of this if you continue doing shows."

Kyle snorted. "I guess I'll have to. I just thought it would be more of a slow progression kind of thing, you know? But damn, I come back to Arcadia and get hit over the head."

"Just think, you are also dating a royal," Emerald pointed out. "It's a double whammy."

"Dating? Is that what you call it?" Kyle grabbed her by her waist, tickling her.

Emerald giggled, slapping his ass. "Well, no. You're more of a paramour."

Kyle eyed her through his shades. "Paramour? What in the hell is that?"

"It's a lover."

"Lover?"

Emerald flushed. "Yes. It's a fancy title."

That didn't sit right with him. Did she really just insinuate that he was a lover? Anger flared up inside, causing him to clench his jaw. Was that all that he was to her? They'd made a child for gods' sake.

"Hey, are you okay?" Emerald said as he hugged his side.

Wanting to avoid an argument, Kyle kissed her. "Yeah. Just nervous, that's all." *I'll talk to her about it tomorrow when we are alone.*

At that moment, Kyle saw Remy from across the way, near the venue. He waved them over. "What the hell are you doing? People will see you out here!" Remy called out.

"What the hell does it look like I'm doing? Jacking off?" Kyle said, shrugging. "Or are you mad that I didn't invite your ass to rock my socks off too?"

"Fucking dick, as usual. Get your ass to that back door. Things are different now," Remy said.

"Well, I do have backup." Kyle pointed to the palace guards in disguise.

"Just get inside. You and everyone else, before you make a scene!"

Kyle shook hands with a few bouncers, then they led them inside. As they entered, there was a man in an expensive and stylish suit. His hair was dark, his skin bronzed, and on his wrist was a huge gold watch. The man was on a communicator talking loudly as he leaned back against the wall.

"Yeah, all right, just make sure you have him call me," the man said, then flipped his device shut. He looked up.

"Kyle Trancer?" said the man, straightening his posture, coming up to him.

"Yeah, that's me. Who're you?"

"I'm your manager. Name's Joe." He held out his hand.

Kyle didn't shake his hand, just stared at it. "Manager?"

Remy walked by, nodding. "He's legit our manager, Kyle."

"We were just fine with you as a manager," Kyle said to Remy as he blew smoke in Joe's face. It was only half true. Remy was kind of a pain in the ass.

"The band hired me to take over," Joe said, trying to pretend that the smoke didn't bother him. "It was too big to manage, and Remy needed to focus on the music."

The fuck were they thinking? Kyle sighed. "If the other band members were cool with it, then I guess I am too." Though he was not cool with a corporate dude managing their band.

Joe held out his hand a second time, and this time Kyle accepted it. "Nice to meet you, Joe." Kyle turned to Emerald, gesturing. "This is…well, I guess you know who she is."

Joe looked confused, and Emerald flushed.

Now Kyle *really* didn't like the guy.

Kyle leaned in, saying, "This is Queen Emerald!" with an irritated voice.

Joe's eyes went wide, then bowed. "Your Majesty! I am so very sorry!" He dropped to his feet, which made Kyle feel satisfied, but only because he was corporate. "I had no idea it was you. Please forgive me!"

Emerald smiled, then waved her hand, gesturing for him to rise. "It's quite all right. I am not dressed in formal royal attire, so it's completely understandable for one to not recognize me."

Joe bowed again. "Thank you, My Queen." Kyle grunted as Joe stood up straight again. "It is such a pleasure and honor to meet Her Majesty in person. It is overwhelming, like the sun itself."

Emerald held out her hand, and he kissed it formally. "Thank you, Joe. You are too kind."

Oh God, please. What a fucking kiss-ass.

Joe smiled, then turned to Kyle, waving. "Let me get acquainted with you while we walk to your dressing rooms. There is much to catch up on."

"All right," Kyle said, biting his tongue.

"So where have you been while supposedly dead?" Joe asked as they walked through the stage corridors.

"He's been at the palace," Emerald answered. "There was a bit of confusion regarding a personal dilemma, but all has been sorted out."

"What she means is that I was in jail for shit I didn't do," Kyle said.

Emerald met his eyes secretly, and he gave her a private wink.

"Wow, really? Worked out in your favor in the long run." Joe laughed, ignoring a call on his communication device. He swiped it off. "People thought you were dead. And look at you now. We can't keep up with the demand for merchandise."

"Merchandise?" Kyle repeated, dumbfounded.

"Yeah, merchandise. Everyone wants a T-shirt, poster, or something of yours. Even with the millions of digital downloads of your music, fans still want vinyl, you know? Something to hold in their hands."

"Vinyl?"

"Vinyl, cassette tapes, and other platforms. It's trendy to be retro."

"Ain't that something," Kyle said bitterly.

"It is," Joe said.

Fucking goddamn corporate bullshit. Remy sold out. The band sold out. All for money and fucking fame.

Each step of the way, Kyle was becoming increasingly irritated. Band manager. Corporate… *Dear God, what have they done?* Joe led them outside of the dressing room, then turned to him. "It was nice meeting you, Kyle." He pulled out a digital card, then handed it to him. "You need anything from me, just give me a holler."

"Yeah," Kyle said. *Not on my life, asshole.*

Kyle and Emerald walked into the dressing room, and he closed the door behind them. "He seems nice," Emerald said.

Kyle snorted. "I guess."

Emerald eyed him. "What? You don't like him?"

"No, I don't." Kyle rubbed the back of his neck, shaking his head. "He seems shady as fuck to me."

"What makes you think that?" Her face frowned. "Because he is a businessman?"

Just then, a voice interrupted them. "Hey, man!" Diego said from across the dressing room.

Kyle leaned in, kissing her on the top of her head. "I'll tell you later," he whispered.

"Okay," she breathed.

"So you met Joe, I take it?" Diego asked as he took a drink from his flask.

"Yeah, out in the hall."

Diego laughed as if he could read his mind. "You excited for the show? It's been a while," Diego said, raising his flask.

"That it has," Kyle said, smiling. He plopped down on a chair, then grabbed his case and pulled the guitar out to start tuning it.

"Dude, give that to the stagehand. He will tune it for you," Remy said.

"No thanks."

"The stagehands are legit," Diego continued.

"I'm not trusting some asshole to tune my guitar."

"Stop being a fucking man-baby and give it to him," Diego said, rolling his eyes.

"It's my fucking guitar, and I'll do whatever I the fuck I want with it!" Kyle snapped. "And I don't want anyone to touch it, so fuck you all!"

"I don't understand what the fuck is your problem," Diego said, taking a swig.

The fucking problem is Joe and you assholes are a bunch of sellouts. My woman is referring to me as a fancy fuck-buddy. That's the fucking problem.

"Just leave him be, man," Kamren said.

"Always a dick," Diego muttered.

"I am *not* giving my most precious thing—the guitar Em got for me—to some fucking stagehand!" Kyle snarled.

Emerald shied herself farther away from everyone.

They all looked at her, then to him. "Have it your way," Remy said, shrugging.

"Fuck, man," Kyle huffed as he turned away.

Kyle walked off into the corner of the room to tune his guitar. Emerald sat near him, listening. The guys drank from their flasks, having a good time as he tried to cool down. Hearing them joke before the show made him realize all the more how much he'd missed this life in Arcadia. All throughout his time as Rubius, he'd played the harp and sang for a bunch of wealthy gifted yahoos. Here, he was his real self. He liked being Kyle, whereas Rubius was a shell of himself. Admittedly, Kyle did like playing the harp, but he would never ever say it to his friends. Ever. Diego would never let him live that down, and Kyle could hear all the jokes already.

A stagehand waved to them. "They're ready for you."

"Let's go," Remy said to the group.

Kyle's palms started to sweat. He was nervous as fuck. He cradled his guitar, tapping it slightly while he fidgeted.

Somehow, it was as if Emerald felt his nervous mind because she beamed excitedly and put her hand on his leg. His leg stopped shaking. He hadn't realized that he was shaking like a tweaker. Her touch had an immediate calming effect.

Kyle grabbed her hand, then raised it to his lips, kissing it.

"You shouldn't be nervous," she said. "You are so talented, you have nothing to be worried about."

"Yeah, you're right." Her comment from earlier about him being her paramour was melted away by her soothing words. It was all water under the bridge.

"My Queen, follow us," one of the stagehands said. "We have a spot reserved for you."

Emerald nodded, then looked over at him. "I'll be watching."

"One last good-luck kiss?" Kyle asked.

Emerald ran over to him and planted her lips on his, kissing him deeply. It gave him a slight rise, but then she pulled back suddenly, waving to him. "Good luck!" She smiled, then followed the stagehands out, along with her undercover guards.

"You gonna wear those shades onstage too?" Kamren asked, glancing at him.

"Yeah."

"Why? You too cool for us?" Diego said.

"I like them, okay?"

"Whatever. You look like a fucking douche." Diego shrugged. "If you wanna look like a douche, I'd say it's your prerogative."

"I guess it is, then," Kyle said under his breath.

Kyle and the guys followed a different stagehand to the stage. There were wild rumblings coming from the auditorium.

Fuck... There's a shitload of people! he thought wildly. Kyle yanked on Remy's hand. "Dude, you didn't fucking tell me it was gonna be like this!"

"Like hell I didn't! I warned you." Remy shook his hand off.

"He's right. He told you we were famous," Diego said.

At that moment, the light from the stage lit up like the high heavens, even from where they were standing backstage. Whistles, screams, and cries came from the auditorium, filling the place with noise.

Holy shit.

Kyle didn't even notice that Kamren was already onstage, starting the intro song of their first set as the other guys' silhouettes walked onstage, grabbing their instruments, starting to play. More wild cheers erupted from the audience as the sounds began to play in harmony.

"Ladies and gentlemen. We have a special treat for you tonight!" Kamren said in his personal microphone. "Please welcome the original lead singer of Disorderly Conduct—Kyle Trancer!"

The crowd went fucking ballistic at his name. Screams, shouts, cries of disbelief…they all screamed *his* name. His fucking name. Holy motherfucking shit. Not just some little hole in the wall, but a fucking auditorium. Screaming his fucking name.

Kyle started to sweat and said a few curse words under his breath. He honestly almost shat himself. The crowd chanted his name while the music got louder.

"Ky-le! Ky-le!"

I'm going to fucking hurl.

"Ky-le! Ky-le!"

Oh God.

"Ky-le! Ky-le!"

Taking a deep breath, Kyle walked out with his guitar.

The crowd screamed, jumped, cried, danced, waved their lighters as he walked across the stage, playing with his guitar.

"Hey," Kyle said into his personal audio set.

More wild screams. "Ky-le! Ky-le!" they screamed.

Kyle laughed to himself as he started to play, joining the guys. More screams…all chanting his name. The musical momentum built up, the crowd getting wilder.

Then he started to sing. The crowd went haywire, screaming and crying, having a good-ass time.

Kyle glanced down. There in the first row, front and center, was his goddess of light.

Emerald smiled at him, cheering him on. Her vivid green eyes glowed, even through his lenses.

I guess it's okay to take these off. Not like the crowd can see my eye color anyway.

The band continued their first number. As they finished, Kyle lifted his shades, and the crowd went nuts. He tucked them into the military side pocket of his pants and waved. The guys nodded to him on stage, approving of him removing his glasses. He tried not to make direct eye contact, just in case they got a flash of red.

From the crowd, Emerald gave him one of her signature smiles. This was what he wanted in life. Being with her. Playing for big crowds. Hell, the band got big! And now he could now make a decent fucking income.

He felt so fucking alive.

Number by number, set by set, the band played. Nearly two hours went by, but to him it was like two seconds. The crowd ate up the performance. With each song, they got louder, wilder, giving him and the band pure, raw energy.

As the band finished up their last song, they waved, then walked offstage.

"Encore! Kyle!" the crowd chanted. "Encore! Kyle!"

Shit...they fucking want me, Kyle thought wildly. Him. Fucking him. It was as if he'd walked into a dream. Literally.

Remy laughed as Diego glanced at them. "Let's give 'em what they want," Diego said.

"All right." Kyle slipped his glasses back on.

"One more," they chanted. "One more..."

More and more, they shouted. The band stood backstage, smirking as the crowd got wilder.

"Let's go," Remy said.

Then they all followed him back onstage.

CHAPTER 25

◆

Reila sat in the bed of the ground vehicle, looking back at the landscape. There was nothing but a sea of black, it being late in the night. Though she was happy to go back to the old wasteland camp, she was conflicted. No matter how many times she tried not to, her mind kept wandering back to Scion.

She snorted, thinking that a woman like her ended up being completely enamored with a cyborg. Never in her wildest dreams had she ever thought it would be possible. But yet here she was, pining over him like a little girl and a fairy-tale prince. She smiled to herself that he thought of her—the only one out of whatever random number he'd spouted off. Maybe he liked a woman in charge. Hell, she was the very definition of that.

The ground vehicles veered off onto a small road, making rocks churn hard against the undercarriage. They had reached familiar territory, the rinky-dink road that led to their camp. She and others would have the bare bones of camp set up within the hour. She wished they had left earlier in the day. Then they could have their dinner and a bit of drink after setup. She sighed. It sucked to set up tents in the dark. She was tired. Tomorrow would be more setup too. But hopefully she and the crew could finish getting everyone back in their old dwellings, trailers, or large tents. She was sure there would have to be some extra work scouting too. A group of Olympian cyborgs might have found the old camp. That was what she'd heard anyway.

As they approached the turnoff, Reila looked over the cab roof. Nothing but the usual pitch black, with the vehicle lights illuminating the rocks. She scanned the camp as far as the light reached. Nothing. She didn't see the usual boulders, which was weird, considering that she would typically see them by now. They must be farther back than she thought.

Reila plopped back down in the bed of the vehicle, zipping up her jacket to get ready to unload.

The vehicle suddenly stopped, causing Reila to fly back, nearly hitting her head.

"Hey! What the hell?"

"Reila, I think you'll want to see this," the driver called out.

Reila rose to her feet, looking over the cab again. She paused, then sucked in her breath in disbelief.

The headlights shone onto the camp. Or what was left of the camp. It was… *gone*. No, gone wouldn't be the right word to describe it. There was a *mountain* in its place.

"What in the fuck?" she cursed.

"What…should we do?" asked the driver.

"Are you sure this is our camp?"

"Do you think I'm fucking stupid? I've been driving to and from the camp for five fucking years. Am I sure… Give me a break."

"All right, I got it!" Reila banged the roof. "Just drive closer."

The closer they got to the mountain, it became apparent that the new mountain had indeed covered the entire area of where the camp should have been.

"Stop," she ordered, tapping the roof once more.

The vehicle stopped, along with the others behind them. She jumped out, then marched up to the edge of the mountain, shining her flashlight on it. Some of the other wastelanders joined her, shining their lights and murmuring in shock.

"What in the flying hell?" Reila snapped, as if cussing out the mountain. "How in the fuck did a mountain just appear here?"

The wastelanders all chimed in, getting rowdy, shouting, yelling, cussing with surprise at the mountain. Reila lit up a cigarette, took a giant inhale, then took a long swig from her hip flask. Her eyes didn't leave the mountain; it was hard not to, considering it was lit up like Arcadia with all their headlights on it.

Chris came up to her side. "Now what? There's a fucking mountain where our camp is supposed to be."

"I'm well aware of that," Reila muttered. A fucking mountain. As if the earth had crapped right on their home. *Wild stuff.* She took another giant inhale of her cigarette, then turned to Chris. "Considering we are all tired as hell, let's make camp here and do a full inspection in the morning. We can go from there. If this thing is really on our camp, we'll radio Victor and see what he thinks. We might just have to make do on the outskirts of this thing, but then again, we don't have all the equipment. Some of the group who lived in the dwellings don't have tents, just sleeping bags and some cooking gear."

"If it came down to it, I'm sure others would be willing to double up in tents until we have it sorted out," he said. "It would be unfortunate to split up the camp if some wanted to go back to the refuge."

Reila took another puff. "Agreed. We need to stick together. We're safer in larger numbers." She eyed him. "After all, just because we had our little victory out in the wastelands, doesn't mean Olympia isn't a threat anymore. Being out here gives them another chance to prey on us. And I don't like being prey."

Chris chuckled. "Prey? You? Never. You're every man's predator."

"Don't you forget it," Reila said, flicking her cigarette butt.

"Never have," Chris said. "Let me know what Victor says, then I'll start getting them situated if that's what he wants us to do."

"You bet."

Chris walked off to the wastelanders, telling them to rest while they waited on their next instructions.

Reila grabbed her communicator. She dialed Victor's number, walking away from the crowd. It took a few times to establish a connection, but her call did manage to go through.

"Reila?" Victor asked on the other end.

"Hey, Victor."

"You made it?"

"Yeah, about that," Reila started, glancing at the direction of the mountain. "We seem to have run into a problem."

"Has the Olympian army taken over our camp?" he asked.

"No, nothing to do with Olympia," Reila continued, hearing a sigh of relief from Victor on the other end. "It's just…there's a mountain where our camp used to be."

There was a pause on the other end. "Reila, what's really going on?"

"Am I the type to waste your time, Victor? You know how I feel about that sort of thing."

"No, I know you wouldn't. But a mountain? Are you serious? It seems so…"

"Impossible, I know," Reila finished his statement. "You see my dilemma? I don't know what you want to do. We could set up a temporary camp where we are, though some of the camp won't last. They were counting on their dwellings…I don't know…being here? Also, I worry about us being one big fucking target for Olympia. What if somehow they were behind this?"

"Forming a mountain?"

Reila sighed. "I don't know how else a mountain just suddenly appears. I mean, you think God said one day, 'this place could use a mountain, let me drop one out of the sky' and placed it here?"

There was another pause. "It's late, let the camp sleep and rest up for a few days, maybe a week. They need some sun. They've been cooped up for too long in the refuge, and need the outdoors to refresh themselves. Give them that. Then if they are up to it, some can go and restock supplies and salvage anything in the area. After that, everyone can come back here, and we can decide as a group what we want to do. That'll give me time to decide on the best course of action."

"Sure thing. I'll radio you in a few days to check in."

"Thank you, Reila. Be careful and take care."

"Will do."

Reila turned off the communicator, dropped it into her utility pants pocket, then walked over to the group. "Listen up, I just got word from Victor," she said. "We are going to take it easy for a few days, maybe even a week. Get some sun and fresh air. Roll around in the dirt. Get drunk as hell. I don't care what you do, but have some fun. We need it after being walled up in that refuge. Boss says if anyone is bored, feel free to restock supplies or salvage crap in the nearby area. After that, we'll go back and decide as a whole collective what our next move is. Those of you with tents, you need to share like you are five years old. The night is old, and everyone needs shut-eye as soon as you all get your tents up."

The camp nodded, with a few outbursts of questions.

"Where did the mountain come from?"

"Is Olympia involved?"

"Do you think it's a trap?"

Reila squinted as a light shone in her eyes. "Stop pointing that at me!" The flashlight turned off. "I have no clue why there's a mountain here."

"It has to be magic," said a little girl. "Only magic can make mountains appear."

Magic.

Reila gave her full attention to the little girl. An impossible mountain suddenly on top of their camp. She herself had witnessed some impossible stuff, with Scion, Drew, and Telly having magical abilities. Hell, even the Olympian cyborgs had some magic.

Bet this little girl called it.

Reila lit a cigarette, then puffed, pointing at the girl. "Magic."

The camp shone their flashlights at the little girl, all mumbling.

"There you have it," Reila said. "I think she's onto something."

"You think magic did this?" asked another.

"It seems more of a possibility than the sky just shitting a mountain," Reila said. Suddenly, she turned to the little girl. "Pretend you didn't hear that."

The little girl smirked and nodded.

"Anyway, forget about the mountain, and let's set up a temporary camp," she said. "I'm tired, and I'm willing to bet the rest of you are too. Let's go!"

The others dispersed, grabbing their camping equipment, starting to pitch their tents. The ones who didn't have tents started drifting through the group, asking others to share.

Reila swooped over and picked up her backpack, tent, and bedroll. She walked through the camp, shining her flashlight in every direction, then spotted an area to pitch her tent on the edge of the camp. Just because she was in charge didn't mean she had to be right in the middle of the camp. She needed some breathing space.

While she pitched her tent, she thought more about what the little girl said. If the mountain was truly magical or formed by magic, maybe Geeta or the others might be able to detect something. Or maybe a cyborg could get an actual reading?

She suddenly had an idea.

She needed to find a cyborg.

CHAPTER 26

◆

BLUE

As he released his magic, Derek heard the phones, communicators, and other devices ringing, with the Corporation secretary answering the calls or placing them on hold.

He was back. Back in his own time. How truly wonderful it was—the sounds of the phones, the electronics, the lights powered by electricity... Derek hadn't realized how much he'd missed Arcadia until now. And Emerald. Just stepping foot into his original time made his heart skip a beat, knowing that he was close to her once again.

What was Emerald facing at this point? What of Olympia? Had Councilor Emerys taken care of the kingdom while he was away? Or had Emerald been ruling in his stead and taking care of business?

First things first, he reminded himself. *I must get the cyborgs in working order.*

Turning around the corner, Derek walked up to the front desk. The woman had a sleek bun rolled back and pinned, with a stylish skirt suit and lacquered nails.

Upon noticing him, her expression went from a bored smile to a startled expression.

"Your Majesty," she said, quickly getting to her feet and bowing to Derek. "What a surprise to see you. We weren't expecting a visit from you."

"I hadn't expected it either," Derek stated. "I have come to speak to Head Director Santiago," Derek stated.

"I will get him right away," the secretary said. "Please, make yourself comfortable. Would you like anything to drink?"

"No, thank you," Derek said as he took a seat on the white leather sofa. The secretary bowed, then touched a few buttons on her headset as she typed on her computer. "Just a moment while I fetch the head director now."

"Thank you."

While waiting, Derek listened to the terrible elevator music playing in the lobby. Did people still listen to that nonsense? It definitely was one of the things that he *didn't* miss from his own time. On the lobby's screen, it showed the latest news of Arcadia. Though he was interested in all he had missed while he was gone, it all seemed so insignificant in the grand scheme of things. He was going to change the world, so why did it matter?

Just as he was about to look away, Emerald appeared on the screen. Derek's eyes were suddenly were glued to the screen, tuning in to the news. Lo and behold, there he was, like the dog that he was. Kyle Trancer. Next to *his* wife and queen.

A flood of rage rocked Derek's body. His hands shook, and his throat was tight because he was so damn angry.

"Recent gossip is said that the Queen has taken a paramour in light of the King being away," said a male broadcaster.

Derek choked at the words.

"That's right, Don," the female broadcaster said to the first, flipping to another video clip of Emerald. "With none other than the hottest celebrity in town, Kyle Trancer, lead singer of Disorderly Conduct. It is said that he has been seen by servants in the palace. Our inside connections recently snapped this photo of the couple." Derek's face darkened as the screen showed Emerald and Kyle together, holding hands. "And just recently, there was a sighting of the couple in the mid-levels of Arcadia—and the Queen attending his concert after his reappearance."

Derek fought back bitter jealousy as he stared at the screen.

"Early reports indicated that Kyle Trancer was pronounced dead several months ago after an altercation with the Arcadian authorities. But now, since his sudden reappearance at his last night's concert, fans have been speculating about his disappearance."

Derek used every ounce of his energy not to lose it.

"I wonder: Where this hunk was all this time?" the female broadcaster continued.

HUNK?

"Rumor had it that he was being contained in the palace prisons for several months. If that's true, there could be more history to this relationship…"

"WHAT!" Derek snarled.

There was a clearing of a throat, and Derek whipped his head around. The secretary stood right before him.

"Your Majesty, Santiago is waiting for you. Please follow me," said the secretary, flushing a little. She side-eyed the screen, then glanced back at Derek.

Derek swallowed hard, trying to clear the lump in his throat. He had known *this* was coming—he had foreseen it in the waters of time. But living in the moment was completely different.

Derek glanced at the screen one last time, showing Emerald and Kyle hand in hand. The secretary bit her lip, lowering her gaze.

"It's not every day that a king sees his wife with some other man," Derek commented, narrowing his eyes.

"Yes, Your Majesty," she said in a strange tone, as if she didn't know how to answer her king.

"Where does the King of Arcadia fit in all of this?" the newscaster said as Derek eyed the secretary nervously standing still.

"Yes. I wonder," Derek said passively, swallowing hard. He side-eyed the screen, then turned to the secretary. "Take me to Director Santiago now. I can't stomach any more of this."

"Right away, Your Majesty," she said.

As the secretary led him through the doors and down into the halls, Derek continued to rage. Everything would work out in his favor in the end. He should just speed up time to get to the part where everything was good. Actually, he *could.*

Derek suddenly beamed. It was brilliant. He *could* speed up time, getting to the parts of time that mattered.

Starting with Emerald's pregnancy.

As they walked through the upper levels of the Corporation, they came to a glass sky-bridge. The entire Arcadian skyline was sprawled out before them. In the distance, Derek saw the palace towers.

He paused, staring at the palace.

"Your Majesty?" the secretary asked.

Derek glanced at her, then smiled. "It's not every day that I get to see a view of the palace from this angle."

The secretary smiled back, though she looked nervous.

Glancing back at the palace once more, Derek gathered the time magic within his soul, then released it. Blue washed across the room, freezing the secretary in time, then the city, all paused like a video. Then, glancing at the palace's tallest turret, Derek focused another wave of magic, pouring more energy and power out with each second.

You will be mine once more, he thought of Emerald. *Forever until the end of time!*

Derek funneled his time magic, fueling his anger and rage into it. Then, in a split second, Derek released it directly at the palace. Then time returned to normal, along with the world, in full color.

Derek turned back to the secretary. "It really is a lovely view."

"It is," she said, then bowed.

They continued across the skyway, then entered a small conference room. Inside was all glass with polished chrome beams as support. Beyond the glass were other rooms, and beyond those were glass lifts.

"Your Majesty." Director Santiago bowed deeply. "Please. Have a seat." The director gestured, waving the secretary away. "To what do I owe this pleasure?"

"Director, I came here to discuss old matters."

The two of them watched as the secretary left, closing the conference door behind her.

"What can I help His Majesty with? Are you here about the parts?" Santiago asked.

Derek blinked. "Forgive me, but I am unaware about parts," he said, then added quickly, "There is a lot going on, and I let others handle some of the other matters of state."

"Of course." Santiago leaned back in his chair. "The Queen personally requested that we assemble new parts for Andrew DiNapoli."

"Andrew?" Derek met his gaze steadily. "You mean the cyborg *Drew*?"

"The very same." Santiago leaned in. "If Your Majesty has a problem with the Queen's orders, then we can forego them…"

"No, not at all," Derek said quickly. "By all means, please proceed with her request."

The damned robot needed parts. The very one he needed to bring back to the future.

Derek gave him a concerned glance. "What is wrong with Drew? I know the Queen is very fond of him."

"He is incapacitated. I'm sure you know about the skirmish out in the wastelands. Apparently Drew was damaged pretty bad by the Olympian cyborgs."

Olympian cyborgs? Skirmish? Derek thought for a moment. Had his kingdom fought against Olympia? They must've, or at least had some sort of squabble. If that was the case, that meant more stress for his pregnant wife. Derek's face darkened at the thought. He would pay back King Renard for meddling in his kingdom, that was for sure.

"Where is Drew right now?" Derek asked casually.

"He is in the Western Wastelands with Telly Hearly. She has equipment set up to stabilize him while we work on his replacement parts. Once the parts are complete, Geeta Sharma will pick up the replacement parts and deliver them."

"Geeta Sharma?"

Santiago leaned in. "You know, your Protector of the Realm. The one who supposedly has"—he lowered his voice to a whisper—"violet magic."

Derek nearly fell off his chair. The violet-gifted Geeta.

It couldn't get any more perfect than this. Drew and Geeta, both in the wastelands—both of the gifted that he *needed*. Though it disappointed him that the cyborg was incapacitated, in a way it helped because Drew wouldn't be going anywhere for the time being. The Corporation could make the parts, as well as his gauntlet. The other scientist could fix Drew up while Derek paid Olympia a visit. When it was time, Derek would be there at the very moment Drew was revived in the wastelands. Of course, he would have to take out the violet-gifted. But by drinking the new gifted's blood, mixed with Elyathi's blood he had—Derek had no doubt that he could overpower that violet woman.

Many ideas swam in Derek's mind about how to get the violet woman's blood…

"When will the parts be ready?" Derek asked. "I expect it will be soon?"

"In the next few days," Santiago assured him. "I will contact Ms. Sharma as soon as they are ready."

"Excellent." Derek smiled at the director, then breathed. "I appreciate you aiding the Queen in the matter. Might I ask for you to send word to me as well? I will give you my personal transmission device."

"Of course. Anything His Majesty asks, we will provide."

Excellent. Derek smiled inwardly. "Good. I hate to impose upon you another palace matter, but I came here for a different purpose. I wouldn't ask you unless it was a matter of urgency."

"Of course. What can we do for you, Your Majesty?"

"There is an old project that the Corporation once worked on. A gauntlet." Derek shifted his eyes. "You know what I speak of?"

Santiago's lips parted in surprise. "Why, yes. But that hasn't been active for a few months now. Last I heard, it was destroyed. I haven't heard about it since."

"Theoretically, would you be able to restore it to working order if you did have it?" Derek asked.

Santiago paused, thinking. "Theoretically, yes, I suppose so. But…you see, it was designed for King Damaris. The cell structure and molecular level was activated by the bloodline of the royal family."

"I am well aware of that fact, Director," Derek said. He thought of Ikaria, how she had used the gauntlet with Emerald's blood. He was going to do the same. "I have the gauntlet in my possession, and you are correct, it is not in working order. I need it to be restored. The Queen is in need of it, and it will give her much protection with the cyborgs that chose to stay in Arcadia."

"It will be done," Santiago said. "I can only imagine the stress that the palace is facing after the recent events with Olympia."

"Indeed," Derek huffed. "I have it stored away at the palace. I'll have it brought here immediately. Once it's delivered, you and your teams just worry about getting it activated again. And quickly."

"I will do whatever His Majesty asks," Santiago said.

"It is of the utmost importance that it be restored—in a timely manner. This project takes precedence over everything but the parts for Drew."

"Yes, Your Majesty." Santiago gave a deep nod.

"How long do you think it would take to restore it?"

"I'll have a better idea once my team assesses the circuitry. Maybe a week?

Possibly two."

He didn't like that answer, as the parts would be ready quicker than the gauntlet.

Derek eyed the director. "I will give a rather large bonus if the gauntlet is done quicker than a week. The sooner, the better."

Santiago smiled. "Understood."

"Thank you, Director," Derek said. "Just one more thing."

Santiago bowed deeply. "Yes, Your Majesty?"

Derek shot out his hand, casting all of his violet energy into Santiago.

"Call your secretary in here," he commanded.

Mindlessly, Santiago picked up his communication device, then dialed the secretary. Within seconds, she appeared in the doorway.

Derek shot out his hands with violet magic, taking hold of the secretary's body and mind. With a jerk of his hand, the door shut behind her.

No one screamed, no one spoke. He had their minds fully.

Closing his eyes, Derek cleared out all memories of their conversations with Derek.

"You will construct the gauntlet without knowing who asked you to," Derek ordered. "You never saw me here."

"You were not here…" they both murmured in unison within the violet light.

"Work as fast as you can. I want it done *now*!"

"Now…" they murmured.

"I will have the gauntlet brought here immediately, then you'll get to work. I expect a transmission once it's ready—and the parts for the cyborg," Derek said. "You will contact me about these matters and not remember any of it once you do. You will only remember when it is needed."

With a yank of his hand, the spell was complete, and the violet magic disappeared.

Both of them were knocked out cold.

"Get up and work! I have much to do!" he snapped while they groaned on the floor.

Before they opened their eyes, Derek summoned his blue magic and flashed away.

CHAPTER 27

◆

RED

Kyle had the world's biggest fucking hangover.

The pounding. The noise coming from outside. The damn light that was shining through thick curtains from the patio windows. Even his bird, making scratching noises from where he was perched.

Fuck me.

How much whiskey had he drank last night?

Kyle groaned. A sharp pain in his head came and went. He needed a fucking headache pill and some water. A smoke too. Anything to get rid of the headache.

He reached across the bed to feel for Emerald, but she was gone. There were soft footsteps in the room, but to Kyle each step was like a hammer, loudly interrupted by Zaphod's caw.

"Gah," Kyle cried out, flinching.

"Hangover?" Glacia asked softly.

"Yeah."

"Thought so. I put some water and a couple of pills on your nightstand. I also put a mini communicator there in case you need to call me for anything else."

"Thanks."

The handmaiden left, closing the door gently, leaving him to the silence of the room mixed with the faint noise of the transports outside. He managed to sit up, his head pounding and the room spinning at the same time. Peeking with one eye, he grabbed the two pills and the glass of water on the silver tray.

Quickly, he downed the pills and the entire glass of water, then managed to pour himself another one, gulping it in one go.

"You." Kyle pointed to Zaphod. "I can't handle noise. Keep it down."

The bird whistled softly in reply as Kyle flopped back down in bed, which was a mistake. Instant pain.

Nope. Guess my head don't like that.

He sat up slowly, as his head felt slightly better when he was upright. Kyle tiredly grabbed his pack of smokes off the nightstand, then put his shades on. It was too damn bright.

Kyle trudged across the room, then went outside on Emerald's balcony, settling into his favorite patio chair, lighting his smoke and watching the sights of the city. As much as he viewed the upper levels with spite, Kyle had to admit that the view from Emerald's balcony was awesome. It was like he was God, watching little ants crawl around throughout the city. Perhaps that was the intent of the palace design, to make the royals feel like God. It was pretty fucked up if that was the case.

A quiet knock came from behind him.

Kyle peeked behind his shoulder, seeing Glacia standing behind the glass.

"You can come out here, you know," Kyle said to her, waving.

The handmaiden slid the door aside, then stepped onto the patio. "You had a transmission come through. I said I'd see if you wanted to talk to them, but then they hung up."

"Who was it? Did they say?" Kyle said, taking another puff with his ringed fingers.

"It was Diego."

"Sounds about right. He hates to be put on hold longer than a minute. Doesn't have the patience," Kyle said through the smoke.

Glacia chuckled. "I brought out the transmission device in case you wanted to call him back." She held out the device, with him accepting it.

"Thanks," Kyle said. He turned to her, leaning back against the chair. "Can I ask you something?"

"Sure."

Kyle looked down at the transmitter, then back to her. "Do you think a guy like me could get used to a place like this?"

Glacia blinked for a moment through her heavy white eye makeup, then gave him a slight frown. "Would you like the honest-to-God truth?"

"Yeah."

"No, I don't think so," she admitted, nearing him. "I've been here for many years, and I'm still not used to it. I miss the mid-levels much of the time. Visiting the mid and lower levels isn't the same as living in them. Why do you think I get along with Remy so much?"

Kyle glanced at her curiously. "You aren't from the upper levels?"

"Not at all."

"No shit?"

"I would've thought a guy like you would have noticed." Glacia chuckled. "Perhaps living here for so long, I've melded into this upper-level world. But I can still make my way through the other levels without being singled out as an outsider."

"How did you get to work at the palace, then?"

Glacia leaned against the railing, relaxing slightly. "My parents had a connection here at the palace. Friends of friends of friends, supposedly. When a job opened up for a servant to the princess, they called in many favors just to land me an interview." She breathed. "They interviewed hundreds of girls, but when they met me, the palace staff said they instantly loved my wit and personality. Supposedly all the other girls were boring."

Kyle snorted. "I'm not surprised." He took a drag, then asked, "Why did they interview only girls, and not women?"

Glacia glanced at him. "Because at the time, the advisors thought it would be good for the princess to have girls in the same age range serving her. They said that the princess needed to have some sort of normalcy. Of course, at the time, they had two handmaidens that were older. But over the years, as I neared adulthood, the women retired and were replaced with younger women." Glacia smiled. "That's how I am the Queen's first handmaiden."

"Huh." Kyle puffed his smoke again. A woman trying to get by. He could relate.

Glacia continued. "You just need to find some shred of happiness up here. Hold on to it and focus on that. Can't be hard for you," she said, jabbing him in the shoulder.

"Em's something, that's for sure." He eyed her. "What do you hold on to? Especially since your man Remy is below."

She gave him a serious glance. "I hold on to the fact that I am helping my family. They have a hard time making ends meet, so I send them a chunk of my pay when I can. I thank my lucky stars that the palace hired me to work with the princess at the time, given where I was from."

Kyle remained silent, taking another drag, then exhaling. He was ever so thankful that he was back with Em. That was enough for him. He glanced down at the transmitter, fidgeting with it.

Guess I should call Diego. "Thanks for the chat," he said to Glacia. "Appreciate it."

"No problem. Just be you, and you'll be happy. If you try and fit into their world, you will find that you lose who you truly are. Don't conform to them, but do make peace."

"Thanks for the advice."

Glacia smiled, then bowed to him. "Good day."

Kyle watched as she disappeared back into the room, shutting the patio door behind her, leaving him alone once again.

Just be me, huh? he thought as he finished his smoke. Kyle looked at the transmitter, then dialed Diego's number.

A few rings went by, then he heard, "Hello?"

"You called?" Kyle asked.

"Yeah, but your ass was still in bed. You should come over."

"I dunno, man," Kyle said. "I'm supposed to be with Em."

"To do what? You got plans?"

"Yeah. I was gonna have lunch with her."

"Just bring her with."

"Em's busy. She's at some important meeting. I'm supposed to meet her after that."

"Well, it's still morning, isn't it?"

"Well, yeah…"

"Then what's the hold up? Just get your ass over here," Diego said.

"Dude, I told you, I have plans with Em," Kyle shot back.

"What, is she your ball and chain now? Do you need to ask her permission? She's not even there with you right now."

"Fuck you!"

"Calm the fuck down, man. But seriously, do you really gotta be a man-bitch to go out with your friends? The fuck kind of relationship is that?"

Kyle clenched his jaw. "Our relationship isn't like that."

"Oh yeah? You just told me otherwise. Guess I'll see you at the next show. Tomorrow, asshole."

Click.

Kyle looked down at the transmitter, a deep wave of anger coming over him. He clutched the transmitter hard, then shot a wave of red magic through his body.

The transmitter suddenly caught on fire, and Kyle whipped it off the balcony with all his might.

God, what the fuck? He was no bitch. Em wasn't like that either.

Kyle took one last drag, smashed his cigarette, then grabbed his jacket.

✦ ✦ ✦

The fuck?

Kyle stood outside Diego's apartment door, still in shock. It was no damn apartment. More like a penthouse.

I guess I shouldn't be surprised, considering how damn corporate the band is now.

He gave it a good knock, then waited. His eyes ran up and down the hallway, noticing how expensive everything looked.

The door didn't open, so Kyle rang the doorbell and waited again. There was some muffled noise, then the door clicked open and Diego was standing there with some chick wearing a dress that barely covered her body. She looked like the type of bar floozy looking for free drinks, free drugs, free clothes, and a good fuck.

Diego glanced at him, then smiled. "Well, look who showed his ass up at my doorstep."

"You surprised?" Kyle said casually.

"I thought you weren't coming over."

"You thought wrong."

"What happened to you needing to be with Em?" Diego said with a sheepish grin.

"I'm proving a point, dickwad."

"And what's that?"

"That Em is not my ball and chain, asshole. She doesn't care what I do," Kyle snapped.

"Then why did you say you had to stay in the palace?"

Because I have to protect her from that fucking asshole and that crazy-ass mother of hers. "Just forget about it. I'm here now, aren't I?" Kyle said, crossing his arms.

"I made other plans," Diego said, eyeing the girl latched on to him. Just then, another girl came from behind him, squeezing his butt and putting her arms around him.

"Apparently." Kyle turned around, about to walk away. "I'll see you around."

"Naw, dude, we were just finishing up, bro." Kyle looked back as Diego turned to the chicks. "Party's over."

"Aww," the girls cooed.

"Don't worry. I'll see you two later this week, remember?"

The girls nodded, then gathered their things, finally slipping out of the apartment. Kyle tried not to roll his eyes. Those types were seriously annoying.

"Have a seat, bro," Diego said.

Kyle plopped down on a deluxe black leather sofa. "You didn't have sex on this just now, did you?"

"Sure did."

Kyle hopped up, then looked around for another seat, moving his ass to another matching sofa.

"When did you pick up those chicks?"

"Last night. They offered, and I couldn't refuse."

"Guess not."

"Easy when you're famous and have money, you know?" Diego slapped him on the shoulder. "Shows are paying so much now. Same with record sales."

"Can't believe it," Kyle mumbled. "By the way, when do I get paid like the rest of you assholes?"

"Talk to Joe about it. He does the financials too."

"That asshole?"

"What? You don't like Joe?" Diego started laughing, pouring himself a drink of whiskey.

"What do you think?"

Diego smiled in agreement.

"If you don't like him, then why have his ass run the band?" Kyle said, lighting a smoke.

"Do you really need to ask that?"

Kyle snorted. "Yeah, I do."

"The man is good at what he does."

"At being a fucking douchey-chode?"

Diego snorted with more laughter. "I don't like the asshole either, but he does do a lot for us. He books us shows we never could have landed before with Remy doing all of it. Man's got connections."

Kyle sighed, taking a puff. "I suppose whatever works."

"You gonna fully be in the band again? Or was last night just for old times' sake, now that you're in the palace?"

"Yeah, I'll do shows again. But Joe needs to consider my schedule too when booking shit. I have responsibilities now, so he's gotta align with the shit I gotta do."

Diego smirked. "Like what?"

"Like do palace shit with Em, you know?"

"Who's the high-and-mighty a-hole now?" Diego said.

Kyle slammed his fist on the coffee table. "You *trying* to make me pissed off? Because it's working."

"Ouch. What the fuck? I was just joking," Diego said as he got up and walked over to the bar. He grabbed another bottle of whiskey, pouring some into his glass. He eyed Kyle's shades. "Seriously, why are you wearing those in here?"

"Because my head is pounding," Kyle lied.

Diego eyed him again. "Come to think of it, I haven't seen you without shades since you landed in the slammer."

"Not true. I took them off for the show."

"It's not the same," Diego pointed out. "What are you, too cool for me now?"

"It's not like that," Kyle said.

"Then what *is it* like?"

"It's like I have vision problems, okay? I don't want people to know. Ball-buster."

Diego took a drink, raising his eyebrow. "That's all you had to say."

"It's kinda embarrassing, you know?" Kyle lied again.

"I got you," Diego said. "Wanna do a line? The girls left this here." Diego sat next to him, holding up a little plastic bag with white powder.

"Naw dude. I quit that shit years ago. You did too, *remember*?"

Diego laughed. "That's what they all say until they do it again."

Kyle eyed the coke, recalling what it was like. He fucking loved that shit, but he also didn't like being a fucking junkie either. Hell, he'd battled that for years. But since most anyone he knew couldn't keep their habits under control, nothing about that shit was good.

Diego dumped the powder on the coffee table in front of them, then took his ID card, cutting a line. Kyle watched more than he should as Diego rolled up a piece of paper tightly, creating a tube. He remembered the feeling, the high…

Just then, Diego handed the rolled-up piece of paper to Kyle. He pushed Diego's hand back.

"Chill with me," Diego said, snorting a line, then rubbing his nose.

"I don't want it, bro."

"You need it."

"The hell I do."

"The fuck, man?" Diego said angrily.

"The fuck what?" Kyle stood, feeling a flush of anger.

"The fuck is your problem? You used to be cool," Diego snapped.

"So that's it? I'm not cool anymore because I'm not doing a fucking line? The fuck?"

"Why are you such an asshole?"

"Why are you?"

"Let's recap your assholeness…" Diego started.

"Hell no, let's recap yours," Kyle interrupted. "Last night, you gave me shit about the guitar. Then today on the phone about Em. And now." Kyle marched up to him, leaning in. "You haven't seen me in months, and this is the kind of shit I get?"

"You want me to roll the red carpet for you?" Diego shot back. "You fucking live in the palace, and now you're better than us? Well, fuck you."

"Fuck you, too!"

"Goddamn, Kyle. If you are gonna be like this, just leave," Diego said. He bent down to the coffee table, snorting another line.

"You know what? I think I will," Kyle snapped.

"Don't hit your ass on the way out," Diego called out as he rubbed his nose.

Fucking Diego.

Bitterly, Kyle stormed out, slamming the door behind him. God, what the fuck was his best friend thinking?

He closed his eyes, channeling his orange magic. It shimmered across his body, making him disappear. Right now, he didn't want anyone to see him. He was too angry.

CHAPTER 28

✦

"Do you see anything?" Reila called out.

One of the rehabilitated camp cyborgs, Xeon, stood motionless as he stared at the mountain. "I am getting a reading, but am running a few others to further detail my initial findings."

"Can you tell me what that all means in layman's terms?"

"My initial scan detected that our camp is intact," Xeon said.

Reila turned toward him. "Intact? Like, the mountain didn't mess anything up?"

"Affirmative," Xeon said. "According to my readings, the mountain is made up of rock. I can get you the precise rock type if you—"

"I don't care what kind of rock that the mountain is made up of," Reila interrupted. If she hadn't, the cyborg would just rattle off more useless information. "I don't understand how the mountain didn't mess anything up."

"The entire camp is enclosed by a hollow mountain."

Reila's jaw dropped. "Well, I'll be damned. So you're saying that we could chip away at the rock and find everything inside?"

"It requires much effort to chip away at rock," Xeon stated.

"Okay, let me rephrase that," Reila said, slightly annoyed. "If we somehow manage to blow a hole at the side of the mountain, we would find everything there?"

"Affirmative."

"Well, shoot," Reila muttered. She glanced up at the mountain. It was huge. It had to be, considering it covered their entire camp. She turned Xeon. "Thanks for your help."

"Of course, Miss Reila."

Reila shot him a dirty look, then sighed. That name. "If you happen to be bored, it would be nice if you could come up with ways to, I don't know, maybe remove the mountain? Chip away at it? Blow a hole on the side?"

"Affirmative," Xeon said. "I will do so. Giving me a job is most preferred."

"Thanks."

Reila walked off, heading toward the camp's cooking circles. Her stomach kept making ungodly noises.

As she approached, Ryan waved to her, holding up an extra plate of food.

"Got you your meal," he said, smiling.

"I'm a big girl, you know," Reila said, taking a seat next to him on a stone. She grabbed the plate, then gave him a half smile. "Thanks, though. I needed this."

"Sure thing. I knew you would be hungry, so I figured I'd grab you some before the pickings were slim."

Reila snorted. "I hope you know that this doesn't mean I'm going to sleep with you."

Ryan chuckled. "Never."

"You sure about that?"

"You offering?"

"Hell no," Reila said. Suddenly, she thought of Scion. His sexy, confusing kisses. It was quite the turn-on. Reila looked away. "Besides, I'm not in the mood for anyone."

"Who are you seeing?" Ryan asked, lighthearted with a hint of jealousy.

"No one."

"Really?"

"Really." Reila scarfed down her food, then handed him the empty plate. "Thanks for the grub. I'm tired and going to turn in for the night."

Ryan laughed. "What's got you all changed? Turning away casual sex and a night of drinking?"

"Good night, Ryan," Reila said, ignoring his last question.

She got up, then headed to her tent. Night had fallen on the camp. The moon hadn't made its way into the sky yet, but by the looks of it, another two hours and it'd be out.

Reila got into her tent, foregoing getting into clean sleeping clothes. She was too tired. She crawled into her sleeping bag, then fluffed her small pillow.

She lay in the darkness, thinking about Scion. Secretly, she missed him. What was that old calculator up to? Probably sitting next to Drew, working his robot butt off to get Drew back into working order. She felt bad for the city scientist. Telly had lost her man and her daughter, all in the same day.

Her thoughts shifted to the mountain and what Xeon said. Maybe Scion had answers. After all, he was magical to an extent. And if he didn't, maybe that city scientist would have answers.

She reached for her communicator, then paused. Would it be weird for her to directly call Scion instead of Victor? As if she were going around the man in charge?

Nah, Victor won't mind. I'm just getting answers. It's not like I'd keep it from him. I'll just tell him what I find out tomorrow.

Reila pressed the button to dial Scion, then lay back down in her sleeping bad. As the communicator's connection tone buzzed in her ear, she stared at the ceiling of her tent.

There was an audio shift in the connection.

"Hello, this is Scion speaking. How may I assist you?"

"Enough of the receptionist talk, Scion. It's me, Reila."

"Miss Reila? What are you doing calling me?" Scion asked. "It is nighttime."

"Really? You can't understand why I'm calling you?" Reila sighed. Why was it these robots could make complex calculations yet couldn't figure out the simplicity of a situation?

"I would assume by my deductions that you need assistance," Scion stated.

Reila sighed loudly. "Assistance? Is that what you think?"

"Am I incorrect, Miss Reila?"

"Reila."

"Yes, Reila."

"To answer your question," Reila said, "I suppose I called you to ask for your advice. But I'll admit there's another motive behind wanting to call you."

There was silence.

"Scion? You there?" Reila asked.

"Affirmative. I was processing your motive."

"And?"

"I was running the scenario of your motive behind your intent to talk to me on an intimate level."

"Scion!" Reila chuckled. "You naughty cyborg!"

"I am naughty?"

Reila laughed so hard, she swore that others outside heard her. "It's just an expression. Yes, I'll admit I wanted to hear your voice again." Reila paused, glancing up at the tent's ceiling. "I miss you already. Dunno why, it hasn't been that long…but you know, I kinda like you."

"Miss Reila…"

"Reila."

"Yes, Reila. I must confess that I had been thinking of you too. However, I knew that the probability of you communicating with me via transmitter was one in one thousand eight hundred and eighty-seven. You have beaten my odds."

"That's my style." Reila chuckled, then cleared her throat. "As much as I want to keep talking, I have to save this battery. There is something I want to ask your advice on."

"I do wish we could interact on a more personal level longer," Scion said. "Are you needing input about the mountain?"

"Victor told you about it?"

"Negative. Xeon sent the records to the other camp cyborgs via our private intranet."

Reila shifted in her sleeping bag. "And? What do you think about the readings? Do you think it's possible that this mountain could have been shaped…er…formed by magic?"

"I do think that it is possible with the energy in six hundred nanometers."

"Six hundred nanometers? What does that mean?"

"It is the technical term for orange in the visual spectrum. It is the wavelength of light that is split into color," Scion offered.

Drew. He had orange magic. And Telly did too, or at least some.

"Is Telly with you?" Reila said.

"She is standing beside me listening. Would you like to speak to her?"

Great. She probably heard every damn word when she was flirting with him.

"Yes, I want to talk to her," Reila said.

There was a muffle, then Telly's voice rang out. "I didn't mean to overhear your conversation. I happened to be next to him when he answered."

Fucking great.

"I'm glad we established that," Reila said.

"I won't…say anything," Telly said. "I heard you asking about orange magic and the mountain. It is possible with orange magic to transmute elements, including objects. Drew did so himself back…" Her voice trailed off.

Reila shook the communicator, wondering if she lost a connection. "You there?"

"Yes, I am still here. I just finally understand everything."

"What?"

"Drew made that mountain. He had to have. Back when we were all vacating the camp before the Olympian invasion, Drew stayed behind. He wouldn't tell me why. He was very secretive about it."

Reila bit her lip. "You really think he *made* this mountain?" The whole statement was weird coming out of her mouth.

"I do, and I sort of understand why," Telly said. "He…he was protecting what he cared about. The camp. It always meant so much to him. He had told me a few times while living in the camp that it felt like home. It was the first time that he got to live his life with me and Gwen… With his transmutation power, it makes sense."

Reila sucked in her breath. There was a long pause between them.

"Do you think…you think you can transmute it…er…away?" She had no clue how to even ask, *Telly, can you get rid of the mountain?*

"I am limited on my powers, Reila. That would be something Drew would have to do."

And Drew was nearly dead.

"You don't suppose you could try?"

"I mean…" Another long pause. "I *could* try. But that would mean I have to leave Drew." There were a few soft sobs on the other line.

"I…I'm sorry to have even asked. I know it's not good for you to leave him. Hell, I would do the same," Reila said.

"Thank you for understanding," she said. "But I will tell you this: I will try once Drew is more stable and I feel comfortable leaving him. And if I cannot do it, then he will be able to once he's back to normal."

"That's a good compromise," Reila said. "Thank you."

There were more sobs.

"Can…I speak to Scion again?"

"Sure."

Another muffle, then Scion said, "What is it, Reila?"

"I wanted to say goodnight to you, that's all."

"Good night, Reila," Scion said in a soothing tone.

"Goodnight, you big lug-nut hunk of a robot," Reila said.

She paused, wanting to say more, but then clicked the button to end the transmission.

Reila got comfortable in her sleeping bag once again, thinking over everything. It would be such a waste to go back to the refuge after they had just arrived. No, they should stay put and wait. They would have to get more supplies, but that was manageable. Everyone seemed happier out in the sun, despite the mountain. After all, the wastelanders were meant to dwell in the desert, not hide in an underground cave.

She'd give Victor a call tomorrow and convince him.

I'm sure he'd agree. Hard not to when my plan makes sense.

Her eyes got heavy, and she dozed off, listening to the camp's wild night party in the background.

CHAPTER 29

✦

Ayera glanced toward the iron bars that separated her cell from the next. She had never realized darkness came in many shades, from the faintest hint of smoky gray to the deepest black reserved for the Lord of Darkness and his minions—it was its own arrangement of colors. Sometimes she would see a flicker of firelight from a torch, or a flash of magic if she was fortunate enough. Other times, she was met with a strong whiff of putrid musk and body stench suddenly, causing her to gag.

She desperately wanted to speak to another person. But if it meant speaking to that letch of a captain, then she would rather live a hundred lives in this darkness. If that commander hadn't shown up, Ayera could only imagine the worst of it.

Choking back tears, Ayera shifted her thoughts to other things. In her time spent here, she had reflected on many things. Her life growing up. Her parents. Her sister. Being empress. Even Lord Kohren, whom she had admired. And the one thing that tore the world apart: magic.

Why was it that the colors of magic that the God of Light granted to the people could rip the entire world apart? It was a heavenly gift from above, yet it could ultimately destroy them all. The irony. The Dark Lord was most likely laughing at the destruction of mankind, reveling in each downfall.

In the corner of her eye, a distinct shadow swept across the other side of the iron bars. Cautiously, she inched her way over, then leaned her head in between two of them. Her cheeks were met with the icy resistance of the bars pressed into her cheeks, causing her to shiver.

She sat silently, staring at the section of darkness where she swore she'd seen the shadow. Nothing. Her mind was playing tricks on her once again.

Crawling back toward the section of prison wall that she felt was most comfortable, she lay against the stone wall, listening to the endless whispers of madness. Sometimes those whispers entered her dreams, forming them into nightmares. Time had no meaning in this place, and her dreams became reality, and reality became her dreams. The variety of voices that echoed throughout the dungeons were almost musical, like an aria of sadness, their notes carrying madness, insanity, pleading, and anguish. Instead of shutting them out, she listened to each of them and felt the emotions behind their cries. Strangely, she heard their thoughts as well.

Each voice broke her heart. The insane, they talked to themselves because they were lonely. Missed their loved ones. The cries calling out the unjustness of their imprisonment. In their thoughts, she felt their rage, their anger, their despair. Voices were in her mind—*their* voices.

I must be losing my wits, teetering on the verge of insanity, she thought.

You are not as you think you are.

That voice. It kept talking to her. It was a man's voice, she knew—or so she had dreamt. Never had she answered him, because if she did, she would be giving in to her insanity. She couldn't let the High Court win.

I have been listening to you, Empress. It is the only thing that gives me hope.

He was so convincing.

I know you think I am a figment of your imagination. At times, I wonder if I am dreaming you, too. The prison that surrounds me distorts time; maybe you are of the past. Maybe you are of the future. Or perhaps you are from my time. I do not know.

His argument was quite compelling. Almost as compelling as her sister's.

Crawling back to the iron bars that separated her cell from the next, Ayera gazed into the darkness. "Is anyone in there?" Ayera called out softly.

I am not in your prison, he stated.

Ayera sat up straight with surprise. This person knew her actions, heard her words. Perhaps I should answer. Dare she speak to her imagination?

Against her better judgment, Ayera answered the voice. "If you are not in my prison, then where are you, sir?" she called out.

I am in the High Court Citadel, same as you, but yet, in a very different location. Please, speak through your mind. You don't want to cause alarm.

Ayera paused as her heart raced. He was in the High Court Citadel, too?

Speak in my mind, she thought. It was lunacy. Perhaps she was making up this man's voice in her mind, and she was talking to herself. But then again, something in this man's voice told her it was real.

What is your name? Ayera asked within her mind.

Suresh Acheya. And you are Ayera, Empress of World Sector Six.

Ayera paused, contemplating. Forgive me, sir, for not properly speaking to you. I am still yet discerning if you are a figment of my imagination.

I can understand, as I have felt the same as you. I have been listening to you within my own prison walls, and have been wondering if I, too, dreamed you up. But I have come to realize that you are real, as I can feel your power.

Power?

Our minds have established a connection. That is how I know who you are and sense what is happening to you.

Established a connection. Ayera suddenly thought of her sister and the power of the violet gift. That magic had the power to reach into the mind.

Are you gifted? Ayera asked quickly, taking fast breaths.

I am, though I do not possess the power of the mind as you think me to. I believe it must be your gift.

Ayera almost laughed. Almost. *Gifted? No, I am not. You are mistaken. I have no gift. I am merely an ordinary human, albeit ruler of my sector.*

There was a long silence between them, then he continued. *Strange that a connection was established, with you not being gifted and me not possessing this kind of magic. Something brought us together. Who or what...I do not know.*

It is strange indeed. Perhaps a higher power has brought us together to speak... Ayera thought. It had to be. It was the very answer to her pleads with the God of Light. *Why are you imprisoned, Suresh?*

There was a long pause. *Because I am green-gifted.*

Ayera felt a surge of excitement that there was a green-gifted, but also a sickening in her gut. A green-gifted, here in her time. No one had encountered a green-gifted in many millennia, with the exception of her people traveling back to the past. A living green-gifted man... Ayera sighed heavily. He was imprisoned in this very citadel.

I am held prisoner under the white-gifted known as Elyathi, he continued.

Her and a blue-gifted man. They have me in some sort of time-dimensional prison, cast in his blue magic.

Ayera's heart beat fiercely at the mention of the white-gifted. *I know this Elyathi that you speak of. She is an abomination. She stole the life forces of my gifted peoples,* Ayera thought.

A heaviness seemed to descend on Suresh's spirit. *I have seen the stolen life forces; she keeps them contained here within the citadel. Thousands of vials, transmuted gems...all gifted life forces. She will not stop until she has accomplished what she has set out to do. To meld the world into one timeline, creating a new earth. She wants to change time—compress all timelines and reshape the world as we know it. Erase memories, pasts, everything that she deems unworthy to enter the new world. And now, she needs only one color.*

If Suresh was a green-gifted, then that could only mean one thing...

Ikaria! Ayera exclaimed.

Ayera felt his spirit stir in agreement. *Yes, your sister is in grave danger.*

Her sister. Knowing Ikaria, she would storm the High Court Citadel in retaliation for what Elyathi had done to World Sector Six, and to rescue her. She was surprised that her sister hadn't already. At least not that she knew of...

Ikaria would fall right into their trap.

Ayera wished with all her heart and mind that her sister would stay back in their sector. Ayera was willing to die in this cell if it meant that the High Court wouldn't be able to steal her sister's magic away, knowing the fate of their existence with Elyathi's vile plan.

Ayera paused, then realized what Suresh had said. *Suresh, I never said anything about my sister having violet magic. How do you know about her and her gift?*

I was there in Arcadia to stop your sister when she possessed the gift of the black. When I arrived, the princess of Arcadia had already defeated her. Everything that I have done has paved the road to decimation. I am the cause of the world about to collapse into oblivion, into Elyathi's fate.

That's not possible. Just because you were captured and she stole your gift—you cannot blame yourself!

Your words are sweet, Empress, but it is the truth. Many years ago, I was searching throughout time in an attempt to find Geeta, my violet-gifted friend. During my time travels, I came across Elyathi many years ago, pregnant and on the verge of death. I took pity on her and healed her with my green magic. I felt compelled by her spirit—so pure and beautiful, one of the most beautiful souls that I have ever come across. I knew at the time, I would be possibly taking a risk by interfering with her life, but I never thought that doing the right thing could lead down this road…to where we are now.

But how did your saving her change time? Just by extending her life?

When I healed her, she absorbed my magic, sending it into her baby, thus turning the child into a green-gifted. Since this child grew up as a gifted— something she was not meant to be—the High Court went searching for her. The sorceress—your sister—also went searching for her. Now, with King Derek of Arcadia leading us down the road of destruction all because of the chain of events, the sorceress would never have interfered with their relationship, and he wouldn't have turned to the darkness with a dark heart… There was a pause. Empress, I am never one to admit defeat or lose hope. But as of now, there is no hope for me. I cannot fight this battle. Elyathi has stolen most of my life force, and I hang on a mere thread. It is almost as if I am non-gifted. What hope is there? I have no power.

We must do something! Ayera clenched her fist.

I am ashamed and dishonored by my gods. I violated the laws of the gods, and this is my punishment.

No! You thought you did what was right.

There was a scoff. *I said the same thing to another a time ago. This man, King Derek of Arcadia, he was ashamed for what he had done through the mind of your sister. He was about to throw himself off a high place, to be no more. I interfered. Again. Now this man lives and is aiding Elyathi! Don't you see? My interference for what I thought was "right" led to this, for both Elyathi and the King of Arcadia! I should die in this prison, my soul disintegrated into the air, resolved as no more. Even if I were to help fix the mess I created, I cannot! This is my doom. I don't have much of my magic left…I am sorry, Empress Ayera, but my hopes are gone, and my spirit is crushed. The only comfort I have now is your spirit to lead my mind into the next life. That is, if the gods allow it so.*

Hearing him say those words frightened her. But also, they made her angry.

You can't give up! We can't give up! There must be a way!

I can't do anything without my gift being on the brink of summoning. I feel that I am merely a normal being with most of my life force drained. Nothing extraordinary.

The words struck her hard. She had felt like that many times, having no gift. But hearing a once-gifted say this…it made her rethink her own ideals. An angry flare struck her body. *That's not true. I have no gift, nor have I ever. I have been able to accomplish many things in my life with no gift. In some ways, it makes me a stronger person because I do not rely on power! Make no mistake, Sir Suresh, I won't go down without trying everything I possibly can to stop that woman from destroying what we know of our dear world! Even if it is at my trial—or execution—so be it. I will do what I can. What say you? You, who blame yourself…make things right if you truly believe you helped cause these events! Why don't you redeem your actions?*

There is comfort in your words. It almost makes me want to believe.

Ayera couldn't understand why this gifted man had lost all hope. It was as if he had already given in.

If you truly believe you cannot do a thing, then why fight it? Why not just give Elyathi what she wants? It seems you've made up your mind.

There was a long silence. *I cannot say why I haven't given up. Maybe I do have hope but do not see it in my eyes or heart. I have fought endlessly, and I am tired. I have fought months, or has it been years? I don't know because I am in a strange dimensional prison. I cannot understand the concept of time or space. My body hasn't been the same since I lost most of my life force. Forgive me, Empress, if I sound as if I have given up all hope. I have struggled with this. But my resolve is still within, somewhere. Hearing your words has somehow strengthened me; my mind has become more sharp just by our exchange of words.*

Ayera peered out into the darkness, thinking on his words. *Let us continue to speak so your strength returns, or more of your magic to summon. If it as you say it is, and Elyathi intends to change all of earth and time, then it is imperative we not fail.*

You are a unique soul, Empress Ayera. You have the strength of a gifted. There is much power in you. More than you know. You remind me of one of my great gods—she is a goddess, the most powerful in my religion. Even without ever using her gift of power, she had the strength of the mind to take on the other gods. It's what one refers to as willpower in this age.

Ayera took a deep breath. *Your words give me strength. I will take them with me when I face the High Court.*

Ayera felt Suresh's spirit approve—there was a tinge of lightness in their connection. *I must go now. Elyathi is coming, and I cannot let her find out about you...*

Surely she already knows that I am in prison?

There was no answer. The connection was lost.

It was strange, as if suddenly Ayera was alone in her cell for the first time. Though she had been alone before, Suresh's mind had made her feel like he had truly been right there in her cell, sitting next to her. The warmth of his soul was gone, leaving her chilly.

Ayera resumed listening to the echoes in the dungeons. But those echoes didn't register.

The only echoes were Suresh's words.

Elyathi had to be stopped.

And Ikaria would fall right into her trap.

Sister...don't rescue me! Whatever you might think is right, don't step foot in the citadel.

All Ayera could do was plead within her mind. Maybe if she spoke the words over and over again, it would somehow reach her sister. It was wishful thinking, but at the same time, it gave her hope.

Please, sister...

CHAPTER 30

✦

VIOLET

It was that time again. Her favorite time of day.

Ikaria laughed as she sat in her favorite chair in her quarters—the very one that Cyrus gave her. It was also the very same one that she had strapped him to with her violet magic. The fool.

Gifted. Oh, gifted...which one shall I select for today's sacrifice? Which one will affect Belinda or that white-gifted hypocrite the most? Ikaria closed her eyes, scanning the minds within the High Court Citadel. She swept through many of the minds, ensuring that she was careful that those gifted weren't aware of her presence. Prior to her finding her color complement in the priest, breaking the mind of a gifted was difficult. But now, having a true complement and using the power of the Spectrum of Magic, it was second nature to meddle her way in.

There were many emotions Ikaria encountered, ones that she preferred not to be in contact with. Despair, pity, love. All things that made one weak. But the anger she felt from some of the minds she came across, it made Ikaria burn with delight, like devouring a delicacy. How she loved to dine on hatred.

Ikaria noted something of interest with these minds that harbored hatred. Some of these souls were in anguish over the High Court's actions. She even detected some outrage at her sister's imprisonment. As much as Ikaria wanted to glean more information from these life forces, she couldn't exert all of her energy. There was much to do, and chasing every little thought wasn't worth it.

Ikaria suddenly burst out laughing as she brushed against a certain mind.

This is too good.

This mind...it recently had encountered Derek and Elyathi. The further that

Ikaria delved into this mind, the more it piqued her interest. It was a woman, one extremely attracted to Derek. But she was terrified of Elyathi.

What did you do, you white-gifted hag?

Ikaria dug deeper and read in between the lines. This woman had come to the conclusion that Elyathi abducted her for her blood—in retaliation for her finding Derek attractive. Elyathi had tied this woman up to offer her blood to Derek to make him grow stronger.

If it weren't so amusing, Ikaria would've made this red-gifted woman today's sacrifice.

I will allow you to live, you little High Court trollop, only because you vex Elyathi like no other, Ikaria thought as she smirked.

Ikaria scanned more of the minds inside the citadel, coming across another red-gifted. This time, it was a close court servant to Belinda. A handsome, strapping young man. *Too bad he has red hair. Such a charmer, that one.*

With a surge of violet magic, Ikaria felt a sudden severed connection. She opened her eyes.

She had killed her daily gifted for the day.

Satisfied, Ikaria waved her fingertip, sending out another surge of violet magic. It glowed around a goblet of wine, filling it up, then floated it over to her. She clutched the cup, taking a deep drink.

As she sat, Ikaria glanced at the goblet, reflecting on Suri. She missed her servant. It was such an annoyance to serve herself. Lord Jiao was a decent man, but he wasn't servant material. He was a court lord. But Suri, she went above and beyond what one would do for Ikaria. That kind of loyalty and dedication was hard to find in anyone.

Suri, be safe, Ikaria thought. *You'd best come back to me.*

Ikaria sighed, pushing her own fears aside. She rarely had fears. That was her old self before Cyrus broke her. Now, she had little fear of anything. And the only fears she had were of people in jeopardy.

Her sister and Suri must remain alive and well.

In the past, all she wanted was the throne. Now, her ambitions had changed. As long as the High Court and Elyathi were wiped off the face of the earth, Ikaria didn't care who ruled World Sector Six. Her revenge would be complete, and she could live satisfied knowing that Elyathi and the lot of them were no more.

But then, Ikaria had another personal vendetta…

Where are you, you fool?

Ikaria set down her goblet, refocusing her magic.

She continued to seep out her energy, pouring into the unknown. She felt more thoughts and emotions. That was when she found him.

I see you, Cyrus. Try as you might, you cannot hide from me, you little arrogant pink-haired fool, Ikaria fumed.

Ikaria felt his thoughts, his comings and goings. His trysts. His desire to become greater. What a waste of a life force. Didn't he know that he could never become great like her? Cyrus was a mere speck of dust compared to her power. Dare she enter his mind completely and be done with him? No, it wouldn't give her satisfaction. It wouldn't even be one-tenth of the payback he deserved for what he'd done to her. No, she had to make him suffer as she did. She would make good on her promise, but she needed to have a detailed plan.

Suddenly, a familiar soul's words rang loud and clear in her head.

Sister…

Ikaria paused. That inner voice was her sister's.

Sister…don't rescue me!

Ikaria paused. How had she heard her words? Her energy had been focused on *Cyrus*, not Ayera.

She flowed more energy into the area where Cyrus was, hoping somehow she heard her sister's mind again. Was her sister with Cyrus?

He better not touch her if he knows what's good for him, Ikaria snarled, thinking back to what Cyrus did to her during her own imprisonment. She would be his living nightmare, sending him to hell and back every day and every night. That, she would make good on.

Ikaria waited.

Nothing.

Ikaria sat in the quiet, waiting for any sort of calling from her sister once more. How had Ikaria heard her? Without any other sense from her sister's life force, Ikaria summoned all the violet magic from her core, filling her mind with her power, then shot it across the dimension to where she had sensed Ayera.

Her violet magic streamed into the unknown, unable to determine where her sister's life force was.

"You wanted to see me?" Auron's voice rang out.

Ikaria opened her eyes, disconnecting her power from the minds she'd brushed against, then drew her power back into her core, focusing on her whereabouts. In the doorway, she saw the priest standing at attention, waiting.

"You have quite a knack for interrupting someone at the height of important matters," Ikaria stated smoothly. "Really, priest, did you not see me in the midst of using my ever-so-desired magic?"

Auron smirked. "I might have been standing in this doorway all day if I hadn't interrupted."

"I don't see the harm in that. Perhaps it would teach you a lesson in patience," Ikaria retorted.

"I have received many lessons in that area. As you recall, I read *The Spectrum*," Auron pointed out. "Perhaps you should give it a read."

"Sarcasm at its finest," Ikaria muttered. She elegantly took a long drink from her goblet. "Mmm, nothing like a sweet drink after an afternoon of planning someone's demise." Ikaria smiled to herself, then waved the priest in casually. "Would you care to drink with me?"

"If it's to someone's demise, then no," Auron said.

"You are missing out," Ikaria said as she shrugged, taking another drink. "It's probably because this individual truly deserves their downfall. It really gives the wine a strong taste of fulfillment." She waved her fingertip with a jolt. A bench across the room was seized by her violet magic, then scooted toward her left side. "Have a seat, priest."

Auron raised an eyebrow, then sat on the bench. "I was told you wanted to see me. Did you find out more about your sister?"

Ikaria furrowed her brow. "I can sense her life force, but past than that, I cannot tell."

Sister...don't rescue me! Ikaria blinked at the memory of Ayera's words.

Auron breathed a small sigh of relief. "Praise the God of Light that she is still alive." He paused. "I worry that time is short."

"I am concerned as well, but I don't think that the High Court will do anything to her yet. She can take care of herself for the time being," Ikaria stated, gulping down the rest of her wine.

"Ikaria." Auron clicked his tongue, his face flickering with anger. "Have you no *heart*?"

Ikaria whipped around to face him directly. "Of course I do. It is right here." She pointed at her chest mockingly.

Auron gritted his teeth. "So you think that she can take care of herself? What if they are torturing her?"

Ikaria leaned into his face, wrath burning in her eyes. "Do you think that I will allow the High Court to get satisfaction from my sister? Tell me, *priest,* is that what you think?" Ikaria spat.

The two stared at each other for a time, then Auron relented. "Not one bit, Ikaria. But I had hoped that you would have some sort of master scheme to get your sister back by now and not be so focused on *war.*"

Never, in all of her years of knowing the *pious priest* had Ikaria seen him so full of anger.

Ikaria's face relaxed, then she gave him a glimmer of a smile. "I like that look on you. You should wear it more often."

Auron's face looked sternly at her, unchanged.

"And as for my sister, she doesn't want to be rescued," Ikaria stated, staring directly into his golden eyes as she took another drink. "She told me herself."

"What?" Auron's mouth dropped open. "You…*spoke* with her? With your magic?"

"Well, I fibbed." Ikaria smacked her lips. "I didn't speak to her directly." She leaned into him, this time giving a serious look. "I heard her through my mind. Her thoughts, her prayers, whatever they were, reached me. For whatever reason, she doesn't want to be rescued. I don't know any more than that." Ikaria leaned away, back into the folds of her throne. "I would venture to say that Elyathi is making moves, as well as the High Court, to get my magic—as usual. I'm sure Ayera knows that it is a trap for me to just show up at her trial. This is nothing new, priest. They will be expecting me one way or another. I am quite sure it's the reason my sister doesn't want me to rescue her."

Auron leaned in, softening his face. "Is this why you have been focused on the war? Because of this?"

"Not at all," Ikaria said. "I only heard her words moments ago. But I know how the High Court does things. As I said, they will carry out a public trial for a grand spectacle for all to witness." She paused. "That being said, my sister's words solidify some of my plans."

"And those are?"

Ikaria smiled with smugness. "You'll soon find out." She got up, then gestured to him. "Walk with me."

Auron gave her a hesitant look, then rose. They walked out of her chambers and into one of the main halls. Lord Jiao bowed to her.

"You have any errands for me, Enchantress?" he asked.

"Nothing as of yet, Lord Jiao. You may go and make yourself useful by checking in on the artifacts that have been coming in from the other sectors. I will meet with you after dinner."

"Yes, Enchantress." He bowed and walked the other way down the hall, disappearing.

Auron eyed her but didn't say anything. Ikaria knew what he was thinking. That "meeting" after dinner meant a wild night in bed. He wasn't wrong. There were no blond lords available lately, so she had to make do with other handsome men, even though they didn't fit her qualifications.

As Ikaria and Auron walked down the halls, they passed by several new artifacts lined on pillars, ones that she needed to activate. "Do you see what we have gathered already? So many gadgets our own court had in hiding." Her violet eyes darted to his, almost in a smile. "One would think this sector is full of sinners."

"Perhaps at one time I would have agreed with that," Auron said.

"Why, Auron, I'm shocked." Ikaria's mouth parted in a surprise. "Something has changed your mind?"

"I suppose you can say that," he answered. They exchanged glances, but he said nothing more as they walked to each display.

Auron eyed the technology lining the halls as Ikaria picked one up. Curiously, she eyed the machine, then twisted a few metal pieces, picking up another, assembling it. The machine suddenly activated. Ikaria smiled, then handed the machine to Auron. "What do you think?"

"It's...incredible."

Ikaria scoffed. "Incredible? Come now, Auron, there are far better words to describe this machine than 'incredible.'"

"I'm just...worried about Vala. She's been on my mind lately." He stared at the activated machine, then said, "Have you heard from her?"

Ikaria shrugged. "Nothing."

Auron paused, then turned to her. "Do you suppose she's in danger?"

"I'm almost sure of it," Ikaria said. "Somewhere down the line, the High Court has caught on to her scent, being the dogs they are." His face dropped. "Lady Vala can handle her own. She's done so for many years now, evading them at every turn. After all, she has a mind like no other."

"I am at a loss as to what you called me here for," Auron stated.

Ikaria ran her hands over one of the ancient technology parts, then placed it back on a marbled ledge. "Your life force. It feels complete now, does it not?"

Auron's face took on an unusual look, then he nodded. "It does."

"And why is that? Is it because you finally found your complement?" Ikaria leaned toward him, hearing his life force ripple with strength. "Or did it perhaps start when the green-gifted princess healed you back in Arcadia?"

He paused, then gave her a knowing nod. "At first, I would have said it was my complement. But when you state it that way, it makes me second-guess. In a way, perhaps it is both. If the princess hadn't healed our life forces back in Arcadia, we would have been 'one' color—without our adjacent colors. But since we have these adjacent colors, our souls have been restored to the way a true gifted's life force should be. To further our life force's desires, my life force has its own soul."

Ikaria nodded with approval. "You are turning out to be quite a pleasant surprise, but don't think your flowery words will convert me."

"I never said—"

"But you're right," Ikaria interrupted. "I have often thought about this. I think it is what you said. You and I—we are the only ones that have been rightfully restored to how true gifted should be: a true life force with its true complement. That is, in our time, at least. We have the power to access the true Spectrum of Magic."

"Sorceress...er... I mean Enchantress," he started, "have you ever wondered how the gifted got to this point?"

"Are you referring to our gift being altered as one color?"

"Yes." He looked deep in thought. "How is it that magic wasn't in existence in the era Princess Emerald resided, but the birth of magic happened with her own birth? And added to that, she had the full potential of her magic. Geeta had it too, but she was at the beginning of time. But us?" He glanced at her. "When was the source of the gift altered? There is nothing referencing the adjacent colors of magic besides in the tome discovered months ago."

"That, my dear High Priest, is the ultimate question," Ikaria stated. "One that I have been trying to answer for many years. I have my theories, but nothing fits." She neared him, feeling her power intermingle with his, their powers like yin and yang, flowing in a circular motion.

His face searched hers. It was as if he was seeing her for the first time, her true self underneath her hatred, jealousy, and past history. All of it was stripped away; no longer was he High Priest Auron and no longer was she Enchantress Ikaria. They were searching each other's life forces, two bare souls underneath the surface, yellow and violet flowing as oil and water, spinning endlessly.

Ikaria knew then that Auron understood her. Her thoughts. Deep down, she knew he wanted what she had wanted all these years.

"You want to heal earth's surface," Auron whispered.

His words broke their concentration, and suddenly, they weren't souls; they were mere people once again.

Ikaria studied him. "Why, Auron, you surprise me. You took the very words out of my mouth…"

"It is why you brought up the healing with the green-gifted princess," Auron stated. "Her life force hadn't been altered…" He paused. "You keep bringing up the old argument that was held at court."

"Because I know it to be true," Ikaria pointed out. "If all of our gifted were healed, perhaps there is a way to heal the planet. And if not us, maybe, just maybe, through an ancient spell. I suspect that it is possible, given that there were ancient prophecies about that white-gifted whore, and we just never heard of it before."

"Mind your tongue," he scolded.

"I do not care to hold back my propriety when it comes to Elyathi. After all, she is the face of that no-good, twisted High Court. So full of herself. So proud," Ikaria said. "Wait until I see her once again. She'll weep like she has never before."

Auron paused, then sighed. "It's just that…isn't that the point of the white-gifted? She is supposed to restore the earth and its magic to the God of Light's true intentions?"

Ikaria snorted. "Well, I don't know any of the prophecies that the hypocrite professes. Through scanning the whispering thoughts of the highest-ranking gifted at the High Court, it is said that she is. Supposedly. Others say that she is to birth a new world. But who knows if there is a prophecy? I, for one, don't believe a word of it." Ikaria glanced at Auron, noticing he was visibly disturbed.

"What is it, priest?"

"It just…feels wrong for me to spend time finding ways to heal our lands and not finding ways to help the Empress instead."

"I know that you are concerned, but do you know who you are speaking with?" Ikaria said. "It's my sister, priest. I am spinning my web as we speak. We will get her back sooner than you think, and then what? Have my sister continue to rule the skies? As you are well aware, I'm getting along in age and would like to see the green earth while I'm living, not be buried in it."

Auron didn't look satisfied, but underneath his exterior, Ikaria could feel his trust in her. "I have dreamed of seeing the earth restored as well. Though I don't understand why, at this moment, you want me to do this. It doesn't make sense."

Ikaria held her head high, giving him a half smile. "I cannot explain why the moon shines at night, nor why the air exists, my dear priest. But consider what you said earlier, about how the gifted have changed over the years. How did they change?"

He raised his eyebrow.

"Does the moonlight change over time? Does air become something else over the centuries?" Ikaria posed the question. "Why is it then the gifted have changed?"

Auron slowly met her eyes. "I see what you are getting at, but how does this affect the here and now? The importance of it?"

Ikaria met his eyes. "Because what if the shift of the gifted's abilities were changed, just like this earth? What if Elyathi is to bring forth a new world?" Ikaria eyed him. "If there is a shift in the earth, perhaps it would ricochet throughout time, and through that ripple…"

"It could affect Elyathi's world?" Auron finished.

"*Perhaps,*" Ikaria emphasized. She held a machine up, showing him. "There is data stored in these machines. Endless amounts of data. What if the people stored endless memories of the past?"

The priest went silent, thinking upon it. "It is quite the far-fetched theory."

Ikaria snorted. "Indeed it is. But we need to safeguard our existence, whether or not the bitch changes this world or brings forth a new one. That, my dear priest, is why you need to find answers now. Take several gifted that are well versed in the ancient texts to the libraries, even some of the ancient temple's vaults. There must be something."

They both paused, then Ikaria turned to one of the broken machines. She could rescue her sister, no doubt. She even felt confident that she could evade that white bitch's power. But Elyathi *had* been growing more troublesome. There had to be a way that led to her undoing. A power that contradicted hers. In case all the prophecy nonsense was true, Ikaria had to be extra cautious. Safeguard whatever the outcome. Especially if Elyathi was in cahoots with Derek, with the power of time. That in itself was problematic.

Auron broke the silence. "I will head to the libraries."

"Take Lord Jiao. He is quite versed in the art of ancient technology."

"Technology? We are looking for answers to heal our earth."

"Do not discount technology, priest," Ikaria said. "It might not only be the key to winning this war but to restoring our lands."

"Yes, Enchantress." Auron bowed.

"Very well," Ikaria got up, smoothing her skirts.

"What will you be doing in the meantime? More battle plans?" Auron asked. "I do hope it involves getting the Empress back somehow. It would certainly put my mind at ease."

Ikaria smiled darkly. "Something like that."

He bowed, then left the room.

She glanced around at the ancient technology, then selected a few of them.

"You and I are going to be best friends," she told the objects, then eyed them darkly. "Do I have plans for you all..."

There was a sudden brush within her mind.

Ikaria paused, then closed her eyes, sending a surge of magic across the skies once more. She searched, trying to find that connection...

Then she shot open her eyes, realizing who she'd come across.

It was the green-gifted. The one Oriel warned about. The very same one that Vala was assured went into the portal to escape this time...

He was there. At the *High Court* Citadel.

Ikaria set the ancient technology back in its place, then sneered. *I'm getting too sloppy!* That gifted man was inside a time prison. She was furious that she had been so lackadaisical with her magic.

So, you think you can have it all, do you? Ikaria thought of Elyathi. *Just you wait. I'll interfere with your plans so hard you won't know what hit you, then destroy you from the inside out.*

That green-gifted needed to be rescued now. Before it was too late.

✦ ✦ ✦

"Get to work, you little good-for-nothing slug scum!"

The masked overseer kicked Suri hard as he walked by. Suri stumbled against the wall of the mine shaft, nearly dropping her pickaxe. She side-eyed the masked overseer, noticing that his weapon was readied to fire at will.

Suri began chipping away at the end of the shaft with a few other prisoners, loading the mine cart behind them. Jude was with her, working diligently. On her ankles and wrists, her enchanted shackles burned. Whenever she tried to summon any magic, the shackles sent a deep wave of pain into her life force. The greater the magic she tried to use, the greater the pain. Jude had experienced the same.

She had been shackled to Jude and a few other sky-dwellers. She never asked the prisoners why they were there, nor did she care. Jude tried a few times to ask the first nights when the prisoners were given the chance to sleep, but it was no use. The overlords didn't let anyone speak a word. The young priest found out the hard way, getting a blunt hit to his back from the overlord's mechanical weapon. Besides, with everyone masked, it was hard to make out what one said through the equipment.

The masks were fascinating in and of themselves. The enchantress would be most pleased to know about the contraptions. Perhaps she did already. It was a relief when she and the other imprisoned got to remove their masks prior to bed. The downside was that it left an impression on one's skin where the mask had been. There was a small metal compound large enough to house the prisoners during sleep, which was a slight improvement. Suri wasn't sure what was worse—wearing the mask or smelling the bad scents of the prisoners who hadn't washed in months…even years. Everyone was given a worn-out plain tunic, bottoms, boots, and gloves. The clothes didn't help the smell in the slightest, given that the prisoner clothes were washed very infrequently.

In the many days they had been captured and taken, Suri thought about every possible way to escape. Without her magic, it was a challenge to come up with a decent plan. And the overseers' weapons made it nearly impossible. The more prominent the overseer, the better the weapon. And the overlords, those in charge of the overseers, they had the biggest weapons. One of her ideas was to locate the shaft that led to the ancient city, thus losing the overlords and finding a way out. It was said that several of the prisoners were working in that chamber. It was also where they had discovered the most ancient technological artifacts. With her skilled movement in the ancient arts, she could easily go undetected without her magic. Her plan seemed weak, though, as she didn't know where the shaft was. And even if there was another way out, losing the overseers was merely a distant dream with her being locked in imbued chains.

"Mistress Suri," Jude said as quietly as he could through his mask as he cleared away more dirt. "When I was using the latrine this morning, I heard an overlord talking to another…"

Suri noticed that an overseer was making his rounds, coming near them.

"Quiet," she scolded him.

They both remained silent as the overseer walked by, his mechanical weapon readied.

When the overseer was out of sight, Jude leaned in again, still cleaning away rock and debris. "The overlord said that there was an attack outside the mines yesterday."

Suri stopped, then eyed him through her mask.

"There must be earth dwellers," he continued.

"Quiet! Before you get us all punished," hissed one of the workers. "I want my dinner!"

Suri nodded at Jude, agreeing that he should remain silent. The young man turned back to his section, clearing away more dirt and emptying it into the cart.

One of the workers that were unshackled started pushing a lever, enabling the cart to wheel away on the tracks.

"Water break!" yelled an overseer. The overseer began to hand out waterskins to each worker. "You get fifteen seconds this time!"

Everyone demasked, then guzzled down their water, some coughing afterward from the toxic air. One had to be quick in the mines; the air seemed far worse than the surface. There was no cleaning the air without their magic, and without the masks, they wouldn't survive.

"Time's up! Get to work!" the overseer called out with his distorted voice.

The prisoners masked up again. Suri noticed that the overseer was staring in the direction of one particular prisoner. Another overseer joined the first, both nodding at the certain prisoner.

The prisoner was putting his mask back on but was interrupted by a huge whack to his back. He cried out in pain, his real voice escaping the mask. The prisoner began to cough as the overseer kicked the prisoner's mask off further, revealing a handsome young man. His features were like hers—dark eyes framed by monolids, smooth skin, and long midnight hair as smooth as silk.

"Haven't you had enough?" the young man said, hacking and gasping for breath.

"This is payback from last night," snarled the overseer, hitting him hard once more with his weapon. Blood splattered across the cavern wall. "Your cousin is a nuisance."

Suri felt Jude's hand grab her arm, as if urging her to do something. There was nothing that they could do.

The man continued to wheeze. "They will come for you. It's only a matter of time."

"No one's coming for no one," the overseer said. Then he blasted his weapon.

Suri jumped back, startled by its power. An intense beam of red light shot right to the man's chest, then through it, melting his body like wax.

The prisoner screamed, then flopped to the stone floor, lying in his own melted flesh and blood. Even with her mask, Suri could detect a hint of the putrid smell of burnt flesh. Jude shifted her way but made no remark or motion.

The overseer glanced around sharply through his mask; though no one could see his expression since everything was covered, Suri knew he was furious.

"That will be you next if any one of you tries to defy us. That goes for anyone outside this mine as well. Let me make myself clear: *No one* will be saving you. Not one soul. Now work!"

Every prisoner scampered back to their positions, clacking away at the stone wall, sifting dirt, sorting debris. The overseer stood for a while with the other one, both laughing maniacally.

✦ ✦ ✦

That night, Suri remained awake in her dirty cot. She couldn't help but wonder what the prisoner had meant. *They will come for you. It's only a matter of time…*

Who were these people this man spoke of?

In the darkness, Suri absently reached for the enchantress's vial around her neck. It was still safe. It was short of a miracle that the overlords didn't see the vial. One would call it luck. Knowing Jude, he would say that the God of Light intervened. Whatever fate had in store for them, it didn't include her losing the enchantress's vial of blood. It did, however, include the overlord taking her enchanted dagger. Every now and then, Suri noticed that same overlord using her blade.

A shadow of one of the overseers could be seen doing their nightly routine of guarding the prisoners. They passed by her cot, strolling through the walkway with their weapon in hand. Always ready at a moment's notice.

I'm sorry, Enchantress, that my task hasn't been fulfilled yet. I promise I will rescue the Empress when I get out of here.

Suri heard Jude shift in his cot, making no more noise than one would when they slept. But Suri knew how Jude slept, and these weren't his normal movements.

After a few moments went by, Jude made another movement. "Mistress Suri," he whispered in the lowest voice. "Are you awake?"

Suri darted her eyes toward the overseer; he was nowhere that she could detect.

"Yes, Master Jude," she whispered faintly.

"Do you think we will be here for a long while?"

"It is hard to say."

Jude shifted in the dark. "I hope not. I've been praying for a way out of here."

"Keep praying, Master Jude, for I have no reliable plans as of yet."

"I will." He paused. "Do you suppose that man's people were the ones attacking the mines earlier?"

"Yes, I do."

Jude sighed in the dark. "Goodnight, Mistress Suri." Jude shifted again without another word. It was good timing too, as the overseer was making his rounds once again.

Suri nodded off into a dreamless sleep.

CHAPTER 31

✦

BLUE

The main palace halls were empty when Vala arrived at World Sector Five's royal citadel. The guards had informed her that there was a royal feast tonight, filled with dancing, drinking, and other sorts of entertainment. Entertainment. Vala knew what *that* meant. World Sector Five was known for its looseness when it came to morality, though they did maintain they followed the High Court and the teachings of *The Spectrum*. It was a fine line they treaded when it came to holy discipline, as Vala had overheard countless times in her homeland's court.

The guards led her to the main dining hall. Upon opening the doors, Vala was met with a picture of a drunken court falling on its face. Lords, ladies, unknowns of lower court positions, all having a great time filled with drink and laughter. Jovial music was playing, and the Emperor and Empress of World Sector Five were together, laughing hysterically. The Emperor looked as though he would bust his gut with laughter. The man was happy enough, though it wasn't the time for laughter. Hadn't they heard of what had happened to World Sector Six?

I guess I'll find out soon enough.

Vala walked through the crowds of World Sector Five's drunken courtiers, weaving her way to the Emperor. A few glanced at her, realizing that she was not one of their citizens by her style of dress. Even more so, she was a blue-gifted, a color that was seemingly rarer these days. As Vala had recently discovered firsthand, it was not because of the rareness of being born with the blue gift, but because of the High Court's order to toss every blue-gifted back in time in a desperate attempt to capture Queen Emerald and bring her back to this era. Vala seemed to be the sole survivor of this, nearly escaping death.

Just as Vala was nearing the Emperor, she noticed an attractive orange-gifted man edging his way near her. He bowed, and she gave a nod in return. It seemed that he wanted to talk to her but shied away as Vala approached the Emperor.

"Emperor Zaro," Vala said informally.

The Emperor whipped around, immediately noticing Vala. His cheeks were flush from drink and his eyes glassy with intoxication. She suspected it but was disappointed that she was right.

"My lady," the Emperor said, lifting his glass in merriment. "Do I know you?"

Vala bowed deeply. "I am sorry we haven't had the pleasure to meet. I am Lady Vala from World Sector Four. I have come on behalf of the Khari Rhamla, and that of the—" She'd been about to say Sorceress Ikaria but decided to switch up her words. "—the temporary ward of World Sector Six."

The Emperor's eyes went wide with surprise, then beckoned her closer. "What a pleasure to meet you, Lady Bala."

"Vala."

"Lady Vala," the Emperor corrected himself. The people around him grinned and smiled at her, and she eyed up the group.

"I have pressing news—news and matters that must be discussed," Vala continued.

The Emperor waved for her to follow him, and she did so obediently. "As you can see, I am not in the most fitting state to hear news, but nonetheless, I will listen. Though I will warn you, I cannot make any decision under the influence of my drink. I will hear it, then any decisions that must be made will have to wait until tomorrow's light."

"Fair enough, as my visit is most unexpected," Vala said. They both walked toward the doors, the guards opening them. They ended up in a small adjacent room down the hall. Vala and the Emperor sat, and guards surrounded the room.

"What is this news you bring?" the drunken Emperor began.

Vala eyed the guards. "I am not sure if you are aware of the recent events surrounding Empress Ayera."

The Emperor frowned. "I am. Word came to me about her imprisonment.

The High Court means to execute her."

Vala nodded. "Her sister has assumed the throne as temporary ward—that is, until she can rescue her sister."

The Emperor almost burst out laughing. "Ikaria? On the throne?" The guards laughed with him.

This is going nowhere.

"Yes, but that is not the point. High Priest Auron, my uncle, has aligned himself with her as well. They have a plan to get the Empress back to safety. However, that is not why I am here. I have come to ask for an alliance between the two sectors, and persuasion of the other world sectors to aid us."

The Emperor's face shifted to merriment to a furrowed brow. "Aid you? With armies? Our gifted?"

"Your ancient artifacts," Vala stated.

The Emperor's eyes nearly popped out of his sockets, leaning forward. "Ancient artifacts?"

"We have a way to activate them, and with your aid, it will be used to help us get the Empress Ayera back." Vala didn't want to say how, especially given the Emperor was drunk and she didn't know his true intentions or alliances. All she knew was his sector was the most hedonistic of the sectors. Perhaps that was what he was truly aligned to.

"Now that is news and certainly unexpected," the Emperor said, taking a drink from his chalice. "And I suppose if I were to give you these artifacts, you would be wanting an oath of some kind?"

"Loyalty is hard to come by these days," Vala pointed out. "I hate to say it, but either you are *all in* as they say, or all out. The High Court has overstepped their reach many times." Vala was going to continue, but there was no point to explain to a drunken Emperor. "There is much more to say in regard to this, but I will spare you the details."

The Emperor gave her a solid look of understanding, as if the drunkenness had cleared from his eyes. "I know all about the High Court," he breathed. There was some silence, then the Emperor said, "Let me finish up my merriment for the night, Lady Vala, for I fear that this will be one of the last nights that I will have the luxury to do so. Tomorrow, you will come before my court, and my advisors and I will hear a full account."

"Yes, Your Majesty." Vala nodded. "I will be awaiting your summons."

"Give Lady Vala the best rooms of our citadel. She is to be our guest for tonight," the Emperor told the guards.

"Yes, Your Majesty," they said, saluting him.

"See you tomorrow at high noon, Lady Vala," the Emperor said. "Feel free to enjoy the remainder of the night's party. It doesn't end until sunup, so there is still much left in the night."

"Thank you, Your Majesty," Vala said.

The Emperor left the room, and Vala followed the guards to her chambers for the evening. Vala decided to get cleaned up, as she did feel a bit sweaty from the day's events. After washing her face and blotting her underarms with a towel, she found a bottle of sweet fragrant oil, dabbing her skin with it.

Vala headed back down to the party. If she could manage to speak to several people within the court just to get a feel of their thoughts on current events, then it would help her when she stood before their court system for tomorrow's meeting.

She turned a corner, noticing an orange-gifted man standing in the middle of the hall. It was the same one from earlier.

"Excuse me, my lady," the orange-gifted man said with a handsome grin. "I couldn't help but notice the obvious. You are blue-gifted."

"How astute you are, sir." Vala raised an eyebrow, then gave him a bright smile. "Do you have the habit of standing in one's way?"

"Only if it's a beautiful woman," he replied.

Vala raised her eyebrow. "A flirt, I see." She liked this one. He had a sense of humor.

"You could say that." The man chuckled, then bowed formally. "My name is Pierre. No formal titles, no pleasantries. Just Pierre."

"Well, Just Pierre, my name is Lady Vala. I am from World Sector Four's court," Vala said. "Though I have been traveling to the other sectors as of late."

The man was rather handsome, though he wasn't her usual type. A mop of soft orange curls, piercing orange eyes. A bit on the scrawny side, but he was tall, which balanced him out. His eyes were round with big lids and soft lips, which gave him a pleasant appearance.

"My lady, nice to meet you," Pierre said. "I won't keep you from your duties for too long. The reason I came to you was that I hoping that I could ask you something, with you being blue-gifted."

"So it is not because of my beauty, then?"

Pierre chuckled. "Well, there is that as well. But I must admit, my ulterior motive is more than that."

Vala eyed him curiously, then nodded. "Sure. I am going to the main hall, so I could use the company while we walk."

"My pleasure." They started walking down the hall as Pierre spoke. "I have a friend that is blue-gifted. Dydrone is his name. He was summoned to the High Court a few months ago. Since then, I haven't seen or heard from him." Pierre shifted his gaze to Vala as they walked. "Do you know of Dydrone? Or have you seen him at World Sector Three? I have heard that all blue-gifted were summoned to the High Court Citadel…"

"I see why you sought me out," Vala said with care. "I am sorry, Pierre, I have not ever had the pleasure of making your friend's acquaintance. I do not know of any Dydrone, nor have I heard his name until this moment."

Pierre frowned. "I see," he said, sighing. "I'm worried about him."

Vala turned to him, stopping in her tracks. "I do know what is happening at the High Court with the blue-gifted. It's not good news, I'm afraid. It's one of the reasons why I came, though I cannot disclose everything to you. What I can tell you is this: All the blue-gifted were forced by the High Court to travel back in time to capture a Queen. All those prior to me that traveled had perished."

Pierre's face morphed with vast array of emotions—confusion to wonder to shock to anger, and back to confusion. Vala suddenly wasn't sure if she should comfort Pierre or excuse herself to give the man some privacy.

"I…I am sorry to be the bearer of bad news," Vala said.

There was a thick silence between them, until finally Pierre said, "And what of you? How did you escape this?"

Vala's voice went cold. "I was threatened, poisoned, and thrown into the flow of time. I nearly lost my life. I was saved by some people back in time." Vala stopped, as she didn't want to say anything more about Geeta, who had healed her—especially that she was violet-gifted. Vala put a hand on Pierre's shoulder. "I am sorry," she whispered. "I do hope your friend managed to escape as I did."

"Thank you," Pierre said, and they continued to walk once again. "One more thing."

"Yes?"

"You mentioned you have been to the other sectors recently. Have you seen High Inquisitor Rubius?"

Vala swung around at full attention. "How do you know *him*?"

Pierre's face shifted, piquing curiosity. "He's a good friend of mine. He also left around the same time Dydrone left. I had heard a rumor that he was in World Sector Six, but after that, nothing."

"Rubius…is your friend?"

"Yes, why?" Pierre looked anxious.

Should she tell him? Everything that she knew of Rubius—or his past self as Kyle—would be hard for anyone to swallow. But these were strange times, and Vala was curious to know more about this man who had befriended an extraordinary gifted like Rubius.

"I have come across your friend," Vala hesitated.

Pierre's eyes widened. "Something has happened. I know it. Ever since my two friends left, nothing has been…right."

There was more silence, and Pierre leaned closer. "Please, Lady Vala. I have been good friends with Rubius since we were teens. I must know what has happened to him. Between Dydrone and Rubius…I have lost much."

Vala met his orange eyes, pleading with her. "Well, I do tell people information in the right circumstances. In fact, I am known to be silver-tongued. I feel compelled to tell you, but I'm also reluctant because I'm sure you will have a hard time believing me, so hear my words and do with them as you please."

Pierre nodded. "I need to know," he whispered.

"Very well," Vala said, gesturing for him to follow her to a bench. Several couples happened to be leaving the main hall, walking past them, Vala and Pierre doing their best to be discreet.

When the hall was clear, Vala leaned in. "Your friend Rubius, he's a different person. I mean, he's not a fraud by any accounts. It's merely that he was reborn as a new person in this time."

Pierre gave her an utterly confused look. The whole thing did sound like lunacy.

"Rubius is and was Rubius—in this time," Vala continued to explain rather quickly. "However, his soul was that of a man named Kyle from thousands of years ago, back in World Sector One. Before he died in the past, a green-gifted queen put a life spell on him. This life spell allowed him to be reborn in this time, though she had originally intended for him to not die in his original time. The queen went into a magical trance after he died and was on the verge of death herself due to her grief for him. When I was thrown back in time to kidnap this queen by order of the High Court, all the pieces fell into place. I was essentially rescued by the gifted back in time, then made a plan to find your friend Rubius to bring him back to the dying queen." Vala sighed, meeting Pierre's eyes. "From my perspective in the flow of time, as a gifted of time magic, this was necessary for the world to not fall apart." Vala sighed. "The last I saw of your friend was when he entered a time portal in World Sector Six. I haven't seen him since."

Pierre leaned back against the wall, a deep frown on his face. It didn't sit right, Vala decided, for such a beautiful and handsome man to harbor such a sad expression. But who could blame him? He was missing two of his friends. Most likely the man Dydrone was dead in the flow of time, and Rubius was never coming back.

"Your words are quite outlandish, and to anyone else it would be hard to believe," Pierre said. "But even so, I believe you. It actually makes a lot of sense and fills in a lot of answers to questions that I have asked myself over the years."

"How so?"

Pierre glanced at her. "Rubius never came out and said it, but I knew he had secrets. A few times, I noticed him bartering with dealers. Tome and book dealers, ones that the High Court would jail if they knew what they peddled. I had overheard him several times, inquiring about ancient texts dealing with World Sector One." Pierre gave a sad smile, then chuckled. "I also do know of his, shall we say…kinks when it came to sexual encounters."

"I don't know how that would tie in to your believing me," Vala said, frowning.

"Let's just say Rubius had a type. Always talked about a green-gifted woman. Since he couldn't have her, he sought out his urges with…erm, let's just say, orange-gifted who…"

"…could illusion themselves," Vala finished, snorting with a private smile.

Pierre nodded, smiling back. "Yes, exactly." He paused in thought, shifting on the bench. "Rubius never said that he was another person, and maybe he didn't know it either until as of late. I do hope he found his love. No woman ever seemed to make him happy."

"I am sure that he found his queen."

"What makes you so sure?"

"Because the world is continuing its flow of time," Vala stated. "If it hadn't, the High Court wouldn't be—" Vala stopped herself. "Sorry, I can't say more."

Pierre nodded. "I understand, say no more. Too many words get one into trouble these days."

"Indeed." Vala gave him a sad but hopeful glance. "I meant what I said, that I am sorry for all terrible news that I have delivered. If I happen to find out more about your friend Dydrone, I will send word."

Pierre smiled sadly. "Thank you, Lady Vala. Though your news is not the most pleasant, it has brought me closure."

Vala bowed to him. "Would you like to join me in the hall for an hour or two? His Majesty has invited me to enjoy the festivities."

Pierre shook his head. "I think I will spend tonight alone."

"I understand," Vala said. Their eyes met, then they nodded. "If our paths do not cross again, then godspeed to you, Pierre."

"You too, my lady."

As Vala left Pierre and walked away, she heard his footsteps trailing in the opposite direction. She sighed, knowing what was to come tomorrow. Lord and ladies with major hangovers. Everyone would be in a sour mood. She sighed. Nothing seemed to be going right for her.

✦ ✦ ✦

The summons came exactly at the time the Emperor had said. At high noon, Vala received a knock on her guest chamber door. Upon opening it, she discovered guards awaiting her.

"Lady Vala," the guards said, bowing. "The Emperor and his council have summoned you."

"Thank you."

The guards led her to the council chambers, near the room where Vala had spoken to the Emperor the night before. It was a decently sized room with a round table to seat the council members, plus a few empty chairs for summoned people to speak. The room was quite plain compared to most of the royal citadel, and it made Vala wonder why they'd chosen to have such a boring chamber. Perhaps so that they wouldn't be distracted during long meetings and could focus on the current task at hand.

"Lady Vala," the Emperor said. "Thank you for joining us."

"Thank you for receiving me, Your Majesty."

The Emperor smiled. Vala was surprised that there was no trace of the night's prior revelry, nor any hint of his drunkenness. It was if he got a full night's sleep with no alcohol.

"This is my council. I have informed them of everything you told me last night," he continued.

Vala bowed, and the Emperor raised his hand for her to be seated. "If Your Majesty needs me to go over any other details from last night's conversation, I'd be willing to do so." *In case you were too drunk to remember,* she thought.

"I am perfectly clear on the situation, Lady Vala, though I am sure the council has questions," he said. "We need all the details cleared up in order to make a formal decision."

Vala glanced around at the council, which consisted of an equal number of lords and ladies. At least it was balanced, compared to her home sector.

"Lady Vala," called out one lord. "His Majesty tells me that you are asking for any ancient artifacts to aid World Sector Six in their confrontation with the High Court. Is this correct?"

"Yes, it is," Vala said with confidence. "World Sector Six has a way to activate these artifacts and plans to put them to use in order to return the Empress to safety."

Many glances were exchanged around the table.

"And how is World Sector Six able to activate these artifacts, precisely?" asked the same lord.

Vala breathed. She couldn't very well lie to them. "The temporary ward of World Sector Six, the enchantress Ikaria, has a way to activate them."

The council members shifted in their seats. "Does she have a certain unique power to do so?"

"At one time, she had gained a magic unknown to us. This magic gave her the understanding of the construction of these artifacts—anything that had to do with technology and machines. Though the power was stripped away from her months ago, her understanding of it remains."

This time, the Emperor sucked in his breath, amazed. "Sorceress Ikaria is quite the woman, isn't she?" He eyed the table, and several of the men chuckled.

"The enchantress is not a mere joke, good lords and ladies of the court," Vala said. "She is of the highest intellect, one of the most brilliant minds that I have ever encountered."

The Emperor smiled. "I fully agree with you, Lady Vala. It was not meant as a joke."

Vala's mouth dropped open. "What?"

The councilors glanced at each other, nodding, with the Emperor continuing. "We have always admired the sorceress Ikaria here in this sector, though none would know it. Never in the open, obviously. You see, Lady Vala, we don't care for the High Court and its laws, and think that the world is not all black and white."

"I don't understand."

The Emperor leaned in. "There is a gray area, Lady Vala. Sometimes, one must follow that gray area to live their life. And currently, life with the High Court confines us in a way that we don't care for."

The council members nodded, and Vala risked a hopeful smile. "Are you saying that you will aid us?" Vala asked.

"Only if Ikaria is truly leading your sector," the Emperor stated. "I was ecstatic to hear of the damage she had inflicted on the High Court Citadel. I only wish she had been able to do more."

This is certainly unexpected.

He leaned forward. "I have heard of the High Court murders." The Emperor then smiled. "It seems that Ikaria is quite the leader, wouldn't you say?"

Vala nodded. "She is undoubtedly in charge. I can say this for certain."

"Then you have our aid," the Emperor said. "We will send World Sector Six our artifacts. In exchange, we would like some of them returned to us in working order."

"You want to infuse technology into your sector?"

"That is our ultimate goal," the Emperor said. "Considering they are our artifacts."

"I think Enchantress Ikaria will abide by this."

"Tell me, does the sorceress plan to attack the High Court once more?" the Emperor asked.

Vala gave a cool, knowing smile. "She does, though I must admit that even I do not know the full details of her plan. I know that she is heavily leaning on implementing these ancient artifacts."

One of the ladies gave a pointed look to the Emperor.

"Tell Ikaria that if she leads an attack, we want to be there," the Emperor said.

"You are serious?" Vala asked, darting her eyes around the table.

"Lady Vala," said the woman, "as the Emperor stated, we are done with the High Court and would like to govern our sector how we see fit. We know of Ikaria's court arguments about technology, and admire her greatly. And as you witnessed from last night's state of affairs, our sector enjoys the fruits of our labor, while the High Court condemns it as indulgence. They have meddled in our sector for too long. Many of our blue-gifted have been torn from us; other gifted have left to serve the High Court in fear of losing their families." The woman stood up from the table, leaning in. "We no longer want to be their subjects."

The council clapped, with the Emperor nodding in agreement. "Tell the sorceress my terms, and see if she agrees. We want the ability to fight the High Court, given we have lost many of our gifted."

Vala smiled. "These sound like favorable terms for both parties. If I might suggest: send a blue-gifted as an ambassador to Ikaria. That would be most helpful. I have other sectors to plead our case with, and time is of the essence. If she and your ambassador agree to terms, you then have the means to send artifacts back and forth immediately."

"We don't have many blue-gifted left, as the High Court claimed most," said the woman, "but we will find one within a few hours and get you both on your way."

Vala nodded. "Thank you."

"One more thing before we disperse, Lady Vala," asked another lord.

"Yes?"

"Why is it that your home sector chose not to take part in this fight?"

Vala gritted her teeth, while the room waited. Finally, she glanced at those in attendance. "I must admit, I am thoroughly disappointed that they have not come to a decision yet. My sector feels quite the opposite as you do when it comes to Ikaria, though I do believe that the Khari wants to join us. He is hearing arguments from all sides of the court."

The Emperor let out a laugh. "If it is controversial, then all the more we will join. I do not like meddling in affairs and getting our hands dirty, but there is only so much our sector can take until we say enough is enough." He looked Vala straight in the eye. "You can count on us, Lady Vala. Hopefully with us joining, it will sway your people as well. I will fetch the blue-gifted I have in mind and send them on their way to World Sector Six."

"Thank you, Your Majesty. If you do not mind, I will refresh myself with food before I depart for the next sector," Vala said.

"You are welcome to anything in our court," the Emperor said. "Stay as long as you like. You will always have a guest chamber waiting here, Lady Vala."

"Thank you." Vala rose from her seat and bowed to the Emperor, then once more to the council. She exited the chambers, smiling to herself. Finally, something was going right for her.

Her stomach growled, reminding her that she had hardly eaten while here. It was unlike her, but she had been anxious about everything.

Hopefully, the dining hall has some jam and cookies, she thought as she made her way to the dining hall. Her mind was already planning where to go next. World Sector Two. She had never been there before, though she knew others who had.

As she entered the dining hall, the smell of warm fresh baked goods and roasted meats hit her nose, making her even more hungry. She eyed the buffet tables, seeing many trays of cookies and tarts with fruit fillings and jams.

Without a second thought, she grabbed a plate, then helped herself to six tarts and a slice of roasted ham, as she did have to balance out her meal with something substantial.

"Lady Vala!" she heard someone say from behind her.

Turning around, Vala faced a courier. "What is it?"

"News from World Sector Four," he said, handing her a small note sealed with the Khari's crest.

Quicky, Vala stuffed the note in her dress pocket, then took the nearest seat. She placed her plate on the table, ignoring it as she opened the note.

Lady Vala, I am sorry to deliver you unfortunate news. Our sector took a vote this morning. It seems that most were in favor of staying out of World Sector Six's business. Though I disagree with their decision, I will go along with it, as there are too many who are opposed to helping the sorceress. Our people are still reminded of the battle back in time, and helping out then. They don't want to continue this fight. If I take complete authority, I am sure there would be an uprising here, and we know that the High Court would use that to their advantage. I don't know what has changed with them, considering that you were able to persuade them in the past. With recent events, they grow more fearful every day. If anything changes, I will send word. I do wish you success with the other sectors, and that they come to their senses, unlike ours. May the God of Light bestow favor upon you. Your Khari.

Vala sat frozen in her seat, staring blankly at the words in disbelief. It was that bad that the Khari couldn't even invoke the call of the warrior. She knew that some of the gifted in her sector had been losing their gifts. Was her warning not good enough? Had they not heard what she had said? She nearly lost her life protecting her sector. And for what?

She fought back a tear as she glanced at her plate. Clutching the note angrily, she crumpled it up, then shoved it back in her dress pocket.

Then she took two full tarts, shoving them in her mouth. She needed energy for the work ahead of her.

CHAPTER 32

RED

Kyle was perched on one of the ledges of the Unimark building, overlooking the entire city of Arcadia. It was so peaceful. The winds felt soothing, the air fresh. It was his place to refocus his thoughts and come to his senses. With everything that happened with Diego, and that Joe guy that was supposedly his band manager, even the stress of the palace. There was no way he would go traipsing back to Em in a bad mood.

This place held so many memories…old memories that seemed like a lifetime ago. Hell, it pretty much was a whole lifetime ago. This building had that nostalgic home feel to it. Maybe it was because it was the same building that he and Geeta had practiced in every day while locked in time. He could probably recite how many bricks or windows were in the damn thing if he wanted.

Kyle smirked at the thought of Geeta. *She still doesn't know I talked to Nym.* He needed to give Geeta Nym's number soon; otherwise she might fuck this one up. *She's busy. I'll wait a few more days and see what's up with her.* He knew she was coming back to Arcadia at some point, when the parts were finished for that cyborg.

In the distance, Kyle glanced at the palace. Since being back in Arcadia, everything was turning out much differently than he could have ever imagined. Not like he had any expectations after gaining his old memories back. But still, not everything was what he had hoped for. The only constants were being with Emerald and playing his music.

Emerald...I want my heart to be yours forever, he thought. He was going to do it. He was seriously going to ask Emerald when the time was right. She was the one. Always the one, in this life and in the life of Rubius. There was no other woman he would want to spend his life with.

He'd been serious when he brought up marriage the first time with her. At the time, Kyle thought that she wasn't really thinking it through, just going through the motions of being queen. But with her pregnancy progressing and her soon to be a mother—and him a father—it made sense. They loved each other, and he wanted to raise the kids with her. It was time to cement their love through marriage.

Kyle rose, then walked around on the rooftop of the building, collecting several scraps of metal and random pebbles. *How do pebbles even get up on the rooftop?* he wondered. Not that it mattered, just a random thought.

After collecting the materials, Kyle sat back down, closing his eyes. He focused on the orange magic within his life force. Slowly, he filtered his energy through his body and into his hands.

Kyle felt the energy transfer to the materials, but he needed more. Hell, it wasn't hard to give more joyful energy. All he had to do was think about how much Emerald made him happy. He thought about her smile. Her pure heart. Her love and adoration for him. And her spirit made him a better man. They were meant to be as one.

The metal and pebbles felt hot in his hands as Kyle clutched them tightly.

Transform to the picture in my mind, he commanded the magic.

The song that he wrote for her came flooding into the back of his mind.

Focusing on his magic, Kyle began to sing their song out loud to the wind. His heart hammered with each word, as if each note of the song pulled more energy from him and into the transmutation spell. The metal became hotter, but Kyle didn't let go. He funneled more magic as he sang, giving it more power. He sang with the entirety of his heart and soul until he was sweating profusely. But he never let go of the materials in his hands.

When the song was over and the last note was sung, the new transmuted creation felt cold, and he knew it was done.

Kyle opened his eyes, then released the tension in his hands.

It just how I imagined! he thought, smiling.

In the palm of his hands was the most beautiful ring he had ever seen. The ring consisted of a platinum band, and set in it were three stones. On the left side was a ruby—for he was the fire and passion. And on the right side, there was an emerald—for she was life and love. In the middle was a giant princess-cut diamond.

Together, we make white light, he thought with a gleeful smile.

He rummaged through his leather vest pockets but couldn't find anything to put the ring in. He yanked out a frayed piece of pocket fabric.

Guess this will work.

Shifting his magic into the fabric, Kyle once more used his transmutation magic. The fabric morphed itself into a plush piece of fabric in the shape of a pouch.

Kyle slid the ring into the pouch, then pocketed it in a small section of his vest. The energy spent making the ring had taken a toll on him.

Kyle lit up a smoke, then smiled to himself. He couldn't wait to find the right time to ask Em.

✦ ✦ ✦

Emerald turned on the shower to a warm setting, then took out a few hair clips, stepping inside. Warm water immediately sprayed on her skin. She wished it was hotter, but knowing that hot water wasn't good for her children in the womb, she didn't want to do anything that endangered her little life-forms.

Looking down at her belly, she could have sworn that it was bigger than yesterday. From what she had read online, her tummy wasn't supposed to get bigger until the later months. Or so she thought.

Grabbing the shampoo, Emerald squeezed a good portion into her hand, then lathered her hair. A few soap bubbles slid down her forehead and into her eye as the water continued to spray from behind. As she washed her hair, she kept wondering where Kyle had run off to. Glacia was off on an errand, and the other handmaidens had heard that he'd taken off earlier in the morning.

Though normally she would have been washed up in the morning and ready for the day, Emerald felt sweaty from being in the Inner Council meeting all morning. Not only had her body started changing on the outside, her chemistry on the inside felt completely different. She sweated more and was lightheaded, dizzy. Then there was that time she fainted at the club; just walking around made her hot and overheated.

Emerald shrieked in surprise. Kyle's face was smashed up against the glass.

"Kyle! What are you doing?" Emerald said as her heart raced wildly.

"What does it look like I'm doing?"

"You scared me!"

He laughed. "Well, what guy wouldn't take an opportunity like this to see his woman in the shower?"

"Kyle…" Emerald suddenly felt acutely aware of her changing body, then crossed her arms across her breasts and stomach in embarrassment.

"You don't want me here? I can leave."

Emerald blushed as the water continued to spray against her back. "It's just…I'm not in the same shape anymore."

"So? You're pregnant. You supposed to keep the same shape?" He smiled behind the glass. "Besides, I think you look even hotter."

"I don't feel that way."

"You might not think so, but I do. And when you gain more weight, you'll still would be the hottest woman alive."

Emerald shook her head. "You're just saying that."

"I don't just make shit up." He pressed his head against the glass. "You're so beautiful, Em. I wish that you believed it, especially now."

Emerald blushed, then nodded, meeting his eyes through the glass. "I guess I'm feeling insecure about my body."

"Like I said, you shouldn't. How about I come in there and prove what I said to you?"

Emerald scoffed and laughed at the same time, splashing the glass with water. "Kyle!"

"What? I'm serious! I need a shower anyways. Might as well get two jobs done at once." He laughed. "What d'ya say, Em?"

She giggled.

"I'll take that as a yes?"

"Yes."

He beamed, then started ripping off his clothes, leaving his jewelry on.

"Where were you earlier?" Emerald asked as he opened the shower door.

"Just out." She saw a flicker of frustration on his face.

"You know, the parts for Drew will be ready soon," Emerald continued.

"Next few days at the most."

"Oh yeah? That's great news."

"Yes." Emerald watched his expression through the foggy glass. "Have you given Geeta Nym's number?"

"Nah, not yet," he said, shrugging. "I'll give it to her when she visits or whenever I talk to her next."

Emerald watched as he stepped inside. His lean body gleamed under the shower light, even more so once the water droplets pelted his skin. Seeing the jewelry against his naked skin made his muscles even more pronounced somehow.

Kyle noticed her staring, and she blushed.

"You like what you see?"

She blushed more. "Of course."

He smiled deviously, then ran his hands down the sides of her body.

"Touch me, Em," he begged in her ear, pressing his wet body against hers.

"Where?"

"Anywhere."

Emerald put her hands around his lean waist, then slid her hands lower. And lower…

"That's a good start. A damn good start," he cooed in her ear.

A hotness surged in her lowers as his body moved against hers, including the twin baby bump. The water ran down their bodies, leaving them feeling slick.

Kyle ran his fingers along the back of her neck, kissing her wildly.

A surge of excitement and euphoria flooded her body, her hormones raging, her body wanting.

"Kyle…" she whispered.

"Goddamn, Em," he whispered in her ear. "You feel so fucking good…"

CHAPTER 33

✦

RED

He had a stupid grin on his face the entire afternoon. The sex was fucking amazing. God, if only they had more time. Kyle smiled again as he stared out the transport window. He had felt the drop in gravity as the transport landed.

"Are you okay?" Emerald asked, leaning on his shoulder. She playfully grabbed his hand.

"Okay? More than okay. God, I'm getting hard just thinking about earlier," he said.

Her bright green eyes peered up at him, then she blushed. "Same."

"Oh yeah? You too?" Kyle smirked.

She giggled in response as he kissed her hand, then gently massaged her fingers with his thumbs.

"Looks like we are here," she stated, glancing out the window.

Kyle looked out the window again. The venue was huge in comparison to the skyscrapers that surrounded it. In the distance, Kyle saw street bikes racing on some of the upper ramps, then disappearing down into the streets below. Just watching them made him a little bit jealous, with him lacking a bike.

Just then, the transport door flung open, and Joe appeared in the doorway. Kyle internally groaned at the sight of his band manager but attempted to look indifferent.

"Hey, man. I got your contracts filed and taken care of. Your account is now set up with the backpay funds," Joe said to him.

"Sounds good, man," Kyle said as he got to his feet.

Joe then saw Emerald, bowing to her. "Your Majesty." He then swiped his communicator to silent.

"Hello," she said softly.

"I'll meet you at the door," Joe said, leaving the two of them alone.

Kyle turned to Emerald. "Wanna go out tomorrow?"

"I think I might have a few meetings, but I can check. What did you have in mind?" she asked.

"I wanna get a bike."

Emerald smiled at him, and immediately Kyle felt his nerves leave. "If I don't have any prior engagements, then I will come."

Kyle smiled at her as she rose from her seat. Hand in hand, they exited the transport.

Immediately, there were screams from crowds of fans, all roped off on both sides of the landing. Photos were being snapped, broadcasters were there taping them as they walked.

"Shit," Kyle murmured under his breath as the fans screamed. A slew of girls bounced up and down, while men shouted and cheered him on.

Emerald gave him a soft smile. "It will be like this from now on."

More screams from the crowd to their queen. They went wild as they threw roses at Emerald's feet and love notes to Kyle.

They met up with Joe, who was waiting outside the doorway with a security team.

They all bowed. "We are overjoyed by Her Majesty's presence."

"Thank you, sirs," Emerald said.

"Shit, Joe," said Kyle. "I didn't know it was going to be like this."

Joe laughed. "It will only get crazier from here."

Crazier? He'd wanted to be famous, but this famous? Now he wasn't so sure.

"Sir, we are to show you the way, with Her Majesty, of course," the leader of the security team said.

"Thanks."

The entourage walked through a private corridor that led to a backstage room. Remy was there, but there was no sign of the others.

"Where is everyone?" Kyle asked, as he set down his guitar case.

"Looks like you finally got your ass here on time," Remy commented. Just then, a familiar face popped out from behind Remy.

"My Queen," a woman said, bowing to Emerald. She was all dolled up in the latest fashions. Her brown hair was done up wildly, her makeup bright green, accenting her golden-brown eyes with glossy lips.

"Glacia?" Emerald exclaimed wildly, running up to her. She'd hardly recognized her. They both giggled.

"Are you surprised? I thought it might be fun!" Glacia said with a giggle.

"I am!" Emerald said.

"Hey, Master Kyle," Glacia said, waving across the room.

Kyle snorted. "Don't call me that here."

"Okay, big guy," she commented.

The girls started chatting excitedly, while Kyle got his guitar tuned. Kamren appeared a few minutes later, but still no sign of Diego.

"Where the fuck is he?" Remy said as he started walking anxiously around the dressing room. His anxiety always gave Kyle anxiety. That was how bad Remy had it.

"He'll be here," Kamren said as he headed to the bathroom.

Remy sighed as he lit up a cigarette, still walking around in circles.

"Stop acting like a crazy person. You're freaking me out," Kyle said.

"You should talk." Remy shot him a dirty look, taking another drag as Glacia came up and hugged him.

"He'll be here, like Kamren said. Don't worry, babe." Remy looked a little more calm from Glacia's touch.

One of the bouncers came back to escort Emerald and Glacia to their seats for the show.

"Guys, you're about to go on. Come on," one of the guards said, gesturing at them.

Emerald looked at Kyle, and he looked back at her.

"You gonna be in front, right?" Kyle said, holding her hands one last time.

"If they let me," she said.

He turned to the guard. "Get a front middle seat for the queen."

"Yes, sir. Anything for Her Majesty."

The guard led Emerald away, and Kyle gave her one last wink. She air-kissed him, then turned away, going out the doors.

As they left, Diego came trudging in.

"What the hell, man?" Remy said angrily. "Do you know what time it is?"

"It's party time!" Diego joked, taking out a flask and drinking from it.

Kyle sighed. Remy always had a stick up his ass, but Diego was no saint either.

"That's not funny—" Remy began.

"He's here now, isn't he?" Kyle interrupted.

Remy gritted his teeth, then turned away, taking another drag.

"Here's to another show!" Diego took another swig, then shot Kyle a dirty look.

Kyle clenched his jaw, turning in a different direction. *What a fucking ass,* he thought.

The venue managers came in with Joe. "You ready?"

"Yeah," Remy said as the guys nodded.

Kyle grabbed his guitar and walked out with the group, down the hall leading backstage. He could already hear the crazy audience echoing throughout the large auditorium.

As the band positioned themselves backstage, suddenly there were screams of excitement, followed by the audience exclaiming, "The Queen!"

Normally, Kyle and everyone else would react differently to a royal attending an event like this. Royals were hated. But not Emerald. The entire kingdom loved her—she was their princess. Hell, she was loved in other kingdoms, too, from what he had heard.

The stagehands waved the guys into position, and Kamren started their first number.

Then, with an explosion of lights, the curtain rose, and the other band members joined in. The crowd screamed, cheered, cried. Kyle couldn't help it. He smiled a stupid-ass grin. They were there for him and his band. For the music. The whole experience was like a drug, but far more seductive.

Kyle looked down, right where Emerald was. She peered up at him with adoring eyes. He smiled at her as the band played.

Pure ecstasy came over him. Between the raw thrill of the crowd, Emerald's excitement watching him with admiration...

Suddenly, he had an idea. Geeta would think it reckless, which convinced him to do it.

Kyle channeled his power as he played, focused on the raw, pure energy in his soul. The fire, the passion, the thrill—everything that made him gifted.

Instantly his soul flooded with energy, sending a stream of fire across the stage and a waterfall of sparks flying everywhere, like a giant display of pyrotechnics. The guys looked startled, and Kyle bit back laughter. The crowd screamed with excitement, but Kyle saw shadows of the backstage workers with fire extinguishers. It wasn't a part of the show.

Quickly, with another stroke of his guitar, water droplets whooshed through the stage, dousing the fires.

The crowd screamed once again while the backstage crew looked bewildered, wondering where all the special effects were coming from. Kyle sent another wave of magic through his mind—telling them internally it would be okay, making them be at peace. Non-gifted minds were so persuadable.

Kyle thought back to Geeta saying it was wrong to dive into one's private thoughts, unless necessary. Geeta always had been a stickler for rules. The stagehands shrugged, and Joe looked ecstatic, excitedly palming his communicator. Kyle glanced down at Emerald; she looked surprised too, but she giggled along with the crowd.

No harm, no foul, Kyle thought.

The band continued to play through the night, number after number. Here and there, Kyle sprinkled in some "special effects," making the crowd even more wild with excitement. He took shots from his flask during Kamren's drum solos.

When their last number came up on deck, he was feeling pretty drunk.

Diego quickly stalked over to him. The crowd was still roaring, excited for the next number.

"Hey, man, sorry about the bad blood between us," Diego whispered.

Kyle glanced at him with drunken eyes. Dude seemed sorry. "No worries, man," Kyle said with a shrug.

Diego slapped him on the back in a friendly gesture, then handed him a drink. Kyle took it, slammed it, then wiped his mouth, starting the final song.

He played like he had never played before. Life was good. Em was there. He was playing for a shitload of people. Everybody loved him. God, how he loved Em. She peered up at him with adoring eyes. He'd missed her all those years being Rubius. Never had he believed in destiny, but how could he not believe they were meant to be?

For a split second, the God of Light's warning flashed in his mind. The warning of how he wasn't supposed to be in Arcadia ever again. As quick as it came, the thought disappeared with the help of another chug of his flask.

As the song ended, Kyle leaned into the microphone, stumbling.

He was so fucked up.

"I have a special thank-you to say. Give a hand to the Queen!" Kyle announced. The whole crowd cheered wildly, while Kyle leaned over the stage, reaching out to her. Emerald, surprised, grabbed his hand, and the guards lifted her onto the stage.

They stood side by side. Kyle, looking at her with drunken eyes, marveled at how beautiful she was. She was his! With her hand in his, he raised it.

The crowd went wild again, everyone raising their lighters in reverence. Emerald nodded bashfully. She raised her hand, and everyone went quiet.

"Thank you, everyone. I really mean it. Thank you. Isn't the band wonderful?" Emerald said with confidence. Kyle could see a hint of blushing under those pale, delicate cheeks.

The crowd yelled again. "The Queen is badass!"

"She is the fucking coolest queen ever!"

Other girls screamed, "I love you, Kyle!" or "Marry me!"

Kyle snorted, then led Emerald, hand in hand, walking toward the edge of the stage. People would know something was up.

Who the hell cares? he thought. *We are together, and I want to show the world she is with me.*

Kyle leaned in, then kissed her passionately. The crowd went crazy. The world now knew their secret. Hell, it was rumored anyway, so now there was no wondering. To hell with it all. He wanted to be with Emerald. He was hers, and she his.

His lips departed hers, Emerald blushing as the crowd continued to scream with joy. Her eyes met his, glowing with green life and light.

"I love you, Em..." he whispered.

"I love you too, Kyle..."

They were led backstage and into their dressing room. Emerald plopped down on the couch.

"I think I need to eat something," she said. "I wasn't feeling good earlier. I couldn't stomach food. Now it's catching up to me."

Still feeling drunk and woozy, Kyle looked for the nearest dude, saw someone, and said, "Can you get her something to eat?"

"Of course," the backstage hand said.

They walked back to the room, where the guys were already drinking.

"Dude, did you see that fucking fire and shit? Whoever was in charge of that, we gotta tell them to do that for the next show," Diego said, slamming his flask.

Kyle smiled. He blinked, feeling lightheaded.

"Here's to the return of our man," Diego said, holding out his flask to Kyle.

"Thanks, man. It's good to be back." Kyle took the flask, and the two nodded to each other. Kyle chugged the rest. It was Diego's best whiskey.

"Get your asses back out there for an encore," Remy snapped. "The crowd is waiting!"

"Oh shit, I forgot. Got distracted," Diego said.

As Kyle walked back toward the stage, his feet felt heavy. The floor was curved. Must've drank way more than his limit.

He made it out onstage, then picked up his guitar. The crowd continued to scream.

"What are we gonna play?" Diego called out.

That was a good question.

His eyes blurred again.

It was the last thing he remembered.

CHAPTER 34

◆

BLUE

The Olympian palace. The decor irritated him, down to the very ornaments. Though it was very beautiful with the golds, white-and-black-checkered marble, and colored glass throughout, the mere thought that this city-kingdom gave him so much grief aggravated him. The only gratification was that the air felt right in his life force, telling him that he was meant to be in this time.

As Derek marched down the halls to the throne room, he was met with frantic servants scurrying about. Other advisors were moving quickly, not even noticing him. There were communicators blasting on about a fire that had broken out in the city. He hoped that this fire everyone was up in arms about would burn all of Olympia to the ground. It would be much deserved after the strain King Renard had put on Derek and Emerald.

The guards standing firm in front of the doors to the throne room noticed him. "The King is not seeing anyone this evening," said one of the guards.

"I am King Derek of Arcadia, and I am going to speak to King Renard now," Derek announced, his thick brows furrowed as he swept his dark blue curls out of his eyes.

The captain bowed to him. "I am sorry, Your Grace, but His Majesty is busy with important matters. I will contact the councilor and see if His Majesty can make other arrangements for a meeting with Your Grace at a later time."

"That will not suffice."

With a loud flick of his wrist, Derek flooded his veins with his analogous magic—blue-violet—then with another motion, he shot the captain with the magic, slamming him into a hall pillar.

The armor clanged loudly as the captain fell limply to the marbled floors, echoing loudly. He tried to move but instead blacked out.

Derek eyed the rest of the guards. "Now, please, inform the King that I am here to have an audience with him."

The guards hesitated.

Derek huffed with impatience. With another swish of his hand, the guards were lifted from their feet into the air, then dropped ten feet, smacking them into the ground. Then he snapped his fingers, and instantly, the room stilled. The captain, the guards, even the very dust particles—all lifeless, frozen in time.

"Insubordinates," he sneered, sidestepping the captain.

Holding out his hand, he summoned more blue-violet magic, using it to yank the door to the throne room open. He could simply appear to the lot of them, but he wanted it this way—to come in unannounced through a proper door. He had at least some propriety.

As he walked inside, the King of Olympia and his advisors turned to him, alarmed.

"You sure know how to make other visiting royals feel welcome. I'd expect nothing less," Derek announced to the lot of them.

"If it isn't King Derek of Arcadia," King Renard called out, his eyebrows raised in suspicion.

"Indeed. I felt it high time to pay you a visit," Derek stated boldly. His boots clacked as he neared the King.

"Come to gloat, I take it?" Renard said. "Really, Derek, we are dealing with a city matter."

"You mean the fire in your city?" Derek snorted. "I am far more important than a fire, Renard…and more dangerous." His eyes narrowed. "We have matters to settle once and for all."

"What matters?"

"Olympian cyborgs. Really, Renard? After you pushed and pushed me to surrender mine? You are a lousy, spineless amoeba of a king. Can't even promote a decent ambassador."

The King's eyes darkened with anger. Behind the King, Derek saw two magical forms masked in orange illusion magic.

"You dare insult me in my own kingdom?" the King said.

"I absolutely do. After all, you insulted me for two months with your lousy terms," Derek shot back.

"I had heard that you went away for some time, leaving your pregnant queen behind," the King said. "Tell me, were you out whoring while you kept your wife locked away?" The King leaned in. "How long have you been gone, Derek? Long enough to not lead the battle of the wastelands?"

"How dare you bring Queen Emerald into this!" Derek snarled, then shot out his hand, blasting his blue magic.

The world was suddenly drained of color, replaced by shades of blue. The court stilled, unmoving. The only people moving were the king and the hidden gifted.

One of them has blue magic.

King Renard was about to shout, but Derek slapped a thick force of blue-violet magic over the King's mouth, then bound his entire body from the neck down with a string of violet magic shaped like a rope.

Derek started to laugh loudly. "Come out, you blue-gifted. Try me! Go ahead, let's see if you can take me down! I dare you."

A blue-gifted man with deep olive skin and startling blue eyes appeared. In the man's hand was an ancient curved sword.

"You do not know what you are meddling with," the blue-gifted man with a heavy accent warned.

"New Blood thinks he knows best," hissed another thickly accented voice. It was the other gifted who was under the guise of the illusion magic.

"New blood," Derek hissed. "Come find out how new blooded I *am.*"

The King struggled in his throne; Derek could hear him. He was desperate to have his gifted defeat Derek.

Not on your life.

The blue-gifted man disappeared, but Derek saw the dimension that he had reappeared in. The world's dimensions were like layers, and he could see right through each one of them simultaneously.

Derek focused on his new red magic and called forth the rage of his frozen heart. Within his hand, glowing blue ice appeared, forming a giant floating ice spike. He hurled it at the man, who deflected it with his sword.

There was a shimmer of illusion magic, masking the other gifted man. Derek turned, then summoned the orange part of his soul, draining away the illusion, revealing a yellow-gifted man. The man's eyes were startling yellow compared to his deep golden skin and wiry long hair and round deep-set eyes.

The man lowered his bushy brows, then summoned a barrier around the two as Derek hurled a round of ice shards at the men. With another flick of magic, Derek drained away the men's barriers, then raised his hands with his blue-violet magic. The violet magic responded, lifting the struggling men to their feet, binding them tightly.

"Now we are going to have a talk and settle matters once and for all," Derek stated. He flicked his finger, and the violet magic loosened around the King's mouth.

The King gasped for breath.

"Impossible," hacked the yellow-gifted man. "Are you from the High Court in the far future?"

"You answer to the High Court?" Derek asked, strutting over to them.

The blue-gifted man's eyes widened, whilst the yellow-gifted man coughed. "I plan to take part in the new world, reborn in a new time."

"Then you know who really is behind the coming of the new world," Derek stated. "Be ready for her."

"Her?" The yellow-gifted man spat. "I don't answer to any woman. No, it is the coming of the colors together—the High Court." He narrowed his eyes. "It is not meant for a *woman* to rule."

Derek struck the man across the face. "Shut up." Then he struck him again. Then again. Leaning in, he said, "If it weren't for you working for our ultimate goal, I would disintegrate you!" He struck the man again. "Make no mistake, she *will* rule," he spat, striking him again.

Blood poured out from the man's nose and jaw, spilling onto the floor as Derek strutted over to the blue-gifted man. The man gazed at him but said nothing. But he didn't need to; Derek knew that the man was conflicted. The man's entire life was full of conviction.

Derek turned around to face the king. "So, did you two give your blood to the Olympian cyborgs? Or did you steal blood from my *wife*?" Derek demanded.

"The High Court commanded us to be staged here in this time," the blue-gifted offered. "We gave our blood freely. It was foreseen in the flow of time in order to get the cyborgs resurrected for the new world."

Derek raised an eyebrow. "Then why attack my kingdom?"

"To draw out the Arcadian scientists," the yellow-gifted snapped. "They are needed for the future."

This time, King Renard gave a thin smile.

"What are you smirking about?" Derek asked.

"We have bait to lure out the scientists." The King narrowed his eyes.

"Do you now?"

"Indeed." King Renard smiled darkly. "A child."

"A child?" Derek scoffed.

"The scientists' daughter. One they had *together*."

Derek's mouth nearly dropped at the news. "You are telling me that the scientists have a *daughter*? And she is here, as your prisoner?"

"Precisely."

Derek hated Olympia. He hated King Renard. He didn't like the yellow-gifted man. But if they had the same goal as he did, why not unite them? If they did have this child, then the cyborg would eventually come for his daughter. And if Geeta was with the cyborg… What if Derek was able to get that violet-gifted away from the cyborg? Perhaps have King Renard do something drastic? It might just bring Telly Hearly instead…but it was a chance worth taking. If Olympia captured the cyborg and the violet-gifted, then he would take them anyway. And if they didn't, then he would do it. Either way, he would have those two hunted.

Derek eyed the king, then strutted around him, his shirt torn with magical friction exposing his strong physique. "The High Court is getting impatient," Derek announced. "They have commanded me to retrieve the gifted cyborg and bring him into the future. And that's what I intend to do." Derek leaned in. "Do everything your damnedest to capture this robot! If you do, I will take him off your hands. And also, there is a violet-gifted out there with the scientists. Do whatever you can to get her crawling out of her hole. Now, I have other matters to attend to for the time being. I will be watching."

The King glared at him. "I do not like you, *pretty boy*. I never have."

"And I have never liked you either. Your face is arranged in such a way that it mirrors the back end of a dog," Derek spat. "But you have no choice now, do you?" Derek extended a hand, then flowed his violet magic around the king, squeezing his body. "Do you?"

The King's eyes were daggers as Derek squeezed his body like a rag doll.

"It seems so."

"Call me Your Majesty, dammit!"

"Yes, Your Majesty," Renard grunted.

"Did you hear me? You must capture that cyborg! I need to have him!"

With the King's eyes wide, he nodded. "Yes, King Derek."

"Good." Derek eyed him sharply. "You cannot fight me. Though you won't remember me after I'm done with you, you remember that when you see me next time," he snarled in his face.

"Remember you?"

Derek laughed. "Didn't I tell you? I am going to wipe your memories."

"You can't!" snapped the yellow-gifted.

"Think again," Derek dared. "I can do whatever I want with you subordinates, for soon, I will be crowned the King of Time. I can make it so that you won't remember your name if I so please. You won't even remember that I came here. You'll just think that you came up with this on your own. Now, who is your master?" he asked. His eyes narrowed, then shot up, glancing at the court. "All of you. Your memories of this will be erased!"

"King of Time!" spat the yellow-gifted.

The blue-gifted looked frightened.

He knows I speak of the truth, Derek determined.

Suddenly, he sensed another presence nearby; it wasn't necessarily a gifted life force, but it did have an underlying power to it. So much that Derek felt its radiance within the air, thickened with energy.

"There is another gifted here," Derek said.

Renard eyed him. "I have a son. He has the power of deep-red magic. But he is miles away from here."

The King has a gifted son? Derek paused, reaching out to feel this strange life force. It wasn't red magic he was detecting.

"You aren't lying to me, are you?" Derek pressed.

"No, no," he said defensively. "He isn't my blood kin. I adopted him…"

"I wasn't referring to your adopted son. There is someone here. Don't lie to me!"

"The only other magics we have are cyborgs, that's it!"

"It is true," called out the blue-gifted. "He only has access to the dark side of the Spectrum in red."

Before the King could answer with his lips, Derek could hear that the King was telling the truth through his mind.

"Perhaps your councilors will tell me more!" Derek loosened the time magic over the court, allowing the advisors to move freely, utterly confused.

"You there! Or anyone in the court! Tell me if anyone knows about another gifted here in Olympia!" Derek shouted.

Everyone remained silent, shaking their heads and lowering their eyes to the floor. They were afraid; they knew nothing.

Derek reached out, focusing on the power. He couldn't quite explain the sensation he was detecting. It was like a gifted life force, but it lacked a gift.

Derek felt another brush of power.

It was the violet-gifted woman.

She had sent a wave of energy over Olympia, but it was gone as quick as it came.

Derek burst out in a deep, dark, ironic laugh. She was in the wastelands.

I will find you, Geeta Sharma!

Derek turned, then drained the court advisors and guards of their memories. The entire court slumped to the floor, the sound echoing against the marble floor.

"Useless." Derek turned to the King and the gifted men. "Now get that cyborg! Get that violet-gifted, too! That is an order!"

No one said anything.

"This court has some serious priority issues. Answer me, dammit!" Derek shouted.

The King and the gifted mumbled, "Yes, Your Majesty."

Derek smirked. "That's more like it."

He then closed his eyes and focused on all minds within the room. The King and the gifted men, even another once-over of the passed-out guards and the advisors. All needed a good mind scrub.

He felt the violet side of his blue magic—it was raging, full of power and authority. He released the power, flooding the men's minds, scouring all memory of this event.

The gifted men started screaming in pain as the King went pale.

With another motion of his hands, Derek yanked the memory out with a stream of violet magic, and both gifted men collapsed to the floor, unconscious.

The wisp of memory magic floated in the air, right in front of Derek, who clutched the wisp in his palm, causing the magic to dissipate instantly.

Shaking off his hand as if it had been wet or dirty, Derek turned his attention to the King and his guards.

Though he'd wiped their memories of him, Derek left the memories of his instructions. As he released their minds, Derek flashed away.

CHAPTER 35

◆

VIOLET

The night was young as Geeta exited the refuge. There were a few stars out, one of the brighter planets in the sky beaming brightly like the morning star. They twinkled as if they had a heart of their own, still beating to the rhythm of light.

Another day of training with Victor. And another day searching for that boy across the planes of the mind. Every day had been the same since the camp left, Geeta teaching Victor all that she knew. It made her feel inadequate, that she couldn't guide him more. But what was she to do? She ever never read about or seen gray magic. It was frustrating trying to teach something she knew nothing about except the basics. Victor wasn't getting anywhere either; he was unable to tap into an emotion to draw out his power. It was as if his power didn't work like the other colors of magic.

Geeta took a breath, thinking about the lack of progress. She was getting nervous. Terrified, more like it, though she never showed it outwardly. If she did, Victor would possibly lose heart too. And then what? The only temporary relief that they had was that if Derek knew about Emerald's pregnancy, it would stall both him and Elyathi. After the children were born, their time would be up, and Emerald would be in constant peril. Her and her offspring.

Geeta glanced in the corner of her eye, noticing Victor's black outline against the twilight sky. She could only assume he was meditating, as he often did at the end of the day. *I hope you find something within your life force soon.* She swallowed a lump in her throat.

She turned to her side satchel, sifting through it, then pulled out a box of incense. She then grabbed a single stick, putting the box back into her pack. Pinching her thumb and index finger on the tip of the incense, she channeled her underlying adjacent magic.

Her fingers began to glow violet with a red undertone, the tip of the incense stick doing the same. Suddenly, the stick lit up with a small flame. Geeta pulled her fingers away quickly, then watched the flame burn more of the stick before blowing it out. The smell of her favorite incense flooded her nose, instantly reducing her stress. Something about this particular scent always soothed her mind, even back in ancient times.

She placed the incense stick upright in the sand, letting the smoke waft in the air, across the wastelands. Images of her homeland from the ancient times filled her mind. Every day, she wondered if the event at the temple had caused a rift in time. What if she had never left that day?

Suresh, I hope you are well, wherever you are. She missed him, more than she admitted to herself. She truly loved him deeply as a friend. He was one of only ones who truly understood her, though she never told him about her attraction to him. But Geeta was sure that he wouldn't even care—perhaps only be a little hurt because of how he felt toward her.

Geeta's heart sank as she reflected on Suresh. They had been apart for most of the past seven or so years, only briefly seeing each other after capturing the sorceress. He left urgently after her capture, then nothing.

Geeta kneeled down, moving the incense stick next to a boulder. The rock blocked the wind perfectly, not letting the power of the wasteland winds blow the incense stick out.

She gently floated upward with her analogous violet-red magic onto the top of the boulder, then sat in her prayer formation.

Goddess of the Violet, please protect Suresh, wherever he may be.

Geeta said a few more prayers silently, then turned to face the direction of Olympia.

The boy. She needed to find him. If she found Gwen instead, it would be even better. But somehow, whenever Geeta reflected on Gwen, there was nothing but a void.

She shuddered at the thought of the boy's mind, full of terror and twisted evil.

Little boy...why are your thoughts full of darkness? What is haunting you?

Taking slow, deep breaths, Geeta closed her eyes and cleared her mind of all her thoughts, hanging on to the ones about the boy. She pictured his face, back from when they were in the wastelands. His strange headset, the type used by gamers. Only this headset and goggles seemed to do much more than play games. What was the purpose of it? Was the headset keeping him under control? And through his goggles, his eyes, the deep redness, like a bloodstone gem.

She recalled his cries out in the wasteland. *I don't want to be here! I don't want to be here...*

No child should ever have those kinds of dark thoughts plaguing them, Geeta thought.

I don't want to be here! his voice continued to echo over and over in her head.

Little boy, Geeta called out to him within her mind.

She focused on her words, sending them out on the mental dimensional plane. Her mind traveled with them, scanning the wastelands within the wind. Her thoughts were in violet; her words became an energy, pure violet within the purple dimensions. The winds continued to carry her thoughts toward Olympia.

Little boy, where are they hiding you?

Her energy reached the vicinity of Olympia. The city was bathed in violets within the mental dimension, and her ball of energy—her words—reached the gates.

Geeta raised her hands in the physical world, feeling the energy of her words. Then, with a hard clap, she pulled her hands apart quickly. Her violet energy in Olympia cracked apart into fragments, heading in different directions across the city.

She separated her mind, traveling with each new ball of energy through Olympia. The violet balls of light left violet light trails behind them, slowly fading away. Each ball went this way and that, scanning the city, feeling out each citizen, anything that Geeta could find that represented the boy's mind. Through crowds of people, through their thoughts—joy, pain, sadness—the balls continued to flow over each thought, dream...

There was something strong at work within the city.

Geeta homed in on the collective thoughts of the citizens. What she could make of it was a fire, but no other details.

Better use this event as a distraction to find this boy…

Geeta searched with her magic, brushing the minds across Olympia. There. A sudden presence. One that she hadn't felt in a long time.

Is it…?

Her communicator rang out suddenly. On the faceplate, she saw the palace's number.

Geeta pressed the button to answer. "This is Geeta," she said.

"Geeta! How the hell are you? Oh God, you won't believe what I'm gonna tell you."

It was Kyle's voice on the line. He sounded like he had been drinking heavily.

"Are you *drunk*?"

"I think so? Hell, I don't know. I suppose so, because I was drinking some powerful whiskey." He laughed, bizarrely out of character. "I just played a show. It was fucking great that I thought to celebrate my return, you know? You should have been there, Geeta. They fucking loved me out there on stage."

"Did I hear you correctly? You played at a show?"

"Yeah."

Geeta blinked in disbelief.

"I'm in the band again."

"I can't believe you played in a show!" Geeta gestured furiously. "You're supposed to be watching over the Queen!"

"Calm down. Em was with me."

"She's with you now?" Geeta asked pointedly.

"Uh, wait." There was muffling. "I don't see her. Damn. I dunno."

Her blood began to boil. "You aren't with Emerald?"

"God, if I knew you were gonna flip your shit, I wouldn't have called you."

A wave of annoyance flared up inside Geeta. "You are only supposed to call me if you have parts!"

Kyle laughed on the other line. "Chill out. God. Didn't you get Em's message? Or did I call earlier? I can't remember… It's all a blur. I think they'll be ready this week? Who the hell knows. I'm so fucked up…"

"I didn't get any call or message." Geeta sighed. This was getting nowhere. "Are the parts ready or not?"

"Wait, I did hear something now that you mention it. Yeah, the parts are ready."

"Are you sure?"

"Yeah, I'm sure. Positive." More laughter. "Oh man, that whiskey sure is strong."

Geeta didn't know if she should be relieved that the parts for Drew were about ready or majorly irritated that Kyle was off being his Kyle-ass self. Though, even with his drunkenness, something was off.

"Are you okay?"

"Why the hell wouldn't I be?"

Geeta gritted her teeth. "Because you just told me that you are screwed up!"

"Did I?" He laughed. "So check this out. Em and I went down to the lower levels. It's a long story, so I'll spare you."

Before or after he got drunk?

Kyle continued. "But we went to eat at this diner, and I happened to talk to this girl…you know, with short pink hair…"

Geeta froze.

This isn't happening. I'm in a nightmare…

"Her name is Nym. She said she knew you, and I told her that I knew you, too. We talked about you for a while, and she gave me her number to give to you!"

"WHAT?" Geeta snapped, jumping up.

Kyle laughed. "I think she's into you."

"I am going to kick your fucking ass!" Geeta clutched the communicator, her hand shaking hard.

Victor jerked his head toward her, breaking from his meditation.

"Why? I did you a fucking favor."

"You don't know anything about anything!"

"The hell I don't! I fucking saw your mind. I know you like her!"

"You didn't have to get your nose in my business!" She was shouting at this point.

"If it were up to you, you'd not do anything for fucking years and let the opportunity fly by!"

"You're an *ass*," Geeta snarled.

"You're fucking welcome!" The line disconnected.

Geeta stood frozen, holding the communicator in her hand. What in the hell was that ass thinking?

Victor stood silently nearby. Geeta knew he didn't know what to do or say.

Geeta sighed, then turned to him. "The Corporation has Drew's parts. I'll go and pick them up tomorrow."

"Good. Hopefully this will give him the boost he needs." In the darkness, his eyes glowed a soft eerie gray. "What is wrong with Kyle?"

She sighed. "Without probing his mind…he's definitely drunk. Maybe more."

"That fool tends to do things without thinking." Victor sat down next to her. "He's probably getting used to…his old self once again. Maybe having some bumps along the way."

He does have a point.

"Any luck locating the boy?" Victor continued.

"I'm not sure." Geeta said. "I felt a familiar mind. My concentration was broken by that jackal's call."

"Familiar mind," Victor said, almost in thought.

She met his question with silence. Familiar mind indeed.

Geeta turned to her communicator, then pocketed it. "Let's duel." She rose to her feet.

Victor sighed. "You'll just be shooting magic at me, and I'll be taking it."

"Maybe. I'm hoping that one of these times you will tap into your magic under pressure." That was what she was counting on, at least.

"Let's hope so," he replied.

✦ ✦ ✦

She was here, in this time.

She was the violet-gifted the blue-gifted man spoke about.

He felt her brush against his mind. All by accident, with her not knowing, of course. His protection magic encircled his thoughts and body, strong against other magics.

I will make you pay for everything! Vihaan cursed. *I will make you beg for my forgiveness on your knees!*

There was a knock on the door.

"Come!"

Bryce opened the door, then bowed, shutting it behind him. "Yes?"

"Ready the boy!"

"He's already having fits of rage." Bryce paused. "We can't get him strapped in in his current state."

"I hate to wait!" Vihaan snarled.

"Heal him in the morning once he's calmed down. Then we can proceed." Bryce eyed him. "What is so pressing? An army?"

Vihaan inched near his face, hovering over Bryce, narrowing his eyes. "We have a violet-gifted to catch…"

CHAPTER 36

◆

Garrett yawned loudly, then made a big catlike stretch as he got up from his keyboard. It was sometime in the morning, and he needed something to keep him awake. Or was it late in the afternoon? Who knew at this point. The radio wasn't helping either, just boring news stories from the area. Usually there were highlights that made him chuckle. Wife charged with assault for beating her husband with an ice cream bar. Some guy charged with arson in the wastelands for making a campfire. A long transport chase in the heart of Arcadia's western sector, involving half the force. But tonight, nothing entertaining.

Lazily walking over to the cooler, Garrett popped it open, seeing he only had two cans of soda left. As much as he wanted to save his nightly fuel, he needed an extra boost tonight. He could barely keep his eyes open.

Cracking open a can of soda, Garrett guzzled half of it down, still in a haze when he flopped down in his chair. Logging into his system, Garrett checked the screens.

There were red dots on the computerized map. Probably Olympian cyborgs. Garrett had figured out how much energy the cyborgs emitted with their yellow magic, eliminating their possibility. But there were dots that looked different than the norm.

As he started pinpointing the dots, Garrett heard the radio mention Olympia.

"Another fire this week in Olympia, according to the fire reports from the Fire Sector Lord," said the broadcaster. "It is the third fire this week in the city, though tonight's fire is the biggest Olympia has seen yet. Police are baffled as to how the fires were started. No leads have been reported…"

Garrett opened a new screen tab on his device, searching for where the fires in Olympia had been reported. According several of the reports from earlier in the week, the fires matched where his program detected bursts of energy.

Holy shit. It's gotta be that boy!

He mapped out where the current fire was. It had already been managed, and no more energies were logged.

Determined, Garrett started pulling any sort of fire reports, then started to edit his program.

◆ ◆ ◆

Gwen hadn't slept all night. There had been a fire in the city that broke out unexpectedly, quickly spreading. She had heard a lot of commotion outside her door the entire night, which made it impossible to sleep. Because of the noise, she decided to watch outside her window as the fire rescue air transports worked to put it out. Though it was far off in the city, it still terrified her and put her on edge. As of this morning, there was nothing but brownish smoke in the city air.

Looks like they put the fire out, she thought. Turning away from the window, she rubbed her sleepy eyes, noticing a breakfast platter set on her table.

Maybe I did get some sleep after all.

Gwen rolled out of bed, wandering over to the table. It was her favorite breakfast food—cinnamon roll sticky toast. Looking at the food made her start to cry. She missed her mom.

I don't care what awesome food they give me! I'm not eating from those a-hole jerks!

She turned away, then flopped back into bed, wiping her tears away.

The door opened, and Mae came in, giving her a smile. "Morning, Miss Gwen."

"Morning."

Mae noticed the full platter. "Not hungry?" she asked.

"Not really."

"Perhaps later."

"Perhaps never, as long as I'm here," Gwen grumbled. "I want to go *home*, Mae!"

Mae was silent. She probably agreed.

Gwen felt slightly bad for the maid. Mae was doing everything she could to help her out.

"I'm sorry. I'm frustrated," Gwen said.

Mae smiled sadly. "I know."

"What happened last night?" Gwen asked. "I heard everyone running around in the palace halls. Did it have to do with the fire in the city? How did the fire start?"

"Palace matter," Mae said casually. Though Gwen did catch Mae's eyes flicker toward the cameras.

"Figures. No one tells me anything," Gwen muttered. "Just like my mom. Just like the wastelanders." Gwen's heart ached mentioning her mother. She would give anything to be back with her mom, even with her mom not telling her anything.

Mae gave her a smile, trying to lighten the mood. "Master Jihyun wants your company this morning."

Gwen sighed. All the kid did was play video games. But at least he made it so she wasn't so lonely. "Fine," Gwen said. "But can I at least dress myself?"

"Sure. Just give a small knock on your door when you are ready."

Mae left, leaving Gwen alone. She eyed the cinnamon roll sticky toast, then ran over to it, shoving almost the entire thing in her mouth. She chewed it hastily, then scarfed down the two sausage links that accompanied it, drank the entire glass of orange juice, and headed to the bathroom to wash up.

After she was changed and ready, Gwen knocked on the door. Mae unlocked and opened it.

"Ready?"

"Yes."

They walked the same route as last time through the palace. Gwen took more mental notes on the layout, looking for stairs, elevators, or lifts. This time, however, Mae didn't dare pull Gwen into that alcove and tell her anything new. Instead, they kept walking, and Mae acted just like business as usual.

As they came to the room with the strange blue portal, Mae jiggled the handle a few times with a curious look. "Strange. The room is locked."

They stood in front of the door while Mae pulled out her communicator, making a few transmissions. Gwen waited in silence, glancing at the hall decorations while listening to Mae's calls intently.

After several communications, Mae turned to Gwen. "There was some confusion. The master isn't feeling well today but still wants to see you. It's why no one is here to meet us."

"Then we wait here?" Gwen asked.

"Yes. Master Radgu will be here shortly."

"The blue magical guy?" Gwen asked.

Mae nodded. "Yes, that's him. He's in charge of Master Jihyun's security. Only he is able to bring people to see Jihyun."

"But why? Is Jihyun far away?"

Mae's face stilled as she turned away. "We shouldn't be speaking of this."

Gwen frowned. Of course she couldn't speak of it. *Why can't I be a mind-reader like Geeta? That way I could at least get some freaking answers!*

They waited a few more moments, then the door made a clicking sound. Gwen turned her attention toward the door, seeing the strange man Radgu in the doorway.

"The portal is ready for her," he said to Mae. It was as if Gwen was invisible.

Mae turned to Gwen. "Go on."

Gwen glanced at the blue-gifted man, then back at Mae. The blue guy made her feel on edge. "You aren't coming?" she asked.

"No, Lady Gwen. I am only allowed if His Majesty the King allows it," she replied as she gestured to the door. "Go on. The master is expecting you."

Gwen turned away from Mae, then followed the man into the portal room, closing the door behind them. Gwen glanced back at the shut door, then, daringly, she looked straight into his eyes. The portal magic was the same within his eyes, glowing a vibrant blue, swirling.

"Get in the portal," he stated firmly.

Without hesitation, Gwen darted into the portal, allowing the color to overtake her body. As the blue magic washed away, Gwen noticed that this time, the portal made her appear in a different place.

At first, all she saw was bright light, so bright that she couldn't see anything. Gwen stood in the same place, unmoved, blinking a few times. As she focused, Gwen realized she was in a bedroom.

She blinked again as tears ran down her cheeks. The light was too intense. As her eyes adjusted, she noticed another light; it had a yellowish-green hue to it. Spherical, almost like a glowing magical ball.

Inside the magical dome, Gwen saw Jihyun's outline and a man next to him. The light swirled around Jihyun, getting brighter each second.

As if it wasn't bright enough in here…

Then with a soft gesture from the man next to Jihyun, the light flecked with green sparkles, settling into Jihyun's body. The power softly faded away until the room returned to normal. If one considered every light in the room *normal*.

"It worked!" Jihyun exclaimed. "I feel better already! Thanks, Vihaan!"

The man was the creepy weirdo that she did *not* like.

Vihaan smiled at Jihyun, then turned and saw Gwen. "Good. I'm so glad you feel better now. And just in time too, as it seems your new friend has arrived."

"Gwen!" Jihyun said happily, noticing her. "You're here! Finally!" He sat up in his bed with much pep and enthusiasm.

"Finally?" Gwen said.

"I've been waiting all morning!"

"I heard that you weren't feeling well," Gwen said.

"I will leave you be now to play with your new friend, Master Jihyun. I have much work to do," Vihaan said, bowing.

Jihyun waved. "Bye, Vihaan! See you soon!"

"Goodbye, Master."

He walked toward Gwen, staring at her, his strange golden eyes giving her a sense of alarm and unease, sending a shiver down her spine. It made her want to run out of the room.

Vihaan walked into the portal that she had arrived in, and it disappeared behind him.

There goes any sort of escape, she thought.

"Gwen, come on! Sit next to me while I eat my breakfast," Jihyun said with his mouth stuffed as he gobbled more food off a bed tray.

"Sure." Gwen walked over to him, then sat down, trying not to wobble the breakfast tray. Another bright light was in her view. "What's with all the bright lights in your room?"

Jihyun spoke through buttered toast. "I get scared sometimes, so I turn on all the lights."

Gwen made a face, then frowned. There had to be a hundred lights at least. "You feel safer with them on?"

"Kind of." He shrugged as he took a large bite of a muffin. "Last night I was scared, so I turned them all on and fell asleep."

Gwen remembered what Mae had told her in confidence. She darted her eyes around the room, not seeing any cameras, leaning in. "Are you having nightmares?" Gwen whispered.

He shrugged. "I always have nightmares. I feel sick after I wake up, so they need to give me medicine."

"Medicine? What kind of medicine?"

"I don't know," Jihyun said. "Bryce just gives it to me, and I feel better. They tell me that I have a genetic condition. I'm missing enzymes."

"What does that even mean?"

"I heard Bryce say a few times to others that I have some sort of genetic metabolic disorder…other times I heard them say I have low-active enzymes… whatever that means." Jihyun shrugged, then offered Gwen a muffin. "Vihaan makes me feel better when I am really sick," he continued.

Somehow, Gwen highly doubted that the yellow-gifted creep made him feel better.

Jihyun turned away, eating more of his food, offering her a donut. "Here, Gwen, these are my favorite! They have chocolate sprinkles on them!"

"I better not," Gwen said, thinking of the sticky roll she'd scarfed down earlier. "I have to maintain my figure." She eyed him. "Why are you always eating junk?"

"Junk?"

"Muffins. Cereal. Chips. Don't you eat any fruits or vegetables?"

"Most of them make me sick."

Gwen raised her eyebrow doubtfully. "Really." It was more of a statement than a question.

"Uh-huh. It's a part of my condition. Why won't you eat, Gwen? You don't need to lose weight." Jihyun took a big bite of the donut. Pink frosting with chocolate sprinkles smeared his face as he chewed. His round cheeks made it extra cute.

Gwen sighed. *Good question.* "I like a boy. When you get older, you will understand." Not that she would be able to impress Garrett beyond a friendship level.

His face turned serious. "You can't like other boys!"

Gwen smirked. "Why's that?"

"Because I'm going to marry you when I get older. If you marry someone else, then it means that I can't marry you."

Gwen chuckled. "You're a kid. You shouldn't even be thinking about that kind of thing anyways. Not until you are at least thirteen."

"It's not funny, Gwen!"

Suddenly, Jihyun's eyes flickered a deep glowing red. Seconds later, a low rumbling came from beneath them. Red energy started to emit from Jihyun's body as the ground shook harder.

It was his magic, just as it was out in the wasteland. It was triggered by anger.

"I'm sorry, Jihyun," Gwen said quickly. "I thought you were telling a joke! Really! I didn't think little…I mean…boys at eight thought about that kind of thing," she said quickly, trying to defuse the situation.

As the words left her lips, she paused. It was a similar situation to her and Garrett, but in the opposite direction. She was almost ten years older than Jihyun; he was just a boy. A brother to her.

Is this how Garrett sees me? Like a little kid, just as I see Jihyun?

Jihyun's face relaxed at her words. The shaking grounded to a halt, and the red energy evaporated. He smiled at her, then chuckled. "You thought it was a joke? I didn't think you were joking!" He started laughing again. "Sorry, Gwen. We should play more games!" He took another huge bite of his donut, then wiped his face quickly, jumping out of bed. He was still wearing his pajamas, not caring. "I got really far into the game. You gotta see the new zone!"

"Sure, I guess," Gwen said, wiping the nervous sweat from her forehead.

Is this why they try to pacify him? Make him happy so he doesn't blow up the palace? It was something to consider.

She followed him out of his room and out into a dark hall. Gwen was making notes once again, trying to ingrain the directions and layout of her surroundings. There were no doors, no strange markings. The only thing decorating the halls were light fixtures every couple of feet.

"Are we in the palace?" Gwen asked.

"No," Jihyun answered. He was uninterested in the subject. But she was.

"Are we even in Olympia?"

Jihyun suddenly giggled. "Of course! Why wouldn't we be?"

"I just thought, if you were the King's son, that you would be at the palace. But since you aren't, I wasn't sure." She held a straight face, waiting to see what he would say.

Jihyun looked sad all of a sudden. "I don't know why I don't live at the palace. Father says someday I will." He looked up at her. "I just have to live in this special lab a few more years."

"Lab?" Gwen eyed the halls. "Doesn't look like much of a lab to me."

"How do you know what labs look like?" he said defensively.

"Because my parents worked in a lab pretty much all their lives." Gwen paused. "And the fact that they froze my dad's body in a lab, withholding him in a lab, etcetera etcetera…" Gwen gritted her teeth. She hated thinking about it.

"Oh," he said as they walked farther down the hall. "Well, this part of the lab is my living quarters. It's built and designed just for me!" he said proudly.

Gwen smiled back as if she thought it was cool, but inside her heart sank to her stomach. It was hard to not feel for the boy. His life was just…sad.

The long hall finally ended with a few doors. Jihyun excitedly whipped the left door open, revealing the video game room she had been to before, then sprinted inside.

As Gwen entered, she saw that Jihyun was already hooked into the system, with his VR goggles on. "I'm getting the game loaded. Oh, it's on now! Can you see the screen?" he said excitedly.

"I can see it," Gwen said, glancing at the monitor. "I'm just going to relax and watch you, if that's okay." She sat down on a chair.

"Okay." He became focused on his game as Gwen watched the gaming avatar run through the world, battling enemies. Occasionally, Jihyun swung wildly with his power glove, doing motions that any kid would do.

She kept thinking about his supposed genetic condition. It wasn't like she was foreign to science; she grew up around her mom of all people. Plus, she was pretty skilled at computers and programming. But really, what kind of genetic condition made him sick from eating vegetables? Sounded pretty far-fetched.

"Hey, do you have a library around here?" Gwen said.

"Why?" he said, still focused on his game.

"I want to read."

Jihyun slid up his goggles, then looked at her curiously. "There is a library."

"Great! Can you ask that guy with the blue magic to take us there?"

"It's right here!" Jihyun giggled.

Gwen glanced around at the empty room. "Here?"

Jihyun slid his goggles back on, then quit his game. All of a sudden, tons of VR computer menus popped up in the air. After many clicks through the menus, suddenly she was surrounded by books. Virtual books.

"Oh my gosh..." Gwen said, standing up. She walked over to the holographic books; they were crystal clear. She could see the spines clearly, reading each title. She whipped her head in Jihyun's direction. "I didn't know you could do that!" she said, amazed.

"They gave me access to this library in case I got bored of games. But I never get bored." He shrugged.

"You...you have access? Like *internet* access?"

"Of course. But it's only good for the library and a few other apps, like my games."

She was finally getting somewhere.

"Can I try and read one?"

"I'll give you my headset. I'm hungry, so I'm going back to the snack room while you use them," he said, handing them to her.

"You're hungry? Again? Didn't you just eat?"

"Yeah, but I'm still hungry."

She blinked as she grabbed the goggles from him. Jihyun ran to the next room, closing the door, leaving her alone. He usually took about twenty minutes to eat and pee. Now was her chance.

Maybe I can hack into the net and contact Mom! Or better yet, Arcadia's palace.

She would prefer to send a message to her mom. But the smarter thing was to contact the palace, because if she could, Geeta could kick some serious butt if she knew where she was.

Gwen quickly slipped on the goggles. Instantly, she was overwhelmed by how many menus were open.

Jihyun must've forgotten to close them. It was fine though; she knew computers and programming like no one else her age, or even people twice her age. She was one of the best in the camp, and those hackers had been hacking since she was born.

Immediately, Gwen tried to access the mainframe, worming her way into their systems to bypass the codes. She needed to get out of their intranet and into the actual internet. But the system was locked tight, and no amount of hacking of her level would break it, unless she had more time.

Drat.

However, some menus were still open, so she decided to at least go through the libraries.

Genetic Metabolic Disorder.

Gwen started digging through some of the genetic files and books. Menu after menu, scrolling until she came across anything that seemed remotely on the same subject.

One generic article popped up about inherited metabolic disorders. She started reading.

Inherited metabolic disorders are defined by a missing or low-active enzyme. In the absence of an enzyme, it causes toxic chemicals to build up in the host's body. The inherited disorder comes from two defective copies of the gene, each one from a parent...

Hmmm...

She skimmed the rest of the article, then continued her search. She kept scrolling until she came to some strange files with numbers. Randomly clicking on several of the folders, she noticed that some of them had names. Names of people.

Gwen glanced over at the door, noticing that Jihyun was still eating. Quickly turning back to the files, she opened the files. Then paused.

Genetic sequencing patient number 8096: Lee, Jihyun.

Without hesitation, Gwen opened the file. Before her was a long list of numbers, with marks for variants, stars, and hashtags. In a strange way, it resembled computer coding, only these were genetic numbers for the body. Human coding.

I might be able to understand this if I could cross-reference these numbers.

She came across two genetic markers that had stars.

Are these his enzymes?

Quickly, Gwen slid off the goggles, looking around wildly for something to write on. She quickly combed the room, seeing nothing she could use. An idea came to her suddenly. Running back to the sofa, she stuck her hand in between the cushions. The trick worked, as there was a pen that had fallen out of someone's pockets at some point at the bottom.

Running back to the goggles, she slid them back on, then memorized the first numbers. Looking around from under the bottom of the goggles, no one was there. She pulled up her long sleeve, then quickly wrote the first number on the inside of her arm. Then she did the same with the second, then slid down the sleeve.

She exited out of the file, then went back to the menus, closing down a few extra, then began scanning the library. Jihyun wasn't around, so she quickly went to the science section, under genetics.

A pop-up window came up, asking her what kind of book she wanted. Gwen looked at the first number, then typed it in. A list generated in front of her, and she selected the first book.

The book auto-highlighted what she typed in, and Gwen turned to the page. It gave some boring information about an enzyme, but she figured that she might as well read it.

This isn't anything like the internet search function. She sighed.

She found an article about the genetic marker, then started reading.

The CYP2A6 gene is a part of the group of P450 genes on the chromosome 19q...

Gwen groaned. Science journals were so dry.

As she read the medical journal, she came upon an interesting insert.

The CYP2A6 gene is responsible for metabolizing many of the common drugs, especially Codeine and Tramadol. With a low-active CYP2A6 gene, drugs cannot be broken down correctly and thus have serious side effects, including coma and/or death. In these cases, the effects of the unmetabolized drug would circulate through one's bloodstream, thus prolonging the side effects from weeks to sometimes months, depending on the individual. If a drug that relies on the gene to metabolize it, the person with the low-acting enzyme would experience all the listed side effects in potent forms. For instance, if the drug has a side effect of mental hallucinations, then the user would be guaranteed to feel this effect.

Gwen stopped. If Jihyun was missing this enzyme along with one other, then what drugs was that man Bryce giving this kid to make him feel better?

Her thoughts suddenly went to the battle in the wastelands. *Jihyun was completely insane out there and says he doesn't remember any of it…*

She froze.

What if Olympia is drugging him? Giving him medicines that his body can't handle? She frowned. To make him do all those terrible things when they want him to? What if the drugs make him forget what he was doing? Like one of those date-rape drugs, but they are using it for different purposes?

What if the video games were a way for him to focus his powers? Drugging him with medicines or substances that his body couldn't handle, then sticking a game in front of his face? It was already the boy's obsession to play games, and it seemed whenever he got upset, they stuck him in front of a game to calm him down. Anger was the key that unlocked his magic…

She recalled the man named Bryce climbing the communications tower…

I wonder what he was seeing in his VR goggles in the wastelands?

There was a tingling in her stomach as her heart raced. She had a feeling that there was more to Jihyun than even he knew about himself.

Quickly, she logged out of the book, then quickly went to the teen romance section, picking a book at random.

She started reading about some stupid emo girl that acted dumb around a guy. Like all the dumb girls in her school back in Arcadia. All they cared about was their makeup, hair, clothes, and being skinny for all the boys. At least she knew how to program a computer and shoot a gun. Even ride a dirt bike.

Dumb, stupid prissy girls.

There was a noise, then the pitter-patter of footsteps.

"What'cha reading?" Jihyun asked from behind.

Pretending to stretch, Gwen said, "Some silly book."

"Silly? How's it silly?"

"It's about a girl liking a boy, and he doesn't like her," Gwen continued. *Sounds like my life*, she thought bitterly.

"It does sound silly." Jihyun nodded. "Let's play our new game."

"That's a good idea. This book was boring anyways."

CHAPTER 37

◆

RED

"Kyle," Emerald's soft voice called out to him.

"Mmm." He couldn't move his face off the fucking pillow. His body wouldn't allow it.

"Kyle," Emerald said again, lightly shaking his body.

"Mmm." His mouth wouldn't work. Had he been hit by a fucking transport? Sure as hell felt like it.

"I'm going to go to breakfast."

Breakfast. That sounded fucking amazing. If only he could move his body off the damn bed.

"Mmm."

"I'll let you sleep. You seem tired," Emerald continued.

"Nnnnnn."

"What was that?"

"Nnnnnn."

Fuck. His head was spinning. He couldn't remember how he gotten to the palace. In fact, he couldn't remember much of anything.

What the fuck is going on?

"Kyle, I'm worried about you," Emerald said softly.

If only I could move my body.

With everything he had, Kyle managed to move his upper torso, but only an inch. He felt Emerald's cold hands on his hot body, giving him a shock. He attempted to move again, this time with Emerald's help, moving to a sitting position. His head was fucking killing him. God, he felt woozy as fuck. He suddenly plummeted back into the bed, his face sinking into the pillows.

"Oh hell…" he muttered in the pillows.

"Kyle?" came Em's muffled voice.

Struggling with all his might, Kyle managed to lift himself out of the pillows. Emerald's face neared his, forcing him to make eye contact.

"Are you sick?" she asked with deep concern.

"How did I get here?" Kyle asked.

Emerald looked confused. "The palace transport."

The concert. He couldn't remember anything about the concert…

Suddenly, a surge of energy ran through him, and his eyes shot open.

"Em, did the concert even happen?" Kyle asked quickly.

Emerald looked lost. "Kyle, are you okay? Of course the concert happened. Everyone loved you. Especially when you sang…the encore," she said, hesitating.

Kyle caught a strange expression on her face for a quick moment.

His mouth dropped open. "Encore?" Kyle said.

Emerald raised her eyebrow, then bit her lip. "You…don't remember singing the encore?"

"No."

Her eyes lowered. "You had me come out on stage, remember? You serenaded me in front of the entire audience." Her cheeks turned flush.

Kyle stared blankly at her. "Is this a joke, Em?"

"Joke!" cawed Zaphod, flapping over to him. "Joke!"

"God, you too?" Kyle snapped at the bird.

Emerald leaned in. "You really don't remember?"

"No."

She studied him curiously.

"All I remember is getting there and being backstage," Kyle continued, then paused. He did recall the floors bending every which way, but that didn't count.

She appeared hurt, glancing down at the floor. Kyle could tell she was trying to hold back tears.

Holy fuck, what the hell is going on? Kyle grabbed her hand, holding it. "Em…I…Did I do something to you? What did I do?" he asked desperately.

"Kyle, I loved that you showered me with attention in front of everyone," she began. "But that song, it was rather personal."

"Song?"

"Our song. You sang it to the entire audience for the encore with me on stage," she whispered. "I…I love your passion, but it was meant for us." She bit her lip, fighting back tears. "For me. Not the audience. Not those… screaming fans."

Motherfucker!

Kyle hugged her quickly, then looked into her eyes. "Em…I swear to God I didn't know I did that. I don't even know what the fuck happened. I don't remember anything about the encore!"

Why the *fuck* couldn't he remember anything?

It was like fucking magic, because in that moment he answered his own question and realized what was going on.

"Oh my fucking god!" Kyle screamed as he shot up to his feet in anger.

Surprised, Emerald leaned back.

His heart pounded in his chest with rage. "You gotta be fucking kidding me! That motherfucker! I'm gonna strangle the shit out of him!" Kyle said, getting up and storming around a few steps. His legs felt like jelly, giving out, sending him tumbling right back into bed.

"Kyle?" Emerald asked quickly, shaking his arm. "Are you okay? Should I call the palace physician?"

Zaphod cawed again, peering down at Kyle.

"Yes. Because that fucker Diego is gonna need it once I'm done with him!" Kyle snarled.

"What?"

"He fucking roofied me!"

"Roofied?"

"Drugged me. I can fucking guarantee he slipped some sort of shit in that flask. Hell. It has to be. It's why I don't remember shit."

Emerald looked hesitant. "Would Diego really do that to his best friend?"

"Yes, he would, to fuck with people that pissed him off." His face darkened. "That fucker."

"I didn't know you'd pissed him off," she began. "When did this happen?"

"When I went to visit him earlier in the day."

"So that's what you didn't tell me in the shower," Emerald said, lowering her eyes.

Kyle noticed her blank face. "I didn't want to ruin the moment."

"But why didn't you tell me? About making him upset?"

Because it was about you…

"I just didn't think it was a big deal at the time."

"Apparently it is a big deal," she said softly, tears forming. "Because whatever happened resulted in this."

Kyle's heart sank as he grabbed her hands, holding them to his chest. "Em, I swear that I had no idea that I sang that song. I would have used better judgment, had I had any. I would never do anything to fuck things up between us. I swear on my life and love that he drugged me. I swear to god that I don't know what I did!" *That fucking asshole is gonna get his ass handed to him.*

Emerald pressed her hands on his chest, blinked back her tears, and breathed. "I believe you. About the song, though it was between us…there is nothing that can be done about it now."

You can say that again. A sudden thought hit him. "Em, maybe we could view it as part of our public declaration that we're together. A turning point, you might say. A new beginning. You and I…the world knows. So why not stand by what was accidentally done on stage? We can even get Joe to make a statement for the broadcasts. Make him actually useful for once. That's what people pay him to do."

Her face hinted at a smile. "Isn't that what you wanted? To be a public couple?"

Kyle smiled sheepishly, rubbing the back of his neck. "Well, yes, though I didn't want it to come out like this. But what the hell, let's ride this out. I mean, people are saying shit anyways about us, so why not embrace what happened?" In the back of his mind, all he could think about was fucking punching that motherfucker Diego.

Emerald kissed his cheek, making him feel slightly better. She sucked in her breath, saying, "The one thing I don't understand is why he would do that to you. What did you say to upset him?"

Kyle thought back to their spat. He couldn't tell her that Diego was making fun of him being at the palace…

"He and I kind of got into it at his place," Kyle said. "He wanted to snort a line, and I didn't. He gave me shit."

Emerald looked taken aback. "He's using drugs?" she said with a great hint of naivety.

Kyle sighed. "Yeah, he's back on the transport." Her face looked confused, so he added, "It's a saying. It means that person is back to using again."

"Oh." She sighed, lowering her eyes.

"That's what a lot of people do in the lower levels, Em," Kyle said.

She remained silent. Goddamn, he needed a smoke. His head hurt from thinking about it.

Kyle broke the silence. "Honestly, he's been an ass to me ever since I've been back in Arcadia, and I pointed that fact out to him. He didn't like me saying so, so he decided to be a fucking dick." Kyle paused, thinking about the lost time. "I'm going to set things straight with him."

"Kyle, don't do anything that will jeopardize your career," Emerald said quietly.

"Oh, don't worry, Em. I won't," Kyle promised. *That fucker is gonna get what's coming to him.*

She breathed a sigh of relief. "Well, don't go after him now. You said you wanted to go get a motorcycle today." Her face softened, making all his problems disappear. "I have no prior engagements."

"Good." He smiled. Kyle noticed Emerald biting her lip. "What are you hiding?"

She giggled, then said, "Tomorrow evening, there will be a big palace event. Since everybody knows about us, I want you to be my escort."

"You thought I wouldn't wanna go to a fancy event, didn't you?" Kyle joked as he nudged her.

"Was I mistaken?"

Kyle laughed. "You're right about that." He kissed her lips. "But I'll do whatever."

Emerald giggled again. "Good."

Pain shot through his head, making him flinch.

"Are you sure you want to go look at motorcycles today? You seem like you should rest," Emerald said, touching him gently.

He gazed up at Emerald, their eyes meeting. Her words were like cool waters, soothing to his fiery soul. "I'm sure, Em," he said, with a smile. "I just love you."

She flushed, then gave him the biggest embrace. "I love you too."

◆ ◆ ◆

Never had Kyle seen so many expensive bikes all in one place. The latest models lined the shop halls, displays, and showroom floor. From shiny chrome finishes to different colors of lacquered paint, engines with custom motors…it was a wet dream come true.

"How about this one?" Emerald asked, pointing to a high-end air bike.

"I'm looking for a street bike, Em."

"That isn't one?"

Kyle inwardly laughed at her naive cuteness. "Naw. That's for the air." Kyle glanced over to the far end of the showroom, seeing a few street bikes. He motioned to her. "Over there."

The two of them walked back toward the street bike section. Most of the shop focused on air bikes, which were popular with the mid to upper levels. Not that they could ride them in Arcadia's airspace—only designated transports were allowed. No, the air riders had to go to special bike arenas designated for that.

As they walked across the showroom floor, Kyle became acutely aware of being on the upper levels as they passed by customers. It felt uncomfortable being in the upper levels shopping for a street bike. There were a few raised eyebrows and stares at him, but he continued just as he normally would with any upper-level asshole: ignore them.

As Kyle hovered over each bike, taking a hard look at them, he couldn't help but be happy. Street bikes were like music to his ears. He couldn't get enough of taking it all in.

Then in one of the corners, he found it. The bike he had to have.

Kyle quickly walked over to the motorcycle, running his hands across it. It had all the shit he could ever dream of having. Not only that, it was his style. Yes. He had to have this bike.

"Can I help you, sir?" a salesman asked from behind, startling him.

"Geez, you scared me," Kyle said. Emerald hinted a smile at the salesman as Kyle continued. "I want this bike," he said, gesturing to the bike.

As he met the salesman's eyes, he could see exactly what all the upper-level assholes thought. The asshole was downsizing him.

"All right," the salesman said, eyeing him suspiciously. "Would you like to know the price on it?"

"No. I just want to buy it."

The salesman paused again, glancing at his outfit. "I will gather the final total for you."

Judgmental asshole. "I don't care about that," Kyle said.

"Wouldn't you like to know how much you are being charged, sir?" the salesman pressed. "Just in case…"

"Just in case *what*?"

The salesman looked flustered, turning red. "I just thought you…"

Kyle neared his face, then lowered his voice with rage. "You think I can't afford it, don't you?" he snarled.

Kyle felt Emerald's hand on his. "Kyle," she said uncomfortably.

"Don't *you*?" Kyle said to the salesman, ignoring Emerald.

The salesman turned beet red.

"Well, fuck you!" Kyle shouted.

"Kyle…"

"This is some bullshit!" Kyle threw his hands up in the air.

"Let's just go somewhere else, okay?" Emerald said, trying to defuse the situation.

"No, Em! This is wrong as fuck!" Kyle shouted for the entire store to hear.

Suddenly, the manager appeared behind the salesman. "What seems to be the matter here?" he asked.

"What seems to be the matter is that your asshole salesman is fucking snubbing me, that's what," Kyle spat.

The manager eyed him up and down. "Is that so?"

"Kyle…" Emerald said with a nervous voice, yanking his hand.

Kyle turned to her. "No, Em. These fucking pricks need to be schooled, hard."

"Sir, I will have to ask you to leave," the manager stated.

As the words left the manager's lips, Kyle became even more infuriated. "Why? Because you all assume that I have no money?"

The manager snorted.

"Fucking newsflash," Kyle said in dramatic fashion, gesturing with his ringed fingers. "I have a shitload of cash ready to drop. In fact, I have so much I could buy this entire shop and fire your asses!"

"Sir, I am going to have to call security…"

"To escort the Queen and her companion out of your shop? That's fucking low."

The manager and the salesman's faces dropped, quickly darting their eyes to Emerald. Kyle could tell they were trying to see if he was bullshitting them, studying her features.

"We don't have to do this, Kyle," Emerald said softly.

"No, we really do, Em." He turned to them. "You wanna call the palace to verify that this is the Queen standing before you? Because we can." He threw his ID, hitting the manager square in the face. It fell to the ground. "That's my ID, in case you wanna check who the hell I am."

The salesman picked up the ID, his eyes wide.

"Yeah, buddy. You see that shit?" Kyle shouted. "That's me, asshole."

"It's Kyle Trancer. He's the lead singer of Disorderly Conduct," the salesman said, turning even redder.

"Fucking got that right. The Queen doesn't have ID, because royalty doesn't need it."

The manager and salesman both fell to their feet, bowing to Emerald. "Your Majesty…"

"Get your fucking chodes off the fucking floor."

Emerald was embarrassed, turning red as her gaze lowered to the polished floors.

"Your Majesty. Kyle Trancer. We are deeply sorry about this situation," said the manager, along with the salesman.

Kyle interjected. "You should be. Fucking judging me like that. The fuck is wrong with you people?" he spat.

"Please accept our apologies by allowing us to gift you the bike. No charge," the manager said.

He could just take the bike. But fucking A! He'd worked for the bike…only to have assholes treat him like shit, then smooth things over by "giving" him a bike? Fuck that.

"I don't want your bike, even if it's free," Kyle snapped. "I earned my money, and it will feel a hell of a lot better riding a bike that I paid for!" He turned to Emerald. "Let's get out of here."

"Sir, please accept our sincere apologies! The bike is yours," the manager begged.

Kyle snorted. "You can take that bike and that attitude of yours and shove it up your ass. Now give me back my ID!"

He quickly handed it back, and Kyle yanked it from his hands. "Come on, Em, let's blow this joint."

Emerald grabbed his hand quietly, embarrassment in her cheeks as they walked out of the showroom, everyone looking at them. He was sure as shit this would be on the broadcasts tonight. Well, fucking good. Show all the assholes that they can't treat people like shit.

They exited the shop, coming onto the upper-level platform, seeing the entire city through the skyways. They walked in silence as Kyle fumed. Through the corner of his eye, Emerald's face was downcast. She looked pretty shaken up by the ordeal.

When he couldn't take any more silence, Kyle stopped and turned to her.

"Hey, I'm sorry I embarrassed you," he said.

Emerald took a moment to respond, still focused on the ground. That wasn't a good sign.

"Please don't tell me that you think those assholes were in the right," Kyle said, getting angry.

Emerald sighed deeply, then finally glanced up at him. "Kyle. You were right in what you said. They treated you wrongly. However." She paused. "You need to control your anger."

Her words just made him more angry. "But you see my point?"

Emerald's eyes darted to his. "Of course I do!" she managed. "But to go off on them? If you are going to be seen with me—as the Queen—you *must* control your temper. I have a lot of business with the upper levels to ensure this kingdom runs as smoothly as possible. If I have disruptions within the city sectors, it could lead to more issues within the levels." She shot him a hard glance. "Like the taxes you so hate."

Her statement was a dig at him, making his blood boil. As much as he wanted to argue with her, Kyle held his tongue. It was Em, and he didn't want to fuck things up with her, especially after this morning's episode. But did that mean that he should he have to play nice when others treated him like shit?

God, no! It pissed him off! But knowing that he'd already upset her with the song, and now this…he had to consider her well-being, especially with her being pregnant.

Kyle took a deep breath, trying to release his anger. "You're right. I was wrong to make a scene. I won't do it again," he said. He glanced down at her belly, placing his hands on her tummy. "I don't want to stress you or them out," he managed.

Kyle could have sworn that her tummy looked even larger than the day before.

Emerald's face released its tension. "Thank you," she said with a genuine smile.

It's still fucking bullshit!

Kyle offered his hand to her, which she accepted with a shy smile. They began to walk again through the city, admiring the view. The sun's beams shone brightly across the city. He had to admit, the city in the upper levels had its own beauty to it.

"You didn't get your motorcycle," Emerald said as they continued to walk.

"It can wait. You being happy is the most important thing on my agenda," Kyle said.

He turned to her as she gave him a smile. He leaned in, then kissed her. Within that kiss, he felt her love and her forgiveness.

As their lips parted, Emerald smiled and tickled his side. "You're so sweet."

"Sweet? Me?" Kyle chuckled. "I was beginning to think you thought me an asshole."

Emerald giggled, then slapped him on the butt.

"Come on. Let's go find you a bike," Emerald said, yanking his hand.

"You don't have to tell me twice."

CHAPTER 38

✦

ORANGE

Telly could barely manage to keep her eyes open as the machine mixed the vials. She hadn't had a full night's sleep since her daughter was kidnapped and Drew had been hanging on by a thread. She was sure that she had slept, but how much, she couldn't say. Telly felt guilty for even trying to sleep, sickened at the thought.

A beep came from the machine. More were finished. Her head perked up at the noise, and she grabbed several of the vials. It was time to test them out in the wastelands with her weapon. She had improved the formula and wanted to see the results. Telly's body, however, screamed with exhaustion.

Pocketing the vials, Telly glanced over at Drew on his makeshift bed. Just like back in Lab 34 at the Corporation, Drew remained inanimate in his trancelike state.

Telly heaved a sorrowful sigh, then walked over to him, sitting on the edge of the bed. Wistfully, Telly ran her fingers over the flesh of his cheeks, to the sockets of his eyes, meeting his cybernetic eye.

"Drew...I—I'm doing everything I can. I hate to admit it, but this time... it's proving to be difficult," Telly whispered.

Fighting back tears, Telly stared at him. He was at peace. She wasn't sure what compelled her to do so, but she climbed into the bed. She wanted that same peace.

As she settled in next to him, Telly was cautious not to bump any bad circuitry or roll over wires that were essential. In reality, there was hardly any room for her, but she didn't care. Just being next to Drew put her mind slightly at ease.

"Garrett has been working hard on a program to find Gwen. As much as I am angry at him, I am indebted to his efforts to find our daughter," she confessed to him.

Drew remained still.

"Reila called about the camp being encased in a mountain," she continued. "According to Xeon's readings, there is orange magic in that mountain. I don't suppose you had anything to do with it, did you?" Telly glanced at Drew, then blinked back her tears as his face stared into oblivion. "Well, I'm going to go back and try to transmute the mountain. I probably won't be able to, considering I don't have power like you do. But I will try. The camp needs their home back. You too, when the time comes."

Telly rolled over to face him on the bed. Her hand softly brushed his skin where there weren't any mechanical parts. Just his soft, pale skin mixed with an old scar from his childhood. A scar that had bothered him before he became a cyborg. Her fingertips traced the scar, remembering the story of how he had been climbing playground equipment as a young boy. He slipped, landing hard on the ground, injuring himself on a piece of equipment. Drew had always been embarrassed by the scar, never wanting to take off his shirt in public. She could never understand why, considering the scar looked so minute to her. As a cyborg, he hardly wore any sort of shirt due to the cybernetic components sticking out of his body. Wearing practically nothing made it much easier to move.

Telly heaved a deep sigh. Just thinking about old memories hurt. Her soul felt like it had been dismembered with Gwen gone and Drew lying in this state.

"I'm so tired, Drew," Telly continued, her heart heavy. "I feel so guilty sleeping when our daughter is out there alone. Who knows what she is going through at the moment..." Her throat went tight. "I want Gwen back. I want you back. I just want us back together again...as a family."

Telly glanced at Drew once more; he remained unchanged.

She sighed, then laid her head on his chest, breathing with the sound of his heart.

"Goodnight," she whispered as she closed her eyes.

She didn't know why, but suddenly, the thought of Jonathan's words came to her mind once again.

Have you considered reading The Spectrum?

Telly rolled over, then whispered to the thin air, "I know for certain that magic exists. But I don't know if *you* exist. But if you do…please let my daughter return to me safely and let my love reawaken once more."

She remained deathly silent after her first-ever prayer, not knowing what to expect.

The only replies were the hums of the machines hooked up to Drew, with their everlasting white noise.

Disappointed, Telly nuzzled her head into Drew's chest and dozed off.

She awoke stiff and sore, confused at what time it was. Telly rubbed the sleep from her eyes, then looked at Drew, giving him a soft kiss on his cheek. Her eyes still felt heavy, swollen, and puffy. Her head pounded something awful, and her joints ached.

Telly slipped out of bed, managing not to kink any wires in the process. After popping a pill for her headache, she downed a bottle of water and a cup of instant coffee, then threw on her jacket and scarf. As she walked over to her workstation, she heard Scion's unique footsteps from behind her.

"I'm going out for a bit. Could you watch Drew?"

"Most certainly, Miss Hearly."

More footsteps scraped the rocky floor, then the cyborg sat down next to Drew. Telly noticed that he had plugged in a wire that connected to his own body to Drew's.

Telly raised her eyebrow. "What are you doing?"

"I am giving him some of my energy. It seems that his body responds well with my unique energy of 565 nanometers. Given that his own energy can accept that part of the wavelength, as his energy meets that number exactly, no lower than that."

Telly inched closer to him. "You've done this before?"

Through the darkness, Scion's eyes began to glow a golden yellow as he nodded. "I have. It seems to be one of the few things that keep him stabilized."

"Why haven't you…"

"Told you before?" Scion finished her sentence, surprising her. "Because,

Miss Hearly, you have a lot to deal with. I am doing the best I can to assist you, even if it means draining my own energy. I wasn't trying to hide the fact; you are extremely busy. I actually have done this in front of you without you noticing."

Have I been that out of it to not notice everything that has been going on? She had been crying every day, depressed, exhausted…it was no wonder she didn't see Scion doing this. If she recounted the past week or two, she hardly recalled anything that anyone had done.

Telly cleared her throat. "I'm sorry I haven't been more aware."

"No need to apologize. We have been through this before."

"I know…" she said, shuffling her feet.

"Go try and do what you can to that mountain," Scion stated. "Reila cannot stop talking about it."

Telly whirled around. "How did you know I was going there?"

"I heard you talking in your sleep a little bit ago," Scion stated. "I also heard you talking to your god."

Telly froze, dumbfounded. "I don't believe in God."

Scion made a small noise, almost resembling laughter mixed with a mechanical sound effect. "You structured your words like a prayer, Miss Hearly. If you do not believe in any sort of god, then who were you speaking to?"

"It's complicated," Telly said with finality.

Scion's eyes flashed a brighter yellow, then stared at her with confusion. "How is it complicated? You are given a power. Though you were not born with this energy, you were infused with it in your adult life. According to ancient texts that I have read through documentation, the energy comes from what some peoples refer to as the God of Light. From the sound of your words last night, it seemed that you were praying to this god, asking for help. That is a very normal response for any human. It gives one hope."

Her head hurt. Her headache medicine hadn't yet kicked in, and she just wanted to go. Rubbing her temples, Telly said, "You realize that hardly anyone believes in that ancient religion anymore, right? There is one cathedral in Arcadia for die-hards, and that's it. No one else believes in that. You sound less like a cyborg and more like a priest." She scoffed.

"That is correct," Scion said. "However, I have been researching where this power comes from. My human side needs answers, and it fights with my cybernetic side after reading answers online and spewing them out. Just like at the Olympian corporation, I sought answers, breaking rules and regulations just to find them. And now, I am still seeking answers. Upon reading about *The Spectrum* and learning where this power comes from, it all has fallen into place and makes sense to me. For when I dream, I see things that one normally cannot see. Is that not the power of the gift in 565 nanometers? Visions? Surely, these powers are derived from an ultimate being."

"You have *visions*?"

Scion remained still, deep in thought. He almost had a hint of fear flicker across his face. "I see the future. Many times, I see the future." His eyes met hers. "I can assure you, Miss Hearly, there is a higher being. Much is about to take place. The question remains: Are you ready?"

Her head was spinning. A cyborg telling her about the God of Light, the future, and being ready? What in hell was going on?

Telly adjusted her scarf, then grabbed some vials, her weapon, then hid it in her jacket. "I'm going now. Like you said, I'm going to the camp to try and get rid of that mountain. I'll be back tomorrow tonight." She glanced at him. "Twenty-four hours, tops. Send me a transmission if Drew's condition turns critical."

"Absolutely, Miss Hearly," he said. "Also, please give my regards to Miss Reila."

Telly snorted, then gave him a half smile, knowing of their secret affections. "I will."

Higher being, she thought as she walked through the refuge. It *was* the best explanation for everything…

She recalled Gwen's words back in Arcadia. *What is this? You actually bought a book?*

Have you considered reading The Spectrum? Jonathan's words echoed in her mind once again. Secretly, she had indeed acquired a hard copy of the ancient text *The Spectrum* several months back, after Jonathan told her to look into it. It was for research, she had told herself. She had read some of the text, and some of it did speak to her inside her heart. It was like she wanted to believe but the concept was unimaginable.

She passed by Garrett's quarters, seeing the glowing monitors with many points flashing in red. He was busy, typing away on the keyboard in another program that showed on a separate monitor. He was completely engrossed in his work, his face stern.

She took in the scene, then turned away.

Exiting the refuge, Telly came to a hidden area where the last few vehicles were, Telly got in one of the four-wheelers, starting the vehicle. Funneling her orange magic, she shimmered with its bright glow, then spread out the power, glazing the vehicle in her magic. The magic turned her and the vehicle invisible, and she drove off.

CHAPTER 39

✦

YELLOW

*S*cion...

Scion looked up from his tablet, startled.

There was no one there according to his readings. Telly had already left. Garrett was several caverns away—too far from him. Victor and Geeta blipped on his radar, far on the other side of the refuge.

It must be my human side that perceived a voice that did not exist. He had to admit, with the amount of work that kept Drew alive and transferring a part of his life force to him, Scion felt a shadow of himself. And after the extreme trials that he had been put through, he had been having strange visions.

"Knock-knock," Garrett called out from the doorway.

"Miss Hearly has stepped out for the time being," Scion stated.

Garrett frowned, plopping down next to Drew on the other side of the bed. "Will she be back soon? I have discovered a location in Olympia that seems promising. I told her that she would be the first to know."

"Miss Hearly stated that she would return within twenty-four hours' time," Scion said.

Scion glanced down at Drew; his readings were satisfactory. The energy that he had transferred to Drew helped stimulate new growth, cellular activity, and internal healing.

"How is he?" Garrett asked, running his hands over a cable, ensuring that it was secure in its socket, then grabbing another tablet nearby, glancing at Drew's statistics. "From the looks of it, he seems better than the last I checked."

"Affirmative. His condition has improved in his cells, organs, and tissues.

But as for his cybernetic side, he needs those parts that we requested."

Garrett sighed. "They'll be ready soon from the Corporation. At least, I have hope. Keep him in a good state until that happens." He got up from his seat. "Let Telly know that I have news about Olympia when she returns, yeah?"

"I will do so."

Scion turned his attention back to Drew as Garrett trotted off.

Scion...

"Did you say something, Mr. Garrett?" Scion called out.

But Garrett was already long gone from the room, and nothing in his scans alerted him of another presence.

Scion...

Scion jumped up from his seat, still clutching his tablet as a bright golden light flashed from behind him.

Whirling around, Scion faced the intense golden light. In its glory was an angelic figure.

The bright light became more intense, then softened to a comfortable brightness for his human eyes.

Then he was face-to-face was his dead wife. But Darcy was not dead. She was alive, robed in shimmering golds, her hair and eyes the color of the sun, and her skin glowed as though made of light itself.

Am I having another lucid vision from my energy in the wavelength of 575 nanometers? he asked himself.

Scion... Darcy's voice echoed in his mind. She smiled, full of love and light.

"Darcy? I do not understand. You are dead. I watched as those men shot you," Scion said, his voice wobbling with confusion.

I am alive, Scion. Death is another part of life, as you are discovering now with your gift.

"I am not gifted, as many refer to them as. I am only infused with a portion of the energy from a gifted subject's blood."

It seems that the gift wanted to blossom inside your life force.

Scion smiled at her, remembering fragments of his past with her. Then suddenly, Reila came into his mind. He felt...guilty.

Scion, I have come with a message. It is very important, as this message must reach another through your power.

"What do you ask of me?"

Before I return to the Realm of Light, there is one thing that I want you to know: In no way will our love ever diminish if you choose to love another. We had our time together before I left the earth. Now that I am not of this earth, do not hold back your love for that woman.

Scion paused. She knew of Reila.

Yes, Scion. I know your thoughts and your feelings deep within. Darcy smiled brightly at him. *You must focus on your current life's love and devotion. It will make you stronger.*

His heart tugged, as if a wire was stuck and someone was yanking it. But at the same time, it was a tug that felt…good and free.

"I love you, Darcy," Scion said, softer than normal.

And I, you. I know that your love for me will never fade, she said in a soothing voice. *Love that woman how you loved me. She desires your affection.*

A wave of peace flowed through his body as Darcy gave him a bright smile. Though the idea of seeing Darcy once more seemed like it should be melancholy—it was anything but. The overall sensation was a joy so great that it filled his heart with peace—and closure.

"Is it required for you to return to the Realm of Light?"

It is. We will see each other once again when you journey to the other side. Her golden eyes brightened to an almost-hot white, her hair softly flowing. Her white robes streamed in the heavenly breeze. *My time is short, and I am called to return. Here is what the God of Light asks of you…*

It was still night when Telly had arrived at the edge of the camp. Dawn was soon to come. The wastelands were painted in black, with the stars glimmering in the sky. The moon was hidden behind the clouds, trying to peek its way through the thickness of the sky's puffy contents. Even through the darkness, Telly could see the altered skyline of the transmuted mountain.

Bonfires from the camp dotted the skyline, one the biggest of them all. As she drove on the familiar road that led into the camp, Telly noticed that the road ended much sooner than it should have, probably due to the mountain. The wastelanders were at the farther rim of their normal settlement.

I hope that I can at least get them back in their dwellings again, she thought.

Her trailer too. Telly could tell that it was most definitely where the mountain was now situated.

As she pulled up, most of the camp was silent. The wastelanders had long retired from their nightly bonfires and drinking, as it was nearing the last hour of the night until sunrise. But there was one that stuck out near the main bonfire. Ryan was on guard duty, approaching her as Telly parked the four-wheeler and killed the engine.

"I didn't know you were coming," Ryan called out, relaxing from his tense position as he holstered his gun.

Telly swung off the four-wheeler. "I didn't make it known. Is Reila up?"

"Nah, she's asleep." Ryan glanced at her again. "Really, though, why are you here?" He inched near her. "Did Victor send you to try to do something about the mountain?"

"I sent myself. But yes, I hope to do something about it." She hoped so, at least. If she wouldn't be able to, she would feel ashamed. People would question what kind of gifted she was if she couldn't cast spells that others could.

Ryan smiled, then raised his hip flask. "Here's to you for helping."

"Don't toast to me yet. I'm not sure I will be able to do anything," Telly said, then scanned the silhouette of the mountain. "I just need ten minutes to rest, then I'll see what I can do."

"I'll go wake Reila," Ryan said.

"No need. Just leave me be, okay? It'll be easier on me."

"Sure thing."

Ryan disappeared into the night as Telly took a drink from her canteen. After a few minutes' rest, she turned on a flashlight and headed to the base of the mountain.

Telly didn't realize the base was farther off from where the camp was situated. Even with the flashlight, Telly stumbled over the rocks and brush. She always was a bit of a klutz, though she tried her hardest not to be in front of others. But out in the wilderness, it didn't matter much. Nothing else mattered except to have Drew alive and her daughter back.

Telly didn't even know why she'd felt compelled to leave Drew for the evening to help the camp. She reasoned that she wanted to give the wastelanders their home back. And when the time came that Drew would arise and Gwen would return to her, then they would have their home, too. It was a shred of hope she could hold on to, which made her hope more *real*.

The mountain's looming figure hung over her as Telly came to the rim. The faint pink light started painting the sky's lower portion. The sun would soon be up—and so would the camp. Knowing the camp, they would all watch, which would make her even more nervous and stressed out.

I can't let it get to that point.

She felt the side of her thigh. Her new magitech weapon was still there, secured in her holster.

Please…I need a win in my life.

Telly narrowed her focus, then closed her eyes, concentrating on her orange gift. Telly recalled the words from months ago. *You didn't fully believe,* the magic once told her.

I need to believe!

The orange magic bubbled within her core as Telly homed in on happy memories. Her first kiss with Drew…the first time they made love…her daughter…the cybernetics that she created with Drew…

I must believe!

More orange magic funneled throughout her body.

Slowly, Telly began to feel a love and joy that made her swell with delight. The power within her began to flutter with enchanted bliss, a euphoric sensation, heightening her emotions. In the back of her mind, she thought of the mountain melting into a puddle, sinking into the earth below.

Her skin was on fire, the burning coming from within. Telly snapped open her eyes, her body embodied with the full power of the orange. She couldn't see anything but her orange light, radiating from her body. Hot winds swept through her hair, her jacket and scarf fluttering in the winds.

I believe! she screamed in her mind as the magic swelled almost to bursting.

Telly jolted, releasing the magic in the form of a powerful beam of orange light.

The light beam shot into the mountain, sending Telly sliding back across the ground several feet, causing her to nearly tumble. As she slid, she grounded her feet hard to the side, scooting to a stop as she funneled more energy and power into the mountain. As her magic poured out, it slowly turning itself orange, glimmering with her energy.

Pure orange magic.

Before her eyes, the mountain was shifting slowly, receding as if a giant hand was smashing putty.

Melt away! she commanded her magic.

In the corner of her eyes, Telly saw the entire camp running up to her, watching in amazement.

Suddenly, she felt terrified.

Telly tried to block out the camp members as they cheered while she poured out more of her magic. But the more they cheered, the more she faltered.

You still hesitate, the magic whispered to her.

Telly fought hard to maintain her focus. But there was a wedge that drove her between her magic in her core.

The mountain began to flicker with orange magic to a lighter tint of orange.

Let go of your fears and fully embrace your power!

How can I let go of my fears? My daughter is gone! My love is nearly dead! These people…they think I'm great, but I'm not! I'm just an ordinary person!

Tears ran down her face as Telly struggled with the immense power shooting out of her hands. Inwardly, it was a war with her magic. The mountain shifted, reshaping, melting, then forming…

"NO!" Telly screamed.

The camp went silent. The more she struggled, the more the mountain slowed its transmutation. It was as if the harder she tried, the more it stopped listening to her commands.

Then the mountain went to its normal color, reforming itself back to its original shape.

"WHY?" Telly shouted through her tears. She flung herself around, then kicked sand.

No one said anything.

"WHY?"

Ashamed to meet anyone's gaze, Telly turned away, storming past everyone before they could get a word in. In the distance, she saw Reila. She gave her a sympathetic glance, then a sad smile.

Telly gritted her teeth through her tears as she kept running. Through the desert as the morning light grazed the sands, past the main bonfire pit, and past Ryan and the other guards, then jumping in her four-wheeler, driving away like a madwoman.

The wind kissed her tears as she rode, but it wasn't enough. She was ashamed, embarrassed, and felt so helpless and empty.

For just a few seconds, she had felt the entirety of the orange magic.

Why? she cried out in her mind.

Let go of your fears, was the reply.

CHAPTER 40

✦

"Gwen!"

Gwen groaned as she snuggled with her blanket. "Huh?"

"It's six o'clock!"

"A.m. or p.m.?" she mumbled.

"You really don't know what time it is?"

"Without seeing a window, I have no idea."

"It's p.m., silly!" He giggled.

"So?" Gwen mumbled again, this time tossing the entire throw over her head and flopping onto the couch.

"That means we can play the new game that is being released tonight—online! It should be uploading onto my gaming system right now!" Jihyun yelled excitedly in her ear through the blanket.

"Are you for real? Didn't you see that I was taking a nap?"

"You can't now! You don't want to miss the first hour of release! They have a special item if you log in the first hour. I want you to see it with me!" Jihyun said excitedly.

"We already played hours of games earlier this morning," Gwen muttered.

"I know!" Jihyun jumped on the couch excitedly.

"How did you get in here anyways? I thought you had to be in your quarters."

"Father gave me permission. The guards brought me here." Jihyun jumped up again, indifferent. "Let's hurry! I don't want to miss it!"

"Fine." Gwen rolled out of bed, barely managing to get slippers on. There was no sign of Mae. Gwen sighed, getting to her feet. Jihyun was standing right by her door, waving.

Ugh. She might not be able to find out anything useful if this kid kept her up 24/7.

Gwen walked out of her rooms, seeing a set of guards.

"Ready, Master Jihyun?" one of them asked.

"Yes. Let's hurry!"

The man gave him a smile that Gwen thought to be genuine, then the three of them walked down the hall, with Jihyun leading them. As they did, Jihyun zigzagged, pretending to be one of the air transports in his games. From time to time, he peeked over his shoulder, making sure they were following him.

Gwen eyed the guards. They were always watching. She glanced back, trying to memorize the layout of the hallways as she always did on her way to Jihyun's room. If she could only remember the layout, maybe there would be some chance of an escape.

The group approached the strange corridor, the one that was heavily guarded where Gwen had been prior. The portal room. They guards saluted each other, then they bowed to Jihyun, opening the door to the portal room. Gwen eyed them as she followed Jihyun inside.

Jihyun had already darted into the portal. The strange man with the glowing blue eyes stood next to the swirling pool of light, gesturing for her to enter. She glanced at him; this time, she didn't feel so threatened or scared of him. If she had to guess, he almost had a good side to him, if it weren't for him taking orders from King Bully.

You have the gift, a soft voice resonated within her. She knew it was the man that spoke to her. But it was inside her mind.

The gift? "Are you talking to me? I don't have…" Gwen fumbled with her words.

It hasn't been activated in your life force, but it resides in you. No one must find out! he warned.

"What do you mean?"

"Were you speaking to me?" he said in a strange accent, giving her a blank stare, as if he didn't know what she was talking about. But she knew she hadn't imagined it.

"Uh, I guess not."

He motioned for her to get in the portal. "The master is waiting," he said.

Gwen broke her eye contact, then stepped inside.

The blue magic faded away, and she reappeared in the halls of Jihyun's quarters, inside the lab.

"What took you so long?" Jihyun said.

Unsure of how to answer, Gwen shrugged. "I don't know."

As they walked down the hall toward the gaming rooms, Gwen kept trying to figure out what the strange guy meant. She wasn't gifted. Did he mean that she would become gifted like her parents? The thought made her excited. And who wasn't supposed to find out? That thought made her nervous.

A man was standing outside the door, waiting. Gwen had seen him before—he'd been on the moving communications tower with Jihyun out in the wastelands.

"Master Jihyun, there you are! I need to give your medicine," said the man, seeming impatient.

"Can we wait? Puh-leeeease, Bryce? I'm about to play that new game that came out today, and I need to log on now! I get a new item! But if I don't log in soon, it will expire, and I can never get it! Ever! If I'll be so sad if I don't get that…"

"Yes, yes. Let's get you that new item. I would hate to make you upset," Bryce said, bowing to him. "But after you log on and collect it, then I have to give you your medicine. Vihaan says it's necessary right away. You want to feel better, don't you?"

"Of course I do. It will only take a second," Jihyun said sweetly. He turned to Gwen. "Come on, Gwen!"

Medicine, my butt.

Jihyun darted inside the room, leaving Gwen with Bryce in the hallway. He gave her creep vibes, just like that weirdo Vihaan, but not as bad. Whatever it was, she didn't like him.

"Jihyun is sick?" Gwen said, playing dumb as she paused before entering the game room.

Bryce gave her a smug look. "You were out in the wastelands. You saw his condition for yourself."

Gwen gave an innocent shrug. "I saw. But what of it? I didn't know magic was considered a sickness."

He leaned in, then lowered his voice. "Why don't you run along, little girl, and play that new game with Master Jihyun? I am sure he is waiting for you," he said with a stern tone.

Something in his eyes set off all sorts of internal alarms, telling her everything she needed to know. If it weren't for Jihyun's attachment to her, she probably would have been in the dungeons.

"Good idea," Gwen said quickly.

"Good." He then melted his face into a pleasant expression. Bryce opened the door, then gestured for her to go inside.

Gwen darted into the game room, and the door shut behind her. She heard a lock click.

These people are terrible, she thought, frightened. She turned her attention to Jihyun, who was already wearing his cyber goggles and logging into the game.

"I'm about to get that item, Gwen!" he exclaimed, jumping up and down, not even aware of the exchange that had happened outside. "Ohhhhhh! It's being sent to my inventory now!"

All she wanted to do was cry. She hated being here. She wanted to go home.

What was she going to do? The idea of his medicine made her even more scared, especially after reading about Jihyun's condition. What kind of medicine were they going to give him?

"Gwen! See what I got?" Jihyun called out, interrupting her thoughts. "They gave me a special blaster! It's red! Dark red, like my magic! It glows when it blasts and shoots fire out everywhere! See? Look at it!" Jihyun gave a demonstration on his VR screen. "Did you see that? Did ya?"

Suddenly, Gwen felt even worse than a moment before. The kid was blind to everything that was happening around him. Olympia was doing their best to pacify the kid, just so they could take advantage of his powers. He was being used by those stupid jerks. They both needed to get out of there. But how?

Gwen casually walked over to Jihyun, smiling as she fought back her tears. She had to stay strong. "That's so cool! And it matches your magic. It was meant to be."

"This game is so cool! When I get to a save point, you'll have to try!" Jihyun said, remaining focused.

"I'd like to."

The door clicked open, and Bryce appeared. "Did you get your item, Master

Jihyun?"

"I did, Bryce! I got a blaster that's red! Do you wanna see?"

"I'll take a look after I give you your medicine. Can you save it, please?" Bryce said.

"Okay, give me one second," Jihyun said. He ran through the virtual world, coming to a glowing circle: the save point. Jihyun lifted his goggles to his forehead, pushing his ear-length fine black hair back, revealing his glowing red eyes. "Done."

"Good."

Jihyun happily hopped over to a chair and sat down. Bryce walked over next to him, sliding his hand into his pocket. Out came a syringe sealed in a plastic baggie.

Jihyun edged back into his chair, eyeing the needle as Bryce unsealed the bag. "I hate getting my shots," he said, making the biggest stink face. He slumped his head against one of his hands in protest.

"It will only take a second," Bryce said smoothly.

"I know, I know," Jihyun muttered.

Gwen watched, biting her tongue. She wanted to say something. But she knew they might hurt her too. Bryce administered the medicine, then nodded, gesturing to Jihyun. "All set."

"Can I play my game now?" Jihyun perked up, swinging his legs back and forth in the chair.

"You can play all day if you like. We aren't going anywhere today," Bryce said.

Jihyun smiled, jumping up. "Great! Did you hear that, Gwen? We can play all day again!"

Gwen groaned internally but didn't show it. Being stuck in a room with a kid that had just been injected with medicine made her on edge.

Bryce nodded to Jihyun, then flashed Gwen one last look. Definitely a *you better behave or you will regret it look*. Then he left, leaving them alone in the room.

Gwen plopped down on the couch, putting her head back. She was so tired from playing games all day with Jihyun. Too much of a good thing made it not enjoyable anymore. *I swear, after this, I'll never be able to look at another video game again.*

"Do you wanna play too?" Jihyun called out, still focused on the game.

"No, you play. I'll watch," Gwen said. "I might take that nap while you play. I'm really tired."

"Okay," Jihyun said, continuing to play as he swung his hands around wildly. He was using the power gloves, making all sorts of movements. Just watching him made her more tired.

Gwen leaned her head back on the couch, zoning out. She couldn't sleep or nap, since it was evening and she wasn't used to napping at this hour. She decided at least resting was enough.

A little time passed, and Jihyun still playing his game. Over time, something in his movements didn't seem right. He was acting lethargic.

"You okay?" Gwen called out.

"Yeahhhh," Jihyun said. "I'mmm sleeeepy."

His speech wasn't right either, slurred and slow. It reminded her of when she saw her friends' parents drunk, or when she watched the wastelanders party at their nightly bonfires from her trailer window.

Gwen sat up straight, eyeing him. "Jihyun?"

Jihyun ripped off the goggles, then stumbled over his legs, tripping to the ground.

"Jihyun?!" Gwen ran over to him as the boy lay down on the ground.

"I'mmm…soooo…hot…hot," he murmured. "I dooon't feel sooo good…"

He closed his eyes, not moving. Gwen's heart pounded hard as she placed a hand on his forehead. He was burning up. She ran over to the door.

"Open up! Something is wrong with Jihyun!" she yelled, pounding on the door. Gwen looked back at Jihyun as he lay there, his body wet with sweat.

The door opened, the guards and Bryce walking into the room.

"Something is wrong with him," Gwen said, frantically, running back to Jihyun. The boy looked worse than seconds prior, with his body entirely drenched in sweat and his breathing irregular. Gwen placed her hand on his palm. His heartbeat was erratic. "It has to be that medicine that you gave him!" she said accusingly.

"I should have given him his medicine sooner." Bryce darted murderous eyes at Gwen as he bent down next to Jihyun. "He just needs sleep," he told the guards. "Move him to his quarters, and get the girl back to her rooms."

"Did you hear me?" Gwen snapped, tears welling up in her eyes. "He's not okay, and your medicine is causing this!"

"Remove this *child* from my sight!" Bryce snarled to the guards.

Gwen's eyes went wide as the guards grabbed her by her wrists, dragging her out of the room. "What's wrong with you people? Can't you see that he isn't okay? He doesn't need sleep! You are the problem!" she screamed.

The guards put a handkerchief around her mouth, muffling her cries. Gwen tried to struggle and drag her feet, but the men were twice her size, with muscles like weightlifters that she had seen on broadcasts.

As they dragged her through the halls, Gwen tried to scream and even bite the big guard's hands, arms, anything. Her muffled cries fell on deaf ears.

Mae's warning entered her mind. *They do things to the boy,* her mind echoed. Gwen fought back tears, struggling every inch of the way as she thought about Mae's words.

They came to her rooms, with Mae opening the door, her eyes wide. The men threw her down, sending Gwen to her knees in tears. The door slammed shut.

Mae quietly walked over, kneeling beside her. She gently untied the handkerchief, waiting in silence.

Gwen blew her nose in it. Secretly, she wanted to keep the snot rag and throw it in the guard's face. Better yet, throw it in Bryce's face.

"Something happened to Jihyun," Gwen choked on her tears.

Mae's face grew concerned, then she placed a hand on Gwen's hair, gently stroking it out of her sobbing face.

Knowing that she and Mae were being watched through the cameras, Gwen said nothing more. Instead, she continued to sob while Mae remained by her side.

❖ ❖ ❖

"Master Jihyun," called out a soothing voice.

Jihyun was sleepy. Very sleepy.

"Master Jihyun."

He managed to open his eyes. The world was blurry, spinning. Strange colors appeared. It felt like bugs crawling on him…

The face. The scary triangle face appeared before him. He was blurry but still there.

Jihyun started to cry. "I'm so scared!" His body felt heavy.

"Shh. Don't be scared. I'm here."

"Vihaan? Is that you?" Through the corner of his eyes, he saw Vihaan glow a soft yellow with his magic.

"I apologize for disturbing your sleep," Vihaan said, his voice sounding muffled. "Your father has discovered malicious men outside the city twenty miles from here, ready to attack. They plan to overrun the city this very night."

"Are they bad guys?"

"Yes, bad guys. Very bad guys," he said. Vihaan sat down next to Jihyun on his bed, leaning in. "The leader is a woman with violet hair."

Jihyun scrunched up his face. "Like the woman out in the wastelands? The evil woman?"

Vihaan nodded. "Yes. The very same woman."

Jihyun paused. Gwen had been with that violet woman, and Gwen wasn't so bad. He turned to Vihaan. "How do you know she is a bad woman?"

"We intercepted a transmission," Vihaan said. "You know what a transmission is, don't you?"

"Yes, silly. What did it say?"

"They plan to attack at midnight. Your father doesn't think he has the power to fight them…"

"What will he do?" Jihyun asked with wide eyes. More bugs crawling on his skin. He itched.

"I do not know," Vihaan whispered, concerned.

"I'm scared," Jihyun said, flailing his arms around wildly.

Vihaan smiled, then put his arms around him. "Don't worry. We will do everything to protect you. We'll think of something. In the meantime, I'll give you something to help you sleep. It seems that Bryce didn't give you enough medicine earlier."

"Yeah, his medicine didn't work," Jihyun agreed. "I itch very badly."

Vihaan gave him a warm smile. "There, there. I will make sure you feel better. We will protect you, as you will protect us from that evil violet woman. She's been sending you those nightmares. That's what her power does—send evil nightmares to her enemies!"

Jihyun started to tear up but tried to be brave. He wanted to protect Gwen from being attacked too.

Where was Gwen?

Before he could ask, Vihaan was gone, and Bryce walked into the room. "Master Jihyun. I have some sleeping medicine for you."

Jihyun looked up at Bryce, who already had the big needle ready. Bryce pushed up his sleeve, then poked him with the big needle.

No matter how often he got medicine, he hated it.

"Get some rest now," Bryce said, bowing to him.

The lights were still on in his room. Feeling tired, Jihyun closed his eyes and dozed off.

A loud sound boomed.

Jihyun suddenly opened his eyes. The room was pitch black. The bright lights in his room were off.

"Bryce?" Jihyun called out.

Faces appeared in the darkness. Faces…faces that were scary. The faces that always came out in the deep red of night. That was what happened when he was scared. The darkness turned to a deep red. The color of his blood when he got cuts.

"Bryce?"

Voices whispered around him. Creepy voices. More whispers.

We will kill you! You will die!

"Bryce!" Jihyun jumped out of bed, running to the door. Hands were all over his body. Three pairs of hands. It was a thousand times worse than the bugs crawling over him. The hands were touching his body all over, floating around him in a triangle. Jihyun jiggled the door handle, screaming. Inside the wood of the door, a face appeared.

It was Questy.

Jihyun screamed.

"Help! Questy is here!" Jihyun screamed and cried, jiggling the handle. "I'm scared!"

No one answered him, and his door wouldn't open.

In the corner of his eye, Questy's face floated into view.

You will die, the triangle apparition whispered.

Jihyun fell to the floor, screaming. Underneath him, the floorboards turned to a deep, dark red hellfire pit. If he fell into the pit, the face would do bad things to him.

Dark red colors swirled in his sight as the hands choked him. He couldn't breathe…

"They are getting me!" Jihyun screamed. "Questy is getting me!"

Fire entered his body, and he was suddenly paralyzed. All he could see was black with red specks. The floor rumbled harder, and the world swirled black. Muffled voices, swirling darkness and reds…

Right next to him, the red shadow was there.

Jihyun screamed again. "Vihaan! Bryce! HELP ME!"

Jihyun couldn't move from the position he was in.

"No one is going to help you!" Questy hissed out loud, not in his mind. "You are my slave!"

Jihyun screamed through his cries. Around him, the red shadow turned the world into blood. Then the blood turned into black fires. Within the fires, he could see red, but the black wouldn't let it come out.

Questy turned into three dark shadows. They floated around him in a circle, making his body feel sick. Even though they hovered above him in the dark, Jihyun knew they were holding him down with their evil powers. They squeezed his neck, making him unable to breathe while they held him down.

His chest felt heavy, as if they'd set a bag of rocks on him, making it so he couldn't move.

Jihyun cried, only because the shadows let him. "I want my parents," Jihyun cried out.

"Your parents are dead. You have no one left," they replied.

"King Renard is my dad now! I have him!"

"The King will die if you don't help!" hissed the voice.

He couldn't breathe. All he saw were the shadows. The scary shadows.

"I don't want the King to die like my father!" Jihyun called out to the red shadows. Below, he saw the fiery pit. The world around him swirled, making him sick and scared. The evil spirits were still whispering to him, and he couldn't escape.

"I want it to stop," he cried. "Please just make it stop…"

"The violet witch," hissed Questy. "She is doing this to you…"

More voices, more dizziness, and more hellfire. The spirits squeezed his neck, saying things he didn't understand. They made him unable to move, holding him down again. He couldn't move his mouth. No one could help him. Because nobody loved him.

Suddenly, his eyesight swirled with confusion, and he fell into the hellfire pit as the voice continued to roar, "We must capture the violet witch and punish her…"

CHAPTER 41

◆

Garrett heard a loud beep coming from his device from across the room. Another fire?

He ran over to it and logged in, sitting absentmindedly in his chair. Red dots were flashing on his screen. But there was one big main red dot.

It's the boy! It has to be!

"I found him!" Garrett said out loud excitedly.

He jumped up with the device in hand, then ran out of the weapons chamber.

Gwen, we're coming!

Garrett turned down the halls of the cavernous refuge, running every which way, hoping to find Telly, Scion, Victor, Geeta…anyone.

"I found the boy!" he shouted as he held the device over his head. He ran down the hall to where Telly would be. Scion was right outside their makeshift lab.

"Scion! I think I found the boy!" Garrett yelled. He stopped in front of Scion, still trying to catch his breath. "I gotta tell Telly."

"It is unfortunate, but she is still gone."

Garrett felt suddenly stressed. Telly still hadn't returned? She was going to miss their rescue operation. "Okay…" Garrett breathed. "I'll find Victor then."

"According to my readings, he is in his tent."

"Thanks."

Garrett ran through the caverns, passing the main hall where the gatherings were held at, past the underground stream, then came to Victor's tent.

"Victor!" Garrett called out.

There was shuffling from inside the tent, then Victor popped his head out.

"What is it?"

"The boy...I have precise readings!"

Garrett flipped the device in front of Victor, his eyes going wide.

"Let's find Geeta, and quickly," he said.

"I'll get the magitech weapons..."

✦ ✦ ✦

Startled from her sleep, Gwen jolted her eyes open.

The palace was shaking violently. The bed, the shelves, every item scattered throughout her room...they all rattled violently. Gwen had never been in an earthquake before. Well, not a big one like this. She could hear the earth *groaning*.

Alarmed, she jumped out of bed, unsure of what to do. The palace ground felt uneven and weightless under her feet. Was it another fire?

Gwen ran over to her door and tried to open it. Of course, it was still locked. "Help!" Gwen screamed as she pounded on the door.

A loud explosion rocked the entire palace.

"Somebody HELP!"

No answer.

Objects rattled off the shelves, some falling to the rumbling floor.

Turning away, Gwen scrambled to a corner of the room, crouching down, then instead she slid herself under her breakfast table.

There were muffled sounds of servants and guards yelling outside her chambers, running back and forth in the hallway.

She tucked her head in her knees, then placed her hands on her head, just like they did in school fire drills when she was young. It was the only thing she could think of doing.

After painstakingly long minutes went by, the earthquake stopped. All went still.

Gwen waited a few more minutes. Then, sighing with relief, uncurled herself and slid out from under the table, getting to her feet. She headed for the door, jiggling the handle. It was still locked.

She knocked on the door and shook the handle.

"Hello?" Gwen yelled. "Hello!"

There was no answer, except more servants yelling at each other, running up and down the hall with loud footsteps.

"Hello!" Gwen yelled, banging the door.

No one answered her.

Did they forget that I'm here?

Dismayed, she slumped her head against the door, listening to what was going on outside. After she heard no more sounds, Gwen sighed and headed toward the window to look outside at the cityscape.

But this time, she saw no city.

The entire thing had been secured by a metal plate. It had to have been activated by the palace security system.

She leaned on the window plate, shaking.

◆　◆　◆

Evil.

Red. Black.

The thoughts were forced.

Screams. Cries. No love.

The number three.

It was forced.

No breath.

Choking.

Evil. Thoughts.

No escape.

Red. Black.

Three.

Three.

Three...

Lost, Geeta wandered aimlessly in her dream. Surrounding her were dark red skies raining blood. The moon was a deep red, casting a terrible eerie redness across the unfamiliar territory. Shadows whispered all around her as she moved through the wasteland. She had to find the boy.

What is the significance of the number three?

The shadows around her grew. If she didn't move, the triangle would consume her soul. It floated overhead, a looming, impending doom, waiting for her to give up so it could take her. The evil that radiated from it hurt her soul. She had to move.

Looking up, Geeta saw the triangle, the transparent darkness forming against the deep red sky. A horrific face appeared within the shape.

She ran.

Keep running, the triangle roared with laughter. *Your power will soon be gone…*

Geeta looked at the triangle in defiance. The face was the stuff that nightmares came from, causing her soul to quiver with fear.

You cannot take my power! You have no authority!

The triangle roared, *Soon your power will be no more, and I will delight in it.*

Geeta's dream broke, and her eyes snapped open. Her body was shaking, her heart wild and her breathing erratic. Sweat poured down her body, and she was soaked. The image of the triangle was ingrained in her mind. Either the camp or the refuge was in danger. Or she was.

Wiping the sweat off her brow, Geeta changed into warm clothes. She felt a strong urge to go outside to make sure the refuge was safe.

Quickly walking down the hall, she heard Garrett's shouts echoing. Whatever he was going on about was indistinguishable, but it sounded important.

Garrett passed by, then saw her. He ran up to her breathless, holding a device in front of her.

Geeta eyed the device, which had all sorts of flashing red on the screen. Red…like her vision.

"Did you hear what I was yelling about?" he asked.

Geeta eyed him. "No, what?"

"There's another burst of energy," he said, then his eyes met hers. "I think I found the boy."

Geeta suddenly felt feverish, and the hair on her arms was standing on end. Was the dream a premonition to the boy?

"Let's get Victor," Geeta said.

"I already told him. He's getting ready now and told me to find you." He paused. "Also, to add to this, some bad news. The camp. It's experiencing the worst sandstorm ever. And the storm is heading this way."

Geeta sighed. "Of course it would be."

There was another beep on his device, and Garrett looked down, clicking the button. "Another burst of energy. It's moved outside of Olympia, twenty miles or so. And it's bigger. Much, much bigger."

They exchanged worried glances, then Geeta said, "Let's hurry."

The two of them ran to the open chamber, where they found Victor.

"Geeta, did you hear?"

"Yes."

"There's a sandstorm hitting the camp right now," Garrett said.

"Dammit," Victor said, slinging his weapon strap over his shoulder, securing it. "Can we still travel?"

"My magic will freeze time while we move through the dimension. It shouldn't affect us," Geeta said. "Garrett said there is another burst of energy at a new point outside Olympia." Geeta glanced at Victor. "Are you ready?"

"Yes." He grabbed the last of his weapons, then nodded. "Did anyone let Telly and Scion know?"

"I told Scion," Garrett said, then he paused. "Telly is gone."

Geeta glanced at him. "Does she know about this?"

"No. Scion said she left a while ago."

What was Telly doing? Through Garrett's loud thoughts, she learned Telly had left the refuge, but he didn't know why. It worked out, though—Geeta had wanted Telly to stay behind. Drew needed to be looked after, and Telly's mind was in a fragile state, her life force shattered. She didn't have the strength that they needed.

"Let's go, then," Geeta said.

Geeta fluttered her hand, pouring her adjacent time magic from her hands. The world painted itself in shades of violet and shimmers of blue. Garrett, Victor, and Geeta moved within her dimensional magic, reaching the outside of the refuge.

The group climbed into a four-passenger vehicle, with Victor driving.

They passed the planes of the wastelands in the night. The moon was violet-white instead of its normal white, and the stars shimmered in the same hue.

"This is really weird," Garrett called out. "Everything is still, and the vehicle seems like it's floating."

"We are moving through dimensional space rather than normal gravity,"

Geeta replied.

"Why can't you use that portal magic?"

"I need to conserve my energy. I'm not as powerful with time magic, so it consumes more of my life force."

"Oh."

They exchanged nervous glances.

"I don't see any signs of a sandstorm anywhere," Garrett continued. "The sky is clear."

Geeta thought back to her dream. Things didn't seem right. But what else were they supposed to do? Was the sandstorm connected to the boy? This whole situation didn't sit well with her.

Garrett's device beeped louder as they traveled closer to their destination. The drive felt endless, just like time had felt the past few weeks. Each day felt like a repeat, with her training Victor from sunrise to sunset. And still, no magic flowed from his fingertips.

"Guys, there's another burst of energy—"

Alarmed by his statement, Geeta realized her dimensional magic was no longer activated.

Then a wave of dark red sand hit them so hard, it knocked the entire vehicle sideways.

✦ ✦ ✦

As Telly drove across the wastelands, she noticed a wall of sand in the distance. It was by far the biggest wall of sand she had ever seen, rippling across the desert.

A sandstorm!

Quickly looking for anything that she could go to for shelter, Telly spotted an outcropping in a nearby patch of rock formations. It was near the pinnacle, which would have been more ideal, but she didn't have that kind of time. It was coming fast, and coming strong.

The moonlight above shifted to a deep, eerie red. As it did so, the wall of sand shimmered a dark red. Cracks of red lightning flashed, while loud thunder rumbled.

The camp is in danger, she thought wildly as she realized it was heading in that direction. Most of those who only had tents would likely be killed in the storm.

It had come to this. She could either live for her daughter and Drew, or she could try to save everyone in the camp with her power. There was a good chance she'd die in the process.

What good does illusion magic do in a storm? I would be foolish to run out there to try and combat the storm.

Let go of your fears, the magic whispered to her.

Telly glanced at sandstorm wall moving across the desert like a tidal wave. She didn't even have time to get to the outcropping.

Let go of your fears…

Telly started to tear up, then looked to the sky. "I need you!" she screamed. "I want to live to rescue my daughter and bring her to safety! I want to live to see Drew alive and well!"

The heavens shook and roared as if responding to her demands. Though she didn't hear a voice, Telly knew it was urging her onward…

Telly got off of her vehicle, then marched toward the sandstorm wall as if facing an opponent in battle.

"I won't let you kill my friends, or anyone else in this godforsaken wasteland!" she screamed at the sandstorm wall.

Suddenly a flurry of energy shot out of her body as Telly slammed her hand against the wasteland ground. Bright, vivid orange light burst from her hands, then rolled across the wasteland, covering it.

Grains of sand began to rise and ripple, faster and faster, as she fed her energy into it. In the distance, Telly saw the sandstorm heading straight toward her.

Oh no, you don't!

Telly screamed, sending all the energy from her heart, soul, and mind funneling straight into the earth. Her magic reached the oncoming sandstorm, glowing bright orange and seeping into the giant wall of sand as it grew in size over her.

Telly struggled with the funneling power, trying to hang on to the magical connection as her life force and the sandstorm fought.

You aren't going anywhere!

Then she began to move the sand in the air. The entire sandstorm.

Telly grunted and cried as she slowly lifted her hands upward, the bright orange magic glowing brighter and more vibrant. With another loud cry, Telly clapped her hands together, feeling the magical friction between her fingertips.

You don't believe… the magic whispered.

"I do believe!" she screamed. Her magic was losing its power, becoming weaker. She was losing the magic…

There was a burst so bright and so loud, it caused her to fly backward. The sandstorm shot right up into the sky, mixing with the clouds as Telly tumbled across the desert sand. She clenched the ground, then glanced up to see rainclouds forming, so thick and so dark, shimmering with orange. There was a loud crackle in the dark sky, and then the clouds let loose a pouring rain.

A transmuted sandstorm… She'd turned a sandstorm into a rainstorm. She had managed to access the full orange magic, but she wasn't able to hold on to it.

Why was it so hard to obtain the full magic? It seemed to come so naturally for Drew, Geeta, and the other gifted she had witnessed in the battle of Arcadia. But for her? She was only able to do it for a few seconds before she gave out.

Why? Why can't I hold on to this power?

You must believe, a voice answered.

Then she slumped to the ground, spent of her energy. She could only hope that it was enough.

✦ ✦ ✦

Panicked muffles could be heard through the sand. In any moment, Garrett and Victor would suffocate. Her as well.

A loud crack sounded above. Sands all around her began pulling away, as if a layer was being peeled off of her, allowing Geeta to breathe.

Gasping, Geeta got to her feet and saw Garrett and Victor.

"What in the hell…?" Garrett gasped.

The sandstorm was *rising up* into the sky.

Then a burst of orange magic knocked the three of them backward.

Geeta heard Garrett and Victor shouting as they were rolled every which way. Rocks, sand, and debris whipped and pelted her bare skin.

Her body came to a halt, and the dark clouds poured out rain, hard and fast.

Within seconds, the entire wasteland was drenched.

"Did you see that? It was orange magic!" Garrett exclaimed. "It can't be Drew, can it?"

"I don't know," Victor said in a low whisper.

Geeta glanced up at the sky, noticing the bloodred moon peeking through the storm clouds. "I don't think it's over. The boy's magic is still active."

Filling her spirit with her protection magic, Geeta cast a shield around her body. It soaked into her skin, glistening and shimmering in the red moonlight in deep purples. She then sent a wave to Garrett and Victor, encasing them as well.

The hard rain pelted their bodies, yellow magic glistening wherever each droplet hit.

Through the storm, Geeta saw another giant sandstorm forming. And it continued to grow, glowing deep red, like burning embers.

"How is it possible for a sandstorm to form in rain?" Garrett said.

"Magic," Geeta said.

Geeta narrowed her eyes, then roared a loud battle cry. She smacked her hands together, then raised her arms, the sand in front of them glowing with deep violet magic.

The sand divided with her magic, pushing everything away from the trio, destroying everything in its path.

A mech stood in front of them.

The rain continued to pour, the mech's machinery glistening a dark red in the moonlight.

The boy was at the center of the mech. He had goggles on, connected to the mech's machinery, which made strange mechanical sounds. The boy was using the mech's hands as an extension of his human hands.

"You are a bad woman!" screamed the boy, using the mech hands to point at her accusingly.

Wet sand crashed against Geeta's body, knocking the wind out of her. Blackness filled her vision with twinkling white stars.

I can't see!

Geeta gasped, then panicked, trying to get what air she could back into her lungs.

Stunned, Geeta felt her body rising above the ground as the boy's magic whipped dry sand at her. Geeta fought, but he was too strong. She tried to reach into her life force, but without air, she couldn't focus.

Her vision and breath returned to her as the mech picked her up entirely, holding her by the shoulders. She was a little speck compared to the big contraption.

I will be dead if I don't get out of here!

Geeta sent a wave of electrical magic through the mech. The yellow magic rippled against the machinery but didn't affect it at all. The mech was protected with yellow magic, too.

Could there be another Olympian cyborg nearby, one with yellow magic?

Geeta sent another wave of magic, this time trying to pry the mech's hand open by force.

"Stop this!" Geeta cried out.

"You cannot invade with your army!" The boy raised his mech hands, his goggles glowing. Sand all around them rose suddenly.

"Army?"

"You and your army are bad people!"

They were about to be buried in the sand once more.

"I am only here to find the girl!" Geeta shouted back.

"Girl…?"

The boy continued to sweep the sand around them. From the corner of her eye, a giant sandstorm rose a mile high above and behind the boy, ready to swallow her and the group.

"Yes! The girl! Gwen!" Geeta screamed as she struggled.

The mech stopped, the sand freezing over them, and Geeta saw the boy's face quiver. Though there was a VR headset attached to him, she could tell that Gwen's name meant something to him.

Geeta seized the moment.

She summoned her mind magic, sending a wave from her core into her mind. Then Geeta jumped from her body into the boy's mind.

Geeta was met with a deep red wasteland.

It was just like in her nightmare. Her spirit heard the boy's soul crying. He was on the ground next to her, sobbing.

Geeta quickly kneeled to comfort him but was startled by screeching screams. Demonic images floated around them. Melted faces, eyes dropping to the ground, long gnarled hands, and the teeth…

They were floating around the boy.

"Away with you!" Geeta shouted at the dark spirits.

Questy will kill you! one hissed.

You must do as he says! another said.

The boy cried harder. "I'm scared."

Geeta's heart hammered. The dark spirits, the evil that emanated from them made her heart ache with disgust. She turned to the boy, leaning over him. "I need to find Gwen! Where is she?"

The boy looked to her. "Gwen is my only friend," he said through his tears. "I don't want her to go…"

Just then, the spirits formed into a triangle.

You will get what you deserve! it hissed.

Geeta trembled. She *knew* that voice.

In the dreamland, a dark blue portal opened up, swirling with dark energy. It was the same as the space-time continuum portals.

You are coming with me!

"No!" Geeta screamed.

The portal swelled in size, flecks of blue magic funneling around it. Then it burst all around Geeta, engulfing her.

Geeta couldn't fight it. She was being pushed into the portal.

"NO!" Geeta screamed.

Geeta turned her head toward the kid. "Boy! Help me!"

The boy ignored her, as if she didn't exist.

Do not fight it!

"I will fight you as long as I have breath!" Geeta shouted, trying to grip her feet in the sand. It didn't work. Her feet were sliding toward the portal, making long tracks in the sand.

More laughter echoed the sky as her body was pushed closer to the portal.

"Stop this!" Geeta screamed. She tried to summon her magic, but her force was weak against its power.

The dark sapphire portal swirled furiously in front of her, as if waiting for her to accept its invitation. The more she struggled, the more the power took hold of her body and mind.

And it was drawing her closer and closer…

✦ ✦ ✦

"Victor!" Garrett shouted. He shot his magitech weapon at the boy, trying to stave him off. It wasn't affecting the boy or the mech. He must have a special magical shield covering the mech.

"Something is happening to Geeta!"

"I know!" he yelled.

The two were suddenly whipped off their feet by a blast of violent red winds. Victor grasped the ground hard, then reached for his weapon, taking a shot.

The red magic within the weapon ricocheted against the golden shield encasing the boy's mech.

A dark blur appeared in front of Geeta, growing in size and sparkling with deep-blue flecks, forming a portal. It felt like all the light of the world was being drawn into this portal. Like a tear in the air, as if someone had torn a piece of fabric.

Victor got the sense this magic was feeding off a source that was far away.

"Geeta! Get away!" Victor screamed.

But Geeta was frozen, as if locked in time, staring mindlessly into the portal. Her paralyzed body was being pushed across the muddy grounds. She was almost to the portal.

He had to do something, otherwise Geeta would be gone.

I have the gift.

There was a soft humming through his life force, as if it agreed.

He had denied it for so long. He couldn't accept that he had the gift—much less a gift that no one else had.

I have been given the gift of the gray.

The darkness and light in his life force stopped fighting in that instant, as if chains wrapped around his heart had broken.

He was *free*. Or rather, his spirit was. There was no more war between them. Victor felt them meld together.

The darkness and light became gray…

In the background, Garrett was screaming and shooting. The boy was screaming. Sand was thrown against them. The dark portal pulled Geeta closer and closer.

"I HAVE A GIFT!" Victor yelled to the darkness.

Then, a burst of gray light filled his eyes, and his body felt like it had exploded.

✦ ✦ ✦

Geeta was thrown out of the boy's mind, her body dropping to the ground hard.

Confused, Geeta rolled her head, grimacing as she looked for the boy.

All that she saw was bright gray light. There were screams mixed with the boy's panic and confusion.

The gray magic continued as the screams faded away.

Then the magic died down, revealing a clear sky with stars and the white light of the moon.

All was silent.

"What…" Geeta whispered as she lifted her head. The mech was gone. The sandstorms were gone. Even the rain. Her body and hair were caked with mud.

Vihaan. He'd been inside that nightmare. He was the cause behind this boy's pain.

Geeta slumped her head in the sand, face down. Her body shook just thinking about her husband from the past. Her stomach felt weak, her body shaking violently.

"Geeta?" Victor shouted.

She couldn't think straight, her mind consumed with thoughts of Vihaan.

Geeta let out a loud scream. Vihaan…he was trying to capture her and deliver her to someone else. If she had been pulled into that portal, she was sure she would have lost her gift.

Elyathi must be behind this somehow. She must need my magic.

The sudden realization of her terrifying husband, her life force so close to being stripped away—it was all too much.

She screamed again, tears streaming down her face.

Then she threw up.

"Geeta!" Victor shouted. She felt his hands on her back, patting it gently. "It's all right. You're here now."

She screamed again.

After a long silence, Geeta turned to face Victor and Garrett. Her eyes were swollen, snot pouring out of her nose, and her hands…they trembled in the sand.

"I *HATE* him," was all she said.

She never hated anyone. But Vihaan…she had a special place for hate in her heart for him.

"Who?" Garrett asked.

Victor remained silent. Both men were at a loss.

"I hate him…" she whispered through her tears, then lay back down in the mud.

She continued to sob until everything in her body hurt.

"Get him back to bed!" Vihaan shouted to the guards as they unstrapped Jihyun from the muddy mech. Radgu helped unstrap the boy, then lifted him in his arms. Their eyes met, and he glanced away, disappearing with the boy in a swirl of blue magic.

Keep running, Geeta, Vihaan thought. *The future wants you, and you cannot defy them no matter how much you try. You will pay for this!*

CHAPTER 42

◆

BLUE

Derek snapped his eyes open, then threw down his wineglass. He ran his fingers through his hair, then shot up from his seat.

Damn you to hell, Geeta Sharma. I will have your power!

Olympia had almost had her. He almost had her. Derek heaved with deep breaths. His hands shook with rage. He was so close. He'd had her under his complete control for a brief moment, but something stopped him. It was as if a cord had been severed from him to his host. But before he was cut off from Geeta's mind, he'd found something that could weaken her to the point of being paralyzed. Her husband from the past.

Derek heaved a few more deep breaths, then glared out at the black wasteland behind the glowing city of Illumina from his hotel balcony. The godforsaken heat of the city made his curls constantly soaked with sweat, even with the cooling air units running at full blast. He'd stripped down to no more than his pants and jewelry. It was too bloody hot. Though he wanted to spend his time in Arcadia while he waited for the gauntlet and the parts, he thought it best to lie low in this city. He could rest in comfort in his hotel while he waited for the parts. Hardly anyone knew who he was in this city. All they cared about were their own royals and home-grown celebrities.

Derek waved his hand, fixing the shattered glass with his new power of transmutation. The glass melded together, then floated over to him. Wine from another dimension appeared in front of him, filling his glass. He wanted that woman's violet magic. That way, if he had the power of the violet before facing Ikaria, nothing could stop him from killing that witch. He wanted to kill her before the coming of the new world. It would be immensely satisfying to know her life force would be no more, and Elyathi wouldn't have to depend on her for the final spell.

He took a long drink of his wine, thinking about Elyathi. Had she faced Ikaria once again while he was in this present time? What was happening in the future? Was she waiting on him to return with the scientists? And was she wondering how far along Emerald was? He had sped up her pregnancy, but it was still going too slow for his liking.

These things take time, Derek thought. *Especially for that lowlife nobody Kyle to crush my Emerald's heart.* He hated the thought of Emerald being crushed, but it would put everything in place for her to trust him once more. To love him once again.

There was a soft brush against his skin, making the hair on his arms stand on edge. Derek felt a presence in this era and dimension. It was smooth, warm, and inviting. The presence was so strong, he could detect the scent of lavender and lilacs. His body felt a sudden desire, following a wave of confusion.

"Queen Elyathi," Derek called out as he stood.

Elyathi appeared in front of him, shimmering in the moonlight, her beauty undiminished.

"Derek," she said with a gentle tone. "Remember, I am not queen anymore." Her eyes glanced at his bare chest but flicked her gaze to his eyes.

He pretended not to notice, but he felt his cheeks burn. "I know. It's hard to forget when I was so used it for years. I meant to contact you soon, but it seems you have done so first."

"Yes. I wanted to see if you had made any progress with the scientist," she said.

"Not yet. But rest assured, it will be anytime now," Derek confirmed. "The Corporation will have the gauntlet ready for me any day now. And," he said, glancing into her pearl-like eyes, "I nearly had that violet-gifted's power."

Elyathi's image smiled. "Oh? Imagine if you are able to retrieve that gifted…" she breathed.

"I have a plan. The next time we speak, I hope to have her power in my life force."

"I know you have the power to do so. I believe in you."

Derek couldn't help the feeling of elation. It felt good to have someone finally acknowledge all his work, his progress. His father and mother never did. His councilors gave him unapproved stares half the time when he was in Arcadia. Even his own servant Silas often questioned his reasons. But Elyathi, she gave him encouragement. Praise. Just as Emerald had when she had been in love with him…

His thoughts shifted to Emerald. He loved her. This lingering infatuation with his complement was a spell…a dark, wavering line. His loss of Emerald had left a hole in his heart. He needed to fill that void.

He needed Emerald now.

"Lady Elyathi, I have sped up the progress of your daughter's pregnancy," Derek said. "This Kyle Trancer she's with will be creating his own downfall with Emerald. That being said…" He paused, suddenly feeling the weight of his guilt—the one that Ikaria caused. "I think it might be best if she had some convincing."

"I agree…" she cooed. "I will play a part in this. I miss her, and I know that she feels the same. I will do what I can."

Derek flushed. "Thank you. I will let you know once she gives birth."

"And I will do the same when I convince her." Elyathi nodded with respect to him. "Farewell, Derek. We will speak again."

Derek's eyes took in her form, more than he should, then he averted his gaze, taking a deep drink of his wine. "Goodbye, my lady. Be safe."

"I will. You as well."

Her image faded away, leaving Derek alone on the balcony once more. He clutched his wineglass, thinking about all that he was up against. The conversation with Elyathi had made him even more impatient. He just wanted to have Emerald back in his arms. Everything would go back to the way it should be. These confusing thoughts would melt into oblivion.

Derek snatched up his communicator, about to make a call to the Corporation, but noticed there was a missed communication. It was from Director Santiago.

Your Majesty,

The project you requested is completed and ready. I also want to inform you that the parts for Andrew DiNapoli are also ready, waiting for Ms. Geeta Sharma to pick up. I have arranged a time tomorrow afternoon for Ms. Sharma's arrival. We look forward to Your Majesty's visit.

—Santiago

Derek snapped his communicator shut. They wouldn't remember why they'd constructed the damn thing until they saw his face. As for the parts…

Just you wait, Geeta Sharma. I am coming for you.

Derek refilled his wine, then took a sip. *Time to pay the Arcadian corporation a visit.*

CHAPTER 43

YELLOW

Auron sighed as he pushed away another tome. Auron was growing increasingly worried about Vala. Was she safe?

Auron glanced down at the book, reminded of his task. Time came and went as he vigorously searched for any writings on restoring the earth as it should be. Unfortunately, only one tome of interest came up—*The Chosen*. It had only one small paragraph mentioning the white-gifted—the one to restore magic to the heavens to purify the earth. Other than that, there was nothing.

Purifying the earth. It seemed the God of Light had created the white-gifted for that sole purpose. Had the God of Light intended to purge the earth of magic or purify the earth of its transgressions to make it holy? Or had the God of Light intended to actually purify the physical earth's ground, knowing that this present era would be in dire need of healing?

Why did the God of Light allow his chosen to become corrupt?

Auron sighed at the thought, then leaned back in his chair. He knew the answer to his own question: because of free will on earth. The people were not slaves to the God of Light; they were created in beauty and given freedom to care for the world and all that was in it. And as Auron very well knew, the Lord of Darkness lurked everywhere in the darkest corners of the earth, waiting for his revenge after being cast out of the heavens. Even knowing this, it still made Auron wonder why, out of all people, Elyathi was chosen to be the white-gifted. She had proven to be anything but of the purest of hearts.

As Auron dwelled on the thought, a strange idea came to him. What if the God of Light could create a new white-gifted? One to take Elyathi's place due to the corruption of her heart. It was an intriguing thought, and one that could fit the prophecy…

I must pray on it, he vowed. It was the only hope. Unless, somehow, Elyathi turned from her sin.

"High Priest Auron," called out a servant.

Auron glanced over at the man. He served the priests but was not a yellow-gifted himself. He did have a yellow-gifted twin brother, a priest. Auron felt nothing but sorrow for the man's twin. For in this man's eyes, he felt the loss of his twin brother. Though the twin was alive, he was mentally crippled, lost in his own mind.

"Yes?" Auron said as he closed the tome in front of him.

"It is nearly sunset," he said softly, bowing.

"Thank you."

He rose to his feet. Auron wanted to say something of comfort to the man, but he felt out of place doing so.

Auron left the library, walking through the golden citadel. Sunlight shone through the small citadel windows, gleaming in its glory.

The power of his gift had transformed the citadel with but a few words. If only he could do that again, but to the earth instead.

Auron froze at that thought. What *if* he *could* transform the earth below, as he had done to the citadel? It was the same thing, but on an epic scale.

By the God of Light! Could I possibly have the power to do so?

Auron made for the temple. It, too, was bathed in gold, with silver accents and encrusted jewels in the pillars. The sun was already setting according to its alignment for this time of year, casting its golden glow across the entire temple. The acolytes had lit the incense, filling its braziers with fire and smoke.

Auron fell to his knees, then closed his eyes in silence. His heart stirred, troubled. He had to purge his worry before he began.

He bowed, his forehead touching the warm floor. In his foresight, he saw green.

Bright, vivid green.

✦ ✦ ✦

A warm flood of sunlight covered his body, relaxing his mind, body, and soul. Birds chirping mixed with the rustling of trees in the wind. A babbling brook could be heard somewhere nearby.

Had he fallen asleep?

Auron watched as the tree branches swayed in the gentle wind, as the sunlight peered through them, highlighting the intense green foliage. The beams of light were powerful, streaming all the way through to the ground, soaking into the grass.

He suddenly looked down. He was on *grass*!

Auron brushed his hands over the grass, feeling the blades against his palms. He leaned closer, taking a long whiff of the fresh scent. It was clean, yet rustic. The sensation delighted him, causing him to chuckle out loud.

From the corner of his eye, he caught the sight of the babbling brook, the stream gently flowing over rocks. Birds soared above, while bugs of the forest chirped. Wildflowers dotted the forest among a mix of strange plants. Were they ferns, the plants he once read about? He had seen very little plant life on the floating isles and citadel, but here, the plant life was lush and natural. The way it was meant to be.

Peace filled his heart in this sacred place. The golden magic within his soul hummed with serenity, and suddenly Auron felt more passion, more fervor in his devotion to the God of Light. Though this was no holy temple, nor a consecrated place, just through the peace and serenity of the place, Auron had felt the God of Light.

The magic had wrapped his mind to a state of enlightenment. Auron took in its beauty, breathing refreshing cool air, and let the gentle peaceful sounds fill his mind. A surge of his magic hummed through his body once again, empowering his life force. It was as if the glen was strengthening his core being. The power was overwhelming, but at the same time, it was as if a piece of the missing puzzle finally clicked into place, one that had been missing in his soul.

Am I on Earth's surface? Auron kept running the scenario through his mind, trying to remember how he'd ended up in the peaceful glen. The last thing he recalled was that he was praying. Was this a dream? Or a foreshadowing of things to come?

Deciding to take a further look around the magical clearing, Auron rose to his feet. He started walking downstream, following the path of the water. The water grew stronger, and the foliage thickened the farther he traveled. The sunlight's golden beams dimmed with each step away from the clearing. Auron noticed the flowers beginning to wilt. The trees blackened, and the waters were violent. Anger, sickness flooded his life force.

He suddenly fell to his knees. Around him, the trees began to hang limp until the branches snapped. Behind him there was a loud rumble, and the earth groaned.

Auron jumped to his feet, summoning the power of his life force. Instead of the golden dazzle surrounding and protecting him, nothing came out. Just a fizzle. He looked down at his empty hands, then up to the sky.

"What is happening?" he asked the God of Light.

A quake in response to his question.

He needed to keep moving.

Auron began to quickly make his way through the darkened forest, with all the trees snapping, breaking, and the flowers turning into mold fodder.

Finally, he came upon a clearing. A clearing of *nothing*. No wildlife, no nature, no water, no nothing. The sky was black, and the air cold.

The ground violently rumbled once again. Auron watched as the ground split open right before his eyes. A long metal tower topped with a spike rose from its depths. There was evil, a dark and ancient evil, coming from the tower. If he weren't a priest of the God of Light, he would have run. But he needed to fight.

"Begone!" Auron commanded as he summoned his holy magic.

Instead of obeying, the tower sprouted machines with flat glass panels lit up with different pictures. Each picture had a different person featured on it.

"I say to you, *begone!*"

Nothing happened.

Auron paused. Something told him to look at the pictures.

Obeying the feeling, Auron walked closer. The pictures were of gifted people.

These pictures moved; it was as if he were watching their daily lives. It was strange, but as he watched them, he knew that something was missing. Something was off about them.

"You see it, too?" said a mechanical voice.

Auron turned to face an ancient machine similar to the ones his world sector had fought back in ancient Arcadia. It had a man's body infused with machine parts.

Auron shivered at the unearthly sight of this abhorrent being. The eyes were lit up in a golden color. Seeing this made Auron hyper aware of what was truly happening to him—he was in a vision.

"You see it, too?" the machine man asked again.

"What do you see?" Auron asked curiously.

"They seem empty, do they not?" the ancient robot asked.

Auron glanced back at the glass panels, watching the subjects. "They are missing a part of their souls."

"Precisely. They are not how they should be," the robot confirmed.

Auron eyed him curiously. "Are you not how you should be either?"

"Yes. I should have died years ago. Instead, society has kept me alive."

Auron walked toward the robotic man, studying him. "Since we are in a vision of prophecy, there must be some sort of message you have for me."

"I have often wondered if I have been accessing other men's files," the robot said.

"Accessing? I don't know what that means. What files?"

The robot cocked his head. "I can feel it within my human mind that you are not of my time era. I don't understand how I know this. I just do." He paused. "I am like you, visiting this premonition, searching for answers."

Auron raised an eyebrow. "You are telling me that you are here, with me, in this God-given vision?"

"It is as you say," the cyborg answered.

Why would the God of Light give a cyborg a vision? The cyborg was a yellow-gifted, but he was still mechanical. Machinery. Was it possible that the machine could have this kind of power with his gift?

"Do you have a name?" Auron asked.

"I am Model 695-b. Some refer to me as Scion," he answered. "What is your name, user?"

"Auron." Auron glanced at the tower. "You live in this tower, Scion?"

"Negative, Mr. Auron. The tower is a figment of this vision. In the real world, I reside in the wastelands."

"The wastelands?" Auron repeated. "Is that on Earth?"

"Yes. The coordinates are thirty-two point three six to be precise." Scion projected a translucent, glowing map into the air from his mechanical eyes.

Auron took a look, realizing that it was a map of World Sector One. "Where you live—in these wastelands—is the earth's surface destroyed?"

"No, Mr. Auron. It is inhabited by many human beings."

Scion was from the past. Could it be that he was aware of Queen Emerald? Had Auron fought this cyborg at one point, just like the others? Hadn't Geeta said she had encountered machines that could do good?

Perhaps this is one of them, he thought.

Auron turned to the machine. "Scion. Do you know anything of the earth getting sick?"

"Negative," Scion said. "But within this distortion of dreams, I can sense a hatred from the earth in this dream."

Auron's heart quickened. "I feel it too. This hatred that radiates from the earth, I can sense that it is the start of the sickness."

"Sickness, Mr. Auron?"

"The earth has been sick for thousands of years—in my time," Auron said.

The robot look over to Auron. "You are searching for a way to heal this evil."

"I am," Auron said. "Our world is at stake. Not only the evil that permeates the earth's surface, but the evil that awaits in the future."

"You must plant a new gift."

Auron froze. "Plant a new *gift*?" he asked incredulously.

He nodded. "The earth needs good soil and clean water in order to produce plants that have a solid root." His words now sounded more human than machine as he pointed in the direction of the vibrant forest, then cocked his head to Auron. "But the earth here, the soil has no nourishment, no nutrients, no water, in order to produce any living green things. Just as soil goes bad, plants die. Is a wayward heart not like a dying plant? It is time to weed out the corrupt gifted and plant a new gifted in its place."

Is he referring to Elyathi? Auron had been thinking of her prior to waking in this place.

Auron studied the half man, half machine, in awe of his words. "Good sir, were you once a priest? I see you have the yellow gift."

Scion shook his head. "I am not a priest, nor do I have the full potential of the gift in 570 nanometers. I have been infused with very little."

"Nanometers?"

"The gift of the yellow, as other users would refer to it," he said, sounding more machine than human.

Scion's eyes glowed a soft yellow, but within the machine's depths, Auron could feel the sincerity of his words. And there was something else: a desire to be whole. The man's spirit was within that mechanical body, along with a suppressed gift.

"Scion, let me try to heal your body. Though I am in a vision, and it's usually not how it works, I am compelled to at least try."

"There are many who could benefit in my time if I were able to access more power." Scion paused, and his golden eyes flashed with concern. "However, I am not the one who should be healed. There is a man…a cyborg, that is. He needs help. It is critical that he wakes. We need his help."

Auron eyed him steadily, then nodded. "I will do what I can. Think of this cyborg, and I will do the rest."

"Affirmative."

Auron gestured for him to come near. When he did so, Auron rested his hand on the robot's chest where his heart would be.

Screams erupted from the tower, startling them both. It sounded like a boy. The louder the screams became, the redder the tower burned. The tower's metal bent and twisted, while the panels of glowing images suddenly projected black-and-white *snowstorms*. The sky matched the color of the tower—blood red, and anger radiated from the ground as it rumbled. Above, shooting stars radiated with red magic. No, not stars. Meteors.

Scion grabbed Auron's hand, shaking it. "Do it now before it is too late, Mr. Auron."

Screams from the boy continued as the ground shook.

"What's the cyborg's name?" Auron asked quickly.

"Andrew DiNapoli."

Auron closed his eyes, keeping his hands firmly on Scion's chest. He focused on this man's name, funneling his healing light through the vision.

In the distance, Auron heard a woman's soft cries. Trying to ignore the sound, Auron grabbed Scion's other hand, then clasped it tightly, closing his eyes. He searched deep within himself through the pounding of magic in his veins, traveling to his heart and into the next dimension, the spirit dimension, to the devotion of his servitude.

He felt a humming of approval within, and the power of the yellow began flowing through his veins.

Heal the cyborg, Auron said to the magic.

The soft cries of the woman interfered with his focus. She was afraid.

He gained a sudden understanding of this woman, and Auron felt a release of a different magic come from within. Holding that thought, Auron continued to focus on the woman's fear.

Through the strange connection, her fear funneled to him, filling his life force with a gift of healing.

The gift of the green. His adjacent color.

"You left me with nothing but a broken heart…" her voice whispered.

Auron began to fear for her, and his heart ached in return. Through the fear, Auron turned it into a healing wave. Within his mind's eye, Auron saw the full color of green, glowing as bright as the leaves in the peaceful glen.

He opened his eyes. The green magic swirled between Scion and Auron with the energy and power of a vortex. He could barely maintain his grasp, holding on to the robot as tight as he could.

Just say the words, a whisper said in Auron's mind.

Auron looked right into Scion's mechanical eyes, then shouted, "Restore Andrew DiNapoli's original life force!"

Green magic exploded across the world. The power ripped Scion and Auron apart, and Auron was flung into the green expanse.

Intense light and power enveloped Auron as he floated in the expanse. Within the vivid light, a voice thundered, *It is not Andrew that needs this power.*

Then who shall receive it? Auron asked the voice.

Do you not yet understand what needs to be done? A pure heart shall replace my corrupt servant. Prophesy and hope shall be born!

"Remember to plant the seed, Mr. Auron!" Scion's words echoed from the green expanse.

Auron spoke, but he didn't know the exact words he spoke. But he did know it was a prayer for one pure of heart.

In his heart of hearts, he put forth his most earnest prayer.

A prayer for a new white-gifted.

CHAPTER 44

✦

ORANGE

Telly rode back to the refuge, mud still crusted on her clothing and hair, making it feel crunchy. Dirt smeared her face. She could hardly see out of her riding goggles.

She felt...*defeated.*

The wastelands felt so desolate after the storm. Deadly quiet except for the sound of her vehicle. Telly didn't see any wastelanders from other camps. She was sure that if it weren't for her last-minute transmutation of the storm, things would be much worse.

Or so she had hoped. But seeing the emptiness made her question herself.

Telly pulled into the refuge area, parking the vehicle in a hidden crevice of the rock formation. Her body ached past the point of exhaustion. She didn't know how much more she could take, from her depression over her daughter, Drew, and trying to do something with her new weaponry or magical attempts.

Trudging up the hill, she entered the refuge, making her way back to her area.

Scion didn't glance in her direction, remaining focused on Drew.

There were new parts that he was replacing.

"Hello, Miss Hearly," he greeted.

"How is he?" Telly asked quickly, coming over to him.

Scion raised his free hand. "Do not come closer, Miss Hearly. Grains of sand falling into his open body would cause more issues."

Telly paused. "I wasn't thinking. I'm so tired."

"You must shower, Miss Hearly. This will help relieve tension in your muscles, causing your brain to release stress," Scion said. "It is imperative you do so if you are to remain here in the lab."

Telly snorted. It amused her when cyborgs got demanding. But he did have a point.

"I'll be back shortly."

Scion continued to work on one of the parts near Drew's open chest. "Affirmative. I do want to let you know that you received a transmission from Director Jonathan earlier today."

"And?"

"He said that he had something he wanted to tell you, but he had a hard time trying to figure out what it was," Scion continued.

"Must be the stress getting to him," Telly commented. "That was it?"

"That was it. No more."

That's odd. He never sends a transmission unless it's urgent. And why would her old boss forget what he had to tell her?

"Did he say he wanted me to reach out to him?" Telly asked.

"He told me to forget about it. As a cyborg, that is hard for me to process."

Telly sighed. "I'm going to shower. Be back in a few to help you."

CHAPTER 45

✦

RED

Winds ripped through Kyle's spiked hair as he drove freely through the streets of Arcadia. The thrill running through his body was like no other. Every second was a high, and nothing else could compare to this.

Kyle laughed loudly and wildly as he rode, like a crazy kid who'd just broken free from his mom for the first time. God, he'd missed riding. It was exactly what he needed with all the shit that had been happening. He was so glad that he had found a bike after the whole shitshow incident in the upper levels. At Emerald's insistence, they ventured into the mid-levels and found the perfect bike.

As he raced down one of the open streets of Arcadia, he made a turn on another street, coming to an intersection. This was what living was like. Crowds of normal people, not arrogant rich assholes. He would take the crowds down here in the lower levels over the palace crowd any day.

Kyle frowned. Soon he would have to be a permanent figure at the palace, being that he would be a father. And what of Derek still being king? The thought pissed him off. He wanted to marry Em. Hell, he had the ring, was just waiting for the right time. He hoped when he proposed to Emerald that she would finally start the divorce proceedings.

Why is she waiting? Did she understand that he was dead serious about marrying her? The thought unnerved him, along with how fast Emerald's tummy was growing. It seemed unnatural. Not that he had any sort of experience in that department, but still…to be as big as she was now was *off*.

What if Emerald's magic was making her pregnancy progress faster? It was possible. After all, she did have the power of life with her green magic.

A realization hit him. If her pregnancy was indeed moving at a faster rate, he was going to be a dad much sooner than the typical nine months. His time being free was short.

Better make the most of my free time while I can. Better yet, I've got to find a good time to propose to Em.

Kyle pulled into an alleyway, parking his bike. He swung off the bike, then headed down the alley and to his destination. He felt his communicator vibrate. Fumbling around in his leather jacket pocket, Kyle pulled out his communicator, seeing a missed transmission from Emerald.

Is she okay? he wondered. He'd left the palace early this morning to take a joy ride before traffic became a bitch down in the lower levels.

Kyle lit a smoke, then called her back. There were a few rings, then a voice on the other end.

"Kyle!" Emerald said over the transmission.

"Em! Everything okay?"

"There was an incident last night in the wastelands," she said as Kyle held his breath. "Geeta nearly lost her magic."

Kyle froze. "Holy shit. I take back everything I ever said about Geeta. Is she okay?" He swallowed. "Was it…your mother?"

"From what she had told me, she is okay and unharmed. She, Victor, and Garrett were attempting to locate the kidnapped girl, but in the process, they came across that red-gifted boy from Olympia. A scuffle broke out, and she nearly lost her magic."

Kyle remembered hearing about a wicked sandstorm last night. "Remember that sandstorm last night? You think it was that boy?"

"It's a good possibility."

"Did Geeta capture him?"

"No. When she was nearly captured, Victor was able to use his magic to save her. Geeta didn't go into much detail except from what I told you. She was very distant, angry, and distraught."

"Fuck Olympia. Fuck all of this," Kyle said, burning with fury. He wanted to go over there and burn the fucking place to the ground. The only thing stopping him was his desire to protect Emerald and not wanting to injure the kidnapped girl in the process. But what was far more concerning was that this reeked of

Elyathi. During his life as Rubius, the High Court had been doing everything they could to get Ikaria's violet blood. Maybe Geeta was their plan B. In fact, he would bet on it.

Kyle gripped his communicator. "Em, you know how hard it is not to leave here right now and go to Olympia and kick some fucking ass?"

"Easy," Emerald said in a soothing tone. "Remember that Geeta wanted us to stay in Arcadia. You are to be with me, and I am in no shape to go out to Olympia and start using my gift. Best you stay in the city to be near me."

"But those assholes…"

"They will be dealt with accordingly," Emerald finished his statement. "With Victor being able to access his power, we have an even playing field. And to think, with the parts ready and with Drew being fixed—it's only a matter of time before we have even stronger reinforcements." She paused. "Speaking of which, Geeta will be in Arcadia today to pick up the parts for Drew."

"Really? Is she going to visit the palace?"

"She's going straight to the Corporation and will deliver the parts right away."

Kyle frowned, taking a puff of his cigarette. "Damn. I wanted to say hi."

"Maybe you could catch her there when she's picking up the parts?"

"Good idea," Kyle said. "I'll try contacting her to meet up."

"When will you be back? I miss you already," she said longingly.

Kyle smiled as a warm fuzzy feeling fluttered over his body. "You miss me, huh? Well, I miss you too."

She laughed. "What are you up to?"

"I was going to finish up my drive and practice with the guys for a little bit."

"Okay. Don't get into trouble."

Kyle paused. Had she read his mind? "Why do you say that, Em?"

"Because I know you. You are still angry about Diego."

Kyle gritted his teeth. "Well, what do you expect? The asshole fucked with my life."

"Exactly. Just…be careful, okay?"

Kyle sighed. "Okay. Will do."

"I love you, Kyle. See you soon."

"Love you, Em."

Kyle pressed the button, ending their transmission. *Don't get into trouble, huh?* Kyle took a long drag of his smoke as he started walking down the alley. *I'll do what I can not to, Em,* he silently promised her. He just needed to sort things out first. Find out why his best buddy was so pissed off and finally put this bad blood behind them.

After walking half a block, he came to the band's warehouse. He slipped on his shades, then busted out the key, unlocked it, and slipped inside.

As soon as Kyle entered, he saw Remy and Kamren. It looked like they had arrived moments before Kyle did.

Fuck. No Diego. It was the entire reason why he'd come here. But there was another guy. Kyle groaned internally. *Fucking Joe.*

Joe saw Kyle, immediately putting away his communicator and running up to him. "Kyle. Good to see you, man."

Kyle eyed him. "Hey."

"You know that song you sang at the last show?"

Kyle gritted his teeth, thinking about his spat with Emerald and her in tears. "What about it?"

"It is the most listened to song online."

"*What?*" Kyle said, feeling ill suddenly. It was as if someone socked him in the gut.

"The song you sang," Joe said. "Some concertgoer illegally recorded the show. Turns out, they uploaded it online. As soon as it was up, it became a mega worldwide hit. It's the most downloaded song."

"You're shitting me."

"No, I'm not."

Joe laughed. Kyle didn't.

How the fuck am I going to tell Em this? Kyle's heart beat with fear at the thought. It was bad enough to slip up and sing the song once. But a fucking number one hit? He was so fucked.

"At least the ads pay us good money," Joe continued. "By the way, you'll be getting a fat check from that." He grinned ear to ear. "You guys are now the top of the top."

Rage bubbled inside of him. The fucking song that he didn't even know he sang because he was fucking roofied!

That fucker Diego! Kyle clenched his jaw. The blood pumping through his veins was full of rage. It was so bad he was choking on it. He had planned to be civil about this whole fucking thing because of Emerald. But this?

"You have no idea how incredibly lucky we are that the illegal upload made it big," Joe continued, excited. "That song is your golden ticket for life. You will be set until you croak."

The statement hit a nerve. Hard.

"Wonderful. Just fucking wonderful," Kyle snarled.

"What are you complaining about?" Joe frowned.

"Because I didn't *want* that song to become a big hit!"

"Too late. You should have thought about that before you sang it. There's nothing you can do now, so you might as well embrace it. Anyway, on my to-do list for you guys is to schedule a studio session. That way there will be a legit release, and we can make some real money off of it."

"Fuck my life," Kyle snapped.

"Fuck your life? Come on, Kyle," Joe said. "You are making serious cash. You should thank your lucky stars."

This was all Diego's fucking fault.

"Will you excuse me for a moment?" Kyle said. Remy and Kamren eyed him curiously as Kyle took a deep breath, then walked over to one of the warehouse walls around the corner. Among all the graffiti drawings on the wall, Kyle saw Emerald's old drawing, the one she drew the first time at the warehouse.

Emerald was going to be hurt by this news. How in the everlasting fuck was he going to tell her? The most fucking downloaded song online? She would never look at him the same. How the hell would he propose to her now with this shit looming over their relationship? Then another thought came to him, making him feel even more like shit. What if Glacia found out and told her before he got back to the palace?

His stomach churned.

"GODDAMMIT!" Kyle screamed as he kicked the wall hard. "FUCK this fucking BULLSHIT!" He punched the drywall, lodging his fist into the wall. He yanked it out, chunks of debris falling to the floor.

He heard Joe, Remy, and Kamren's footsteps from behind.

Fucking Joe. The fucking song. Fucking Diego!

"FUCKING piece of goddamn FUCKING shit!"

"Hey, man, what—" Joe started.

"I made a fucking mistake, and now I'm FUCKED!" Kyle yelled at him.

Joe stepped far back from Kyle. "Okay, buddy, calm down."

"CALM DOWN? How the FUCK am I supposed to CALM DOWN when I am royally FUCKED in the asshole?"

"Kyle?" Remy said. "Why are you so pissed off?"

Kyle eyed Remy. "Because I'm gonna lose the most important thing in my life! All because of fucking DIEGO!" He punched the wall again, with an added kick.

"What did that asshole do now?" Remy asked.

"He fucking drugged me, that's what! That song that I sang at the concert…I don't remember singing it. It's a private fucking song that I wrote for Em!" Kyle shouted. "And since that fucker fucked with me, I am now fucked with Em!" Saying it out loud made him even more pissed off. "FUCK!" he shouted, kicking the wall.

"Fucking Diego," Remy said.

"That's *right*," Kyle snapped. "Fucking Diego!"

"Damn, dude," Kamren said. "We know Diego can pull some stupid-ass shit, but this is pretty low."

"Low? That doesn't even begin to describe how terribly he *fucked* with my life!" Kyle shouted. "I'm gonna *kill* that motherfucker!"

"Whoa there, buddy," Kamren said. "I know you're angry as hell, but you gotta watch yourself!"

Kyle whipped around, getting in Kamren's face. "Well, then what the fuck would you do if he'd fucked you like this? Huh? Tell me!"

"I—"

"Exactly!" Kyle snapped. "Now I gotta explain everything to Em! As if that wasn't going to be hard enough! And speaking of that asshole, where the fuck is he, anyways? Isn't he supposed to be here?"

"He said he was running late." Joe inserted himself carefully. "He'll be here soon."

Rage poured over Kyle's body. He just wanted to explode.

"Kyle. Please, don't do anything stupid," Remy said. He knew what Kyle was thinking. Hell, Remy would probably think the same thing too if the circumstances were switched.

Without acknowledging Remy's statement, Kyle took a deep breath, then walked away from the wall, passing the guys and going back to where his guitar was. He lit up a smoke, shoved it in his lips, then puffed away while playing.

From the corner of his eye, he saw Kamren and Remy return to their instruments, jamming to their music. He didn't feel like singing. Just playing. He wanted to see Em, but hell, he couldn't return to the palace like this.

Almost two hours went by as the guys practiced. Kyle joined in, not saying a word. He was too fucking pissed. Joe had already left for another meeting, leaving the three of them alone playing. Kyle went through a whole pack of smokes just trying to calm his nerves.

Suddenly, a loud slam came from the main door. Kyle side-eyed, seeing Diego appear in the doorway. But in no way did he move his head. He continued to play as if he hadn't seen him.

Diego walked over to his bass, picking it up. "Sorry I'm late," Diego said.

"You can't keep being late," Remy scolded him. "We have to start coming up with new songs. And that takes time."

"Yeah, I know," Diego said.

Kyle heard Diego strum his guitar. "How are you feeling, man?" Diego called out with a snicker.

A hot surge of anger flooded Kyle's veins as he ignored him.

Diego noticed, then sneered. "What? You not talking to me?"

The guys looked wary, continuing to play their instruments, hoping music would defuse the situation.

"Oh, I see. You pissed at me?" Diego said, starting to laugh. "You should have seen all the crazy shit you pulled that night!" He began to laugh.

Without a word, Kyle put down his instrument.

"Kyle…" Remy warned.

Kyle silently walked over to Diego, looked him in the eye, and puffed his cigarette. Then he swung hard, clocking him in the face. Diego was knocked to the floor, blood spurting from his nose.

"What the fuck, man?" Diego yelled, touching his nose. Blood ran down his fingers and mouth. "That fucking hurt!"

"Hurt?" Kyle repeated. He dropped his cigarette to the floor, smashing it under his boot. "Hurt doesn't even *begin* to describe how much you fucked with me."

"It was a fucking joke!" Diego shouted back. He jumped to his feet, ready to fight.

"Some fucking joke!" Kyle shouted in his face, then punched him again, this time hard, straight in the gut. Diego doubled over in pain.

Remy yanked Kyle away, getting in between them. "No, no, no, you guys!" Remy started.

"Stay the fuck out of this, Remy!" Kyle snapped.

"You've changed, you know that?" Diego yelled at him, still grimacing. Blood ran down his chin and onto the floor.

"Changed? You're the one who's back on the transport! I'm still the same fucking person!" Kyle shouted. He pushed Remy aside, but Kamren held him back.

"Fuck you, man!" Diego shouted back. "You have changed! You and all your upper-class bullshit. You think you're better than us!"

"Is that your problem with me? Really? I came here to sort this shit out. Well, you know what? Fuck you, Diego! I ain't upper class. Never was!"

"Oh, really? Because all it is lately is 'palace this' and 'Emerald that.'"

"Because she is my *life*, asshole!"

Diego snorted through his bloody nostril. "Oh yeah? If she is your life like you say, then why hasn't she divorced the King?" he shouted.

Kyle froze in place, the guys still holding on to him. Diego's insult hit below the belt. It hurt.

"I can't believe you went there," Kyle said in a low, angry whisper.

"Yeah, I did. High and mighty Kyle Trancer! Too cool for us. Wearing shades like an asshole! All you are is the Queen's piece of ass!"

Kyle swallowed hard, giving him a hard stare. What Diego said were his own thoughts. God, he hated his best friend.

"I see it in your face. You know it's true," Diego continued. "Instead of taking out your shit on me, why don't you fucking look at your 'perfect' life."

Rage pumped through Kyle so hard that he wanted to explode. Every word hurt. It was a like a match to his soul, now ignited, and he was going to blow. And if he did, he would regret what would be the result for Diego, and ultimately his relationship with Em.

It took every muscle in his body for Kyle to jerk away. "I'm fucking done for the day," he shouted.

"That's right," Diego yelled. "Go back to being the upper-class bitch that you are!"

Kyle kicked a wall furiously. He quickly grabbed his guitar, threw it in his case, then flung it across his chest.

Then kicked the door open hard with his boot, fuming. The door swung shut behind him with a loud boom.

As he exited, he immediately thought about Emerald.

He was so fucked. No, he was beyond fucked.

CHAPTER 46

✦

GREEN

Emerald walked down the hall, returning to her quarters. After the morning's meetings with the Inner Council, she was exhausted and wanted to nap. Her legs and feet were swollen, her belly protruding, and her energy was spent.

A sudden kick fluttered in her belly.

Startled, Emerald stopped and put her hand on her belly. Another kick and a movement.

Her handmaidens paused, then eyed her curiously with excitement.

"Are you okay, Your Majesty?" asked Cyndi.

Emerald paused, then with a smile on her face, said, "Yes. I am," she said, delighted. "I felt them kick."

Her handmaidens gasped, and Emerald waved them over to feel. Each girl exclaimed when they felt it, as well as Emerald. There was a lot of movement.

"I beg your pardon, My Queen," Glacia said. "Isn't it early to feel them kick?"

Emerald thought about it. She had a point. "I did think it would happen later," Emerald agreed.

"Should we call the doctor?" Glacia asked. "It's only been a couple of months."

"Her Majesty *is* larger than typical at ten weeks," Celeste pointed out.

"Twelve weeks," Glacia corrected.

Emerald glanced around at the women, their eyes agreeing.

"Yes, call the palace physician. Better to be safe," Emerald stated.

They continued to her rooms, where Emerald climbed into bed. Immediately, she felt relief from the swelling of her feet. But it was exchanged with the uncomfortableness of her protruding belly on the mattress. Glacia noticed, helping her get in a good position with her pregnancy pillow.

"The palace physician should be here shortly," she said. "Do you want me to tell him to wait while you take a nap?"

"No, send him in when he gets here," Emerald said.

Glacia nodded, then darted out the door. For some reason that Emerald couldn't place, Glacia seemed different. Not as chipper or nosy.

Maybe she and Remy had a spat.

Just as Emerald was about to fall asleep, the door opened and the palace physician walked in.

"Your Majesty," he said, bowing.

"Doctor," Emerald stated, sitting up in bed. "Thank you for coming so quickly."

He smiled. "Your Majesty's health is the utmost priority. Your handmaidens informed me that you are experiencing kicks already?"

"Yes."

"But you are at twelve weeks?" His face was concerned. The doctor walked over to her, sitting on the edge of the bed. "May I?" he asked, holding a stethoscope.

Emerald nodded, and he placed it on her belly, listening. His face tensed. "I'm going to have the staff bring in an ultrasound machine to further examine them."

Emerald felt another flutter in her stomach. "Is everything all right?"

He went quiet. "More than all right," he said, pausing. "For some reason, it seems that the children are growing inside of you at a rapid rate. I'll be able to get an accurate assessment after the ultrasound."

They looked at each other, neither of them knowing what to say.

"Doctor, do you think it's due to my gift?" Emerald dared ask.

"I was thinking that exact same thing," he admitted. "It's the only explanation."

The doctor got up, then bowed. "I'll send a transmission for the ultrasound tech immediately. Sit tight and I'll be right back."

"Thank you."

Emerald sighed. She wished Kyle was with her.

From across the room, Zaphod cawed.

Emerald looked to him, then waved him over. "Come here, my friend."

Zaphod fluttered over to her, landing on her blanket near her knee. He cocked his head at her, then whistled.

Emerald smiled sadly. "I know. I thought Kyle was going to take you to Rosie already," she said. "Maybe he doesn't want you to leave."

The bird cocked his head again, listening, then hopped closer to her.

"Perhaps you are meant to stay with me so I'm not so lonely when he's gone."

Zaphod purred once again.

"I know I gave him my blessing about playing in his band. But I feel like… it's a bit too much." Emerald paused, thinking how late he was. It was just a band practice. But then he did mention Diego…

Emerald swallowed at the thought. Hopefully Kyle hadn't gotten into trouble. He promised he wouldn't, but his best friend did know how to push his buttons.

Kyle had said that the band wouldn't interfere with their life. But now he'd missed his baby's first kick. Not to mention he was completely neglecting his pet.

Emerald picked up her communicator on her nightstand, then dialed the number for Kyle's communicator. She let it ring and ring until she got tired of holding the communicator.

Where are you?

Emerald flopped the communicator on her bed, then stroked Zaphod's feathers, as he purred.

Lying in the bed felt so good, making Emerald realize how exhausted she truly was.

It was only moments later when the ultrasound tech appeared with the doctor, rolling in the machine.

"Your Majesty," the doctor greeted her again. "This will only take a few minutes."

The handmaidens changed her into a robe, then the doctor had Emerald raise it to expose her belly. He squeezed clear jelly on her stomach, then put the machine's smooth reader against it.

Emerald watched as the children on the screen appeared. The babies were *large.*

The doctor studied the images intently on the screen, then printed them out, handing them to Emerald. He looked flustered. "Th-they are perfectly healthy. Although, I'd say they are the size of children in the seventh month of development."

Emerald's jaw dropped. She knew her handmaidens had done the same. "*Seven* months?"

The doctor had the same expression, then shrugged. "It's definitely something I have never seen before," he said. "Considering the measurements I took of your belly, I'm not surprised. Don't worry, though. All is well."

Emerald, still wide-eyed, swallowed hard. "Thank you, Doctor."

He bowed. "I'm going to do checkups three times a week now, just to monitor them."

"Okay," Emerald said.

"Good day, Your Majesty."

He left, rolling the machine out, and most of her maidens left as well. Glacia remained. *She looks tired,* Emerald thought.

Just as Emerald was about to ask her if she was okay, Glacia bowed. "You must get some rest before this evening's event," she said, then darted out the door.

What is going on with her?

The room was silent, leaving Emerald to her thoughts.

Where is Kyle? Emerald thought. *He was supposed to be back by now.* They had planned on getting ready for the evening's event within the hour.

If it was true that her babies were measuring at seven months, then she needed to prepare now. Kyle too. She had thought that they had more time for him to embrace his musical success before he became a father, giving him time to live his life. But that time was almost gone. In the back of her mind, all Emerald could think about was Kyle not being there for her.

A noise at the door startled Emerald.

Celeste came in, bowing. "I'm here to do your hair, My Queen."

"Thank you, Celeste," Emerald said as she sat up.

"First, though, you must splash your face with cold water," Celeste said.

"I look that tired?" Emerald asked.

Celeste didn't say anything, just smiled at her as she helped her out of bed.

Emerald walked over to her bathroom sink and splashed icy water across her face several times. The cold water did make her feel more alive and definitely awake.

Cyndi came in after her, bowing. "Glacia picked out a couple gowns for you. I put them on the bed. Several of them are new."

"Okay, I'll take a look." Emerald walked over to the bed, sifting through the gowns. "This one," she said, pointing to a dark purple gown. She turned to Celeste. "I'd rather do my hair first. The less time I'm sitting in a gown the better."

"That's fine. The gown has a long zipper in the back, so it will be easy to step into it rather than slipping it over your head."

Emerald sat down at her vanity as Celeste started to get to work on her hair.

"Have you seen Kyle today?" Emerald asked.

Celeste shrugged. "I saw him early this morning on the back lift but haven't since."

A knot formed in Emerald's stomach.

Celeste brushed her hair thoroughly, working through the wavy tangles. The feeling of Celeste styling her hair always gave her chills down her spine, in the best sort of way. If it were up to Emerald, she would have Celeste style her hair most of the day, every day.

As Celeste continued to work, the bedroom door opened, and Kyle appeared.

Emerald cried out, causing Celeste to let go of her hair.

"Hey, gorgeous, what's going on?" Kyle said casually.

Emerald noticed one of his hands was behind his back.

"Master Kyle," Celeste said, bowing.

"Kyle! You startled me," Emerald breathed, beaming at him in the mirror.

"Sorry 'bout that."

Suddenly, her worry fled her mind, and her stomach wasn't knotted up anymore.

Kyle chuckled, walking over to her as Celeste backed up, giving them space. Kyle leaned in and kissed her. Just then, he pulled his hand out in front of her, a deep red rose in its grasp.

Emerald gasped with a big smile. "Kyle! You shouldn't have." She blushed as she smelled the rose.

His ruby eyes sparkled as he kissed her. "I want you to know how much you mean to me, Em," he whispered in her ear, kissing her once again.

A hot flush ran throughout her body as she smiled shyly. Their eyes met, then he began rubbing her shoulders and neck. His touch felt so soothing, releasing all the tension she had been feeling. Emerald breathed a sigh of relief. Why had she been so worried in the first place? After all, it was just a dream.

"That feels so good," Emerald said.

Zaphod cawed.

"Enjoying the show?" Kyle asked the bird.

"Should I come back later?" Celeste asked.

Emerald nodded. "Yes, let me tell him the news."

Celeste smiled, then bowed as Kyle said, "What news?"

When Celeste left, Emerald leaned in. "The palace physician did a scan on me."

His face suddenly turned concerned. "What? Are you okay? Oh my God, Em, what happened…"

"I'm fine," Emerald said, then quickly, "They are fine too."

Emerald watched as Kyle's tension melted away. "Whew. What a relief."

"But there is something you should know," Emerald said, as her eyes met his. "The babies are measuring at seven months."

"What? *Seven* months?"

"They are growing at an alarming rate, that's all."

"Oh my God, Em, stop scaring me! Are they going to be all right?"

"The doctor said they'll be fine," Emerald said. "It must be my gift."

Emerald could see a hint of worry and stress on Kyle's face, but he played it cool. He gave her a hug, then kissed her forehead. "I'm just glad you are okay, and them too."

Emerald smiled at him. "Same."

He gave her a charming smile, then strode over to her bed, kicked off his combat boots, and plopped onto it.

"Where were you?" Emerald asked.

"You know I went for a ride then to practice," he said almost defensively.

"Yes, but I didn't think it would be that long."

There was an awkward silence between them. "I didn't mean to upset you." Kyle glanced at her, giving her a smile. It made her melt the way he looked at her. "I didn't think you would mind, that's all."

"Did you see that I tried sending you a transmission?"

Kyle's face drew a blank. "You did?"

"Yes. Several times."

He quickly grabbed his personal communicator, then looked at the faceplate. "Oh shit. I didn't see it. It looks like you tried during my practice. I guess I couldn't hear it over the music. I'm sorry."

His apology made her feel bad for even having frustrated thoughts about him.

"It's fine. I'm glad you are here now," Emerald said, flushing. She pressed the button on her vanity. A second later, Celeste appeared.

"My Queen," she said, bowing, then returned to Emerald's hair.

"By the way, did I tell you that I love the hairstyle?" Kyle called out.

"No, you didn't."

"Well, it's beautiful on you," he said, coming over to her.

Emerald smiled. "Thank you."

"Must you wear clothes to this event?"

"Kyle!" Emerald grabbed a makeup brush, playfully throwing it at him. Celeste laughed.

"Sorry! My mouth just starts talking without my brain," he admitted. "Kidding aside, you really do look stunning." He kissed her cheek sweetly. "Have I ever told you how lucky I am? Beautiful woman with the kindest spirit. And a creative master painter."

"All right, what are you buttering me up for?" Emerald asked teasingly.

"I'm not!" He chuckled. "Can't a guy give praise when praise is due? I mean, look at your most recent paintings," he said, pointing at her easel, then to the wall. "These are spectacular."

Emerald blushed. "Thank you."

"I mean it."

They exchanged loving eyes, until Celeste said, "Master Kyle, what are you wearing for tonight's event?"

"This, I guess." He gestured to his black leather pants with silver spikes and studs. "Don't got much else."

Celeste moved her eyes up and down, her eyebrows moving up.

"I will send Cyndi out to get you something," Emerald said. "Just tell her your size, and she can go now and be back in time for the event."

"All right." He reached into his jacket pocket, searching. Then he started getting frantic. "What the hell? Where is it?"

"Where is what?" Emerald asked.

"My wallet! It's gone! I put it in my jacket…"

"I'll just have the palace pay for it," Emerald said.

His face turned serious. "No."

"What? Why not?"

"I don't want you paying for my stuff, that's all."

Celeste froze, while Emerald turned around to face him. In the ruby depths of his eyes, anger simmered.

Emerald tensed up. "Celeste, will you please excuse us for a moment?"

"Yes, My Queen," she replied, bowing.

Emerald turned to face him. "What is going on? Why are you so upset? What did I say?"

"Who says I'm upset? I just don't want you to pay for my things."

"Why?"

Kyle sighed, then began pacing. "Em, the last thing a guy wants is for a woman to pay for his shit. Men are supposed to support their woman, not the other way around."

"Kyle, you realize that society has progressed past such notions, haven't you?" Emerald said.

"It's a pride thing, okay? I should be making a shitload of money to support you, because that's what men are supposed to do. It's wired into our nature," he urged. Kyle came up to her, leaning in. "You mean everything to me, and I want to do everything to make you happy. That includes me working hard to support you and the children."

"I guess if it means that much to you…"

"It does. I am serious. I want to make my own way and not have my girl pay for me. I don't wanna be a mooch. Ever."

"You aren't being a mooch, whatever that means," Emerald insisted.

"But I would be if I kept leeching off you. Not gonna do it."

Emerald sighed. "But you aren't 'leeching' off me. You have money, it's just tied up." She paused. "And given your current circumstances, you can't very well go to the event like that." Emerald put her hand on his leg. "Please, just let Cyndi get you an outfit. It's just one. If it makes you feel better, you can pay the palace treasury back."

Emerald sat in silence as he thought about it. Kyle frowned, then sighed. "Fine. But I *will* be paying back the treasury."

Emerald went to the door, opening it. "Cyndi, could you please come take Kyle's measurements?"

She smiled, then hopped up. "Yes, My Queen."

Kyle appeared at the door with his arms crossed. "Guess I gotta get this over with." Cyndi grabbed a measuring tape, then started in on him. "Just so you know, I like wearing black. I don't want to look like the other assholes at the party, okay?"

Cyndi smirked, then nodded. "I think I understand your style, Master Kyle. I'll pick out something that will suit you, you have no need to worry."

"All right." His eyes met Emerald's. "The things I do for love," he said jokingly.

Emerald smiled, then came over to him, kissing him. "Thank you. I mean it."

In his eyes, there was still much anxiety.

Cyndi finished up, then left them alone once again.

As soon as the door clicked shut, Kyle looked at her. He seemed *off*.

"There's…something I have to tell you," he said, clearing his throat.

Emerald perked up immediately. "What is it?"

"Well, you see…" Her eyes were glowing green. He gulped. "So, remember our whole conversation about that song I sang?"

"Yes." Her face was serious.

"Uh, well, there was an illegal sound recording of it when I sang it. It's become the number one song online…"

Emerald's heart stopped, and she stared blankly at him.

"*What?*"

Kyle quickly came over to her, getting on his knees. "Em, I swear to God that I never wanted any of this to happen! I was seeing red when I found out. I just…you know…I know we smoothed it out and all. I did not expect this. I can't even begin to tell you how sorry I am. I've been shitting bricks about it since. I don't want to lose you over this, but it seems that this keeps coming back and biting us in the ass."

"So that's why you gave me a rose."

"No! I gave it to you because I love you!"

"You were buttering me up."

"That's *so* not *true*," he said pointedly.

"How did it happen, then?" Emerald's face went stone-cold.

"Some fucking asshole recorded the song illegally at the concert, then uploaded it to the internet," he said quickly. "After that, the song spread like wildfire online." Kyle gritted his teeth. "I found out right before I came back here."

"Can't Joe take it offline by talking to the Corporation?"

"He could, but that won't stop all the copies that have gone up. Joe said everyone has been demanding a legit copy."

A wave of anger and jealousy came over her. Emerald shot up from her vanity, walking toward Zaphod. Anything to let her avoid looking at him.

"Em…"

It was as if she couldn't hear him. She didn't want to hear him. It was as if she had entered a bad dream. The one thing that had upset her came back to haunt her. And now, his mistake—if she could even blame him—would always linger. Even worse, that knotted feeling in her stomach returned.

"Em…say something," he whispered.

Her lips parted, then Emerald blinked again.

"Anything."

"What do you *want* me to say?" Emerald snapped as she slowly sat on the edge of her bed.

His face dropped. Even she surprised herself.

"I didn't know any of this was gonna happen," Kyle continued. "After our talk the other day, I thought, just like you, that this whole thing would be behind us." He paused. "But it's not. I know you're pissed off at me…"

"I'm not pissed off at you…"

"Okay. Pissed off that this is happening. It's not my fault," he finished. "But I'm scared. Every day, you are gonna resent me. Resent me for something I had no control over. And your resentment is how I am gonna lose you."

Emerald paused. She tried hard not to show emotion on her face, and instead closed her eyes. He was right—if she harbored her resentment over one mistake, it would put a wedge between them. What was she angry about? Why was she so jealous?

"I'm just upset that the song was between the two of us, and now the whole world—literally—is part of our private moment," Emerald said. "It's one thing for it to happen at the concert. But now…it will live on forever."

"I know. I wouldn't have done it if I hadn't been drugged by that fucking asshole! I already beat the shit out of him…"

Emerald jerked her head toward him. "You *beat up* Diego?"

Kyle gritted his teeth. "That's putting it mildly."

"Kyle…"

"Well, what the fuck should I have done? Let it go? Hell no!" Kyle dropped to his knees again, grabbing her hands. "I can't lose you, Em. I love you. I want to be with you the rest of my life!"

"But what does that have to do with Diego?"

"It has everything to do with Diego! Look at us now. If that asshole hadn't roofied me, we wouldn't be having this talk!"

I must let this go, she thought. Emerald faced him, placing a hand on his chest. "Kyle…"

He put his hand on hers. "Please. Please don't be pissed at me."

His eyes flickered with worry as she studied them. Suddenly, she felt bad. Maybe she was overreacting. But then, he did miss the babies' kick, the doctor scare…

Emerald put her hand on his face, guiding it up. "I'll be fine. What's done is done. You couldn't help the entire situation, and for that, how can I be angry? It isn't fair to you. The song…yes, it means so much to me. But now that it's out, like you said before, we should embrace it and let it be our declaration of love for each other. Just…sing it for *me* each time you sing it to your audience." His eyes locked on to hers, and she smiled at him, playfully running her hands down his cheek. "That's all I ask for."

"But what you told me earlier…" he started.

"The situation has changed," Emerald said softly. His eyes radiated with energy as the situation melted away. "And as for what's online, make a better recording of it."

Kyle gave her a confused look. "Is this a trap?"

"What do you mean?"

"First you ask me not to sing it anymore. Now you are asking me to make an official recording?" Kyle said. "Sounds like a fucking trap to me."

Emerald sighed. "Kyle…I'm not one to 'trap' anybody. I am trying to make light of the situation that we find ourselves in. All I ask is that you think of me when you sing that song."

There was a long pause between them. "And you won't be pissed off at me? You won't be fuming in secret?" he pressed.

Emerald shook her head. "No. I'm mostly over it now." She leaned into him.

"Really? That quick, huh?"

"Well, not that quick. But I'll be all right." Tension melted away between the two of them. "Kyle, I am giving you permission. It is okay."

Kyle glanced at her. "I love you."

She breathed. "I love you too…"

He leaned in to kiss her. His lips felt soft, warm, and plush against hers. Warmth ran through her body, warming her center…

Zaphod cawed, startling them from their kiss.

"He's always got to make a comment," he whispered.

Emerald giggled, and the mood lightened. "Indeed."

Their lips met again as he held her cheeks tenderly. "Let's get this damn party out of the way, shall we?"

She nodded. Everything would be okay.

CHAPTER 47

◆

Elder Moon watched the monitors. On them, the sandstorm blew across the planet's surface. The patterns made strange motions overhead. According to the other underground citadels, the ones they had connections to, they had seen the same occurrence. The world was in upheaval.

She had been watching the sandstorm patterns every day since she had met Rubius, or rather, Kyle. Elder Moon was by no means gifted, but even she could feel the unrest within the earth. It was as if the earth had changed since Kyle had appeared to her people. Though he was a red-gifted, even Elder Moon knew that no one had that kind of power to change the natural elements for this long of time. Even the green magic that pumped through their citadel felt different. Maybe it was due to his connection to the ancient queen of long ago.

I wonder if Kyle ever fought the High Court or made his way back to Queen Emerald, she thought. Somehow, she knew that something had happened—the wind patterns were proof. But what?

Something else had disturbed her since meeting Kyle. He spoke of the white-gifted. The very gifted who was prophesied to save the earth. Restore it to its former glory. But now, the High Court had her, and she seemed to have a very different perception of what she was supposed to do to fulfill the prophecy according to Kyle the sky dweller. Had the High Court brainwashed her? Or had she turned of her own accord?

Browsing the glowing monitors, Elder Moon sighed.

"What is on your mind?" Elder Stone's voice called out.

Elder Moon glanced over her shoulder. "Can't you feel it? Something is happening."

Elder Stone gave her a long sigh, then eyed the screens. "Yes. The magic within our citadel…it's almost as if it's calling us to help. A sadness, if you will."

She frowned, turning back to the monitors. It was like a switch had been flipped inside of her, causing much anxiety and unrest just like the earth itself.

"Do you suppose these storms are tied to the white-gifted Kyle spoke of?" Elder Moon asked.

"Why would it?" he asked. "She has no control over the earth, or him."

"But suppose that because of the events that transpired, this is a way for the earth to warn us. As if our time is near," she said. "Maybe this white-gifted is about to fulfill the prophecy."

"I can't accept that." Elder Stone's face turned serious. "As keepers of the ancient earth's knowledge, we know this planet. The anger that it radiates…it's not ready to accept the final ending."

Elder Moon sighed. "You're right." She got up, her old bones aching from sitting too long. "I need some rest." She turned away from the monitors, walking through their underground citadel, her thoughts still fixated on the white-gifted Elyathi. Elder Moon had been in her late teens when news of the white-gifted child was rampant in all the underground citadels. All the earth dwellers knew that one day, a white-gifted would restore the earth to its former glory. That she would be the one to bring peace…

But now, the white-gifted child was a woman fully embracing her power. And the earth was angry.

Where did we go wrong? Elder Moon wondered. According to what Rubius told her of Elyathi, this white-gifted was not the hope that every earth dweller had dreamed about. Maybe it was all a mistake.

As Elder Moon walked back to her quarters, her uneasiness grew. If what Rubius said about Elyathi was true, that woman had to be stopped. Did Elder Moon and her people dare fight against a chosen destined to fulfill a prophecy? It was all counterintuitive. She needed a sign.

Elder Moon entered her quarters, then walked to her bookshelf. She didn't have much, but the tomes and books she did have were important. She did have other data from books in their screen data readers, but what she wanted was to hold the holy book.

Clutching the only copy of *The Spectrum* ever found on the earth's surface, Elder Moon carefully slid the book from the shelf, then held it within her frail hands. She slowly walked over to her favorite chair, then sat down, her knees twinging in pain.

Gently, she caressed the cover with utmost care. Elder Moon dared not even open the book, for the pages could crumble, given how old it was. But there was power just in holding the holy book.

Laying both hands upon the book, she prayed in earnest.

What are we to do as a people? We feel your anger upon the earth. Shall we pay for the High Court's sins? For what the white-gifted woman is doing? Is she truly your servant, taking away all the magic of the world? We need...I need a sign...

And she continued to pray.

Prayed all night until she couldn't remember falling asleep.

CHAPTER 48

♦

WHITE

From across the room, Elyathi watched in secret as Samir drank from his chalice. Seated next to him for the dinner was the duke of Montez, the Arcadian overlord of the southern sector. The two were exchanging laughs in between bites of dinner. What they said, Elyathi couldn't tell.

The evening sunlight that shone through the windows hit his face perfectly, bathing him in golden-orange hues. Even from a distance, his dark eyes and lush lashes captured the light perfectly, his chiseled face and dark curls standing out.

Elyathi lowered her gaze to her own dinner. Her husband was watching her like a hawk, and the longer she stared, the more Samir was in jeopardy. Damaris would start to question her loyalty to him, her devotion to him, and she couldn't endure his questioning. It wouldn't matter what was true and what wasn't; he would make up his own mind and hand out consequences. And those consequences were always extreme. She couldn't let that happen, especially to Samir.

She twirled her fork, staring at the intricate designs etched on the dinner plate, lost in thought. Her heart longed for Samir. She couldn't think of anything else but him. Every whisper of his name made her jump inside. Even his name on a document made her blush. But no matter how much she wished for a glance from him, how much she dreamed of a private smile, it never happened. He treated her just like how he treated any other woman. Perhaps even less. What did she expect? It was not possible for him to show her any sort of affection, regardless of what he felt. She was married to his best friend.

It was wrong of him, and wrong of her to even think such things…

Elyathi said a sudden, silent prayer, asking the God of Light to forgive her for her heart straying. She was supposed to love her husband. Supposed to be devoted. She had to be faithful. It was so hard in her current state. Her marriage, her love…it had all turned out so differently than what she had dreamed growing up.

"What is wrong, my sweet Elyathi?" Damaris asked, seated next to her.

Elyathi looked up to him, her so-called "beloved," and mustered the most genuine smile she could. "I'm just not fond of this dinner," she said. She couldn't very well lie, and roasted chicken wasn't her favorite.

Damaris's face suddenly darkened. "I should fire the cook."

"No, please don't do that," Elyathi said. "Perhaps have them make me another dish?"

Damaris turned to a servant, pointing to Elyathi's plate of food. "The Queen is unhappy with her dish. Summon that insubordinate cook immediately!"

"Yes, right away," the servant said, then ran off.

Elyathi frowned to herself privately, then gave another false smile to Damaris as he turned to her.

"My King, there is no need to summon the cook," Elyathi said hastily, her heart racing. She knew what was coming.

"No, he needs to hear the words from my own lips and correct this situation. I *cannot* and *will not* have my wife unhappy. You are the jewel of Arcadia, for all the world to behold, and my beloved. You deserve everything your heart desires," he said, his cold green eyes angry.

Elyathi gripped the armrest of the chair, trying not to shake. As she did, the cook appeared with the servant.

"Your Majesty, you have called upon me?" the cook asked nervously.

"The Queen is unhappy with her dinner," he said sharply. A few people seated near them pretended not to notice.

"I am very sorry, Your Majesties." The cook bowed low.

"Unforgiven," Damaris said coldly.

The cook fell to his hands and knees. "Your Majesty, I beg of you, please forgive me. Let me rectify the situation."

Damaris snarled, then grabbed her plate of food. Elyathi wanted to stop him, but if she did, it would be much worse for her later.

The King hurled the metal plate of food at the cook's head. It hit the cook hard, knocking him over, while the food went everywhere.

People at the table were dead silent. The cook struggled to his knees, lowering his head in shame. "I'll make a new dish for the Queen. Anything that you wish, Your Majesty. I could make a roasted herb chicken with wine sauce…"

Elyathi wanted to run. Scream. Cry. But she sat motionless, as if under her husband's spell.

Damaris shot up from his seat, and Elyathi could no longer look.

"I didn't realize that I had an imbecile for a cook!" She heard Damaris pick up the metal plate. Then a loud thunk followed by the cook crying out in pain. "The Queen does—"

Whack.

"NOT—"

Whack. Blood splattered in her view.

"LIKE—"

Smack.

"CHICKEN!" he shouted.

Elyathi's throat tightened as the word *chicken* echoed in the dining hall.

Damaris snapped the plate square in the cook's face. "No chicken! You understand, you pea-brained, insignificant, worthless piece of filth?"

"Yes! Yes!" cried the cook. Elyathi saw blood running down his face.

"Yes? Yes? Have you forgotten to how to address your king?"

"I'm sorry, Your Majesty. Your Majesty, I'm so sorry, please forgive me," the cook begged, tears mixing with blood.

Elyathi turned away.

As she looked down at her chalice, there was another loud whack, another cry from the cook. "Get this fool out of my sight and throw him in the dungeon!" he roared. "And someone make the Queen an acceptable dinner! Otherwise heads will roll! You hear me? I will have their HEADS!"

The servants all said in unison, "Yes, Your Majesty."

Footsteps, then shuffling as the cook struggled.

"Please, Your Majesty, I beg of you…" the cook cried as the guards dragged him off.

The doors to the dining hall shut, while Elyathi continued to stare at her chalice.

Her stomach churned. She just wanted to cry. She had to hold it back, otherwise he would even get more upset.

"All will be better now," Damaris said, putting his hand on her shoulder. She wanted to throw his hand off, get away from him. His touch made her flinch inwardly. She was supposed to love him. She was supposed to support him…

"Let us finish the evening with more joy," Damaris stated to the table. "I would hate to have that no-good lemming of a cook ruin our evening. In fact, bring out one of the finest palace wines to compensate for everyone's poor evening."

Elyathi's eyes flicked to the bloody floor. She looked up; everyone at the table gave her smiles. Whether they were false or real, she didn't know. They raised their glasses and cheered.

Damaris leaned over her shoulder, whispering in her ear hotly, "I will have you tonight." His violent behavior always made him want sex. The more infuriated he was, the worse her night would be.

As he kissed her neck, she cringed in her mind. Just then, her eyes darted to Samir. Or where he had been. Samir's seat was empty. Elyathi trembled.

Damaris swept her hair aside, running his fingers across her bare back.

"You bring me much pleasure, Elyathi…" he whispered hotly. "I will always make you happy…"

She just wanted him to stop touching her, kissing her, but he continued.

His hand ran down her neck and into the top of her dress, right in front of their guests. They pretended not to notice, but she knew they saw.

She remained frozen. Damaris let out a private laugh, taking pride in his control over her. His *doll*.

I will always make you happy, echoed his voice.

She just wanted to escape, but his hand clutched her bosom. Murmurs started.

I will always make you happy…

Tears formed, her husband fondling her in front of everyone, exposing more of her breasts.

Always make you happy…

Samir suddenly came into view, peering behind one of the hall's pillars. His dark eyes met hers…

Elyathi opened her eyes to the white of the ceiling. She sat up from her bed, noticing she was in the safety of her room. Far, far away from Damaris…

No matter how much she tried to forget all those years, they kept coming back to haunt her. She wiped a few tears away. All those years, she was so alone. Not even her best friend Victor had come and visited her. Not once had he responded to all the letters she had sent to him.

He didn't care. No one did.

Birds chirped from outside the window as the sun's rays poured inside. Turning her head, Elyathi glanced outside the window. Something in her soul was restless. What was it? Why had her dream come back to haunt her once again?

Her soul had been feeling restless ever since seeing Derek. The years of locking away her feelings for Samir, then seeing his son. Derek was very much like his father.

She had spent so many years…wanting. Yearning.

How many years had she denied her true feelings for Samir? How many nights had she lain awake, thinking about him? How many times had she thought of him while Damaris had his way with her? To escape the pain, to escape her reality. Samir was her comfort.

Elyathi ran her hands down the front of her white lacy nightgown as she thought about Samir. She had fantasized about him countless times. How would he touch her body? Would he be violent like Damaris? Or would he be gentle? What would he kiss first? Her lips? Her neck? Or lower?

Elyathi was supposed to get out of bed. She had much work to do in World Sector Four. But somehow, the dream of Samir made her immobile, and her thoughts continued to linger on his beautiful dark eyes, the color of onyx stones…

Her hand moved slowly from her neck down to the tops of her breasts. Nothing but the sheerness of the fabric covered her. But instead of her hand, she imagined that it was Samir's, touching her breasts. She imagined him being aroused by her, his member hard.

What am I doing? But everything felt so good. Her body had never felt this elated in her life.

Her hands trailed down her body. She had never touched her body like she was now. Her fingers reached her center. Her sheer undergarment was slightly damp and sticky to the touch. She focused on Samir, as if he were the one touching her below.

Slipping her fingers below her undergarment, she slid her fingers inside of herself. But it was not her fingers, it was Samir thrusting into her.

Her body arched in ecstasy as she continued.

But then, something happened.

Samir's image changed. No longer were his dark eyes peering at her. They were replaced with crystal blue ones, burning with desire. Firm hands, desperate, longing to touch every inch of her flesh. The hands were paler than Samir's, and much younger. The body, the one she imagined in her mind, was very much was aroused by the sight of her. His muscles gleamed with sweat, glistening in the light, his flesh aching for her.

This was Samir in a different form. Her mind released what she had wanted secretly, and for the first time, admitted her desire.

She *wanted* him.

Her lowers ached with desire. She squeezed her thighs shut, tensing as she focused on the image of him. His crystal blue eyes desired her, lusted after her, hungered for her, needed her…

Elyathi kept her hand in place as she writhed in her bed. The image of him… releasing his sexual tension…

She wanted him. She needed him…

In the new world, you will be with me.

A hard shudder came over her, her mind in complete ecstasy.

Slowly, her breathing returned to normal, and her core calmed. She removed her hand, her fingers completely sticky.

What had she done?

Elyathi snapped upright, her long wavy snowy locks of hair falling in her face. Her forehead beaded with sweat.

She wanted *him*.

The worst of all, she knew she couldn't have him.

Trying to clear her mind, Elyathi walked over to her bedroom's washbasin, rinsing her hands free of her guilt. Her hands became purified as the stickiness was washed away. But this feeling of desire, it felt so right, though it was so wrong to pleasure herself the way she had.

Elyathi splashed her face, then toweled her face and hands. Then she turned to her vanity, seating herself. She grabbed her brush, combing the tangles out of her hair. The light hit her face, accenting yet another fine line to add to the collection. She moved this way and that, seeing how the light highlighted that line. She couldn't unsee it.

She frowned, massaging her skin between her brows, hoping that it was just how she slept. But no amount of massaging rid her of the new wrinkle. She was getting old.

Never in her life had she worried about her looks. She was always deemed perfect, praised by the world for her beauty. And never had she let that go to her heart and become vain by it. It was sinful. Not only that, but one should not be judged on their looks, but how pure of heart they were.

But now, something inside of her had changed. She didn't know what, but it was different. The lines on her face, the faint age spots, even a little loose skin around her neck…it was glaringly obvious to her, as if it was the first time she had truly looked at herself in twenty years. And for the first time ever, she cared about her appearance.

Fear stirred deep within. *He* had said she was beautiful. But if more wrinkles appeared, and age marred her face…she would be less beautiful. And less desirable, especially in *his* eyes.

Another wave of panic came over her.

Pushing the vain and sinful thought aside, she applied her makeup in a delicate manner. Violets on her lids, pink blush on her porcelain skin, and deep ruby lip creme on her small lips. She looked like what everyone described her as…a living doll.

The thought made her angry. That was how Damaris had viewed her. His doll.

She took a look in the mirror again. But she was no longer a young, youthful beautiful doll. She was an *old* doll, one aging into an old maid.

She leaned her face close to the mirror, inspecting each flaw in her once-perfect face.

Thoughts of moments ago returned to her. His hands gently gliding across her breasts…

I must purge this sin from my mind!

But she couldn't help but return to those sinful thoughts.

She could never have him. Could never speak his name in her mind. That is, unless it was in her new world…

I will take Samir for myself in the new world and finally fulfill my desires.

Elyathi clutched her eyeshadow in the palm of her hand, then crushed them angrily. No, Samir wasn't enough.

For once, it was her time to put her own desires first.

She needed *him*. She needed her new world. And quickly.

Loosely shaking off the dust on her hands, she carefully rinsed her hands, then held her chin up high.

Grasping her blue gem necklace, she filled herself with its magic.

It was time for more sinners to pay, and for the gifted to bring forth *her* new world.

CHAPTER 49

$\blacklozenge$

Khari Ramla shot up from his sleep. A flood of screams and shouts pierced his ears. Bloodcurdling screams.

Suddenly his door slammed open without any formalities, his personal guard rushing in.

"Oy! What is happening?" the Khari shouted.

"Everywhere…all the gifted everywhere are sick!" the guard said breathlessly. "All of them!"

The Khari jumped up from bed, not caring that he was in his nightclothes, and ran out of the room.

Chaos filled the halls as the Khari ran past frantic guards and into the stairwell. More screams echoed through the stone tower. He glanced down the down the circular staircase, catching a glimpse of two women writhing in agony on a step in the orange lamplight.

It was the plague.

"Find the other guards and spread out amongst the citadel! See if there are any other victims and bring them to the central courtyard!" the Khari ordered the guard.

"Yes, Khari." The guard saluted and ran down the stairwell in the direction of the courtyard.

A flood of thoughts came into his mind as he ran down the stairs. Lady Vala had warned them. The other lords had thought to stay out of World Sector Six's business with the Empress. Some didn't believe Vala's story of the High Court ordering her to kidnap a green-gifted from another time. They all said that Vala was simply telling a ludicrous story and shouldn't be trusted. Some said that

High Priest Auron, her uncle, lost his wits when he aligned with the Empress Ayera and not the High Court. Yet there were others who had wanted to help Vala and the sector. Some of the court gifted spoke out—they were there at the time of traveling back to Arcadia. But these warnings fell on deaf ears.

And now, it was too late.

The Khari made his way down the stairs to the women. Both were rolling dangerously, about to tumble down the stairs, screaming. He kneeled down, grasping one of the women. It was Lady Wamaba, an orange-gifted.

"My lady," the Khari said loudly, giving her a shake, hoping that it would cause her to snap out of it. Instead, her eyes were clouded with white as she threw her head back, crying and screaming.

She was losing her *gift*.

"MY LADY!" he yelled again, clutching her.

Tears streamed down her cheeks. "My son has walked the surface!" she cried out. "Flowers of orange. Fields of orange!"

The Khari knew that Lady Wamaba's son had died many years ago. He never went to the surface.

"My lady," he whispered, "you must snap out of it."

The woman stared at him eerily, but her mind was elsewhere.

"Did you know that the ground has machines? I have seen them!" she cried. "All in the color of orange. It's so beautiful, and yet terrifying…"

Behind him, the other woman wept uncontrollably, mumbling nonsense. The Khari crawled to the other woman, then pulled her back to a safe position. She looked at him with empty eyes.

"My face has melted off," she cried. "No more can I show my face…" She screamed. "It hurts so much!"

Her face was smooth and beautiful. But her eyes were a cloudy white, like the other woman.

The Khari shed a tear as he watched the two gifted women lose their gifts right before his eyes.

✦ ✦ ✦

An orchestra of screams played out all across World Sector Four. It was the great symphony of the heavens, for the time was drawing near.

Elyathi sat in silence as she kept her hand outstretched toward the royal citadel. Magic from every gifted funneled straight into her body and settled deep within her life force.

I will have you, she said in her mind, thinking of Samir. *All those years I wanted you! You have never once wanted me. That will all change…*

She flared open her eyes, thinking of all her lost time and regrets.

All my friends abandoned me, she continued, thinking of Victor. *You never cared.*

No more. She would suffer no more.

There will be no more hurt…no more pain!

The moon was full, shining its white light across the scattered floating islands, the tops of the golden citadel shining white. She had chosen this night because it was *her* night—the white light of the moon. Her life force was fully refreshed, her energy vibrant. She had consumed more life forces on her way here—making her more powerful this night. For she had gained a higher level of understanding of her magic each time she used her white gift. She no longer needed to touch a body to gain their gift unless her energy was spent.

Let them know who I am! she thought, raising her chin. *I am the chosen!*

With a flurry of anger, Elyathi closed her eyes, using all of her life force's strength to suck all the magic from the citadel. No gifted stood a chance against her, even Lady Vala. That defiant fool. If Lady Vala had brought her daughter back through the portal, Elyathi would have had her new world by now! And yet, Lady Vala had thwarted the God of Light's plans again by assisting that wicked sorceress in the battle of World Sector Six.

Lady Vala ruined everything. Not once, not twice, but *three* times.

She will pay for her treachery.

Elyathi's hand shook furiously as she consumed all the magic that flowed into her from World Sector Four in a stream of color. All the power coursing through her veins, intermixing deep within her core being.

She was the most powerful. She was the chosen one. This was meant to be. No one else, just her and her complement. Derek suddenly entered her thoughts. He was so like Samir in every way.

A flicker of confusion, quickly squelched.

Derek is the ideal of a true ruler for the new world, she thought. Derek would lord over everyone, with her by his side.

Elyathi laughed. Laughed in the face of the Lord of Darkness, of all those wicked people.

The righteous shall overcome...

CHAPTER 50

♦

VIOLET

"Enchantress Ikaria," Lord Jiao called out from her chamber doorway.

It was the early hours of the morning, but Ikaria had already been up, working on activating the new artifacts. She sighed, then put the ancient artifact down as she glanced over her shoulder.

"Lord Jiao, what brings you here at the precise moment I need full concentration?" she said, annoyed. "You know that it's not my time to fulfill my vow. In a little bit, I'll be on with it."

"I am so sorry to disturb you, Enchantress, but it has nothing to do with that. I have important news from World Sector Four," he said with nod. "News that I thought you should hear from my own lips."

"Have they finally come to their senses?" Ikaria huffed. That sector. Out of all the sectors, she had thought Vala's sector would come to their aid. They needed blue-gifted, and that sector was the one with the most.

"No, Enchantress," he said quickly. "The entire sector's gifted..." He paused, finding his words.

Ikaria glanced up at him, searching his face, finding mourning and sorrow. It told her everything she needed to know.

"They have no more gifted, do they?" Ikaria whispered in disbelief.

He nodded, in solemn silence.

Ikaria clutched the artifact in her hand, shaking it in her grasp. She didn't know who she was more angry with—Elyathi or World Sector Four's court. They hadn't wanted to align themselves with her, which aggravated Ikaria to no end. It was a blow to her plans, but she would make do.

But now, with Elyathi draining all the remaining gifted, Ikaria had to admit that it made her sweat. Not that she couldn't take on Elyathi—of course she could—because she was a violet-gifted, and she could take on anyone if she wanted to. But if Elyathi was stripping away powers around her, isolating the remaining gifted, that would make it harder for anyone to stop her. And for Ikaria to save her sister. Ikaria didn't know what was worse. Her own flesh and blood imprisoned by the High Court or Elyathi gaining yet another entire sector's gifted's magic.

That white bitch!

Ikaria clenched her teeth, then shoved all the artifacts off the table in a furious rage. With another sharp movement, Ikaria held out her hands, streaming all of her hatred toward the objects in the room. They levitated for a beat.

Then furniture, objects, papers, lamps, even the artifacts, everything went crashing against the walls as she heaved with hatred. Lord Jiao remained in the doorway, silent. Everything shattered, the pieces smashing against the floor.

Breathing hard, her heart pumped wildly.

After several moments, Ikaria gathered her composure. She straightened in perfect posture, smoothed her skirt, then flicked her fingers with a violet fizzle. Soft violet magic swept over her, fixing her hair, makeup, ornaments, and anything else out of place. After the magic dissipated, Ikaria eyed the room as if she had not been the one to make such a mess.

"Now that I have that out of the way, please let High Priest Auron know that I am not to be disturbed at this time. There are a few things that I need full concentration on in my chambers. Have him make decisions for any further ambassadors that Lady Vala sends our way," Ikaria called out.

"Yes, Enchantress," Lord Jiao said. "How long shall I tell the High Priest you will be indisposed?"

"Perhaps a day. Possibly two. Just have a servant leave food and wine near my study." Ikaria eyed the broken artifacts on the ground. "Also, please have someone gather all these broken artifacts and give them to the World Sector Four's ambassador. Have him deliver them to Khari Ramla and his court as a token of our friendship."

Ikaria shot Jiao a look, and she knew he understood. "As you command."

"One more thing, Lord Jiao."

"Yes, Enchantress?"

Ikaria glanced toward her chamber window. "The full moon was last night, wasn't it?"

Jiao raised an eyebrow. "It was indeed."

"Hm." Ikaria narrowed her eyes, thinking about when the new moon would be. Pure blackness in the sky. Ikaria glanced up at him, then gestured in dismissal. "Thank you, Lord Jiao. That will be all."

He bowed from the doorway, then was out of sight.

Just you wait, Elyathi. I will have you begging at my feet, wishing you'd were never named the chosen.

Ikaria snarled as she stepped across the floor, crunching the artifact debris under her feet. This was how it would be when she was through with Elyathi.

You want to make moves, you old hag? Let's play, shall we?

✦ ✦ ✦

After a carafe of wine and a decent meal, Ikaria locked her personal study and undressed. Normally, Suri would be there helping her undress and either drape a sheet gently on her body or dress her in light robes. Ikaria missed Suri greatly, the only being in this life who actually tended to her needs on a level of great respect. A respect that she deserved.

Suri, I hope you have found a way to retrieve my sister, Ikaria thought. Everything would be so much easier if she had. Though she knew Suri always found some way to fulfill Ikaria's tasks, this one was more difficult than anything before.

Fully nude, Ikaria walked over to her favorite chair, then leaned back in its folds. It was Cyrus's chair, the one she'd bound him to. She loved this chair because it helped her channel the jealousy, hatred, and malice in her heart. Her long violet hair flowed over her body, soft and free. Then with a gentle lift of her fingers, Ikaria floated a light sheet of fabric over, guiding it with her magic, then had it wrap gently around her. She needed to be comfortable and free for her spell.

Closing her eyes, Ikaria reached down in the depths of her life force. She submerged itself within her gift, embracing her violet magic. The sheer force of it, the influence on the mind—nothing could stop its power.

Bathing herself in pure violet energy, she focused on seeking one target.

Her energy seeped out across the multitude of life forces, brushing against all minds as she searched.

Time had no meaning with this spell. She searched until she came upon *that woman*.

Gritting her teeth, Ikaria suddenly shot all her power into this soul's mind like the edge of a blade piercing flesh, so precisely that they wouldn't know until it was too late.

But there was resistance, a thick layer of mental protection around Elyathi's mind. Since having Auron as her complement, breaking into the mind of a gifted was simple. But with Elyathi, it proved quite difficult. Ikaria was not going to stop until she had entered that bitch's thoughts.

Let's see how much you can resist my power.

Ikaria's mental force hummed with a foreign sound as her energy attacked with all its might against Elyathi's mind barrier.

Within her mind's eye, she saw all the colors of the Spectrum flicker in response. The host was not aware of her presence. Yet.

I must enter a different way.

Ikaria smiled as an idea came to her.

Sending another wave of violet magic, this time she didn't try to pierce the barrier. She transformed her energy, sending a wave of thought as Elyathi's favorite person: King Samir of York.

The barrier inside the mind softly melted away to reveal Elyathi's mind in the form of a radiant crystal. It shimmered in all colors of the Spectrum of Magic, so beautiful even Ikaria had to admit it was beyond words. The crystal formed itself into a long tunnel of light. If she reached the end of the tunnel, Ikaria would be in control. And that was where she needed to be.

Shooting her violet magic, Ikaria's life force renewed her mental capacity. The light in the tunnel dimmed to an acceptable level, and then Ikaria saw details that she hadn't when first entering.

The tunnel was all one giant crystal, chiseled away to a gateway of light. Within the many angles of the crystal walls, it displayed imagery.

Elyathi's memories.

Ikaria neared the closest memory, running her fingers across the smooth surface. It was as if the crystal had drained her into the memory, showing her all of the important memories that were ingrained into the host's mind.

Ikaria placed her spirit form's hand onto the memory's surface, and suddenly, she was transported to a new time and place. It was the Arcadian court, for she recognized the audience hall. There was a grand celebration of some kind. The hall was filled with lords and ladies. Damaris was seated at the royal table with a man that resembled Derek, albeit with dark eyes. It was Samir—the King of York, the very man Ikaria had used to trick Elyathi's mind to allow her inside.

Let's see what this man truly holds over her.

Behind her spirit form, Ikaria noticed that Elyathi was hiding in the shadows, her eyes locked on Samir. Damaris and Samir were talking, but all Ikaria could distinguish were muffles. Perhaps Elyathi had not caught this conversation in the moment it happened years ago.

Elyathi adored Samir. Ikaria knew this from prior encounters with Elyathi. She lusted after him. Dreamed about him. This woman could hardly contain her sexual desires. He was everything to Elyathi.

This would be her weapon. But she needed more ammunition.

"Elyathi!" Damaris called out.

The table guests glanced at her empty chair as the King scanned the hall. The servants started frantically running about in search of Elyathi.

Elyathi remained hidden, even though she had fully heard Damaris, Ikaria noted.

"Where is the Queen?" Damaris demanded of the closest servant.

"I believe she went outside to the balcony," the servant offered.

"*Find* her."

Samir of York leaned over to his friend. "Friend, perhaps it can wait? The night is young, and we are just getting started."

"Do not interfere, Samir," Damaris snapped. "Linger in this merry place, and I will return in time."

The servants were frantically looking for her. It was only a matter of time. The longer Damaris was kept waiting, the worse it would be for her.

Wiping a small tear in the corner of her eye, Elyathi bravely walked out from behind the pillar and approached Damaris. "I heard you were looking for me," Elyathi said politely as she curtsied to Damaris, disdain hidden within her empty eyes with fake blue lenses.

"*Where* were you?" he sneered.

"I was conversing with our guests."

Damaris took a deep drink of wine from his chalice, noticeably drunk. His shirt was halfway undone, exposing his chiseled chest. He was a beautiful man. Ikaria had always thought so, even at the age she had met him. But a young Damaris full of rage—Ikaria's lowers stirred just watching him.

"Time to fulfill your wifely duties," he ordered.

Elyathi's hands trembled as she placed them behind her back.

As Damaris rose from his seat, her eyes locked with Samir's, giving him a silent plea for help.

Suddenly, Damaris was in front of her, smiling. "Let's go."

Ikaria felt a wave of anxiety and great fear radiate from Elyathi; she was in a heightened state of panic.

The two walked, Damaris occasionally speaking while Elyathi remained silent. It was apparent to Ikaria that Elyathi's mind was not focused.

After what seemed like seconds, they were in Damaris's chambers. Elyathi walked as though marching to her death, into a side chamber, the King following. Ikaria didn't remember seeing that secret room when she had been in Arcadia.

Inside the hidden room was a soft feather bed. Lights glowed softly in eerie greens, blues, violets, and the occasional reds.

"On the bed," Damaris ordered as he locked the door behind him. "Do not speak."

A tear formed in Elyathi's eye as she climbed onto the bed, kneeling with her hands placed in her lap. Damaris walked over to her, then pulled down a pair of chains that were bolted to the wall. Elyathi fought back tears as Damaris locked the chains upon her wrists.

Satisfied, Damaris took a few steps back, then smiled darkly at what was before his eyes. He grasped a nearby chalice, downing it contents. Ikaria knew from Elyathi's mind that what he was drinking was far more potent than his nightly wine. In the hues of the colored lights, Damaris looked like the face of pure evil in the form of a beautiful man.

In his mind-altered state, Damaris walked over to Elyathi. She crawled back in fear until she was up against the wall. Tears were streaming down her face.

"Please don't…" she said under her breath.

"Did you just speak?" Damaris snarled, getting in her face.

There was a long pause while Elyathi tried to put on a brave face, though it was useless. The violet light reflected the moisture of her tears, while the blues glimmered in her eyes. He placed a hand on her neck, gently studying her body, admiring it. Fear of being choked came from Elyathi's mind. Slowly, the hand slid down the tops of her breasts, then latched on to the front of her gown.

"Never speak unless I say so!" Damaris shouted in her face. With a sharp force, he yanked the front of her dress, tearing it away, exposing her.

Damaris laughed loudly, walked over to his chalice, and downed another glass. Chained to the bed and half naked, Elyathi cried.

"You are so beautiful when you cry," Damaris said as he threw off his shirt, then unlaced his pants. "So very beautiful. The only woman who matches my beauty…"

His words trailed off while the lights of the room melted into a blur. All Ikaria could hear were Elyathi's thoughts of Samir—she was replacing Damaris's physical body with Samir in her mind to escape the pain. To Elyathi, Samir loved her and would never harm her…

The colored blur of lights faded into a crystal…

Ikaria was standing inside of Elyathi's mind tunnel once again. Staring back at the crystallized memory, Ikaria narrowed her eyes.

So Damaris was a violent sexual deviant. Ikaria had seen and done many kinks with countless men. But seeing this, she was sure that Damaris had gone further at other times. It was terrifying looking at this memory through Elyathi's mind. But it would be even more terrifying if she were to warp it further…

You will soon learn how far I will go to pay you back for your charade, Ikaria hissed at the memory. *You hurt my sister, stole my people's gifts… You have no idea what is coming to you…*

Ikaria glanced down the hall of crystals. So many memories. Ones that she could weaponize.

Ikaria sent another wave of violet magic through her life force. Elyathi had not yet detected her.

Moving on, Ikaria stopped in front of the next crystal memory. Derek's image appeared, and Ikaria stopped.

Oh my. I've never seen Derek look so good, Ikaria thought deviously. Derek's image was enticing, exciting…and addictive. His chest was bare except for a large jeweled pendant that kissed a spot between his pectorals. His muscles gleamed with sweat, making her thirst for his flesh. Dark curls framed his face, accentuating his chiseled chin, kissable lips, and long dark lashes. And his eyes, like ice, so pale blue they cast a spell.

So this is how Elyathi sees Derek... The bitch wasn't necessarily wrong. Derek was an irresistible guy. But seeing Derek through her eyes, Ikaria couldn't help herself.

I must know more...

Ikaria belted out laughing as she fully immersed herself in the memory.

CHAPTER 51

◆

The hall was so filled with heavy emotions that one could cut it with a knife. Anger, despair, depression, fear, anxiety…

Khari Ramla sat on his royal pillow, staring at the room before him. The gifted—or those who once were—were no more in his court. Their minds had been declared past the brink of insanity, and for good reason. Knowing how this "plague" worked, those gifted would hurt themselves, so he had ordered them to be cared for in a private visiting section of the citadel.

Now, all that remained of his court were the non-gifted lords and ladies. Their voices shouted over one another, while some wailed in mourning for their gift.

The Khari clenched his jaw, fighting the anger inside of him. He knew that they'd made the wrong decision. He should have overridden the vote. But too many of his council members had opposed joining World Sector Six.

The Khari rose from his pillow.

"Silence!" he shouted.

The flurry of conversation died down, and eyes of the court gave him their attention.

"Now that the traditional time of mourning is over, we must address the situation at hand," he continued.

Uproar filled the hall, with everyone on their feet, shouting and crying to get their say in. He turned to his advisor Garcia, then nodded. The advisor exited hastily and returned with a set of guards.

Slowly, the voices died down as the string of guards followed Advisor Garcia in. One by one, each dumped a pile of metal in front of the throne, then formed a line behind the Khari.

"Do you see what is before you?" the Khari asked with a hint of spite in his tone. "Take a *good* look."

The lords and ladies looked at him curiously.

"Go on. *Look*," he dared.

The people shifted around, trying to peek at the scraps of metal.

"Yes. That is ancient technology that has been destroyed," the Khari stated.

"What does this have to do with what has happened to our gifted?" challenged a lord.

"*Everything*!" the Khari roared, startling the entire room. He narrowed his eyes, then gestured to everyone in the room. "This is a reminder from the sorceress Ikaria of our *folly*! If you would have heeded Lady Vala's words, none of us would be sitting here now, grieving the loss of our *gifted*!"

The room erupted with cries of protest. The Khari walked toward the piles of ancient technology and chose the most mangled piece he could find, picking it up. With the room still shouting, the Khari threw the metal piece into a burning brazier, and the clanging of metal against the brazier startled the room.

"I SPEAK AS YOUR KHARI!"

The lords went silent while another lady of the court wept.

The Khari narrowed his eyes. "I didn't want to overrule everyone, since every council member has a vote. But this? Because of your blind hatred of the sorceress, and the words of a woman, this is where it got you all! Your gifted family members trusted you! And this is what you did to them. They writhe with insanity, never to be who they once were." The Khari sneered in disgust. "Oh yes, they will eventually return to normal thinking. But they will never have their gift again. Do you understand? They will have to live with that fact once they become coherent—whenever that is. Days. Weeks. Perhaps months?"

Tears formed in his eyes as he thought about watching those two gifted women lose their magic.

"*No more*! I will be your leader no more!" the Khari declared.

More chaos, until one voice rose above the others.

"You cannot just quit being a khari. You are our leader!" insisted a lord.

"Am I?" the Khari asked. "No one wanted to do the right thing for this court, even with Lady Vala putting her life on the line for yours. I have failed."

"We need you, Khari," said another council member.

"No, you don't."

"But we do," argued another lord. "You have led us for many years now. We don't want anyone else."

The entire hall nodded and murmured in agreement.

"I'm done with the lot of you."

"You mustn't step down," another lady of the court pleaded. "I voted in favor of joining World Sector Six. Does that mean you will punish those who agreed with the Lady Vala? Will you also punish those who, in good conscience, voted for what they thought was the right thing for their sector? How were they to know the outcome? Yes, we tread a fine line, Khari. But to give it all up for a mistake?"

The lady did have a point, making him pause.

"You need me, you say?" the Khari said.

"We do, now more than ever," the woman replied.

The Khari darted his eyes around the room, meeting the gazes of all the lords and ladies.

"I have one condition: until we have our vengeance, I make all decisions. Without the votes of this council," the Khari declared.

The whole room mumbled, with another lord calling out, "And what is the end to our vengeance?"

The Khari stared back evenly. "Until the High Court is destroyed."

Noise filled the hall like never before as the lords debated, argued, and shouted.

"What shall it be?" the Khari asked over the slew of voices. "Shall I sit back on my pillow? Or shall I walk out of this room, never to return? This is your last chance, because I promise you, never again will I witness a gifted lose their powers on account of your foolishness!"

It had a slow start, but each lord sat on their pillow—their way of voting that he remain as their Khari. Finally, the entire room was in unison.

"World Sector Four has spoken," announced the mediator. "Long live the Khari!"

"Long live the Khari! Long live World Sector Four!" they shouted.

While they shouted, he bowed, then walked back to his platform, seating himself on his pillow.

The room waited.

"Now that we are united, it is the time for vengeance."

The room shouted in agreement.

"Now is the time for war!"

More shouts of agreement.

His eyes met those of a lady toward the back of the room. It was one of the lesser ladies of the court.

Then it dawned on him. This lady's sister was one of those he had witnessed losing her gift…

Tears streamed down the woman's cheeks, and she mouthed the words, *Thank you.*

The Khari nodded in respect, suppressing his own tears.

CHAPTER 52

ORANGE

"You there," an overlord called out to a group of prisoners that included Suri. "You will be working down there today." He pointed to one of the main shafts, one that Suri had never worked in prior.

Suri eyed the shaft, then turned to collect her tools with the other prisoners. Her energy was spent. Same with Jude and the other prisoners. They had run everyone ragged, and there was no stopping to rest. And the imbued shackles seemed to drain her physical and magical energy. The more it drained, the stronger the pain if she tried to cast a spell.

An overseer waited at the entrance, then yelled with impatience, "Hurry before I blast you all!"

The prisoners gathered their tools quickly, then followed the overseer down the shaft, following a set of mine cart tracks. Behind them, Suri detected a group of overseers, all aiming their weapons at the prisoners.

The air became cooler the lower they traveled into the earth. Suri could only imagine the wooden planks that held up the tunnels. Old stonework peeped through the shaft every now and then. Jude was behind her, walking in silence, like the others. It was strange seeing the young talkative priest being so quiet. Suri missed Jude's liveliness.

The shaft split into multiple directions, with the overlord taking the leftmost tunnel. The tunnel became wider and taller—until the full-grown men could stand up straight. In the distance, glittering orange lights illuminated a small chamber.

As they neared the orange light, Suri realized that it was not small at all.

They entered through a main doorway that opened up to a large cavern in the earth. Suri couldn't help but gape in amazement.

It was an excavated section of an ancient city.

As the group traveled closer, Suri realized that the orange lights were enchanted, scattered throughout the ancient city. Stairs, old towers, tunnels, half-buried buildings—some in a state of ruin but others nearly intact.

"This is incredible," Jude whispered.

"QUIET!"

Jude was smacked hard in the back, making him grunt.

The overseer positioned himself in front of Jude. "If you talk again, you will be buried here, like this city."

Jude hung his head in obedience.

The overlord followed the set of mine cart tracks, leading the prisoners to some mining equipment in carts.

"You'll be working here for the day and every day thereafter until we say so," the overlord ordered. "Unless you slug droppings get trapped like the last crew. And if you do happen to get caved in, know this: no one's going to save your backsides, so you best watch yourself. If you happen across an artifact, show an overseer. They will send a more skilled prisoner than you lazy slugs to extract it." The overlord pointed to a dimly lit area with a table and wooden shelves, "I'll be there logging everything. If any of you good-for-nothings try to steal from us, you are stealing from the High Court. The penalty is death by firing squad. Now get to *work.*"

Suri started carefully chipping away at the debris at one of the upper sections of the ancient dwelling. It was an old structure that seemed to have many levels to it; the previous workers had already uncovered a large portion, revealing walkways inside. They had secured weaker sections of the structure so it wouldn't collapse on the workers. That is, until they made a fatal mistake in their last moments.

Time had gone by quickly, with several of the prisoners finding artifacts and flagging down an overseer. Elevated prisoners would move into that area, then work to remove the artifact from the stone around it. The group would then take that piece into a brightly lit area and use small tools to clean the artifact.

As she worked, Suri thought about the same things she always thought about: escaping, the enchantress, and rescuing the Empress. But a new thought came into her rotation: how to slip an artifact into her possession without notice. Though she was a master of deception, there was no denying that being under constant watch made it impossible, especially with her magic being subdued and her feet in shackles, which made so much noise that it sounded like the heavens rumbling.

"All right, time for you slug droppings to sup and sleep," called out an overlord. "I logged a good number today. Keep this up, you get an extra water break. Now pick up your tools and get your backsides out of my face!"

The group gathered their tools and followed the overseers out.

As they ascended, there was a loud rumbling of earth, followed by a hard shake. The shaft rained dirt and small rocks.

"What was that?" said one of overseers in their mechanical voices. He had his weapon at the ready.

"Up there," said another.

The overlord turned to the group. "You," he said, pointing to one of the overseers, "and you. Stay with these slugs. The rest of you, get your backsides up there."

The overlord disappeared up the shaft with a few overseers, leaving Suri, Jude, and the other prisoners with a couple of overseers.

The group waited in darkness. Suri's eyes began to adjust to the faint grays and darker shades of black. An outline of the nearby prisoners could be seen. More scattered rocks, pebbles, and dirt rained on them as the ground shook again. Suri felt the fear growing amongst the prisoners.

Suddenly, the ground split, knocking the group down. Some smacked against the shaft walls, hitting planks. Others tumbled into each other, tripping over their shackles and falling to the ground. The shaft made a loud groaning noise.

"The tunnel is about to cave!" one of the prisoners screamed.

A loud crack boomed as the ceiling of the shaft collapsed on the back of the group, crushing them. Screams filled Suri's ears.

Another quake hit, and more dirt rained on them from above.

"MOVE OUT!" screamed an overseer. He disappeared upward into the shaft, the other overseer joining him. The other prisoners began to trample each other, fighting and climbing over each other like rats—screaming, clawing, biting, anything to get out of the tunnel first.

In the mass hysteria, Suri heard Jude. "Mistress Suri!" he managed to cry out.

She could leave him behind and save herself. But if she felt protective of anyone beside the enchantress, it was this boy. He was a younger brother to her.

Master Jude…

Suri whirled around. A prisoner was choking Jude, who stood in his way. Suri climbed back with a cry. The ground shook violently again, more dirt raining down on them.

Suri slipped next to the man, unnoticed. Using an old fighting technique, Suri thrust out at the man's collarbone.

The prisoner cried out and stumbled, leaving Jude gasping in the dark. More dirt poured on them from above.

"Thank you."

"There's no time," she said. "Hurry."

They were stuck behind the escaping prisoners as the tunnel caved in once again. More rumblings quaked below their feet. A faint light was coming from her imbued shackles, magic radiating from it. Up ahead, she saw the main shaft's familiar lighting.

The terrified prisoners kept ascending, but Suri and Jude were still in the back of the group. She hoped the prisoners knew where they were going, because she didn't. Neither she nor Jude had been that far up in the mines, at least not in this tunnel. With no overlords or overseers, no one cared. They were running for their lives.

They came to a large open section with several tunnels. The prisoners kept heading in one direction, but Suri noticed some signage for another tunnel— leading to where the overlords slept. Suri turned to Jude.

"You go on. I need to get something," Suri said quickly.

"No, I'll wait here. Hurry," he said with a hint of anxiety.

Suri nodded, then darted down the tunnel and into the overlords' quarters. Suri scanned the metal room, spotting a large wooden desk with papers and other objects scattered about.

Suri ran over to the desk and shoved the papers aside, opening any drawer she could find. There, in one of the middle drawers, was her enchanted dagger. She sheathed it, slipped it inside her tunic, then bolted outside, back into the tunnel.

Jude was waiting, but he got knocked to his feet as another quake rumbled. "I have what I need. Let's go."

They darted up the tunnel, then turned into a wide, open rocky stretch. Then Suri saw the light of day at the end of it. There were no signs of the other prisoners. Maybe they had already exited the tunnel? They ran as fast as their shackles allowed them, and Suri noticed the daylight was mixed with bright flickering colors.

"Magic!" Jude cried out with joy.

She squinted as they neared the light. It was painful, as she had been down in the mines for quite some time. Her breathing increased, making a strange noise as she exhaled.

As soon as they exited, they found themselves on a tall platform on the edge of a rocky plateau, facing a rocky ravine that had been mined and worked. A crowd of prisoners were standing on the platform. Many other wooden platforms dotted the cliffs—other tunnels leading to other excavation sites. Down below were blasts of magic. Magic from *weapons*.

A large group of masked people were shooting down the overlords and overseers. Their masks glowed with power—imbued with magic but not glowing like typical enchantments.

An overlord with a group of overseers came into view on the platform, aiming his weapon at the prisoners.

"Get down there and fight those rebels," he snarled.

"With what?" asked one of the prisoners.

The prisoner got whacked with the blunt side of the weapon as the overlord screamed, "With yourselves!" He then pushed the group down the stairs, sending many knocking into each other.

Suri stumbled but quickly got to her feet, then turned to Jude, helping him.

"I don't want to fight, but I don't want to get blown up either," Jude confessed.

Suri eyed the fighting in the ravine, then an idea came to her. She turned to Jude. "Follow me." She led him down the wooden stairs and into the ravine, being careful with every step. They moved to the side, trying to get as close as they could to the opposing side.

Ahead of them, Suri noticed a large, imposing man who seemed to be leading the opposition charge. He was thick of frame and well-built. His skin was the color of warm golden sand, and even with his mask on, Suri could see he had no hair on his head, the top of his head shining as brightly as his muscles. The man held a bow staff that glowed with a magical effect.

The man whacked and cracked skulls with his bow staff, making it glow red. But suddenly, he stopped, his masked face turning straight to her and Jude. He was most definitely not a friend.

"I think he's going to kill us," Jude commented.

"Agreed," Suri said.

"We can't even use our magic!"

The man was already upon them, swinging his bow staff. Suri rolled, his staff hitting the link between her shackles hard. Then they burst into orange light, disintegrating.

Suri eyed him evenly. "We don't want to fight you! We want to join you!" she said through her mask.

"Join us?"

"We come from the skies…"

"Sky-dwellers! Ha!" he barked through his mask. "You are just as rotten as the overlords! And now, you die with them!"

The man became enveloped with power, in a color that Suri had never seen. The color of tree bark, dirt, and wood…

"It's brown magic!" Jude screamed.

The man grew taller, bigger, more muscular as the brown magic burned.

Suri shot a wave of orange magic into Jude's shackles, transmuting them until they exploded. With another flick, Suri tapped into her foreign color, violet, which had been bestowed to her as a gift from Ikaria.

The dark orange magic funneled around her, then became a ring of energy. Jude's yellow magic surrounded her as well, giving her extra protection.

"A sky-dwelling gifted," snarled the brown-gifted man.

Suddenly, the man's brown magic swirled just as hers did. He laughed as he raised his bow staff, twirling it in his hands like a child's toy. The more the staff spun, the more brown magic it gained.

Then, at the same time, the two of them released their magics.

They collided with such great force that it caused Suri and the man to lose their balance, sending them sliding back, far apart from each other. But Suri held her concentration, continuing to blast the man.

So did he. The man pushed more power into his forceful blast.

More and more, she funneled more energy into her beam, feeding it. The brown-gifted man did the same. The friction grew, causing everyone in the area to be swept off their feet. Thankfully the priest boy kept her encased within his protection.

"He's mimicking your magic!" Jude cried out.

The priest was right, but this man had more power than her. *Maybe it's because I was so subdued for so long...*

Men who sided with the brown-gifted man stood behind him and his power, all making cheering motions. Suri heard nothing but the sounds of the intense friction between their magics.

Suri closed her eyes, gathering more energy and magic. The power swelled deep within, until she no longer could contain it. She released it against the foreign brown magic, both forces colliding with a giant blast.

The ravine rattled with such magnitude that for a while there was nothing but sand filling the air. Men in both parties flew back like flimsy scrolls, smacking against rocks, boulders, or each other.

Using the distraction, Suri melded into the landscape, also casting her invisibility on Jude, as the dust was settling. Through her mask, Suri noticed that brown magic flowed over her. Then, in a flash off in the distance, the brown-gifted man went invisible.

The caster was copying her magic again.

He is able to use my own magic against me!

Whatever she was going to do, he was going to mimic her abilities. Darting her eyes, she wondered if she was going to be able to detect him like she could a normal orange-gifted. But this was no normal caster.

There was a brown wave of magic dispelling her magic over Jude. The priest stood fully visible; he realized it too, so casted another layer of protection over himself.

Suri began shifting the landscape with her illusion magic, warping it into a new reality, but in mere seconds, the landscape shifted back into reality.

Never had she felt so frustrated with an opponent as she did now. She couldn't even detect this brown-gifted who was leeching off her magic.

Irritated, Suri yanked her enchanted blade from her tunic, then ran toward the man nearest Jude.

Suddenly brown magical barriers surrounded them. Suri ran into the barrier, hitting her body against the metal-like bubble.

Another brown wave of magic flowed over Jude, melting his barrier—and her own.

There was a hard yank on her mask, and her face was suddenly exposed to the elements. In the corner of her eye, Suri saw Jude's mask being pulled off, too.

"Mistress Suri…" Jude wheezed.

Involuntarily, she took a breath. She knew she shouldn't, but it was second nature to breathe. It was choking her…

In the corner of her eye, she caught a strange movement.

Hovering over her was the thick brown-gifted man. In the golden sun, his muscles shone like pure oil. She still couldn't see his face under the mask.

"Get these two on the vehicle for interrogation," he ordered the others.

"Sir…" Suri choked. "We must get back to the skies…"

"So you can suppress more of my peoples?" the masked man said with spite.

"We…must save…our Empress from execution…" Jude hacked, then slumped over, unconscious.

"I care not for any Empress."

"The…High…Court…has…imprisoned…our…Empress…we…must…" Suri couldn't manage any more words. Her head felt light, and her vision was turning black.

"Mask them before they get infected and get them loaded," the man said. "I will finish the overlords off and return shortly."

Suri tried to speak, but the harsh air became too much. Her lungs locked up, and she coughed. She slumped to the ground, crawling next to Jude.

"Jude," she whispered.

The brown-gifted man stood over them, unmoved as several other masked individuals kneeled beside them. The next thing she knew, something extremely heavy was being placed on her face. Then she blacked out.

CHAPTER 53

♦

VIOLET

The Corporation was like every other major corporation in Arcadia. Glass skyways, glass lifts, glass reception desks, everything mixed with machinery. The escalators, the computers. Scientists came and went from the upper departments and labs, filtering out into the main entryway. In the corner were doorways that required key cards. Geeta noticed they went down instead of up.

Geeta walked up to the receptionist, who gave her a once-over.

"May I help you?" she asked as she typed with catlike fingernails painted with high-gloss red lacquer. Her blonde hair was pulled back tight into a French roll, pinned to perfection.

Geeta leaned forward, and the secretary rolled her chair back slightly. "Yes. I'm here on behalf of the Queen. There should be parts ready for pickup."

The receptionist raised an eyebrow. "Name?"

"Geeta Sharma, Protector of the Realm."

The woman's jaw dropped in disbelief. "Give me a moment," she said. "Have a seat."

"Thanks, I'll stand."

The news played on the screen, flashing to the next segment.

Geeta sighed as the screen showed Kyle and Emerald at his latest show. The paparazzi were at it again, chasing down the couple to get the latest gossip. What was ridiculous was that Kyle seemed to be enjoying the attention.

For someone who is all about not being the norm, he sure seems like he wants to become the norm in Arcadia.

She was still irritated with him about Nym. But Geeta knew, Kyle being his numbskull self, that he really was trying to be helpful.

"Geeta Sharma?"

Breaking contact with the screen, Geeta turned to see the receptionist standing behind her, startling her.

"I didn't mean to frighten you," the receptionist said. "The shipment is ready on one of our back platforms. Someone is coming to meet you now."

"Thanks," Geeta said. She turned back around, glancing at the screen once more but saw nothing of interest.

"Geeta Sharma?" called out a voice.

Geeta turned and saw a man in a lab coat standing there.

"Yes."

"I am Director Jonathan. I'm here to take you to the deck with the shipment," he said with a smile. "If you will follow me…"

✦ ✦ ✦

Reila marched through the temporary camp. Mud still caked the ground from the strange sandstorm or rainstorm or whatever it was. It clung like glue to her combat boots, and made sleeping unbearable for those who didn't have cots.

Since the storm, some of the wastelanders wanted to go back to the refuge. Others wanted to stay and wait it out. And a handful were distraught that a giant mountain still remained over their original camp. Everyone seemed to have an opinion. Reila felt like throwing her hands in the air and telling them to do whatever the fuck they wanted. But that would be pointless, and real shitty of her, being a leader and all. That would be stooping lower than Garrett or even that bucket-head, Kyle.

Glancing over at the mountain, it made her think back to the city scientist. Telly really had tried to use whatever power she had. Reila felt bad for her; she knew that Telly was embarrassed and ran off in a fury.

Hope she's calmed down by now.

In one of their recent communications, Scion told her that Telly had seemed her usual self since, but that wasn't saying much. The cyborg was terrible at perceiving one's emotions.

Scion… Reila smiled. It was hard not to think of him. The longer she was away from him, the more she missed him.

Reila chuckled to herself as she explored the idea of getting it on with Scion. She glanced over her shoulders, seeing that no one was in view. Good. Couldn't have people getting in her private business or seeing her acting all giddy.

In their last transmission, he told her that Geeta was traveling to get Drew's parts. If so, maybe that cyborg would finally wake up, and the mountain could be eradicated and everyone would be happy. If only people would have some damn patience and stop bitching to her.

I should call him. He won't know what to do with himself.

Reila fumbled through her pocket, pulling out her transmitter, then dialed as she lit a smoke.

A few rings went by, then someone on the other end picked up.

"Miss Reila?" Scion's voice asked.

"Hey, Scion," Reila said. "How are you?"

"The same as the last time you asked."

"Of course. How silly of me." Reila rolled her eyes as she puffed her smoke. "Actually, I wanted to ask your opinion." *And have an excuse to call you.*

"I can give you my opinion, Miss Reila…"

Reila sighed loudly. "Reila, remember?"

"Yes, Reila," Scion said. "What I was saying is that I can give you my opinion, but it might not be the best assessment. It is best to get all the input before finalizing an answer."

She didn't want to admit it, but all that gobbledygook made her kind of horny. "Scion, I want *your* opinion. Nobody else's. You see, everyone here at the camp wants different actions to be taken. Some want to go back to the refuge. Some want to stay here. Some just want to bitch and moan because that's what they like to do." Reila paused. "They want their home back. I know that you will be fixing Drew up soon with the new parts, but we don't know how long it will take for him to be stabilized. And you know, if he's fixed, then maybe he can fix this mountain situation."

"Hmmm." There was a moment of silence.

Reila let him process it like any computer from thirty years ago—painfully slow.

Just as she was about to ask him if he was still there, he answered. "By my estimation, I think Drew will be functional within weeks, with the exception of a few abilities."

Reila groaned. Weeks of putting up with the feisty group? That was too long.

"But Miss Reila…"

"Reila."

"Reila. You must consider that you are in a position of authority. Victor has granted you this responsibility. As a leader, you must tell them what they must do with firm instruction. They must abide. If you do not, the group will do all they can to get what they want. I have studied your leadership firsthand."

"You have?"

"Affirmative. You have what humans call talent. But I have observed that they listen more when you yell at them."

"Yell at them? Shucks."

"You should yell and lead, Reila."

Reila sucked on her smoke, thinking about his words. What he said was true. She was being a bit wishy-washy lately. People saw that, and they walked all over the head honcho. She took another puff. How the hell was he so wise?

"You know," Reila said, "you would make an excellent sidekick."

"I do not know if you mean this to be a compliment or not, Reila."

Reila chucked. "It's a compliment, you silly cyborg."

"Thank you, Reila."

Reila glanced over her shoulder, ensuring no one was looking at her, then she leaned in. "You know, I was thinking dirty thoughts of you before I called." She felt her blood grow hot.

"Dirty thoughts? Are these ones that you must purge?"

"God, I love the way you talk to me," Reila said. "I want to hear about what cyborgs fantasize about…"

"Miss Reila…" He chuckled.

Reila froze as her heart leapt in her chest. He actually laughed.

This was going to get good.

"Hold that thought…" she said as she headed to her tent.

CHAPTER 54

◆

BLUE

Derek shimmered blue as he entered the Corporation's upper levels, appearing in an inconspicuous part of the corporate bathroom. Soon, Geeta would be there, and he wanted to be ready prior to her arrival.

As Derek went to exit the bathroom, he passed by oversized mirrors, pausing. He hadn't truly taken in account his appearance as of late. He had been busy with acquiring magic and hadn't been in the presence of Emerald. Derek sighed as he took a long look. His eyes looked more sunken in, with dark rings, making his pale blue eyes look dimmer.

Best get myself together before seeing Emerald again. After fixing a loose curl that went astray, he walked out.

Derek made his way down the familiar gleaming white marbled floors. Many of the walls were pure glass. On the other side, Derek saw scientists going up and down escalators and lifts, chatting in the halls, or hurrying to their next meeting. He was in the corporate side of the building, so there were no true labs. Here, everything was for show. The executive offices were more private.

As he neared the head secretary's office, Derek spotted the head director. Santiago noticed him too, approaching Derek and bowing.

"Your Majesty," Santiago said. "You are here a little earlier than expected."

Derek felt his spell permeating the area. Everyone, including the director, was under his spell. *Good.*

"Indeed I am. I can wait while you get the project ready for my departure," Derek answered.

Santiago smiled. "It's ready now. I was just about to message Your Majesty, but here you are. Impeccable timing."

"I am very punctual when it comes to time," Derek stated.

"This way, if you please," Santiago said, gesturing to Derek.

Derek glanced to the side, hoping to see Geeta. He followed Santiago. "I was hoping to see Miss Geeta," Derek said casually. "Will your secretary let us know when she arrives?"

"Miss Geeta already picked up the parts an hour ago," he said.

A shot of fury went through Derek.

"*What?*" Derek said loudly, causing people nearby to dart their eyes at them nervously. His hands began to shake.

"I would have sent word to you, but I was under the impression that Miss Sharma would inform the palace upon receipt of the parts," Santiago said, confused.

Derek took a deep breath, trying to compose himself. He wanted to crush the director for being such a clod, but he needed to get the gauntlet.

"I have an urgent matter that I needed to speak to Miss Sharma about right away," Derek stated coolly. "It had to be delivered in person. However, seeing that she is gone now, I will reach out to her by another means."

"Forgive me, sire," Santiago said with a bit of a nervous tone.

Half-wit. Derek smiled through his clenched teeth. "What's done is done. Let's see the project."

The director led Derek into the very same conference room they had met in the first time. On the black glass table sat a metal box with four glowing green numbers in its faceplate. The sheen of the metal reflected in the glass as the director entered a combination of four numbers.

Four, six, nine, two, Derek heard Santiago's mind say.

The box made an electronic beep, then opened. "The combination is four, six, nine, two," Santiago stated.

"Thank you, Director."

"Here it is. The gauntlet."

Director Santiago held it up, inviting Derek to inspect it.

Derek strode over. It was the same design as before. Perhaps with a little extra polishing of the metal, but it was the same device. Deep silver metal made of god knew what substance. In the center of the outer hand was an orb.

"May I?" Derek asked.

"Of course."

As Derek grasped the gauntlet, the orb faintly lit up with green power. He then proceeded to slide the gauntlet on, while Santiago watched him curiously. The orb burned brighter with green energy—Emerald's magic, within his blood.

He couldn't detect what it was, but Derek felt Emerald's spirit within the gauntlet. Perhaps it was the old saying, *"Absence makes the heart grow fonder,"* and he missed her so terribly that it could be felt within this old contraption.

Santiago blinked, as if confused by the orb lighting up. But the director knew better than to ask.

"Can I test this on one of your cyborgs below?" Derek asked. "That is, if you happen to have any cyborgs left that didn't want to be freed by the Queen's decree."

"I do have several, in fact. Some of them felt they needed guidance, so they stayed. But I do want to point out that, as you know, the gauntlet was made for use by the royal family…ones that have the Queen's blood."

"Just take me to your nearest lab."

"Absolutely. Follow me," Santiago said, looking slightly hesitant.

If it doesn't activate for him, I will surely lose my job, Derek heard Santiago's mind say.

Let him think that, Derek thought.

Derek snatched the box, holding it in his arms as he followed Santiago through the halls, entering one of the glass lifts.

As they traveled down, Derek observed the floors showing different activities of the labs. It was slightly entertaining, but at the same time, he felt that all their work was in vain. The old world was about to fall, and none of this science mattered.

Derek glanced down at the gauntlet, clenching his hand within it. Damaris loved the damn thing. Ikaria too. But him? He hated everything about it. If it were up to him, he would burn it. This was just another fascination of Ikaria's, that meddling witch.

The lift arrived at the basement level of the Corporation, as the view changed to one of concrete and glowing machinery. The elevator tinged, and the doors opened.

Santiago led Derek down a dark corridor lit only by the glowing of machinery and screens.

"Why is it so dark down here?"

"The cyborgs don't like a lot of light, especially when they are getting used to their cybernetic parts. Dimmed lighting helps them get adjusted to their new life quicker."

"I see."

They came to a lab, and the director scanned his key card. The door opened, and the two stepped inside. Glowing capsules contained resting cyborgs. Thick tubing and wires connected to the capsules, while several scientists worked at each cyborg station.

"I thought you said that they don't like a lot of light?" Derek said as he took in the glowing capsules.

"They don't. However, these cyborgs are in a cryogenic sleep. The light won't affect them because they will never awaken. That is, unless we choose to wake them."

Derek took in the sight, a chill running down his spine. These cyborgs were once men. But in these capsules, they looked like circus freaks. Naked and embedded with machinery.

At the end of the aisle of capsules was a large metal door.

"Are there more cyborgs through that door?" Derek asked.

"That is Lab 34," Santiago said. "It's where the cyborg Andrew Napoli used to be while at the Corporation."

Derek raised an eyebrow. "He got his own room?"

"Because of Drew's special circumstances, as you know. It helped contain his *abilities*."

"May I see this lab?" Derek asked.

"Sure thing, follow me."

The director used his key card once more, and the metal containment door slid open. There was an office that contained a workstation, machinery parts, and some lab equipment. A window was inset in one wall, allowing a view into a containment room with a metal slab that Drew most likely lay on, with a slew of loose wires.

"Uh, Your Majesty," Santiago called out from behind him.

Derek turned around, seeing another scientist.

"This is Director Jonathan. He was head of this project," Santiago finished.

"Pleased to meet His Majesty." Jonathan bowed.

"You as well," Derek said. "Wasn't there a Miss Hearly that worked with this cyborg?"

"She was the lead scientist on the project," Jonathan stated. "More like the only scientist. I was head of the project, nothing more. Miss Hearly did all the grunt work." He smiled brightly.

If Derek couldn't find Geeta in Arcadia, Telly Hearly would be the next best thing. It would lead to Drew…where Geeta was heading. After all, she was delivering parts for the damned thing, and he needed to be fixed before Derek captured him. Now that she had those parts, she'd go to him. He could just capture Geeta after she delivered the parts.

Hmmm…

Reaching into the director's thoughts, Derek searched Jonathan's mind. Through his mental connection, Derek gave him the idea to think about Drew and Telly. And just like a dog trained by its owner, Jonathan thought of the two scientists. They were out in the western wastelands. They lived in a camp…

Derek broke his connection, then smiled. "Thank you for indulging me by showing me this room. I would like to see the other cyborgs now."

As Derek and Santiago left, and Derek reached into Jonathan's mind once more, wiping the memory of Derek showing up here. Derek felt Jonathan's mind go numb as the metal door shut behind them.

They came back to the central capsule room, with Derek stopping at the center.

"Is there something else Your Majesty would like to see?" Santiago asked.

"No. But I do want to test this out."

"Your Majesty…" the director began.

Reaching out his hand, Derek felt the presence of Emerald's blood in the gauntlet, as if her life force flowed from the device straight into his heart.

He missed Emerald with all that he had.

I will soon have her back.

He felt the flow of her magic—and the presence of the cyborg collective who shared her blood.

"Your Majesty…?" the director repeated.

Derek glanced at the cyborg in front of him.

Open your eyes! he commanded.

The cyborg opened his eyes from inside the capsule. None of the other scientists realized it, as they were all focused on Derek. But he saw it.

Derek turned to Santiago. "You're right. It will only work for the Queen." He smiled. "I must get going now."

Santiago gave a relieved smile. "I will escort you to your vehicle."

"That won't be necessary," Derek said.

With a jerk of his hand, Derek funneled the entire room with his time magic. The entire room was tinged blue, with light flecks floating in the air. With another jerk of his hand, Derek wiped the minds of every person in the building for the entire time he had been there.

Can't have you tattling to the Queen that I am back.

Derek released time, and all their bodies slumped over, sending a light vibration through the building from the combined body weight falling all at once.

Derek glanced at Santiago, then stood over the director. He clenched his teeth, then kicked the director over, flopping him face down.

"That's for meddling with my plans for Miss Sharma," Derek sneered.

With the metal box in his hand, Derek flashed away.

✦ ✦ ✦

The diner was busy as usual. A slew of customers came and went from the door, the bell making its usual ting sound. Passersby paid no attention to her. The mid-levels were flooded with Arcadians going about their daily activities. Loud advertisements blared whatever they were selling, and glowing images played across the screens, showing the latest products.

Geeta glanced at the doorway as it flung open. Two more customers walked out, nearly brushing her elbow as they passed. The pack that was slung over her shoulder dug into her body. The bag was heavy, laden with the parts for her to deliver. It was critical she deliver them right away, but she couldn't help making one more stop.

Minutes went by as she debated whether to go inside.

Damn you, you son of an ass, Kyle! Geeta swore. *The idiot probably made a muck of everything, sticking his nose where it doesn't belong.* Geeta glanced in the window. *I shouldn't even be here right now. I should be back at the refuge, not chasing romance.*

Geeta kicked a piece of trash, clenching her teeth. She paced in circles, then stopped in front of the diner window, glancing through it again.

She froze as she saw Nym inside.

Geeta swallowed hard. Nym looked so happy, bustling around the diner and chatting with customers. It was cute how bubbly she was—something that Geeta was definitely not. Being around Nym just made Geeta so…happy. Cheerful. That was a hard thing to do, considering her life was anything but that.

Taking a deep breath, Geeta reached for the diner door. At that moment, her communicator dinged.

Grabbing the device, Geeta answered it. "Yes?"

"You got the parts?" Garrett asked on the other end.

"I did." Geeta glanced in the window, seeing Nym wave to another customer.

"You coming soon? Telly and I are prepping Drew for the next replacement…"

"Yes, I am on my way now," she said.

"All right, see you shortly."

There was a click, and the communication ended.

Geeta sighed. *The gods will that I don't go in there right now, it seems.*

As Geeta put her device away, another couple exited the diner, the door swinging open wildly. Geeta caught a glimpse of pink hair inside. Nym was happily walking back to the kitchen. Of course, she didn't notice Geeta, as she was busy working.

Geeta turned away from the diner. *After all this…I'll gather my courage.*

◆ ◆ ◆

As Geeta shimmered away, Derek watched from a distance, cloaked in his own magic. She hadn't detected him. Was it due to her lack of orange magic? Or was it due to Elyathi's infused blood with his? Regardless, he now knew he could remain undetected and use it to his advantage.

Derek released his magic, dark blue shimmers vaporizing away as he stood before the diner.

It seems Geeta has a love interest. Derek eyed the pink-haired woman.

Then Derek stepped inside the diner.

CHAPTER 55

◆

RED

Some banquet, Kyle thought as he stood against one of the pillars in the banquet hall. The gaudy oversized room was packed with a bunch of yahoos, and he had no fucking idea what their names were. He would bet money that they all had no fucking idea who everyone was either. They were all mingling in their little social circles, laughing, drinking, and talking. What he needed was a drink in one hand and a smoke in the other to get through a night like this. This was exactly how he had pictured snobbish upper-level parties.

Kyle sighed as he yanked on the hem of his sleeve, feeling uncomfortable in his getup. He then fidgeted with his rings and necklaces. He had to admit that Cyndi did a damn good job picking out something in his style—black leather outfit tailored with studs and spikes. Around his neck, he wore the gemstone from Elder Moon—the gemstone with a fragment of Emerald's soul. He loved wearing it, as if Emerald were right next to him. Sometimes, memories of being Rubius came in full force. Other times, it was as if he made the whole thing up in his head, as if he had drank far too much in an evening and had a bad dream.

Elder Moon…I wonder what the old lady is up to? Kyle hoped that the underground citadel remained safe, far away from the High Court. Kyle grasped the stone around his neck. As much as he wanted to forget everything in his past life, he couldn't ignore the help that Elder Moon gave him. Without the stone, Kyle doubted that he would have escaped that pit of hell. Literally.

Kyle straightened his shades, shivered at the thought.

"Drink, sir?" asked a servant, holding out a tray.

"Thank you." Kyle quickly grabbed a drink, slammed it, then set it down on the tray again. "Thanks, man. I'll take another while you're here." He quickly finished off another.

The servant looked at him, raising an eyebrow.

"Just one more." Kyle grabbed another one, then raised the glass. "For the road," he added with a wink. He turned away, probably leaving the servant staring for a moment. The servant likely wasn't used to people like him. He couldn't blame the guy. Lower-level folks hardly ever crossed the social boundaries into high society Arcadia.

Kyle spotted Emerald across the room. She was mingling with lords, a bright smile on her face. Kyle knew that smile—though it was genuine, it was also an *I'm done talking to you* smile.

For some reason, she looked even more pregnant than when he'd seen her earlier in the day. Fatherhood was just around the bend. He was running out of time as a free man. He wanted to be a dad. But it was all happening so quickly. His current life would come to an end, and he would regret not being able to do all that he wanted to do before becoming a dad. Playing at shows, late into the night, drinking with his buddies. And Emerald, she would change too. Would she become unreasonable like all the other ball-and-chain wives out there? Telling him that he couldn't do anything anymore because of their twins?

Speaking of wives... He patted his inner jacket pocket. The ring was still tucked away safely. He just needed to find the perfect time to ask Em. That way, they could finally be official.

Em's gonna love the ring, I just know it. Kyle smiled to himself. He couldn't wait.

Kyle flagged down another server, grabbing a drink from the tray, then scanned the room once more. Councilor Emerys stood next to Emerald across the room. Out of everyone in the upper levels, Kyle thought the councilor seemed like a stand-up guy.

The councilor bowed to Emerald, then made his way to another partygoer. Kyle made a mad dash toward her, hoping that no one else got to her before he did.

Emerald saw him approaching and burst into a bright smile. "Kyle. You look quite handsome tonight," she said, placing a hand on her very pregnant belly.

"You're telling me that I don't usually?"

She playfully slapped his arm, then smiled, eyeing his shades. "It's such a shame that you hide your cute face behind those sunglasses."

"Well, you know, don't wanna scare the shit out of anyone with my freaky eyes."

"I suppose." She smiled. "It might help make you less identifiable, Mr. Rock Star."

"That's definitely a plus." He took a drink. "So how's it going?"

Emerald slipped her hands playfully on his leg, then smiled. "It's 'going' as you would say. However I'd rather be somewhere else with you. I'm thinking… another adventure in Arcadia," she said dreamily, leaning her side against him.

"God, I'm a lucky man." Kyle leaned into her. Her scent was everywhere around him, arousing his senses, driving him wild. God, he wanted to kiss her right there. Make it known that the world's most beautiful woman was with him. She was a vision, a moving painting, and her smile was especially bright tonight.

From the corner of his eye, Kyle saw several flashes. He stood up straight, seeing that several guest photographers were taking their photo. Next to them were a handful of reporters.

"Excuse me, but are you Kyle Trancer?" asked one.

"Yeah. What of it?" Kyle asked. More photos snapped.

Emerald gave a blank stare as if caught off guard, then blinked, smiling for the camera.

"How does it feel now that your new song is a worldwide mega hit?" asked a reporter.

"What is your business at the palace?" asked another.

More photos.

"Are you here on behalf of the lower-level citizens regarding the tax?" questioned a third.

"Will you be performing for the event?" asked a fourth.

He didn't know what to fucking say. Kyle glanced over at Emerald. If he opened his mouth, it would probably damage whatever story she had in place for the lords.

She caught on quick, facing the group of photographers and reporters. "Master Kyle Trancer is here regarding the new tax cut. He was well-spoken about this cause, so the palace invited him for a visit."

Her words made him freeze. More snaps. Something about her saying that he was there for some tax cut and not there for her didn't sit right with him.

"Could you tell us when you started lobbying for the tax cut?" asked another reporter.

"Are there any plans for a new song?"

More questions, more pictures.

Fury bubbled inside of him. Kyle stood next to Emerald, putting his arm around her. He gritted his teeth, using every ounce of energy not to shout at these assholes.

More cameras flashed.

"Please, that's quite enough," Emerald said. "Leave us be."

But they kept snapping photos. And snapping. And snapping…

"She said leave, assholes!" Kyle barked loudly.

The photographers all stopped, staring at him.

"Have respect for Her Majesty and the palace, why don't you!" he continued.

The photographers blinked in disbelief.

"Leave!"

They all scrambled in different directions of the party, eventually leaving them alone.

Kyle took a deep breath as she placed a calming hand on his arm.

"I'm impressed," Emerald said. "I had expected you to blow your top at them entirely."

That stung a little. Was he always that much of an asshole? "Yeah, well, you told me to check my head, remember?" Kyle said, meeting her eyes. She half smiled at him, then touched his hand lightly, brushing the top of it.

"Why are they all here anyway? Don't they have other things to report, like the news?"

"Unfortunately, we are the news. All socialite events are reported. Usually, my friend Haze does all of the palace photography, but the palace couldn't get him for tonight's event. Instead, we got fill-ins."

"Well, if he's a friend of yours, I'm sure he at least respects your privacy when needed." *Any photographer would be an improvement than those bastards.*

"That he does."

"Why couldn't he be here for tonight?"

"He was supposed to be, but he's been having relationship issues," she added. "His partner is getting more jealous. Troy is a good guy, but he gets upset over petty things."

"Been there," Kyle said, then quickly looked at her. "Not you, of course. My ex."

Emerald laughed. "You mean the one I knocked some sense into before?"

Kyle laughed. "God, I love you."

She leaned in, staring up at him with sparkling green eyes. "I want you," she whispered.

Immediately he had a raging hard-on, and a stupid smile spread across his face. "Oh yeah?" he whispered in her ear.

"Come on," she said softly, waving for him to follow.

Emerald led him down one of the rows of pillars, leading away from the main party. She giggled as she tugged at his hand, leaving him flushing with excitement. They darted down another hall, where they were completely alone.

As he went to kiss her, she playfully rubbed her hand against his thigh.

Kyle raised an eyebrow at her, and she smiled at him. Leaning in, he said, "Are you trying to get a rise out of me? Cause if so, it's working."

"Perhaps." Her eyes sparkled.

"Do it again," he whispered in her ear as she giggled.

At that moment, he caught Emerys in the corner of his eye, staring at them. It was so quick that Kyle almost questioned whether he had seen the councilor, because a moment later, he was out of sight.

"Did you see him?" he whispered in her ear.

"See who?"

"Forget it," Kyle said to her as he grabbed her hand. "Follow me."

"Where are we going?"

"You'll see."

Kyle remembered seeing an even more private and remote hall in the palace, trying to recall the location. He had accidentally stumbled across it when he got lost and had always thought it was a perfect area to be more discreet.

"Kyle, I can't leave the hall."

"It's only for a few minutes," he said, yanking her hand as she giggled.

Finally, they reached a small nook in the small hall, oversized pillars blocking the nook. Without a moment to waste, he smashed his body against hers. It was a little awkward considering how incredibly pregnant she was, but it didn't matter. He loved her and wanted to feel her lips against his.

He kissed her wildly, and she kissed him back, slipping her hand up the back of his jacket. Her breasts pressed up against his body. They felt so fucking good. Kyle ran his hands down her sides, traveling lower and lower.

"Do you think it's proper…here?" She laughed softly in his ear.

"Proper?" Kyle kissed her neck. "Who said anything about proper? To hell with proper. Weren't you the one that started this in the first place?"

She giggled. "I did…"

"I just want to kiss you all over," he said, his desire burning, pumping blood in his loins. "Here, in this room…who gives a fuck where. If someone walks by, then to hell with them. We'll give those servants a good show."

Her lips were sweet, making him hunger for more. The flesh of her neck, her earring playfully dangling. Kyle leaned in, kissing her neck. The scent of her floral perfume smothered him, leaving him wanting more. He caressed her down to her waist, smashing into her as they kissed deeply. He pressed his hardness against her, and she let out a small moan.

Suddenly, she let go with alarm.

Kyle looked over his shoulder. Several servants were passing by, trying to pretend they hadn't seen anything.

They both waited until the servants were gone. "God, haven't they ever seen a couple kiss before?" he muttered. "These people are like damn flies."

Emerald smiled, leaning against him. "Now you know what my whole life has been like."

"No wonder you ran away that time."

"That wasn't the reason."

"I know, bad joke," he said. He kissed her lips again, tenderly this time. He was still hard, his leather pants now tight.

Emerald lowered her eyes, as if she knew he was thinking. She grabbed his bulge, then squeezed gently. "You must oblige me later."

"You don't have to tell me twice," Kyle said. He straightened up, adjusting his erection. God, how was he supposed to just walk away from this?

She kissed him one last time, then said, "I've got to get back. People will notice if I'm gone too long. I still have to make my rounds and speak to several of the sector lords." She patted his butt playfully, then smiled.

From behind, Kyle could hear voices and scuffles of feet.

He glanced over his shoulder, noticing another photographer. It was one of the ones he'd scolded earlier. The photographer held his camera up, ready to snap a photo of them alone.

It took every ounce of his energy to choke back his irritation.

"*Didn't* the Queen tell you no more photos?" Kyle said, gritting his teeth.

Emerald had a blank look.

"Yes, well, since the others are gone, I figured that I could quickly just grab one photo…" the photographer said.

Seeing the asshole's face, the camera, Emerald's flushed face…

He couldn't fucking help it.

Without another word, Kyle stormed over to the photographer, yanked the camera from him, and threw it against the ground. The lens shattered, and the camera split into a few pieces.

"There's your fucking photo!" Kyle yelled at him, kicking the camera fragments all across the floor.

"My camera…" the photographer said, running to grab the camera parts, slipping Kyle angry looks as he snatched up the broken pieces.

Calm…I must remain calm for Em…

Kyle readjusted his shades. "Come on, Em," he said, pulling her away.

"Kyle…" she breathed.

The two walked down the halls, with Emerald being silent.

He just couldn't take it anymore. Turning to her, Kyle said, "Em, I know what you said before, but the dude deserved it! You gave him an order, and he pressed his luck."

"That I did," she said, then looked at him. "But that was completely uncalled for."

"Oh God, here we go again," Kyle said. "You're defending him? Homeboy literally disturbed a private moment between us. You should be glad that I didn't unleash my fury on him. You have no idea how reserved I was!"

Emerald stared at him. "I'm not defending his actions. But this? This is the second time you have lost your temper with these people."

Fuck, here it is. "So you are defending them."

Emerald leaned in, then grabbed his hand. The coolness of her touch calmed him, but he was still raging. "Kyle, you *must* control your *manners* up here. These people help run the kingdom smoothly. The more you upset them, the more problems there will be for me…and for *us*."

"The photographers? They run the kingdom smoothly? Tell me how."

Emerald's face darkened. "They don't. But they show everything that goes on here. And if up here is a mess, then everyone down there gets upset."

Her reasoning suddenly made sense, like everything clicked into place.

"I…I guess when you put it like that, I can see your point," Kyle said with an angry sigh.

Emerald gave him a hard stare. "I'm glad that you get it."

Seeing her angry face made him wonder.

"Em?"

"What."

"Do you regret being with me?"

At that, Emerald let out a surprised but uneasy laugh. "*Regret*? Of course not. Why would you say such a thing?" She placed a hand on her belly, rubbing it.

"Because I am who I am. And you are who you are." Kyle took a deep breath. "I feel like I don't really belong in your world." *Because apparently I can't do anything right.*

"Kyle, stop doing this."

"Doing what?"

"This. Questioning my love for you," Emerald said. "Unless… you question it yourself?" Her voice shook as she said it.

Quickly, Kyle leaned in, holding her hand. "No, no, no! That's not it at all."

"Then why do you say these things?"

We are completely different, that's why. "Because I'm a scumbag, and you are queen," Kyle continued.

She raised her eyebrow. "Again, you are putting yourself on a different level."

Everything was coming out wrong. Why was he so terrible with his words when it came to her?

Kyle placed her hand on his chest. "Em, I'm sorry," he whispered. "I will do everything to keep my cool. For you. For me. And for us."

Her eyes met his. So beautiful. He did not want to lose her over some dumb differences. It wasn't worth it.

She gave a smile, the kind and innocent smile that he loved so much. He knew by that smile that she wasn't upset or worried.

"Thank you," she said in a whisper.

"I love you," he whispered back. "I mean it. I don't want to lose you. I lost you once, and I can't lose you again."

"You won't lose me." She rubbed her belly, looking down. "You know, we are going to be parents."

God, didn't he know it.

Emerald gave him a determined look. "I want us to be strong. On the same page."

"Em…" Kyle said. He put his arms around her, and she embraced him, leaning her head on his arms. How he loved her. "I want us to be solid too, you know?" he whispered in her ear.

She smiled shyly. "I love you, Kyle."

"I love you too."

They kissed softly, then she pulled away. "Really, I must go back to the party now."

They exchanged one last kiss.

"See you tonight," she said, giggling.

Kyle watched as she walked off, talking a deep breath. God, he needed a damn drink after that fiasco. That and a smoke to clear his head.

Kyle walked back to the hall. As he entered, he saw Emerald from afar, seated on her throne. She was engaged in conversation with some important dude by the looks of it. He strolled through the party, coming to another servant with a drink tray.

"I'll take two," Kyle said, grabbing them off the tray.

"Yes, my lord."

"I ain't no lord, but thanks anyway, man," Kyle said.

"Of course not. You are Master Kyle Trancer, lead singer of Disorderly Conduct," the servant said. "I am required to call everyone lord in my duty as a servant."

Shit. It seemed everyone did know who he was. He wasn't sure how he felt about that.

"Makes sense," Kyle said with a shrug.

The servant was about to leave, but Kyle interrupted him. "Don't leave yet." He slammed the first drink, then the second, then placed the glasses back on the tray. "Now you can leave."

"Yes, sir," the servant said, and bowed, looking confused.

He noticed a large exit with a balcony, and headed in that direction. His head had started spinning, the buzz of the alcohol finally kicking in. It felt good, making him not think about all the lords, people knowing who the hell he was, and his latest fight with Emerald. Not really a fight, but it was definitely something.

Kyle walked outside, immediately lighting up a cigarette. He took a giant inhale, then relaxed against the railing. Outside on the balcony were several other lords, smoking their tobacco pipes, cigars, or fashionable e-cigarettes.

Kyle snorted. *E-cigarettes. The hell is that shit anyways?* Nothing beat the real thing. A few of the lords looked at him, nodding. Kyle waved back at them casually. He suddenly felt like shit judging them. Wasn't that what they did to him?

There was a soft clearing of a man's throat near him. Kyle turned to find Emerys approaching him.

"Hey, man, what's up? Coming out here for a drag too?" Kyle asked.

"No, Master Kyle. I don't smoke," he said. "Might I have a word with you?"

"Sure," Kyle said, taking another drag. "I've noticed you've been kind of keeping an eye on me."

"Indeed. You are quite keen to your surroundings."

Kyle laughed, flicking the ash of his cigarette. "Yeah. Kind of comes with the territory when one lives in the lower levels."

Emerys gave him a half smile, nodding in understanding.

"So…what do you want to talk to me about?" Kyle already knew where this was going.

"It's about the Queen."

Bingo. "What about her?"

Emerys raised his eyebrows. "My loyalties have always been with Arcadia, especially pertaining to the Queen herself."

"I'm glad to hear that," Kyle said, taking another drag. "It's good to have someone watching Em's back in this joint. Emerald is lucky to have you, man."

"Precisely." He eyed him, leaning in slightly. "That is why I wanted to express my *concerns*."

"What's going on? Is it Olympia again?" Kyle played dumb, taking another drag.

"No. It is with you."

"Ah. Straight to the point. You don't fuck around, do you?" Kyle said, eyeing him.

Emerys ignored his statement. "I have only just met you, but you seem to care fully for the Queen, which I appreciate. She is quite taken with you." He lowered his voice. "However, you two must be more guarded with your *behavior*."

"The Queen has already talked to me about my behavior. I promise I won't get out of hand with the other lords."

"That is not what I was referring to." Emerys gave him a stern look. "I am referring to your forward affections."

"Oh, really?"

"*Really*. Because, Master Kyle, you parading your affections for the Queen in front of the lords can reflect negatively on Arcadia's relations with the other kingdoms, especially with the Queen still being married. His Majesty King Derek has connections with the other kingdoms, and you don't want to destroy Arcadia's relations, do you?"

"Don't I know it." Kyle sighed, then leaned in. "I love her, Emerys."

Emerys gave him a sad smile.

Kyle sighed. "Then you realize my dilemma, right?"

"I do." He lowered his voice. "What you two do behind closed doors is none of my business. As the Queen's paramour, however, you must not show displays of public affection. It could cause more damage than you can imagine."

Paramour. That was how people viewed him. A side piece.

Suddenly, Kyle felt anxious and angry. He looked at Emerald inside the glass patio window. She was talking with some important lord. She glanced over at him, and he saw a smile in her eyes meant only for him.

Emerys blotted his forehead with a handkerchief. "It is hard not to notice the Queen's affections. And if it were to come out that the Queen, pregnant with the King's child, is now traipsing around with a lover while he is away… how do you think the Queen's reputation would fare, especially during these tough times? It's already being destroyed by the press."

"What if I were to tell you that one of the children is mine?"

Emerys didn't flinch. "I am well aware of that fact. It still doesn't change the situation. She is still queen, and she needs her kingdom, and her *house*, to be in order."

Kyle clenched his teeth. "Who's to say what the Queen gets to do and not do? She's gotta live her own damn life! It's not fair for her to hide herself. She's done it her whole damn life. And what now? She's gotta do it all over again? That's fucking bullshit! Why should she have to hide who she is? I mean, that's the whole reason why she ran away from this place in the first place, right? She had no say in anything! Now, she finally does, and she should be able to be who she wants to be!"

Emerys smiled sadly. "I agree with all your passionate words. The life of a royal is a hard path to live. But unfortunately, she does not get to live her life how she wants to…publicly."

Kyle fumed. "I don't like it," he said under his breath. "That's about the shittiest thing I've ever heard."

"It is indeed the *shittiest* thing," Emerys agreed. "But for the sake of your affections for the Queen, please be more discreet."

"God, well, there goes my night," Kyle muttered.

"I am sorry to be such a damper to your evening," Emerys stated.

"I'll say."

Emerys put his hand on Kyle's shoulder. Kyle could sense his thoughts; Emerys was genuinely concerned for the Queen, and for their relationship. He also could feel the fear gripping the councilor. He was terrified of Derek returning to see what was going on.

"I do mean it when I say that what you two do is entirely up to you," Emerys said.

Kyle stood still, sucking in his breath. He glanced up at Emerys through his shades, then nodded. "I know. You're doing what you should be doing. Can't blame you, man. I'm just pissed as hell."

"I can relate. Just…consider what I have said." He turned to leave.

"I will. Thanks, man." Just then, Kyle called out, "One thing."

Emerys turned to look over his shoulder. "Yes?"

"What if I told you that I serenaded the Queen in front of an audience at one of my shows, and now it's the number one song?"

Emerys frowned. "I've already heard. That incident is the very reason why I was prompted to keep a closer eye on you, not to mention your *affections* earlier at the party. Good evening, Master Kyle." Emerys bowed, then walked away.

God, what bullshit. Kyle hated the idea of living in the palace. Living in the upper levels. Now he had to live by their rules, hiding like a couple of damn horny teens. Fuck that. He loved that woman, and she shouldn't be treated like a caged bird. And like hell was he going to have a kid grow up in that bullshit too.

It's fucking decided, he said to himself.

He was going to ask Em to marry him. She could divorce Derek. No more stress with the kingdom.

Then they would be free to do whatever the fuck they want in peace, raising their children.

CHAPTER 56

◆

RED

Kyle finished up his cigarette, taking one last deep inhale of smoke. He rubbed the butt of the cigarette on the new ashtray on the patio, exhaling as he did so. Apparently Glacia had placed one there just for him.

Before entering the bedroom, Kyle watched as Emerald removed her jewelry piece by piece. She was still in her evening clothes, starting to get ready for bed. He couldn't help but watch her. The way she gracefully moved as she removed her necklace. Her neck swayed as her hair swept over her shoulder, leaving it bare.

Kyle stared as a wave of burning desire swept over him.

What a mess, he thought, his mind going back to his conversation with Emerys.

Emerald saw his gaze through the patio glass and gave him a smile.

Kyle mustered up a smile as he slid open the patio door, entering the bedroom.

"Tired?" Emerald called out from her vanity.

"Very," Kyle answered. He neared her, then gave her a hug from behind, fully embracing her in his arms. In return, she clutched onto his arms.

"Unzip me? That is, if you don't mind," she said in a soothing tone.

"If I do, I can't promise I'll be good after…"

"You are supposed to oblige me anyways, are you not? After all, I requested that of you earlier."

"Is that a royal command?" Kyle joked.

Emerald glanced over her shoulder, then gave him a bright smile as she lifted her hair off the nape of her neck. "It is," she said as she waited for him to unzip her.

Kyle smiled as he slowly unzipped her dress. As he exposed her back, he got a glimpse of her side breast. He slipped her dress to her waist, then pulled her to him, kissing the back of her shoulder. She reached to touch the side of his face, then gently ran her hands down his face.

Emerald turned to face him. Her eyes were glowing with her mysterious beautiful green magic. Her beauty was so unreal at times, as if she were a heavenly creature that didn't belong in this world.

She slipped off her dress, leaving her naked except her underwear.

Kyle couldn't help himself, pushing her gently to the bed, Emerald giving him a devious smile. He unbuckled his belt, then unzipped his pants, pushing them off and to the floor.

He crawled on top of her, feeling her wetness through the fabric of her panties. God, it gave him a raging hard-on. Looking at her once more, he saw the desire in her eyes, he knew right then and there that he was the luckiest fucking man alive.

He kissed her chest, then her pregnant stomach, her hip, sliding off her underwear, then came up to her again. He grabbed her ankles, slowly dragging her to the edge of the bed for her to be comfortable. Then he pushed himself in. She gasped in response, then gave a small moan.

There was nothing sweeter than being in that moment with Em, the woman he loved, having her.

The faster his movements became, the louder her moans grew. He wanted to explode, but he wanted her to have her way too.

"Em," he said softly. "What do you want me to do for you?" He continued thrusting, until she held a hand up on his chest.

"My favorite thing…"

He knew exactly what she wanted.

She ran her right hand across his chest, then down to his fingertips as his motion began to slow.

Her hand never left his as he let himself out of her. Kyle climbed onto the bed, sitting over her. With her guidance, she traveled his hand down to her hot spot, with him slipping two fingers inside.

She moaned, then slid her leg upward in pleasure, giving him an invitation to continue. Just when he thought he couldn't get any harder, he did.

He started slow at first, his fingers playing with her, traveling inside and out. With the other hand, he cupped her breast, rubbing it in a circular motion, focusing on her nipple.

Emerald let out another seductive moan, this time louder.

Another strong surge of desire swept over him.

Kyle became mesmerized by Emerald as he watched her in her trancelike ecstasy. His movements became faster as he made a steady circular motion with both his hands—one between her legs, the other on her nipple.

"More…I want more…" she said breathlessly.

Faster and faster his movements became, with her wanting screams approving.

Then, with a sudden pulsating, she cried out with her eyes rolling back. She shuddered as his fingers slowly withdrew from between her thighs, then he blew out a slow breath. She pulled herself upward and leaned against a pillow, still dripping. She used her panties and wiped herself.

Kyle knelt over her, then tenderly kissed her lips. He loved her so much.

"Did you like that?" he asked.

"Most definitely," she whispered as she played with his earring, then nibbled on his ear.

"I'm glad," Kyle said, kissing her neck. "God, I'll need to smoke a pack now after that."

"I could use some wine after that." Emerald leaned back in her pillows.

"You know I would get you some in a heartbeat…"

Emerald pushed him playfully. "There will be plenty of opportunities after the birth of the twins."

Kyle fluffed a pillow next to Emerald, then he flopped down, putting his arm around her. She rested her head on his chest, combing her fingers through his necklaces. It felt so right being next to her. It was as if all his other issues with the palace, the stuffy old upper-level hags, the tax…it all melted away with her touch.

Kyle felt Emerald's hand slide to the green-jeweled pendant on his chest. She lifted it carefully, staring at it. The jewel glowed a vibrant green with her touch. "It's strange. I can feel my life force within this jewel. You never told me how you got this."

"A woman in the future gave it to me. She lived where Arcadia was at."

"You've been to Arcadia in the future?"

Kyle snorted. "What was left of it."

Emerald's face went pale. "Tell me about it. I want to know about the future," she whispered.

Kyle eyed her, then held her tightly. "It's pretty bleak."

"I still want to hear about it."

Kyle sighed, taking in a deep breath. "In the future, there is no kingdom of Arcadia, Em. All of the United Kingdoms are no more. The land is unlivable, and most of this land, called 'World Sector One,' is destroyed. That is, the time when I lived as Rubius."

"How was it destroyed?"

"From what the future teaches of history, there was a meteor that crashed into the planet."

Emerald shot up. "A meteor?"

"Yeah. A toxic one at that," he said. "They say that it was the God of Light punishing them for using technology."

She had a curious look on her face. "Technology? It's considered a bad thing?"

"Apparently." Kyle sighed. "Anyways, when I was trying to find my way back to you, I visited the ruins of Arcadia. I found an underground group of people that had been hiding from the sky people for centuries. They had been mining in this kingdom, and found weapons with magic in them." Kyle paused, thinking about the underground citadel and Elder Moon. "It was incredible. You should have seen it. They were able to somehow take the magic from these old-ass artifacts and use the magic stored within them. One of the elders of the group had this pendant. She knew I was looking for you, and when I realized who I was, the pendant responded. She gave it to me then." Kyle looked at her. "With this, we were connected through time."

"I think somehow, it guided my spirit to yours down in Hell," Emerald said. "It was like...a path in my dreams." Her face turned solemn. "But what you said about our future makes me sad. All this that we work so hard for...gone. I wonder if we can stop the meteor from coming?"

Kyle shrugged. "Who knows. But who knows if it even happened during our lifetime? It could be years after we die. Hundreds of years."

"Still," she said, laying her head back down on his chest.

"No one should be altering time. I'm sure I'm already fucking it up by being here."

"Why do you say that?" Emerald asked, perking her head up.

Kyle suddenly thought of the God of Light's warning.

"I dunno, it seems like something Geeta would go on about," Kyle said, not meeting her gaze. "Hey, forget the future."

She settled her head back down on his chest and clutched his necklace. The gem glowed brightly in response. Through it, Kyle felt her fear.

"What are you afraid of? Is it what I said about the future?"

She quickly glanced at him, shaking her head. "Not about the future. I guess everything? I will soon be a mother. My own mother is a completely different person than what I expected. The kingdom's tensions are rising with Olympia. That girl hasn't been saved yet. And Geeta nearly losing her magic…" Her glowing green eyes darted to him. "What if my mother was behind it?"

Kyle put his hands over hers, clasping the life gem in both their hands.

Emerald gave him a worried but loving smile. Everything in that moment felt right. Her softness, their closeness…

"I will always protect you," Kyle said. The gem glowed brighter in her hand as she smiled. "Always. From *any* harm."

"I know that you will."

The time felt *right*.

Kyle sucked in his breath, then fumbled around in his pocket.

Emerald looked at him curiously as he nervously withdrew the velvet cloth from his pocket, unwrapping it carefully.

Kyle smiled at her, Emerald smiling back in anticipation. In the folds of the velvet, Kyle held up his creation—the ring he had made with his gift.

Steadily holding her hands with one of his, Kyle lifted the ring in Emerald's view.

Her face turned white as she realized what it was, and suddenly, Kyle felt the air thicken.

"Em…I made this for you," Kyle said nervously. "See the stones? The ruby represents me, and the emerald obviously represents you. In the middle is the diamond. Because together we make white light."

Emerald smiled at him, but Kyle could tell that it seemed forced.

"Em, I love you," Kyle continued. "I would die for you. I pledge my life to you. I want to be bound to you not only by our love for each other, but by also marrying you. I mean, if we traveled through dimensions of dreams and of Hell together and back, I think we will do just fine being married." He chuckled nervously.

Kyle watched as her face flickered through a series of emotions, staring at the ring. Each second felt like an eternity, and his anxiety began turning into anger.

This definitely wasn't how he had thought this situation would go.

Emerald took a steady breath. "Kyle, you know I want to marry you." Her eyes looked serious. "But you know I cannot. I have explained why before."

She *had* said those words before. But somehow this time, her words were like soul fire, burning all the way to the depths of his heart. A wave of physical aching, gnawing pain came over his chest.

He felt like a fucking fool. Like, the fuck were they doing if she didn't want to ultimately marry him? The ultimate kick in the ass was that Emerald really had chosen to remain married to Derek. He was second to that asshole.

Kyle grabbed the ring, then pocketed it. Fury struck his heart, and he could no longer contain his rage. Wordlessly, he got up and grabbed his jacket, because if he did say anything, he would say the wrong fucking thing.

Emerald got in front of him, her eyes wide. "Kyle? You know I would do anything to marry you."

"Really? Because it sure as hell seems to me that you wouldn't," Kyle sneered. Her words dug painfully deeper.

"I would!"

"Then *divorce* Derek! How hard is it?"

"With all my heart, I do not want to be tied to Derek! But I cannot divorce him," she said firmly. Her eyes narrowed, tears forming. "You want my kingdom to slip away from me and my people? Have Derek's father rule in its stead?"

Kyle whirred around. "Have you ever once thought about yourself? What you want?"

"Of course!"

"Then why are you always sacrificing your dreams for some random-ass people that don't mean a damn thing! How about thinking about your soulmate, your complement, instead? It's your fucking life!" Kyle stared at her. "And have you ever considered how I feel in all of this?"

She blinked, as if she had never posed the question to herself.

"Em, I don't want to be just some 'guy' to you forever."

"But you're not."

"Yeah, I am. Because by not divorcing Derek, and wanting me around, you are basically telling me that I'm just that. How do you think I feel? I mean, I have Emerys telling me to be guarded with my behavior. Do you know how hard that is, when all I want to do is love you? Be with you? Laugh with you? Hold you?"

Kyle could tell that Emerald was angry, confused, sad, hurt, and stressed. Her eyes were like glass, and her face pale as porcelain.

"You don't understand my life," she whispered spitefully through angry tears.

"You're right, I don't. I've been doing everything for you, and it's not enough." Kyle stared right into her soul. "I will never be *enough* for you."

Kyle headed for the patio. Emerald reached out to him. "Where are you going?"

"I need to breathe. I said that I would protect you, so I won't be gone long. I promised that," Kyle said bitterly through his teeth.

With that, he threw on his jacket, then cast his adjacent orange magic over himself, turning invisible. He could hear Emerald's light sobs, and he hesitated.

His heart ached at the idea of leaving.

He just needed to think. Em too. Maybe she would reconsider everything.

A deep ache hurt his heart once more as he summoned the wind, then took off from her balcony.

CHAPTER 57

◆

GREEN

Emerald lay awake, sickened by what had transpired earlier. There was no possible way that she could sleep. Inside her belly, she felt the babies kick, almost in response to her distress.

He'd asked to marry her. It was a dream come true, Kyle proposing. But with all the tension of her current situation, it made her more uneasy. How she wished that Kyle understood what she had been going through. It was such an easy thought for her to divorce Derek. But actually doing so was a whole other issue. There would be so many repercussions with the kingdoms—especially with York. Her people would most likely not care—but the other kingdoms would definitely not favor her or Arcadia. And the legality of it?

She could talk to Emerys and see what could be done. But she didn't have a lot of hope for it—she knew the laws of the land and what was in place. And if Emerys had already spoken to Kyle about his behavior, it wasn't a good sign for their future together.

Suddenly, the melody of their song played within her mind.

Kyle…I'm so sorry I can't give you what you want. What I want…

Getting out of bed, Emerald cradled herself as she walked over to the patio, looking out the window. The night sky was so very beautiful. But her heart was a mess.

Tears streamed down her cheeks as she looked at her kingdom.

The more she and Kyle had these arguments, the more uneasy she became. At times, she questioned if he wanted to be a father, or even be with her. He said he loved her, but…was it enough?

He is trying to do the best he can, she told herself.

Kyle's singing flooded her mind once again. The beautiful melody that was special for them. Instead of lulling her into a peaceful state, it did the opposite.

Emerald couldn't be in her room any longer. Her mind was too active.

Suddenly, there was a warm presence in her room. It brushed her skin, soothing her.

"Kyle?" Emerald whispered as she turned around.

No one was there. But the warmth continued to embrace her, calming her with its familiarity.

I can't bear to see you hurt, her mother's voice whispered within her thoughts.

Emerald froze. "Mother?"

The warmth fled her room, leaving Emerald cold and alone by her window.

"Mother?" Emerald called out once more.

No answer.

I need to get some air, she thought. Emerald threw on her robe, then left her chambers, coming upon the sitting room. Cyndi shot up, bowing.

"Is everything okay, Your Majesty?" she asked.

"I'm fine. I just need to take a walk," Emerald said.

Cyndi bowed as Emerald let herself out. The guards down the hall noticed, but Emerald gave them a sign that all was well, then made her way to the lift. Though she greatly wanted to be alone, it was the duty of her handmaidens to accompany her.

Emerald stepped onto the lift, Cyndi standing in silence next to her. As the lift descended, Emerald said in a whisper, "Love is so hard, Cyndi."

"It really is, Your Majesty," Cyndi replied.

Emerald turned her, taking in her sympathetic expression.

The lift opened, and Emerald walked out into the gardens. Turning to Cyndi, she said, "Let me be."

Cyndi bowed, then remained at the doorway as Emerald wandered off.

Fragrant smells permeated the air, soft whispers of the wind mixing with the transports overhead. The night sky was illuminated with the city's neon lights below, creating a vivid pool of colored lights. From behind, the palace panels were electric green, highlighting the gardens.

Emerald turned to a more private area of the garden, where goldfish swam freely in a mini stone pool. She fell to her knees, trying to calm her mind as she watched the fish swim in the illuminated pond.

As much as she tried, she couldn't shake her anxiety.

Please, let everything be all right, she thought as she watched the fish.

Emerald didn't know why, but suddenly Derek crossed her mind. Thoughts of him had always come and gone, but this was the first time in a long time that those thoughts were anything other than anger or confusion.

What if things had turned out differently, without the sorceress interfering with time? Would she be in this same predicament now? Not likely. Kyle wouldn't have perished months ago, and she wouldn't have married Derek. Prior to the sorceress, Derek was kind and devoted to her. Attentive in many ways that Kyle wasn't.

Stop it! she told herself. *Kyle is doing the best he can. He isn't used to being in the upper levels and dealing with all the royal expectations.*

Emerald got up, then glanced into the night sky once again.

Kyle, where are you? I miss you.

"Kyle," she whispered aloud, half hoping that he would appear. "Come back. I'll try and make it right."

✦ ✦ ✦

Emerald opened her eyes and glanced up from where she'd fallen asleep. The world was bright, the air warm. Palaces from every corner of the world rose high like crystals, gleaming. The sun had a holy presence, as if its rays disintegrated evil itself. Songbirds sang happy tunes, while bubbling brooks soothed her mind.

I'm in a dream, she thought, amazed by her surroundings.

"Emerald."

A wisp of warm, soft air blew against Emerald's skin.

"Who's there?" Emerald called out.

More warmth surrounded her. Arms embraced her.

Light suddenly blinded her vision, with the air growing hotter.

I can't bear to see you hurt…

Emerald perked up; she knew that the voice.

"Mother?" Emerald called out into the blinding light.

The light dimmed to a comfortable level, suddenly revealing her mother's face. Elyathi's face shone like an angel, holy and bright. The warmth that came from the light, Emerald felt love within its rays.

Men steal women's hearts as if they are toys, worthless, then utterly destroy them, leaving the woman heartbroken, her mother whispered.

"Mother?"

I cannot let that happen to you, my daughter...

Her mother's face wisped away as a hand shook her shoulder.

"Emerald."

Emerald opened her eyes. She was still in the gardens.

Mother... she thought. She had felt the presence of her mother and couldn't shake it. Men breaking the hearts of women? Was she warning against Kyle? Had she foreseen what would happen between them? No, it couldn't be. Her mother was a threat to the world; she couldn't be trusted. Besides, Kyle told her that she'd had it out for him since day one. But still, Emerald couldn't help but wonder. The mixed feelings and emotions that they had been experiencing being back together wasn't what she'd expected. And in her dream, her mother hadn't seemed evil at all. Quite the opposite, in fact. Warm. Loving. Caring.

Should she tell Kyle about it? She wasn't sure, especially after their last exchange. But one thing she was sure about: how much she truly missed her mother.

CHAPTER 58

◆

GREEN

Time. It was nonexistent. Never ending, with no beginning. It gave Suresh all the time he could have wanted to think about what would happen. And yet, he didn't have much time left. It was dwindling like a dying star.

All colors create the light of the world, Suresh. Elyathi's words echoed in his mind.

Everything was his fault. If he hadn't time traveled in the first place, Elyathi would never have been able to activate her inner power, thus never causing her daughter to be born with the green gift. Every time he thought about it, more guilt came to him. And in this timeless prison, there were no escaping his mind. He needed to redeem his sins. There was a reason why the gods had made their laws in the first place.

For days, weeks, however long it had been since Suresh last spoke to Ayera, he had thought about their last exchange: that being without a gift, one could still accomplish many things. She had argued it made her stronger in some aspects.

If only I could apply that ideology here, he thought. Suresh glanced upward, seeing the streaming light with the dancing specks of dust, floating gently like soft feathers. Ayera's words did have wisdom in them. But how could he apply that thinking here? He was locked away in this time prison, unable to use his magic, not even able to move his physical body. Derek of Arcadia was much too powerful with time magic, and he was only going to get more powerful. There seemed to be no hope.

His thoughts flickered back to the time he had come across the storage room in the citadel, with all the blood and gemstones. The empty shelves of the green and violet. This High Court, as they called themselves, wanted those gifts especially. And now, they certainly had his power—or nearly all of it. His life force was hanging by a mere thread.

A warm gust of air pricked his skin. Suresh knew it was not a physical wind, but within his thoughts.

Ayera? Can you hear me? he called out.

Yes.

He smiled weakly. She was the only thing that kept him fighting. *How are you faring?*

As best as any prisoner can, I expect. I don't think I'll ever feel the warmth of the sun again, she replied. Despite her sorrow, her voice was soothing to his soul.

You will, he assured her. *You told me so yourself, remember?*

A lightness touched her tone. *I know deep in my heart that my sister will somehow come for me, though I am anxious.* She paused. *Suresh? May I ask you something?*

What is it?

Tell me…tell me what Earth's surface is like. What was it like in the ancient days of your homeland? I want to hear of it. It will help take my anxious thoughts away.

Suresh breathed. He hadn't thought of his homeland in a long time. The dust in the air. The cattle. The small huts and stone temples…

Where I lived, it was the center of the known world—at least, in my region. The land was different from other parts of the world throughout time, as I have come to have seen.

Were there trees?

Suresh laughed. *Yes, but not like the forests that you read about. The area was dry, with dust in the wind. There were trees scattered about, bushes, lush in their own sort of way. There was a main river, where the source of water was for the farms, cattle, and drinking. Most everyone lived in huts, except the highest caste of the land.*

Caste?

Different social levels in our society. Suresh paused, closing his eyes. He could envision the ancient city now. Sounds of his people yelling in the streets.

Cattle roaming the city. Children playing. The sunlight was golden, casting a holy glow across the city. Suresh could almost taste the dust on his tongue, with the hot winds, dry air…

One did not cross the caste system, Empress. It was forbidden. I was one of the exceptions.

Because you were gifted?

Yes. My family was poor—the poorest of the poor. But when I was born with the gift, I was considered a miracle. I was dedicated to the temple at birth, raised by priests. My father was paid a large lump sum because I was the only one born with the green gift. You see, the people born of the gift, there was only one of each color. We were considered guardians of those gifts. Gifts that the Gods of the Spectrum bestowed upon us. There was a temple of the Spectrum, and I was a Priest of the Green when I became of age.

You were a priest?

It is not like the priests you see in this time, nor other parts of the world. The yellow gift had always meant to be a holy color, bringing forth dedicated priests for all future generations. But at the beginning of time, us gifted were all considered priests in our own right. People all over the region traveled far to see us for blessings and prayers. Since I was the representative of the God of the Green, I had the task of healing the sick who were brought to the temple.

The image of the temple came into Suresh's mind. Tall, thick stone pillars, the circular room plated with gold, the incense streaming from the braziers. The sick in the outer courts of the temple, crying out for healing. Blood, sickness, disease—those smells and sounds had never left him.

Geeta was from your time, was she not?

She was. And a good friend. Suresh suddenly thought about Geeta. How much he cared for her.

Was she a priestess like the others? Ayera asked.

Suresh sighed. *You must know, in ancient days, men had all the power, and women had none. For Geeta to be discovered a gifted… There was much uproar within the temple and my society. Of course, she was brought forth to the temple at birth, presented just like the others. But she grew up with a much different experience than the other gifted. She was expected to serve her husband—a yellow priest. She did all the wifely duties expected of women, on top of her priestess duties. Her husband reveled in that fact, knowing that he was the only gifted that had another gifted as a mate. She had no say in anything.*

Why did she marry him?

It was an arranged marriage between the families, and expected since he was a yellow and she was violet. It was a picturesque explanation of why a woman was born with the gift. She was made an example of what a complement should be. A marriage of submission that created "harmony." Suddenly, his thoughts were bitter, and his arm injury flared in pain.

Memories of that day flashed into his mind. The last time he was at the temple. Vihaan beating Geeta. Blood… And Geeta controlling their minds as payback.

I am sorry… Geeta's past words echoed in his mind.

Suresh shuddered as he looked down at his arm—the one he had bitten under her influence. He was still scarred. Just by the sight of it, Suresh felt Geeta's bitterness, her jealousy of the other priests—being favored because they were men and of high caste…

Are you still there, Suresh? Ayera called out.

Yes. Suresh blinked. *Why do you ask about my homeland?*

There was a pause, then Suresh felt a sad heaviness. *I have dreamed of the earth's surface, and have imagined what it's like, how it used to be before its destruction,* she answered. *I think every one of us in this time dreams of Earth's mountains, streams, forests, deserts, snows, and oceans. It is nice to hear you speak of it, having seen it yourself. It makes me feel as if I am thousands of miles away from this place.*

I am glad that I can give you some comfort, Suresh said. *I had thought I was distressing you.*

How?

Because of my words. I spoke with bitterness.

I felt your emotions, but I wanted to hear it all. By listening, it makes me understand the depth of what you have gone through, and of the world at its beginning. I hope one day, my world in this time will be restored as it was in the ancient days.

Without the caste system, Suresh added.

There was a soft laugh. *Yes, most definitely without the caste system, as you say. I just wish the earth could be restored. I want to live on the land once more, as my ancestors did.*

Ayera was so pure of heart, so beautiful with her thoughts, dreams. And so wise. Suresh realized how truly beautiful her soul was. He wanted to know more of her.

Tell me of your homeland, Suresh asked.

You want to know of mine?

Yes. I want to know of you as well. It will ease my mind of the troubles, just the same as you.

My upbringing isn't fascinating like yours, Ayera started.

I beg to differ. You were born into a world of magic, Suresh pointed out. *Magical enchantments crossed with other magics…very different and remarkable.*

Very well. I grew up in the royal citadel of World Sector Six. That was mostly all I knew other than the surrounding floating isles. It was the same citadel that my ancestors before me ruled, and the very citadel that was raised from our earthly lands. Of course, over the centuries, the citadel has been improved and enhanced. As for travel, I have been to other parts of the world—all of it in the air. I have traveled in our airships or with the use of blue magic from the court. As you know, the High Court rules all the sectors, and they are supreme.

She continued. *According to historical records, my family line has ruled my sector for thousands of years. The throne was to go to my sister. All her life, she was raised as a true court princess, with expectations of taking over the throne. I was treated as unimportant, but still a member of the royal family. Because my father did not think of me having a knack for ruling or being quick witted enough for any court position, I embraced traditional dance in our sector's theaters.* There was a pause. *It looked like the God of Light had a different path for me.*

Your father was very wrong.

About what?

You not being quick witted, Suresh pointed out.

There was another quiet chuckle. *Thank you.*

It is strange how our life comes out in a much different way than what we envision in our younger years, Suresh said.

It is.

Suresh looked around at his watery time prison. Her words warmed his heart, and for the first time, he felt this soul actually could make a difference—a true difference—against Elyathi.

Ayera?

Yes?

Should he tell her?

But before he could think any further, a flash of white caught his attention. Behind the time curtain, Elyathi's form blurred.

You should go, he warned.

Go?

Don't think of me right now, or anything about me…

But…

The white came closer.

Please, I am begging you! Suresh argued. *Now! Do not think of me!*

There was a sudden disconnect, and he could no longer sense Ayera.

The white blur paused, almost in hesitation. Elyathi lingered for a moment, then disappeared again. He breathed hard with relief.

No one could know about Ayera's gift.

✦　✦　✦

Elyathi watched Suresh's reflection distort like a strong water current as she parted the magical walls of his time prison. Suresh weakly shifted his eyes toward her but otherwise made no other movements.

The life forces from World Sector Four were strong, making her far more powerful. The collective of their powers felt beautiful and alive. She kept many of them for herself, though she didn't like handing any over to the High Court.

"Have you thought about all that I have said?" Elyathi called out. She clutched his green vial, holding it on display. Perhaps it would put some sense in him. Why was he resisting her? She had thought that he, out of all people, would be with her. They were one and the same in many ways.

"I have thought endlessly, as this place makes me do so," he said softly.

Elyathi smiled, then plopped down in a chair next to him. "So tell me, Suresh. What is your conclusion to this all?"

His forest-green eyes glanced at her, though the luster was gone. "You will never find what you are looking for in the new world. It will never bring you healing, only sorrow."

Elyathi flinched at his words. They burned, sparking a deep anger within. Elyathi swallowed, pushing that fire back. She had to resist it; persistence would pay off in the end. He needed to undo all of his thinking.

"Suresh," she whispered, "I do not understand where all this hatred of me comes from. I only want to give you what you truly deserve. You saved my life, and I owe you everything."

"If that were true, you wouldn't have stolen a part of my life force," Suresh stated firmly.

His words sparked fury. Why was he resisting?

Elyathi gracefully placed a hand on his head, then softly swept it over his hair. "It was not taken with malice, it was taken for God's good work. I only did what I was called to do." Elyathi grasped the vial with part of his life force. It glowed vibrant green as she held it up. "This…this is yours. It will be returned to you in the new world. I am merely borrowing it until the world is recreated." She leaned toward him as she dropped the vial necklace down her dress. "Suresh, I have never forgotten about you. From the moment I knew my purpose, I have thought of you and your kindness. I wish…I wish you could see the world through my eyes for just a moment, what the new world will be like. I have it perfectly created in my mind, waiting for it to be unleashed. Purity, harmony, love, laughter, joy…it's all there."

Elyathi watched as his face flickered with thoughts. Were her words finally getting through to him? Even if it was a little bit?

There was a long pause, before he said, "Tell me more of your new world."

A warm flood of emotion came over her, and she smiled. "With pleasure…"

CHAPTER 59

◆

BLUE

World Sector One. The land of nothingness.

Vala sighed, staring out in the distance. Nothing but scattered rock formations floating in the sky as far as the eye could see. There were a few islands with ruins on them, but as for civilization, Vala doubted that anyone had made their home in these desolate skies.

This is a waste of my time, Vala thought. If it were up to her, she would have moved on to World Sector Two from her last appointment. But since it was at Ikaria's request, Vala had no choice but to at least try and see if there were any people before moving on.

It had been nearly two days now, and she'd found no one. She had searched many of the large islands, checking ruins, dwellings, or anything that could be considered a shelter. There was no trace of life other than a lost passenger from an airship or some dead fool who decided to make their home on a floating island. Since she was down on her luck, she swore that by sundown, if she still hadn't found anyone, she would move on. That way, at least she could report to Ikaria that she spent two days in this sector searching.

Vala glanced at her next target—a small island in the distance with ruins. She closed her eyes, then summoned her magic, fully immersing herself in the blue gift. She felt the flow of the dimensional space wash over her as her mind concentrated on that specific island. She felt the magic dissipate, and she opened her eyes.

Crumbled ruins lay before her, as if they had been destroyed by a large rock. If she had to guess, it was from the Great Cataclysm. The island was much larger than she had anticipated, with other ancient dwellings dotting the island.

I suppose I'll have to have a look before moving on.

Vala walked through the ruins, moving around several collapsed stone pillars. A mixed strange metal was strewn all over the ground. Metal had been used thousands of years ago in the ancient cities, and some of it had survived for several millennia, but this metal looked recently scavenged.

Bending down, Vala touched one of the metal pieces and picked it up, examining it. It was no different than any other metal piece, except it was old. *Hmmm.* She tossed it back to the ground.

Just as she was getting to her feet, Vala noticed a crack in the stonework of one of the ruins, and a white flash came from inside the split.

Going over to the large crack, she realized the white flash was from metal inside the rock. Running her hand down the crack, the rock itself was smooth, with its own shine to it. She admired the rock, wishing she had all the time in the world to find out more about the strange metal inside. But there was no time to explore and satisfy her curiosity.

Turning away, Vala noticed three towers, all in different directions but at the same distance. Choosing the one that looked the least corroded, Vala headed in that direction.

She walked through a grassy clearing, passing many wildflowers and even mushrooms. As she got closer to the tower, she noticed it stood in a group of pine trees.

She paused, then did a double take. The flowers appeared to have been planted purposely. The pines opened up to a path, with more flowers, mushrooms, and vegetables lining the way.

Someone lives here, she thought excitedly.

She paused. Even if she found a family living in the tower, what could they do? It wasn't as if they were in charge of World Sector One. But perhaps they knew where more people lived.

Might as well find out.

Quickly heading down the path to the tower, Vala walked along the path until she came to a small bridge that crossed over a dried-up stream. On the other side was the tower.

Giving the tower a once-over, Vala took a deep breath and crossed the bridge. She came to the tower's doorway, then paused.

Should I knock? Or should I just push it open?

Looking over her shoulder, Vala shrugged, then knocked. She waited a few seconds. The door opened, making a loud scraping sound against the floor.

A man her age stood before her. He was taller than her, with ebony skin like hers. He had short hair, not even a quarter of an inch from his scalp. Vala couldn't help but think the man was extremely attractive. But what surprised her was that he had water-blue hair and bright blue eyes.

He had the blue gift like her.

Both of them sucked in their breath at the same time, exchanging curious glances.

"What are you doing here?" the man asked, standing in the doorway.

Vala was suddenly self-conscious, fixing her necklace absentmindedly. "Erm, well, I don't know where to start, but are you in charge of World Sector One?"

"Me?" The man laughed, making Vala feel foolish.

"Let me rephrase that," Vala said. "Are there any others that live nearby? Or that you know of?"

"My answer depends on your answer to this: Are you from the High Court?" he asked.

"Not at all," Vala answered, then raised her eyebrow. "Are you?" she whispered.

The man laughed again, then opened the door further. "Come inside and get warmed up. I'll make you some tea, though I'm not very good at it."

Vala smiled, then nodded. "Sure thing." *I hope he has cookies or biscuits.*

She followed him inside, shutting the door. The base of the tower was basic, with a fireplace equipped with a cauldron for cooking. Wooden shelving adorned the walls, stocked with herbs and dried goods. Other shelves held tomes. Near the far end of the room was a spiral staircase.

"Have a seat," the man said, pointing to a couple of wooden chairs by the fireplace. "Tea will be ready in a few minutes.

"Thanks," Vala said, taking the nearest seat at the fire. She hadn't realized how cold she was until she was warming up at the fire. Of course, she always braved the cold—she should have been born a red-gifted—but feeling the chill in her hands was a sobering reminder that she was indeed a blue-gifted.

"Before having some of my terrible tea, would you give me your name at least?" the man asked with a bright smile.

"Oh, my bad." Vala blushed as she laughed awkwardly. "I am Lady Vala from World Sector Four. Who are you? I know many blue-gifted, but I have never seen you before."

The man's face turned serious. "My name is Dydrone. I worked for World Sector Two's court for a time but then was ordered by the High Court to go to World Sector Five. I worked there for several years."

Dydrone handed Vala her tea. The steam warmed her cheeks as she took a drink. "Orange spice, my favorite," Vala said happily.

"Mine too."

They both chuckled. She took another drink, then held the cup in her lap. "Aren't you a long way off from World Sector Five?"

Dydrone sat down in the chair next to her, then stared into the fire. "Being blue-gifted, I am sure you were aware of the High Court's summons, no?"

Vala knew that all too well. "It's a hard subject to speak of."

His blue eyes met hers, and they began to glow. "It is. They started slowly, summoning us one at a time. Blue-gifted went to the High Court, but none returned."

Vala's hands began to shake at his words, remembering the horror of it. "You're right. No one returned, because they all perished back in time."

Dydrone went wide-eyed. "How do you know this?"

Vala paused. "I was the only one to survive." She glanced down as she drank her tea, not wanting Dydrone to see her watery eyes. "In short, the High Court injected me with a poison, then threatened me and my entire sector if I didn't try to find the green-gifted queen back in time. I found her and was healed by her blood."

"Healed by her blood?"

Vala smiled sadly. "I'll spare you the details, but I survived and made it back. Let's just say the High Court was furious. Since then, they have been doing everything to retrieve green and violet magic with their white-gifted."

"*White*-gifted?" Dydrone said incredulously. "Now that's a new one."

"She can extract one's gift from their life force. They hallucinate for days, weeks, months…until they snap out of it. And once they come back to their senses, they have to deal with the loss of their gift." Vala gritted her teeth, thinking of her father. "Sometimes, the loss of your gift is like losing a loved one. A part of your heart and soul is severed from your being."

"Damn." Dydrone sucked in his breath. "She must be the cause of the plague, then."

"Yes." Vala watched as his face shifted through an array of emotions. "You still haven't told me how you came to this place. I assume you had orders from the High Court?"

"Not exactly," he said. "I was in World Sector Five, minding my own business, drinking with my friends like I did every night after court was dismissed. A blue-gifted woman showed up, demanded that my good friend return to the High Court on a new mission. She mentioned that I should check in with the High Court as well." He sighed heavily. "I don't understand it, but she was extremely weak. She couldn't even port herself, my friend, and his harp. What kind of blue-gifted working for the High Court is that weak?"

Vala frowned, trying to recall anyone that terrible with their gift, but no one came up. "That's odd."

"Yeah," he agreed. "I went to deliver my friend's harp to his quarters at the High Court. That's when I heard that more official summons were being delivered to more blue-gifted. Since I'd heard the rumors of the blue-gifted never returning…"

"You came here to hide," Vala finished.

Dydrone nodded. "I did. Maybe I'm a coward, but I'm no fool." He met her eyes, then said, "I found this place. It was stocked with the essentials. Someone even planted all that you see out there. I don't know where the original owner is, but it was good enough for me."

Vala leaned back in her chair, lost in thought. *He's one of the few blue-gifted left,* she thought. Many more had lost their gift, and it seemed that Elyathi was on a rampage.

"Why don't you come with me?" Vala said.

"And do what?" Dydrone asked. "You have yet to tell me why you came here."

"I have taken a vow to serve World Sector Six in their war against the High Court," Vala said, holding her head high. "I am their ambassador, traveling to all world sectors to convince others to join us in return for the sorceress activating their technology to aid in the war."

Dydrone spat out his tea in surprise. "War? Against the High Court? Are you mad?"

Vala chuckled. "I think so." She turned serious. "But if the High Court threatened your life, your people, your gift, and stole your father's gift… wouldn't you fight?"

Dydrone turned away from her, looking back into the fire. "Your words are powerful, Lady Vala, I give you that. Like you, I despise the High Court. But it is foolish to go against them. They are too powerful."

Vala snorted. "That may be. But I now work for the sorceress Ikaria. She is the key to winning this war."

"Sorceress *Ikaria*?" Dydrone blinked. "The one with the violet magic?"

"Yes, that one." Vala nodded. "Do you know that the High Court is about to execute her sister, Empress Ayera? They have been after her gift for many years, and since they cannot get it, they are using her sister as bait—using the justification that she was not abiding by High Court's laws," she said bitterly. "I have pledged to the sorceress that I will do what I can do make sure the Empress is safe—and before the world comes to an end."

Dydrone's face went still. "Time compression, you mean," he whispered.

"Oh? You know of it?"

"Are we not masters of time? Have you never peeked into the flow of time just to see certain outcomes?"

"Well, yes," Vala admitted.

"I have too, recently," Dydrone stated. "If I decided to stay on this island, I wanted to see where all of this was heading."

"And?"

"I think you know there are many outcomes when it comes to the flow of time," Dydrone said sadly. "Truthfully, I don't like most of them. So I'd rather live my last days in peace, drinking tea and reading in the daylight, saving the hard drinks at night."

"Really? That's how you choose to spend your last time here?" Vala fumed, shooting up to her feet. "You intend to *drink* it away?"

Dydrone's face turned red, furious. He got to his feet, meeting her gaze evenly. "Like I said, I hate the High Court, but I am no fool."

Vala neared his face, her breath hot. "Then you truly are a coward."

She whirled around, then stormed toward the door as Dydrone called out,

"Lady Vala, I do not mean to upset you. When I say that I am truly sorry, I mean it wholeheartedly. In fact, your cause is very noble. But as you know, one person is just a small ripple in time. There is nothing that I can do personally—not if I want to survive."

"I beg to differ. You can always change the course of time. Always." Without turning to face him, Vala called out, "I am going to be a ripple that turns into a wave that will change the flow of time. You will see."

Vala marched out the door and shut it quickly behind her before he got another word in. She heaved angry breaths as she walked across the bridge. It was frustrating to find someone with a gift that could help them, but instead they chose to remain in hiding. Didn't Dydrone see? With all of them working together, they could have a winning chance against the High Court.

Why didn't I say that when I was talking to him? Vala wanted to slap herself for forgetting that part of her argument, which was unlike her. But it was too late now. She would be wasting her breath. It was too bad, because the guy was handsome as all get out. In fact, he was definitely her type, someone she'd consider chasing for a date after all this was said and done.

Too bad he's a milksop.

Vala turned to face the other two towers on the island, wondering if she should see if others lived there as well. Instead, she summoned her magic, focusing on World Sector Two.

She was too upset to spend another moment in World Sector One.

CHAPTER 60

ORANGE

Suri lay in a bed not of her own, looking up at the pipes. Her body was spent of energy, and her muscles ached. Her entire body felt heavy as lead, and she was lethargic. She knew her body was trying to recover from all the toxic air that she had inhaled earlier.

There were loud, constant hums mixed with a sporadic clanging of metal. The humming created strong vibrations, leading all the way to where Suri lay. She was in a metal room that consisted of a bed, some sort of water closet, and a few other oddities. There were pipes above her, which filtered fresh air into her room. No windows, but there was one door. No sign of Jude anywhere, nor any other people either. The metal door appeared to be sealed shut by a mechanism, as she didn't see any handle.

I hope Jude is safe.

She moved her hands to her collarbone, feeling for the enchantress's vial. There was no cord, no vial against her skin…

Suri shot up, frantically checking the inside of her tunic. The vial was gone.

Panicked, she forced herself to slip out of her bed, wobbling to her feet. She scoured the blanket, then moved on to search the floor. There was no sign of the vial anywhere.

The brown-gifted must have taken it! Already, Suri started running scenarios in her mind. She had to get out of this place and retrieve that vial.

Suri walked swiftly to the door, inspecting the mechanism thoroughly. A few buttons glowed in different colors, with numbers displaying a glowing square above the buttons.

Picking the button nearest the door, Suri pushed it. The mechanism beeped, then the door slid open. She paused for a moment, wondering why she wasn't being held in confinement as a prisoner.

I best be on guard.

On the other side of the door was an all-metal hallway, lit up with some sort of machinery infused with magic. A group of men were casually gathered down the hall, chatting and laughing. They looked over at her, noticing her immediately.

Jude popped out randomly from the group, noticing her. "Mistress Suri?" He called out, then smiled. "Mistress Suri! Thank the God of Light you are okay!" He ran over to her, hugging her with joy.

Suri wasn't used to any sort of physical affection. She didn't hug. Never had she. But Master Jude…she felt a unique affection toward the boy.

"Master Jude," she said softly, giving him a side hug. Suri gave him a half smile, relieved that he was okay. But the vial…

"What's wrong?" Jude asked, reading her face carefully.

"Nothing."

Jude leaned in, then rotated his body with his back facing the men, then lowered his voice to a whisper. "Looking for this?"

He opened the palm of his hand, revealing the enchantress's vial.

Suri snatched it from his hand, making no expression so the men wouldn't be alarmed. "Do you realize what this is?" she whispered.

"I know exactly what it is," Jude said in a low whisper. "I've seen you discreetly care for it. I can feel the power coming from it." Jude eyed her evenly. "I first felt its presence during our battle on the airship. I didn't mean to; it just happened that way," he admitted. "But I noticed it again from time to time on the island, and in the mines." Jude's eyes cautiously looked around, continuing to whisper. "When these men brought us here, I woke up before they separated us. I had to do something in case they found it. I may not be as stealthy as you, but I think by watching your movements, I have learned a few things. Besides, with the brown-gifted man knowing you have access to the violet gift, I had to take it for safeguarding."

"Do I dare ask how you hid it?"

Jude smiled proudly. "With orange magic."

Her eyebrows rose in surprise. "I do not know how to thank you, Master

Jude." Suri paused, then carefully slid the necklace around her neck, tucking the vial in her tunic. "Do not breathe a word of the vial to anyone."

"I wouldn't dare. What you carry is dangerous for the wrong person."

"It is." Suri side-eyed the men in the hall. "What is happening? We are not prisoners? Why are we able to roam free in this place?"

"There was some sort of misunderstanding. These people thought since we were from the sky, that we were supporters of the High Court. I finally convinced them otherwise." He leaned in, golden eyes glimmering in the magical light as his voice dropped to a whisper. "Their leader said that Kang is hot-headed and makes assumptions."

"Their leader? He's not the brown-gifted?"

Jude shook his head as one of the men came up to them, startling them both. "Ma'am. Would you like some rations?"

"Oh. Yes."

The man handed Suri a small bag. Suri eyed it curiously.

"Go on. Open it," he urged.

Suri opened the bag. It was packed full of dried meat.

"Should last you a few days out in the wilderness," he added.

Suri sheepishly looked at the man, then bowed. "Thank you, Master…"

The man laughed. "I'm not a master of nothing." He waved to her and Jude. "This way. Our leader has been anxiously waiting to talk to you." He paused, then leaned closer. "And although we have never had any outsider gifted in our citadel, we have a rule: No magic in the citadel."

"Citadel?" Suri murmured. "Are we not on the surface?"

"This is an underground citadel, ma'am. You are far beneath the earth."

Almost on cue, Jude chimed in, "Isn't that something, Mistress Suri?" he said excitedly. "I've never been to the earth's surface, let alone inside." The boy was much too enthusiastic given their current situation. The enchantress would have been impressed too.

The men led them down the metal corridors. Some glowed in cool tones, others burned in warm tones. After a series of hallways, they came upon a large metal door, where the man pressed a series of buttons.

"Your citadel has technology," Suri pointed out.

"Why do you think we hate the High Court so much?" another of the men said.

Suri nodded as she and Jude followed the men into a large metal room glowing with different colors. Flat glass filled the walls, brightly lit up with colorful pictures. Some pictures were moving, others were still.

Suri slowly walked inside, each step a wonder. She gasped, taking in the sight.

"This is remarkable. I've never seen anything like this," Jude said under his breath.

"It truly is a great feat." Suri nodded. *I can see why the enchantress is so fascinated with technology.*

Suri recalled what Ikaria told her about the past. The kingdom of Arcadia. Was this like what the enchantress witnessed?

Jude suddenly had a serious look. "All my life, and especially during the priesthood, I have been taught that technology is evil." His golden eyes glowed. "Now, finally standing in the midst of it, there is no evil coming from it, nor do I sense it in my life force. On the contrary, it feels wonderful and exciting."

"You must follow what you think to be true," said one of the men.

"Good sir," said Jude, "I only follow the God of Light. He has given me a gift of discernment, and through this, I hear it in my heart. If I followed myself and what I thought to be true, I would be following foolish desires. That is why there have been so many corrupt priests and High Court members throughout the ages, desperate to cling to their truth, their desire, thus in turn—their power. That is now apparent to me." Jude glanced around in wonder. "The High Court has technology all wrong."

"I agree, gifted sky-dweller," called out another male voice.

Suri turned around, seeing a surprisingly handsome man approaching the group. Even she, who had no interest in men, felt he could be one of those who persuaded her otherwise. He had waist-long dark hair that flowed like silk, pale skin, and narrow eyes like hers and Master Kang's. His pupils were so dark that they appeared black. He was wearing a finer tunic than the other men, though it was still practical. Around his head was a simple metal circlet—no gemstones, just a plain band.

Behind the handsome man was a small group of men, one of whom was the notable brown-gifted from earlier. Suri hadn't gotten a good look at him prior, but in the light, she saw his features perfectly. Deep lines etched his face with weather and age. He had to be in his late forties, possibly even fifties. He had narrow eyes like her and the younger man, with irises glowing a soft brown. He was bald, the top of his bronzed skin shining in the light. He had arched eyebrows and a pointed beard and mustache. Around his thick neck was a beaded necklace.

Suri stared at him, her face unchanged, the brown-gifted eyeing her steadily.

"Please forgive Kang from your earlier exchange. He can be overambitious at times," the handsome man said. "He thought you were lying earlier in the mines."

Kang grunted. "Most prisoners do." The thick man turned, placing his hand on his heart, bowing. "Please forgive me for our skirmish. I realize now that we fight for the same cause."

"I thought that I made it apparent when we were using our gifts against each other," Suri said coolly.

The man bellowed out a loud laugh. "In the heat of battle, I tend to overreact. Not my best quality." He held out his hand. "You are Suri, correct?"

"How do you know my name, Master Kang?"

"I told him your name," Jude butted in. "Hope you don't mind. He asked after I healed him."

Suri raised an eyebrow at Jude, and he smiled sheepishly at her.

"Please, sit with us," the handsome man said. He pointed at a short metal table surrounded by sitting pillows. "I am curious to know more about your background."

Suri eyed the fine man. "I do not sit. It is not my place as a servant."

"Hmph," Kang grumbled beside her.

Jude happily sat, glancing at all the screens. "You're not a servant here, Mistress Suri."

"Yes, Mistress Suri," Kang said in a gruff tone.

Suri eyed one of the cushions, then gracefully knelt in a traditional position, then looked at the handsome man. "You are the leader of these people. May I know your name?"

"I am Tekka, the leader of this citadel. Master Jude informed us earlier that you were on your way to the High Court to stop your empress from being executed."

Suri nodded. "You are correct. It is imperative that I get to the High Court. That is, if it is not too late. I fear the worst for the Empress."

"According to the word in the skies," Tekka said, "Empress Ayera remains in prison. She is scheduled for a public trial soon. I believe a few days? It will be a farce, of course. We do not know if the execution will take place that day or thereafter."

"How do you know this?" Jude asked curiously. "Did…" He pointed to the glowing glass. "Did these machines tell you?"

Tekka nodded. "Word traveled in the sky sectors, and then to the mines and workers."

Jude scrunched his face. "I don't understand. How, then, did it get to these screens?"

"Sympathizers. There are many down here that are loyal to the cause—even several of the mine guards. When word spreads about anything in the mines or the earth's surface about news from above, people talk through all the underground citadels."

The mines were the last thing Suri wanted to think about. "Master Tekka," Suri said, changing the subject, "do you have means to get to the skies?"

"That we do. However, if you were to go to the High Court Citadel, what will you do? Use your orange magic against the High Court to rescue your empress?"

Suri sighed. "Admittedly, I have not yet formulated a plan. I work best when I know my surroundings. I can assure you that I will use my gift to the fullest extent to save the Empress from her doom—or die trying."

"You have more than the orange gift," Kang pointed out.

Suri eyed him steadily. "Was it my orange magic being a shade darker that gave it away?"

"No. It's because I have sapped orange magic off other gifted before meeting you. This has made me well aware of orange magic and its abilities of illusion and transmutation. However, I know of no one with force magic."

Suri remained motionless. She wasn't going to reveal anything unless it was necessary. It appeared that Kang wasn't going to say more on the subject either. That was good, as she didn't feel like clashing with that man.

"Mister Kang," Jude said, "I have never heard of the brown gift. Brown isn't in *The Spectrum*."

Kang gruffed. "It's not."

"How is that possible, for you to have brown magic? Are there more like you?" Jude asked.

"I am the only one that I know of."

"Were you born with brown magic?"

"You are pretty nosy, aren't you?" Kang huffed.

"I just want to know," Jude said innocently.

Suri looked at Kang, wanting to know too.

"I was not born with it," he said, relenting. "When I was young, the elders in this citadel injected the entire populace with blood they had stored from many centuries ago, using dried components. They tried the colors they had at the time—blue and orange, hoping that someone would get magic. And now, here I stand, with brown magic."

Blue and orange. That makes brown if you mix the colors together, Suri thought. "Blood magic is different than pure magic from the life force."

Kang shot her a look. "What do you know of this type of 'blood' magic? Is not all magic the same?"

Suri shook her head. "The enchantress studied many magics over the years while I served her. Blood magic consists of magic color pigments."

"Pigments?"

"You mix blue and orange pigments, in this case, blood, you get brown." Suri eyed him. "But my mistress never heard of brown magic. It seems very unlikely that the blood colors would collide as a new color."

"Must be the result of the experimentation," Jude said. "Brown magic—it can copy other magics?"

"Only to an extent. I do not have the benefit of accessing it fully," Kang said.

"Like how you couldn't see me as invisible."

"Correct, Miss Suri," Kang said. "I am not a true orange-gifted, so I was unable to detect *your* orange magic with my brown magic imitating orange. I only can mimic certain aspects of the power. What power is it that you hide?"

Jude made no expression, while Suri remained still. "I do not hide any sort of power."

Kang laughed. "What a beautiful liar you are. Stone-cold with a delicate face. Smooth as clay." His face turned serious. "I know you hide something. Perhaps I might even can make a good guess what it is. The raw power radiates from your neck."

Tekka glanced to Kang, then to Suri.

Suri glared at Kang evenly. "Do not say another word, Master Kang, or you might not wake up tomorrow."

Kang's bright brown eyes narrowed. "Is that a threat?"

"If you know what's best for you, for this sector, and for all that we cherish, then yes," Suri said.

Kang burst out laughing again. "You are a feisty one. Are you taken?"

"Kang, manners," Tekka scolded.

"Sorry."

"I have a question," Jude said. "Master Kang, why are you down here? The law requires all gifted to live in the skies, in the royal citadels."

"This is my home."

"We hid him from the High Court," Tekka explained.

"Tekka is saying in flowery terms that we are rebels," Kang added.

Tekka nodded. "Us earth dwellers despise most sky people, for they uphold the High Court laws and twist the words of *The Spectrum*. Though recently, there has been word across the ground citadels that some of the sky people do not like the High Court either."

Suri leaned in. "My empress and the subjects of World Sector Six were planning to break away from the High Court. There were whispers that it was to happen soon. That is, until she was captured."

Tekka folded his hands on the table delicately, grinning. "That is why we are going to help you, Suri,"

"You want to help us?"

"Absolutely," Tekka said. "For many years, us earth dwellers have been developing weapons, planning to rise up against the High Court. Though they do not know how many of us exist down here, we wish to be united with our people."

The enchantress would like this one, Suri thought.

"Would you then live in the skies under Empress Ayera's laws?" she asked.

"Master Tekka is and will always be our leader," Kang stated, unwavering.

Tekka sighed. "That may be so here on the ground, but if we live in Empress Ayera's sector, perhaps she will be able to provide us lands above to house us...or we could work in unison between the land and skies," Tekka said to Kang, then paused. "We want to coexist again, and we hope to figure out how to transform our earth."

"Heal it, you mean?" Jude said incredulously.

Tekka nodded. "Precisely."

It was something that the enchantress had always desired. Healing Earth's surface. These people were aligned in many ways with her enchantress's wishes.

Tekka looked at Suri. "We will help you rescue the Empress. We will take you to her."

"To the High Court Citadel?" Jude asked, surprised. "How?"

"With our airship, of course," Tekka answered.

"I didn't know you had airships down here."

"You didn't know our citadel was down here either."

"True." Jude flushed, rubbing the back of his neck.

"I thank you for your help in advance," Suri said.

"I wish with everything in me to live on a peaceful earth, how it was at its creation. Our peoples are not meant to live above or below the earth. It's not natural."

"Indeed, Master Tekka."

Tekka met her eyes. "There is something you should know. There was a report from another citadel, a sky citadel that is secretly aligned with the surface dwellers. There is a blue-gifted ambassador asking for aid. This ambassador claimed they were from World Sector Six. They were gathering allies from across the sectors to go to war against the High Court."

Kang glanced at them. "Do you know anything about this? That is your sector."

Suri remained motionless. "I cannot say. I do not know of any blue-gifted in our sector."

"Are you sure it was World Sector Six?" Jude repeated.

"Someone is lying," Kang grumbled, turning to Tekka. "Either that blue-gifted is not from World Sector Six or they aren't." He pointed to Suri.

Tekka raised his hand, indicating silence. "Do you know the enchantress Ikaria?"

"She is my master." It was the first emotion Suri showed them. "The Empress is her sister."

"Interesting," Tekka said. "From what my reports tell me, the enchantress

Ikaria is orchestrating this war of the sectors. The blue-gifted was her ambassador, making her way to each of the sectors to gather help. We have been discussing whether to join her war. All of the ground citadels have been."

Suri stepped forward and bowed deeply. "Master Tekka, I am not in the habit of swearing on anything." Suri rose, meeting his gaze. "But know this: the enchantress Ikaria will prevail. Never have I met anyone so passionate, dedicated, masterful, and cunning as I have her. She can outwit the witted. She can make the intelligent appear foolish. She can rise against an enemy with her army of one and win." Suri paused. "She has the gift of the violet. The only one in this world. The High Court has desired her power from day one—and since day one, she has been on the defensive, moving into offense to ensure she never loses her gift to them. Have you ever seen one as her?"

"Gift of the violet," said Tekka as he rubbed his chin in thought.

Kang turned to him. "You know the whole world will fall on its face if the High Court gets to her."

"They will use her sister to get to her," Suri pointed out. "It is why I have been on a mission to rescue her. The enchantress is the one who sent me."

Tekka remained silent, then folded his hands. "The timing of this seems to coincide with the other report."

Kang turned to him. "What other report?"

Tekka paused, taking in a breath. "A citadel located in World Sector One made a wild report that a man recently appeared at their citadel. A man with great magic who knew many things. It was said that he could recount the age of the machines of the great kingdom of Arcadia, and he knew of the green-gifted queen. Even more so, the elder of that citadel said that he claimed to be from the kingdom of Arcadia, that he'd been reborn in this time. A gifted, nonetheless. A red-gifted who claimed he was in love with the Queen and needed to find his way back to her. It all read like some ancient myth…"

"Do you know what this means?" Jude jumped up, interrupting him. "The God of Light is incredible!"

"What are you talking about, boy?" Kang said.

"I went to the kingdom of Arcadia! I fought in the battle against the cyborgs and the sorceress myself. It has to be the red-gifted man back in time who fought against the sorceress!" Jude seemed very excited at the prospect.

"*You*? You traveled back in time?" Kang said, unconvinced.

"I did! With a whole group of gifted! A blue-gifted from World Sector Three cast her magic to send us back in time to stop the sorceress."

"Sorceress?"

"I mean…the enchantress," he corrected himself.

"But why would you stop her?" Tekka asked. "I thought you just said she will be the winning side."

Jude bit his lip, then shrugged. "It's a long story. But what's important is that when we were in the kingdom of Arcadia, we were injected with the Queen's blood. The green-gifted Queen," Jude pointed out. "The Queen's lover died during the battle. The green-gifted Queen cast her life magic over him, but he never woke up." He paused. "Don't you see? That red-gifted man from the other citadel seems to fit the same story where we left off back in time!" They were silent for a moment, while Jude had a silly grin on his face. "I have never heard of anything more fantastical in my life than this! This is the God of Light's doing," Jude said without hesitation. He turned to Suri. "I think the timing has aligned in our favor."

"That is what the elder from that citadel said as well," Tekka said.

"See? It's a sign!" Jude said excitedly. "Now is our time! This moment has been given to us!"

Tekka continued. "But there is something else for us to concern ourselves with."

"The white-gifted woman," Suri said quietly.

Tekka eyed her evenly. "You know of this unique gifted woman?"

"I have seen her with my own eyes, and the sheer power she possesses," Suri said.

"She took away all of World Sector Six's gifted powers," Jude chimed in. "All except us two. They arrested our empress after stealing everyone's gift. We barely escaped."

"And now World Sector Four is powerless as well."

Suri froze. The woman got to another entire sector and stole their gifts?

"Shocking, I know. We have felt the same." Tekka folded his hands. "This is what concerns us. Elyathi is defying the prophecy."

"Prophecy? What prophecy?"

"There are many sky people who have never heard the prophecy of the white-gifted," Tekka said. "But it is well known down here. The prophecy says they will be the one to restore the earth."

Jude crossed his arms. "I have studied the ancient scriptures and holy texts. Sounds heretical to me."

"One to make the heavens and earth anew. Restore magic to its rightful place in the heavens."

Jude didn't look convinced.

"You might not believe, but it is true. I am willing to show you the ancient texts myself if you'd like to see them. But our people hold this prophecy dear to our hearts. Elyathi was born in the ground citadel in World Sector Three. As you can imagine, with the elders knowing of the prophecy, there was much excitement. At the time of her birth, it was the law to give up any gifted babies to the sky people, so that they could better the world by assisting the High Court. The earth dwellers didn't want to give up the white-gifted child, for they knew the High Court would want the magic for their own selfish reasons. There was a group of dedicated people against the High Court, and they hid her until she was a small child. By chance, a blue-gifted that became disenchanted with the High Court joined their cause, then traveled with the child to another time, hoping that the High Court would never find her. And we thought we never would hear of her ever again. And we hadn't. That is, until this recent transmission from World Sector One citadel."

"This white-gifted is not holy," Jude said. "She stole our whole sector's magic."

"She is just as corrupt as the High Court, that I can assure you," Suri said. "She will continue to steal all magic until there is none left. Including the enchantress's violet gift."

Kang glanced at Suri. "I now understand the burden you carry."

Suri eyed him steadily. Kang knew exactly what her vial held.

"I will do whatever I can to protect you and your power," he said, lowering his eyes to her neckline. Then, he gave a deep bow.

Tekka stood. "It is decided. We will do everything to stop this woman and rescue your empress. We will join your enchantress's war. One thing—if we were to help you, all we ask is to be reunited with the sky people after this is over. My wish is to live side by side, land and sky. And perhaps with us reunited, we can figure out a way to heal our earth together."

"I cannot promise all those things, Master Tekka, since I am but a lowly servant," Suri said. "I can put in a word for you to the Empress once we bring her home."

"Then as you said, let us waste no more time," Tekka said, then turned to Kang. "Ready the weapons and our people. Send communications to all the other citadels. Tell them we are joining this war. It's about time we take back the heavens and earth as one people. Perhaps there might be a restoration foretold in the ancients manuscripts after all."

Kang bowed, then turned to the men. "Let us prepare for the skies," he announced. "We must save the Empress!"

CHAPTER 61

◆

Strange lips were on his, drinking deeply of his desires, having their way with him. He couldn't resist those luscious lips, nor the naked flesh against his. Making love to this intoxicating woman was everything he desired. Exciting, new, and…almost as if he had wanted her for years. He didn't know this woman, but oddly, she was strangely familiar.

"Samir," she whispered with a moan. "How I wanted you. I waited years for this."

The woman cried out in orgasmic ecstasy. He rolled his eyes back, waiting for his own climax.

Just as he was closing his eyes, a long lock of white hair fell across his bare chest. He wanted to ignore it, but the hair color was unique.

Only one person he knew had that hair…

Samir glanced up at the woman moving in a rhythmic motion, making his loins ache has she had her way with him. Her neck stretched upward, revealing her perfectly engorged breasts and the long white hair moving gently with her body. Her hips swayed all in the right ways.

"Samir…" she moaned again. The woman's bloodred lips were parted as she gazed down at him with lustful eyes.

Her eyes were blank, the color of empty skies.

His heart beat quickly. "Elyathi?"

Her eyes were like mirrors, and Samir saw himself in them. His eyes… were pale blue…

Terrified, Samir cried out.

"Samir?"

Samir blinked.

"Samir?"

Samir blinked once again, realizing that he held a communication device in the palm of his hand, and he was sitting in his favorite chair. He was in his study, sending communications to the other kingdoms.

"Have you heard from Derek yet?" asked Allena, placing her hand on his, leaning over.

Allena's words went in one ear and out the other, his pounding heart drowning out her voice.

It was so real, he thought. Sweat beaded his brow. The dream was beyond disturbing. He never had daydreams or had his thoughts wander off like that. That is, not since his youth. It was not normal—for him anyway.

"Darling, are you all right?" Allena neared him, folding her hands over his.

Samir looked up at his wife, her eyes sparkling like the ocean, her long thick midnight-blue hair framing her pale face.

He frowned as he ran his fingers through his black curls. He couldn't tell this wife and queen that he'd had a sex dream. Her wrath was not something to take lightly. It wasn't his fault, but she still wouldn't understand.

Samir sighed. "I'm fine. A little distracted."

"Fine?" Allena said, fixing his curl. "I don't think so. Whenever you are troubled, even I cannot see your thoughts behind those dark eyes of yours. They are like mirrors to your soul."

Mirrors... The word made him think of his dream. His heart pounded loudly. "I'm worried about Derek," he admitted.

"Still no answer from him?" she asked.

"No," Samir said, then met her gaze. "There have been some disturbing rumors about Queen Emerald as well."

Allena raised her eyebrow. "Oh?"

"According to certain outlets, the Queen has taken a paramour," Samir said. His daughter-in-law, the one he promised to keep safe from Damaris.

That has all changed, he thought.

Allena's eyes turned fiery. "I have heard too. But really. Emerald? A paramour? That's a serious allegation. Emerald would do no such thing. She's so innocent of the world."

Just like her mother.

"I agree with you. But others don't. It's hard not to spread rumors, considering her circumstances. Being left alone."

Allena sighed, then rose to her feet, pacing. "What could be so important for our son to leave Arcadia and our dear precious daughter-in-law alone? And especially with her being pregnant?" Allena sighed. "He's always been so selfish."

"That's not fair, Allena. Don't bring him into *that* again," Samir countered.

Allena stopped in her tracks, her back to him. There was a moment of silence. "I know."

It was always like this. Allena wishing for their unborn daughter to be alive. Allena misplacing her hurt and anger on their son. She was always extra tough when it came to Derek.

"He must know something that we don't in order to leave the kingdom at a moment's notice," she said, tempering her words, soothing the situation.

"Don't forget how much Olympia has been weighing upon Arcadia," Samir said.

"I've never liked Olympia."

"Neither have I, but I couldn't very well stand against the alliances of the kingdoms. I was trying to advise our son, but like always, he never wanted to hear my advice."

"I'm afraid for him," Allena continued. "He hasn't been the same since leaving York. He was so determined to marry Emerald, no matter what. And all that Damaris put him through? To think, at our son's own wedding. I myself am still shook up by the whole thing," she said. "I know that Damaris had changed over the years…but I never would have thought the man would commit suicide in front of us all."

"I know." There was nothing more to say of Olympia, or his best friend. Or his one-time best friend. Samir had been holding on to hope for years, waiting for Damaris to be his old self. Instead, his best friend went down a dark path. A very dark path, taking Elyathi down with him.

"What Damaris did was…horrendous and saddening. I…"

"I know he was once your best friend," she whispered.

Samir paused. "I must say that we can breathe a bit easier now that Damaris is gone," he said quickly.

"Which is why I worry about Derek," Allena pointed out. "What if that kingdom is cursed?"

Samir eyed her, shaking his head. "Impossible."

"Think about it. Damaris changes over the years as he sits on the throne. Elyathi dies suddenly. Then Damaris gets worse, leading to his suicide. Then the strange attack at the palace's upper levels by cyborgs. Derek leaves the kingdom in the hands of Emerald—who is now rumored to have a paramour? Is it so hard to think Arcadia is cursed?"

"You make an excellent case."

"I usually do," Allena said with a hint of a smile. "Emerys can give you a better idea where Derek has gone. With Olympia and Arcadia's squabble in the Western Wastelands, I am afraid without Derek there, the other kingdoms will hop on board. Perhaps you can reason with him about the cyborgs."

"Perhaps," Samir muttered under his breath.

Her communicator beeped, then she eyed him. "I must take this," she said, walking off to an adjacent room.

The whole thing was disconcerting. Especially knowing that his son was the same as Emerald.

Gifted. That was the term Elyathi used. And now, his son had magic too.

For all those years, he'd kept quiet about Elyathi's secret. She had confided in him about everything. The day Elyathi told him everything, Samir had never seen her so terrified and desperate. That was saying something because he had witnessed Elyathi go through some serious situations. Elyathi had come to him for protection because she was afraid for her life, and for Emerald's life as well. He had been even more afraid of what Damaris would become with such a weapon that he would possess. She had been sobbing in his arms pleading with him for safe and secret passage into his kingdom. He had to help her.

It made him sad to think of how Elyathi's life had ended. If circumstances had been different, he would have courted her himself. If he had, she would still be alive today, that he knew for certain. Elyathi had been kind and sweet, one who thrived off love and affection—one Damaris should have never been paired with. To see her over the years endure such violence from Damaris, and the sadness in her eyes—Samir could see it himself. Her innocence was long gone.

A sudden flash of his daydream came to him.

How I wanted you…

Samir flushed, then moved the thought out of his mind.

Allena was the one he loved. Yes, it was true, he had thought of Elyathi, but that was a long time ago. When Allena entered the picture, it wasn't a thought anymore. He was truly content with Allena.

Only once had Samir brought up how Damaris treated his wife to his friend. It was the worst thing he could have ever done, because it threw Damaris into a full-on raging tantrum. They had been drunk, which made matters worse. Damaris accused Samir of plotting to steal Elyathi, wanting her for himself, threating war upon York. Knowing his friend, Damaris *would* start a war with the other kingdoms if anyone dared to seduce his wife, or even be kind to her. As if someone would offend him by being kind to his "property."

And so it was, to keep peace with Arcadia and York, Samir ate his own words, apologizing profusely, because Arcadia was the reigning kingdom over all others. They had the power. And if it meant that he had to swallow his pride, he would do so for peace in his own kingdom. After that, Samir never brought Elyathi up to Damaris again. Never glancing at her, never even acknowledging her unless he came face-to-face with her. He had risked his kingdom and peace that day when Elyathi came to him. He was lucky it hadn't been more.

Allena came back in the library, pushing a long lock of midnight hair out of her face. "Great timing. That was one of the lords from Arcadia," she said. "There has been another sighting of our daughter-in-law with some famous rock star." Allena sat on the armrest of his chair, gently touching his shoulder.

Samir glanced at her, then eyed his communicator. "I think I will make a visit to Arcadia. I want to see for myself. Besides, I would like to see how the Queen is faring with Derek leaving her in the middle of a mess with Olympia. I should see if there is anything I can do and dispel these rumors. Give her some advice now that Derek is gone for the moment. He was being so unreasonable before he disappeared. Always combative."

"I will go with," Allena said.

"No. You must stay here. Someone needs to rule in my absence," he said.

Allena gracefully walked toward him, then held his hand, kissing him. "I will miss you, darling."

His heart warmed. "Likewise, my darling love."

"Emerald has always been reasonable. But so was our son at one time. I hope she hasn't changed," Allena said.

That was always a possibility.

"Give our daughter-in-law my love," Allena said.

"I will. And give our lords a run for their money," Samir added.

Allena kissed his cheek sweetly. "Of course, darling. You know I set everyone straight while you are away."

Samir smiled at her. "I think they like it."

"I think so too." She laughed, then smoothed her skirts. She smiled one last time, then turned to leave.

He watched as his wife walked away, her long, thick dark hair swaying down her back. She was so powerful in the way she moved. In the way she did everything. So very different from Elyathi. Complete opposite personality, down to the hair color…

Samir took one last drink of his coffee, then dialed his communicator for Councilor Emerys of Arcadia.

CHAPTER 62

◆

GREEN

Emerald sat in her favorite spot in the open balcony garden, sipping her morning tea. She felt wiped, having gotten hardly any sleep. There was still no sign of Kyle, which made her feel worse. Adding to her anxiety was a slew of new stretch marks; her stomach was now a giant balloon, and she could barely walk without becoming completely exhausted. It was possible that she could go into labor any day now.

The thought of motherhood was exciting but frightening all at once. She loved the idea of being a mother soon, having her offspring. She would do all the things that her mother didn't do, mostly spend time with her children. But as for the father figure… It seemed the closer she got to delivering her twins, the deeper the wedge was being driven between them.

Kyle, please don't be angry.

Emerald sighed, taking another sip of her tea, thinking about her last exchange with Kyle. From his perspective, Emerald could understand how he could feel. Was it reasonable for her to expect him to stand by her side, still married to Derek while she ruled her kingdom? The more she thought about it, the more confused and hurt she became. Hurt that she'd hurt him. Kyle was trying his best to be happy at the palace. But deep down, Emerald knew he was miserable. Kyle was like a wild animal, one that could not be caged or contained. He loved his music and having the freedom of living life—a life that she could not have being queen.

A servant came by and filled her cup. As he walked away, Emerald noticed a small folded piece of paper on her teacup saucer.

Her heart suddenly hammered as she unfolded the note.

I love you, Em. Be back later. Don't want you to worry.

Emerald darted around, looking for any indication of Kyle being nearby. There was none, but he had to be somewhere close for him to deliver the note.

In the corner of her eye, Emerald saw Councilor Emerys approaching.

"Good morning, Your Majesty," he said, bowing, then eyeing the empty seat next to her.

"Good morning, Councilor," Emerald greeted him, setting down her teacup.

"I am sorry to disturb you, but you have an unexpected visitor. King Samir of York arrived early this morning. He has requested an audience with Your Majesty," he continued.

"King Samir? *Here?*"

"Yes."

A bit of bile surged in the back of her throat at the thought of Derek's *father* here to see her. Her nerves shook her, and it felt like the children in her womb were doing somersaults.

"Where is His Majesty now?" Emerald asked as she dabbed her lips, then rose from her seat.

"In the Inner Council room. I felt it appropriate to not make it such a formal appearance, as it might stress Your Majesty," Emerys said with comfort.

Emerald nodded with gratefulness. "Thank you, Councilor. Let us be on our way."

The two of them left the gardens, making their way toward the Inner Council chamber. "I noticed Master Kyle wasn't with you this morning for breakfast," he said as they walked.

"He is at a band practice," Emerald said. Or so she assumed.

"I see. Since the King is here for a visit, this works in your favor."

Emerald flashed him a look. "What do you mean?"

Emerys turned back, pausing in his tracks. "To be blunt, I believe that the King of York is here because of your behavior with Master Kyle."

His words hurt. But she knew they were true.

"Is it because he kissed me on the open stage? If so, many rock stars do that as part of their act," Emerald said defensively.

"Do you think the King of York will believe that?" Emerys asked.

Emerald's eyes shifted to the floor.

"I warned Master Kyle. Unfortunately, my warning came too late," Emerys said under his breath. "I hope you can persuade the King of York otherwise. Otherwise, this may result in consequences between our two kingdoms once again."

"Councilor, do you think it was okay for Derek to abandon me? Our kingdom? Our children?" Emerald said with an edge. "Do you know all that had happened?"

"I do not agree with His Majesty's abrupt departure. But then again, I am not privy to all His Majesty's business." Emerys gave her an apologetic look. "That being said, I do care for Your Majesty more than the kingdom itself. I want you to be happy." He paused. "But you must be careful how you display your affections toward Master Kyle. As I said before, there could be dire consequences."

Emerald remained silent for a moment, gathering her composure. Indeed, she was stressed. Very much so. What to say to Derek's father?

"Let's go," she said.

He bowed, then they both headed toward the Inner Council chambers.

As they arrived outside the doors, Emerys bowed once again, then said, "I will be right outside if you need me."

Emerald nodded. "Thank you, Emerys," she whispered. Her legs began to shake with nerves. All she wanted to do was vomit her breakfast all over the floor.

Inside the glass room sat Derek's father. His dark curls looked a bit longer, but other than that, he hadn't changed much since the last time she had seen him. He had been at the wedding, or so she had been told, but she didn't remember anything about it or anyone there, since she'd been under Ikaria's spell at the time.

Her father-in-law immediately saw her as the doors opened, nodding to her in formality. Emerald returned it with a deeper bow, in respect for her elders, though it was hard with her protruding stomach.

"Queen Emerald," Samir said.

"King Samir. What a surprise to see you here," Emerald said as she shuffled to her seat. Her feet hurt, and her legs were swollen.

He eyed her belly. "With all due respect, you look far more pregnant than a few months. Are you feeling okay?" He gave her a sympathetic smile.

Emerald flashed him a nervous smile. "I am. The royal physician says that the children are growing at an alarming rate." Emerald shifted her eyes nervously to the floor.

"Hm. I see." His dark eyes flashed with knowing. "Is it because of your gift?"

Emerald gave him a curious glance as she sat down. "Why, yes, my gift. How did you know of it?"

"Your mother. She told me about your power," Samir said, meeting her gaze. "And about hers. Right before your father had us banished from his sight."

Emerald's lips parted, gasping. "You know of my mother's gift?"

"I do," he said, meeting her gaze evenly. "She had confided in me about it the last time I saw her. She begged me to take you, keep you safe, because of what your father had been doing—using your blood for experiments. But your father caught on to our plan to send you away, and that was when he accused us of inappropriate relations."

A sudden peace came over her. Finally, after all these years, she knew what had happened. In a way, she felt almost...sorry for Derek and her friendship. Their relationship had suffered because of her father. Though it didn't change the facts, it gave her a new understanding.

"I had always wondered why," Emerald said.

The King nodded, then folded his hands. "I always cared for your father— that is, when he was a decent man. In our youth, he was always a bit selfish, but I chalked that up to being a spoiled royal. But a little before marrying your mother, he became...unbearable." Samir paused, lost in thought. "I think that your power became an unhealthy obsession. One that's similar to an addict. He became addicted to your power, and through that, he became addicted to other cruel obsessions. It was fortunate that your father never found out about your mother's power..." Samir sighed. "I will leave it at that."

All the pieces were suddenly coming together, or at least illustrating a clearer picture of what happened that day.

"I see," Emerald said, shifting in her chair. It felt more uncomfortable than ever. "It's unfortunate that you have come to visit now. Derek is away for the time being. I am sorry you have wasted your time."

"So I heard," Samir said. "I did not come here to visit my son, though I miss him terribly. I have heard he is out on kingdom business."

"Indeed, that is correct."

"Queen Emerald, I have come here to discuss other matters."

Emerald suddenly felt small in her chair, as if she were a child. "And what matters are you referring to?"

Samir cleared his throat. He looked rather uncomfortable, but his face didn't falter. "There are rumors that have reached my kingdom, rumors that I hope to put to rest. Rumors that my daughter-in-law, the Queen of Arcadia, has been sighted with a rock star." His dark eyes stared at her intensely. "More than that, it is said that he is your paramour. I told my council, 'surely my daughter-in-law wouldn't behave in such a way.' But they pressed the issue, and the rumors grew. The broadcasts show you and this rock star on a daily basis now." Samir leaned in. "Tell me. Do these rumors have any merit?"

Emerald felt like she'd been pushed into a corner, and there was no way out. She wanted to scream, cry, shout…anything to escape.

"Forgive me, Your Majesty, but is this really your business?" Emerald said with an edge.

King Samir frowned, then folded his hands on the table. "It is. Because it will be a monumental issue if the child you bear in your womb is not of my son's blood."

Emerald was furious. Her own father-in-law, grilling her about her personal life.

"King Samir, that's quite the inquiry," Emerald shot back.

"It's not an easy one to bring up in a conversation." He raised his eyebrow in disappointment. "The United Kingdoms are unstable right now, as you are well aware. The cyborgs here caused alliances across the kingdoms to fall apart, namely your kingdom, and to some extent mine due to my son being involved with Arcadia. The war of the wastelands didn't help, and now Olympia is a mess. The alliances are in uproar over your behavior with some unknown, unruly punk rock star, and they question the validity of the child in your womb. I inquire because I have to deal with the mess of Arcadia, my son, and now my daughter-in-law.

"There are only two options I see at this point. You drop your relations with this rock star, have your child in peace, and wait for my son to return. In turn, this will squelch the rumors, put the kingdoms at peace, and we can progress our talks about the cyborgs—furthering your relations with the kingdoms.

There is talk of a DNA test for you, in regard to the child's parentage. They are pressing me to do so."

Emerald looked at him in shock. "What? *Who* is requesting you to do so? And *would* you?"

"I would never do such a thing," Samir said pointedly. "But the other kingdoms are in an uproar, demanding that I do, as I am your father-in-law and tied to Arcadia. You know how they feel about bastards on the throne." He sighed. "I don't know exactly what your status is with my son and how well you two get along. Really, as you say, it is none of my business. And if it a lonely marriage, I am sorry for that. Perhaps, if this is the case, in time, you might find love in my son. But that is a mere hope of a father-in-law." He paused. "The other option is this: You continue your relations with this rock star. Damage your reputation and your alliance to the United Kingdoms. More war could possibly come to you, as most side with Olympia."

"They have cyborgs too!" Emerald shot back.

"Is that so?" Samir raised an eyebrow.

"Yes," Emerald said. "Not to mention they have taken one of my citizens hostage."

"I know nothing about a hostage."

"I have kept it secret from all the kingdoms, as we are dealing with it discreetly for the time being."

"Hm." Samir paused. "Well, be that as it may, the other kingdoms are not aware of the Olympian cyborgs or the hostage. If you bring this up officially, it would have to be investigated, and it would take a while for other kingdoms to change their mind about Olympia. But for now, they still see you as a threat. Knowing what you and my son are—I see it as a threat as well. You and my son are, after all, most powerful—wielding a power that no one else has."

"You see us as a threat?" Emerald asked, saddened.

"Wouldn't you if you were in my position? And from what you have told me, what would happen to Arcadia and the rest of the United Kingdom if someone else had magic and used it for a nefarious purpose?" Samir folded his hands, his face solemn and serious.

"I see your point," Emerald said in a low voice, "but know this: I will never give in to the United Kingdoms' demands to dismantle the cyborgs permanently. They are part human. That was one thing I made clear to Derek, and which he made sure of."

Samir leaned back, almost chuckling. "Really? Well, now it makes sense."

"What does?"

"He truly loves you, and is doing anything to make up for everything," he breathed. "Though I do not know all that transpired between you, it is obvious he wants your favor. Why else would he be so vehemently opposed to the United Kingdoms' request to dismantle the cyborgs? I know my son, and he wouldn't do that."

It was Emerald's turn to breathe in, sitting back in her chair. She knew that Derek was trying to win her back. That he had been remorseful…

He'd been under the influence of the sorceress for the majority of his decisions, including…

Emerald glanced at her father-in-law.

"If you choose to be 'seen' with the rock star," Samir interrupted her thoughts, "I will be forced by the United Kingdoms to request a DNA test. If found to be carrying a bastard, the life of the child would be a terrible one. Not raised in the palace, away from you. And if you don't submit to the United Kingdoms' ruling, more war will come to you. Your kingdom in still in much debt, not trusted by the others…" He glanced at her. "Surely you see the reason why I came to you now?"

Emerald felt sickened. Kyle's child would be humiliated, under public scrutiny forever, because of his parentage. And as for Derek's son and the treatment he would receive because of his parentage? Kyle would hate her, hate everything that she stood for.

"I understand, but I do not like it one bit," Emerald whispered. A tear rolled down her cheek, and she quickly wiped it away.

Her father-in-law noticed but did not say anything. Samir eyed her evenly, then rose from his seat. "I am sorry to put a damper on your day. Never have I liked to be the bearer of bad news. I have always cared for your family. I will take my leave," he said with a deep bow of respect.

"Thank you for your visit, Your Majesty," Emerald said bitterly through angry tears.

Samir paused. "Emerald, I wish…things could have worked out differently for you. I want to let you know that it pains me to see you follow in your mother's footsteps in a similar fashion…sad and alone."

Emerald stared at him but had no words.

They exchanged glances one last time, then Samir left the room.

Emerald sat at the table, fuming with anger, but also feeling sad and confused.

Why is everything that I do so difficult? Kyle was right. Why can't I just live my life? Her life wasn't her own. It was her people's…her kingdom's…

Would it start a war with the other kingdoms if she tried to divorce Derek?

What she needed was some solid counsel.

CHAPTER 63

VIOLET

The sun was shining across the courtyard while a cool breeze gently glided across her cheeks. The High Court Citadel was bustling with activity, with news of the upcoming trial of the Empress Ayera. The adjoining isles that floated nearby had bridges constructed for the event to accommodate all the people who wanted to attend the high-profile trial. Carts with pastries, fruit drinks, and magical-enchanted knickknacks were being sold.

Ikaria adjusted the hood over her face, narrowing her eyes. The entire display of getting ready for the event gave her even more resolve. Because of their insolence, Ikaria made sure she offed two High Court officials today instead of just one.

The audacity of the citadel celebrating my sister's trial. It will turn into their funeral.

"Just look at them, priest. So merry," Ikaria said mockingly. "I can assure you they won't quite so merry once I'm through with them."

"Are you sure about this?" Auron whispered from behind her, dressed in red High Court garb.

"About rescuing the green-gifted? Come now, priest," Ikaria hissed. "I thought you more intelligent than that."

Auron sighed. "No, about entering the red quarters. The trial is soon, and we might lose the chance to rescue your sister—and that green-gifted."

Ikaria smirked. "Oh, going to the red quarters is a high priority."

"I just don't want it to end up like how it did last time."

Neither do I.

Ikaria shifted her stance. "I know you are frightened. Just act as if you normally would at court. It's not that hard for someone as mundane as yourself." Ikaria eyed the courtyard, then whispered, "Let's go."

Auron nodded silently, then the two of them moved quickly through the courtyard. Ikaria headed toward the red quarters of the citadel. She had dressed specifically in red robes, as was custom for red-gifted at the citadel. Her robe pockets sagged under the weight of a few technological artifacts. The only thing keeping them somewhat secure was a thick leather belt.

In the corner of her eye, she saw an enchanted portrait of her sister, advertising the trial. A magical poster, listing all the charges that her sister faced. The stars must have been aligned in Ikaria's favor, as it was to be a new moon the night of the big event.

There was a strange shift in the air. Ikaria paused for a moment, trying to sort out where it was coming from.

"What is it?" Auron said from behind.

Ikaria glanced down the hall from both directions. This sense…it was the same magical presence she had detected from the green-gifted.

"I feel something. Wait." Ikaria reached out with her mind to sense where it was coming from. Her mind's energy poured out across the citadel. For a split second, she felt a certain direction it came from. Then in a flash it was gone.

"I lost it."

Auron frowned. "Were you able to detect where it came from?"

"I think I have a good idea."

"I hope it doesn't involve Elyathi," Auron said wistfully.

"Oh, it does. Her pride permeates the air of this entire citadel so thickly that I am choking on it." *And I cannot wait to make her eat her pride until she vomits. Then I will make her lick it up and vomit again.* Ikaria smirked at the thought, then turned away and cautiously entered the red section of the citadel.

Gleaming marble in all sorts of reds shone brightly, accented with whites, blacks, silvers, and golds. Rubies, garnets, and beryls were encrusted in the stonework sculptures of the God of Light and his angels. Other sculptures were famous red-gifted people of the past. She moved swiftly through the corridors, ensuring each step she took made no sound. It was a shame she didn't have her orange magic anymore; she had gotten so used to it masking her every move. No matter. She was just as skilled without that garish color.

I wonder if Suri is lurking in the shadows here in the citadel. She could only hope.

They came to a small corridor with a few chamber doors. No one was in the other rooms that she could detect. Only her target.

They moved down the hall, stopping in front of a specific door.

Ikaria turned to Auron. "Stay put and I'll be right out."

Auron's eyes glimmered gold from the depths of his hood. "I hope you aren't doing anything to put us in a bind," he said in a harsh whisper.

"Don't worry, priest. I just need to remove some rubbish from this place," she said. Before Auron could get another word in, Ikaria opened the door and slipped inside.

Once inside, Ikaria shut and locked the door behind her. Cyrus was seated at a desk, composing a message. His quill stopped when he heard the sound of the door locking.

"Who is it?" Cyrus called out.

"How disappointing. I expected to find you with a whore's mouth locked around your manhood," Ikaria said as she pretended to inspect her lacquered nails, then darted her eyes at him.

Cyrus jolted from his seat. "Ikaria!" he spat. "I should have known."

"Have you no manners, Cyrus? After all we've been through, this is the greeting I get?" Ikaria pouted.

Cyrus frowned. "I am surprised that you are here, considering your sister is heading to her trial now."

Ikaria lowered her hood, then smiled. "If you thought I would forget my threats, I promise you, I haven't, even for a split second. I make good on my word, Cyrus. It's a shame you don't."

"I know you've come for her."

"Oh? What makes you think I suddenly have a heart for her?"

He wrinkled his eyes. "Don't toy with me, Ikaria. I know you better than anyone."

Ikaria belted out a loud laugh. "Do you?" Her vicious eyes flared as she strutted toward him.

"I'm more powerful now," he warned. "Not one step closer."

"Perhaps you are right. I simply cannot be here just for you. It would give you a bigger ego than you already have."

"I mean it!" Cyrus threatened.

"I'm quivering in my shoes," Ikaria mocked as she flailed her fingers dramatically. She gave him a smug look, then sat down in midair, her magic flowing around her, as if on an invisible throne. The magic danced around her long tresses, floating every which way. "You know, Cyrus, I have great plans for you. I think you will admire the beauty of it. After all, you have such excellent ideas when it comes to revenge."

Cyrus gritted his teeth, starting to burn with his bright pink magic. "I hate you."

Ikaria kicked up her legs, relaxing, as her violet magic cradled her. "You hate me because I am a woman who rules over you."

"Your sister will die at the hands of the High Court. Who will be victorious then?"

"Certainly not you." Ikaria laughed, narrowing her eyes at him.

His magenta eyes suddenly lit up with magic. With a sharp motion, he summoned a slew of ice shards and sent them at Ikaria.

Ikaria held up her hand, countering them and sending them right back to him. He cast a fire spell, melting them into water puddles on the floor.

"How cute. You have fire now?"

Another round of ice came at her, but this time it was a line of frost mixed with ice spikes on the ground. A couple shot up at her thigh, but she dodged them effortlessly, floating in the air with her magic.

She laughed again, slapping the ice shards like flies. "I like games. Let's play some more, shall we?" With a snap of her fingers, violet magic swirled around Cyrus, lifting him up from the ground, then binding him tightly.

Cyrus's body glowed a brighter pink, engulfed with pink flames. But the flames didn't burn through her violet magical cords. Instead, he sent a pink wave of flames shooting straight toward her.

Lazily, Ikaria waved her hand, dousing the flames with violet-red water. "I must admit, as weak as your pathetic pink magic is, it is pretty. In fact, would you like me to dress it up in a bonnet and call it your child?"

"You bitch!" he shouted at her.

"Really, Cyrus, you should have gone the way of the theatre. There are dreadful actors these days. They need fresh and exciting talent such as yourself."

"You truly are the most horrendous person that ever walked the skies!"

"Thank you for the most delightful compliment. I will wear it upon my heart proudly," Ikaria said, standing. She raised her hand, and her enchanted dagger appeared, floating in violet-blue magic.

"You don't have the courage," Cyrus spat.

"Courage? Is that what you call it?"

This time, he laughed. "That's precisely what I call it. You never did. Always did what your father told you to do. Cried yourself to sleep when you couldn't wed me. Cried because you didn't become empress. Well, I don't blame anyone for not seating your fat ass to the throne. Nobody wants to see a dog rule the sector!"

Ikaria smiled, laughing to herself. What a lie. She could hear his thoughts perfectly. She was the best thing he ever had, including the most beautiful *thing*.

She held her enchanted dagger higher, then Cyrus blurted out, "They are going to execute your cunt of a sister no matter what the outcome of the trial is."

"Did you honestly think that I would believe otherwise? You were always such a disappointment." Ikaria lowered him to the floor with her magic. Still bound, he struggled, and every so often a pink flame shot out from his hands or a pink jolt of lightning filled the room.

"I knew you didn't have the guts." He laughed.

"That was merely for fun."

"You've always been a terrible liar. You have proven me right!" he sneered.

"Well, we can't have that."

Ikaria stood over him, watching him wriggle. It pleased her greatly. Then, she positioned her feet on either side of him, right over his face.

"What are you doing?"

She lifted her robes, baring her privates for him to see.

Then she pissed all over his face.

"You BITCH of a CUNT!" Piss landed in his mouth as he screamed.

Ikaria moaned. "I've been holding that for *hours*." Ikaria stepped away, admiring what she had done.

A pink electric shock of magic jolted her body, but she welcomed it.

"You SLUT! WHORE!" he screamed.

"That's right. I am. Say it again for me," Ikaria stated. "Please. I *beg* of you." Then she laughed as she raised his body with her magic, meeting him eye to eye. His face was sopped with her piss.

"I HATE YOU!"

"The feeling is mutual."

Cyrus snarled with a smirk on his face. "Deep down, you'll always love me. I was your *first*."

She struck him across the face. "You're absolutely right, Cyrus."

"You have always been so attached to me." He sneered, spitting at her face but missing.

"I can't honestly say why," Ikaria said, striking him again, this time harder. "But I can say that I have no qualms about taking your pathetic life."

"You can't do it."

"You are absolutely right. I cannot. That is to say, not if I want you to watch from the back of your mind as I take control of your body. I want you to see the power I hold over you. I will possess you, force you to watch me pretend to be you. I will make a fool out of you in front of everyone you deem important. I will make them laugh and mock you, just as you made others do to me. And after that, I will take your pathetic life so you cannot save what's left of your reputation. No one will remember you as anything more than the most pathetic emperor that ever lived."

"IKAR—"

Ikaria sent a solid flow of violet magic across his lips, sealing them shut. Cyrus's eyes opened wide, then narrowed, exuberating hatred for her. It made her proud. She wafted more of her violet energy into his mind, establishing a connection.

Then she broke through.

Ikaria opened Cyrus's eyes. In the back of his mind, she heard him cursing all sorts of profanities at her. At least she had entertainment in the background. She sent a wave of violet magic back to her original body, allowing the host to move freely. Now that the violet magic released Cyrus's possessed body, Ikaria went into the adjoining bathing room. The smell of her piss was strong, which disgusted and pleased her all at once. Cyrus had a small tub. She presumed it was meant for the red-gifted to draw their own baths.

Filling the host's body with her magic, Ikaria summoned hot water from her fingertips. The liquid ran through her fingertips as she rinsed him off.

My, I forgot how big that fool was when it came to his man parts. It was about the only thing that pleased her. She towel-dried Cyrus's body, then slipped on a fresh robe from his closet.

Through Cyrus's eyes, she saw her own body standing, staring out at space. Never before had she noticed the wrinkles near her eyes, the darkened circles and aging of her body. It was startling from this angle, seeing herself with a new set of eyes. Was this how Cyrus viewed her now, since she was in his body? Or was it the first time she had come to this sort of conclusion about herself?

Flowing magic through her body, she made her own body fix her hood back in position over her face, sitting down in the study chair, then she left Cyrus's chambers.

Outside in the hall, Auron looked up in alarm and flung out his hand to send a wave of magic, but Ikaria grabbed his wrist.

"It's me, priest," Ikaria said through Cyrus's body.

Auron paused, then flinched. "How do I know it's really you?"

She leaned in. "You want proof, priest? You're such a disappointment sometimes. Can't you sense our bond as complements? Can you not sense my life force?"

Auron studied Cyrus's eyes—her eyes.

Impatiently, Ikaria rolled her eyes. "Really, priest? Can you not sense how much I hate you, the High Court, the white bitch, and let's not forget my sister. Especially Lord Wellington."

Auron shook his head. "That's what you have to say? Can you not hate anyone for two seconds?"

"Not in the slightest."

Auron sighed. "Come on. We have to get to your sister."

"You must go inside and guard my body."

"What if Cyrus gets a visitor?"

"The High Court is holding the most important trial of the century, and you are worried if someone will come knocking?"

Auron sighed, then said, "Don't be too long."

"Oh, don't you worry, priest." Ikaria smiled darkly. Everything was going according to plan. "I will make excellent use of my time."

Laughing, Ikaria headed for her sister's trial.

✦ ✦ ✦

Ayera saw a soft orange light outside her cell as she wearily raised her eyes. Seeing light was always welcoming, as it brought warmth. But it also could mean her impending doom.

"Get up," a man's voice commanded.

Ayera saw within the flicker of orange light that there were two guards. One was red-gifted, the other was non-gifted, the one holding the torch.

"I said get up!"

Ayera struggled to get up. She hadn't realized until this moment how weak she was from lack of nourishment.

The red-gifted grasped her hands firmly, pulling her to her feet. He then shoved her long matted hair aside as the other man locked iron shackles around her wrists behind her back, securing them.

"Don't try anything foolish," the red-gifted guard warned.

A burning sensation radiated from the iron shackles. Ayera knew these types of shackles; they had been imbued with a fire enchantment. If she were to try to get them off without the one who had put them on her, they would burn her deep into her bones while melting her skin in the process.

"Am I to see the High Court now?"

The guards ignored her inquiry, pushing her out of her cell and into the prison hall. As her eyes adjusted to the torchlight, Ayera saw more detail in the facility. She had seen the prison briefly when being led to her cell, but she had been so terrified at the time that she hadn't paid much attention. The dank halls were filled with iron cells, and within those, magical enchanted chains and torture devices. Occasionally they passed guard stations. Seeing all the torture devices suddenly made Ayera grateful that she hadn't faced them—yet.

The guards led her down a main hall lined with cells. Mutterings came from the cells, prisoners pressing their faces against the iron bars as they walked by.

"The walk of death," whispered one prisoner.

"No, it is the path of righteousness," said another.

"It's the Empress of World Sector Six!"

"Empress Ayera?"

"It is her!"

"Empress Ayera, God bless you," said another prisoner.

"The Empress of World Sector Six?" questioned another.

"Stick it to them!" shouted another. "Tell them all to go to hell for what they did to us!"

"Help us, Empress!"

The non-gifted guard smacked some iron bars. "Shut up, you pea-brained imbeciles!" he roared. "Otherwise you get no rations for a week!"

More yelling and maniacal laughter, this time louder. A lunatic voice came from another cell, yelling loudly, "Do you think we care for rations? Worms! Bottom feeders of the earth! You are a disgrace! You will burn in hell!"

"Empress Ayera, you are our saving grace!" cried out another prisoner.

"That white-gifted is sick!"

"SILENCE!" commanded the guards.

Ayera's heart leapt in her chest. *He said white-gifted*! She turned to look over her shoulder to see the who had called out about the white-gifted, but she couldn't make out where the voice had come from.

"Tell the white witch that the heavens will fall on her face!" shouted the same prisoner.

"I said SILENCE!" The red-gifted guard shot out his hand, then filled his hand with red lightning. With a jolt, he released it upon the prisoners. They screamed in pain, and the guard released another handful of lightning. "That will teach you vermin to shut up," he said, yanking Ayera's shackles. Just then, he sent another bright red storm of lightning throughout the entire prison, and everyone screamed louder. The guard kept feeding the red lightning energy, lighting the prison up like the pits of hell itself. The screams kept going, and the magic kept getting brighter.

"Stop it!" Ayera pleaded. "You have done enough!"

The guard side-eyed her, then sent another wave of red magic, the screams reaching a fevered pitch before finally cutting off.

The guard gave her a cold look. "Get *moving*."

Ayera's heart sank, feeling completely powerless. She was their saving grace? The very thought made her feel ill. How could she, one with no power, be someone's hope?

I am sorry that I cannot help you, she thought.

The guards led her up the flight of stairs, reaching the ground level of the

High Court Citadel. As they emerged, more guards formed around the group, one of them casting a magical barrier around them. Whispers came from the crowd as they passed, while lords and ladies gave her condescending stares. Some in the crowd laughed, while others snorted in disgust.

I must be headed to my trial. Or my execution.

The bigger the crowd grew, the more rowdy they became, hurling insults at her. Heretic, witch, possessed demon, they called her. What was disheartening was that everyone had already predetermined their idea of her. Regardless, Ayera held her head high, just as her sister would. If she was going to die, she would do it with the dignity of an empress. If she were heading to her trial, then she would defend herself with that same dignity. That included not backing down on her actions or her words. She would fight to the bitter end.

The guards came upon an all-too-familiar set of grand double doors: They had arrived at the High Court's judgment seat.

God of Light, give me strength.

The doors opened, and the group was suddenly blinded by a bright light coming from within. The guards yanked her in place, then stopped her.

"Do not move," a guard warned.

The light faded, and Ayera saw that she was standing in the middle of the circular room. Whispers surrounded her. She had never seen a chamber so full of people. High officials of the court were seated nearest to her, ones with the most influence. Other important lords, ambassadors from other sectors, were also in the chamber. Staring at her from their high seats in a semicircle, the high justices sat in their thrones with cold, calculating glances.

As her eyes darted around the chamber, Ayera noticed a woman with long wavy white hair and glowing white eyes standing next to High Justice Belinda. The white-gifted woman. The woman gave Ayera a hard stare, her delicate chin held high.

A glimmer of light came from the white-gifted woman's neck, then it was gone. Ayera saw the woman grasp a necklace, fix it, then stuff it down her neckline.

"Ayera Suzuki," a red-robed clerk of the court announced off to the side. He opened a magical scroll, which shimmered brightly as it unrolled. "You have hereby been charged with treason, leading rebellion, insubordination of the High Court, and attempted murder of a High Court official." When he'd concluded, the scroll magically wrapped back up. "Do you have anything to say in your defense?" the clerk called out, his voice echoing across the chamber.

"I do," Ayera stated. "Every single one of those charges are false."

The chamber audience buzzed with snickers and surprised voices.

"Quiet in the court!" yelled High Justice Nyrden of the Red.

The audience quieted down, and Ayera held her head high. "You say I am leading a rebellion? I say that I am standing up for what is right for my people. At every turn, my people have been oppressed by your rules—rules that have been made up by your court and previous courts before you. Your interpretation of the God of Light's laws are just that—interpretations. You twist these words of truth into laws of mankind, making them the opposite of what the God of Light intended. Then, under the guise of a 'plague' of wickedness, you send that white-gifted to strip my people of their magic." Ayera looked directly into the white-gifted woman's eyes. "My people have made it clear—they no longer want to be under the High Court's rule, and want to return to the ways of our ancestors. If you label that as rebellion, then so be it."

The white-gifted woman remained unmoved by her words, glaring coldly at Ayera. She then called out, "You are being formally questioned by the High Court. I strongly suggest you choose your words wisely, as your life, or your *death* depend on it." The woman's eyes glowed a bright white. "This is your moment to repent of your sins, to set your crooked path straight."

Ayera remained strong. "You should eat your own words, you vile woman. You, who stole all of World Sector Six's magic from my gifted. I think it best for *you* to repent, for your time is coming to an end."

"You see?" the white-gifted woman called out. "This so-called *empress* has no remorse for her sins. She is just as wicked as her sister. The root of evil comes from the same bloodline."

"Indeed," Belinda said. "There is much evidence that she took matters into her own hands. She *coerced* the other sectors into helping her gifted in the past. That is criminal in itself."

"Criminal?" Ayera called out. "I find that hypocritical considering you were the one who asked me to take care of my sister."

Shouts erupted from the lords.

"ENOUGH!" called out Tyllos of the Yellow as he stood.

The court went silent, and Belinda resumed. "As I was saying, the former empress coerced gifted to travel back in time to stop the sorceress against High Justice Tyllos's warning. Furthermore, we sent the High Inquisitor to investigate matters of her sector. She had Emperor Cyrus imprisoned without formal instruction from this court."

More whispers from the audience while Ayera scoffed.

"If you have forgotten your own laws, let me remind you, for I made sure that my scholars looked into the matter before I took action," Ayera said. "It is the law that any gifted must disclose their gift to their sector. The emperor Cyrus hid his power from our entire sector, including me, his spouse, mother to the true bloodline of the ancient royals of World Sector Six. I reminded High Inquisitor Rubius of this as well." Ayera stared down Belinda, unwavering. "He knew the law and had nothing to say to counter it. Just as you do not now."

Nyrden sent a magical icy blast at the Empress. Her dirty kimono and long hair fluttered about momentarily in the red flurry, then settled. "We, the High Court, directed the Emperor to do so."

"How was I to know?" Ayera shot back. "I was only following the law that your predecessors wrote. If you told only my husband, I cannot abide by orders to the contrary."

The white-gifted woman sneered as Belinda clenched her throne.

"We sent a directive to release the Emperor," Nyrden announced. "*That* was no hidden order."

"Indeed, I received it," Ayera said coolly. "I burned it after reading it, for what it asked of me—to release the Emperor—was not done in accordance with your laws. There was only one seal, that of the High Justice of the Red. For it to be official, it must have all colored seals. I thought it was a fake."

"You dare—" Nyrden roared, losing his composure.

Belinda held up her hand to silence Nyrden. Wild whispers flooded the chambers. Some nodded at Ayera, while others looked incredulous. Ayera felt strengthened by the support, which fueled her hope. Ayera met Belinda's cold, angry eyes.

Ayera turned and felt the white-gifted's voice inside her mind. *I will make the Empress kiss my hand. I will enjoy every second of her begging while she cries out for mercy. I will make both those vile sinner sisters pay! They will have no place in the new world.*

Had Ayera imagined that? Perhaps she had been in the darkened prison for too long and her mind was going?

Ayera? Why are you using your power? Suresh called out within her mind.

Suresh! Ayera's heart suddenly was uplifted. *I have no power, nor am I using any… Please help me. I am terrified.*

Be firm. Do not waver… I believe in you.

Thank you, Suresh. Thank you for believing in me…

More voices flooded her mind, while Ayera spun around in confusion. Suddenly, a clear voice rang out in the chamber.

"If the High Court will allow it, let me clarify a few matters to corroborate High Justice Belinda's story, to show that the Empress is a heretic," called out a familiar voice.

Any and all hope that Suresh gave her left Ayera instantly at the sound of Cyrus's voice. Things were about to get much worse.

"You have our permission to proceed, Emperor," Belinda called out, a daring, calculated smile on her face.

Cyrus approached, bowing to the court, then turned to Ayera, staring directly at her. His magenta eyes gave her a hard stare, sending a shiver down her spine. He turned to address the crowd. "It is true. The Empress imprisoned me wrongfully, against my will, working with her sister to capture me!" he said in a dramatic fashion.

The crowd whispered wildly.

"Working with my sister? No, you fell right into her trap! That was your own doing. I had no idea she was there until I found you in your naked state!"

The crowd buzzed with loud chatter. Was that…a smile on Cyrus's face? Did he think this was humorous?

"How can I, a man that embraces the very nature of being created in the divine image of the God of Light's beauty, pass up such a delicacy and not sample the sorceress Ikaria with my manhood?" Cyrus stated boldly. "That unearthly body was created to drive a man's sin further into lust, a magic so evil and so powerful that I could not escape her wickedness! Even the God of Light couldn't have created such luscious breasts or backside curves!"

Ayera furrowed her brow in confusion. She darted her eyes around, seeing that many of the lords and ladies suppressed their laughs or looks of surprise.

"Emperor Cyrus, what is your *point*?" Belinda said with an icy edge, narrowing her eyes.

"My point, High Justice, is that it couldn't be as she says. She had been working with her wicked sister to plot my demise. The two of them are inherently evil, I say!" he boomed. "They are cunning tricksters. Why, if it wasn't be for my deep love for my well-endowed manhood, I wouldn't be here telling my tale of my heroic victory!"

"Emperor Cyrus!" scolded the white-gifted. "How dare you say such filth in this court!"

Cyrus turned to her, then nodded. "Forgive me, Lady Elyathi."

"Thank you for your testimony," Belinda stated with a hand gesture. "You may be seated now, Emperor."

"But I am not done yet."

Ayera raised an eyebrow, enjoying the fury on the high justices' faces, including the white-gifted.

"You have been excused, *Emperor*," Nyrden sneered.

"I implore you to allow me one last statement, if you please, high justices," Cyrus said, turning back around, facing them.

Belinda, Elyathi, and the other members of the High Court glanced at each other. "This is a trial, Emperor. Does what you have to say pertain to the defendant? Or does it have to do with her sister?"

Cyrus narrowed his eyes. "Quite so."

The group of high justices eyes each other, then Belinda said, "You may proceed."

Cyrus stood front and center, his voice booming across the audience hall. "High Justices, the hour has come for me to fulfill my oath," he said, then lowered his voice. "However, I can be convinced to save Emperor Cyrus's life if you kindly hand over my sister and that green-gifted."

"IKARIA!" screamed Nyrden, pointing to Cyrus. "SEIZE HER!"

Screams, shouts, and confusion rang out in the audience hall, with many people scattering.

In that split second, Ayera saw her sister in Cyrus's eyes. Her sister—she was *here*.

"SISTER!" Ayera screamed, meeting her gaze through Cyrus's eyes. "Get out of here before the *white-gifted* gets your magic!"

Cyrus's eyes met Ayera's. *I am sorry that I cannot rescue you today, sister.*

I promised Auron that I would, but there is someone here that needs to be rescued before you. I needed this as a distraction.

Ayera immediately understood. *Suresh! He is the one you are looking for!*

A burst of fire magic singed Cyrus's arm. Ikaria flinched in pain as she tried to counter the magic with her host's magic.

Do you know of his whereabouts? Time is of the essence.

He is being held in Elyathi's quarters under some kind of time-dimensional spell. I don't know much more than that.

Thank you, sister. Once I have him in our sector safely, I vow to return for you.

I...I thank you, sister.

You can thank me when it's all said and done.

"Since it seems you do not like my offer, then say goodbye to your sweet emperor," Ikaria said aloud.

"You wouldn't dare!" snarled Tyllos.

"Oh, but I would."

Before anyone could stop her, Ikaria slit Cyrus's throat, and he slumped to the floor in a pool of blood.

There were screams, shouts, and bright white light.

"That bitch!" Nyrden screamed.

Ayera felt thick hands latch on to her arms, holding her in place.

"GUARDS!" called out Belinda. "Take Ayera back to the prison immediately. Make sure she *stays* there!"

"She is not to see the light of day until her death!" Tyllos added.

The guards snatched her upper arms, digging their metal gauntlets into her flesh.

Ayera jerked wildly in their grasp as she turned to face Tyllos. "You condemned me before the trial was even over! Some justice you serve. May the God of Light condemn you as you have condemned me."

As she was being dragged away, Ayera saw the white-gifted woman, her eyes narrowed at Ayera.

This would have never happened if I had my complement, Elyathi's mind spoke loudly. *I must compress time, and quickly!*

Ayera sucked in a breath. She'd heard the woman's thoughts again.

Do I really have power as Suresh suggested?

The white-gifted flitted away in anger as Ayera was dragged away.

✦ ✦ ✦

Ikaria blinked, seeing the world through her own eyes once again. She was back in her own body, sitting in Cyrus's chair. There were no sounds coming from outside his chambers, but she knew that everyone would be trying to find her now.

Auron was standing next to her, where she'd told him to wait. "Well?" he asked.

"I know where the green-gifted is," Ikaria stated.

His eyes went wide. "Where?"

"In Elyathi's chambers." She flashed Auron a satisfied look. "Just keep us shielded as we move about. And I have upset the entire High Court, so try to stay quiet."

"Of course you did," he said sarcastically. "Dare I ask?"

"No time, priest. Let's go."

Auron sighed, then the two of them moved silently throughout the halls, making their way out of the red quarters. As they passed through halls, guards ran past them, screaming about Cyrus, her name, her sister's name. Auron flashed her a look each time he heard a guard curse her.

You are looking for me…I can sense it, a man's voice said within her mind. *Are you Ayera's sister?*

Ikaria paused, gesturing for Auron to stop. *Indeed I am, on all accounts. I am pressed for time. It would help me greatly if you could open your mind to me.*

It will be difficult, as my life force has been mostly extracted from my soul. I am in another dimension.

Do not worry about that. I have dimensional magic. Just hurry up!

The man's mind suddenly opened, and she felt Suresh's clear and concise path of consciousness.

Ikaria turned to Auron, whispering, "Be on guard. I can assure you that we will see our dear friend Elyathi."

His eyes were determined. "This time, we shall get retribution for her crimes."

"This new side of you is more becoming, I must say," Ikaria said with a small chuckle. She narrowed her eyes. *Yes, you will get what's coming to you...*

Using the man's mind as a guide, Ikaria and Auron quickly moved through the maze of hallways. They exited the main part of the citadel, which opened up to a large courtyard with a garden. The roses were in bloom, and the smell of lilacs filled the air with its sweetness.

"We are definitely heading in the right direction," Ikaria huffed. Only Elyathi would surround herself with delicate things like flowers, a garden, and...

Ikaria glanced across the garden, noticing a part of the citadel that she had never seen before. It was the highest tower in the entire citadel, toward the far back. Though it wasn't very big, it was lavish, constructed of ivory and gold.

"Talk about humble," Auron muttered.

"I would expect no less from a hypocrite such as her," Ikaria sneered. "I feel sick just looking at it."

The two of them quickly walked across the garden, evading many of the passing guards scurrying about, acting like any other citizen.

They made it to the tower's entrance, which was open, leading to a spiral staircase made of white marble. They made it to the top, Auron wheezing breathlessly beside her.

"Ready, priest?"

"Absolutely."

Flicking her finger, Ikaria burst it open with her magic, stepping inside.

White marbled floors instantly beamed in her eyes, so bright that Ikaria could have sworn the God of Light himself was smiting her with his holy power.

What garish taste.

The white room was empty of any living being. Lavish objects glimmered in the light, while lavender curtains swayed in the open window.

Ikaria felt Suresh's presence in a room down the hall. Turning back to Auron, she gestured for him to follow, keeping silent.

Ikaria felt the green-gifted life force grow stronger with each step as the two of them walked down one corridor, then another.

Suddenly, a young female servant came around the corner. Her eyes went wide as she noticed Ikaria, then let out a loud scream.

"Hush!" Ikaria snapped. She flicked her finger, slapping violet magic across the woman's lips, sealing them. Ikaria neared her, leaning in, smelling the lousy cheap perfume the woman wore. "I will send you to the God of Light if you move from this spot. I make good on my word, believe me."

"She does," Auron agreed.

The maid nodded energetically in agreement, standing against the corridor wall.

Ikaria gestured to Auron, and they moved down the hall.

"You think she will stay?" he asked.

"Oh, you can count on it." Ikaria smiled. "If she moves, my magic will rip her apart."

Auron didn't protest, but she could tell by the priest's expression that he didn't like her methods.

At the end of the hall was a door. With a flick of her wrist, the door opened. Inside, a magical blue wall, similar to a waterfall, shimmered. Ikaria couldn't see anything beyond the wall. It looked empty.

"I'll be a minute," she warned Auron.

"Wait," he said, holding out his hand. "You need protection, just in case."

Without a word, Auron swept his hand across her forehead, casting a powerful barrier over her body, its power soaking into her skin.

After Auron had finished, Ikaria summoned her violet-blue magic, turning it completely blue. Suddenly, the waterfall-like wall of blue magic rippled. Embracing the full power of her blue magic, Ikaria cast it over herself, sending her body and being into another dimension. Her vision was suddenly cast in hues of blue.

Ikaria held out a hand, wafting the blue power aside, and the waterfall-like curtain parted. As she stepped inside, her gaze landed on Suresh.

Bound by magic, the green-gifted man looked up at her weakly. His life force was nearly gone.

"You are Ikaria," he whispered.

Ikaria knelt down beside him. "No time for proprieties. We are leaving. I am sure that Elyathi is on her way here."

"I can hardly move," Suresh whispered.

"Just hang on to me."

Suresh weakly clutched onto her sleeve, and Ikaria wrapped her arm around his waist. With a sharp flood of blue magic, Ikaria filled her life force, pouring it over them both. The man began to glow a bright blue.

Suddenly, her magic around him flickered violently. The blue magic shifted to black, the energy sparking wildly through the air. It began to shock Suresh, jolting him. It was the magical vortex. Apparently this dimension didn't like her interfering, or perhaps it didn't want him to leave.

"Picture using your adjacent blue magic!" Ikaria hissed, assuming he knew how to use it. "You will need to do whatever you can to help. It's hard enough with this spell to leave; it's made with strong magic."

The green-gifted man didn't respond, but he closed his eyes, still jolting from the painful shocks. Green-blue magic surrounded them, and Ikaria joined in, sending another wave of magic. Together, they formed an exit portal.

A sudden burst of bright solid-blue light overpowered the portal spell. The portal froze in time, and Suresh slumped over on the floor as Ikaria whipped around.

Shimmering in the light was none other than Elyathi herself. She held her head high as she clenched one of the vials around her neck—the one that glowed with green magic.

"I *knew* it," Elyathi said as she yanked her hand on one of her necklaces.

Ikaria gave her a smug look. "Well, well, well, if it isn't the High Hypocrite herself."

"You evil witch," Elyathi spat.

"Did you miss me? I daresay, I had so much fun last time."

Elyathi screamed as she soaked in yellow magic from a gemstone. "Do not think that you can break my vials again," Elyathi warned. "Because it won't work. I made sure that if I encountered you again, I wouldn't make the same mistake twice!" Her eyes and hair turned yellow, glowing with the light of the sun. "His power is mine! And now your power is mine for the taking."

"How selfish of you. And here I thought you had dedicated your life to fulfilling the God of Light's prophecy," Ikaria said nonchalantly. She whipped a violet magic spell around Elyathi's neck, trying to yank it off with force. Something was interfering.

Elyathi laughed at her attempt, then raised her eyebrows, tutting. "I am the chosen, and nothing stands in my way! Begone, witch!"

The golden barrier that surrounded Elyathi glowed brighter, her power growing. With a jolt of her hand, she cast a bolt of yellow magic, eating away Auron's spell of protection.

Ikaria needed to break that vial, otherwise she wouldn't be going anywhere.

Elyathi's anger intensified, then she turned red, hurling a flame strike at Ikaria.

Ikaria raised her hand, creating an ice barrier around her. The flames hit, melting the ice into water, soaking both women's robes.

"Tell me, how is the King of York faring?" Ikaria asked innocently. "What was his name? Oh, that's right. Samir?"

Elyathi didn't answer, and instead cast another spell, this time a bolt of red lightning.

"Were you not his mistress?" Ikaria asked. "I could have sworn that you were as I watched your memories."

Elyathi twisted her face in hatred, ignoring her jabs.

"How was he in bed?" Ikaria called out. "He did have a body of a god, full muscles, ringlet curls so dark, tempting, handsome."

Without a word, Elyathi cast another red lightning strike at Ikaria.

"I'd love to have a piece of that. Mm-hmmm, those muscles and dark curls," Ikaria said as she deflected her spell.

Elyathi's face darkened. "You twisted memories that you tried to control me with. It won't work. I have all the power and all of the control!"

"Really? And what about his son? Talk about being in control." Ikaria's eyes flickered with devious delight. "Why, I wouldn't be surprised if you two have already done the nasty deed. I mean, Derek seems just as confused as you do."

Her statement caught Elyathi off guard. She blinked in surprise, then narrowed her eyes. "You *sick, disgusting, filthy, wretched creature!*"

"Now we are getting somewhere!" Ikaria chuckled. "He is quite handsome. I daresay one of the finest I have ever laid eyes on. If I can't get a good romp with him, then maybe I can always try the father instead. He's getting on in age and could use younger meat for his manhood. Perhaps I could have both at the same time."

"WITCH!" Elyathi screamed.

Ikaria laughed wickedly.

Elyathi emptied herself of the red magic, becoming white once again.

This was the moment.

Ikaria surrounded herself with a whirlwind of violet force.

Right as Elyathi cast her white magic, Ikaria hurled a violent, violet burst of force magic fueled by her mind and body. It was enough of a mental push in Elyathi's mind to break her concentration. Her violet power ripped everything inside the chambers back against the wall, including Elyathi. The woman was flung back, sending her tripping on her dress.

Elyathi's mind…it was all hers to have fun with…

Ikaria watched as Elyathi stretched out a hand.

Let's see how much you can withstand, hag! Ikaria hissed. *I will warp your memories until you won't know what's real or fake…*

Ikaria shot out her hand, then flung her consciousness straight into Elyathi's mind. She knew the way—she had visited Elyathi's mind before. Ikaria took the most hurtful memory that she could have ever pulled from Elyathi's mind.

White light.

Silence.

White light.

Pounding.

More pounding.

"OPEN THE DOOR!" screamed Damaris through the white expanse.

Elyathi felt Samir's arms around her, his hot breath on the top of her head as she sobbed. She never wanted to leave his arms. His touch was all that she desired from any man.

"Don't worry, I will protect you," Samir said. "Both you and your daughter, I will bring you to safety."

Ikaria could feel Elyathi's attachment to this memory, as it was the only time she got to feel what it was like being in Samir's arms…

Ikaria changed the memory.

Samir brushed her cheek softly, wiping away her tears. Elyathi slowly met his gaze as he gave her a reassuring smile, then held her close.

Suddenly, Damaris opened the door with his string of guards.

"My own wife and best friend," he sneered.

Samir positioned himself in front of her, getting in between the King and Queen of Arcadia.

Guards grabbed Samir, holding him back.

"No!" Elyathi cried out. "Don't hurt him! He didn't do anything!"

Damaris walked silently up to her, pinned in the guards' arms, inspecting every inch of her body. Those eyes. They were full of hatred and evil.

Fear wracked every inch of her being.

"Please…"

He slapped her across the face.

"You vile wife! Your body belongs to ME!"

Elyathi's lip quivered, fighting back the tears.

"Are you crying?" Damaris slapped her again, this time hard.

She let out a loud cry, her cheeks flooding with tears.

"You *are* crying. What a whore you are," Damaris sneered, smacking her cheek hard. Blood poured down her lips, chin, and chest.

"STOP!" Samir shouted.

Damaris laughed, focused on Elyathi. "You love him, don't you?" he sneered.

Elyathi shot a glance to Samir, surprise hitting his face when she shook her head in denial.

"No," she said quickly.

Damaris slapped her again. "Don't LIE!"

"No…" Elyathi glanced at Samir. She saw his eyes. They held sympathy, but no love.

"You want him to love you?" Damaris said. "Let's show him how much of a whore you are!"

Damaris grabbed her dress, then tore it down the front. She sobbed louder.

"SILENCE!" he shouted as he tore more of her dress. Her entire torso was exposed, only the bottom half of her dress still hugging her hips. Samir averted his eyes as she stood weeping with shame while he fought the guards holding him back.

"Isn't she beautiful, Samir?" Damaris commented.

Samir remained still, in shock.

"No? I didn't think you had such fine taste as I do," Damaris said.

"Stop…" Elyathi whispered.

"Stop? We are just getting started."

"Please stop…"

Damaris glared at her, then he turned to Samir. "Since you were so eager to lay with my wife, let me show you the kind of fantasy she *really* likes."

"Damaris…" Samir said, mortified.

"Shut him up," Damaris ordered his guards.

Elyathi watched as the guards put a cloth around Samir's mouth while he struggled.

"Let's give your man a good show, shall we?" Damaris called out.

"Please…don't…"

Damaris came over to her, then leaned in, guiding his hands down her naked flesh as she cried. He then whispered, "You stole the very heart of *my gifted*, so I shall steal *your heart* in return."

"STOP!"

Ikaria was suddenly disconnected from her host, flung back out of her body.

"STOP!" Elyathi screamed and sobbed as she cradled her forehead.

"How dare you ruin my connection! The *nerve*!" Ikaria screamed in frustration. She then let out a loud scream, shooting a blast of violet magic to Elyathi. How had she broken the connection?

Suresh lay against her legs, half dead. The only reason she knew he was still alive was that he held her skirts tightly.

I best get him out of here.

Elyathi angrily jolted her hands toward Ikaria, eyes bloodshot and wet with tears. "You *dare* interfere with my memories, you wicked, vile, soulless filth!"

"It is the least you deserve for what you have done to me, my sister, and my entire SECTOR!" Ikaria screamed.

Ikaria began glowing blue again, summoning her dimensional magic. The area flickered with dark blue flecks of energy, shocking her.

Elyathi had a smug look mixed with her angry tears. "You aren't going anywhere with Suresh unless you get past me. The spell doesn't allow him to leave unless he has permission." She grasped the green-glowing vial. "I've had enough of this."

Green magic flowed out of Suresh, as if he were bleeding magic. Elyathi was doing this without touching Suresh, just standing with a smug grin as his life force drained out of his body into hers.

"Since I cannot have him willingly, neither shall you," Elyathi snarled.

"You sure enjoy outdoing me when it comes to toying with insanity." Ikaria pulled Suresh to his feet, but it was no use. The man was dead weight.

"Insanity?" Elyathi cooed. "No. It makes perfect sense. He will live a perfectly normal life in the new world—without his gift. I am just doing my godly duties as the chosen."

Ikaria, get out of here! Suresh's voice pleaded in her mind. In the corner of her eye, Suresh appeared dead, unmoving.

Not without you! Ikaria answered. *She cannot have your gift!*

And she won't.

What?

The only way for her to lose, and for the world to remain safe, is without me in it.

Ikaria cast a time spell, slowing Elyathi's magic sucking Suresh's life force. *Our world cannot lose your magic!*

I will lose my magic regardless. It is the only way for you to leave this place. Not only will she not have my gift, she will be distracted, and you can get out of here.

He was right. It was the only way. She didn't like it at all. In fact, it went against every fiber of her being. Yes, she had murdered gifted before, but those gifted deserved it. This man certainly did not.

Suresh, I...

Ikaria felt as if time had slowed down in that moment. Elyathi was moving at a snail's pace, and she herself was locked into place. Was it the shock?

Suresh physically tugged at her skirt. Looking down, Ikaria took in his sad smile. *Your sister must be rescued at all costs.*

My sister?

She...is...

Their eyes met in the slowed time.

...special...

His green eyes gave one last knowing twinkle.

Special? Ikaria gritted her teeth while fighting back bitter tears.

Suddenly a dark green burst exploded from Suresh's body.

After the green energy burned off, Ikaria saw Suresh. Or what was left of him.

He was no more.

Elyathi screamed, desperately grasping at the green vial, attempting to tap into it in order to keep him alive, but it was too late.

Suresh was dead, and her vial was empty.

While Elyathi was distracted, Ikaria filled her life force with her blue magic, then drew back the time curtain, hopping through.

On the other side, Auron looked startled.

"Ikaria!" he said, then looked at her empty hands.

"No time. We are leaving now."

He clasped her hand, then they both flashed away. Far, far away…

◆　◆　◆

Her hands trembled. The delicate glass vial that held his soul, it was no more.

Elyathi wept, slumping over Suresh's lifeless body.

"Suresh…" Elyathi pleaded with his corpse.

His eyes were wide, staring out into the void.

"Why…?"

A fresh stream of tears came streaming down her cheeks. This wasn't supposed to happen. Suresh was to be the key to the next world, her guardian. He was to be *hers*. And even if he didn't want to help her, she was going to let him live happily in the new world.

Elyathi let out another scream, weeping as she held his body.

Now I have no choice.

She had to use her daughter instead. All because of that vile, twisted, sick violet-gifted woman.

"I *hate* her," Elyathi snarled under her tears. "I *hate* that witch." It was forbidden to hate a person. According to The Spectrum, only hatred for the sin was allowed. But she hated Ikaria with all her being.

She looked to Suresh one last time, then knelt over him, kissing him gently on his forehead.

Goodbye, my dear friend. How I wish I could have called you that.

Grasping the red gem around her neck, Elyathi soaked in the elemental magic, then stepped to the corner of the room. With another stroke of her hand, a whirlpool of magic formed underneath Suresh's body, burning bright red. Then the red magic burst into flames, consuming Suresh entirely.

"She's going to regret she ever had been born with her gift," Elyathi sneered, as she got up and wiped away her tears.

Elyathi angrily yanked the blue gem from her necklace, then filled herself with its power. She missed her daughter. And it seemed her daughter missed her just as much, so the two of them were about to have their long overdue reunion. All she'd ever wanted was to live in peace with her daughter. But now?

It has to be done.

Filled with blue magic, Elyathi fought back tears as she wafted the time-dimensional magic around her. The boundaries melted away before her eyes, disappearing and forming into a doorway to her time and plane of existence.

✦ ✦ ✦

"Ikaria!" Auron called out, shaking her body.

The priest.

Ikaria swatted thin air aimlessly to shoo him away.

"Ikaria!"

"Go away, priest," Ikaria murmured.

"Are you okay? Let me heal you…"

"NO!" Ikaria her head up, meeting his gaze. "I don't need healing." Her eyes began to well up with tears, then she took a proud breath.

With a sad, heavy sigh, Ikaria sat up, finding herself on a sofa. She was still wearing those godawful red robes; they were slightly tattered, and her skin felt grimy. She swept her hair out of her face. Auron was kneeling beside the sofa at her side, still in his disguise robes too.

She didn't want to look at Auron, because if she did, he would see straight into her soul. She wasn't up for that nonsense right now.

"What happened in that time prison?" Auron pressed.

The green gift was gone from this world.

"Ikaria?"

No reply.

Auron's face turned ghostly. "Was it Elyathi?"

Ikaria couldn't find the words. Of all the people that had lost their lives, this one felt so *wrong*.

"Did she almost take your magic?"

Ikaria sighed heavily, plopping back down in the sofa. "I don't feel like chatting right now."

Auron gave her a hard glare. "Normally, I would back down and be on my way. But this time, absolutely not. I went to the High Court with you in hopes of rescuing the green-gifted, or even the Empress. The least you can do is let me know what transpired while you made me stand aside doing nothing. I feel that I am owed at least that."

Ikaria side-eyed him. He didn't move, nor did one inch of his face change. She gave in. "His name was Suresh."

"What? What do you mean was?"

Ikaria met his eyes, and suddenly Auron sucked in his breath.

"The green-gifted. He ended his life to stick it to Elyathi." Ikaria rolled over on her side, away from Auron, fighting back her tears. "Sounds like my kind of man. It's a shame, really. I had so dreamed of having a green-gifted on this court, so we could heal our ancestral lands."

"I'm sorry that—"

"Don't apologize. I hate when men get all sappy." Ikaria still faced the other direction, choking on a lump in her throat.

There was a long silence between them. Suddenly, she felt a gentle brush of healing magic within her body, down to her spirit. It soothed her body and relaxed her mind a little. But knowing that the green-gifted man was gone made her realize who was next.

Queen Emerald.

"What now? The Empress is still at the mercy of the High Court," he said softly.

She is special... Suresh's words echoed in her mind. Was she gifted?

Ikaria took a deep breath, then faced Auron. "We still proceed with our plans," she said, acting as if she hadn't been emotional a moment earlier. "We will go to war on that corrupt citadel, that I can assure you, priest. I make good on my word."

"It's just...you were there. They will expect you even more so than before."

"They are always expecting me, especially with my sister in their clutches."

Auron paused. "You must know that the green-gifted Queen in the past is now in danger. Perhaps we should focus our attention on her."

"I'm well aware of that, especially since she's her daughter."

"God of Light help us," he said under his breath.

"You best pray hard, priest. Because rest assured, Elyathi will get her daughter. I just bought us more time, that's all." Ikaria paused, thinking about her sister. Suresh warned her that she must be saved at all costs. Of course, she was planning on it. But he'd seemed rather insistent about it. He knew her true power. Why hadn't he just told her? Ikaria paused. "You know what? I'm feeling rather lucky. Let's move up our date, shall we?"

"Date?"

Ikaria sighed, annoyed. "The *date* when we will storm the citadel with all our might."

"I can only imagine what you are about to say…"

Though she was in a foul mood, she snorted. "You know me best. Talk to Lord Jiao and the ambassadors that have come at Vala's urging. Let them know the time. Now, where is a servant? I need wine. And lots of it."

"Perhaps you should try praying instead drinking at a time like this," Auron suggested.

"*Praying.* I don't pray to anyone or anything except to my blessedly good looks." Feeling a little bit more like herself, Ikaria rolled over, then sat up on the sofa.

"If you prayed as much as I did, then perhaps you could get a new gifted to aid us."

"What?" Ikaria froze on the sofa. Did he mean her sister? She shook her head, then said, "What new gifted? What are you talking about?"

"In the past."

"What about the past? What have you been hiding from me, priest?"

Auron held his Spectrum pendant, which clung to his neck. "I'm not hiding anything, just haven't had a chance to speak of this until now." He paused. "I had a vision prior to leaving for the citadel. In my vision, I met another yellow-gifted from the past. He told me that I needed to plant a gift."

Ikaria blinked with curiosity. "Plant a gift?"

His eyes shifted downward, slightly flustered. "I've never been good with words, not of my own accord. Only when the God of Light speaks through me."

"I don't have time to listen to priestly ideals—"

"I'll spare you the ancient parables," he cut her off, surprising Ikaria, then meeting her eyes. "All I know is that it was imperative that I plant this gift—by prophesying—to heal the earth."

"And did you?"

"I did."

Auron locked his gaze on hers. "A new *white-gifted*."

Ikaria shot up, grabbed on to his vestments. "Are you sure, priest? You are telling me there is another white-gifted somewhere?"

Could my sister be white-gifted?

He eyed her hands, raising his eyebrow. "I can't say exactly for sure. But it's just…I felt it in my vision. I saw a prophecy for a new white-gifted, then everything went white."

Ikaria searched his thoughts. Though at many times she could feel them since he was her complement, these thoughts were now void.

Perhaps I cannot feel his thoughts because it's only meant for him alone, she thought.

"I see," Ikaria said, slumping over in slight disappointment. "Well, we'd best hope that your vision is correct, though I don't know why we need another white-gifted walking around and mucking things up. We already have one of those. Two sounds much worse."

"You're not a priest, so I cannot explain to you the full aspect of my vision."

Ikaria snorted. "That is for sure."

"I myself don't quite understand it, and didn't know what to make of it," he admitted. "It's why I need to meditate on it further."

"I see," she said, plopping back down on the sofa, waving her hand. "Go meditate so you can fill me in more later. I need some rest before I wage my war."

"I'll be at the temple for the rest of the day, perhaps sleep there tonight."

"Yes, yes," she said. "I'll see you when you're done with your holy meditation."

Auron left. Now, more than ever, she needed to get to her sister. If Ayera was the new white-gifted and imprisoned at the High Court Citadel, things could get murky.

Lazily summoning a glass of wine from across the room, Ikaria took the chalice, then downed the contents. A fine wine always made her think clearer about any situation and less about her innermost thoughts.

She needed to win this once and for all and be done with Elyathi and the High Court. Her mental weapon worked wonders, but still, Elyathi had been able to break free from the nightmare she'd been feeding that whore.

Ikaria poured herself another glass, taking a drink. Samir had been locked away in Elyathi's heart. But Derek…he lingered in her thoughts.

Ikaria narrowed her eyes, reassessing Elyathi's most personal thoughts. Elyathi felt a deep draw to Derek's life force, often misplacing her desires on him. Who wouldn't? Derek was the spitting image of his father, except for his pale blue eyes. Derek was in his prime, so what wasn't there to desire? It gave Elyathi all the reminders of Samir in his youth.

That was my mistake!

She had used the wrong man as a weapon against Elyathi. She should have used Derek. Interestingly enough, Derek was so hell-bent on Emerald that his heart would never sway away from her. But there was some confusion on Derek's part… She had felt it the last time they confronted each other in battle.

He is confused because Elyathi is so much like Emerald. Unlike Emerald, Elyathi had a void in her heart, so desperate for love and to be fully desired …

Ikaria smiled darkly to herself.

She downed her wine, then held out her hand, refilling it with her magic.

There was a soft knock. One of her temporary servants. She scoffed. None could ever compare to her Suri. None.

Stay safe, my dearest Suri, Ikaria thought, as if in prayer.

Prayer. That was laughable.

Another knock.

"I am not to be bothered by anyone!" Ikaria barked.

"Yes, Enchantress," murmured the servant.

Silence once again, and Ikaria sighed in relief.

Your sister is special…

Ikaria poured another glass of wine, fighting back tears. There was much planning to do. Because to hell with the High Court if they thought they could keep her sister.

CHAPTER 64

◆

GREEN

"Your Majesty?" Emerys called out from across the Inner Council room. "You sent for me?"

Emerald blinked, then glanced over at him. "I did. Please, have a seat."

The councilor was dressed in his usual deep gray robe, with pressed pants and knee-high leather boots. The silver streak in his hair shone against the rest of his dark hair.

Emerys bowed, then walked across the brightly lit room. The city of Arcadia was bustling outside. Transports flying to their destinations. Glowing lights that even outshone the daylight. Emerald could have sworn she saw an advertisement on top of a far-off building featuring Kyle's concert.

Her heart sank at the thought.

"Your Majesty, did your meeting with the King of York go well?" Emerys asked cautiously. "I can see that you are out of sorts."

Emerald glanced out the window at her kingdom, pushing a lock of hair out of her face. "No, it didn't, and now I'm a mess."

I can't bear to see you hurt, her mother's voice echoed in her mind.

"It's just that…" Emerald bit her lip as she glanced into Emerys's dark eyes.

I have seen some of the things that have transpired, and I worry for you.

"What am I to do, Emerys?" Emerald breathed. "King Samir says the other kingdoms are questioning if my child is a bastard! He doesn't even know about the twins. Can you imagine the extra trouble that's going to bring? The United Kingdoms are still pressuring us to dismantle the cyborgs, questioning

Derek and my gift, and siding with Olympia. Nobody understands what all has transpired with the hostage Gwen—and Samir thinks that the other kingdoms wouldn't even bat an eye about it due to my kingdom being overpowered." Emerald shot him a look. "And now, the only source of my happiness is about to be crushed."

Emerys looked grim. "Master Kyle?"

She nodded. "Wait until I tell him. He's going to be so upset." Emerald placed a hand on her stomach. "King Samir says that he will be requesting a DNA test on my child as soon as it's born in order to establish that it is Derek's. That is, if I choose to remain with Kyle. If I want to avoid the test, then I must cut all ties with Kyle."

Emerald felt the stress just thinking about it. Her stomach hurt. The babies were doing flips inside her. She placed a hand on her belly to try and calm them.

"Everything is all my fault," she whispered.

"It is not your fault."

"Sadly, it is," Emerald said. "I was born a royal. I knew the life I am required to live. Councilor, I love Kyle with all my heart. We are meant to be as one— that I do know for certain. However…" She paused, fighting tears. "Palace life does not suit him. And with me being pregnant and him being a wild soul, it's all too much for him. Can you cage a wild animal? Can you capture fire and contain it in a bottle?" Emerald sighed bitterly. "Now I must tell him that our love is causing further erosion between the United Kingdoms. I can see his reaction now."

She fell back into her chair. Emerys moved next to her with a deep look of concern.

"Emerys, I cannot bear this secret," Emerald began. "One child is His Majesty's, and the other is Master Kyle's." She looked at Emerys to see his reaction, and it was as she expected. He couldn't contain his surprise. "This, in particular, was not my doing, Councilor. Yes, I fell in love with Master Kyle while I was away from the palace. But with His Majesty…" Emerald paused. "It was under different circumstances."

Emerys frowned. "You needn't say more. His Majesty was *different* while his advisor was here."

For a long while, they sat in silence.

"Kyle wants me to divorce Derek. I cannot lose him, Councilor. But if I do stay with him, Arcadia, the United Kingdoms…everything would fall into chaos. What am I to do?"

His dark eyes met hers. "In regard to Master Kyle?"

"Everything."

Emerys sighed, then took a long pause before continuing. "As much as it pains me to say this for Your Majesty's personal pursuit of happiness, I would highly advise against divorcing His Majesty, and I think you know that as well. You will lose this kingdom, as the law in effect would grant King Derek the entire kingdom since Damaris made him his heir. Can you imagine what the United Kingdoms' reaction would be? We cannot lose you. You are the fiber of this kingdom. If we lose you, we lose Arcadia. And if you choose to keep Master Kyle as you are doing now, the kingdoms would fall into chaos as you said."

She felt even worse than before because in her heart of hearts, she knew he was right.

"I know," she breathed. "You can see my dilemma. I cannot lose this kingdom or destroy the United Kingdoms, even for love."

"That is why kings take consorts."

"Not queens," Emerald emphasized.

"Not queens, as it would put into question the parentage of the children."

Emerald bit her lip.

Emerys sucked in his breath, then continued. "Though I am not usually in favor of such things, it has been a thing in many kingdoms throughout history. I see only one option that could somewhat please you."

Emerald perked up, wiping away her tears. "What is it?"

"You do not see Master Kyle—in public. I can arrange private meetings, in the same place, perhaps once a week. Master Kyle will be flown in secret to the arranged place. There you can spend a few hours a week with him to satisfy your love. No other contact."

Her heart sank down to the pit of her stomach. "Master Kyle will not like it."

"Neither will the United Kingdoms if you continue down your path," Emerys pressed. "This entire situation could shatter Arcadia. I worry about our alliances." They exchanged glances. "The world is watching *you*, Your Majesty." Emerys rose from his seat. "I will leave you to your thoughts. Send a transmission when you have made a decision so I know how to proceed from here."

"I will need to speak to Kyle about everything," Emerald said. "Whatever I decide."

"Understandably so."

He bowed, then paused at the door. "If it is any consolation, the citizens of Arcadia love the idea of you with the rock star. They support your love."

"It's just not enough," Emerald said, not glancing at him.

"Indeed. Just not enough to convince the royals of the United Kingdoms."

He left Emerald alone. She got up from her seat. Another kick in utero. They were moving.

Glancing out at her kingdom, she leaned her forehead on the glass.

"What am I to do…" she whispered under her breath, a stream of tears running down her cheeks.

✦ ✦ ✦

Kyle was outside on her patio when she returned to her chambers, smoking a cigarette and staring at the view of Arcadia.

Emerald managed a deep breath, terrified. She couldn't lose him. She couldn't subject their child to a humiliating life. As she walked toward the patio door, Zaphod cawed. Sadly, Emerald looked at the bird, then walked toward him. Stroking his feathers.

"I'm scared," she confessed.

Zaphod cooed as if understanding.

Blinking back fresh tears, Emerald wiped them away, then headed to the patio. As she slid the door open, their eyes met, searching for what the other would say.

Silently, Kyle put out his cigarette, then came up to her, giving her a long and warm embrace.

Emerald leaned her head into his chest, tightly hugging him in return as he softly ran his hands over her hair.

"Em…"

"Kyle," she started, glancing up at him. "I'm really sorry about last night. I didn't mean to hurt you."

His fiery eyes sparkled as his face released tension. "Em, I'm sorry too. I know you are under a lot of stress, being pregnant and ruling a kingdom." His face turned serious. "It did hurt hearing that…you won't marry me. I'm not gonna lie, I'm still torn up about it."

Emerald bit her lip. "There is something that I need to talk to you about."

Kyle stiffened, his face solemn.

"I just met with Samir," she said.

"Samir?"

"Derek's father."

"Ah, fuck, here we go," Kyle said, turning away from her, leaning against the railing.

"He heard about you and me, so he decided to make a visit," Emerald said as she came up next to him, leaning with him against the railing.

"Did you tell him that you're with me now?"

"Kyle, I'm serious."

"So am I!" Kyle snapped, turning toward her. "We are *together*, Em. People are going to have to come to terms with it, including Derek's father."

Suddenly, her stomach jolted, the babies seemingly sensing her anxiety. "Kyle. Our relationship is affecting our relations with the other kingdoms."

Kyle's eye flared. "And there it is," he shot back, gritting his teeth. "You are embarrassed to be seen with me by *your* people."

"Not at all!" Emerald said defensively. "Kyle, I love you. I want to be with you."

"Then *be* with me, Em. Why are you worried about all this bullshit?" Kyle held her hand up to his lips, kissing the top of it as his face melted into compassion and love and warmth. "I'm yours. I want to marry you. I want to raise our children. I fought my entire future life to be with you. I don't want anything else but you." His eyes sparkled with his own tears. "And when you said last night that you 'couldn't' marry me…well, it hurt. Real bad. It was a knife to the heart."

There was a churn in her stomach at the mention of marriage. "Kyle…" Emerald paused, then sighed. "It's impossible for us to get married."

His eyes burned a deep fiery red. "*Who* said that? *Samir*? *The councilor*? Or *you*?"

"I am already married…" she began.

"To a *jackass* who's done some godawful things to you, Em," Kyle fumed. "Let's not forget the fucking asshole is conspiring with your mother to change the face of the world!"

"I haven't forgotten that."

Kyle began pacing. "Then why do you want to remain married to him?"

"Have you even thought about your child, or the children, for one moment?" Emerald countered.

"Of course I have! I think about it constantly!"

"If I stay with you, the United Kingdoms will force the children to take a DNA test right after I give birth. When they find out that one of the children is yours, the child's fate will be decided by the Arcadian court. They might rule that our child is taken away and raised in a royal house. Maybe not, and they will be raised at that palace, but not with every luxury of a prince. Meanwhile, Derek's child will always be above ours!" She was shouting at this point, not even realizing it.

"You mean *I* don't have *any* say over my child? A fucking court does?"

She couldn't avoid answering, but she really wanted to.

"Yes…" Emerald started. "It can be all avoided if I am not subjected to the DNA test."

He looked like he'd been hit by a ton of bricks. Kyle suddenly got quiet. Really quiet. Scary quiet.

"I can't bear that, Kyle," Emerald sobbed in a whisper. "I cannot bear to have *our* child's fate revealed to the *world*. Can you imagine what our child will go through? What we will go through? To have *our* child treated lower than Derek's." Emerald searched for any sort of reaction from him, but he remained still. "On top of it all, if I did divorce Derek, I would lose the entire kingdom, and it would belong to Derek. I cannot have that either. Councilor Emerys advised that we should not be seen publicly anymore, that he can arrange a time and place for us to meet in secret."

"In *secret*," Kyle repeated.

"Yes…" Emerald bit her lip. "He would make all the arrangements for us to meet, once a week."

He walked up to her, making Emerald keenly aware of his fury. "Are you listening to yourself right now?"

Emerald stood in silence.

"*Once a week*? And oh yeah, by the way, I can't see my own kid if I don't agree to this once a week bullshit? I didn't fucking sign up for this, Em! Why would you do this to us? I fucking went through hell and back. For what? So I can see you fucking once a week? So I can't see my child grow up like a normal father?" Kyle's body radiated more magic. "You know, I'm starting to think you *want* to stay married to him!"

"No, I don't!"

"Well, then why is it so hard for you to make the right decision? To be with the one you love?" Kyle yelled. "Seriously! I don't understand!" His body shook with rage. "I don't want to be your paramour! I don't want to be your 'fuck buddy!' I want to be your man! Your husband! I am not one for marrying, Em. I swore I'd never get married in my previous life. But you? You mean the fucking world to me. I am committed to you! And for what?" He raised his voice even louder as he turned away, pacing. "So you can remain married to that fucking asshole fuck while I'm some side piece of cock? Is that all I am?"

"No!" Emerald cried.

"Then *divorce* his ass!" Kyle shouted. "Leave this fucking place permanently and live your life with me! I will take care of you. I will take care of the children. I have money now and can get whatever we need to live our fucking life. Just leave!"

Emerald flinched as her whole body shook.

"I'm serious, Em! You have a choice to make, even if you think you don't."

There was a long, hard silence between them. He didn't move from his spot, just stared at her, his eyes radiating fury, anger, and disappointment.

"It's not that easy…" she whispered.

He didn't say anything, which made everything worse.

After a long pause, Kyle said, "I'm going. I have a show tonight." He stormed away, then went invisible.

Emerald fell to her knees, then buried her face in her hands, sobbing. Snot ran from her nose, and bile ran up her throat. The children in the womb kicked furiously, squirming from the stress.

CHAPTER 65

♦

WHITE

The citadel gardens were in high bloom. Thousands of roses of all colors furled open, their fragrance lingering in the cool air. Perfumes of the blooming roses lingered in her nose. The manicured shrubs had just been cut, adding to the fresh garden smell. Vines entangled the magnificent sculptures of the ancient justices and the God of Light, as well as the symbol of the Spectrum of Magic.

Elyathi admired the many varieties as they passed by. She picked a blossom, smelling its fragrant petals. It reminded her of Samir. She placed the rose next to her heart.

In the new world, I will finally see you, Samir. For now, your son will have to do.

She paused, reflecting on Suresh's last moments. Her soul still hurt from the loss. She fought back a tear as she gritted her teeth. *I will make you eat your vile filth, Ikaria.* She couldn't believe that she wasn't able to take Ikaria's magic. She had the power to hold out her hand and cast her spell to drain life forces…yet still that witch defied her once again!

Another thought came over her. Something that Ikaria had told her while imprisoned.

Elyathi glanced at the rose one last time, holding it close, then continued on through the gardens. She moved along the path, choosing the one that the high justices would take. As she did so, she saw High Justice Belinda from afar, near her favorite spot in the gardens.

Though she did truly believe that Belinda was devoted to the God of Light,

Elyathi felt that she had been always hiding her true self. But it was nothing more than a hunch.

"High Justice Belinda," Elyathi said as she approached.

Belinda glanced up, then gave her a closed-lip smile. "Lady Elyathi, what a pleasant surprise."

"What are you doing here? I thought that the High Court was making preparations for the execution."

"They are," Belinda said. "I have done my part and wait for the others to do theirs."

"I look forward to ending the life of that wicked, sinful witch's sister," Elyathi said, raising her chin.

"Yes. We'll be one step closer to capturing that woman's power once and for all," Belinda said. She rose to her feet. "Might I walk with you? The gardens are quite lovely, and I would like the company. There are a few things to discuss."

"Of course."

Belinda smiled, this time a true and bright smile. "Come. This way."

The two women followed the path, Elyathi holding her rose close to her.

"What is it that you want to speak to me about?" Elyathi asked.

"It is about your daughter," Belinda said. "The trial is soon. With your daughter being able to utilize the dark side of the Spectrum to drain life out of anyone she chooses, I think it would be most fitting for her to be at Ayera's trial. Ikaria will be there no doubt." Belinda turned to her, her eyes glimmering a deep red. "We'll have Emerald make Ikaria stay put as she sucks her life away for you to finally take ahold of the violet magic."

Elyathi didn't like that one bit. She wanted to be the one with the power to overcome the witch. But there was truth behind Belinda's logic.

"I will contact Derek about Emerald and see if she has given birth yet," Elyathi said.

"Just have him go to the time right after the birth."

"It's not as easy as one thinks, High Justice," Elyathi said. "Some have said that splitting time is like splitting hairs."

"Certainly not for Derek," Belinda said, then breathed. "In any case, please send word to him. It is imperative that he brings Emerald to this time *before* the trial begins."

"I will," Elyathi said with a nod.

"Also, was he able to retrieve the scientist?" Belinda asked curiously.

"Not yet, but he's close," Elyathi said. "He has a device to control the cyborg scientist. All he needs to do is wait for him to be repaired and awake, then he'll have him."

"Awake?" Belinda said, then shrugged. "Technology is so fickle. I pray for his success. I'm sure he will follow through and return victorious."

Elyathi couldn't tell if Belinda was being sarcastic or sincere. She paused, looking down at the rose, thinking about that memory of her crying in Samir's arms…

Belinda eyed her, giving her a knowing smile. "Lady Elyathi, I've now known you for many years now and can see that something is on your mind. You don't typically come wandering around these parts of the gardens without purpose."

"Indeed, you know me quite well."

"What is on your mind?"

"When I was in World Sector Six with the High Inquisitor, Rubius, the sorceress told me something. Something that I have been troubled with."

"The sorceress? I am sure that whatever that woman said, it was all planned to sow seeds of contempt. That is what she does."

"Be that as it may, I have come to ask you if there is any truth to her words."

Belinda furrowed her brow. "What did she say?"

"That back in time, my husband, King Damaris, ordered my daughter's blood to be extracted for the purpose of experimentation, ultimately to be infused into the cyborgs. A magical army, made of magic and machinery."

"Of course he did," Belinda said. "That is why we have been after the cyborgs infused with magic. You can see why we want to know all about them. They have much power and are easy to control, unlike a human. I fail to understand why this troubles you so."

"But how did he get that idea?"

"Lady Elyathi, I hope you aren't insinuating what I think you are."

"You know how much my past hurts me, High Justice. So when my past is brought up and the reality of it is in doubt, I must know." Elyathi stopped walking. "The sorceress had seen it in Damaris's mind. Dreams of creating the army. That in his 'vision,' he would rule all kingdoms for all of time. I was with Damaris for many years. He was always a wicked man, obsessed with *The Spectrum* and the idea of magic. But when my daughter was born, he became beyond delusional, with visions that I now know to be from the dark side of the yellow. The sorceress herself said that these visions were 'planted.' Tell me, is this true, and was Tyllos the one to do it?"

Belinda raised an eyebrow. "Absolutely not, Lady Elyathi. That would be heresy," she said firmly. "I can assure you that neither Tyllos, nor anyone in the High Court had a part in Damaris's delusions. You should know that every word that comes out of Ikaria's mouth is a lie. I am disappointed that you even entertained the notion, thinking that there was a shred of truth to her falsehood. Do you doubt our loyalty to the God of Light and his prophecy? Have you ever been witness to us being swayed by others?"

Elyathi eyed her. "I never doubted your loyalty, High Justice."

"Then close your mind to these doubts, Lady," Belinda said. "We are on your side. Always have been. We want the God of Light's new world to rise, for it is his will, is it not?"

"We all must discern truth from time to time, High Justice." Elyathi bowed. "I am sorry I wasted your time on such a trivial matter."

Belinda folded her hands against her dress. "Nothing from you is trivial, nor wasted."

"Thank you, High Justice," Elyathi said in a regretful tone. "I will head back to my quarters and make contact with Derek."

Belinda gave a soft smile. "Please send word once you do. The trial is soon, and I do not want to delay."

"I will. Thank you," Elyathi said.

As she turned away, Elyathi clenched her necklace, the one with the blue gem. She filled her soul with the blue magic, felt it pouring over her as she walked before flashing away.

CHAPTER 66

◆

Loud wails were coming from the Queen's chambers.

Alarmed, Celeste ran over to the door, knocking. "My Queen! Are you all right?"

More wailing sobs.

Celeste let herself inside and stopped.

A shimmering greenish-yellow magical barrier covered the Queen as she sobbed and choked on her tears.

Celeste, panicking, immediately ran over to her, kneeling beside her. "My Queen! What happened? Are you in pain?"

Emerald continued to sob and sob. The harder she cried, the brighter her magic became.

"Do you need me to call a doctor?"

Emerald shook her head. "Kyle…" she said through choking sobs.

The magic around Emerald became more intense.

Celeste noticed that the magic shifted to a dark green. She knew what that meant.

"Your magic!" Celeste warned, as she took a step back. "It's dark green…"

Emerald didn't hear her warning, sobbing uncontrollably.

The dark green magic streamed to Celeste, piercing right into the depths of her soul.

Celeste screamed. Uncontrollable pain, hurt, sadness, despair…her life was being torn from her body.

Emerald didn't move, didn't hear…or didn't care…she was too deep in her sorrow.

Celeste screamed once more, struggling with all her might as she crawled her way to the doorway.

"Your Majesty! Please! You're hurting me!"

The magic weakened its grip on her body and soul for an instant. Immediately, Celeste bolted for the door, then slammed it shut, shaken.

She grabbed her communicator, then pressed speed dial.

CHAPTER 67

◆

RED

Kyle rode fast and hard through the streets of Arcadia. It was raining, but he didn't give a fuck. In fact, the rain cooled his hot temper. He was pissed as fuck. At this point, he didn't know what the fuck to think or do. Be the Queen's forever lapdog? What if Derek returned? And their child…They didn't even get to figure that shit out because he left. What was Emerald even thinking?

He drove as if he were on autopilot, thinking about what the God of Light told him. The big man upstairs had warned Kyle that he would face consequences and hardships if he returned to his original time.

Kyle didn't want to think about it. Any of it. He needed to take his mind off everything. Play at the show. Have fun. Get bombed. Every time he got bombed, Kyle always thought clearer in the morning. This whole thing would blow over, and they would talk in the morning. Maybe at that point Emerald would tell him that she chose him over appeasing those asshole fucks in the United Kingdoms.

Kyle rode to a parking structure to where the main event was for the evening, driving up the ramps until he hit the middle level, then swung a left over to the valet section. A valet approached as Kyle got off his bike.

"Here, man," Kyle said, gesturing to his bike.

The valet's eyes went wide. "You're Kyle Trancer."

"In the flesh."

The valet handed him a ticket. "I'll take care of your ride, man."

"Thanks."

Kyle stuffed the ticket in his leather vest's inside pocket, then grabbed his pack of cigarettes. He exited the structure, quickly getting drenched in the pouring rain. He managed to find some cover for a second, then lit the smoke. At that moment, his personal communicator buzzed.

I'm not fucking answering anything, he thought. *Tonight is for me.* He continued to puff his smoke as he headed toward the event.

It wasn't as big as the last event, but it still was no small gig. The event was in the mid-levels, a large club that was very popular with the eastern sector.

He went to the backstage door, then knocked. No answer.

Kyle kicked the door angrily as he puffed his smoke.

The door opened, the bouncer recognizing him. "You're all wet, man."

"You think?"

"Come on. Let's get you dry." The bouncer waved him in, then shut the door behind him.

The two walked down the backstage hall, heading to a room where the band was already at. All his bandmates, and several women, noticed he was sopping wet.

"What happened to you? You get flushed down the toilet?" Diego snorted.

He was so angry about Emerald that he couldn't make a snide retort.

"About the other night…" Diego started to say, coming up to him.

Kyle felt Diego's mind. He was searching for the right words to apologize.

He could be a complete asshole and punch Diego in the jaw. But after all the shit that he had just gone through, Kyle couldn't handle another fight. Instead, he mustered up his energy and cleared his throat. "Water under the bridge, my man."

Diego smiled as he gave him a bro handshake. "Good man."

Kyle sighed as he plopped down on the couch, still wet as fuck.

"Glad to see you girls work it out," Remy said.

"Ha-ha, Remy," Diego said.

Remy eyed Kyle's outfit. "You might wanna put on another outfit before the show. We still have some time."

"Does it look like I have another outfit?" Kyle said, irritated. He popped open his flask, taking a drink. He didn't want to think about anything anymore.

"What happened now?" Diego said.

"Don't wanna talk about it," Kyle said, finishing his cigarette and lighting another.

"Em, huh? You two get in a little tiff?"

His face darkened, then took a drag. "I said I *don't* wanna talk about it."

"Probably the pregnancy. That shit makes women all sorts of crazy," Diego said, taking a swig from his flask.

Kyle narrowed his eyes. Rage, anger, wrath radiated from them from behind his shades. God, he was so angry.

From the corner of his eye, Kyle watched as Diego cut a line. He followed the trail as his friend snorted it up. Next to the line Diego snorted was another line of coke, untouched.

It was calling his name, tempting him to take his mind off all the shit that had happened.

"I know you don't do this shit anymore, but I cut this for you. Peace offering, you know?" Diego said. "It's yours if you want it. You don't have to, though."

Kyle stared at it. God, he fucking wanted it. Just to take away everything he felt on his broken inside.

"You look like you could use it," Diego said, giving him a friendly tap on the arm.

Kyle looked up, seeing the other band members doing lines. Except Remy. He'd always been the sober one of the group. On the other side of the room, Kyle watched as Glacia did a line, unashamed.

"You too?" Kyle called out to her.

"Yeah. Twice a year," she said, shrugging like it was no big deal.

Wonder if Em knows.

"Sometimes, you just need to let go of the stress," Glacia said, then came over to him, plopping down. "I know you are with her, but please don't say anything. Nobody knows except these guys and a good friend in the mid-levels."

"I won't," Kyle said. He felt a sharp pang of guilt, but this secret wasn't for him to tell. Was it? Did it matter right now? He was beyond angry.

"Remy, you don't mind her doing it?" Kyle asked.

"She can control her usage. Unlike *others*," Remy added.

"Remy always gotta ruin the fun," Diego said, laughing.

Kyle watched as the group snorted their lines, getting completely fucked up. He wanted to be just as fucked up as they were.

I don't want to feel anymore. It hurts too much.

"Pass the glass," Kyle said.

Diego smiled.

"But no one can know about this," he added.

"You think we would tell the Queen we were doing illegal shit?" Diego scoffed.

"No one will say anything," Kamren said.

Kyle looked straight at Glacia.

"What? You think I would tell her? Especially when I've been keeping this from her myself?"

Diego pushed the mirrored plate over to him. The line stared back. Waiting for him.

Then Kyle pinched his left nostril and snorted the line of coke just as his communicator vibrated again.

CHAPTER 68

◆

GREEN

All around her was dark green energy. She didn't care. All Emerald could do was continuously sob. She could have sworn she heard Celeste at one point, but she must have imagined it.

It didn't matter. Nothing mattered. Kyle was gone once again. And this time, it was her doing. *Again.* But she'd made that conscious decision. He didn't understand anything of what she had to deal with. Their own child would suffer tremendously.

More sobs. Her dark energy swirled around her.

Sharp and sudden excruciating pain shot through her body as a burst of energy exploded from her.

Emerald stopped mid-sob, then looked down. A gush of liquid began running down her thighs, soaking into her dress, followed by another excruciating pain.

Her water had broken.

"Help!" Emerald screamed. "Help!"

There was a scuffle from outside her door. More pains.

"Help!"

It's all right, said a voice inside her mind. *I'm here.*

Emerald glanced around wildly, not seeing anyone. More pain.

Celeste flung open her bedroom door, looked at the water all over the floor, then gasped.

Emerald, helpless, looked at the large water stain, then at Celeste. "I—"

"I'll get the palace physician!" She turned away. "Cyndi!"

Cyndi appeared with a stunned look on her face as she ran to Emerald.

"Here, let me help you get to your bed." Cyndi wrapped her arm around Emerald's waist, the other arm over her shoulder.

Emerald mustered all her strength and got to her feet, then shuffled to her bed with Cyndi's help.

Celeste appeared in the room again. "The doctor is on his way. In the meantime, we are to get you in a light robe."

"Thank you," she breathed.

"At least you aren't casting that dark magic now."

Emerald shot her a look. "It was real, then? I thought I imagined it."

Celeste nodded her head.

"Did I hurt you?"

"Yes. But I'm fine now. I know you didn't mean to," Celeste said.

More pain. Emerald groaned then cried out. After it faded, she glanced at Celeste. "I'm sorry, Celeste."

"I know. It's all right." Celeste smiled, then eyed her belly. "Do you want me to call Master Kyle?"

Kyle had been so very angry when he left. But it was his child…

"Yes, please let him know. I want him here," Emerald said in a breathless voice. "I know he has a show…but I want him here…"

"I did try to call him earlier when you—" She bit her lip. "When the green energy attacked me. I couldn't get ahold of him, so I dialed Emerys."

Kyle hadn't picked up the communicator, even when Celeste called him. She felt sick at the thought.

"I'm sure Master Kyle will pick up this time. He was probably on stage already," Celeste added.

Another pain, and Emerald flinched. "Call Glacia. I know she has tonight off, but I would like her with me."

Celeste left the room as Emerald's next contractions started. She heard muffled words outside. The doctors would arrive soon, if they hadn't already.

A few minutes went by, then Celeste came back. "My Queen, I cannot get ahold of either one of them," she said. "I'll keep trying if you want me to."

Emerald nodded her head. "Yes. I want them here."

The birth pangs kept coming, harder and faster. Emerald cried out in pain, her handmaidens doing all that they could to comfort her as Cyndi helped her out of her clothes, putting a silk robe on her.

Emerald was in and out of sleep when the doctor showed up. He assured her that she would be okay as he directed the other nurses who came with him, as well as to the other handmaidens.

Celeste appeared at Emerald's side as Emerald cried in pain, holding her hand.

"She is fully dilated," the doctor said to a nurse.

Emerald darted her eyes to Celeste, but she looked downcast. "I've been trying all night, My Queen. I haven't heard from either of them."

A wave of tears flooded Emerald's eyes at Celeste's words. The pains kept coming harder and faster. The nurses helped Emerald up, exposing her back. An assistant shot something in Emerald's back, then laid her down. They assisted her into a birthing position. Everything was such a blur…though the pain seemed to have subsided.

The voices all blurred together, but one voice rang out. "I still can't get ahold of them. I must have called him nearly thirty times now…"

Kyle wasn't coming. The birth of their child, and he wasn't here.

Emerald started sobbing.

"You're doing great," called out the doctor.

She couldn't help but cry out in desperation.

"Keep pushing!"

Emerald turned her head to the side as she cried and suddenly sucked in her breath. Derek stood next to the wall, watching her with anxiety, worry, and concern.

"Derek?" Emerald whispered through her pain and tears.

"The King isn't here, Your Majesty," the doctor told her. "Keep pushing!"

The world was tinged blue with bright blue sparkles wisping in the air. Emerald blinked, staring at Derek. Was she imagining this? Was it the drugs the doctor gave her?

Derek's image neared her, as if he were a transparent spirit that no one could see except her. "Derek? You are here?" she said.

"Do you want me to leave?"

"No. Please don't leave," Emerald answered. "I don't want to be alone."

"I'm not leaving," the doctor assured her.

The world slowed to a crawl. Derek knelt beside her, then held out his hand. "I…I'm so sorry…"

Emerald accepted his hand, then held it close. His eyes went wide, then his face flushed.

"I know it's not entirely your fault," Emerald said, new tears forming. "The final result of this…it was because of the sorceress."

Angry and confused, tears trickled down his cheeks, and he wiped them away. "I've always loved you. I still love you," he said. His blue eyes radiated deep sorrow. "You are my everything."

"I never thought it would be this way," Emerald said. "Please, stay with me. I'm scared…"

Derek gave her a hopeful smile. "Gladly."

The world returned to full color, the speed of time returning to normal. Derek knelt by her side in his dimensional spirit form—which only she could see—holding her hand. His hand was warm, soft, and strong. Reassuring.

His blue eyes sparkled as he held her hand, stroking her hair.

"It's coming!" the doctor yelled. "Push!"

Emerald squeezed Derek's hand tightly.

Then a baby's scream rang out.

CHAPTER 69

◆

RED

He was so fucked up. He didn't know what the fuck was going on, but did it matter? He was having a damn good time. The crowd fucking loved him. He was their idol. Everything he did, they went wild. The song, they loved the song. The hot girls screaming to marry him…they *wanted him*. Professing their undying love for him. Their praise gave him the ultimate high. He felt like he was on top of the fucking world. He was here, famous, as he'd always wanted to be.

Why couldn't Em be happy for him? Why couldn't she be just as excited to marry him as those chicks?

Fury bubbled up inside of him just thinking about it.

"Fucking sing, dammit!" Diego said, laughing. "I know you're fucked up, but come on!"

"Yeah…" Kyle said. The crowd was fucking all over the place, swaying here and there. God he *was* so fucked up.

He started singing the song. The one that people couldn't get enough of. The one that people idolized him for. Made him fucking legend.

The one for Emerald.

Oh God, Emerald.

As he was singing, Kyle thought about their fight. He wanted to marry her, goddammit. Why couldn't she just divorce the asshole fuck? She was embarrassed by him, just like all the other fuckers in the upper levels.

More girls screamed at him.

"Marry me!" screamed one woman.

"I wanna have your babies!" screamed another woman.

They all screamed that. They were horny as fuck for him and wanted to marry his ass. But all he wanted was to be with Em. But she wasn't there and didn't want to fucking marry him. She didn't give a fuck about him. How could she suggest that they only see each other once a goddamn fucking week? Not to mention their *child*…he had no say in the whole fucking matter? The thought made him seethe.

Everything became a blur as he sang. Faces, the stage floor. Images of her angry face haunted him. He'd lived a whole fucking life searching for her.

Kyle suddenly stopped singing mid-song.

He'd fucking gone through HELL for her.

"FUCK!" he screamed.

He finally found her and came back for her.

He smashed the guitar.

Emerald didn't care.

Kyle grabbed the guitar, then swiped it into the ground, smashing it.

Em…I fucking love you!

"FUCKING FUCK!"

Smashed the guitar again. More pieces flew everywhere.

"Dude…" Remy whispered as the audience went silent.

I want to marry you! I want to live by your side my whole life!

"FUCK ME!" he shouted, smashing the guitar again.

But no, I'm just a fuck buddy to you! Some fucking nobody!

Rage flooded him, pounding his temples. His heart beat fiercely as he continued to smash the guitar over and over again.

The guitar she gave him.

Smashed it again.

It all meant nothing.

The band stopped playing. The audience gaped at him.

"FUCK!" he screamed again. This time, he let the guitar go, then he kicked it. Pieces scattered across the stage. But he didn't give a fuck.

Kyle turned, then bolted off the stage.

CHAPTER 70

◆

His machine beeped. Sandstorm detected.

Thaddeus clicked the button on the device, then took one last look. In the distance, the sky had a deep red patch against the orangish atmosphere, almost like a bloodstain on a bandage. Soon, the sandstorm would hit where he stood.

He checked his mask, making sure the straps were secured, then turned to the men. "Sandstorm heading this way," he said through the mask, his words sounding mechanical. "About two hours until it hits."

The group he was with nodded, then grabbed their scavenger bags, throwing them into the vehicle. He did the same, grabbing his sack and tossing it in. His was much heavier than the others; he had found some old metal devices and chunks that they could melt down to make new machinery.

The driver waved to the group, gesturing for them to get seated. Thaddeus jumped into the back bed of the vehicle, along with the others, and the engine started.

They drove through the empty terrain, seeing the old remnants of the kingdom of Arcadia. Ever since that man Rubius—or rather, *Kyle*—had appeared to them, Thaddeus couldn't stop thinking of him.

What were the chances that a gifted man, who claimed to be from another time, just showed up at their citadel? Rumors after Kyle left circulated that maybe, just maybe, this was a sign for their time. For as long as Thaddeus could remember, the earth citadels had dreamed of overthrowing the High Court and reuniting with the skies.

Everyone had been waiting for a sign.

He frowned. By the sounds of it, the white-gifted that Kyle spoke of was extremely dangerous. Even a powerful gifted like Kyle seemed frightened of her.

I wonder what the strange man is up to, he thought.

Their vehicle drove up to a set of iron doors in the side of a giant mountain. After it fully opened, the vehicle drove inside, the doors closing behind them.

When the vehicle parked, the group split up to shower. He stripped down, throwing off his mask, then stepped into the warm water. He wasn't that dirty, but the healing, glowing green water felt good on his body, and it would wash away any toxic materials on him.

After the shower, Thaddeus threw on a fresh set of clothes and walked to his station. One of the other citadel members came up to him, slapping him on the back.

"Heard you found some good scraps out there. Even an intact machine," he said.

"It was where we had been digging before. Just went a little lower and found the sucker. I think it was a computer case."

"Computer?"

"Isn't that what the ancients called it?" Thaddeus shrugged.

"No idea." The man smiled, then took off as Thaddeus reached his own station. He sat down, then dialed into the communications device. His screen device glowed brighter, and the map of the underground citadels came up onto the device. All the icons were red except one, which was blinking green.

They had a message.

Thaddeus flipped the switch, hearing the connection being established.

"Hello, hello? Citadel Fifty-Two? Hello?" said a voice.

Thaddeus reached for his input sound device, flipped it on, then set it close to his mouth. "Hello. I hear you. This is Citadel Fifty-Two."

"Copy. This is Citadel Twenty-Five from World Sector Six."

"What can I do for you, Citadel Twenty-Five?"

"We have been trying to reach your citadel for days."

Thaddeus sighed. "Sorry about that. There have been several sandstorms interfering with our reception."

"That is all right. The important thing is that we finally reached you before the assault."

"Assault?"

"Elder Tekka has declared an emergency. The sky Empress of World Sector Six has been arrested by the High Court and will be publicly executed. Tekka has deemed it imperative to rescue the Empress and is calling for any reinforcements to help stop the execution at all costs."

Thaddeus's heart pounded. The sky Empress? Executed by the High Court?

"Hello? Citadel Fifty-Two? You still there?"

Thaddeus turned to the input device. "Yes, yes. I'm still here."

"We have two gifted from the skies with us. They are from the World Sector Six citadel. They barely managed to escape from a gifted of the High Court. They claim it is a woman with the white gift. Says she can steal magic permanently."

It was exactly what Kyle had said. A white-gifted.

"Did you say white-gifted?" Thaddeus reaffirmed.

"Yes."

"When is this assault? Who is leading it?"

"We were contacted by our sources above. The sorceress Ikaria, the sky Empress's sister, is leading the assault on the High Court Citadel. She has declared the time is near. Everyone is preparing as we speak. I will send the coordinates and details of when the charge will take place. If you are to join, ready any and all weapons you have. The two gifted with us are prepared to fight—including our one and only gifted from this citadel."

Thaddeus's heart hammered in his chest with excitement and worry. "Copy. Let me get in contact with the elders here in the citadel and get back to you."

"Make haste, Citadel Fifty-Two. Our leader is planning on leaving shortly, with or without reinforcements. Our elder wants to make it in time before the Empress's execution."

"Right away," Thaddeus said.

White noise, then the transmission ended.

Thaddeus jumped out of his chair, running to the elders' meeting chambers, knocking loudly on the iron door.

There was a clank, then Elder Nile appeared, looking rather startled.

Thaddeus tried to catch his breath.

"Thaddeus? What has happened?" Elder Stone called out from inside the room.

"Excuse me, elders, but there is an urgent message from one of the other citadels," Thaddeus said, coming into the room.

"What is it?" Elder Moon asked. The other two elders looked at him. "Which citadel?"

"A ground citadel from World Sector Six. Far west of their sector," Thaddeus began. "They are gathering their entire citadel and leading an assault on the High Court."

Elder Stone jumped up, nearing him. "They are doing *what*?"

"They are heading to the High Court? Have they lost their wits?" said Elder Nile.

Thaddeus thought of the Empress. She was about to lose her life. She must be some empress if she stood up to the High Court. It could be their chance. A chance to rise up against the High Court once and for all. All those years of planning, and this could be it.

"What is it, Thaddeus? Tell us!" Elder Moon said.

"They are going to stop the Empress of World Sector Six from being executed."

The elders exchanged glances.

"They have two gifted with them from the skies to help them lead the charge." He paused. "And a third gifted from below."

"Below?"

"He resides in the underground citadel," Thaddeus continued.

"I cannot believe they are going to the High Court," Elder Nile said. "They are fools."

"I don't believe them to be fools. They are doing what is right," Elder Stone said.

Elder Moon stood up. "We are going to help them."

"But the High Court has many gifted with them. What are a few weapons against an army of gifted?" Elder Nile argued.

"Weapons with magic, lest you forget," Elder Moon said.

"And what of the white-gifted?" he countered.

"When was the last time we stood up to what was wrong? Why must our people live in fear throughout the centuries, living like worms under a rock? I say we help them!" Elder Moon said. "There have been too many signs recently, all at the same time. Rubius—or Kyle—seeking the green-gifted queen...the very one who dwelled in these lands centuries ago. And the white-gifted has been found within time itself, but she has turned to evil. And a sky empress rebelling against the High Court?" Elder Moon paused, staring at them all. "This is our time. This is our chance to align ourselves with gifted who think like us!"

Thaddeus smiled brightly. "I think, Elder Moon, there are many that would gladly go and fight."

Elder Nile frowned. "So be it. I cannot stop you from fighting. But there will be causalities."

"And that is a risk that we must take," said Elder Stone.

"Thaddeus, gather everyone in the citadel that is willing to go. Arm them with magitech armor and weapons."

"Aye-aye!" Thaddeus said.

Just as he was about to leave, he heard Elder Nile say, "Madness. Utter madness."

"Is it? Or is it madness living under oppression? Sacrificing our gifted to the skies? Afraid of their power?" Elder Moon said.

Thaddeus opened the door, and footsteps echoed behind him. He turned around, then heard Elder Stone call out, "Where are you going?"

"Do you even need to ask?" Elder Moon said.

Elder Stone rose from his seat. "I'm coming too."

Thaddeus walked out of the door, but heard Elder Nile say firmly, "I am staying behind. I'm not going to get myself killed over an impossible battle."

Elder Moon hmphed behind Thaddeus as he walked down the hall, the other elder following.

They were going to rescue the Empress of World Sector Six.

CHAPTER 71

◆

GREEN

Time wasn't as it was. It wove in and out. Was she asleep? Or was she awake? Perhaps she was caught in a twilight sleep, unsure of what was happening. Emerald remembered the fight, going into labor, the doctor, and Derek.

The children. Had they been born?

Confused, Emerald tried to move, but she felt like lead. There were muffled voices, then gentle hands leading her back down in a sleep position. Her mind drifted to Kyle. He had missed the birth of their child. All for what? Because of their fight earlier? Tears formed in her eyes at the thought. He hadn't even bothered to answer the communications from her handmaidens.

In her twilight state, Emerald noticed a sparkling lavender flower next to her bedside. It had a strange glow to it. She weakly reached over to pick up the flower and immediately felt its life force within its stem. It had been made with life magic.

Had Kyle shown up while she was out?

Emerald darted her eyes around the room, still weak. There was no sign of Kyle.

Suddenly, she remembered seeing Derek during the birth. He had been there with her. Was it Derek who left the flower for her?

Emerald recalled the time Derek had surprised her with purple flowers when she woke up after their night of dancing. How happy she had been at the time. Emerald smelled the flower. Its fragrant bloom brought back memories of her and Derek. The innocent feelings that they had toward each other. They were, after all, best of friends growing up.

Do not blame Derek, the sorceress had said to her.

Derek had done everything he could to make it right. His mind had been compromised by the sorceress. It was a lousy excuse, but so was hers. She was the one who killed Kyle under the sorceress's influence. Was that any different than what Derek did to her?

Fresh tears formed in her eyes.

No, it wasn't. It was one and the same.

Derek was trying what he could to counter it...

Any man would have stopped and moved on. Derek had plenty of opportunities. And yet, he didn't, always professing his unwavering love and devotion to her.

In a small way, Emerald felt guilty. But then again, she didn't. Where *was* Kyle in all of this? Missing the birth of their child was unforgivable. What kind of love did they have? Kyle couldn't understand her duties as a queen. He said that he would do anything for her but wouldn't compromise on her queenly duties. She compromised for his music. There wasn't a middle ground, it seemed.

I love him so much, Emerald thought. But was love enough to survive?

She already knew the answer within her soul.

"I made a mistake. A terrible mistake. Why was I so naive?" Emerald whispered under her breath as she cried, staring at the glittering flower.

"Because we are fed lies by the very people who we love and care about most," whispered an all-to-familiar voice.

Suddenly, the world around Emerald faded into nighttime, with Derek's flower glowing at the center. Stars shimmered in the sky, and the ground was of glass.

Emerald lay still in her bed as a figure strode toward her and caressed her hair. Emerald glanced up to see her mother shining down on her, as bright as a star. Her mother looked as beautiful as ever.

"Mother...? Is that you?"

"It is, my daughter." Her mother's gift glowed from her eyes like light streams from a crystal prism.

Emerald breathed. "I can't believe you are here."

"Unfortunately, this is only an illusion while you are asleep, just as you saw me the last time we met," Elyathi said softly. "I used a combination of magics to come back and speak with you. You've been sedated due to a difficult birth."

Emerald paused. "Then it did happen. Everything."

"Yes. And what beautiful children you have."

"I haven't seen them yet," Emerald said, suddenly realizing. She needed to see her children.

"You will when you wake." Her mother smiled, continuing to stroke her hair softly.

"I dreamt of you recently," Emerald said.

"You felt me calling you through my magic."

"You seem so real. Right here in this moment, I swear that I can feel you."

Elyathi touched her chin, gently guiding it upward as she sat next to her. "It is my magic you feel. And do not doubt, I am alive. I have been living in the future. Did you not get my letter?"

Emerald's eyes shifted away from her mother. "I did, though it's been hard to believe at times. Everything that I ever knew about you isn't as I was told."

"I have been through so much, and there is much to discuss. But know this: I have been doing everything in my power for us to be reunited. The portal to travel back to Arcadia has been hidden for a long time. Now, it is finally open, and you are able to travel," Elyathi said. "I want you with me, daughter. You and the children. We can finally live in peace."

"The other time I saw you in a dream, you—"

"I had to warn you." Her mother tenderly touched her hand. "I felt a deep sorrow in your soul. I am crushed knowing that you are in pain." Her eyes turned down in sadness. "Who has done such a thing to you to make it so?"

Emerald's eyes lowered to the pond. How could she look her mother in the eye and tell her what was going on?

Elyathi stared intently, waiting.

Emerald's eyes welled up with tears.

Her mother's face darkened. "A man has done this to you." It wasn't a question, but a knowing fact her mother was all too familiar with.

Emerald's lip quivered as she suppressed her tears. "He said he would help raise the children. He promised to take care of me. I supported his choice to play music, to give him time to himself, so that he can be there for me and the children—so that there would be no regrets and animosity toward me. But the more he did things on his own, the more it broke my heart." Emerald sucked in her breath, then put on a brave face for her mother. "Mother, he wanted me to marry him. But I cannot! I will lose the kingdom. The United Kingdoms will be in an uproar, and I will bring calamity to Arcadia. He was angry, and now he missed the birth of the children."

As the words left Emerald's mouth, everything became real to her, even in her twilight sleep. It had really happened. Kyle wasn't there for her. The writing was on the wall the entire time. How could she have been so stupid?

Emerald looked up at her mother through her tears. "What hurts is that I think he despises me because I am who I am, the complete opposite of him. A royal. Comes from money. Proper. Does everything by the book."

Elyathi held her neck high. "Women like us are unattainable and powerful. And that scares any man, as it should." She leaned in. "You see, my daughter, you have all the power in this situation. Like you, I was in this very position, but I never realized that I had all the power. You are a true gifted—the God of Light chose you for a purpose. You are beautiful in every possible way, and most powerful. There is no gifted like you."

"You think so, Mother?"

"Oh, yes," her mother answered. "This man, he sees your power, your strength. And he knows, deep down, he cannot match that, so he tries to acquire you through marriage. He is selfish in his own desires of the flesh. Momentary passion. And now, since he cannot marry you, he is taking it out on you. Tell me, is it not sinful, what he asks of you? He is asking you to divorce Derek so he can possess you."

Emerald flushed, looking downward, unable to meet her mother's eyes.

"Not only that, this man is asking you to ruin an entire kingdom just to have you."

Her mother was saying what Emerald had been feeling this entire time. Finally, after a long pause, Emerald whispered, "You're right."

"You cannot stay here. For if you do, you will experience more pain, more anger, more dissension. This man will turn away from you and your children." Her mother paused, then said, "Why would you subject yourself to all of this heartache when you have someone that has appreciated everything about you since adolescence?"

Her mother's words echoed in her ears. It was true. Emerald's eyes filled with tears, thinking about Derek. Indeed, he had loved her since her youth. He was there for her. The more she thought about everything, the harder she cried. Her mother held her tight, stroking her long hair, trying to calm her. She kissed her on the top of her head.

"I wish I could make everything right for you, my dearest," her mother said. "But in this world, I cannot. Corruption fills the hearts of mankind, and they are swayed by darkness, as you very well know from reading *The Spectrum*."

Emerald nodded. "I do, Mother. I just didn't realize how bad the world was until now."

Her mother looked at her sadly. "I know of the pain you feel."

"I recently came to understand why you were so sad all the time," Emerald said.

"Indeed. In this world, there are many trials we are put through. What you are facing is one of the hardest, no doubt. These are a testament to our faith and our character. What are you going to choose to do? You have the power to change the outcome. Do you wait for this man to let you be the woman you were meant to be? For you to be a powerful ruler and queen in Arcadia? For him to stand back out of the spotlight and help raise your children? Do you think he has it in his soul to do so? You could be waiting years. Perhaps it will never happen. Or do you do something greater?"

Emerald blinked, listening fully to her mother's words. "You…you want me to change the world with you?"

Elyathi smiled. "I see you know about the God of Light's prophecy."

"I was told…by the very man who broke my heart."

Her mother's eye twitched in anger. "I have known this man who has broken your heart. I know him very well. I watched him for many years in court in the future."

Emerald met her mother's gaze. "He told me that he knew you too, and that you were dangerous. That you can take magic away from others, and that you wanted to change the world. Can you take away magic, Mother? Is that what your power can do?"

Her mother brushed a lock of hair out of Emerald's face. "That I can. I have the power to completely strip someone of their gift. It is my God-given gift, and it is intended to be used for the good of mankind." Her mother leaned in. "As for this man who has hurt you, Rubius—or the one you refer to as Kyle Trancer—I am sad that you have become entangled with a man such as him. A man who pursued pleasure instead of true faith. I watched the High Inquisitor as he gambled all his money away, drank every night until he hit the floor, pursued women like they were his next meal…"

Emerald's heart twisted as her mother recounted Kyle's faults, especially the last one. She felt sick.

"I…I didn't know what he did in his life in the future," Emerald whispered. Her mother's description rang true. It was essentially what he was doing now, and had done in his past.

"I am only telling you this because I love you," she whispered.

"I know," Emerald said as tears flowed down her cheeks. Though they had been separated during a rift in time, it was a hard pill to swallow.

"I did not approve of his *unwavering* love for you. What kind of man who does these things would truly be by your side?" She breathed. "I forbade him from ever trying to reach you, because I did not want to see you hurt. I have seen what has been happening. The arguments, the out-of-control anger, the wild behavior. Missing the birth of the children… He's still the same no matter what time era he lives in."

Emerald sighed. She was tired of being everyone else's shadow. Kyle's complement. King Damaris's daughter. Derek's wife. No. She wanted to show everyone that she could stand on her own two feet. She was Queen Emerald of Arcadia. The first gifted in a thousand years born to mankind. Green-gifted. The power of life and healing.

It was time for her to be her own person.

"What must I do?" Emerald whispered.

"Travel to the future. Let us complete the holy and ancient prophecy together. Through your power, using your true gift of the green, we will change the world to a place of no more tears. No pain. No hurt. No sorrow. All of this will be wiped away, and a new earth will appear. You will be queen of the new land, and a mother to strong children." Her mother leaned in. "And you will forever have a man who truly worships you for the powerful woman you are, and will be a true father to your children."

Emerald slowly met her mother's eyes. "You speak of Derek."

Elyathi nodded. "I have never in my life have seen a man so in love with a woman. You should use that to your advantage. You have all the power, and you can be happy forever with a man serving and worshiping *you*."

"Is that not sinful, Mother? To hold such power over a man?" Emerald asked.

"Not at all, my daughter. For in *The Spectrum*, is it not taught that women, just like men, have their own strengths? And did not the God of Light choose me, a woman, to be the chosen one? Woman are blessed with power and strength to help guide men to their true path of righteousness. Without us, they would be reckless, sinful, prideful, and weak. Through our inner strength, these men become better people. Do you not see? You are a righteous guide for Derek. He would do anything for you—you already hold his heart. He was under the influence of a wicked woman with a wicked power over him. A false woman leading a man to do evil things. But you, you hold the true power, pure and virtuous. Support him as king, and you will be queen, equals in power and strength—in the new world. But in the end, you hold all the power. It shows your true heart how to hold fast to him. That is wisdom."

"What of Arcadia? I fought with Kyle not to lose it."

"Arcadia matters not in the end," her mother countered. "For the world will be made anew soon, and you will finally be able to rule in peace without the troubles of this world."

Her mother was right. She had the power to change everything. What had she done recently? Sit and cry in her palace after Kyle was dead? And now, when he was alive, do more of the same?

"Please, I beg of you, come to the future. Let us do great things and change the course of time. Why should you live a life of pain and hardship, and raise my grandchildren in misery? Why not have a bright, happy, and holy future for them?"

Emerald hesitated. "I…just don't know. I'm so confused," she admitted. "This all is so surreal."

"It is the effects of the twilight sleep. It will wear off soon, and you'll be able to see all that has happened. You must do what you think is right. If that means staying in Arcadia and raising your children, then you must. But my daughter, do pray on this. Ask the God of Light for direction, for he will light your path."

Emerald wiped away her tears. "I will."

"Do not linger, my daughter. You must come to a decision. Time waits for no one," she warned. "The longer you wait, the more pain you will endure, and the harder you will fall."

"Yes, Mother."

Her mother smiled at her. "Whisper my name, and I will make the necessary arrangements."

"I love you, Mom," Emerald cried as her mother faded away.

"I love you, my daughter…" her mother's words echoed.

Derek's flower's glow dimmed, and the starry world melted away to its original blurred state. Emerald heard murmurs, indistinguishable, mixed with babies' cries.

✦ ✦ ✦

Emerald was awakened by a baby's cry. She bolted up, suddenly realizing where she was. Nurses, her handmaidens, all filled her room. It was morning, as the golden morning rays shone through the patio's glass windows.

"My Queen, you are up," said Emerys. "Congratulations of the birth of your twins." He bowed with a big smile.

Her mother. She had been with her moments ago. Or had it been hours?

Confused, Emerald's eyes skimmed the room, then locked onto two portable hospital cribs. "Councilor, I need to see them," Emerald said, as she tried to get up, holding out her hands.

Celeste came over with one child in her arms. "Isn't he beautiful?" she said as she handed off the child to Emerald with admiration.

Emerald smiled with tears of joy, cradling him in her arms. The baby was so small and tiny, sleeping so peacefully. The little one's life force surged through her body, and immediately, Emerald felt her son's magic flowing through him.

Emerald unwrapped the swaddled blanket, then immediately saw a lock of dark blue hair.

"Look at him, Celeste," Emerald said in wonder. "He's so beautiful."

"He is," she said with a smile.

The baby cooed in her arms.

"It seems that His Highness takes after both parents," Emerys said with a grin.

Emerald glanced up at the councilor, then nodded. "Indeed." She turned to see her beautiful boy's face. "My Alexander," Emerald said, cuddling with the baby, kissing his forehead.

"He looks like an Alexander," Celeste said happily.

Emerald smile, then turned toward the nurses. "Where's my other baby?"

A nurse came forward, presenting another baby boy. Celeste took baby Alexander from her while the nurse placed the other newborn in her arms.

Just like with the other child, Emerald felt an immediate flow of magical energy coming from the baby's life force. The baby cooed, while Emerald smiled, inspecting the child's hair. Vibrant orange hair.

Emerald smiled widely. "My Nathan," she said, kissing the baby on his head.

Celeste and the others smiled. "Note their names on the birthing records," Councilor Emerys said, and the staff nodded.

Emerald held her children, admiring them. After a little while, she allowed her handmaidens to hold the children, with them taking turns with them, laughing and giggling. Yet there was still no sign of Kyle or Glacia.

"Did anyone get ahold of Kyle?" Emerald asked.

The room became eerily silent, aside from the babies making noises. The situation felt weirdly similar to the wastelands.

Councilor Emerys cleared his throat. "I believe that Master Kyle was contacted on multiple occasions without any success."

"And Glacia?"

Emerys shook his head.

Where was her supposed best friend? As Emerald had those thoughts, little Nathan's life force flowed through Emerald, as if detecting her hint of spite and anger. Emerald glanced down at the baby sadly, then held him close to her chest, kissing his precious little forehead.

A thought crossed her mind. Had her mother been right about Kyle all along? Was this to be her destiny, filled with sadness and despair, if she stayed in Arcadia?

Emerys bowed. "I will leave Her Majesty to her children. And congratulations once again. The kingdom will be most excited to hear the news. There will be much celebration here in the streets, I am sure."

"Celebration?" Emerald blinked.

"Why, yes. All of Arcadia has been excited for the birth. And when they hear of twins—this will be talked about for weeks and bring much cheer to our kingdom. Perhaps, with this news, the United Kingdoms will be open for talks and we can negotiate for that hostage in Olympia. Since we have the birth in our favor, more kingdoms will be receptive to our cause."

Her kingdom. More talks. Emerald felt the warmth of Nathan, holding him close. He cooed in her arms, and she kissed his head once again. It was as if nothing mattered around her. Kyle had already broken her heart—he didn't understand her. Her best friend hadn't been there for her either. Derek, on the other hand…she knew that he was waiting for her, making way for a peaceful and everlasting happy future.

Emerald glanced up at Emerys, then smiled forcefully. "Thank you, Councilor. While I am indisposed, I grant you necessary authority to run the kingdom in my stead. You have always been loyal to the kingdom, and a good friend."

Emerys bowed deeply. "Anything for you and your family, Your Majesty. I will leave you to it."

As the councilor left, Celeste set a decaffeinated coffee next to Emerald's bedside. "I thought My Queen would like to have something to warm you up."

Emerald smiled at her. "Very much so."

Celeste bowed. "I'll bring you something to eat."

"Celeste, where is Glacia? You must know something that Emerys does not."

Celeste looked flustered, shifting her eyes.

Emerald put down her cup of coffee, then said to the room, "Everyone, please step out to the sitting room while I have a moment alone with my handmaiden. You may take the children too. It will only be a minute or two."

Everyone in the room bowed, then filed out.

When everyone was gone, Emerald gave Celeste her full attention. "Tell me."

Celeste glanced about nervously. "This morning, Glacia returned from being out all night. She does this on occasion, and we don't think twice about it. But she was acting odd. Not her usual self. She said that she didn't get much sleep due to the concert. But knowing and working with her for years, I know that she can always manage herself, even after getting no sleep, whether she goes out or stays in." Celeste began to shake. "I told her about Your Majesty's birth. She said she was feeling unwell and left, which I thought very odd, considering how close she is to Your Majesty. She forgot to grab her communicator before she left, which is also unlike her. It kept ringing, so I went to put it to silent mode, and happened to see a message on the faceplate of the device." At this point, Celeste started trembling. "It's never my business what others do, but when it comes to Her Majesty, it is my business."

Emerald suddenly felt sick. But at the same time, a flicker of fury came over her. "What did it say?"

"I can't remember the exact wording, but it was a message from her boyfriend Remy. It said something about Kyle being so messed up from 'doing a line.' It also asked how she was this morning after doing it too."

"Doing a line?"

"Hard drugs, My Queen. The kind that one gets easily addicted to and can't stop. It is probably the reason why we couldn't get ahold of either one of them."

Muffled babies' cries came from the sitting room while Emerald remained frozen in shock.

Kyle. And Glacia. Doing *drugs*? Emerald shook with rage, clinging to her blankets. The offense alone made her furious. The horrible exchange between her and Kyle the last time they had spoken…it was painful. But for him to go and do drugs? What was he *thinking*? This was why he had missed the birth of her children. Their children.

Never had she felt as betrayed as she did now. And her best friend too.

How *could they*? Tears mixed with a deep anger came over her. The two people she trusted most. Emerald took a deep breath, fighting back her rage.

"I…I am sorry to tell you all of this," Celeste began, looking pale.

"No, you shouldn't be sorry. I'm glad you did."

"I felt that Her Majesty should know all that was going on."

"Do not tell anyone what you have told me. Not a soul. I will deal with this in my own manner."

"I will not breathe a word of it, Your Majesty," Celeste said, bowing. "Before you call in everyone again, there is…something else."

Emerald glanced at her. "*More?*"

Celeste shifted her weight nervously. "I saw on the broadcasts this morning that during last night's concert, Master Kyle smashed a guitar onstage and walked off, ending the concert abruptly."

"What?"

"It fits with him using, Your Majesty. It seems the drugs got to him. It's been all over the news."

Was it the guitar she gave him? *This is how he views our love? By destroying it?*

"Again, I-I'm sorry, My Queen," Celeste said, biting her lip. "I hate to put such a damper on your mood after Her Majesty's wondrous birth."

Emerald glanced up at her, then held out her hand. Celeste held it immediately, then kissed it in sign of respect and sympathy. "I will take any extra shifts if needed for the children and your recovery."

"Thank you, Celeste," Emerald said, fighting back tears of rage. "You did right by telling me. When Glacia returns to the palace, please send her on an errand to the palace boutique shop."

"Yes, My Queen."

"Please send in the staff again. I want to see my sons," Emerald said.

Celeste went into the sitting room, gathering the staff. A deep, unsettling anger shot through Emerald, growing with every moment. Kyle was supposed to be a father to their children. How could he if he's out, playing at concerts—which she agreed to—and getting *screwed up* by using drugs! What in the heaven's name was he thinking?

I did not agree to this! Any of this!

Yes, she was sometimes naive to the ways of this world. But being abandoned by the people she cared about the most? It hurt. All of it really hurt.

Her mother was right. She had all the power.

I am queen. It's high time that people respect me and my position! I am not going to be the pushover they think I am.

All she had done was give love and affection to everyone she truly cared about. What had she gotten in return? Nothing. They disregarded her feelings, treating her like a piece of trash to be balled up and thrown aside.

Mother, Emerald whispered. *I need you.*

There was a humming through her mind, then suddenly an image appeared before her once more as the world melded into a blue tint.

Her mother appeared, summoned by Emerald's words, like a spell she cast. Her mother reached out her ghostly hand, and Emerald took it. Though she knew it was just an image far across the sands of time, she felt her mother's love and warmth.

"My daughter…" a whisper went through the air.

Emerald looked over at the empty cribs, tinted in blue. *I need to do the right thing for them.*

Emerald met her mother's eyes. "I want to come to the future to be with you," she said with certainty. "The children and I will come."

"I knew you would decide quickly." Her mother smiled. "I will send Derek, as he has the power to get you to here. In the meantime, you must ready your sons for departure to the future."

"My blood?" Emerald asked.

"Yes. The power of your green gift will allow them to reside in the future."

"Tell Derek to hurry," Emerald said bitterly. "I cannot stand to be here a moment longer."

"Expect Derek very shortly." Her mother smiled. "How I've dreamed of this very moment…"

Emerald watched as the image melted away and time was restored.

More babies' cries as her servants filed back in.

Emerald held out her arms, wanting to hold her sons. "Bring me both of my sons," she said.

The nurses came over to her, situating each of her sons on the comfort pillows, caressing them. "Do they need to be fed?" Emerald asked.

"They seem hungry, yes."

Emerald nodded, then held her sons close to her, the nurses helping her latch each of them onto a breast. A deep sadness came over her as she thought of Kyle, but at the same time, it sharpened her resolve. He was her soul mate—her true complement. But was he, truly? Would a true love do something as unforgiving as what he had done?

It's over, she told herself.

Just thinking those words were freeing, bringing her hope. For the first time, she felt like she was in control of her life. Kyle had given her the first taste of freedom, but her mother opened the door to her life—one that she finally could be in charge of.

No longer would she be the victim. No longer would she cater to everyone else. No longer would she chase after people who didn't love or care for her.

No.

She was Emerald, Queen of Arcadia.

She was finally going to rise up and be the queen that she was.

But first she needed to take care of business.

Gathering her composure, Emerald pressed her communicator button, and moments later, Celeste came into her chambers, bowing.

"Yes, Your Majesty?"

"Celeste, would you please send a transmission to palace security?" Emerald called out.

Celeste locked eyes with her, then nodded in silent understanding.

"Send the agents to the palace boutique. Have them escort Glacia out and revoke her status to the upper levels. If she chooses to visit the upper levels, have Emerys fine her twenty times the old tax."

"Yes, Your Majesty."

"And gather her things and get them out of here."

"Right away."

Not that she would be there long in Arcadia anyway, but still, Emerald wanted to end it with finality. Show her that she was not to be trifled with.

Emerald looked down at her sons. They were her life, they were the future. Then she thought of her mother. Derek. And the true power within her.

Emerald glanced at her nightstand, seeing Derek's magical flower. Leaning over gently, she picked it up and smelled its fragrance. Even the scent reminded her of her first attractions to Derek. Her eyes trailed off the bloom and down to the stem. To the thorn. She pressed hard, allowing it to puncture her thumb. Blood appeared, then she placed it to Alexander's lips, then to Nathan's.

Her sons needed to be ready.

CHAPTER 72

◆

Councilor Jason was standing in the doorway, peering inside. "You two have been playing all day," he called out.

Gwen glanced over at the councilor, trying to avoid his glare as Jihyun jumped up excitedly.

"Hi, Jason!" Jihyun said.

"Well, hello there, Master Jihyun," Councilor Jason said with a half-sincere smile, remaining poised. "I heard that you got a new video game."

"Yes! I got a new item. You wanna see?"

"Perhaps another time," he said. "It's time for Gwen to leave now."

Jihyun let out a loud sigh. "Already?"

"It is nearly time for dinner, Master Jihyun," Jason said, then turned to Gwen. "I've come to fetch you. His Majesty wants to dine with you this evening. I am to escort you there." He eyed her outfit. "Your maid will help you dress properly first."

Gwen's heart sank into the pit of her stomach. Dinner with the King? She had a feeling that her time at the palace was going to take a turn for the worse.

Jihyun had a conflicted look, then said, "Can you tell Father that I'd like to see him sometime?" He paused. "I haven't had dinner with him in a long time."

Jason came over, giving Jihyun a fake pat on the head. "Don't worry. You will have dinner with your father soon. He's just really busy with kingdom business. There are a lot of evil people trying to take over our kingdom."

Jihyun sighed as Gwen let out an accidental scoff.

Jason glanced at her sharply. "Did you want to say anything?" he said with an edge through a fake smile.

Gwen looked straight into the handsome man's phony grin, then took a deep breath. "Yes, I do. Your teeth are crooked."

Jason's eyes flared, but said no more while Jihyun giggled.

"You'd best be on your *way*," the councilor said.

Gwen got to her feet, turning to Jihyun. "See you later, Jihyun."

"Bye, Gwen!" Jihyun smiled back at her, then slid the goggles back down around his eyes, getting back into his game.

Gwen followed Jason outside the gaming room, and suddenly, Gwen felt tired. She remembered that she'd only gotten two hours of sleep, then was stuck inside the gaming room again for many more hours. The air felt different in the corridors as they walked back toward the portal room.

"It's kind of stuffy out here in the halls," Gwen said.

"Stuffy?"

"The air is thick. I don't know how to explain," Gwen continued.

Jason fiddled with a jeweled ring on his finger, straightening it as they walked. "Perhaps being stuck in that room all that time you got used to the air in there."

"Must be."

They walked into the portal room, with the blue-gifted man awaiting them.

"I will send the girl directly to her chambers," he said with no emotion. "You will be on the outside."

Jason nodded, then he stepped in.

Suddenly, the portal burned a bright blue, rippling and swirling. The gifted man gestured to Gwen, and she eyed him for a moment before stepping through as well.

The blue magic danced around Gwen, melting away the portal room, then she fell into an endless blue void. It was a different sensation than the last time, sending her falling hard and fast. Just when she thought she was either going to pass out or crash, her surroundings melted away, forming her chambers. That is, prison in Olympia.

Mae was already in the room next to a chaise, a frilly dress laid out on it. She grabbed the dress, coming up to Gwen and offering it to her.

Gwen sighed, glaring at the garment.

"What's the matter?" Mae asked.

"I don't like wearing those dresses. They make me look stupid."

"This again?" Mae said. "Do they not fit your style?"

"No," Gwen said. "I just hate wearing dresses. They remind me that I'm not skinny and pretty like the other girls."

Mae raised her eyebrow, then gestured to her. "Gwen, I wish you would see yourself in a better light."

"Mae…all of those girls are like a hundred pounds."

"So?"

"So! Mae, I can never be a hundred pounds, even if I stopped eating for a lifetime," she said angrily. Gwen looked at her reflection, her eyes watering. Her gaze moved down her face, to her chin, her thick neck, down to her thick body. A body that was different from the other girls in Arcadia and broad. A body she hated.

Gwen suddenly burst into tears, turning away from her reflection. She fell to the floor, crying. "I'm not going to the stupid dinner. Tell the King to go suck it."

Mae sat down next to her, putting her arm around her. Gwen fell into her arms, and Mae held her as she continued to sob, slowly wiping her hair out of her tear-stained face. After a long while, Gwen whispered, "Why can't I be like the other girls?"

"But why would you want to be like the other girls?" Mae asked softly.

"Because then maybe boys would like me."

Mae glanced at her, this time with a stern face that Gwen had never seen on Mae. It was almost like her mother's stern look when she was in trouble.

"Gwen, why must you lie to yourself?"

"I'm not lying!"

Mae narrowed her eyes. "You are. You tell yourself things that are untrue," Mae continued. "There are many types of people in this world, Gwen. I know it is hard to believe since you only see one type of 'look' of women on the broadcasts."

"But that's what guys like, Mae!"

Mae snorted. "Really? Tell me, what do you like about this boy Garrett?"

Gwen thought about all the times she was with Garrett, especially their more "special" times. "Well, I guess he's funny, cute when he talks about programming, and has the most killer eyes with tattoos lining the side of his brows."

"He looks like all the other men on the broadcasts, then, I take it?"

"No, he's different…"

Gwen stopped mid-sentence, then met Mae's eyes.

Mae raised her chin in victory, giving her a smile. "Everyone has their own uniqueness to them that makes them desirable." She leaned in with a bigger smile. "Use that to your advantage."

"But what about me? What's my advantage?"

"From the little I know of you, you are one of the strongest girls I know. I don't think half the palace guards have the muscle that you do." Mae chuckled. "I've seen you handle some of the equipment and shift your furniture around your room."

"I don't think a guy wants a girl who can kick their butt to be their girlfriend," Gwen muttered.

"You'd be surprised." Mae laughed. "But not only that, you are one of the smartest girls too. Programming, computers…not to mention your beautiful smile, golden hair, and your ocean-blue eyes. You are a shining star."

"What's that supposed to mean?"

"You light up the room."

"You're just saying that."

Mae shook her head. "It's true."

"How is that true?"

"Look at Master Jihyun, how well you two get along. He doesn't get along with anybody. I have never seen him so happy—ever. And that is saying a lot, considering I have known him since he was four."

Could what Mae said be true? She found that hard to believe, but she did so want to?

Gwen rubbed her nose, sniffling.

After a few moments, Mae said, "Now, I want you to take a quick shower to reset your mood. I'll blow-dry your hair and get you dressed and ready for dinner. We don't have much time, so only take a few minutes to shower."

Gwen nodded and went to shower, making the water as hot as she could without scalding herself. When she was finished, she realized Mae was right. Taking a shower had improved her mood. It broke her sadness. Not all of it, but at least she could get through dinner.

What could the King possibly want to talk to me about? As soon as she had that thought, she had her answer. It had to be about her dad. They said that they would exchange her for her dad. They wanted his magic. Or possibly her mom.

"Finished?" Mae called out from behind the door, interrupting her thoughts.

"Yes," Gwen called out.

Mae came in, then started blow-drying her hair. As she did, Gwen watched her in the mirror.

She thought about Mae's words once again. She had to admit, she could kick a lot of the wastelanders' butts. In arm-wrestling matches against the twenty-something-year-old men, she won most of the time.

Mae finished up her hair, styling it in a ponytail the way Gwen liked it, adding a hair decoration on the side of her head. Mae gestured for her to step into the dress.

Gwen took a brave, deep breath. She just had to get through one night.

Mae zipped her up. As she was putting on her shoes, there was a knock at the door. Mae answered, then bowed.

"Is Lady Gwen ready?" Councilor Jason asked from the doorway.

"She is putting on her shoes right now," Mae said.

"I'm ready," Gwen called out, coming up to him.

Councilor Jason had on another green velvet robe, similar to what he had been wearing when they first met, but this one was in a different cut. "Come. His Majesty awaits."

Gwen nodded, then followed him out of her room. There was a group of guards standing in position.

"Check her," Jason said as soon as the door was closed.

Two guards grabbed each of her arms tightly.

"What are you doing?" Gwen said, yanking her arms. They were locked tight in the guards' grip.

"It will only take a moment," Councilor Jason said as he looked down at her. He grasped her face firmly, yanking it up to his. She looked about wildly as he studied her eyes. Then his hands moved to her head, looking at her hairline.

"Do you see anything?" Jason called out.

"Nothing. The girl does not have the gift," said a deep male voice.

Where had that voice come from?

Jason suddenly let her go and motioned to the guards. "Let her go."

The guards released their grip. Gwen spun around, wanting to see who had spoken to Jason, but didn't see anyone.

"Who were you talking to?" Gwen asked, still looking around.

Councilor Jason gave her a half smile, then gestured to her. "Let's go."

"No. Who was talking, and why did you do that?"

"Must I remind you that you are a prisoner here?"

"I haven't forgotten," Gwen said. "But if you want me to comply, then at least answer my questions."

Councilor Jason smiled, then sucked in a breath. "You don't give up, do you?"

"No, I don't. I usually win all the arguments with my mom."

"Let me assure you, I am *nothing* like your mother." He smiled insincerely. He then shoved her, and she complied. How she hated him.

The group walked down the hall, turning into a corridor that she had yet to see. This corridor looked far more expensive and pretty compared to the other parts of the palace.

They made another turn, entering a corridor made up entirely of glass and mirrors. Gwen gasped. It was like walking in the clouds. She *almost* felt happy. Then the feeling died out as they stepped out of the glass corridor, entering the King's dining room.

King Renard of Olympia was already seated, drinking from a chalice of wine as the group entered.

"Your Majesty," the group murmured and bowed. Gwen did the same, mimicking them.

"Be seated, the lot of you," King Renard said, making a grand gesture. "What took you so long?"

"We had to do another check," Councilor Jason said as they all began to seat themselves. A servant guided Gwen where her seat was, and Gwen took it. "Our guest has a lot to say."

"Is that so?" The King turned in Gwen's direction. "Finally I have the chance to speak with you, Lady Gwen," the king said. "Are your quarters comfortable?"

She had been a prisoner all this time, and the first thing he wanted to know was whether her quarters were comfortable? She wanted to kick him where the sun didn't shine.

"I guess," she said, biting her lip. *Although I miss my parents and want to get out of here, you big dummy!*

"Good," he said coldly.

Dinner was served as they talked, a plate placed in front of her. The smell of roast meat made her stomach growl. She hadn't realized how hungry she was for real food, not the snacks and sandwiches she had been eating for days with Jihyun.

"It's too bad that Jihyun isn't here," Gwen said, slipping in the comment. They all looked at her as if she'd spoken out of turn. *Might as well commit now.* "He keeps saying how much he wants to see you."

The King smiled. "My son is such a sweet boy," he said. "We will have him join us next time." There was a falseness in his tone.

"I am sure that would make him very happy," Gwen said stiffly.

"Indeed," the King said, swishing around his glass. "Enough about Jihyun. Gwen—I hear that both your parents have the gift."

Gwen picked up her fork as she contemplated what to say. Of course they knew about her dad having magic. But her mom? She wasn't there in the wastelands. Olympia would have no idea about her mom's power, but how much did they know?

They're blowing smoke.

"What of it?" Gwen answered finally.

The King smiled. "It is incredible. To have two parents with magic. And for them to have orange magic."

"Who says that *both* of them do?" Gwen said.

"You deny it? Because my sources witnessed your father using orange magic."

"He does. But why would you think that my mom has orange magic?" Gwen said, playing it cool.

The King stared at her, then narrowed his eyes. "Just a hunch."

Gwen stared back at him evenly. "Your hunch is wrong."

"You deny your mother having magic altogether?" the King asked.

"She's just a normal fuddy-duddy like all those other mid-level science dorks. Nothing special about her at all." Gwen shrugged.

King Renard and Councilor Jason eyed each other. Gwen couldn't tell whether she had fooled them, but she could only hope.

"The violet magic," called out the deep male voice she had heard in the hallway.

Gwen looked around in alarm, not seeing who the voice came from.

"I was getting there," the King said, then looked back at Gwen. "Who was the woman with violet magic? The one that fought out in the wastelands with your father?"

Gwen didn't know what to say or do. It was obvious that they were talking about Geeta, so if she lied, they would know.

"She is Arcadia's official Protector of the Realm."

"What is her name?" the King pressed, lowering his brow.

Gwen's heart raced in her chest. "I don't remember."

"She's lying," the invisible voice hissed.

"Greka? Greeta?" Gwen pretended nervously.

"I knew that cow of a bitch was working with them," the invisible voice snarled. There was a loud slam on the other side of the room, like someone had thrown something, or their fist, at the wall. Then the door slammed shut behind her, with more noise and commotion in the hallway beyond.

Whoever that is, he sounds very unhappy with Geeta. Maybe she kicked his butt, and he didn't like it.

Breaking up the commotion, Councilor Jason slid a communicator over to her, then smiled. "We would like you to call your mother," he said.

Gwen stared at the communicator in shock. "And say what?" she asked, peering up at them as her heart raced.

"It's simple, really. Just tell her that you are here in Olympia and that you are being treated well," he continued. "After that, you will hand the communicator over to us, and we will do the rest of the talking."

Her heart raced as she stared at the communicator. The people at the table watched her in silence. She didn't want to do anything for these a-hole jerks.

"After you do, we will give you anything you want. Electronic gadgets. Clothes. Money to spend to shop online," Jason continued.

It was the same way they pacified Jihyun. Giving him stuff. It made her sick. Furious, more like.

"Why?" Gwen asked. "So you can try and make my mom more anxious? To get her in a frenzy in the hope she'll exchange my dad for me?" Gwen narrowed her eyes at Jason, then slid the communicator across the table. "I'm not a stupid kid. I don't want your stuff. *Stuff* doesn't replace my mom and dad!"

Jason clenched his jaw, and the King gave her an even stare. "I don't think you realize the severity of the situation, Gwen," he said as he leaned in. "You must do as you are told like a good little girl. Haven't you ever faced the consequences for your actions? It seems to be rare nowadays, but I can assure you, we live by morals here."

Fear pumped through her body, making her shake, just like out in the wastelands when she confronted Jihyun. She had no power. She wasn't even eighteen yet.

No! I can't be afraid.

The King nodded at Jason, and the councilor gently set the communicator back on the table in front of her.

"You can threaten me all you want, but I'm not calling my mother," Gwen said sharply, rising. "You people all suck!"

One of the guards struck her across the face, knocking her to the ground. Her face pounded, and blood ran down her nose. Gwen looked up, and the guard struck her again.

"Just because you are a teen and a girl, doesn't mean we won't hold back," King Renard continued.

The guard struck her hard across the face a third time, sending her slamming back into the floor. Her vision blurred, and stars sparked in her vision. Blood had run onto the front of her fancy dress.

"Now get up," the King said.

"Never!" Gwen shouted from the floor.

A hard kick to the face.

"UP!"

Tears flooded her eyes. She attempted to move, but she hurt so much.

"His Majesty commands you to get up," Councilor Jason said.

Just then, Gwen heard the door slam again, and pounding footsteps approached. "I will beat you to a pulp, *little dog*, if you don't make that call." It was the mystery man.

I'm not as strong as you think, Mae, I'm not a shining star…

Tears ran down her face. "Okay," Gwen whispered as her lip quivered. "I will. I'll make the call."

"Good," snapped the male voice.

Gwen crawled toward her chair, using it to stand, then struggled to get back in her seat. The communicator stared back at her.

With all of them staring her down, Gwen nervously picked up the communicator, then dialed the last known number of her mom's as blood ran out of her nose and down her chin.

CHAPTER 73

ORANGE

Telly entered a few changes in the tablet, adjusting the frequency of the electrons in Drew's inanimate body. His vitals weren't doing as well as she had expected after several of the parts were replaced. They had to take it slow with a partial transfusion; if they did it all at once, Drew's body could go into shock, and then he would really be in trouble.

You can't leave me behind, Drew, Telly thought sadly. The thought of him gone made her eyes well up, and she quickly wiped a tear away from under her glasses.

"How is he?" Garrett's voice called out softly.

"Not good."

Garrett's footsteps approached. Telly noticed that he had another part in his hand. It was the next one to be replaced on their list.

Garrett paused, then sat down next to her. "He will pull through. He always does," he said, then proceeded to make Drew's arm level, resting it on a small rolling metal table with tools. He started opening up the circuits in his arm, cleaning out the frayed ones.

"I know," Telly agreed. Although, she wasn't sure if she believed her own words. The longer he remained in this condition, the harder it would be to restore him. If it went longer, it would be weeks…months…

Her communicator rang, startling them both.

"Must be Victor or the palace," Telly said, grabbing it absentmindedly. As she was about to press receive, Telly looked at the number on the screen. There was no number; it just said *PRIVATE*. Not even the Arcadian palace said private. Her eyes suddenly streamed tears, knowing who was on the other line.

"Who's—" Garrett stopped, noticing her face.

She hit receive.

"Hello?" Telly said frantically.

There was no sound.

"Hello? Hello?" Telly said again quickly, shooting up from her seat. She started pacing.

There was static on the other line, then nothing.

"Hello!"

"Mom?"

"GWEN!" Telly screamed. Fear wracked her insides, and her guts felt turned inside out. She started sobbing. "Gwen! Where are you calling from? Oh God! Gwen! I miss you!"

"I'm safe, Mom. I love…" Gwen's voice said as it trailed away. There were loud shuffling sounds and deep voices talking over her. It sounded as if the phone had been ripped away from Gwen.

"Gwen! Where is Olympia hiding you?" Telly screamed. Her legs turned to jelly, and her whole body shook with disgust and sorrow.

"Hello, Miss Hearly," said an even man's voice. "I am Councilor Jason, advisor to King Renard of Olympia."

Telly froze, her blood pounding with rage. "I don't care who the fuck you are! I want my fucking daughter back now! You hear me? Now! I will raze your kingdom to the ground if I don't have her back immediately!"

"As exciting as that sounds, the King has a better proposal."

"There is no better proposal than me getting my daughter back, you sick twisted fucks!" Garrett looked at her, stunned. She had never sworn like this before.

"You can and will have your daughter back," Jason continued calmly. "But you must in turn hand over your cyborg husband and the violet-gifted."

Telly blinked, caught by surprise. "Violet-gifted?"

"Yes. The one they call Geeta." Telly and Garrett exchanged glances. "Both the orange-gifted cyborg and Geeta must show up at our front gates. Once they do, your daughter will be returned to you."

"That is impossible!" Telly said. "Drew is not stable. He hasn't even woken up from the damage inflicted by your wicked gifted child."

"You can present his body. We don't really care what kind of shape he is in—just as long as he has a heartbeat. We want him and the woman," the councilor said. "The longer you wait, the longer we have your daughter."

"I don't have any say over Geeta!" Telly countered.

"You'd best figure a way to persuade her, then."

"Please," Telly whispered. "Don't hurt my girl."

"I'm afraid we already have," Jason said. "Don't take too long."

Click.

The call had ended.

Telly clutched the communicator tightly, shaking. Then she screamed, turning around and kicking a pile of old computer scraps.

They. Hurt. Her. Girl.

"Telly?" Garrett said.

Her. Baby. Girl.

Telly screamed again, her entire body trembling with rage. Tears streamed down her cheeks as she stormed over to her desk, grabbed her new magitech weapon, then holstered it. She spun around wildly, heading to the door.

Garrett suddenly blocked her way with a concerned look.

"Telly, where are you going?" he said.

"Where do you *think*?" Telly began to push her way through, but he stopped her.

"Wait!"

"You don't understand? They hurt her, Garrett!" Telly got in his face. "I'm going to *raze* that city to the ground so fast they won't even know what hit them," she snarled.

"We *are* going to get her, but we can't just storm Olympia!" Garrett shot back. "Otherwise they'll get us too! Remember the plan? We got to get Drew up and running again. We need to go as a group! The more of us, the better chance we have against them—"

Telly narrowed her eyes. "You don't think I have the power to go against them, do you?"

Garrett looked resigned. "I think you have the will. But against an entire city? Telly, *nobody* has that kind of power."

"Just you watch!"

"We don't even know where Gwen is exactly."

"I don't care! I want my daughter!" Telly cried. "I'm tired of waiting for Geeta. I can go find her myself."

"Geeta *will* find her!" Garrett said, blocking the door.

Telly stared him down. "Either help me or get out of my way," she said in a low voice.

They stood there frozen.

"Move," Telly whispered.

There was a flicker of approval in his eyes, then he stepped aside.

She darted out the door, Garrett running behind her, perhaps to help. She didn't know, nor did she care.

She headed into the supply room, glancing around hastily, then started grabbing all that she needed. Garrett did the same thing, pocketing various devices and gadgets.

As she finalized stuffing her pack, she realized that she had forgotten her new vials back in the lab. She headed back to the lab, Garrett still in tow, and moved toward her workstation.

Scion was there now, adjusting some code for Drew's new replacement equipment watching them curiously. He watched them, trying to make out what was going on.

Telly grabbed all the vials that she had made and placed them in a padded pouch, then into her side pants. She could hear the clicking from Scion's head and knew the cyborg was trying to work things out. He knew better than to speak of her secret vials, especially with Garrett around. He'd find out soon enough.

She began changing into military pants and a tank top. Garrett turned away as he slid on his detector goggles and special location energy device.

"Are you going on a mission, Miss Telly?" Scion asked as he continued to punch in code.

Garrett looked over at her. She gritted her teeth. "Yes, Scion, I am." As soon as the words left her mouth, Telly exploded in anger, grabbing an old scrap part of Drew's and hurling it across the cavern. It slammed into the wall, breaking into three pieces.

Then she started sobbing.

Garrett continued to pack objects while Scion approached her.

"How can I rectify this situation, Miss Hearly?" he asked. "Is there anything that you would like me to do?"

His words somehow were an instant balm, causing her to snap out of it. His words were full of kindness, as much as they could coming from a man who was half machine. She just wanted the two people that made her happy. The love of her life was hanging on by a thread. Her other love, her child with the love her life, was being held hostage. They made her full, and without them, her heart was empty.

"You are doing everything for Drew," Telly whispered. "That means everything to me."

A hint of compassion flashed on his face, melting her heart.

Warmth flooded her body as he placed his robotic hand on her shoulder. His touch eased her heart, filling it with strength. The two loves of her life made her complete, and she would get them back. She'd been given this power, this magic, for a reason. Though it was forced by her, the magic chooses the person.

A strange sensation came over her. A sense of peace…

The magic chose me. There is a reason I was given this power.

It pumped through her veins.

I have the power to make everything right.

Her life force hummed with approval, flooding her heart, mind, soul with power. The full power of the orange, embracing every aspect of her core being. In her mind's eye, she saw that power wash over her thoughts…

The power is yours to command, whispered the magic.

And I plan to use it wisely, she told the power.

Telly took in a breath, feeling the power within her life force. It was as if she was a new person. For the first time in many weeks, she felt a sense of control. Control over her destiny, joined with the power of the orange magic within her soul.

She opened her eyes, realizing that she was glimmering with pure orange magic.

Garrett stood in awe as Scion stared at her intently.

Telly took a heavy, deep breath, wiping away the tears in her eyes, releasing the power, sending it dissipating into the air. A strange calm resided in her, as if her new power was telling her that she now had the ability to do what she needed to do.

"Telly…"

"I'm fine."

Glancing down at her pants pocket, Telly grabbed the pouch of magitech power vials. She held one in the palm of her hand, clutching it tightly as Garrett looked at her curiously. He had never seen her secret experiment before.

"What is that?" he asked.

"I'll explain later."

Closing her eyes, Telly focused her thoughts on Gwen. The first time she held her baby girl. How she loved her dear child.

Gwen, I love you.

Telly gathered the power within her life force, then released it into the vial. When she looked, bright orange light surrounded the vial, then seeped inside. The liquid bubbled, then settled.

Telly grimaced. The vial needed more energy.

Pulling from her life force, she sent another surge to the vial. Suddenly, the room was bathed in hot orange light. With another flash, the orange magic was gone, and she had ten vials in her hand. They were too big for her to hold, so they began to fall. Scion swiftly reached out, catching them.

"Oh my God…" Garrett breathed. "Is that what I think it is?"

"Probably," she stated.

Scion held one of the vials close to his cybernetic eyes, inspecting it thoroughly. "It appears you copied the vial's precise components. My scans tell me that there is no difference between the original and the copies," he said.

"That's enough for me," she said, palming one of the vials. Focusing her magic once again, Telly multiplied the vial, creating many more vials. She kept copying the vials until she had no more space on her ammo belt and in her pants pockets.

An image flashed in her mind. She knew exactly what she needed to do. Telly jolted her eyes to Scion. "How stable is Drew?"

"My readings indicate that he is at sixty percent stability with his new updates."

Telly frowned. "Not enough to leave him."

"Actually, Miss Hearly, I can send him into a sleep with some of our sedatives. It should give us twenty-four hours."

Telly glanced at Drew, sighing. "I don't want to leave him, but Olympia has given me no choice."

Telly took her new weapon from its holster, loaded one of the vials, then slammed it back into her holster.

Garrett gawked at her. "You've been making new weapons without me knowing?"

"I told you I'd explain on the way," Telly stated. She turned to Scion. "Get ready and power up. We are leaving."

"What is our destination?" Scion asked.

Her eyes narrowed. "Olympia."

"Shouldn't we tell the others, at least?" Garrett asked.

Without answering, Telly left the lab, the others following behind.

CHAPTER 74

RED

Kyle drove like a bat out of hell, weaving in and out of traffic, trying to get his mind straight and figure out what he was going to say to Em. He was so fucked. The news was everywhere: The Queen had given birth to twins.

As he turned a corner, he sped down the street, seeing that the light was about to turn red. But he wasn't fast enough, and of course it turned red.

While waiting, he kept thinking about their last spat. To avoid a clusterfuck of his child's future, he would have to quietly stand back and see her once a week. He was beyond pissed about the whole thing. Like, what the fucking hell was Em thinking, expecting to see him once a week for a few hours so what? So she could rule with Derek, whenever that fucker returned?

I don't understand how hard it is for her to live her own life. Why wouldn't she want to raise the children with him? It seemed so simple, but apparently not to her.

Kyle's gut churned, feeling sick about missing the birth. He'd needed just one night to gather his thoughts after she told him that she essentially chose to be queen to her people rather than a lover to him. And the one night he took away from her to gather his thoughts, she gave birth. *The one* time.

There was a loud vibrating rumble in the lane next to him—an engine revving.

"Hey, look who it is. It's that pansy-ass pretty boy!" taunted a familiar voice.

Kyle glanced over, then gritted his teeth. It was Jaxx, of all fucking people. And of all the fucking times too.

"Hey, jackass! I heard you sold out. I knew you were a vagina-bitch. You just couldn't say no to those suits." Jaxx laughed.

He wanted to clock the motherfucker, but the light turned green, and traffic was moving again.

Fuck this guy. If he gave Jaxx any attention, things wouldn't end well. He was in no mood to put up with bullshit.

Kyle continued onward to the palace, clearing his mind. *I'll just say what I mean to say to Em. Whatever fucking happens, happens.*

Deep laughter rumbled in the back of his mind.

Yeah, you won, he swore to the Lord of Darkness. *You warned me that you would get back at me, take control of the earthly realm. Well, you sure showed me.*

Kyle made it to his usual parking spot in his apartment's garage. Then he walked out an open stairwell and flew off to the palace.

◆ ◆ ◆

"My Queen," Celeste said, bowing. "Master Kyle…is here to see you."

Anger rose within her chest.

Glancing down, Nathan fed on her breast. His life force was strong. Emerald situated her robe, covering herself. "Send him in, and make sure none of the doctors or nurses enter while he's inside."

Celeste bowed deeply. "Yes, Your Majesty." She was about to leave, then turned around. "Please press the button on your transmitter…if you need anything."

"I will. Thank you."

As Celeste left, Kyle entered, standing in the doorway. His face was firm—matching hers.

After a long pause, he bowed to her, then asked, "May I?"

"Do come in," Emerald said.

The babies suddenly cried in her arms. Emerald assumed they felt the tension. Emerald watched as Kyle's eyes trailed to the babies, especially Nathan.

Silently, he walked up to Nathan, brushed his ring finger softly against Nathan's cheek, then kissed him gently.

After a long silence, he straightened and looked at her. "I came as soon as I heard the news—"

"Yes, so good of you to come," Emerald cut him off.

His face turned into a deep frown, his eyes burning with anger. "Is this how it's going to be? Are we just going to be angry at each other?"

Emerald held her sons, as if shielding them away from him.

"Can you blame me?" Emerald said.

Emerald watched as an array of emotions flickered across his face. Then he sat down on one of the sofas next to the bed, composing himself. "I was a jackass for leaving you the way I did. I never wanted to leave on an angry note. But had I stayed, I probably would have regretted anything I said. But what hurts most is that I left you to give birth to our sons alone. You didn't deserve that. Our sons didn't deserve that." His eyes flickered like fiery coals. "I am sorry for everything."

Instead of feeling relieved, Kyle's words made her more angry. Emerald held her head high. "Are you sorry you chose to do a line too?"

Kyle's eyes went wide. Emerald waited for his response. The babies cried, and Emerald kissed their heads, shooting Kyle a vengeful look.

Kyle remained still. She could tell that he was angry.

"Do you think I'm stupid?" Emerald asked. "That since I am naive about the world, that you could do terrible things like this and get away with it?"

"Hell NO!" Kyle shot up from his seat, pacing.

"Then *why*, Kyle? Why did you do this to me? To our children!"

Kyle scoffed. "You know what's sad, Em? You think you're right in all of this," he said with an edge. "But just remember this: You chose Arcadia over our love." He snorted with disgust. "And yeah, I am not perfect. Yes, I fucked up and did drugs. I'm not blaming you, but hell, you have not made it easy." Emerald saw a glimmer of a tear form in the corner of his eye. "Fucking hell, do you realize you broke me?"

"Broke you? Broke *you*?" Emerald spat. "You broke *me*."

Kyle snorted again, shaking his head. "Broke you, huh? When?"

"You missed the birth of our children!" Emerald's heart pounded with rage.

"Yeah, after you chose to remain with *Derek*!" Kyle shouted.

The babies started crying.

Emerald's eyes narrowed. "I supported your music career to make you happy. But this? If I knew it was going to be like this, I wouldn't have! Did you not see the thirty missed transmissions from the palace? Celeste tried to get ahold of you all *night*!"

"Like I said, I'm not perfect. I am really sorry that I'm not. I chose one night to give to myself, to think about the fucked-up situation that the woman of my dreams asked of me! You know, to see her for only a couple of hours a week! Not to mention our child's future is on the line because of your royal rules. Do you know how fucking ridiculous all of this is? But I am sorry for missing the birth. I do feel like shit. There. Does that make you feel better? That I feel like shit?" He stood with his arms crossed, unmoving.

"You treat me just you treated the guitar I gave you. You don't care about me, my feelings, or our children!" Emerald shouted.

Another tear rolled down his cheek, his face remaining stone-cold.

There was a long silence as the babies fussed. It was as if all her concerns were falling on deaf ears. Her words had no effect on him. There was no seeing his side of things either.

"You know what's even worse? Is when I said that you chose to remain with Derek, you didn't even deny it," Kyle said in a low tone. "I think you made up your mind a while ago. You never wanted to marry me. You just wanted to stay married to your kingdom."

Emerald flared her eyes. "Whatever you say, Kyle."

Kyle sighed. "Em…I love you. I love you with everything that I have."

"I love you too, but we can't do this. I can't do this."

Another long pause. "And our child?"

"Nathan will stay with me."

"That's not fair, and you know it," he snapped back.

Nathan started wailing, while Emerald soothed him. "It is. He needs *me* more than *you*."

Kyle gritted his teeth through his tears. "I don't want to fight you anymore. If this is what you choose, then so be it. I can't change your mind." Angry tears began streaming down his cheeks. "I will love you from afar, watch over you. But I cannot remain just another guy to you. You chose to be queen and be with Derek. And now that I know, I can move on. I will hate every moment of my life, but I will live it to protect you."

Kyle gripped her mattress, eyes full of tears. Emerald felt the despair in both their hearts.

"I love you so much, Kyle," Emerald whispered. "But I can't live like this. I can't take it. We clearly cannot see eye to eye. We live in completely different worlds."

"I know," he said, then pointed to the babies. "But I don't want to lose them too. Oh God, Em. Why? Please reconsider. I love you…"

Emerald rocked the babies, closing her eyes. Her soul ached with sadness. Blue magic flooded her heart, and more tears came. She felt the sadness within Alexander flow through her too.

I just want to leave this place and time forever. I want to forget.

"Em…" Kyle choked out.

Emerald opened her eyes, looking upon Kyle's face one last time. Soon, she wouldn't have to endure any of this.

"I stand by my decision," Emerald said, her voice shaking.

Kyle blinked away tears from his swollen red eyes, then rubbed his face. "Then I guess this is goodbye." He held out his hand, and his staff flew into his hand. With a whistle, Zaphod flew over to him, landing on his shoulder. Then he gave Nathan one last look, then turned to her and bowed deeply. "I will be watching over you, *My Queen.*"

Emerald swallowed hard. "Goodbye, Kyle," she whispered.

He stood watching her for a moment longer. Then with a jerk of her hand, greenish-blue magic appeared, funneling straight into Kyle's body.

Kyle stood looking at her, unwavering, as her magic turned pure blue, shimmering. Then the magic flashed him away. Kyle was gone. He was really gone.

The sudden realization made her sick with grief. Emerald sobbed quietly as she held her babies.

Kyle was really gone.

CHAPTER 75

◆

VIOLET

Geeta sat in her favorite spot in the diner, waiting for her food. It was packed like it was every other morning. Nym was serving coffee to her assigned tables, hustling back and forth from the kitchen as they called out orders.

"More tea, Geeta?"

Geeta turned just as Nym placed a giant plate of food before her. As always, Nym was peppy with a bright smile. She was stunning.

"Ah, sure, I'll have more," Geeta stammered.

Nym grabbed her cup. "Geeta, why haven't you called me? Didn't Kyle give you my number?"

Geeta's nerves began to take over as she lowered her gaze to her food. "It's…complicated."

Nym gave a confused look. "Dialing my number? How hard is it, really?"

"It's just…" Geeta looked back up at Nym, but she had disappeared.

Where did she go?

Geeta looked around, but Nym was nowhere. The diner was still bustling, with customers yelling for more coffee.

Geeta got up from her table, looking around wildly.

"Nym?" she called out.

You want her? Come and get her! yelled a man's voice in her mind.

Geeta shot open her eyes, seeing the wasteland before her. Sweat poured down her forehead, then a chill shot down her spine. Her senses rose in a panic, and the hairs on the back of her neck stood on edge.

Nym was in trouble. She just knew it. Could it be that the Olympian boy was behind it?

Her hands began to shake. Closing her eyes, Geeta called upon her violet magic, filling her body and mind with its power. Releasing her mental energy, she sent it flowing across the wastelands, reaching toward Arcadia, right to the diner.

Geeta searched, trying to locate Nym's mind. She couldn't sense her. Geeta sent another wave of energy, this time expanding the area, then farther out, all the way to the edges of Arcadia. Still, Nym's presence couldn't be felt.

Her stomach twisted, recalling the man's voice in her dream. *Come and get her!*

Olympia. Could it be…?

Geeta changed the direction of her mind magic, flowing toward the direction of Olympia.

Suddenly, Geeta felt the brush of a familiar presence in Olympia. One that she knew. It wasn't the boy. It wasn't Gwen. It wasn't Nym either.

This doesn't make any sense.

Sending another, more powerful wave of magic, Geeta focused her thoughts on the connection, flowing around this person.

Suddenly, a violent strike hit her energy, cutting deep within her mind.

Geeta screamed as she cut her connection, shaking with fear. She knew who that was. Someone she never wanted to see again.

Geeta let out a loud sob.

Gods, I cannot face him. Not him…

"I hate you! I hate you!" Geeta screamed as she thought of *him.* "You made me understand what it is to hate…something that I don't want to feel!"

Angry tears flowed down her cheeks, and she whipped around to another nearby boulder, smacking her magic against it, blowing it into thousands of pieces.

Geeta sank to her knees once again, then laid herself flat on the sands, sobbing.

"Geeta!" Victor's voice called out. Boots trudged over to her. "By God, what happened to you?"

She couldn't even say his name. An irrational part of her mind told her that if she did, it would summon him to her, and fear would consume her.

"You don't have to tell me," he said, then breathed quickly. "But you need to know something that just happened."

Geeta's eyes shot to his, fear pounding in her heart. He looked anxious. "What is it?"

"Telly, Scion, and Garrett are gone."

"They left?"

Victor nodded. "There was a note left by Drew's bedside from Garrett. It said that Drew is under sedation for twenty-four hours and that they left for Olympia."

It had been a premonition.

"We must head to Olympia now," Geeta said. "Get what you need, and we'll leave as soon as we can."

Victor ran off while Geeta headed to get a few supplies.

Victor better be ready. We are going to need his power.

Then her communicator rang.

It was Emerys. The Queen had given birth, and Kyle was nowhere to be found.

A glowing red raindrop fell on her hand.

CHAPTER 76

RED

Emerald's dimensional magic faded away as Kyle found his bearings. By the looks of it, he was sent to the eastern sector of Arcadia. He wasn't sure if Emerald had thought of this place, or her magic just chose a part of the city. Whatever the case, it didn't fucking matter.

His life, his love…all that mattered to him was stripped from him.

Kyle wiped an angry tear as he swiped his hand in front of him, summoning his red winds, while the other cradled Zaphod. His power funneled around him, then he made himself disappear, heading toward higher ground.

He reached his familiar spot of the Unimark building, looking out toward the palace in the distance. Dark clouds swelled across Arcadia. Forceful winds swept across the city. Zaphod buried his feathery body against his inner jacket flap.

He should be near the palace, keeping watch over Emerald. But in his heart, he felt defeated. This place was his refuge from Arcadia.

Angry tears streamed down his cheeks as he began to sing. With every note, the dark clouds thickened and thunder rumbled. He sang with his entire life force, his magic intertwining with the melody, sending his power up to the skies.

What did it matter if he unleashed his magic into the atmosphere? Life without Emerald's love was meaningless. And now, he would sing one final song to her and cut the cord to his heart. Because it fucking hurt so much. His insides held nothing but pain. Even his bones ached.

Rage and sorrow funneled through him, pouring out into his song. The earth rumbled, and the metal around him began to hum, bending slightly. Glowing red droplets of light rain fell, then grew into a downpour of deep crimson rain, drenching the entire city in his sorrow. Red lightning shot across the sky as he finished his song.

Kyle looked in the direction of Emerald's tower, his view now blocked by the rain and thick red fog.

Em…why?

A deep sorrowful ache wrenched through his chest as he thought of her. It was over. Life was over, because what was his life without her and his own son? The worst was knowing that all his imperfections had caught up to him. He could go on living, sing, ride his bike, and eventually find another woman. Kyle sniffed an angry tear back. He didn't want another woman. He wanted Emerald. She was made to be his complement, just as he was to her. Besides, all those things carried memories of her.

Zaphod cawed, climbing up on his shoulder. The rain continued to pour, with his feathery friend getting drenched too.

"I'm sorry, bud. I've been a shitty master to you," Kyle said as he wiped his face. "I never took you to Rosie. I wanted you to meet her."

Zaphod purred.

"I know. It hurts bad, buddy."

Kyle grasped the staff next to him, then climbed up on the building's ledge.

Emerald…I will watch over you and Nathan, Kyle thought. It fucking sucked. She didn't want him, but he'd sworn to protect her. Could he bear the thought of living each day knowing that she didn't want him? That his child was being raised without him?

Anger and hatred for himself, for what he had done…it burned inside of him. It was a deep and terrifying feeling, one that he had tapped into before as Rubius. But it was also comforting.

It was all he had left.

A bright burst of red magic flared from him, streaming a vibrant power unlike anything he had ever seen. It funneled his fury, his hatred, his self-loathing, his ultimate desire to change everything that he had done. Then the magic shifted, turning a dark red as it streamed back and forth between him and the orb on the staff. The orb absorbed his energy, turning black like onyx mixed with red flecks of power and energy.

Yes. The dark energy felt comforting.

The magic between his body and the orb fed him more rage, more wrath…

Zaphod cawed in warning, but Kyle didn't care. Consuming the rage made him feel like he still had a heartbeat. The magic listened to his hatred, making his blood pump wildly. The moon shifted to deep red behind the storm clouds. Rumbling came from the earth, and a deep crackling sound came from the heavens.

"COME ON, GOD!" Kyle screamed at the sky, holding the staff up high. "JUST FUCKING KILL ME! YOU WON!"

An odd groaning sound boomed across the heavens.

"COME ON! WHAT ARE YOU WAITING FOR? YOU TOLD ME I WASN'T MEANT FOR THIS LIFE! SO GET ON WITH IT! I'M WAITING!"

There was a loud thunderous crack from the sky as the rain poured harder. Deep red lightning shot every which way in the sky. Then, another strange sound rumbled.

A dark red glowing meteorite flew across the sky, striking the earth in the distance, and an explosion of dark red energy followed.

"YOU MISSED!" he said, taunting the heavens.

Kyle pointed the staff to the heavens, bursting with all the dark energy he had within him.

Another meteor shot down from the sky, landing outside the city limits. Rain poured harder, and the furious flashes of red lightning were relentless.

Suddenly, his body flew back, and he was smashed against the floor of the building. He grasped the staff, using it to slow his roll.

"WHAT IS THE MATTER WITH YOU?" a woman shouted.

As he looked up, Geeta's face was right in his.

She flung out her hand, shooting a large burst of violet-blue magic into the sky, sending one of them back the other way. Another meteorite was about to crash right into a nearby building. Geeta cast a protection bubble around the building. On impact, the meteorite disintegrated on her shield.

Geeta shot another beam of her violet force magic at him. Kyle blasted his own magic back at her, using the staff.

A dark red wave knocked Geeta off her feet.

"What are you DOING?" Geeta shouted. "I was supposed to be heading to Olympia."

"Then why don't you?" Kyle snapped. He turned away. He couldn't look at her. In the distance, Kyle saw another stream of dark red energy trail across the sky. Another meteor.

"Because I knew something was wrong. You weren't with Emerald for the birth of the children? You are supposed to be protecting her! If she isn't protected, then Elyathi can get to her!"

Her words stung him, causing him to tremble.

"Who told you I wasn't there?" Kyle said bitterly. "Emerald?"

"No, it was Emerys."

Kyle gritted his teeth, glaring out at the weeping heavens.

"Kyle, do you hear me? You must go and protect Emerald! This is the perfect opportunity for Elyathi to take her!"

Kyle whirled around, then slammed a spell of lightning against the building next to them. "YES! I heard you!" he snarled, then blasted another beam of lightning at the opposite building. "Newsflash, Geeta: Emerald doesn't want me around her!"

Geeta whipped another force beam at him, and this time he was knocked to the ground hard. His nose started to bleed. "So you are telling me that because Emerald doesn't want you around, you will let Elyathi win? That people will die because you're standing here destroying the city?"

"That isn't fair," Kyle snapped as he hurled a stream of fire at her. She countered with a wall of ice.

There was a sudden blast from the dark heavens, then the earth shook hard.

The two of them stumbled, and Geeta glanced at him. Her face went white, as if she had seen a ghost.

"Kyle," Geeta whispered softly. "I can't believe it…"

"Believe *what*?" Kyle rose to his feet, clutching the staff. It still had his dark red magic in it. It fucking felt good holding it. It was making him forget his pain.

Another quake was under their feet, and the building began to shift. A building collapsed in the distance, while the rumbling of debris echoed.

"KYLE!"

"*What*?"

Geeta shot out her hand, blasting him with her full power of violet magic. It broke his concentration, sending him tumbling to the ground. Kyle jumped up, summoning more magic.

"You…will be the cause of the apocalypse if you don't STOP!"

Kyle went dead silent. He turned to face the sky…

It was as if her words had lifted a spell from his mind. As if he had known all along somehow. During his old life as Rubius, he'd known of the apocalypse. He'd had dreams of it—very real dreams. It was like déjà vu. He had done it before, like a ripple in time…

"You must stop this now before it's too late!" she screamed.

"How? HOW do I stop the pain in my heart?" Kyle shouted through his tears. "Do you understand? Emerald doesn't want me anymore…"

He slumped to his knees. Somewhere nearby, Kyle heard Zaphod caw.

"Kyle…let go of the staff," Geeta whispered as she knelt beside him.

Kyle looked down at the staff in the downpour. The staff shimmered a dark red energy, the orb still black. Just by the touch of the metal, Kyle felt the power within. The power that made him not feel his hurt, his loss.

"Kyle…please," Geeta continued, nudging him. She laid a hand on his shoulder. "I don't know all that has transpired between you and the Queen. But be the man you should be—be true to your oath to protect her. By protecting her, you protect the world."

He was doing a fucking lousy job at that. He was nowhere near Emerald, and raining havoc on the world…

His eyes stung with tears, but he dropped the staff. Geeta kicked it away, then sat down next to him.

For a while, there was silence between them as the dark red rain poured on them. The lightning continued, but the meteorites lessened.

"I still don't know if I can stop the earth from feeling what I'm feeling," Kyle finally said.

"You must try," Geeta said softly.

There was another long pause. Finally, Kyle rummaged in his pants pocket, pulling out a flask.

"Shouldn't you be helping rescue that girl right now?" Kyle said, taking a drink. The liquor didn't help. At all.

"Shouldn't you be watching Emerald right now?" Geeta answered back.

Kyle sighed. He rose to his feet, then glanced back at her. "I promised that I would protect her, so I will. I just will do it at a distance…"

Geeta nodded, then got to her feet. She held out her hand, summoning her violet magic. The staff flung right into her outstretched hand. "I need to borrow this while I'm in Olympia."

"Keep it for all I care," Kyle said.

Geeta shook her head. "No. I will return it." She flashed another wave of her magic, and a violet-blue portal appeared before her. "Victor is waiting for me to return. I must go now, just as you must go watch over Emerald."

"Easier said than done," Kyle said, gritting his teeth.

Geeta gave him a sad smile.

"Geeta?"

"Yes?"

Kyle paused, then looked down. "Thanks."

"Anytime."

Then she vanished into the portal. Kyle was left standing in the rain.

Zaphod flew over to him, then cawed on his shoulder.

"Yeah…" Kyle said, sucking in a deep breath, heaving with sadness. "I'll get close enough but still stay out of her way."

Zaphod cawed in agreement.

Kyle glanced back at the palace. Instant pain dug deep into his heart.

He really didn't know what he was going to do.

✦ ✦ ✦

As Emerald lay in bed feeding her sons, she glanced out her patio window. Deep crimson rain pounded the palace, with intense red lightning flashing every few seconds. Thunder rumbled, shaking the palace. Her handmaidens said all the palace staff were talking about the terrible storm, the worst one they had ever seen in their lifetime. There had been mentions of red hail falling from the skies—even a couple of meteorites—damaging buildings and transports. It was advised by the city not to travel anywhere, as there had been many accidents due to the storms.

Emerald sighed with a deep heaviness. She knew it was because of Kyle. But no matter how upset or disheartened Kyle was, it wasn't going to change her mind.

Go ahead...rain down on Arcadia. It doesn't matter because I will change it for the better with my mother.

Emerald glanced down at her newborn sons. She was going to the future with her sons, to live a peaceful life in a new world. She wanted to forget everything. It hurt too much.

Nathan squirmed in her arms as she tried to calm him. He, too, could sense his father's sorrow. Derek would be here soon, and then they would be traveling.

The last few times Emerald had thought of Derek, she couldn't help her old feelings for him resurfacing. The more she thought of everything that she had with Derek in the past, the more she forgave him for his being unable to control his body and mind against the sorceress. For she had been unable to as well—she had killed Kyle under the sorceress's influence. In a twisted way, it made her realize that her and Derek's fate were the same, that they could relate on a level that no one could understand.

Derek. He had also bent over backward for her. He had traveled back, given her that flower, reminding her how much he loved her. He had traveled across dimensions for the birth. As for Kyle, he didn't even answer his communicator.

Her face darkened at the thought.

The ominous crimson storm paused outside, and everything was silent. Too silent. A flash of red lightning had been locked in time. Emerald jerked her head up, then noticed the color of the bolt change, like blue water pouring over the bolt. The entire world changed, all tinged in blue, with light magic sparkles dusting the air.

Emerald held her sons close to her, then whispered, "Derek…? Is that you?" she said in a low whisper.

Emerald watched as a flutter of the magical sparkles formed together, then flashed. When the flash subsided, Derek stood before her.

She studied Derek as if she hadn't seen him for many years. He was well-dressed, head to toe in his royal garb, adorned with necklaces, rings, a circlet, his dark blue curls framing his face. His face was smooth as marble and cut like the statue of a god. Her gaze drank in his striking eyes, jawline, and moved lower to his muscular form…

"Derek," she whispered, blushing.

Derek bowed deeply to her. "Emerald…My Queen." As he rose, their eyes met. In them, Emerald could see the yearning. "I…I was summoned by your mother. She said that you are ready to travel."

"I am."

Derek's eyes moved to Alexander. Alexander cooed at Derek, and he smiled in awe.

"Would you like to meet your son?"

Derek smiled. "Yes, I would love to."

Emerald gestured to him, and Derek approached, sitting at the edge of her bed. Emerald held out Alexander, and Derek proudly took the child, holding him gently.

As Derek held his baby, the two of them emitted magical blue energy, creating a transparent, vivid blue glow around them.

"He's so perfect," Derek said, tearing up. "So very perfect."

"He is," Emerald agreed, smiling warmly. Boldly, she leaned into him, meeting his gaze.

Derek's eyes searched hers, his cheeks flush. "Emerald...I..."

"Derek, thank you for watching over me," Emerald said softly. "I know that I said this earlier, but I know it wasn't your fault."

Derek paused, then flushed red. "Do you know everything?" he whispered.

Emerald nodded, and his eyes welled up with tears.

"Did Kyle finally confess to you about it?"

"Kyle?" Emerald asked, suddenly dumbfounded. "How would he know? It was the sorceress who told me the truth months ago. I just...came to peace with it."

Derek stared at her as the baby cooed.

Something didn't sit right with his last statement. Kyle had known about the sorceress taking hold of Derek's body? Her blood began to boil.

"Derek..." Emerald began. "What did you mean about Kyle confessing? How can you be sure he knew about it?"

"The sorceress," Derek muttered, sighing heavily. "She and I...we were facing off with each other. I had traveled there in hopes of...*undoing* the damage that she had caused. I couldn't have her do that to anyone else..." His voice trailed off. "Kyle heard me as I confronted her about the whole thing. Ikaria admitted it to me—all of it. Kyle got upset too. Wanted to kill her as well." Derek's face darkened. "She got away. Neither one of us got to put an end to that miserable witch."

Kyle knew the entire time? Not once had he mentioned it. Why wouldn't he have told her? The thought of him hiding it sickened her. It was as if he'd done it on purpose to make Derek look bad.

Emerald paused. *Perhaps he worried that if he told me, I wouldn't want to divorce Derek.*

"I…I thought he would have told you," Derek aid.

Anger rose in her chest as Emerald swallowed hard. "No, he didn't." She glanced up at him. "I don't want to think or speak of him anymore. All is in the past. All is forgiven between us."

Derek cheeks were still red and flush as he smiled sadly. "Hearing your words, my precious queen, mends my heart in so many ways." Derek glanced at Alexander in his arms, then kissed the baby's forehead.

In many ways, it did for her as well. It was as if her eyes had been opened to the world for the first time. Yes, they had been opened when she left the palace. But this…it was opening her heart and soul for the first time—as if she now understood humankind.

She understood Derek's downfall. He'd done everything for her. Because he loved her.

"Derek. I want to personally see the sorceress's downfall, just as much as you do. For what she has done to the both of us." Emerald gestured for him to come closer.

Derek slid closer to her on the bed, until he was right next to her.

Emerald reached and brushed his cheek, then lower to his heart. Emerald could feel his heart racing, beating hard through his chest.

You have all the power… her mother's words echoed in her mind. Both babies made cooing sounds.

Emerald leaned in. She guided her fingertips against his lips. He gave a shy smile, and his cheeks went flush.

"Emerald…you don't know how happy this all makes me…" he breathed with delight.

"I know."

Daringly, Derek softly combed his fingers through her tresses, then brushed his fingertips on the back of her neck. She knew he wanted to kiss her.

"You may," Emerald said.

"Is this…a command?"

"It is a command from your queen."

They smiled at each other, then looked to the babies. They both cradled a child in their arms carefully as they leaned toward each other.

"I want to feel loved," Emerald whispered.

"I will love you always."

Their lips met, and she responded with eager wanting. Emerald felt an intimate energy transferred between their bodies. In it, she felt his immense desire for her. His yearning for her. His unfailing love for her. Their kiss deepened. His plush lips tasted so good, quenching her sexual thirst.

He needed her, wanted her.

Emerald hadn't felt this since the day Kyle returned. Not like this.

She felt *loved*.

As if he had heard her thoughts, Derek gently moved his head back, releasing her lips. "I give you my heart, my soul, and pledge my life to you. Emerald, you always had my heart. Always."

"I will wear your pledge upon my heart," she said softly.

It was what she needed. To be empowered. She was the one in control of her life and destiny. A thought of Kyle came over her, but she pushed it aside.

Emerald pulled away softly, then gently held his hand. "Shall we go?" she said.

Derek smiled. "Do they have the green blood in their life force?"

"I have taken care of it."

Emerald rose from the bed, along with Derek, both cradling a child. Derek stretched out his free hand, then swirled it gently. Glowing blue magic appeared, rippling into a magical portal.

She heard a faint sound, one that wove a deep spell behind magic…

"Wait," Emerald said, halting mid-step.

A familiar tune lingered in the air, as if kissing her lightly.

It was Kyle's song for her.

Goodbye, Kyle. Perhaps in another life, we will live as we should have, without the pains of this present world.

Emerald turned to Derek, then smiled. "I thought I forgot something, but it's okay."

"Are you sure?" he asked. Burning blue magic highlighted his face as his eyes glowed with energy.

"I am more than sure," she said, holding his hand reassuringly. "Let's go." They both stepped inside.

✦ ✦ ✦

Kyle was on his way toward the palace, flying on his red winds when he felt a sudden sharp pain in his chest. The pain struck him hard, as if he'd been punched in the chest.

Zaphod squawked loudly.

"I can't breathe…" he told Zaphod.

He was wobbling in midair, fighting with the wind as it started turning against him. Below him were the tops of the Arcadian skyscrapers, taunting him to fall to his doom.

The pain continued, reaching straight into his heart as Zaphod squawked frantically.

Kyle shot out his hand, finally able to conquer the bizarre feeling in him—summoning more red wind. The magical winds obeyed, carrying him safely to the closest rooftop. He gasped for breath but couldn't find the air that he needed.

The pain in his heart twisted and turned so sharp, it was as if he'd been stabbed in the heart. But this pain was deep, like a profound emptiness in his soul, as if half of his body had been cut away permanently.

Then, he knew. Emerald was gone. She had left this world.

"Em…" Kyle rolled over, gasping for breath. She was gone from this world. That's why his life force had gone haywire…she left this world. And he knew the only place she could have gone.

The future. With her fucking mother and Derek.

Kyle lay on his back, letting the red rain drench him as he continued to find his breath. He felt fucking sick.

"EMERALD!" he screamed, rolling to his stomach, pounding the roof with his fist. The earth quaked suddenly, the metal twisting nearby until it could no longer twist. Zaphod remained near him but made no noise.

It was too late to protect Emerald. She'd made her choice. She had chosen to go of her own free will to her mother. Just like how she didn't want to divorce Derek. No. She wanted it.

Kyle shouted again in defeat.

Emerald had gone with Derek.

With their child.

The skies bled more red rain. All he wanted to do was go on a wild joyride and crash his bike. That would be a way to go out once and for all. Or maybe he could go live under a fucking rock.

But if Elyathi got her fucking way, there would be no one who knew him.

Kyle paused, fuming about Elyathi. He recalled all the fucked-up shit she'd done in the future. He would have to face Elyathi to upset her future plans. Possibly Emerald too.

*Dammit all to hell...*Kyle stood, then grasped Zaphod. He needed to get to the future to stop Elyathi. He paused. Could he travel to the future? Was it possible? Could he survive?

Kyle stroked Zaphod's wet feathers. "This time, you are coming with me."

Zaphod whistled.

"That's right. We are going to the wastelands to wait for Geeta."

CHAPTER 77

◆

ORANGE

Garrett's and Scion's motorbikes hummed loudly behind Telly as they drove through the wastelands. The skies were overcast, crackling with red lightning. In the distance, it looked as if large explosions were being detonated. Behind them, the rain had already started pouring on Arcadia. Soon it would reach them. The wind from the storms was fierce, creating sand formations, making it tough to cross particular sections. Underneath her motorbike, Telly felt the ground shifting.

It had to be the Olympian boy.

Hold on, Gwen!

"Two point three miles, we will arrive," Scion's voice hummed in her earpiece.

"The red storm," Garrett said through his device.

"I know. Be prepared," Telly said.

"Affirmative."

The wind whipped through her stubby ponytail as she closed her eyes. *Get me through this! she begged the magic. I need my daughter back!*

In her mind's eye, Telly saw Gwen's smile; it was a from a recent memory when they had been getting along. *Gwen...*Telly latched on to that memory. *I love you, my daughter. I love you with all my being. I am coming...*

Telly felt the orange magic flow through her veins, pumping hard. *I need more! she cried to the magic. I need much, much more!* The magic obeyed, like a giant tidal wave surging through her soul.

Flashing her eyes open, Telly released the magic, funneling it over Scion as the cyborg drove. The magic ribboned over him, changing his appearance right before her eyes. Her magic melded him into a new person—giving him the form of Geeta. Scion had a special gadget that Garrett had crafted for him, which made it so that the other cyborgs would have trouble detecting him as one of their own kind. With another burst, Telly swirled her magic around Garrett, and he took on the image of Drew.

Telly narrowed her eyes, readying herself.

"Miss Hearly," Scion called out.

"I see it!"

In the distance: the cityscape of Olympia. It was near sundown, the city lights flickering on, readying for the night. Storm clouds thundered while deep red lightning crackled.

It was only a matter of time before the rains hit. Or worse, the boy would cause a massive quake and endanger everyone inside the city, including Gwen.

With another shimmer of Telly's orange magic, her weapons became invisible to everyone but her.

The road to Olympia widened as they approached the city gates. Industrial buildings rose to the heavens, similar to Arcadia, but with a different style of architecture. Iron gates wrapped around the city for miles, dwellings dotting the sides, making up small wasteland settlements.

They approached the city gates, and Scion and Garrett slowed to a stop on their dirt bike. Guards were standing out front. Hybrid soldiers, maybe? They were armed, with body armor and cybernetic parts grafted into their bodies. They noticed Telly, Drew, and Geeta, drawing their weapons.

"State your business!" they ordered.

Scion planted his feet on the ground, still seated on his bike. Garrett did likewise.

"I said state your business!"

Telly hopped off and marched over to one of the guards. He raised an eyebrow, watching her as she stormed up to him.

"You get your king on the communicator right now and tell him I have what he wants!" Telly shouted. "But if the king wants them, I want my daughter first!"

"You the prisoner's mother?" one of the other guards called out.

"You bet your ass I am!" Telly snapped. Garrett and Scion got off their bikes, then approached behind her, still in their disguises.

"I need to confirm if her story checks out," another guard said, giving them a once-over before walking away while using his communicator. As he was talking on the communicator away from the group, the other guards kept a watchful eye on them. Especially Telly.

A few minutes later, the guard came back with another high-ranking guard.

"These are the ones?" he asked.

"Yes, Captain."

The captain turned to Telly. "Your daughter is en route right now with His Majesty for the exchange."

"Good. We'll wait right here," Telly said.

Telly watched as the captain punched a message into his communicator. She glanced up at the imposing buildings' tops reaching to the skies. Her eyes took everything in, noting the city's sewage and electrical lines running inside the gates from both sides. They were drawing power from an underground source. To the side, the guards made small gestures.

In her pocket, Telly grasped one of her magitech vials in her hands.

Half an hour later, something caught her eye from above. There was a break in the thick clouds, revealing the moon. But instead of a whitish light, it was blood red. The clouds quickly covered it again, and a flash of crimson lightning was followed by a loud crash of thunder.

Garrett gave her a look in warning.

Finally, a transport neared the gates overhead, its floodlights nearly blinding her.

"Here they come," said the captain.

Scion sent a message into Telly's goggles. *My scans indicate that your daughter is not on that transport.*

Telly narrowed her eyes. She wasn't surprised in the least.

"I always knew you lot were liars," Telly called out.

The captain snorted. "Excuse me?"

Telly drew her invisible magitech weapon. "Go to hell, assholes."

She cocked it, then fired at the transport.

A giant blast of fiery magic shot straight into the transport, bursting it into flames. It twirled down in a loose spiral, then crashed into the city behind the gates.

Telly loaded and fired again.

Another blast rocked the gates, the guards incinerated in the magical fires.

There were sounds of men shouting mixed with weapons firing. Scion threw up a protective barrier around them, reverting to his true form. The bullets shot into his barrier, getting lodged into it.

Garrett, also in his true form, blasted his magitech weapon. "So that's your new weapon?" he asked as he took out a guard.

"It is."

"Why didn't you let me help you build it?"

"Because I was pissed at you."

Garrett shrugged. "Fair enough."

More bullets tried to pierce Scion's shield. Telly glanced at the gate. There was too much debris to get through.

"Scion!"

"Yes, Miss Hearly?"

Telly grabbed another vial from her pocket, loaded it into her weapon, then cocked it. "Get ready for another round!"

"Yes, Miss Hearly."

Scion released his barrier quickly, allowing Telly to aim her magitech weapon and fire.

A blast of fire exploded all around them, filling the entire area with deep flames of red and orange, the fire blazing wildly against Scion's shield. There were glittery golden flecks and a dome barrier shielding them.

She blinked as the fires slowly died down.

The gate was open.

"Let's go!" Telly yelled.

Garrett readied his gun, and Scion refreshed their shields. Just as they were about to move, their golden barriers melted away.

"Who's the liar now? Presenting a false image of the violet-gifted!" hissed an invisible voice.

A hard blow landed on Telly's face. One of the lenses in her glasses cracked.

"Telly!" screamed Garrett.

Telly whipped around, seeing a shimmer of yellow-orange in the shape of a man. It was hard to make out the full details with her damaged glasses.

He's a yellow-gifted. Suddenly, she thought of Scion. *This man...maybe he was the one who had donated his blood to Olympia!* Whoever he is, he is going to get blown away if he doesn't move.

"Out of my way, asshole," Telly snarled, pulling the trigger.

"I move for no one."

Hmph.

Telly cast an illusion on herself, then her comrades, their images becoming like the shifting sands and winds.

"Where are you, you bitch!" the man shouted.

As the man stalked about, Scion recast more barrier magic over them, this time pairing her magic with his.

"I don't have time for childish *games.*"

Telly funneled her orange magic to the unknown man. It ate away at his own magic, making him visible to all, revealing his features. The man was tall, lanky, and had a menacing, sunken-in, elongated face with deep-pitted eyes and an extremely pointed nose. Because of his yellow gift, he had yellow eyes and hair, a wiry beard, and deep tanned skin.

"I want Geeta!" he screamed.

"And I want my *daughter*!" Telly screamed through the translucent barrier.

The man flung his hand out, streaming his magic against Scion's barrier, which melted away.

Scion sent another surge of power to the barrier, but it was no use. Scion only had the energy that was given to him through cybernetics and magic combined. This man, on the other hand, was a true gifted.

"My turn," Garrett whispered. Then he shot the man straight in the chest with his weapon.

The man flew backward, bleeding.

"Asshole!" Garrett shouted.

The yellow-gifted man smiled, putting his hand over his chest as he coughed up blood. Then they watched as the man healed himself. It was a shoddy job, but it was enough to stabilize him.

"This man has power in the frequency of 565 nanometers," Scion stated. "But it appears he utilizes other frequencies."

There was another crack of lightning, then a roar of thunder. Glowing red rain started to fall.

With a flash of magic, the yellow-gifted man disappeared.

"Scion, is the man still here?" Telly asked.

"Negative," Scion confirmed. "He has left the vicinity."

Telly sucked in her breath. "We've no time to waste. Let's move."

CHAPTER 78

◆

There was a small knock at her door. Gwen figured it was Mae checking on her, seeing if she needed more ointment for her face, another bandage needing cleaning, or some tea. She couldn't move, her body still in agony from the beating.

Another knock.

Why doesn't she just come in? It wasn't like she needed permission to open her door. They kept her locked up.

There was another small knock, then a pause. After a moment, the door handle clicked, then cracked open.

"Psst, Gwen. Are you there?" Jihyun said in a loud whisper, poking his head in her room.

"Jihyun?"

He quickly closed the door. "Gwen!" he said in a happy whisper.

"What are you doing here? Aren't the guards out there?"

"They are all distracted. Something is happening outside the palace!" he said, sounding excited. "I heard them talking about other gifted people, and even a red rainstorm! Isn't that exciting?"

Gwen's heart stopped. Gifted people? Red rainstorm? Somehow, she had a strong feeling these events were tied to her mom or dad.

Gwen grimaced as she sat up in bed. "What gifted? Do you know?"

Jihyun ran over to her excitedly, then began to slow as he neared her, eyeing her. "Why is your face all like that? Did you fall?"

"Not exactly," she muttered.

"What did you do? I can ask Vihaan to heal you! He always heals me when

I'm hurt. He can heal almost anyone unless they are very bad." Jihyun leaned close, inspecting her face.

Vihaan. The last person she wanted to see. "I doubt he will heal me," Gwen mumbled.

"Why do you say that?"

"Because he was there when this happened." Gwen jutted her jaw out, angry tears forming.

Jihyun stared at her, his face going from concern to confusion. "He…he saw this happen? Did you bump into something? Why didn't he help you?"

Gwen flinched in pain.

"Why, Gwen?"

"Because!"

Jihyun was startled. "I don't understand."

Gwen looked straight into his eyes. "Jihyun, your father ordered to have me beaten if I didn't do what he said. I didn't, so the guards beat me. And your 'friend' Vihaan…he beat me afterwards too."

It was as if the kid's world suddenly collapsed. Jihyun's face went through a range of emotions. If it weren't such a terrible time, it would be almost comical seeing his strange facial expressions. Finally, his eyes simmered into deep red behind his narrow slits.

"My dad ordered you to get hurt?"

"Yes."

"What did he want you to do?" Jihyun asked, sounding older than a normal eight-year-old kid.

"He wanted me to call my mother. I didn't want to do it because it would make her irrational, and that would cause her to run right out here. The king wanted to trade me for my father and another violet-gifted."

"Trade you? You mean, you would leave?" he said, angrier than before.

Finally, she was getting through to him. It was a revelation for the boy.

"Yes. I would leave and never come back," Gwen continued. "They would do bad things to my father and my friend Geeta. I didn't want them to hurt my dad and my friend, so they hurt me instead." Gwen leaned in. "And with you coming here to see me, they will definitely punish me again."

Jihyun was visibly upset. She had to keep pressing on him.

"What's the matter?"

"I don't want you to go, Gwen! I don't know why my dad hurt you. You are my best friend! Why would he hurt you? I don't understand!" he wailed.

"I want to go home, Jihyun, but I don't want to leave you. You are my best friend too," she whispered. "But you must understand that I can't stay here forever."

He cried harder. "You can't leave!"

"I don't want them to hurt me again, and I don't want them to hurt my dad either," she whispered. "This place…it isn't good for me." She paused. "Not for you either."

"What do you mean?"

Gwen gave him a big shoulder hug. "Jihyun, a good man wouldn't beat people. Bryce, Vihaan, Councilor Jason…they are bad men too. They are drugging you! Your medicine is bogus!"

The boy's lip quivered. "I don't get it."

"It's your genetics. The medicine they are giving you is too potent for your body to metabolize. It makes you flip out."

"You mean…I'm not sick?"

Gwen scoffed. "Well, not technically. You do have a genetic abnormality, but it's nothing that actual medicine can fix. They use your power while you are jacked up on meds. I've seen it."

"They…they're using me?"

"Yes. And they are using me too. I'm a prisoner, and they will continue to use and hurt me until they have my parents." Gwen stared at him. "My *gifted* parents."

"Is that who's outside?"

Gwen nodded. "I believe so. They are coming here to save me."

Jihyun's eyes glowed more intensely.

Good. Let him explode. That way I can get out of here quicker.

"I don't want you to leave!"

"Come with me. You can live with me and my parents," Gwen said. "We'll take good care of you."

Her chamber door swung open, startling them both.

"Jihyun!" said Councilor Jason. A string of guards followed him in. "There you are. We were worried. We looked all over the palace for you. How did you get in here?" Jason frowned. "You know you shouldn't be running off like that!"

Jihyun shot his head in Jason's direction, his eyes like hellfire. "You hurt Gwen…" he said, pointing at her.

"We did no such thing."

The boy wasn't convinced. "YOU HURT GWEN!"

"She didn't want to help us, Jihyun…" Jason said, backing up. "She was not being very nice."

The boy answered with a deep, red-hot glow surrounding his body.

"There are bad men outside," Jason continued. "They are going to kill your father. He needs your help."

Jihyun's eyes narrowed. "NO! You're lying!"

"It's time for your medicine now. We can talk about this after you've had your medicine," Jason said, trying to defuse the situation.

"I don't want my medicine! You are tricking me!" Jihyun screamed, bathed in his magic. "You are a bad man! You all hurt Gwen!"

"She's the one that's tricking you!" Jason yelled, pointing at Gwen.

"Gwen cares about me, but you, you don't!" he screamed.

Jason turned to the guards. "Get Vihaan and Bryce. Now!" he shouted.

Jihyun's body was entirely consumed with his magic. His eyes were pure red burning coals. The floorboards started rattling as dark red energy radiated around him.

Oh crap…

Several guards bolted, while Jason backed up. "Now, now. You don't want to have another nightmare, do you? Think how scary they are."

"You are *giving* him nightmares with your medicine!" Gwen shouted.

Jihyun's magic swelled in size around him, swirling faster.

"Nonsense," Jason said calmly. The man looked like he was going to crap his pants.

"YOU ARE A BAD MAN!" Jihyun repeated as the floors shook harder and the walls creaked. More red power funneled around him, swirling violently.

Gwen didn't know if she should get near him or far away, because he was about to blow.

"Jihyun, please, calm down. You don't understand. Gwen attacked your father," Jason lied.

Gwen turned to Jihyun. "He's lying!"

"Gwen is my best friend! You are a liar…" Jihyun repeated. Gwen's instinct told her to get close to Jihyun, so she edged closer. "I'm going to hurt you just like how you hurt Gwen!" he screamed.

Suddenly, anything that was metal in the room shot up in the air.

The rest of the guards bolted, while Jason screamed, "Where is Vihaan?!" He ran toward the door. As he grabbed the handle, Jihyun raised his arm like a move in his video game. The metal handle shot out, straight into Jason's gut.

Jason cried out in pain, slumping to his knees and clutching his stomach. "Jihyun! Stop this insanity!"

There was a glimmering yellow bubble of light, then a flash, and Vihaan appeared.

"About time," Jason snarled, trying to stop the bleeding.

Vihaan ignored the comment and yanked the metal out of his gut. Jason threw up in response, his vomit mixing with his blood all around him. Vihaan laid a hand on him, sending a wave of yellow magic swirling around Jason. The yellowish-green magic grew brightly, then began mending Jason's stomach.

"That's the best I can do. Now get out of here. You've done enough already," Vihaan snapped. Jason sprinted out the door, and Vihaan turned to the two of them. "You. You are just as insolent as Geeta!" he snarled, pointing at Gwen.

Gwen gulped.

Just then, Jihyun stepped in front of Gwen, entirely consumed with his magic. "No. You are the bad one!" Jihyun screamed. His power grew brighter, as the foundation of the building began to shake. Outside, it was pouring deep red rain.

Vihaan funneled his magic around himself. "Jihyun. You need to stop this nonsense now!"

A blue flash of magic appeared next to Vihaan. "What has happened?" said a voice.

"It's Jihyun," the yellow-gifted man snarled. "Where have you been?"

A whirlpool of blue magic appeared in front of them, and a man stepped out. Vihaan expanded his magic, protecting them both. The second man glanced at Gwen and Jihyun, then lowered his brow. "They are ready for the boy…" the blue-gifted man said.

"We can't bring him in the middle of this, now, can we?" Vihaan snapped.

Gwen turned to Jihyun. She wasn't sure if she should interrupt him, considering she could be an innocent bystander in the process if she did so. But it was now or never, and she would chance it.

"Jihyun! Did you hear that?" Gwen called out. "They're going to take you somewhere. Then we will never see each other again!"

"NEVER!" Jihyun screamed. "I won't let them take you away from me!"

Jihyun raised both his hands, screaming in a rage. Was he focusing his magic for the first time…without the mech? Could the kid finally control his thoughts to cast a spell coherently?

Outside, the storm continued, with loud thunderous quaking. The city buildings began to groan…

Suddenly, Gwen was struck in the face as Jihyun screamed in pain.

CHAPTER 79

◆

ORANGE

M*om never tells me anything! You all treat me like a child!*

Malfunction.

Memories of his daughter flashed through his mind. Programming. Building weapons. A three-year-old girl. A seventeen-year-old girl. Riding a dirt bike. Fighting the boy with the power of 750 nanometers…

Malfunction.

She was gone.

Malfunction.

Drew jerked his eyes open.

Gwen. She was gone.

Malfunction.

Drew slowly turned his head; his neck felt heavy and his body lethargic. He was keenly aware of the wires attached to him, giving him hardly any slack to move.

Drew moved his humanoid hand, feeling the cool, smooth surface that he lay on. The only visible light was the blinking of his grafted cybernetics dancing back and forth against the walls. Water drops echoed in the cavern chamber.

He was in the refuge.

Drew struggled as he sat up, glancing at the monitors nearby. Telly was nowhere in sight. Seeing the tablet next to him, he picked it up, then scrolled through all the data. According to the data log, he was supposed to be sedated for twenty-four hours. Scrolling through the file, he determined that he was functional enough without support.

I wonder where Tell-me-lots is.

Using his human hand, Drew ripped the wires from his body one by one, then yanked the cords from his body, arms, legs. With each rip, his head felt fuzzier and weaker. The only cable left was the largest one—the one plugged into the back of his neck.

His cybernetic hand didn't have the same strength as his human hand. Drew tried many times to grab and turn the cable out of his neck socket, but it resulted in failure.

He couldn't stay here any longer. He had to get his daughter.

Cannot compute.

Drew jolted.

With all of his might, Drew stood up with the cable still attached. His neck ached and twisted oddly from the weight. He had to get that cable detached.

Grabbing the cable with his human hand, Drew shot orange-red ice into the cable, freezing it. The cable became incredibly cold. His neck and head felt numb…

Then with a loud grunt, Drew pulled himself forward like a mule in a yoke. The cable shattered, and he went flying into a desk full of equipment.

Shaken, Drew glanced around, seeing another device. Telly's log.

He grabbed it, scanning her notes quickly.

There wasn't much, but it did give him what he needed.

Gwen was being held against her will in Olympia.

A foreign emotion flooded his body, sinking deep into his heart. Fury.

Drew set down the tablet, shaking with this feeling. He summoned his illusion magic. Within the shimming orange magical dust, he disappeared.

CHAPTER 80

GREEN

Derek's blue magic pulled away from the two of them, revealing the most magnificent structure Emerald had ever seen: the High Court Citadel.

Emerald held Nathan in her arms, while Derek held Alexander. With a silent gasp, Emerald took a step forward, marveling at what lay before her.

Before them was a sprawling circular courtyard, full of citizens walking through a magnificent garden with white marbled sculptures and a giant water fountain. Surrounding the outer court were different sections of the citadel, flags displaying the colors that housed those gifted. In the distance, many towers with long turrets rose to the heavens.

"It's beautiful, isn't it?" Derek said, smiling at her as he cradled Alexander.

"It's more than beautiful," Emerald said. She turned to Derek, then blushed. "Is this where you have been the entire time?"

He shook his head. "I have been here, but also been traveling throughout time. I was in Arcadia for a while before you saw me."

Emerald glanced at him, then paused. "I…I'm sorry if I made you hesitate."

Derek grinned brightly. "There is no need to apologize. Now, let's go see your mother."

Emerald and Derek held the babies as they walked through the citadel. There were a few gasps and disbelieving stares.

"Why are they staring at me?" she whispered to Derek. "Does the citadel know who I am?"

"No one has ever seen a green-gifted before. You are the very first."

Alexander gurgled.

Emerald walked closely, clutching Nathan. "Are we going to my mother's chambers?"

"Your mother is at the High Court. They are all waiting for you," Derek said.

"They?" She suddenly felt anxious at the thought of a panel of gifted—the ones deemed the most powerful—all waiting to meet her. But she shook off her fear, knowing that she had power that none of them had. They should be scared of her.

"Yes, all of the High Court." Derek leaned in, whispering gently, "Emerald. Just…be careful when talking to them."

Emerald shot him a look. "Why?"

He glanced at her, voice still lowered. "Your mother…" He bit his lip. "Your mother told me in confidence that she doesn't entirely trust them. They all have the same goal and purpose, and nothing has happened between them. She just has an inkling."

Emerald stopped. "What do you think?"

"Me?" Derek said. "It's hard to say. But I do feel differently about Belinda, the red justice. I can't put my finger on it, and I don't know if it's necessarily bad or good. Her life force seems…unique?" He paused. "Maybe that's not the right word. I just don't know."

Emerald held Nathan closely, then nodded. "Thank you," she said in a low voice. "I'll be careful."

They continued walking. Gifted, guards, lords, ladies, courtesans—they all fell to their knees, bowing low to both of them. Many of them spoke words of reverence as they passed. Emerald felt a little shy being put up on a pedestal as she was, but it was time for her to accept her position. She deserved to be held in high regard.

They turned another corner, and Emerald saw her mother talking to one of the courtiers. Her mother paused, seeing her, then brightened into a big smile.

"Emerald," her mother said, tears swelling in her eyes as she hurried up to her.

"Mom," Emerald said.

Emerald and her mother embraced, crying, laughing, carefully with Nathan between them.

They parted, with her mother glancing at Alexander, then Nathan, then back to Alexander. "They are precious," she cooed.

"Would you like to hold one of them?" Emerald said, offering.

Her mother glanced at Nathan, then her eyes moved to Alexander. "I'll hold him, since Derek must be on his way." She took Alexander from Derek, and he bowed.

Her heart sank a bit hearing that Derek was leaving.

"What?" Emerald turned to Derek. "Where? We just got here."

"In order to complete the spell, there is a little work left to do," he said.

Complete the spell? He had to mean violet magic.

Derek perked up, as if he heard her thoughts. His mind gently brushed against hers, and she opened her thoughts to him.

Emerald suddenly understood. He needed to get back to Arcadia. Geeta was there.

It's not easy telling you this, but by now you must know that we need Geeta's power, he told her in her mind.

Just don't hurt her.

I will do everything in my power not to. All we need is her blood and her gift. She will remain alive. But if it comes down to fighting her, I must.

The thought made her uneasy. But once the new world came, Geeta would be alive and well, happily living in eternal bliss.

I understand.

"Wish me luck," he whispered.

"Okay," Emerald said, tearing up. She held out her hand, and he kissed it gently.

"I'll be back soon."

Derek bowed to both women, then formed a portal. After he stepped through, the portal disappeared, the blue sparkles shimmering away.

Her mother looked at her. "Don't worry, my daughter. Derek is strong." Alexander burbled, and her mother kissed him on the forehead. "Isn't that right? Your father will be back," she said to Alexander in baby talk. She turned to a court attendant. "Summon the handmaidens that I assigned for the children."

"Right away." He bowed, then was off.

"I can take care of the children, Mom," Emerald said.

"I know, but for your High Court appearance, someone else must watch them. You can't bring them in with you."

Emerald didn't want some strangers watching her children, even if it was few a short while. But she didn't protest either. It was hard to push back against a mother she hadn't seen in years.

The court attendant came back, followed by five handmaidens.

Her mother smiled. "I have a little surprise for you. I chose five handmaidens, all in white." Her mother's white eyes glowed. "Just like Arcadia."

The handmaidens took Alexander from her mother, while Emerald glanced down at Nathan. She felt guilty leaving him.

"He will be all right, my daughter, rest assured."

Emerald handed Nathan to one of the women, who smiled at the baby. They turned to bow at her and her mother, then walked off.

"Let's go."

They walked to the High Court's audience chamber, the double doors opening before them. Emerald entered with her mother, and the doors shut behind them.

Inside, Emerald stood in awe, pausing to take it all in. Six thrones, aligned in a semicircle, spread out before her. Each throne had a jewel above the throne—each color of the Spectrum was represented. Behind the thrones, grand marble pillars rose to the ceiling, framing the open sky behind them. Wisps of clouds blew gently by.

Enchanted urns, spaced out evenly, burned incense around the room.

"Where are they?" Emerald whispered to her mother.

"Have patience."

As if on cue, fuzzy images began appearing on the thrones. Five individuals sat on each throne—all but the green throne.

Elyathi nodded to the high justices, while Emerald followed suit.

"So it is true. The Queen of Arcadia is here," a woman with long red hair stated.

"High justices, let me formally introduce my daughter, Queen Emerald of Arcadia," Elyathi said. She gave Emerald a little gesture, and Emerald stepped forward.

"Ah, finally. At last," an old man with wispy white-blue beard said.

Emerald recognized him. She had stumbled upon him when she saw the sorceress Ikaria back in time.

The red-gifted woman eyed Emerald curiously. "Queen Emerald," she said, "I have been anticipating this moment for a long time. I am High Justice Belinda of the Red. Next to me is Perserine of the Orange, Tyllos of the Yellow, Borgen of the Blue, and Nyrden—temporary ward of the violet throne."

Nyrden scoffed. "*Permanent* in the new world, Belinda."

Belinda smiled. "Yes, indeed."

She was curious what made Nyrden a permanent violet-gifted, but didn't want to ask during her first meeting.

"A pleasure to meet you," Emerald said, bowing. She avoided looking at the blue-gifted Justice Borgen.

"My daughter, there is no need to bow to the high justices," her mother said, pulling her to her feet. "You are equals to them, as you have the power of the green gift."

Emerald noticed that several of the high justices appeared miffed at her mother's words, especially Nyrden. Her mother noticed too. "Isn't that right, high justices? Emerald is here to claim the green throne."

Emerald cast a questioning glance at her mother. This was entirely unexpected. Emerald eyed the empty throne and felt a sudden sense of longing—to be a part of a new way of life, surrounded by other gifted and ruling with them.

"You say that she is most powerful, Lady Elyathi, and I do not doubt your words," Tyllos said. "But does she have the will of the God of Light? Does she have the heart? Does she truly want to be seated on this throne?"

"I say we test her power," Nyrden chimed in. "Let us see if she has the full power of her gift. For only the most powerful is worthy of it."

"Yes, let us test her gift," Belinda said.

"As payment for the test, you must give us a taste of your blood," Nyrden stated.

Emerald's heart raced suddenly. What kind of test?

"What is the meaning of this?" her mother demanded. "How dare you demand her blood, after the many years that I have served you!"

"Do not take offense, Lady Elyathi. We test anyone who is to be seated on a throne," Tyllos continued. "Surely you know of our shared power?"

Her mother fell silent with a stone-cold face. "I do. But must we now? We are so close to the new world."

"We do not know if your son-in-law will be successful in the past, nor now with our present situation," Tyllos continued. Present situation? Was the sorceress causing havoc in this time too? Then again, Derek had said that Kyle battled the sorceress as his past self…

A renewed surge of anger came over Emerald. She still couldn't swallow the fact that Kyle didn't have the audacity to tell her about the sorceress. That he knew what she had done. She knew about it…but him? He kept it from her.

As she fought back her bitterness, Emerald told herself to cut ties from her pain. Her hurt. To move forward. To show these justices her full power.

This was her chance. This was the time, here and now, to show everyone that she was not just some frightened young girl. After all, she'd been the one who put an end to the sorceress back in Arcadia. She was the one who battled in the depths of Hell.

Emerald gracefully stepped forward. "I will take your test," she said.

"I knew you'd see reason," Belinda said.

"But only on one condition," Emerald said.

The justices gave her a curious glance. "You…have a condition?" said Nyrden.

"And what's that?" Borgen asked in a wispy voice.

Emerald turned to stare at them all, evenly down the line of thrones. "You want my magic. You have been pursuing me ever since you knew of me. I know you—especially you, Borgen of the Blue. You cannot dismiss me or my words. You saw me in time, when I came here by accident."

"Nonsense. You must have had a dream," he countered her sharply.

"Do not lie. It was no dream, that I can assure you," Emerald continued. "You have sent blue-gifted after me while I was under a sleep. And don't get me started on my father, Olympia, and other events that have transpired in my time over my magic," Emerald said, with her mother casting a sharp glance at Belinda. "And once again, you are attempting to get my blood."

Belinda folded her hands in delight.

"You'd best watch your words," Nyrden said pointedly.

"I'm not finished, High Justice," Emerald said. Her tone surprised her mother, even herself. She had newfound strength. No more was she going to cower to anyone. No longer was she going to be afraid. "I will be put through your trial. Test me. Know my heart. It is strong and true. The purest of hearts, devoted to the God of Light's will. Though I have faltered at times in my life, I cannot be blamed. Everyone falters at some point. It is the path of life." Emerald took a deep breath, continuing.

"If I fail your trial, you all can have a taste of my blood, and I will be subservient to your will, for it would be the God of Light's will, though you will live in the new world with a fraction of my power."

The high justices' eyes went wide, then they exchanged glances. Emerald could tell they approved. "However, if I pass, and I am seated on the High Court as a green justice, no one will have my blood. My power belongs to me, and I alone will choose who to give its gift to. And those of you who try to take my power, your magic will be sucked out of your marrow by my mother, and I will drain the life out of you until you are no more." Emerald glanced at them evenly.

Her mother's eyes burned a hot white, pride filling her.

The high justices' faces burned with anger, all except Belinda's. The red justice seemed amused.

"You speak confident words, Queen Emerald of Arcadia," stated Tyllos.

"Do not misunderstand me, High Justice," Emerald said. "I am merely stating my position of power. You want to bring a new world into existence? So do I. We are working toward the same cause. If we are to have peace, we must have understanding."

This statement appeared to have some effect, because their faces relaxed. "Indeed, you are correct," Tyllos said.

"Well, I for one don't like it that you've come in here and changed our rules, Queen Emerald," Nyrden stated.

"And I did not like it when you came into my kingdom to try to snatch my magic from me," Emerald stated coldly. "Sending all those blue-gifted, then Lady Vala? You should have known better. You would be on the offense too if you were in my position, wouldn't you? Like I said, I am trying to make peace, but I will make peace through the demonstration of my power. My power is sacred, like every other gift. No one has a right to my green blood. It is mine to give to whom I choose."

"She is definitely your daughter, Lady Elyathi," Belinda said.

"She has the God of Light's will instilled in her," her mother answered.

"A wild card, she is," added Perserine.

"Yes, indeed." Belinda nodded, staring at Emerald in thought. She brushed her long hair aside, sweeping it back, then leaned forward. "So be it. Let us begin our trial now, for there is no reason to delay. Let there be judgment from the God of Light now." There was a deep red sparkle in her eyes.

"I am ready," Emerald declared.

Belinda rose from her throne, and the others followed suit. "Lady Elyathi, would you please step away from the circle?"

"Yes," Elyathi said coolly. Her mother put a hand on Emerald's shoulder, both of them staring at each other. With a formal bow to her, her mother vanished, then reappeared in the far back of the room.

I will show them what I am truly made of.

Emerald watched as the other high justices rose from their seats. The room dissolved away, forming an empty dimensional void.

She was in complete blackness.

Emerald took a deep breath. Before she finished exhaling, there was a sharp squeeze in her lungs, and all the oxygen fled. She gasped, her body numb from lack of air. There was no air, no *nothing*, in this dimension.

A desperate rage filled her life force, and Emerald tapped into her adjacent magic. With a surge of powerful vibrant blue magic, she screamed in her mind. She pictured the dimension disappearing and reappearing in the High Court chambers.

The void instantly melted away and returned her to the chambers. Breath entered her lungs once again.

Angrily, Emerald quickly searched for the blue-magic life force within the chamber—there was still a ripple in an unseen time portal. Throwing out her hand, she shot blue magic into that ripple, then yanked back, throwing old Justice Borgen into the chamber.

He went rolling, tumbling hard against the marble. "How could you?" he cried.

"How could I?" Emerald question. "Like *this*." With another flash of her hand, she shot out her dark green magic. It funneled over Borgen, draining away his life slowly.

The justice screamed, but it was short-lived, as a severe red ice-shard storm funneled through the room. Quickly, Emerald cast a yellow protection spell, deflecting the ice shards hurled at her. Then she called upon time magic, shooting the ice shards back, finding the invisible Nyrden.

The high justice screamed. With one hand maintaining her shield, Emerald funneled another dark wave of green magic and sucked the life out of Nyrden, all while still draining Borgen's life force.

The two justices screamed as they writhed on the floor.

Just as Emerald was about to sever her magical connection, a yellow shield funneled around Nyrden and Borgen, and there was a flash of bright red before Emerald.

Belinda's body became pure fire as she enveloped Emerald. The woman held on tight as Emerald's shield melted away. Tyllos had dispelled it.

Emerald's clothes caught on fire, her skin burning in hellish pain. Deep hellish burns marred her body as Belinda's fiery form held her tight.

Crying out in pain, Emerald called upon her green magic, funneling life and healing back into her body. As Belinda's magic fought to incinerate her, Emerald's body repaired itself, soothing her insides.

Then Emerald began draining Belinda's life away, fast and furious.

Glaring into Belinda's fiery eyes, Emerald said softly, "You cannot win against the power of life."

Belinda burst out laughing, then inched near her face. "I know."

Emerald was taken aback by her statement, but then Belinda let out a loud scream as Emerald's dark green magic ripped the life force from her. Tyllos desperately tried to save her. Instead, Emerald shot dark green magic against him, sucking his life out too.

A flicker of bright orange magic blinded Emerald. Perserine was nearby.

Emerald funneled more life-giving magic into her flesh, repairing it fully. Her tattered, burned-up clothes barely covered her.

A sudden crack, and her shield shattered, then an enchanted sword pierced her chest, just missing her heart.

"Your blood is mine!" cried Perserine.

The pain was too great, and Emerald flopped to the ground, crying out. She screamed while the sword pushed further through her body. Emerald called upon her green magic to heal herself.

Except it didn't work. There was no healing.

"I got you, Queen of Arcadia. Give up," called out the orange justice.

Emerald thought wildly. Why wasn't her green magic working?

Heal me! she cried to her magic.

There was no response.

Emerald's eyes filled with tears as another sharp pain slammed against her head. Slowly, she blinked, seeing the high justices' faces above her. Then, their faces flickered into nothing for a split second. Was she imagining it?

There were hands over her, and more pain.

They were going to get her blood.

Another flicker in their faces as hands came over her.

The flicker.

It was all an illusion!

The sword, the pain…it was why her green magic didn't work. Her body was in perfect condition.

With sudden rage, Emerald shouted, raising her hands toward Perserine's image.

A surge of dark green magic shot out of her hand, draining the orange justice quickly, restoring the world to what it truly was.

"NO!" screamed Perserine.

There was a sharp pain in her back. Emerald screamed, falling to her knees. It was an ice shard.

"You need a lesson in humility!" screamed High Justice Nyrden.

"You're killing her!" screamed Elyathi's voice.

"This is a trial!" shouted Nyrden.

"Her power is needed for the new world!"

"She is not WORTHY!" his voice boomed.

Emerald felt weakened, flopping over. Nyrden was really trying to kill her.

A flood of rage filled Emerald as she rolled over. Her mother didn't need Nyrden for her spell. Derek was going to bring Geeta here to this time. Determined, she grabbed the ice shard on the floor, meeting Nyrden's ice shard in a swordplay fashion.

"You won't win." He narrowed his eyes with a flash of anger.

"Only the righteous will survive," Emerald said.

With a weak attempt, she tried to counter his blow. Her icicle hit his, deflecting his blow to her heart, causing it to hit her shoulder instead.

She funneled dark green magic into her icicle and stabbed him in the thigh.

Nyrden screamed and stumbled back; the dark green magic exploded in the chamber, and his life force dissipated into the air like a cloud of dust. Nyrden's body slumped to the ground, then smoked as it melted away, his bones materializing from the melted puddle of flesh.

Through the corner of her eye, Emerald saw that Belinda had no emotional reaction to what had transpired.

With another flick of her hand, Emerald rippled a dark green wave of magic throughout the chamber, sucking all the justices' life forces, then funneling it back into hers. More and more flowed into her, making her stronger by the second, while the justices became weaker.

Through this process, Emerald detected something that stunned her: their lives were unnatural. They had lived long, extended lives—ones they were not meant to live. And with Belinda, her life force did feel odd, as Derek had mentioned. But like Derek, she couldn't tell what was different about it.

More life drained out of the justices, until they were on the brink of death. Emerald knew she shouldn't take their lives, so she held her power steadily, waiting for them to admit their defeat.

"Say it," Emerald demanded.

There were no answers, only desperate screams.

"I said say it! If you want to survive, say that I passed your trial!" Emerald demanded, still holding on to their fragile lives.

"My daughter has bested you!" Elyathi called out from the edge of the room. "Call it before you lose your lives; I must have your power to complete my task. Don't be prideful, high justices!"

"Swear it!" demanded Emerald. "All of you!"

The high justices continued to be obstinate, struggling with their magic. Emerald noticed that Belinda stood with a sincere smile. Her body appeared transparent, slowly disappearing and reappearing. But it did not appear to be suffering like the others. Emerald bit her lip, furrowing her brow in full concentration. The more she concentrated, the more Belinda's magic faded, but she remained standing.

"Emerald. We need them alive," her mother reminded her.

Belinda, though faint and weakened, stared directly into Emerald's eyes. There was no malice, hatred, or evil. In fact, it was quite the opposite. Through their connection, Emerald felt a submission. Belinda wanted her mother to succeed. More, she wanted *Emerald* to succeed.

"Enough of this," called out Belinda. "Take your throne, Queen Emerald of Arcadia. I welcome you to this court, for I have been awaiting your arrival. I cannot best you." Belinda's eyes flickered, as she lowered her hands in submission.

Her mother turned to her. "You cannot take their lives, my daughter, even to prove a point," she said.

"Mother, I am only trying to prove that I am no one's pawn," Emerald stated.

"Nor should you be," Belinda called out. The high justice gestured to the green throne. "Please, if you will."

"I will gladly assume the green throne," Emerald said.

"I swear on the God of Light's will, you have won. We will not touch you, nor attempt to get your blood. You will be seated on the throne," Perserine said. The others agreed.

Emerald lowered her hand, releasing her dark green magic. The justices relaxed on the floor with relief, still breathing heavily.

She walked by the writhing justices, half naked but full of energy and life. She paused in front of the green throne, taking it all in. The green gem became radiant, activated by her power.

Emerald turned around, then looked at the justices, all watching her from their spots on the floor.

She smiled, then seated herself on the throne, holding her head up high. Her mother's face was gleaming with pride.

"High Justices, I hope you have learned a lesson in humility," Emerald declared.

"It seems that High Justice Nyrden has," Belinda stated, eyeing the man's remains.

Her mother glanced at him too, then to the remaining high justices. "Now bow before the new High Justice of the Green. Submit your will, just as you have done to each other and to the God of Light himself. You have a new equal."

All bowed to her, even her mother. As they rose, they looked to her with a hint of fear. Stretching out her hand, Emerald sent a wave of healing to their bodies. Nyrden's puddled remains still lay on the marbled floor.

"Let Nyrden be a lesson on the folly of pride," Emerald said. "I was only doing what you asked of me."

"Indeed," Belinda said. "You were right to do so."

"Nyrden's faith always teetered on the line," said Borgen.

"Do not dwell on Nyrden's downfall. His ego got the best of him," Belinda continued. They all nodded. "Let us take a brief break for the new green justice to refresh herself. It is almost time."

"Time?" Emerald said.

"Why, yes. The execution of the empress Ayera," Perserine stated in a chipper voice. "Her sister, Ikaria, is sure to show up."

The sound of the sorceress's name made Emerald full of rage. Emerald glanced at the justices. "Then we will ensure that her power is stripped from her. Once and for all." Emerald rose from her seat with her head held high. "I must get ready."

The justices gave her an approving smile. Her mother waited by the doors.

Emerald stepped down from her throne, still bloody, her clothes tattered and torn. It mattered not. She had been reborn by Belinda's fire—her childishness and naivety purged by flames. *Let them all see their new justice.*

This time it would be different. This time, she would show the sorceress who had the real power.

She wasn't afraid. In fact, she welcomed the opportunity to confront the sorceress.

Because Emerald had all the power.

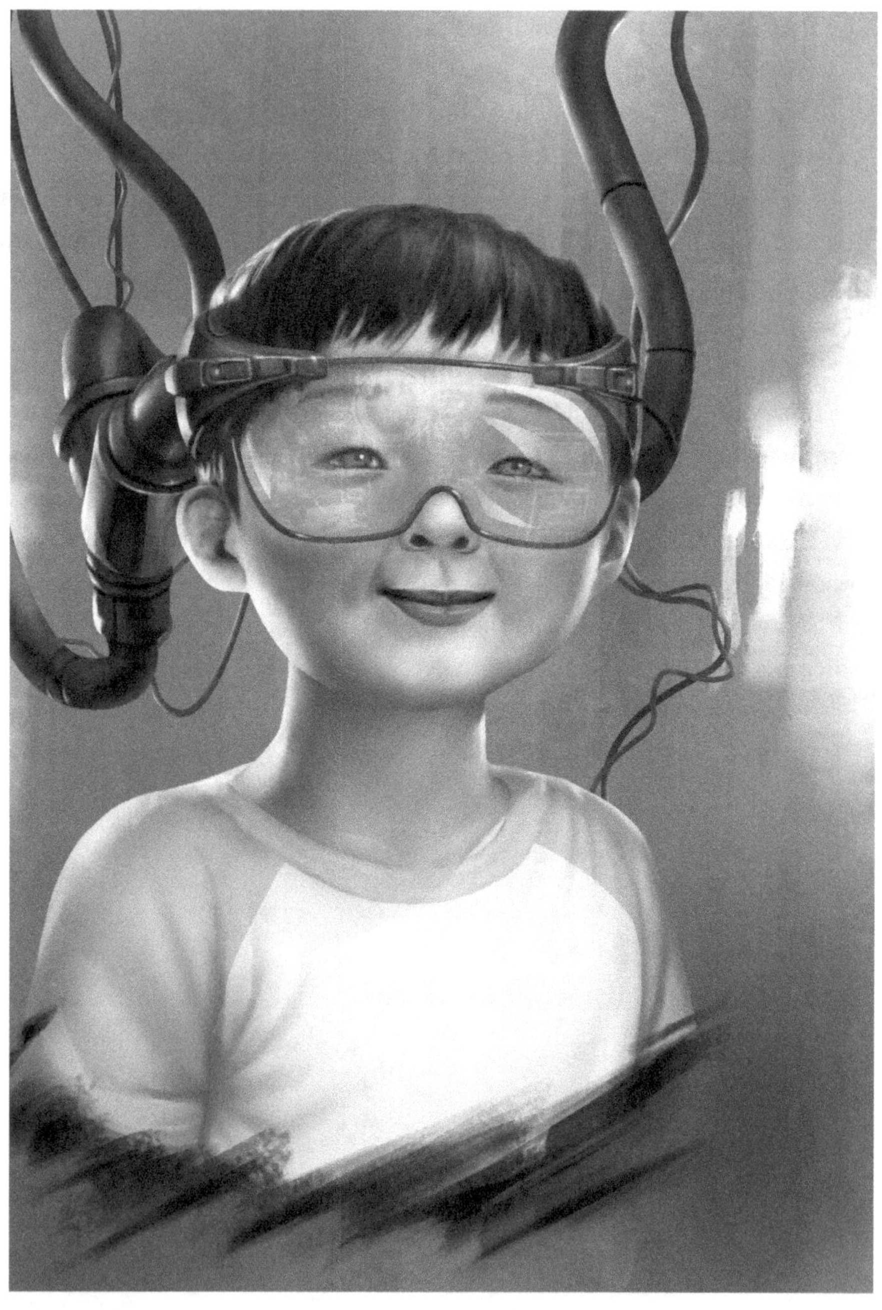

CHAPTER 81

♦

DARK RED

Everything was blurry. He itched. His back, his arms, his neck. It really bugged him! How could he sleep when he itched so much?

Jihyun scratched his neck hard, wondering where he was. Some sort of metal room with lots of lights? He couldn't see that clearly.

The itch was stronger, and Jihyun scratched himself again. It relieved the itch on his neck, but then the itch traveled farther down his back. He tried to get it, but his arms weren't long enough.

Where was he? He remembered he'd been in a room with Gwen. Jihyun thought about it, but he couldn't remember what happened. How did he get here?

Jihyun glanced around, still confused. His body felt strange.

Then he remembered Gwen's bruised and bloodied face. Anger came over him. Why had they hurt Gwen?

There were sounds all around him in the weird metal room. Creepy sounds.

"Are you there, Vihaan?" Jihyun called out.

The only answer he got was the muffled sounds of men, voices, and machines. They were distorted, like a battery dying in an old music machine. Were they answering him?

Suddenly he remembered what Gwen had told him. That Vihaan was a bad man. His skin became more itchy as he thought about it, and he absently scratched his forearms until they hurt. He looked down, seeing they were red from his scratching, but also blurry. There was something brushing against his back, and it wasn't his itch.

Jihyun twirled around to see who or what was there. The scary sounds turned into whispers. Louder and louder until he couldn't take it anymore.

"Someone help me!" Jihyun cried out to the muffled voices and the metal blobs. "Please, I'm scared!"

There were touches against his skin, but he didn't see anyone. More scary whispers called his name, telling him horrible things.

He felt straps against his hands and ankles, his neck unable to move.

More voices.

Jihyun pounded his hands against something metal; his hands were restrained.

You will die…

Jihyun screamed.

Die…

"It's Questy! He's coming to get me!"

No one answered.

DIE!

His skull felt like it was coming out of his head, making him throw up. He didn't know if he threw up on himself or in a metal container. Everything was so confusing, moving in a strange motion. The world was dark, in deep reds. The dizziness made him throw up again. He scratched so hard that he could tell he was bleeding.

"Help…I'm so scared…" he cried. Through his tears, Jihyun saw a floating white blob. He jolted his eyes away, but there was no escape. It moved with his eyes wherever they went.

"Someone help me!" he screamed. More touches, more floating images around him. "Please don't hurt me!"

You will die!

Jihyun wailed, "I don't want to die!"

You will die! Your body wants to die!

"Leave me alone!"

Jihyun blinked hard, seeing a large floating triangle above him. It was the only clear thing that he could see. It was hovering, covering his entire body. Pink, transparent, warped with brown and yellow. Then the triangle was melting.

It was Questy.

"Go away!" Jihyun cried. "I hate you!"

I will kill your soul. I killed your father. I killed your mother. I killed everyone. I will kill Gwen! the triangle laughed at him, floating right on top of him.

Jihyun couldn't breathe. Questy was taking his breath.

More laughs came from Questy, along with other voices.

"Don't hurt Gwen!"

Too late. I already have!

"GWEN!"

Questy's face melted off, pouring all over Jihyun's body like puke. Jihyun's skin started burning. He was on fire.

"Stop it!" Jihyun shouted. He looked at his arms, lying on his back while locked in place. They were on fire. His entire body was on fire. It was red fire, but so dark that it looked black. More images floated behind Questy. They were ghosts. Scary ghosts. They whispered scary things to him.

The ghosts turned into red demonic monsters.

Jihyun screamed.

You must slay the evil monsters! Questy screamed.

"I hate you!" Worms were crawling in his brain. He couldn't see them, but he knew the worms had gotten inside his head. The worms were crawling inside his body. He threw up again.

More laughs while distorted images floated around him. Wherever he looked, he saw Questy and his droopy face melting all over him.

"Get away from me!"

Questy laughed. *I will kill you if you don't kill the monsters! They will kill you! I will kill Gwen! You will die!*

Jihyun wept as the fire burned his body. The red monsters scratched their long black nails against his skin. The worms were crawling everywhere in his body.

Then, suddenly, he felt goggles on his face.

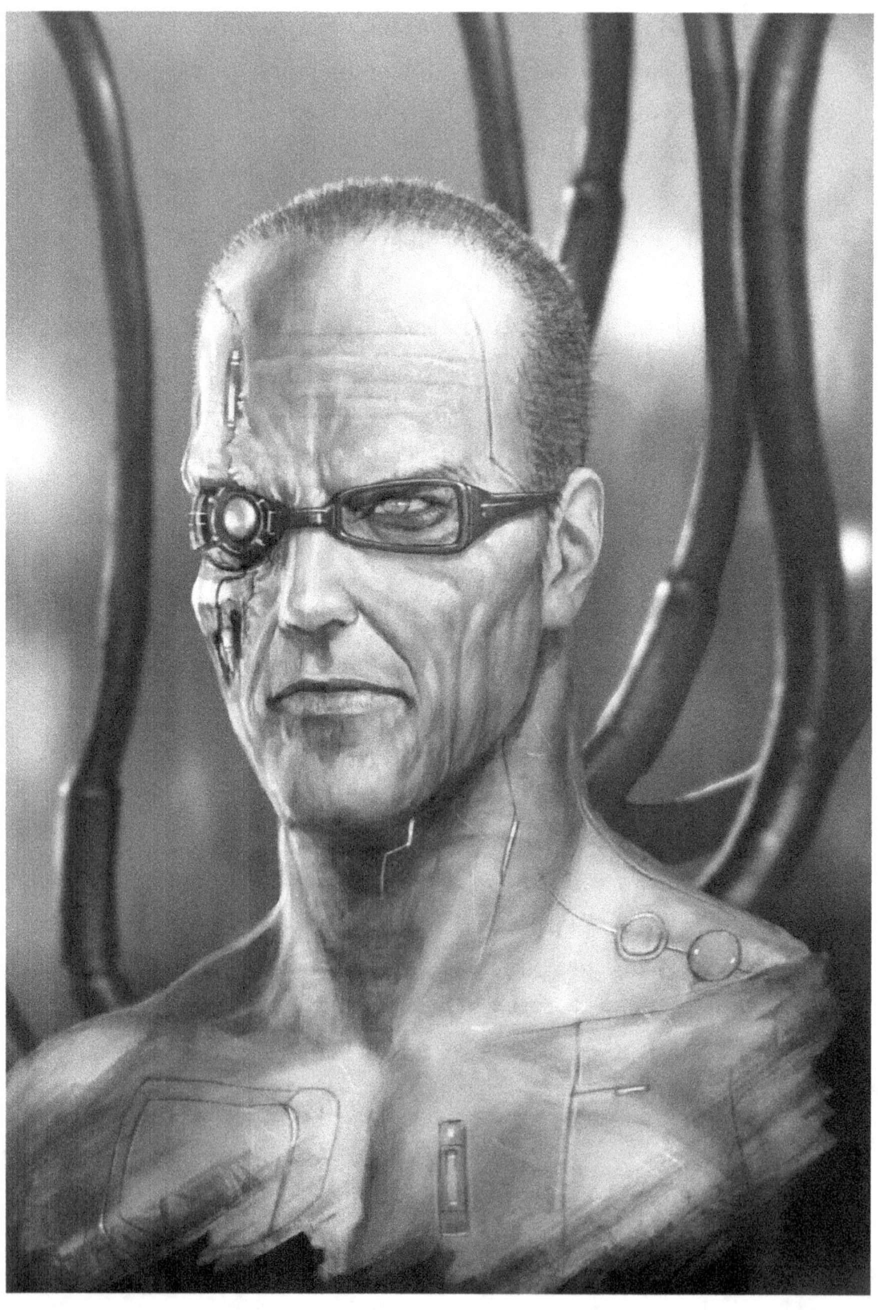

CHAPTER 82

◆

THE DARK SIDE OF THE SPECTRUM

Deep red rain pounded the Olympian city streets, making the visibility next to none.

Telly cocked her weapon again.

"Something major is going down," Garrett said. His goggles lit up brightly in the darkness of the stormy night. "I am picking up an energy source on the north side of the city."

Suddenly, Garrett screamed.

There was a sudden whoosh to Telly's side, and she fired her weapon on instinct.

A golden magical barrier shimmered brightly, her bullet ricocheting off it. The magic died down, revealing the same yellow-gifted man they had confronted moments before.

"Miss Hearly, watch out!" Scion called out.

The yellow-gifted charged at her, knocking her to the ground and pinning her.

Telly looked around. They were in the man's barrier. Would her magic work in here?

He clenched her wrists, making it impossible for her to move.

"Who's in control now?" he sneered.

Telly struggled as the man's magic shifted to a dark yellow. His magic sprinkled on her like dusted snowfall, sending thousands of shocks throughout her body.

Telly screamed in pain. She wanted to escape, but her legs wouldn't cooperate.

I'm not done! I must rescue my daughter! Telly begged the magic. *I want a happy and peaceful life with her and Drew…*

And so you shall, Telly Hearly, the magic answered.

"Women are powerless, didn't you know? They are unclean, menstruating their vileness upon our earth. It is shameful. The only reason they were created was to give birth to powerful men," the yellow-gifted man bellowed. "Even a goat is higher than you."

Fill your soul with ungratefulness, whispered a voice.

That's hard. I am grateful for a lot of things.

But are you not ungrateful for the situation you have recently been put through?

Telly snorted. *Of course.*

Channel that when you release your orange magic…

Telly felt that dark, lonely feeling of being alone…being physically separated from her daughter and mentally apart from Drew. Darkness filled her soul, then there was a shift in her life force, and the floodgates of her soul poured out.

She radiated pure orange magic, burning brightly.

The man stopped laughing, then narrowed his eyes, sending more negative yellow energy, causing immense pain.

"Goat?" Telly snarled. "Did you call me a *goat*?"

"He called you a goat," Scion confirmed from afar.

The vibrant orange magic turned dark orange, and Telly concentrated it all in one area of her body. The giant surge of energy flowed to her wrists.

The man's hands smoked and sizzled, then he realized what was happening. "You WENCH! STOP!" he demanded.

"*No,*" Telly said, narrowing her eyes. She poured more power to his body.

His body started mutating, then his bones began to twist. Fur began to sprout on his skin.

"What are you doing?" he screamed.

"Nobody calls me a goat!"

The man fell to his knees, writhing in pain. Bones were jutting out of his flesh as he continued to transform.

"Holy shit," Garrett said in surprise. "Is he…?"

The man was transforming into an actual goat.

"Ge-eeeee-t her!" the man-goat bleated in the pouring rain as he sent a wave of yellow-green magic to his wrists. The man-goat had cast a bright shimmering layer of protection on his skin, fighting the effects of her dark orange magic.

In the corner of her eye, Telly saw a wave of blue magic, with cyborgs running toward them.

Garrett blasted them with a giant flare. Scion cast his own barrier, pummeling the cyborgs within range. But more were coming.

A blast of dark red energy lanced across the sky.

She closed her eyes, focusing on the sand below her feet. She felt its form, its texture. Each grain of sand was unique, having its own desire…

She wanted to mold it, transform it into something else. It also wanted that.

Get angry, her magic instructed.

I already am!

Release your anger…

Telly shot open her eyes and raised her hands, commanding the sands. "Transform!" she roared.

With a giant surge of orange magic, it flooded the sand everywhere around the city, glowing, and Telly shot up in the air. Power flowed around her, embracing every aspect of her soul. The ground below was melting.

Telly opened her eyes, seeing the city streets below her. She was floating on orange-red magical winds.

Raindrops pelted her body. She was completely drenched, but she didn't care. All she cared about was finding Gwen.

Looking down at the havoc, she saw Scion running to a motorcycle. With another surge of power, Telly shot orange-red winds at Scion, lifting him and Garrett up off the ground with her.

"Get that woman!" roared the yellow-gifted man, enveloped with yellow-orange magic. His half-goat transformation was wearing off.

The sand under the guards, the gifted man, the station, even the gates to the city, transformed into quicksand. The rains made it worse, forming a giant muddy pool of wet sand within the city. The men hopped into their transports, but the sand was already taking them, growing around them transmuting them into stone sculptures.

Suddenly, a violent wind pushed Telly, hurling her to the ground. The ground sank in around her. Telly sent a wave of orange magic below her, trying to stave off her being transmuted as well.

There was another sharp blow, this time twisting the metal components of her weapons. Scion screamed behind her. Objects all around Telly started swirling in a cyclone as all the metal in the area twisted like tinfoil.

A giant moving structure materialized before her in the heavy rains—a mech outlined in a wireframe made of a strange material. At the top radiated dark red energy.

It was the boy.

The gifted child sat within the mech, plugged into the armor with VR goggles strapped to his face. It radiated bright red, sending red power throughout the mech.

The giant mech ran quickly toward Telly, twisting everything in its path. Jolts of dark red energy shot directly at her.

Telly rolled over, narrowly dodging the beam.

"You are bad!" screamed the boy through the pounding rain.

"I want my daughter!" screamed Telly.

With another surge of dark red energy, her body was whipped to the ground. She tumbled over, hitting her head on a rock.

"Get her!" a man's voice said.

Telly weakly opened her eyes. A shimmer of orange-yellow magic cloaked the gifted man in invisibility. The boy's goggles radiated red power, surrounding him.

He blasted his power toward Telly.

Help me! she cried to the power.

Just as the dark red blast was about to make contact, Telly's body was whipped up to the sky. Below was another blast, and through it Telly saw a yellow shimmer.

Scion had encased them all in his magic, half mangled but alive.

"Scion! Watch out!" Telly screamed.

Though his body had sustained a lot of damage, he had some working parts. His arms extended, and spikes slid out. Then he charged at the boy.

"I'll get you, monster! You do bad things to me all the time! I'm going to get rid of you!" the boy screamed.

Monster?

Telly shot orange magic into Scion's spikes, making them radiate with her power, transmuting them. His spikes stabbed into the boy's mech like a hot knife through butter.

The mech fell over, and the yellow-gifted man cast a protective barrier around the boy.

The boy was tangled in the wires, the goggles still over his eyes. "Stop hurting me! Stop hurting my family!" he wailed, kicking wildly. "Don't hurt Gwen!"

"*Gwen?*" Telly turned at the sound of her daughter's name, flying toward the boy. "Did you say Gwen?" she called out as she neared him.

"Gwen is my best friend!" the boy said with confusion.

She and Garrett exchanged looks.

"I wouldn't hurt Gwen! I'm her mother. I want her home with me! I love her very much," Telly cried.

The boy stopped mid-tantrum, almost in a blissful lull. "You're Gwen's mom?"

"Gwen is my friend too," Garrett added.

"Gwen…is your friend?"

"Yes!" Telly nodded quickly. "I love my daughter! Where is she? Can you tell me?" Telly begged.

The boy blinked as if he didn't know where he was. There was something off about him. It was almost as if he was…drunk?

"Please," Telly pleaded. "Where is she?"

The boy glanced down at her, still glowing with deep red energy. "Gwen plays video games with me."

"And where is that?" Garrett pressed.

"She's not there right now. She's in her room, I think?"

"Where's her room?" Telly cried.

"The palace…"

Another wave of magic shot into the boy. Telly saw a yellow-orange illusion next to the boy. It was that yellow-gifted, tapping into his orange magic. She could see him as clear as day.

Telly aimed at the man, but it was too late. A syringe plunged into his skin, and the boy cried out.

"Get the monsters, Jihyun!" the yellow-gifted man screamed as he hurled the empty syringe. The man had completely turned back into his original form. Her transmutation hadn't completed itself in time.

"Telly did you see that?" Garrett shouted, pointing at the boy.

They are drugging the poor boy! Telly thought wildly.

"I did!" Telly shouted back.

The little boy Jihyun grasped a strange handlebar inside his broken mech. With a blast of energy, the sky went pitch black with a deep glow of red on the horizon. Metal shrapnel began to rise into the sky.

Telly embraced the anger in her. It didn't make her fly like the last time, but it did give her an extra boost of air under her feet to steer clear of the boy. She sent another wave of air to Scion and Garrett, pushing them to a safe distance.

As the group slid closer to the heart of the city, a bright yellow energy sparkled against the dark sky. Olympia was surrounded by a golden barrier, the inside looking like any other day. It was an illusion. The citizens didn't see anything that was going on around them.

Telly looked over at Scion; he could still move.

"Scion! Can you melt that barrier?" she said in her transmitter.

"I will attempt to do so, Miss Telly!"

From the distance, the gifted boy in the mech was nearing them once again.

Telly surged all her magic into the city's piping and electrical grid. It burned orange, growing brighter until it was white hot. Then the pipes melted, and the city went black.

"You will not leave this city *alive*," taunted the yellow-gifted man.

"Just you watch," Telly called out. She went invisible and pulled out her magitech weapon. She watched as the yellow-gifted man came toward her.

Telly aimed right at the man, then fired.

A magitech blast consumed the area, this time as a blast of fire.

"It hurts!" the boy screamed. Within the flaming walls of fire, the boy snuffed the fire to a minimum, his hands outstretched, his goggles still glowing bright red.

The yellow-gifted man crawled toward the boy, sending a wave of healing to both of them.

Telly ran toward the heart of the city. Toward the palace.

From behind, she heard the man shout, "Get them, boy!"

Telly poured magic over Scion and Garrett while they ran after her.

"What now?" Garrett asked.

Telly readied her weapon and cocked it. "Keep moving."

◆ ◆ ◆

Violet energy wavered around Victor and Geeta as the violet dimensional tunnel crackled.

"It's fading now! Be ready!" Geeta called out to him. In her hand, she clutched the staff. "Any moment now…"

Victor cocked his weapon. His face remained calm, but Geeta knew that he was nervous. She was too.

The time tunnel dissipated, and the streets of Olympia came into view all around them.

As the magic faded, they were pounded with hard red rain. In the distance, she saw a faint a magical blast in another section of the city.

Geeta perked up, and she and Victor exchanged looks.

"We have to help Telly," Geeta said.

"How do you—"

"I feel her life force within that energy," Geeta said. "Hurry."

Just as they were about to move out, the Olympian city military came marching into the perimeter, made up of military men and cyborgs.

"Get them!" one called out.

Victor fired at a group of cyborgs, electrocuting them. One of the cyborgs caught on fire. Geeta shot a blast of wind, fanning the flames. The fire quickly spread from cyborg to cyborg, with the magical rain intensifying the magical fire, feeding off its power, spreading throughout the soldiers. Some screamed, others tried to run.

Then a golden magical barrier appeared around the injured soldiers, with a healing wind coming from within.

The cyborgs are casting their own barriers.

Geeta summoned her own barrier with the staff, covering her and Victor with a violet shimmering layer of protection. "Telly is northeast of the city," Geeta said. "We need to group up with her and help them retrieve Gwen. I will get us over to her."

Victor nodded as Geeta released a wave of violet-blue magic over them.

◆ ◆ ◆

Through the orange shimmer of her magic, Telly, Garrett, and Scion dodged down a city alley, slipping into a nook in the building.

Telly breathed hard, glancing at Garrett.

"That kid…" Garrett said. "They keep jacking him up with some kind of drug." He reloaded all of his weapons.

"He said he was friends with Gwen," Telly said, recalling the look on the boy's face. There was an innocence when he cried out for Gwen. *Maybe she's been keeping him company during her imprisonment.*

Suddenly, the overhead city speakers blared an announcement: "City of Olympia. A group of terrorists is in the city. His Majesty King Renard has ordered all citizens to stay inside their residences. Do not leave your homes. I repeat, do not leave. These are armed and dangerous terrorists who will kill anyone on contact."

Terrorists? Telly snorted. *I'll show them terrorists!*

"Guess we really pissed them off," Garrett said, turning to her. "You think we lost that yellow magic man?"

"Doubt it," she said. "If he tries to go invisible or cloak himself, I can detect him."

"My readings indicate the boy is heading in this direction," Scion stated.

"Then let's get moving," Garrett said.

"Hold on. I want to do something," Telly said. "You still have access to Olympia's mainframe, Garrett?"

"Whatever still has electricity, I do," he said. "My readings indicate that a portion of the power grid is offline."

"I need you to broadcast across Olympia on one of our communicators. Can you do that?"

"Telly…"

"Please, Garrett," Telly begged, eyeing him through their orange illusions.

He sighed. "Okay. Give me a sec."

As he began hacking the system, Telly heard the military transports overhead. More cyborg units were being deployed.

"Ready?" he asked.

Telly nodded.

"Okay, your communicator will be broadcasting in five, four, three, two, one…"

Telly's hands shook as she raised the communicator to her lips. Scion studied her as she breathed heavily.

Then she spoke.

"Citizens of Olympia! This is your so-called terrorist. I am anything but. Your king captured and kidnapped my daughter, and I want nothing more than for her to be returned to me. Unfortunately, your king has not done so, so I am left with no choice but to raze this entire city to the ground to get my daughter. This is what any mother would do to get their child back. So if you want to call me a terrorist, then so be it. You have fifteen minutes to vacate this city. If you don't, I cannot guarantee you will live through the night. The fifteen minutes starts right now!"

She ended the communication, hanging up.

There was a sudden buzz of noise as people began running out into the streets, military units trying to shove people back into city buildings.

"Citizens of Olympia! Do not come out into the streets! Do not leave the city!" blared a message across the city communicator. "I repeat! Do not leave under any circumstances. If you do, there is no guarantee that you will be safe!"

Telly loaded her weapon. It was an excellent distraction.

"Miss Hearly," Scion said.

"Yes, Scion?"

"It hasn't been fifteen minutes yet."

"I know," Telly said. "Just getting ready." She eyed down the alley, seeing that citizens were having a hard time leaving with the military there trying to stop them.

Telly leaned against a wall, looking up at the Olympian palace. Tears formed in her eyes, but she wiped them away. She had to focus. Failure wasn't an option.

"My scanner says that the boy is within Olympia's perimeter," he answered.

Telly breathed heavily. "That's reassuring."

This life of fighting, of magic…it wasn't her. *Our true selves emerge when the important things are stolen from us,* she thought.

"How many more minutes?"

"One minute and thirty-nine seconds…"

Telly grabbed another vial from her pack, loaded it in the weapon chamber, then cocked it. She eyed Scion until he said the word.

"Fifteen minutes," he stated.

Then she fired. The vial shot across the barricaded main street of the city. The area exploded in a loud fiery rumble, the earth quaking underneath it. Buildings shook around them.

Scion pulled Telly close, summoning a barrier. The barrier encased them as several buildings collapsed to the ground. Large debris flung across the city, with a billowing dust sweeping across the streets, dampened by the rain in seconds. Screams rang out, echoing alongside the blasts of violet magic in the sky and the air transports that fought them off.

Through the smoke, Telly saw the deep red radiating with intermittent blasts of violets throughout the sky.

"Geeta," Garrett breathed as he noticed the violet blasts too.

Telly nodded. "Let's go."

"Don't you want to wait for them?" Garrett asked.

"No. I want Gwen now. If we wait around, the boy and that yellow-gifted might find us," she said. "Geeta will be fine. We need to get to the palace."

"I will direct us with my maps," he said. His eyes flashed yellow, his machinery glowing. "Head north."

"I have the palace architect plans loaded in my screens," Garrett added. "There are several entrances on the ground level, unless we climb."

"Look for best way for us to get in undetected."

Garrett nodded, his lenses glowing with scrolling information.

Telly nodded, running out of the alley with Scion trailing behind her. The guards ran past them, as they were still invisible. Intercom speakers could be heard telling the Olympian citizens to remain calm. More blasts, gunfire, and strange sounds were woven throughout the city's broadcasts.

They came upon a street of ground transports, all abandoned.

"Can you unlock one of these?" Telly asked.

"Affirmative." Scion made a few clicking noises, his eyes flashing yellow. "Get in," he said as one of the transport doors opened.

Suddenly a metal hand grabbed her, pinning her in its grasp. It was an Olympian cyborg.

"Target locked," it chimed.

Telly panicked, her eyes flicking to Scion.

But Scion was fighting his own battle with three other cyborgs.

I can do this, she told herself. Telly closed her eyes, funneling her orange magic, sending it into the cyborg.

The metal hands warbled, then it twisted and morphed. "Warning, warning," the cyborg said mechanically as it watched its hands melt off.

With that, Telly was free, so she grabbed her weapon and shot another blast of orange magic, this time aiming it at the other cyborgs. It blasted right into their chests, taking over their bodies. Suddenly, the group of cyborgs morphed, their metal forming into a street sign.

"I did not know you were capable of this," Scion chimed, running back to the transport.

"You can do anything when you're pissed off," she answered, glancing at him. "You okay?"

"Yes."

They finally climbed inside the transport, with Garrett in the pilot seat. Telly slapped on her seatbelt as he started the engine, Scion behind them.

"This transport has air capabilities."

"Looks like we will be entering the palace from the sky entrance," Telly said.

The transport hovered in place, then shot up into the air. The sharp upward motion made Telly feel like vomiting, but she pushed it down. Garrett was no better of a driver than Reila. The spires of the skyscrapers came into view, the glowing red magic radiating from a nearby palace tower.

"Hold on," Garrett said. "Olympian transports are heading in our direction."

She closed her eyes, trying not to think about the jerkiness.

"They are zero point nine miles from us," Scion called out.

Telly opened her eyes. Through the wet windshield, she saw the Olympian transports getting closer. "I would cast a spell of invisibility on our transport, but the cyborg units can detect us. Is it possible to cast a shield over our transport?" Telly asked Scion.

"Affirmative." Scion clutched his hands and began to radiate with yellow energy. It seeped into his seat, then spread across their transport.

Telly's eyes went to the oncoming transports.

Then there was an explosion. It narrowly missed their transport as Garrett made a hard jerking maneuver with the steering wheel. The transport shot upward, then rolled several times. Her glasses were flung off at some point during the barrel rolls.

Garrett gave the wheel another jerk, then steadied the transport. Telly grabbed an old paper food bag from the floor, opening it quickly. She vomited. The old smells of the food mixed with her bile, and she vomited again.

As she looked up weakly, she saw purple magic flooding their windshield.

"Geeta!" Telly breathed.

"It appears she's clearing a direct path for us!" Garrett said excitedly.

Thank you, Geeta. I will never forget this.

You're welcome, she answered in Telly's mind. *Sorry we are late. We'll hold them off. Go get your daughter!*

We will.

They had a few more minutes, so she took the time to search for her glasses. They were slightly cracked, but it was better than not being able to see at all.

Garrett went in to land the transport, and it wavered as they neared the tower. The closer they got, the more friction they felt.

"The boy…" Garrett said.

They must have moved him closer to Gwen.

"Are you able to land this thing?" Telly asked.

"The chances are 86.6% probability," Scion said from behind them.

Garrett's face was purely focused on the landing. Telly could see he was struggling. From outside her window and through the storm clouds, dark red energy swirled around the tower, with eerie screams and noises.

The transport lowered and finally docked at the nearest platform. They group let out a sigh of relief. Telly unholstered her weapon and shivered, momentarily afraid of the state she'd find Gwen in. She pushed the thought aside as Garrett hit the release button and the transport doors popped open.

They exited the transport, and oddly, there were no guards on the platform.

"Watch out for the boy," Telly said.

"My readings say that the energy signature is this way," Garrett said as Scion popped a yellow energy shield around them.

As they ran across the platform, a vibrant red light burst from the palace, and it began to shake. Anxiety ran through her body. Dark red energy pulsed around the palace.

"Holy shit," Garrett said.

There was another loud blast that shook the palace violently. More eerie noises echoed above.

"There they are!" someone called out.

A battalion of palace guards ran into view, all lined up to stop them. "It's the orange-gifted!" the commander called out. "Protect the palace!"

"Go to hell!" Telly shouted, then fired several vials. A deep freeze blew wildly against the battalion, encapsulating them in ice.

Suddenly, the ice cracked and shattered, freeing them. They had a golden shimmer of magic on them.

Above the platform, dark red energy continued to pour out of the palace like a bleeding wound.

That's how her heart felt without Gwen. Empty. She wanted her daughter back. Now.

Telly screamed, flinging out her hands. These people stood between her and her daughter. They wanted them separated forever.

A dark power emerged from within her soul, a void that she had never known before. She had felt it, but never truly known this darkness.

The pure orange energy swayed around her, emboldening her. Then, there was a deep shift in her soul, allowing that darkness to take over. Suddenly, the orange magic shifted to a deep dark orange, almost black, with orange sparkles within the energy.

Telly swept her hands in a grand motion, screaming at the soldiers. The magic shot out of her body, then encased them.

"Telly!" a familiar voice called out to her.

She ignored the voice. It was time for revenge against those who had done wrong to her and her family.

Telly funneled more of the dark magic at the soldiers. They began to scream. Their bodies—bones, skin, gear—it all began to melt like butter into a puddle.

Telly yanked her handgun, then fired. Then fired again.

"Stop!"

It was Garrett. Her hand shook, realizing what she had done. She looked up, noticing that all that was left was a giant flesh puddle on the ground.

Telly walked over to the melted puddle, her hands trembling. These men had families too…

There is no coming back from this, she told herself.

"Damn," Garrett said, staring.

She ignored him. Then she headed inside the tower, Garrett and Scion following. As they entered, they faced a giant hall, pausing.

"There is a set of stairs down the left hallway," Garrett said, pointing in that direction.

Another loud blast came from above. The ceiling cracked, then spiderwebbed across the top.

"We must vacate this area," Scion said. "It will hold for ten point three seconds."

"Go!" Garrett said.

They all ran toward the stairs, then turned the corner just as a loud cracking sound rang out behind them. Telly turned, seeing that the ceiling had completely collapsed behind them.

"Hurry!" Telly said.

"Up three more flights of stairs," Scion added.

The trio darted up the stairwell.

✦ ✦ ✦

She had to hold them off long enough for Telly to get her daughter. Behind her, Victor blasted a group of cyborgs with his weapons. Her violet magic sensed that the girl was close; she could hear her thoughts.

Hurry, Telly!

Turning back toward the cyborgs, Geeta summoned another blast of energy with the staff. It hit a group of cyborgs, exploding them on contact. A fiery blast rocked the platform, sending smoke billowing. Eerie screams came from the cyborgs. Geeta noticed dark yellow magic coming from the billowing smoke. More screams, this time from the soldiers.

"What are you doing?" yelled a familiar man's voice.

It was a voice she hadn't heard in years…

"We can still fix this! The High Court—"

Geeta's ears rang in alarm at the mention of the High Court.

"No matter…we have what we need right here," the voice called out. "Don't we, *Geeta*?"

Geeta shook, realizing who it was.

The fire, smoke, and blasts cleared as the magic subsided. Geeta saw two men's silhouettes against the shimmering blue and gold magic. The details became clear. A man stood defiantly, strong against the magic. It was Vihaan.

"Geeta. Have you come to beg for your husband's forgiveness?" Vihaan boomed.

The sound of his voice disturbed every bone in Geeta's body, causing her to falter. She summoned a barrier, readying herself. "You…You were behind Olympia?" Geeta said angrily. She sent a bolt of violet-red lightning at Vihaan.

A blue shimmer flashed over the bolt, halting it in place. Then another shimmer of blue magic, and Radgu appeared.

"You should be ashamed!" Geeta shouted at Radgu.

"And so should you," he said.

Vihaan laughed, then moved out of the way of Geeta's frozen lightning bolt. "I have been here for many years, working with a purpose."

"You are working for the High Court," Geeta stated, narrowing her eyes. "And you claim *I* am unholy, *husband*? You seem to have your blood mixed, as you have traveled here and have not faded into the lifestream. Now who is the hypocrite?"

"You know nothing, and you never will." Vihaan began to glow a deep yellow, embraced by his magic. "It's time I teach you a lesson and put you back in your place! You are coming with me!"

"Never," Geeta growled.

"Let's see how powerful you really are now, wife," he snarled.

Darkness loomed over the area, creating a deep blue energy. The landscape started shifting.

Radgu had cast a spell to send them to another dimension. The dimension blinked wildly, forming new images around her. A golden barrier encapsulated her, then began hardening. It was going to trap her.

Geeta summoned her own violet force, blasting it against the golden barrier. It cracked once, spiderwebbing across the barrier. She did it again, this time using the staff, pushing a large amount of force against it. It cracked.

Desperate, the only way she knew that she could go against those two was possessing them.

But as she turned, Geeta saw only Vihaan. Radgu was gone.

Geeta summoned her violet magic once more, this time using violet-blue magic, ready to shift into her own dimension.

Vihaan fueled his yellow magic, gathering more and more power to his barrier. Suddenly, he released it, funneling it over Geeta.

The barrier shifted to deep yellow, pausing her in place.

"We can't let you have all the power, can we?" He laughed. "Stay there like a good little wife."

She struggled with her motor skills, her mind forming a magical force to break the time pause. She couldn't even call upon the power of the staff.

Finally, her mouth moved. "Screw you!"

Vihaan laughed, flinging her paused lightning bolt. It flew backward, hitting her square in the chest.

She flopped like a fish, screaming while Vihaan laughed. He summoned another barrier, this time deep black with flecks of gold. The barrier started tearing at her flesh.

By the gods!

More cracks of Vihaan's dark power shot straight into her, as the barrier continued to rip her soul apart.

"I'll be taking that staff now…" Vihaan said, nearing her.

Suddenly, the pain stopped.

Geeta opened her eyes. Vihaan's magic was gone. There was no alternate dimension… In its place, there was a glowing color. No, it was no color.

It was gray.

Vihaan looked confused, then tried to summon his magic. No magic appeared.

"What is the meaning of this?" he demanded.

Far off, the gray magic radiated, encircling the entire area. Within the light, she saw another man's silhouette fall to the ground, struggling.

"What is happening?" the other man asked. "My magic isn't working!"

"Neither is mine!" screamed Vihaan.

Still weak, Geeta got to her feet, then ran. Vihaan shot out his hand again, trying to tap into his magic.

Without a moment to lose, she ran straight toward Vihaan, then swung the hardest punch she could, decking him across the face. His face shot to the side, and he was ready to hit her back until she kicked him in the balls. Hard.

Vihaan doubled over, grimacing. "You bitch!" he shouted.

From behind, she felt a punch to her back, nearly missing her kidney. She stumbled forward, managing to keep her balance. She whipped around to see Radgu.

Radgu's eyes softened, then he whispered, "The girl is special…"

Geeta froze. "Which girl? Gwen?" she asked softly.

He gave a small nod, then suddenly gray magic filled her sight. It was so bright that she couldn't see anything. Knowing where the men were a moment prior, Geeta looked toward the source of the gray light.

"How did you steal my magic?" Vihaan screamed.

"She didn't," Victor called out. "I did."

"You! Where are you?" Vihaan yelled. Geeta saw a dark outline of Vihaan stumbling around. "I will destroy you! Did you hear me? I will skin you alive and eat the very power from your flesh."

"Very holy and devout of you," Geeta said.

"You know nothing of holiness, you worthless woman. You will all be powerless soon, and your magic will be stripped from you."

Suddenly, a shot rang out, echoing across the platform. Then another.

The gray light suddenly subsided, and Radgu's body slumped to the ground.

Victor's spell was cut short, as he also slumped to his knees, wounded from a bullet.

✦ ✦ ✦

The palace floors rumbled again, splitting. She had to get Gwen, and fast, before the whole building collapsed. The atmosphere was a deep red, pulsing with an immense negative energy. She wasn't one to sense the supernatural, but this was hard to ignore.

"This should be it," Garrett said.

Telly yanked the handle, but it was locked. With a swift motion, she summoned a burst of orange-red wind and blew the door to shreds. Shrapnel went flying, and the two of them barged through the door.

Inside the room, Telly paused, looking around wildly.

"Mom?" Gwen said, sticking her head out from under the bed.

"GWEN!"

Telly ran over to her daughter as Gwen scrambled out, and they crashed into each other's arms, sobbing.

"Mom!"

"Gwen," she whispered.

They gripped each other hard, not wanting to let go.

"Mom, I'm so sorry," Gwen said into her mother's shoulder.

Telly hugged her harder. Her daughter's words were a cure for her broken heart. "I love you so much, Gwen," she cried. "There is no need to be sorry. I'm so sorry that I've been so hard on you. I've been a crappy mom."

"You're not a crappy mom. I love you."

The building shook hard, snapping them out of their embrace. Both exchanged glances, then Telly said, "We have to go."

Telly gave Gwen a quick once-over, and in that moment she saw how beautiful her daughter had truly become. She loved her so much and was so proud of her. Once they were out of there, she was determined to set things right and be a better mom.

There was another shimmer of orange magic in the corner of Telly's eye. Telly couldn't believe what she was seeing...

"DREW?"

Telly shot up, with Gwen doing the same.

"DAD?"

Drew's magic shimmered, then he assimilated right before their eyes. His cybernetic eye glowed, his true human eye smiling with joy.

"G...Gwen...Tell-me-lots..." he said with joy, his arms outstretched.

They both ran into his arms, embracing each other in a group hug. Telly clung hard, burying her face in his chest while all three of them sobbed hard.

"I...I...I...love you, Tell-me-lots..." Drew said, jolting as he said it. "A... annd...I love you...too...Gwen."

"I love you, Dad," Gwen said.

"I love you, Drew..." Telly said. "I promise that things will be different when we get out of this mess."

"A...affirmative," Drew said.

At that moment, Garrett appeared, nearly toppling over the group as the building shook.

"Sorry to break this up, but the building is unstable," he said. "Geeta is trying to fend off those gifted, but it's only a matter of time before they get here…"

"Too late!"

The group of them turned as a large blast of dark yellow magic surrounded them. A wave of pain surged through Telly, and she screamed.

"Get the orange-gifted cyborg!" screamed the gifted man. "He must go to the future!"

With his words, suddenly everything made sense. Drew was about to be taken. Her daughter was just a way to draw him out.

These gifted men caused this!

"You aren't taking anyone, assholes!" Telly screamed, stepping in front of them.

There was another giant flash, this time in blue. It was too late; a giant blast of dark yellow magic with a flash of blue surrounded her.

"MOM," shrieked Gwen.

"TELLY!"

She blinked as immense pain shot through her gut, tearing at her from the inside out.

In shock, Telly glanced down. A huge metal spike was lodged in her stomach, jutting out her back.

"You weren't supposed to hurt the scientist!" the man screamed.

Who said that? she wondered. Telly glanced around, her vision impaired.

"MOM!"

"Did you think we would leave your daughter unattended?" another man said. "Grab that cyborg NOW!"

She was so confused. She glanced down at her hand, trying to move it. It should move…her brain was telling it to move. But it wasn't.

Pain wracked her body. She had to get it out, but how?

"Miss Hearly!" yelled a familiar cyborg's voice.

Telly looked up. Everything was blurry. Was she wearing her glasses? She couldn't remember. Why couldn't she see…?

Blasts of magitech weapons blinked in her vision, along with orange magic.

A lot of orange magic, mixed with purple, blue, and yellow.

"DREW! Get Gwen out of here now!" screamed Geeta's voice.

Telly's face felt numb. She blinked. She couldn't feel her face, her body…

Images of Drew and Gwen flashed in her mind. No sad memories came, only happy ones.

Telly blinked again. More orange flashes. Yellow. Purple. Blue. Dark red. What was going on? Olympia had her daughter. That is what was going on. They had her daughter.

Suddenly, a familiar face stared at her. Drew's face.

"Tell-me-lots," he whispered. She felt cold metal on her body. The coldness of his metal brought her vision into focus. Glowing orange eyes—one human and one cybernetic. "Don't leave me."

Telly felt him cradling her body.

Drew was really there with her.

Behind him, she saw Geeta fighting, while Victor and Garrett blasted their weapons. Victor looked wounded.

Telly focused. "Drew," she breathed. "You have to get out of here. Take Gwen and yourself far away from here. You have to. Take care of our daughter."

His body trembled as tears trickled down from his human eye. "I…I am sorry."

"Why?" Telly asked.

He jolted, shaking her body too. She wanted to sleep. Sleep forever. The pain. It hurt.

"I…I never asked you to marry mmm…me," he confessed, then jolted. "I wanted to ask…askkk, but I was too afraid before the accident."

"We can get married after this, silly," Telly said. Her mind felt fuzzy and numb. "After we are safe."

"Y-yes. We can," he said, still full of tears.

She needed to get to her feet, to stall so Drew and Gwen could get to safety. But her body wouldn't move.

"Why are you crying? Let's get out of here," Telly continued. Swirls and patterns danced in her line of sight. Where was she again?

"Mom," Gwen said, kneeling beside her. Tears ran down her face.

"Gwen…" Telly whispered. More pain shot through her body as she tried to stretch her hand to Gwen.

"Y-y-y…you will make it worse," Drew said quietly.

Gwen took her hand and sobbed. Her head was spinning. More pain coming from her stomach. Telly glanced downward…she'd forgotten about the pole.

"You have to get out of here. They need your magic," Telly breathed. "I'll be in the trailer with you soon."

"I'm not leaving without you," Gwen said, fighting back tears. "It will only be a short while."

Telly looked into Gwen's ocean-blue eyes as her daughter kissed her cheek. She glanced over at Drew. It was as if she couldn't see his cybernetic side anymore; all she saw was his smooth face before the accident. He gave her a bright smile, but even she could see that something was very wrong.

"I love you both," Telly said.

Telly mustered all her strength, getting to her feet. She wobbled, hearing familiar screams. More violet fuzzy magic against blues and yellows…

The pole shifted in her body, but now her body was so numb she couldn't feel it.

Suddenly, the yellow-gifted man came into view. The one behind all this madness. With him was a blue-gifted.

He was the cause of everything. Of her daughter's capture. Of this nightmare.

"You asshole fucks are going to pay!" Telly screamed as she fell to her knees. "I'm going to kill you, and you will die a slow and painful death!"

"Tell-me-lots!" Drew screamed.

She was so weak, but she had to make sure Gwen got to safety. Drew too. She had to make sure that these men didn't take her family…

Pulling the last of her remaining energy, Telly got to her feet, wobbling as she cried out in a sorrowful scream.

Then she ran straight into the flashing blue and yellow.

I want them dead! she commanded the magic.

It comes with a terrible price, it whispered.

I'm not going to survive this, am I? she asked.

No…your time is at an end.

Then so be it!

Bright orange energy filled her, then went all black. She ran straight into the opposing magic.

"TELLY!"

"NOOO!"

Telly ran fast and hard until she felt her body smash into something.

As she made contact, she released her magic like a violent earthquake.

The black swirled into nothing.

Then white. Bright pure white light.

✦ ✦ ✦

Emptiness filled the air; a spirit was gone from this world.

Telly's life force was no more.

Geeta fought back angry tears as she blasted a shockwave of violet energy.

In the midst of the magic, Geeta heard Gwen let out a bloodcurdling scream. The violet magic subsided, revealing Vihaan's and Radgu's bodies lying lifeless, with Telly right next to them.

"MOM!"

All dead.

Drew leaned over Telly's body, clutching it tenderly as he sobbed. Never had Geeta seen a cyborg sob.

The palace continued to quake, rocking and swaying, making loud groaning noises.

Geeta snapped to attention.

We are all going to die if we don't get out of here!

"By my estimate, the building's structure will collapse in approximately ten minutes," Scion said. "My readings also indicate that there is a meteor shower happening outside."

"A meteor shower?" Victor said, gasping with pain.

That was the last thing they needed.

"I will summon a portal. Just get everyone to safety," Geeta said. She held out the staff, then swirled it around, her hand burning with violet-blue magic. The magic formed a portal, floating a foot above the ground.

Turning, she made her way to Gwen and Drew. "We all need to leave now," she told them.

"What about my mom?" Gwen choked, blinking through her tears.

"I will carry Miss Hearly's body," Scion reassured her.

"Please save Jihyun!" Gwen pleaded. "He's my friend! Please!" There was a moment of silence, then Gwen yelled, *"Please*, Geeta."

Victor grimaced in pain, then glanced at her.

Geeta nodded quickly at Gwen. "I'll see what I can do, but you two go now into the portal!"

Drew nodded, then picked up Gwen in his arms, then entered, followed by Scion carrying Telly's lifeless body.

"Let's find the boy," she told Victor. "I might need your magic."

He grunted in pain. "It would be easier if this bullet was out of me."

Geeta got to her knees, then laid a hand on his wound where the bullet was lodged. Victor grunted again. "This will hurt for only a moment," she warned.

Then she sent out a wave of healing magic. Vivid violet magic glimmered over his wound, then mended his flesh.

Victor let out a loud sigh of relief. "Thanks," he said, getting to his feet.

"Don't thank me until we are out of here. The boy must've unleashed this unnatural disaster. We must stop him from destroying the earth."

"My readings show me that the boy's last point of energy was upstairs," Garrett said.

Geeta turned to him. "Thank you. We can find the boy. I can…hear his fear."

"Okay," he said. "Please be careful, you two."

"We will."

Garrett gave them a quick salute, then turned toward the portal.

Geeta turned to Victor. "Let's go."

The two of them ran down the hall, hearing loud groans coming from the structure itself; it would collapse soon. Cracks split the walls, and loud booms came from outside.

Geeta turned to Victor as they ran. "I think this boy is the cause of the meteor shower outside. If that's the case, he is using an immense amount of magic." She eyed him. "You might have to draw upon whatever energy you have in your life force."

"I will do what I can, though I don't know if I have any more in me before I pass out again," Victor said. "I nearly did so with that last burst of energy."

"If you use the full effect for an extended time, you pass out?"

"It is a part of the price I pay to use it."

Geeta's brow furrowed. "I think I can help with that," she said as they continued to run.

The palace continued to crumble. From one of the glass corridors, Geeta noticed that the moon was blood red.

And comets. Raining from the sky.

By the gods! It was far worse than what she had thought.

"The boy will make the world collapse," Victor said. "I will try and snuff out his magic before it's too late."

"Yes, before he kills us all."

Filling her life force with whatever energy she had left, Geeta burst with violet-blue light. The world began to shift from full color to violets and blues.

Time went still. All were safe. For now. All except her and Victor.

They ran until they came to an empty section of the palace, a hall devoid of objects, though it looked important.

Four pillars…

…and the boy.

Releasing her magic, the world began to shake violently as the boy screamed.

"Jihyun!" Geeta cried. "Jihyun!"

The boy continued to scream while blood ran down his eyes. He tore at the goggles connected to his head.

Victor bathed the room in a pure gray light.

The ground continued to quake, and a comet hit the side of the palace, splitting open a wall. The sky swirled with dark red energy, the moon like an angry red eye.

Victor looked weak, sweating, nearly passing out. He had no effect on the boy's magic…

"Victor, it's not working," Geeta said with alarm. "Cut it off!"

Victor's magic faded, and he went to his knees, breathing heavily. "What are we going to do?" he said over the boy's screams.

Yelling at the boy wasn't working, but she needed him to be aware of her presence…

Jihyun! her mind screamed. *Jihyun!*

There was no answer.

Geeta closed her eyes, finding her deep strength within, using the power of the staff. *I'm so sorry,* she prayed to the gods. *I don't like using this power.*

The gods answered with a whisper, and she felt their power. It filled her insides, allowing her core being to release the evil—to do good.

Violet energy filled her mind, turning into the purest black. Flecks of violet light appeared within. She had command over the dark power.

Enter the boy!

Geeta flicked open her eyes. As soon as she did, her mind jumped inside the boy's. Terror filled her as dark whirling images filled her mind, floating around the boy's spirit.

Leave me alone, Jihyun's life force pleaded with the images. *I want to go home! I wanna see my parents! My real parents! I wanna see Gwen!*

Jihyun, Geeta called out. I can bring you to Gwen. *But you must calm down!*

I'm so scared. He always tries to get me.

Who is he?

Questy. He scares me and says bad things to me. I'm so scared. Gwen makes me feel better…

I can bring you to her! Geeta promised.

I don't know you! You could be a bad guy like them! Like Questy!

Dark images floated in front of Geeta, making her weak and shaky. These images, these shadows, they were frightening…

Jihyun screamed in his mind. His world swelled up with more red energy.

Everything was going to blow, and these images were inducing his fear.

Geeta's mind brushed his, then she sent a healing wave, hoping to bring some sort of peace. Suddenly, one of the dark images disappeared. The healing wave worked.

She sent more healing waves from her mind to his. The red energy became less and less, until there were no more dark images, no more darkness, no more evil.

Jihyun's dark red energy became pure red. He was a true red-gifted—as he was meant to be.

Geeta jumped out of his mind. As soon as she blinked, she saw Jihyun on his knees, the goggles ripped off. His face was stained with dirt and tears. The moon was still blood red with meteors still showering across the skies, but the palace was stable, albeit in shambles.

Kyle. Though she calmed him down, Geeta knew his heart had deep hurts that continued to reflect in the elements around them.

Victor was sweating, breathing hard as she glanced at him.

"Are you the one that saved me from my nightmares?" the boy asked.

Geeta came up to him, crouching down to meet him face-to-face. "I am."

"Thank you," he cried, then gave her a big hug. Geeta returned his affection. He needed it, and though she didn't want to admit, she needed it too.

"Jihyun, right?" Geeta asked, releasing him.

"That's me." He looked over at Victor. "Who's that guy?"

Victor smiled at him. "I'm Victor, friend of Gwen's."

"Do you know where Gwen is? I need to find her…"

"Gwen asked me to save you and bring you to her. Do you want that? To see Gwen?" Geeta asked.

Jihyun smiled and cried, "Yes!" He shot up.

"I'll take you to her now, but we must leave quickly. The palace is about to collapse," Geeta said. "That is, if you want to. You may not see anyone here for a long time."

"All these people are mean. I like Gwen. She said I can live with her and her family."

Geeta suddenly thought of Telly, and she tamped down the sadness. "And you will. Hold my hand." Geeta outstretched her hand, and the boy took it.

Victor walked over, taking her hand as well. "The red magic in the sky," Victor said. "It's not the boy's."

Geeta glanced up at it, worry creasing her forehead. "Yes, I know."

Victor gave her a look. Then she waved the staff.

The violet magic burst, and they disappeared in a violet-blue flash.

✦ ✦ ✦

Red rain poured down on her, her face down in the mud. The ground shook violently, but she didn't care. Nothing mattered.

There were sudden voices all around her, familiar voices, with the smell of cigarette smoke.

"Gwen?"

Gwen managed to turn her head in the mud. Reila stood above her in full gear, drenched. Behind her was Geeta's portal.

"You're alive," Reila said as she bent over her.

Tears stung her eyes as Gwen laid her head back down in the mud. "Where's my dad?" Gwen murmured.

"Your dad?" Reila looked surprised. "Is he awake?"

Gwen nodded. "I was just with him before Geeta used her magic to send me here."

"Was your mother with you?" Reila asked as she reached out to lift Gwen out of the mud.

Gwen clutched her arm, getting up, fighting back tears.

The ground shook again, sending Gwen and Reila stumbling. Nearby, the violet-bluish portal radiated, and Scion and Garrett flopped out of it and into the mud.

Scion clutched her mother's body.

Reila's jaw fell open, her cigarette falling right out of her mouth. The camp went ballistic, crying and shouting.

"Oh my God!" Reila said as she ran to Telly's body. Scion put her down gently, and Gwen crawled over to her mother's body.

"Mom…" Gwen cried, then she looked up. "Where's my dad?"

"He has not shown up yet, Miss Gwen," Scion said.

She was with her father in the portal. He should be here.

Another radiating flash, and Jihyun rolled across the camp. Mud splattered everywhere. Another giant flash of red lightning shot across the sky, with a crack of thunder following.

"Jihyun!" Gwen said, wiping her tears.

"Gwen!"

Jihyun ran over to her, then slowed as he neared. The boy blinked at her mother's lifeless body.

Gwen looked down sadly. "Jihyun, this is my mom…"

Jihyun blinked again. "Your mom… Is she…?"

"Yes," Gwen whispered.

Reila and Scion could be heard talking quietly, with her giving him a soft kiss, then leaning her head on his shoulder.

"Is Geeta or Drew here?" Garrett asked. "Where is Victor?"

The portal faded away.

There was no Geeta or her father.

"WHERE'S MY DAD?"

Everyone went silent.

She had her answer.

Gwen covered her face with her hands.

✦ ✦ ✦

Geeta was falling. Falling endlessly.

Something wasn't right with her portal. It wasn't how it should be. Somehow the staff was missing too.

A dark energy was coming from the dimension, making her unable to cast her magic. Far down below, falling at the same speed of time, she saw a speck—it looked like Drew.

"Drew!" Geeta shouted.

He suddenly disappeared in the dark dimension.

"Call out all you want to whoever will listen. It's too late," said a voice.

Suddenly, she smacked against a hard surface, though there was nothing there. There was nothing *anywhere*.

"Victor? Drew?" she called out aimlessly.

"Geeta?"

Geeta froze, recognizing the voice. It was Nym's.

"Nym?"

"Help me! Some guy is holding me hostage!" Nym pleaded.

Geeta whirled around, trying to find Nym. There was nothing but the void. She then tried to find her with her mind, but her magic was depleted. Or not working.

"NYM?"

A dark spell flowed over her, like a stream of water, submerging her entirely. Her mind was stuck, and her body no longer listened to her. Instead, a smug, stern life force held her hostage.

I didn't think it would be this easy, the voice said within her mind. It was King Derek of Arcadia.

Let me go! Geeta cried out.

Why would I do such a thing? After all the trouble you have caused me? I think not.

Geeta wanted to scream. Nym was just a weakness he needed to get inside her mind…

Do not do this! Geeta pleaded. She struggled with his magic inside her body, but his force was too strong. *Think of the future! Think of your wife… your children!*

Little do you know, I am thinking of them. And your blood is exactly what I need to ensure their happy future.

I won't give up, Geeta said.

You'd best do it; otherwise your girlfriend won't see another day.

You wouldn't hurt her!

You bet I would, if that's what it takes to subdue you. But not like it matters anymore. I have control over you. But I will keep her anyway to make sure you stay in line.

Geeta gasped, suddenly feeling dizzy. Nym… A feeling a dread came over her. She had the premonition of Nym, but never had she thought that Derek was behind it.

That's right. I have her somewhere safe with me. If you choose to fight back, you also choose to end her life for the new world. Your choice.

No!

Derek melted into view, with Drew appearing alongside him.

He raised his hand, then summoned a new portal. The portal flashed brightly for a moment, then died down. It remained swirling, as if waiting for them. She wanted to fight, she tried, but her arms…muscles…nothing would respond to her command.

Please, Derek, don't do this…

"I must. For the sake of us all. There are plans in place for him." A dagger appeared from his belt, and he put it in front of her face. "Do you see this? This is the very dagger that pierced the violet-witch's heart months ago. And now, it will pierce your skin to give me what I need so Emerald and I can live in peace, away from that evil witch and all those who have made our lives a living hell." He gave her a sympathetic look. "Believe me when I say it gives me no pleasure to inflict pain and subdue Emerald's friends, or hold your loved one hostage."

Geeta couldn't move. She couldn't even cry or scream, only watch what was about to happen.

"And now, you will live in the back of your own mind while I take control." Derek grasped her hand, then guided it out it a straight motion toward her. Then, with a flick of his wrist, the dagger slid across her arms, sending her glowing blood trickling down her arm.

His lips met her arm, then licked her blood off them. As he continued to drink her blood, the dimension warped wildly, flickering between blue and black.

Derek paused, breathing hard, burning with dark blue energy. His portal wavered as the dimension had, turning from blue to ebony. His body began to be shadowed with the ebony magic, with deep blue flecks of energy. His heart beat loudly, as if the world and his life force were one.

Black magic swirled around her, completely enveloping her in darkness.

Now she understood. They couldn't get violet magic unless it was through his adjacent violet magic. Through Derek's possession.

She was going to be the means to Elyathi's new world.

As Derek's magic grew to the purest, deepest black, her thoughts, her memories, her soul…her life force began slipping away under his newfound possession…

Her soul was slipping away to her own mind prison…for good.

Derek laughed with delight as a rippling tide of dark energy shot straight through his body, down into the depths of his life force. The ebony dimension teemed with dark energy, humming. Immense black energy begged to be released. His body, mind, soul, and spirit…all felt *right*.

In the black dimension, Derek shot a giant wave of energy, releasing its power. Geeta and Drew stood mindlessly next to him as they watched with empty eyes. He now had Geeta's mind and Drew's body to command with the gauntlet.

Everything was finally working in his favor.

More black magic rippled through the dimension. He felt it growing inside his life force.

What power do you wish to have, Derek of Arcadia? echoed a powerful deep voice.

I want the ultimate power in the new world. I want to rule over everyone and be the master of all the colors of magic. I want time to bend to my will, for I am the King of Time! And I want all my memories when the new world is formed! Derek said. He narrowed his eyes. *I have yet to get my revenge on those who have wronged me, and it's past time.*

A deep laughter rumbled through the dark dimension. *You ask a lot of me. I have yet to accomplish it.*

More dark laughter. *Granted. The God of Light gave Elyathi the chosen the ultimate power in this world, I will give you the ultimate power in the next...*

Wait! Derek cried out. *I also want to keep the color of my eyes.*

More laughter. *You may have what you wish, King Derek of Arcadia.*

The darkness swirled around him like water, then pierced his heart. Instead of pain, he felt a flood of power that he had never felt before.

The power...

It was unmatched.

It was godlike. No mortal could come against him.

The black surge of energy consumed his soul.

There is much work to be done... the darkness whispered.

Derek stretched out his body, allowing the darkness to take him completely. "That's right. There is still much to do..." he called out.

Bringing his hands together, Derek pushed all of the black energy together, and he laughed.

✦ ✦ ✦

Victor had landed in some strange dimensional world. The others weren't there.

Where am I?

He looked all around and saw nothing.

Did Elyathi get her new world? Somehow, he knew that wasn't right.

In the distance was a dark source of energy. Strange, unearthly sounds rang out. Inside, he felt a push, telling him he should head toward the ominous magic.

Giving in to his instinct, Victor headed down a path of dark stars in an endless void of night.

"Geeta?" he called out. "Garrett? Scion?"

Not a single one of his friends were there.

Maybe they're by that magic, he thought.

As Victor drew closer, his heart began to race erratically. It reminded him of a nightmare he recently had.

Then he froze. Maybe this was the time for him to intervene. What he was called to do…

The black magic grew in size as an unearthly laugh echoed in the dimension.

Am I too late to save this earth?

Quickly, Victor sprinted toward the black light. In it he saw Geeta's shadow; she was standing next to a man surrounded by black magic. There was another shadow—a cyborg. Was it Drew?

The dark magic swirled all around the man as storms of energy rumbled. Negative energy permeated the air, making Victor feel sick. He finally realized who was in the center of the black magic. It was someone he hadn't seen since the day their wasteland camp was ransacked.

King Derek… Why did this man have black magic? Victor gritted his teeth. It didn't matter why he had black magic. He was holding Geeta captive. He then realized that Drew was indeed the cyborg.

He had to stop Derek.

Derek summoned a rippling black portal of magic. He raised a hand wearing a metal gauntlet. "You are to wait for me on the other side," he commanded. He flicked his hand, and Drew went inside.

Geeta was next.

Let's see what my power holds… Victor focused, picturing the light and darkness spinning inside of him. The darkness and the light did not want to mix together, but Victor surged all his energy, all his might, to make it so.

The white and black within him screamed at him in unison for doing so, but Victor kept pushing them, forcing them to become one.

You are a part of me, and I command you to bend to my will!

Obeying, the magics twirled together, becoming one color: gray.

Victor's body surged with a wild gray energy, pummeling across the dimension like a storm in the middle of an ocean.

Derek's black magic dissipated into nothing, and Geeta slumped to the floor, smacking against the tiles.

Derek snapped out of his ecstasy, suddenly noticing Victor. He tried to summon his magic, but nothing happened.

"You! You did this?" Derek snarled.

Victor's eyes met Derek's sharp gaze. "You are not taking her to Elyathi!"

"Who is going to stop me? You? Certainly not!" Derek said, as he yanked a dagger from his belt. "You might have disarmed my magic temporarily, but your age will determine your true strength. Come at me, old man!"

Victor basked in his gray magic, keeping it activated.

Derek charged toward Victor, lunging at him, nearly stabbing him in the chest square on. But at the last moment, Victor dodged to his side.

"You are more fit than I thought, but not fit enough."

The King grabbed him, then bashed him in the face with his elbow and slammed him in his ribs, hitting Victor hard. The breath was knocked out of Victor, but he continued to radiate gray magic.

Determined, Victor yanked Derek's ankles, sending him stumbling.

After Derek hit the floor, the two men wrestled each other. Victor felt his age, just as Derek pointed out. The King of Arcadia was strong and fit. He was fit too, but not as he was in his youth.

The men continued to roll around, with Derek getting solid punches in, and a few knee kicks. Victor delivered blows too, but he didn't have the stamina.

Then, Derek positioned himself, getting Victor into a headlock.

"Don't make me do this," he said. "I don't want to hurt anyone not involved."

Victor managed to say, "But…I…am…involved."

Derek let out a sigh as he raised the hand with the metal gauntlet. "You aren't worth it. Stay out of my way."

Then Derek struck him hard.

His eyesight went black, and Victor knew his gray magic had diminished.

There was a loud whoosh, then Derek said, "Get in *now*."

"Yes, My King," Geeta's voice answered.

"Geeta!" Victor struggled, still blind. He tried to focus his gray magic but couldn't.

"Her power belongs to Elyathi. Don't even bother."

Then it went silent. He was alone.

Victor sat in darkness, breathing heavily in pain. Slowly his eyesight returned from Derek's powerful blow.

How was he going to get out of there? How was he to stop Derek from bringing Geeta to Elyathi?

Elyathi cannot succeed, a powerful voice spoke in the dimension.

"I know! But I cannot do anything. My power wasn't enough…"

That is false. Your power is more than enough…

"How am I to stop Elyathi from here? I cannot even summon a way out of here."

There was a musical laugh. *Did I not create the earth, and all that is in it, including your magic? You ask the Almighty how you are to get out?*

He was talking to the God of Light? Victor gulped.

Just then, a metal object clanked next to him, as if something fell from the sky of the strange dimension. Eerie gray light shone from it.

Geeta's staff.

I will send you back into the original portal you were on your way to—to the wastelands. Stay there at your camp. There will be many important gifted seeking you out. Keep them safe until it is time to use this staff…

CHAPTER 83

◆

THE LIGHT SIDE OF THE SPECTRUM

"Lady Elyathi?" a servant girl called out from her personal chamber doorway.

Elyathi put down her pen and sat back in the folds of her chair. "What is it, dear girl?"

"The King of Arcadia has returned."

Just the thought of Derek made her stomach flip. Her heart even skipped a beat.

Elyathi rose from her seat, then waved the servant away. "Thank you."

"He also has informed me that he brought a gift."

"A gift?" Elyathi's cheeks flushed.

The servant girl bowed, then stepped aside. Curiously, Elyathi watched as a woman appeared in the doorway. The woman had strange clothing and hair cut very similar to an Arcadian man.

Elyathi's eyes sparkled and went wide. It was the violet-gifted.

The woman bowed obediently. "I am yours to command."

Elyathi giggled with delight. The violet gift, and Derek was giving it to her. A warm, delighted feeling shot down her spine, and she couldn't help but smile.

The servant girl bowed again. "The King of Arcadia says that he has other matters to attend to before seeing you. I believe he is on his way to see High Justice Nyrden."

Nyrden was dead, but no one else knew, as they hadn't announced it. Elyathi said, "If it's not too late, please advise him that he must speak to Nyrden's assistant."

"I will inform him now."

Elyathi nodded, then dismissed the servant girl, waving her hand.

"Come here," Elyathi commanded the violet-gifted.

The violet-gifted woman obeyed, walking up to her, then bowing.

"What is your name?"

"Geeta, my lady."

"Well, Geeta, you cannot go to the execution looking like that. You are going to meet the High Court. The least you can do is look *presentable*."

"Yes, my lady."

"First, I must do what I was born to do," Elyathi said, raising her chin. "Geeta, I want you to give me your life force so I can complete my spell."

"Yes, my lady. I am your servant."

"Good." Elyathi smiled brightly, then held out her hand. Violet magic bled out of Geeta, funneling straight into Elyathi's hand.

As the violet magic flowed in her hand, circling around like an orb, Elyathi grasped her orange gemstone, then absorbed the magic from within. It soaked into her, and slowly, her hair and eyes morphed into that color.

Then she balled her palms into fists, and orange magic flashed brightly from them. When she opened her hand, a brilliant violet gemstone lay in the palm of her hand.

Elyathi couldn't help but laugh with delight. The hour was nearing. She would finally fulfill her destiny.

"Now, let's get you cleaned up," Elyathi told Geeta.

"Yes, my lady."

Then she laid her hand on Geeta. New clothes began to form on the woman, her purple hair growing long past her waist…

✦　✦　✦

Bells rang throughout the courtyard. Crowds had gathered in the citadel to attend the execution.

Emerald had just finished bathing and wore a new gown. Her handmaidens combed her hair and sprayed it with a light hair perfume, her long tresses flowing down the swell of her back and gracing the floor. On her forehead was a circlet of gold with a green gemstone, and on top of her head was a jeweled headpiece, encircling her head like a halo. Her elegant gown was emerald green, with gold thread designs woven throughout, encrusted with green gems. Her shoulders were bare, and the rest of the garment clung tight to her, then flowed out like water from her hips and elbows. She truly looked like a queen of the green gift.

More bells rang out, reminding all that Empress Ayera's execution was soon. Since it was a big public affair, her mother had made it clear that she would be on display for all to see—the first High Justice of the Green in the history of the High Court. She didn't want to make a grand appearance at an execution, but she would do what was necessary.

Emerald was conflicted about the execution. She did feel sorry for the Empress, but at the same time, with all that had taken place, Emerald could understand why the woman had received her sentence. The way her mother explained it, the Empress had defied the High Court at every turn.

Emerald recalled seeing her when Ikaria left Arcadia. It was a brief moment, through a time portal, when Ikaria left imprisoned in her magical barrier. Emerald sighed. At this point, all she could do is pray for her soul. Her fate was sealed.

On the other side of the room, she heard her babies. She glanced back, smiling at them.

The door opened, and her servants announced that her mother had arrived.

"Emerald," she said. "You look radiant, my daughter."

"Thank you, Mother."

Her mother smiled, then headed over to a crib, then picked up Alexander. He gently touched her arm with affection.

"I am sad that I have missed so much of your life," her mother said to her. "If only I could have that time back." Her mother gave a sad smile. "But you are here now, and we will soon live freely and happily in the new world. And I get to see them grow up."

"Yes." Emerald flushed again, but confidently raised her chin. "I'm so happy to be here, Mom. I missed you so much."

"I have been dreaming of this since the day I left," she said. "I wanted to take you, but there was no time before my passage was gone." Her mother's eyes watered. "It was my biggest regret."

They both hugged. "We have lots of time to catch up," Emerald said.

"Indeed. More than enough time." She paused, then rubbed her nose against Alexander's nose. "Did you know that Derek has returned?"

Emerald's heart skipped a beat. "He has? When?"

"Just before I got here. I got the message."

"*And?*" Emerald asked in anticipation. Did he drink Geeta's blood? Her stomach did flips at the thought.

Her mother continued. "He is on his way to see Clarissa."

"Clarissa?"

"Nyrden's assistant. She's in charge of the deceased cyborgs. There were a slew of them that Ikaria sent through the portal months ago. Nyrden was working on a solution to revive them." Elyathi flashed a daring smile. "And now, since he's not here, Clarissa has assumed full control."

Emerald paused. "But why did he go and see Clarissa?"

Her mother was about to say something, but Nathan started fussing in his crib, interrupting their conversation. Emerald walked over and picked him up, then began to soothe him. She momentarily thought of Kyle, frowning. He had hurt her terribly.

It's not our son's fault, she thought as she gazed at Nathan. *He's innocent of this.*

As she held Nathan, Emerald walked back toward her mother, then the two of them sat, holding the children.

"Soon the world will see you as the new high justice," her mother said proudly.

Emerald flushed. "I suppose. It's just, this world is so new and strange to me. I have hardly left this wing of the citadel."

"Do not worry about that. Besides, the new world is nearing its dawn."

Emerald peeked outside her window, seeing the gardens. There were a group of red-robed citizens. From what Emerald had learned, those servants served the red justice.

Belinda. There was something off about her.

"Mother, do you know why Belinda's life force is different from the others?" Emerald asked, turning back toward her mother.

Her mother shot her a curious look. "Different?"

"Well, yes," Emerald continued. "Didn't you notice when I zapped her life force?"

"I did not," her mother said. "Though Belinda and the High Court are very much for our cause, their purpose is not fully aligned with the God of Light's." She leaned in. "For them to terrorize me with your father's delusions, you know perfectly well where that came from."

Emerald looked up at her mother, understanding. "Tyllos."

Her mother nodded. "Do not think for one moment they don't have a different agenda. All they want to do is distract from the true power."

"True power?"

Her mother smiled proudly as she continued to hold Alexander. "Why, me, of course. I am the chosen, and they are not. They have gotten a taste of my power, and they want more. I do not blame them." She paused. "You'd best keep your guard up."

"You have nothing to worry about," Emerald said firmly. "I put them in their place during my test. Besides, I am done being pushed around, used, and taken for a naive woman. I have seen the holes in the hearts of mankind, and am tired of believing in the best in people. Like you have told me, I have all the power."

"Good. But there something else you should know—something that pertains to the prophecy." Her mother paused. "Only if you are willing, my daughter. I don't want you to feel like you must."

"I am more than willing, Mother," Emerald said. "I want you to fulfill the prophecy. I want to live in a world at peace. I'm tired of being depressed. Tired of being sad. Tired of being hurt. I want this more than anything."

Her mother's face turned serious. "Please take the children for the time being," she called out to the servants.

The handmaidens came, gently taking her sons. They cried in protest.

"We will feed them," the handmaidens said.

"Good. We would like some privacy," her mother continued.

"Yes, my lady." They bowed, leaving Emerald and her mother alone.

After they left, her mother leaned in. "Do you know what it requires? The spell?"

Emerald poured herself a cup of tea, taking a sip, then put it down. She watched as her mother jangled her necklace out of her dress's neckline. Gemstones of different colors clung to it, along with one empty vial.

Emerald met her mother's gaze evenly. "You will take a part of my life force, won't you?"

Her mother didn't take her eyes off her. "In exchange for your power, I will grant you some of mine," she whispered. "Since you would lose a part of your life force, I will fill in the void, giving you even more power than before."

Emerald smiled at her. "I will gladly do this for you, Mom."

"I knew you were always faithful." Elyathi gave her a smile in return. "Be still and calm your heart."

"I will," Emerald said.

She remained silent as her mother's eyes closed. Slowly, Elyathi held out her hand, placing it on Emerald's chest where her heart was.

Emerald felt her life force begin to flow; the power draining out of her core, then flooding to the spot where her mother was touching her.

Give my mother the power she needs to overcome this terrible world! Emerald said, closing her eyes.

In a flash, the sensation stopped.

Emerald opened her eyes to see her mother with long green tresses and bright green eyes. In her hand was a piece of her green gift. Though she knew that her mother had extracted a piece of her life force, Emerald felt like the part that her mother had taken had been fully restored in her body, and that she was no longer missing that part of her life force.

The green gift flowed gently in a circular fashion in her mother's hand, almost creating a sparkling green orb of life. With a clench of Elyathi's fists, Emerald watched as her mother drained orange magic from her gemstone, burning brightly. A wave of power fluttered around her, changing her hair and eyes to a bright tangerine. With another sharp movement, Elyathi's hands clenched the green orb within her fist.

With a burst of green and orange magic, the orb vanished.

Emerald watched as her mother opened up the palm of her hand, revealing a beautiful vivid green gemstone.

From the gem's glow, Emerald felt it radiating power and life.

They glanced at each other, exchanging smiles, then bent over to look at the gemstone.

"It's so beautiful," Emerald said.

"Of course it is, my daughter," Elyathi said. "It came from the most beautiful soul I know."

Emerald smiled again as her mother cast another spell, making a charm around the stone. After the silver clasp was formed, Elyathi strung the green gemstone on her necklace, then slipped it inside her dress. Emerald watched as her mother pricked her finger, squeezing it hard, creating a large drop of blood on her fingertip. She squeezed it again, causing more blood to ooze out of the tip. With a glassy white gaze, her mother raised her bloody fingertip to her lips.

"Drink," she commanded.

Emerald began sucking the blood out of the fingertip. Suddenly, a loud pulse of life rang through her ears. Her mother's heartbeat. Louder it grew as she consumed the blood.

"Keep drinking. I want you to be the most powerful queen there ever was," she said.

Emerald kept drinking. Her mother's heartbeat began matching her own. Wild heartbeats, fierce and free…

Everything in her vision turned a vivid green as her mother pulled her fingertip away.

The connection was broken, and silence fell over the room.

Emerald blinked. No more green, just the light of the room. But in her heart, she felt strong.

"I am truly glad that you have returned," her mother whispered.

They hugged each other tightly.

"I am too, Mother," Emerald said.

How good it felt to finally feel love. Genuine love. She never had to feel lonely ever again.

"I must get going," Elyathi said as she rose from her seat. "I will see you at the execution."

"I love you, Mom," Emerald said, getting up and meeting her evenly.

Her mother placed a hand on her cheek. "I love you too, my precious daughter." Her mother stroked her cheek, then turned away, walking out.

Emerald walked over to her mirror and fixed her dress, quickly wiping under her eyes before her eye makeup smudged. Outside her window, people started to pour out of the citadel, readying for the event.

Everything will be different soon, Emerald thought.

There was a knock at the door.

"Who is it?"

"It's me, Derek. May I come in?"

Emerald's heart quickened at his voice. "You may."

The door opened, and Derek entered. Immediately, his eyes locked onto hers. He walked up to her and bowed deeply.

"Emerald…" His voice trailed off as he stared at her in awe. "You are the true definition of beauty," Derek said gracefully. He knelt before her as she held out her hand, kissing it. Emerald's blood ran hot through her veins as she admired his godlike beauty.

One of his hands was behind his back, then he brought it forth. In it was an elegant rose in the color of a soft purple. "I saw this and thought of you," Derek said.

"Thank you, Derek," she whispered. "It's very lovely." She softly coiled her finger around a single curl of his, admiring it.

"Yes." He smiled. "Just like you."

She blushed, then snuggled against his firm chest.

Emerald suddenly thought of Geeta. "Were you…successful? In the past or wherever you were?"

Derek paused, meeting her gaze once more. "Emerald, I wanted to tell you that whatever happens when this is all over with, I will always love you. Always."

He held her tighter in her arms, almost as if he was reassuring her. She broke away, seeing a flicker of emotion on his face.

"Is everything okay?"

"It is." He paused. "I…I guess I am nervous?"

"About what?"

"I had to take the power from Geeta," he admitted.

"But I knew that," Emerald said. "Is she okay?"

Derek lowered his gaze. "She is. Well, in fact," he said. "I have her under my control." He paused, then quickly looked to her. "I'm…sorry. I had to do it, though, for your mother's spell."

Emerald smiled, even though she didn't like it. She put her hand on his cheek, feeling his underlying guilt. "I understand, Derek. If it's needed, you have to do it," she whispered.

Derek breathed easier. "I also wanted to let you know I brought you another present."

Emerald blinked curiously. "What?"

"Your cyborg. He is here."

Emerald paused, then understood what her mother had meant earlier about Clarissa, Nyrden's assistant. "Drew? He is here?" Her heart beat quickly. "What for?"

"There's a lot to explain," he said. "He needed to be here to get working on the cyborgs that came into the portal with Ikaria. Without him, our new world wouldn't be secure. He is the key."

Emerald breathed in, excited. "Drew will be with us? In our kingdom?"

"Indeed," Derek said. "I knew you'd be happy."

Emerald beamed. "I am." She kissed him. Startled, he kissed her back, then they deepened their kiss.

The clang of bells outside startled them. They turned to each other, laughing.

"Could those bells get any louder?" he joked.

"I suppose they could." Her face turned serious. "I'm getting nervous. My mother said that it's possible Ikaria will show up at the execution." Emerald's eyes narrowed at the thought of Ikaria. Emerald was not normally for revenge, but she definitely welcomed it for Ikaria. In fact, she couldn't wait for it.

"What are you nervous about?" Derek pressed. "The new world?"

Emerald shook her head. "No, definitely not. I welcome it gladly with open arms," she continued. "I just…I don't like the idea of anyone being executed. It reminds me too much of my father. But if this leads to the new world, then I know it's the right thing to do."

"Taking a life that isn't justified is a terrible price."

Emerald turned to him suddenly. "Derek?"

He turned, looking at her with concern. "What?"

Emerald paused, then stared into the depths of his eyes, the color of ice. "Kiss me once more. I want to feel loved, as if it will be the last time on this earth."

Derek smiled devilishly. "Your wish is my command."

Immediately Emerald felt the heat of his breath mixed with his strong cedar scent, driving her wild. His soft lips brushed hers, then he slowly kissed her. She felt his longing, passion, lust, and soul…his desire.

She never wanted to let go.

After a good long while, they pulled away gently. "If you sent me to my death, I would go willingly," he whispered, kissing her lips once again. Through his lips, Emerald felt his unfailing love and devotion. It made her feel safe.

Then a sudden foreign thought entered Emerald's mind, making her shake with anxiety.

Derek pulled away, looking at her curiously. "I…I know you were happy with him. Do you truly want to do this?" he dared to ask.

Kyle…the mere thought of him hurt her deeply. Emerald blinked. He felt long gone and a just distant memory.

"I do want this, with all my heart." Emerald looked at him. "I want to forget everything about him." Her eyes began to water. "There is so much pain associated with him. He made a fool out of me. That is not love. Love is…pure devotion." Emerald shook with a quiet rage.

Derek went quiet.

Emerald glanced at him, then held his hand. Their eyes met once again as her lips came within an inch of his. "I was such a fool to pursue love elsewhere. Meanwhile, the entire time, you only wanted me. I realized this now, and truly my heart hurts because of everything. I only want you. You and the children eternally, in the new world. That is my wish and my desire."

Derek smiled with soft tears in his eyes. "That is my desire as well." His gentle lips met her once more, awaking her passion. Her body burned for him. All she wanted was to make love to him, feel his body against hers, flood her mind with his love, his desire…

In the background, she heard the bells again.

Their lips parted, then he whispered in her ear, "Let us live in the new world, loving each other eternally," Derek said softly as he held her close.

"Yes."

They rose to their feet, then Emerald walked to the door, then called out to the handmaidens. "Prepare the children. They will join us on the High Court platform."

"Yes, Your Majesty."

The handmaidens presented their children, with Derek and Emerald kissing them once more. After they'd left, Emerald couldn't help it—she already missed her babies.

Derek turned to her. "I will keep watch over on them on the platform."

"Thank you."

He bowed to her, then cast a black protection spell over the children. "I will meet you on the platform. I must check on my possession."

"Be safe," she said.

"I will," he said.

They kissed each other one last time before he flashed away in black magic.

✦ ✦ ✦

As Emerald walked down the green halls on her way to the execution, she noticed Belinda standing in the middle of the hall, front and center. She was dressed in a grand gown made of crimson silks and elegant fabrics trimmed with gold. Encrusted throughout were rubies and garnets. Her long, wavy red hair graced the sides of her body, nearly kissing the floors, and she bore a golden circlet with a red gem and a gilded headpiece encircling her head. Her skin looked especially pale against the vivid green halls and bright red fabrics that she wore.

"High Justice Belinda," Emerald greeted with a nod.

"High Justice Emerald."

"The hour is near for the execution," Emerald said. "Is everything all right?"

"I wanted to have a word with you before the ceremony."

"Of course," Emerald said. She thought back to Derek's words about Belinda. Was this another warning for her to look out for? Was this a deviation from the plan?

"What is it?" Emerald asked curiously.

Belinda lowered her voice. "I wanted to warn you before time takes us all."

"Warn me? Of what, exactly?"

"Of your mother."

"What of her?"

Belinda eased her head, then continued. "Please, make no mistake, I do want your mother to succeed in bringing forth the new world. It is why I had this court do anything and everything to make it happen." She smiled. "It uplifts my soul knowing what is to come."

"High Justice," Emerald said, "I fail to see what the problem is."

"Be wary of your mother, Emerald. You do not know this yet, but you will.

She will use you for her selfish desires. That is all she cares about."

Her mother? Selfish? Emerald blinked, then became flustered. "Why would you *say that*?"

Belinda's face hardened. "What brought you here, exactly?"

"Derek brought me here…"

Belinda gave a half smile. "No. *What* brought you here? Was it your mother's convincing words? Or was it heartbreak from Kyle?"

Emerald's eyes widened. "*How* do you know about him?" she whispered in a low voice.

"Or was it Glacia and her betrayal?" Belinda continued. "Or was it to get revenge for Ikaria's interference?"

It was as if Belinda knew every secret of her heart.

Emerald shook her head in disbelief. "How do you know all of this? Did Borgen scry time and tell you?"

Belinda smiled at her, a dark smile filled with sadness. "Did you notice that Borgen seemed surprised to see you when you accidentally traveled in time, to where Ikaria was at? You know, the very moment we discovered the green gift. We had searched countless tomes on the subject, to find out what era of time you lived in."

"But you knew of me through my mother. You had been searching for me throughout time, sending blue-gifted," Emerald pointed out.

"Time is a fickle one, wouldn't you say? So many possibilities."

"You aren't making sense. What is the truth of it?"

"All of it," Belinda said. "You see, Queen Emerald, I was once a sweet, innocent young princess, just like yourself. Born with the gift of the red—the first in a thousand years with the *gift*. No one had ever seen anyone like me. I was once good, kind, and innocent many ages ago. Everyone took advantage of me, thought less of me, though I had the power to destroy them all. Through my kindness and love, I held back because wisdom granted me the ability to do so. But over time, everyone who I cared most about took from me. My love, my dignity, even my power…" Belinda's voice trailed off, an edge to her voice.

It sounded exactly like what she had experienced. Everything.

"They made me out to be a villain. All of them, though it was *their* doing. They tried to make me forget. Return me to my innocence," Belinda said bitterly. "This time, it is your chance to change everything. You, and *only you*, will have that power in the new world. Do not forget it."

Emerald shook her head. "I don't understand why you're telling me this. If I understand correctly, I will forget your words in the new world. My pain, my hurts…it will all be erased."

"But will it?" Belinda raised an eyebrow. "I do hope so, for your sake."

Emerald studied her, taking two steps closer. "Who…are you?"

"The better question is 'Who was I?'" Belinda's eyes met hers.

"I sense that you are ancient, and that your life force is completely unique," Emerald said.

"Time. It cycles itself. We are stuck in a constant loop. When my eyes were opened to the reality of time, and of the hurts that the world brings forth, I wanted to do what was right." Belinda paused. "None of that matters now. I look forward to the new world. Things will be different, rest assured. You will have your love, life, and power intact. Everything will be yours."

"But what about you? Won't you tell me anything more?"

"My only advice is to look for the tear in the fabric of time."

"Tear? Fabric of time?" Emerald echoed, confused.

"You will understand when the time comes. Godspeed, Emerald. See you at the execution."

Belinda then flashed away in red magic, leaving sparks behind in the green gemstone halls.

Another loud bell rang. It was nearly time.

On her way outside, Emerald kept thinking about what Belinda said. How was it that her life mirrored her own? Or that Belinda knew so much of hers? Had the woman scried time? And how would she remember Belinda's warning in the new world? It seemed unlikely that she would. It didn't make sense.

As she approached the Colosseum, the crowd in the stands roared at her arrival. Word had spread like wildfire throughout the citadel: There was a green high justice. Many showered her with flower petals or confetti, all while giving shouts of praise for a true green-gifted justice. Emerald even heard some claim that the God of Light had shone his light on the earth because of her.

Though she was used to crowds back in Arcadia, those crowds revered her in a way that those back in her own time never had. It was because of her magic, and not just her beauty.

Emerald walked toward the High Court box, the closest to the center stage of the Colosseum where the judgment circle was located. Several high justices had already taken their seats, drinking chilled wine or eating delicacies. Derek was there, holding Alexander, while a handmaiden held Nathan behind the thrones. Another maiden stood ready to help with the children at a moment's notice. To Derek's left was Geeta.

Emerald couldn't believe it. Though Derek had told her that Geeta was there, it didn't seem real until that moment. Geeta sat proudly on the violet throne with her head high. She was dressed in violet garb similar to Emerald's, including a circlet and headpiece. But what made her unrecognizable was her hair; Geeta had extremely long locks of hair, with thick curls adorned with golden ribbons. She was, no doubt about it, compromised by Derek. Though Derek had warned her, the sight was alarming. Though she wasn't as bothered by it as she thought she would be. After all that she had gone through—between Kyle and her best friend—it was as if she cared much less about others, her heart had been hardened. Or maybe it was that she just didn't want to feel anything anymore. And if she cared, she would feel…and she just didn't want to anymore.

"My Queen." Derek bowed, the compromised Geeta doing the same.

"Derek," Emerald said as she held out her hand. He kissed it. She glanced over at Geeta.

"I can move her out of your sight if it pleases you. Her throne is on the other side," he said.

Emerald shook her head. "This will be over soon." Emerald darted her eyes back at Geeta, as her friend stared out into the crowd. "Her hair is long," Emerald pointed out.

"Elyathi wanted her to fit in as close to this time as possible," Derek stated. "She sped up time to make her hair grow."

"I see," Emerald said, sitting in her throne. "How is our son?"

"Here he is, High Justice."

The maiden handed her Nathan. His little body lay against her chest as she held him close. She gave him a gentle cuddle, then kissed his forehead.

Emerald turned back to the maiden. "Please watch over him until the event is finished."

The maiden bowed, then took Nathan in her arms.

As the crowd gathered, Emerald couldn't help but think about the Empress.

"What's on your mind?" Derek said as he sat down next to her, taking a sip of wine.

"Do you think Ikaria will come?" Emerald asked.

Derek's brow furrowed. "She will," he answered. "I cannot wait to face that witch."

"Same here," Emerald said, also narrowing her eyes. "She will get what's coming to her."

Derek glanced at her, then they both laughed. "Never did I think we'd be in this moment. Not even in my wildest dreams."

"Neither did I."

They clinked wineglasses. "It is…like old times."

"Indeed."

"What shall we toast to this time?" he asked, his dark eyes taking in her beauty.

"To ridding ourselves of the sorceress, and to the new world," Emerald said.

"I will drink a full cup to that," he said.

"Don't drink too much; you want your wits about you," Emerald said.

"Believe me, I do too. Just one cup," he said.

They toasted, drinking their wine fully.

Her mother appeared on the platform, walking toward them. She leaned over behind their thrones. "It is nearly time."

Then the trumpets blared.

✦ ✦ ✦

A loud clanking sound came from her cell's iron door as it opened, waking Ayera. Light shone in her face, causing her to squint.

"Lady, it is time," one of the guards said.

The guard's words startled her awake.

"Time?" Ayera repeated, hoping that the guard would give her a different answer.

His face was solemn in the torchlight. "Time for you to say your final prayers."

Ayera choked on a fresh set of tears as she drew a courageous breath. She rose to her feet, holding her head high. At least she'd have a martyr's death.

"I am ready," Ayera said bravely, and the guards shackled her wrists. Her heart beats pounded through her entire body. These were her final moments.

God of Light, give me strength, she prayed.

The group of guards moved her out of her cell, leading her out of the dungeons. There was a pair of guards on each side of her, and several guards in the front and back. As they walked down the dank path, there were cries from the prisoners.

"Mercy!" screamed one prisoner.

"You slaughter the innocent!" called out another.

More and more cries came from the dark cells, but all went ignored. Ayera fought back her bitter tears, trying to focus on the last moments of her life.

The group came to a guard station, which had a bright blue portal swirling with magic.

"They are waiting on the other side to begin the execution of the prisoner," one of the guards said to the leader of the group.

"Excellent."

The first set of guards entered the portal, with Ayera being dragged by the guards at her sides. Vivid blue magic swirled around her, and the dungeons melted away. As the magic twisted and morphed around her, new shapes and outlines appeared within the blue shifting magic.

They were angelic creatures, shimmering with sparkles of white light. There was a multitude of them, swirling around her, forming a long tunnel of light. Their bodies were completely transparent, lighting up the atmosphere around them.

Am I imagining this?

Ayera stared at the creatures; they all had multiple wings that were long, wide, and grand. They were fully armored, and in their hands were different weapons—swords, spears, and bows. She couldn't make out any details of their faces or their clothing.

In her childhood, she had read accounts of people seeing angelic creatures before they died. Her time was truly over. That realization gave her more determination to speak out at her execution.

So be it.

As the blue magic faded away, so did the angelic beings. The world became clear and vivid—and she was standing at the High Court Citadel's execution arena, at the beginning of the bridge. It was the walk of death.

The bridge led into the Colosseum itself. From far across the floating arena and sky-bridge, Ayera saw the crowds of people. Thousands of people filled those stands, waiting to spectate her death. It sickened her even more that her death was considered entertainment. Perhaps they were enraged by the High Court's list of charges, regardless of their validity. The farce of a trial already showed that.

Ayera took one final look around her. The clouds were beautiful. The sun's beams were bright today.

Soon, I'll be one with the sky.

"Get on with it," said one of the guards.

Taking a deep heave, she began her walk of death.

As she took the first step onto the bridge, the audience roared with applause.

Ayera bit her lip in anger, disgust, and sadness as she continued across the bridge, the guards in front and behind her. The crowd's roars crescendoed wildly as she crossed the sky-bridge, then entered the floating arena. The dots of color in the stands became clear; people could be seen in more detail. Screams, cheers, boos filled the Colosseum. Trash, food, and books were being thrown at her, now that she was in range of the crowd.

The crowd was mainly from the High Court Citadel itself; Ayera could tell by their fashion. Nowhere did she see representation from the other world sectors. That in itself spoke volumes to her.

As she walked onto the main floor of the Colosseum, the crowd roared, calling her all sorts of obscenities.

"Evil unbeliever!" someone screamed from a crowd.

"Go to hell, you wicked woman!" another voice called out.

A book pelted her in the face. From the corner of her eye, she saw it was *The Spectrum*. The very book that she believed in, thrown in her face.

"You and your demonic sister! Exorcise the demons from those witches!" called out a yellow-robed cleric.

More and more objects were thrown at her, with many insults mixed in. It didn't matter to her; what she did and believed in was true and justified.

"Well, look who we have here. It's the ex-empress herself," said the captain of the guard. He sneered at her, then leaned in. "You should have went along with what I wanted. I would have made your death swift."

"You disgusting letch," Ayera snapped back.

The captain took off his gauntlet, then struck her hard across the face. Cheers erupted from the entire stadium as he put it back on. "Now who's disgusting," he said, laughing through his sour breath. The rest of the crowd laughed and cheered with him.

"You people are sick. All of you. I am ashamed that I went along with the High Court for so long," Ayera said, spitting in his face.

"Worthless bitch!" The captain struck her again, this time giving her a bloody nose and lip. Ayera raised her head high, trying not to let her resolve weaken. Far off, she saw the thrones of the High Court with the justices seated upon them.

Ayera paused, noticing there were several new faces in the High Court area—two seated on the thrones. Her eyes trailed to the green throne, causing her heart to skip a beat. It was the green-gifted princess from Arcadia!

What is she doing here? Ayera thought wildly. Behind her stood a man that Ayera did not recognize. He was young like her, perhaps even younger by a few years. Dark black curls, dressed in blue. He stood at full attention behind the Arcadian gifted princess. Both of them held a child.

Ayera's eyes shifted, her heart dropping into the pit of her stomach. Was that Geeta on the platform? It looked like her, though her hair was long and formal. She was seated on the violet throne. *Why would Geeta join them?* Ayera felt her stomach churn. *And why is the gifted queen on the green throne?*

Off to the side, Ayera saw the white-gifted woman, with a vivid smile on her face. They were all there, awaiting her death.

The captain gave her a hard push. "Stand on the circle," he commanded. A circular design was inlaid in the stone floor below, designed as the symbol of the Spectrum. Ayera stumbled, avoiding the circle. "What's wrong with you? I said stand, you bitch." The captain gave her another shove, and this time she happened to be on the circle.

"Don't make a bigger fool out of yourself. You don't want people to remember you as a traitorous bitch," he whispered, laughing again. "Oh wait. They already do!"

Far above, Belinda of the Red rose from her seat. She lifted her hands upward.

Suddenly, the marbled circle that Ayera stood on lifted upward. She yelped, her stomach sinking—she was on a rising platform. As it levitated upward, the crowds of people got to their feet as she became level with them, cheering louder at the captain holding her tightly.

Then the platform was level with the High Court, a deep space between her and the High Court. They all stared at her with stern expressions. The white-gifted woman had her nose in the air, while the handsome dark-haired king gave her a cold icy glare.

"Let us begin," High Justice Belinda stated.

The crowd cheered wildly.

The truth...

Within the skies from afar, Ayera saw black specs in the skies. How was it that birds could fly this high up in the skies?

"Lady Suzuki. You have been sentenced to death for treason to the God of Light, and of this High Court," called out the captain of the guard.

The audience roared.

"Any last words?"

"Yes." Ayera glanced around at the entire stadium.

The audience booed, with Belinda raising her hand in silence. The Colosseum went still, allowing Ayera to speak.

"People of this audience, I not only speak to you, but people of this earth. You have been deceived by the very people that sit on those thrones over there. The so-called high justices should be ashamed of the lies they tell you. They preach of the God of Light, but under the guise of their beliefs, they control you all to do *their* will, not the God of Light's. I stopped a great evil from happening, and yet I was labeled a rebel and a wicked woman. You allow the white-gifted to steal the magic of the gifted, the ones the God of Light bestowed favor to. That is theft of the heart! Not only that, it is theft of the soul! Who is the wicked one now? Me? If you think that a woman stealing gifted souls is right, and for me to stop a great evil is wrong, then so be it. I will die a martyr's death, and go down in history as a heroine to mankind. That is, if our world survives. For our earth is now doomed in the hands of this High Court."

The audience roared with laughter mixed with boos.

"Pretty words," the Captain mocked. He whacked her on the cheek again, causing her to stumble on her feet.

Glancing up, Ayera saw black specks in the skies. They weren't birds—they were *airships*. A whole multitude of them, surrounding the citadel and the Colosseum.

Ayera's heart beat wildly.

Suddenly, a blaring, amplified voice echoed across the sky, coming from the airships:

"You are to end this farce immediately and return the Empress to us or face the consequences!" the amplified voice warned.

Someone was here to save her! She didn't recognize the voice, but she didn't care. Maybe, just maybe, she wasn't going to die this day.

"What is the meaning of this?" Tyllos called out sternly, rising to his feet. The high justices did the same as chaos erupted within the amphitheater. "Those ships are from the earth's surface!" he yelled. "I knew we should have obliterated them when we had the chance!"

"Silence!" ordered Belinda, her voice amplified as well. Meanwhile, Tyllos chanted loudly, filling the entire stadium with his golden magic, shielding them with protection against the airships.

"This is your last warning!" said the loud voice from the airships. "Give us the Empress!"

"Absolutely not," snarled Belinda loudly. She glared right at Ayera, then turned to the captain. "Captain, proceed!" she ordered.

Ayera's heart beat quickly at the command. Deep within her body, a powerful feeling grew. It spread throughout her body like wildfire, causing her heart to beat fiercely.

She heard the sword of the captain being unsheathed. "Lady Suzuki, to your knees," he ordered. A wave of magic shocked her body—red lightning from the captain.

Pain rocked her body. She was going to die before they rescued her.

"ON YOUR KNEES!" the captain shouted, sending a huge blast of red lightning.

Ayera yelped as she fell to the ground. Her limbs were numb, her body could hardly move, and she could barely catch a breath. The pain was too great for her frail body to take.

Ayera glanced once more up to the captain, then past his face to the airship-filled skies. Her people. Other people of the sky sectors…

They had come for her.

She glanced up at the sun, then whispered in her heart, *God of Light, give me strength…*

Use your gift.

The words didn't surprise her; it was as if she had known for some time. Perhaps it had been Suresh's words that made her look inward.

Determined, Ayera slowly rose to her feet. Her knees felt weak and shook with nerves.

Welcome me into your never-ending paradise…

With those final words in her mind, there was a huge explosion of bright light across the stadium, knocking everyone back with a gigantic powerful blast of energy. Cracks from pillars, crumbling foundations, screams from the audience echoed as bright energy flowed out of her heart.

It was her life force—in *color*! It was bluish…and…violet? It radiated the most brilliant power and light from her life force.

Ayera suddenly felt her soul, light and free.

Within the power of light, Ayera saw the shapes of the angelic figures. The same figures she had seen earlier.

"Who…or what are you?" she breathed.

The God of Light chose to release a new magic upon this earth, given the timing of your prayers, they answered.

"New magic?" Ayera whispered.

You will be the wrinkle in time, allowing one gifted to pass through dimensions, with a chance to stop the corrupted chosen…

What is this color? Ayera asked in her mind.

Indigo… they said in unison as they disappeared. *Indigo…*

✦ ✦ ✦

The entire area blasted with indigo magic, rocking the entire airship wildly.

"Brace yourselves!" screamed Kang.

Everyone on the airship grabbed hold of whatever they could as the airship spun madly. Jude held on tightly to a rope that swung from the mast, as he summoned his bright gold magic, covering the entire airship with his glittering barrier magic. A monstrosity of indigo magic rolled through the entire Colosseum, rippling through the crowds, tearing them aimlessly from their seats. The indigo power violently slammed against the golden barrier of their ship. Jude's shield rippled erratically, making wavering sounds as the indigo magic collided.

"Move in close to the Empress's platform!" commanded Tekka to the airship's captain.

Magic in all colors was cast all around them—from the High Court, guards, and any other gifted that were in the area. Magic burst like fireworks. None came close to the powerful blast of the indigo magic.

Within the center of the powerful magic, Suri saw the source. It was Empress Ayera.

Suri climbed to the edge of the airship's deck, holding on to her own rope. "Master Jude, please shield me."

Jude held up his hand to stop her. "I'm coming, Miss Suri!" he said.

"Count me in," Kang said.

Suri glanced at them quickly. "If you must, but do not slow me down."

Kang chuckled at her statement, as Jude nodded.

A gigantic fireball roared their way, targeting their entire airship. The men on the ship shouted as they aimed their own weapons—ones that were outlawed by the High Court.

Glowing red ice shards and red hail shot out from their weapons, all aimed at the fireball. As the fireball neared, it got smaller and smaller from the icy blasts. The fireball shrank in size until it was the size of a sportsman ball, plopping on the airship's deck like a child's toy. A man blasted one final wave of ice on the fireball, putting out the fire on deck.

"Everyone, fire!" yelled Tekka, then he turned to Suri, Jude, and Kang. "You better get down there now before it's too late."

"How are we going to get down there?" Jude asked. "We are still too far."

Suri lightly laid her hand on his back. "We must jump like last time."

"HURRY!" Tekka yelled as the indigo winds whipped his hair wildly, knocking everyone back. Suri and Jude swung wildly on their ropes. Every muscle in Suri's upper arm burned as she held on for dear life.

Suri turned to Jude, then yanked his hand, leading him up to the railing of the airship. It was in no way steady, but they didn't have a choice.

There was a flash of bright blue light nearby in the sky.

"You aren't planning on jumping, are you?" a man asked within the blue light.

"We were…" Jude said, then blinked. "Where did you come from?"

"I have come to help rescue the Empress," the man said. "And you aren't going to jump. I won't let you."

Suri sucked in her breath at his statement. "Please sir, we must get down there."

The blue light faded, enough to see a man with deep ebony skin and royal blue hair and eyes. He shook his head. "That magic down there is too powerful; it's messing with the dimensions, including all magic in the area."

"What do you suggest? The Empress is at the center of it," Suri said. "We must get to her."

"I'll port you as close as I can and follow," the man offered.

Kang turned to them. "I'll extract some of the indigo magic. It might help us to have a bit of that energy."

The man nodded, then summoned a bright blue portal in front of them as the airship continued to sway wildly.

Kang held up his hands, summoning his brown magic. The brown energy turned indigo as he sucked in the continuous wave of indigo magic being emitted from the Empress.

"This should help us," Kang said as he held a ball of indigo energy in his hands. It seeped into his body.

"Jump into my portal before it fizzles away," the man urged.

Then they jumped.

❖ ❖ ❖

The indigo magic rippled through the skies fast and hard. Her airship, along with all the others in the sky, rocked and teetered chaotically.

Ikaria cast a giant force around the airship she commanded, trying to steady the giant contraption with all her magical might. Grunting with the amount of force, Ikaria's extended arms flexed hard, the veins popping out. Behind her, a huge amount of golden magic intertwined with hers, creating a barrier of protection.

As she was casting, magical wind ripped through her long tresses, and her robes went flying every which way. Through the barrier, Ikaria saw airships flung about like toys. The indigo winds tore through the Colosseum, blowing the spectators back violently against the stands. The pillars cracked, and a loud groaning echoed in the air.

Ikaria cried out, trying to control the airship, scanning to find the source of the magic.

Her sister…

…had magic!

A *new* magic!

Ikaria laughed wildly with delight and lunacy as she continued to try to steer the ship with her violet force. "Well, isn't that something? My sister!" Ikaria shouted with a smile.

Suddenly, another of her flying airships went off course, blocking her view. She had to protect her people so they could fight.

"I can try and port those ships, but my magic feels different with this magical blast!" Vala called out in the winds.

"I have an idea," Ikaria called back, then turned to Auron. "Priest! Funnel magic to me! And no questions!"

"Coming your way!" Auron's magic flowed through her body, seeping into her life force. Focusing on his magic within hers, she mixed her life force with his.

I'm not a saint, but help out these innocent souls, at least, she said in the back of her mind.

With her complement's magic combined with hers, suddenly her magic burst into pure light—the white light of the Spectrum. With a sweeping motion of her hands, Ikaria screamed, then released the magical white force, sending it off to each of the airships dotting the skies.

The white beams of light enraptured the entire fleet of airships, then steadied the crew while safeguarding them too. The allied airships started descending into the Colosseum, safely landing.

"Just you wait!" Ikaria screamed at the High Court guards below. "I'm coming for you all!"

Warriors from all the sectors started funneling out of the ships, meeting the High Court army and guards head on in battle.

"You did it! Our allies are safe," Auron said from behind her, then he cleared his throat. "I mean, the God of Light did it."

Ikaria glanced over her shoulder. "You can give me praise, priest. In fact, I welcome it," Ikaria said. "Now get ready, because we are going in. We can't let the other sectors have all the fun."

Auron gave her a stern glance. "Elyathi is down there."

"And so is my sister," Ikaria snapped back. "Do you think that uppity white-gifted hag is going to sit idly by while my sister oozes a new color of magic?" She turned away, then shot out her hands. *I'm coming, sister!*

Throwing her hands down in a quick motion, the entire airship dropped. They were falling fast and hard.

"We are going to smash right into the Colosseum!" screamed Vala, clutching the railing of the ship.

"No, Lady Vala. We are going to smash right into the High Court thrones!" Ikaria laughed maniacally.

"This is madness!" Vala yelled.

"I like to make a grand entrance!" Ikaria called out. "Time to put an end to the High Court once and for all!"

"Ikaria!" Auron said in a panic, gripping one of the sail's ropes.

"Don't you worry, priest," Ikaria said as the wind whipped her hair in her face.

No one was going to get her sister, nor her magic.

The airship was just about to make contact with the ground, so everyone braced themselves as Auron burst with golden light, creating a shimmering golden barrier over the area as they crashed.

The people of the airship were knocked to their feet, tumbling every which way. Getting up quickly, Ikaria saw her sister up ahead. The platform had been lowered by half, still reachable to anyone. There were all sorts of magical spells being cast in an array of colors: High Court gifted against her people of the skies, along with the ground people that somehow seemed to show up unexpectedly. All were fighting for her. For the future.

Ikaria saw the High Court platform in the distance and sneered at who was on the platform: Queen Emerald. Then her eyes quickly found a familiar face. Ikaria's jaw dropped at the sight of the violet-gifted on the platform. The High Court had every color.

For the first time—possibly ever—in her life, Ikaria felt impending doom. She'd been outplayed in this game.

It's not possible. She wouldn't join them, Ikaria thought. Next to Geeta was Derek.

"Ikaria!" called Auron.

Ikaria glanced over to him and looked to where he was pointing, seeing her sister in the distance. Her platform had lowered by half, though she was still standing on the raised pillar.

"I know!" she hissed, then pointed to Geeta. "But I must do something about that violet-gifted!"

Auron's face jerked to the platform, and panic washed over his face. "Geeta? It can't be!"

"Best we stop her now before we dine tonight with either the God of Light or the Lord of Darkness. I still have some years left in this flesh of mine," Ikaria called out. "I'm going over there. I need protection. Don't fail me now."

Ikaria closed her eyes, focusing all of her magic toward Geeta. She had been in her mind before back in Arcadia; though it would prove to be difficult to break into her mind, Ikaria was sure she could do so, and quickly, for their minds had made a prior connection.

Ikaria gathered everything she had in her life force, then shot herself straight into Geeta's mind.

Black void instantly surrounded her. No doors, no stairs, no nothing. Just a blue-violet barren wasteland of nothingness.

Suddenly, Ikaria felt Derek's presence.

This is my power, not yours, Derek, Ikaria thought. Within the barren wasteland, Ikaria began to stream more of her power in the void at a fast pace. The world shifted to a violet, and a delicate glass barrier could be seen in the sky.

Just as she was about to break Derek's possession, Ikaria's consciousness was shot back into her own body.

Pain rocked her as her life force was being ripped from her.

Ikaria screamed as dark green magic seeped into her body, tearing apart her soul. As Ikaria looked up, she saw Queen Emerald looking down on her. Behind the Queen was her sister's magic, still filling the entire area with her indigo power.

Just when Ikaria was going to cast a spell, Emerald flicked her hand, casting dark green magic all over her again.

"You aren't going to get away from me, or any others you have meddled with, ever again," Emerald said coldly.

The pain was excruciating. It was as if a knife was filleting her life force from her body…

"You thought too much of yourself," Derek said as he walked up, towering over her. "Thinking you were the only violet-gifted."

"Let this be a lesson of humility," Emerald said. "What you are experiencing is nothing compared to the mental pain you caused me. For both me and Derek."

More life force was torn from Ikaria as she struggled. She didn't want to give them the satisfaction of knowing how much she suffered. But it was hard not to, and she cried out.

"I'm sure she likes your magic," Derek spat, "considering how much she got off on tormenting others."

"Indeed," Emerald agreed. She filled her hands with more of her dark green energy, sending it flowing hard and fast into Ikaria's body.

"Auron…" Ikaria called out softly. "Where are you, priest?"

"A priest?" Derek laughed. "The one you are paired with? I sent him away. Far away from you!"

"I did feel sorry for you," Emerald said. "But my sympathy doesn't cover the multitude of hurts you have inflicted on me."

More life ebbed away from Ikaria as she grimaced in agony.

There was a sudden bright blue flash, and Ikaria's pain ceased.

Confused, Ikaria glanced up, seeing a blue-gifted man she had never seen before. With him was Auron and Vala.

The man held out his hand, pulling Ikaria to her feet.

"For the sake of formalities, I would ask your name, but I have a sister to rescue," Ikaria said.

"Dydrone," the man said. "But yes, my little trick will have them coming back in five seconds. Get out of here now."

He flashed away in blue magic as Auron encased them in a golden barrier. Ikaria's soul was weakened, but she was alive. There were noises of battle, flashes of magic, screams, disorder, panic.

"For once, I am listening to the advice of a stranger," Ikaria said.

"I encased the green-gifted queen and her partner in my own dark magic within the blue dimension, but we don't have much time before she breaks it."

"Then let's hurry."

The three of them ran across the platform, nearing the indigo light. There were two silhouettes, of two women. Suddenly, Ikaria's breath was stolen from her. It was Elyathi next to her sister, sucking her sister's gift away.

The indigo magic began fading away, with Ayera slumping to the ground.

"BITCH!" Ikaria screamed as she sent a time flash of blue magic surging into her soul. Instantly, the magic transported her right to her sister.

"Sister!" Ikaria screamed again. Ikaria turned and narrowed her eyes as she faced Elyathi.

"If it isn't the sinful, wayward witch herself," Elyathi said, raising her chin up high. "Your sister's power is refreshing to my soul." Then she laughed as she held up her necklaces. "Do you see, sorceress? I have all the magic I need— which doesn't include yours."

"You…" Ikaria whipped her hand out to Elyathi, sending a forceful blast of her magic against Elyathi's body. It didn't even faze her.

My life force is weak from the dark green magic.

"Sister," Ayera called out softly from under Elyathi's feet.

Ikaria narrowed her eyes, sending another violet energy blast to Elyathi, but she held firm.

Then, there was a giant blast of black magic, knocking Ikaria back as she rolled on the ground.

"You thought you could get rid of me?" Derek chided.

Metal shards shot through the air—guided by black magic, sinking into Ikaria's flesh. Ikaria screamed in pain.

There was a sudden blast of indigo magic once more. Derek, Elyathi, and anyone in the area disappeared in the indigo light.

For a moment, Ikaria saw Derek's strong form shadowed against her sister's indigo magic, then he disappeared.

The magic faded away. Elyathi was screaming as she held her stomach. Blood gushed down her white gown and through her ripped dress—her insides were spilling out.

There was only one person who had a move like that.

"Suri!" Ikaria cried out with tears of joy, ignoring her pain. The metal shards were lodged deep into her flesh.

"I am here, Enchantress," Suri said as she shimmered a bright orange, coming into view.

At that moment, Ikaria had the thought that Suri had the most beautiful smile she had ever seen. Ikaria's heart melted at the sight, causing a deep stir of emotion within her.

The moment was short-lived. There was a terrifying deep green glow around Suri's body, then a loud metal scraping. A sword appeared through Suri's chest, hitting her heart.

"Suri!" screamed Ikaria.

Behind Suri, a beautiful feminine figure stood bathed in eerie green magic. Emerald.

"SURI!" Ikaria screamed as she crawled toward her servant.

Emerald's eyes were lit up as power drained out of Suri and into the green-gifted queen.

"Mother…stay still," Emerald commanded. She held out her hand, flowing pure, vibrant green magic over Elyathi. Quickly, her flesh mended, and the white lady got to her feet.

There were bells chiming in the distance.

"Now is the time," her mother called out.

"Just a moment," Emerald said, pouring her dark green magic over Suri. "I must ensure they stay put."

There was a flash of white light, then a young man's voice cried out, "Mistress Suri!"

"It hurts, doesn't it?" Emerald stated as she neared Suri.

Ikaria cried. "You bitch! You green-gifted bitch!"

"Enchantress…" Suri murmured.

More power drained from them as Ikaria screamed. Suri didn't make a sound, merely grasping the sword in her chest.

"It's too bad that I must leave. I would kill you if I had the time," Emerald commented.

"You wouldn't have the strength, bitch!" Ikaria screamed.

A giant rip of pain from her insides tore at her life force. Ikaria screamed.

"I have all the power," she said confidently. "Unfortunately for you, you won't get to witness it. You won't be in the new world."

There was a flash, and the green-gifted queen was gone.

Ikaria wailed as she inched her way toward Suri. Every movement was painful, as the metal shards were still lodged in her.

"Suri…"

"I'm here, Enchantress…" Suri said softly.

The two women held hands, both breathing heavily.

"Enchantress…your gift will always be protected…" she whispered. Her bright orange eyes fluttered back into her lids, then she slumped to the ground.

"SURI!" Ikaria screamed.

A sudden wave of greenish-yellow healing came over her. The metal shards fell out of her flesh abruptly as the wounds closed.

"SURI!" Ikaria shook Suri's lifeless body, hoping she would return. Instead, Suri flopped over to her side.

Auron shook Ikaria's shoulder. "Your sister! We must get her out of here!"

"SURI!"

"IKARIA! Did you hear me? Your sister needs us now! Elyathi has been fully healed!" Auron screamed, shaking her again. "They are going to cast the final spell. Your sister is in danger!"

Ikaria screamed and cried, and in the corner of her blurry, tear-stained vision, she saw a golden blur of magic running over to Suri's body.

She couldn't believe it. She just couldn't believe it…Suri…

She was gone.

Ikaria screamed.

"IKARIA!" screamed Auron. "Now's not the time! Your sister! Think of your sister!"

Ikaria froze as she glared at Suri's lifeless body. All around were magical blasts from the High Court gifted against the strange ground people with their weapons. Her sector was fighting against the High Court too, along with all the others. Everyone was fighting for this world…

Auron was right. She had to rescue her sister. They were probably going to use her new magic to call upon the new world…

Ikaria choked on her tears as she turned back and saw that her sister lay on the ground, nearly dead with no magic.

Auron cast a golden shield around her. "GO! We will be right behind you!"

Ikaria stumbled to her feet, then focused on her sister. Then she ran with everything that she had left in her body.

More golden magic poured over her barrier from multiple gifted as she ran past them.

"Save the Empress!" cried out one yellow-gifted.

"For World Sector Six!" cried another.

"For the future of our world!"

"For Mistress Suri!"

Someone also held Suri dear to their hearts…

Every single one of their words renewed her strength, revitalizing her life force.

"Hurry!" called out another.

As she neared her sister, Ikaria stopped as she became acutely aware: Her sister was dying.

"Sister?" Ikaria breathed.

Quickly sliding to her knees and grabbing on to Ayera, Ikaria cradled her sister in her arms. Around her, Vala and Auron held off many of the High Court guards.

"Sister…they have green magic. The Queen of Arcadia has joined with them…" she breathed hard. "Violet magic too…"

"Shh, don't talk," Ikaria said. "We are getting you out of here."

"I am going to die, sister," Ayera whispered, breathing hard.

Ikaria bit her lip, fighting back tears. "Don't talk like that."

Ayera's indigo eyes glowed as she looked right into hers. "You know it's true…"

"That is nonsense!" Ikaria said. "You cannot die, sister! Suri already left me!"

"Suri?"

Ikaria's eyes swelled with tears. "Don't talk. I'll take you somewhere safe. Auron and Vala will send the High Court to their graves!"

"I know now that I was always meant to be a martyr," Ayera said breathlessly as her eyes radiated vivid indigo.

Ikaria shook her head. "Nonsense. You will live and rule. I mean, look at you—you have a new color of magic. That says something in itself, sister."

"No, it's a sacrificial magic. This world must continue on its original course of time. If I don't unleash this magic, Elyathi will corrupt all of the timelines and rebuild the world with corruption. I must sacrifice myself to release the magic into the flow of time."

"And you know this how, sister?"

Ayera's eyes sparkled the color of deep blue with flecks of purple. "I hear the whispers of the angels as they near this dimension. Now is the time…they are gathering," she spoke softly, her eyes meeting hers. "The green-gifted…"

Ikaria held Ayera close. "What about the green-gifted?"

Ayera's eyes were weak, slowly closing.

No!" Ikaria whispered, shaking her sister's body. "You can't leave me here all by myself! Suri is dead, and you will leave me too? I won't allow it!"

"You must, sister," Ayera said with a weak smile. "Take up my seat after I am gone. Restore our lands on the earth. Rebuild…"

"Sister…" Ikaria cried.

"I love you, sister."

Ikaria was about to say the same, but Ayera went lifeless. Indigo magic burst from Ayera's body, sending a giant shockwave across the earth as far as Ikaria could see through her blurry vision filled with tears.

Ikaria held her sister tightly as she screamed. The people she loved most were dead.

"Sister…I'm so sorry," Ikaria whispered, holding Ayera's body close.

There were loud shouts coming from others, saying her name, but it was gibberish. She didn't care.

More shouts, then bursts of magic; this time it was bright green and flashes of blue.

Auron suddenly came into her vision. "We must get you out of here!" he shouted.

"I don't care!" Ikaria screamed. "I will die here and now!" Streams of tears rolled down her cheeks as she clutched her sister's dead body. Her soul felt empty, and she didn't care about anything. As she cried, she felt her violet magic leave her body, streaming away like the tide returning to the ocean, leaving her bone dry inside.

Auron screamed again.

There was a sudden sharp pain within her mind, and Ikaria slumped over. She saw herself within her mind's eye, falling to the ground, and she had absolutely no control over her own body. Derek was in control. She didn't care. Her sister was dead. Suri was dead.

So this is how it is going to end, oh great Derek, King of Arcadia? Ikaria said within her mind.

It is payback, witch, for all that you have done to me. All that you have put me and Emerald through…

Have it your way, then, Ikaria answered. *I will not resist. I am done fighting. Take my magic. Take my life force. Just take me quickly.*

There were deep laughs within her mind as she felt her life force drain away.

You make it too easy. How am I to get satisfaction from this? I expected a grand fight, witch.

Sorry to disappoint you, Derek. I have no fight in me because you and your white bitch took everything from me. There. Does that satisfy you?

Immensely…

"Lady Elyathi!" Derek called out. "She's yours."

There was another bright flash of white. Then she felt her magic being torn away from her soul.

✦ ✦ ✦

Derek flashed onto the high justices' platform, holding Emerald's hand. He smirked at the mere thought of Ikaria having no more magic. He felt no sympathy for her losing her sister or her trusted servant. For all he cared, the witch could keel over with them both.

The high justices stood farther down the platform, with elite High Court priests on guard, protecting them. With them was Geeta; he was very much still in control of her mind.

"Derek," Emerald whispered.

"What is it?" Derek said, turning to her.

Emerald looked shaken, but she gave him a brave smile as she lifted her hand in his and kissed it. "I'm just nervous, I suppose."

Derek gave her a reassuring smile, then leaned in, kissing her hand as well. "It will be okay. I will be there to protect you. We will be together."

Emerald nodded, then leaned on his shoulder as they walked toward the group. Secretly, he stalled only a few seconds, just so he could relish in the satisfying moment—being with his true love and seeing the downfall of the sorceress.

As they approached, Elyathi flashed in front of the group. She held up a gemstone as her own personal trophy. Ikaria's life force had been converted to a gemstone.

"You have Ikaria's life force?" Tyllos said with a smirk.

"I do, not that it matters," Elyathi said, glancing over at Geeta.

"Still, it is immensely satisfying," Belinda said.

Derek glanced at Emerald, exchanging glances in agreement.

"Derek, you have the violet-gifted secured?" Elyathi asked.

"I do." He gestured to Geeta, making her bow before Elyathi.

"Then it is time, high justices," Elyathi announced. "A new dawn begins."

Elyathi turned to the High Court priests that surrounded the area. "Shield us with your complete life force. I will ensure you will have a high position in the new world if you keep all distractions away from us."

The priests nodded, then began to cast a giant golden barrier. It glimmered over the entire platform. Derek sent a wave of violet magic to Geeta's mind, forcing her to join them. They all formed a summoning circle around the Spectrum symbol.

"Get in the middle," she called out to Derek.

Derek walked inside the circle with Elyathi beside him. Derek noticed that beyond the golden barrier spell, the world was in utter chaos. Magical bursts, weapons being fired, airships flying every which way, stones from the Colosseum toppling over and crushing people, but the priests kept their area free from disaster. It truly was the time for a new world to come forth.

Elyathi clutched the gemstones around her neck, draining them of their power. "Channel your magic into me," she commanded the circle. "Now!"

The high justices lifted their hands toward Elyathi, then funneled their colors of magic into her. Faster and faster, Elyathi began to glow, first with the surrounding colors, then turning prismatic. The magical light that emitted from her body was radiant and vivid, causing Derek's eyes to water. He glanced over at Emerald, who was lit up from her own green magic.

She looked so beautiful in that moment.

"All of your life forces!" Elyathi screamed from the light. "I must have them!"

Their energy funneled into her life force, mixing into one color.

White.

Vibrations hummed through the area as Elyathi's power echoed across the magical field. Loud cracks, thundering, quaking echoed all around them.

It is your turn next, Derek, her mind whispered to him.

Then a loud white blast of light came from Elyathi, followed by screams and cries. Derek heard the sound of shattered glass on the ground—it had to be the gemstones. The screams dissipated, but the light did not. Derek saw shadows of bodies slumped to the ground through the white-hot light.

"Emerald!" Derek screamed. Frantically, looked around. Emerald was not standing in her summoning spot. "Emerald!" he shouted again.

"She will be with us in the new world, Derek," Elyathi called out from the light beyond.

"Where is she?"

"You must cast your spell now!" Elyathi screamed.

Derek's eyes began to water. Was Emerald okay? She wasn't in her spot…

"You must hurry, Derek! Time is short! Cast the spell now!" Elyathi snarled.

Hesitantly, Derek rose to his feet from behind the white light. Staring into the light, Derek lifted his hands, ready to funnel his dark magic. He now understood Elyathi's intent. She'd fully taken the magic that was tied to their life forces.

Will Emerald have her gift in the new world? Derek thought woefully.

It is gone forever, whispered the darkness.

Derek choked on his thoughts, turning angry. He was so blind to everything! Why did he make the same damn foolish mistakes every time?

I will never trust another. Only Emerald, he thought as he stared into the bright light.

Nor should you, whispered the magic. *They have manipulated you at every turn…*

I will never forget this. Ever, he told the black magic. *Elyathi taking Emerald's life force. Ikaria and what she's done. The scientist…the robot… everything and everyone! They will pay! All of them!*

*That, they will, King of the Black Gift…*whispered a voice.

Derek gritted his teeth, fighting back a tear as he thought of Emerald losing her gift forever. *I will make their lives a living hell. They will utterly regret crossing me ...* He then lifted his hands out to Elyathi, casting a beam of black magic into her.

"I feel your power!" Elyathi called out, laughing delightfully.

Derek narrowed his eyes as he surged his black magic into the light. Black magic glittering with sparkling energy like a riptide, shooting right into Elyathi's heart.

That second, Derek felt his life force intertwine with hers. Their life forces were one.

I feel you, Derek, Elyathi's soul whispered.

A giant white magical explosion ricocheted across the circle. Elyathi's hair went loose from her tight buns, flying wild and free within the wind currents of their magic. She held out her hands, and a white ball of light formed within her grasp. She raised it above her head, the white energy growing larger with each second. Her dress flew wildly, shredded and torn, and her white glowing eyes looked wild and feral.

"The time has come!" Elyathi shouted, almost in a command against the earth itself.

Loud vibrations rocked the entire area as the outside world began to melt.

✦ ✦ ✦

Emerald struggled to lift her head, but a wave of nausea and confusion hit her hard. Voices flooded her mind. Strange whispering voices.

"Make them stop," she whispered to herself, as if she had the power to. Only, she didn't. They kept whispering in her mind. There was so much noise too. Burning white light. All she saw was white.

Her eyes shifted downward as she tried to clutch something, anything, as the ground shifted. Her long tresses came into view, her long locks of wavy hair spread out all around her. Her hair...it was *red*. The natural deep red that she had known whenever she had sucked her green magic into her core being. The color she was meant to have without the gift.

Why...?

Confused, Emerald looked up into the white light. Her mother was screaming in the midst of a large magical ball of white energy.

Emerald looked back down at her red hair, holding it delicately. Her mother… She *stole* her magic.

More voices overlapped inside her mind, but they were incoherent. She glanced back down at her red hair once more.

She. Took. Her. Gift.

Emerald screamed.

In the distance, Derek cried out her name. There were more shouts coming from him, but they were muddled.

Her mother *tricked* her. Her gift was missing from her life force. And now…she was empty, as if she'd lost herself completely.

Emerald curled up in a ball, wailing. She was such a fool. Everyone took her to be a fool, even her pious mother. The world's biggest fool that ever lived.

Through her tears, Emerald watched as the sky melted. Was she going mad? Or was this truly the end of the world as she knew it?

More tears were shed as voices filled her mind. One of them Kyle's name. *Kyle…*

Kyle had been right about one thing: Her mother did sincerely want her to come to the future. Not because she missed her, but because she needed her magic to fulfill her purpose. Her mother had told her that she needed her magic—a *part* of her life force, but she had never said she would remove it from her life force completely. Kyle knew her mother was extremely dangerous, and had warned her so. But she didn't listen because of his other offenses.

Kyle…I am so sorry. Emerald started to weep, placing her head against the tiled floors. *Kyle…I am such a fool…*

Blurs, strange shadows, voices…she couldn't focus. She had thought she had finally had control over her life. Instead, her naivety got the best of her— in the form of her mother. Her mother was truly evil.

Emerald continued to sob. *You were right, Kyle…though you broke our love, you were right about my mother…*

Emerald watched as the sky melted away while she clutched her red hair, weeping. Soon, she would be reborn as Derek's wife in the new world and never remember Kyle again. Forever. Was it a bad thing? She'd been starting to become infatuated with Derek all over again. He remained true and loyal. But her heart, deep within, told her she still loved Kyle. It hurt thinking about him…

She glanced over at the other bodies. Belinda's head tilted toward her, almost lifeless. The high justice's hair was red, the same red as hers, a normal human color and not gifted. Their eyes met…Belinda's were pale aqua, like the morning dawn mixed with ice.

Emerald blinked, suddenly aware of something she had never noticed before. Belinda looked like her, but an older version of her.

Why hadn't she realized it before? She had come face-to-face with her before and never noticed. Neither had anyone else. Not her mother, not Derek, not Kyle's former self. Why?

"Belinda?" Emerald whispered.

"Emerald," Belinda said softly. "You should see your true color of eyes."

Emerald grasped her hair, then realized she must not have green eyes as well…

"Are you…me?"

Belinda searched her expression. "Time can be altered, twisted, and morphed into different planes and dimensions. Sometimes, it creates alternate timelines, fragmented in the stream of time." Belinda gasped for breath. "I am you in an alternate timeline…without green magic," she whispered in a hoarse voice.

"I don't understand! Any of it!" she called out through powerful wind.

"I did this for you," she whispered. "The new world wasn't pure, the one I was in. I vowed to change it, but I failed the first time. It is now your chance to make things right. Crush everyone that is corrupt under your feet this time around. You have the inner strength to overcome and rule them all."

"Will you die?" Emerald said, forcing back her tears.

"It was meant to be this way…I am not meant to be here." Belinda looked up at her. "As for you, you will live on. Remember my words."

"But how am I to remember this?"

"The fabric of time…" Belinda whispered. Then her head rolled over as her body went limp. Her hair and dress garments flapped furiously in the white energy. Emerald glanced around in a panic at the other bodies. All lifeless.

She screamed as her vision went black.

Suddenly, Emerald felt strong hands lifting her head.

"I didn't know, Emerald," whispered Derek's voice. "I swear it! I didn't know…"

Emerald cried as she reached out aimlessly. "I know, Derek. I know. Please, keep me safe and hold me. I don't want to remember this. Any of this…"

"As you command. But know this," he said softly, "I will protect you in the new world. This I swear upon my soul."

Derek brushed her hand softly as he kissed it, then propped her up in his arms, holding her.

More voices poured out inside her mind as he held her. The warmth of his body felt safe. It was the only thing that kept her safe from the madness that was taking her away.

Kyle…

He was her last thought before she passed out.

✦ ✦ ✦

Bright white light rippled across the sky, wavering like violent waters as the sky melted like candle wax. Through the atmosphere, Vala saw a transparent layer of another dimension forming, with different timelines overlapping each other. Ghosts of the past, present, and outlines of the future were all around them as time went haywire. Massive panic gripped the citizens, who scurried out of the area like frightened children.

Straight ahead, Vala saw the white-gifted woman Elyathi basking in her energy. Near her was a violent black energy funneling around a man, though Vala couldn't see anything more.

Vala felt a shift deep within her life force. The rules and laws that once applied to time magic had *changed*. And there was nothing that she could do to stop time from slipping away…

Vala turned swiftly to see her uncle, fighting hard to cast more barriers of protection across their group. It did nothing, as much of their magic fizzled, affected by the ending of the world. Ikaria was still on her knees, cradling her sister as she screamed over and over again.

Guards, some of them being gifted, were wearing down Auron's spell and disarming Vala's. Other guards, fearful at what was happening, had run in panic. Above, the airships veered away, others trying to land to fight against what remaining time was left.

"Uncle!" Vala shouted.

"I know!" Auron called out.

"Is there any way to interrupt her spell?"

"I don't know! Their spell is taking away my magic!"

Vala felt it all too well already. Some spells worked, while others didn't. It was as if the balance of magic was hanging on by a thread.

Nearby, she saw the same ghostly people from across all timelines, confused while running in terror.

*If Time were to collapse…If you see time fall upon itself, it is imperative that you find a man in the time rift and get to him…*Oriel's warning echoed in her head.

All Vala knew was that this man had no magic. But how would she find this man when the world had only a few minutes left? Vala scanned the entire area. She saw no one that could help.

I must do something!

"I am going to port us to the white magic source," Vala called out to her uncle. "We'll see if we can stop them!"

Ikaria was heaving with sorrow while holding her sister's body. "You're too late. It's finished," she said through her tears. Then she looked up at them. "Don't you see? You're late. We all are."

Vala and Auron exchanged startled looks. Her violet magic was gone from her eyes.

"That's right, priest," she continued. "They took everything from me. Time for everyone to die."

Auron turned to Vala. "We must find that man Oriel spoke of before we all perish!"

"I know. But where?"

Auron reached down, grabbing on to Ikaria.

Ikaria fought him off. "Let me go, priest! I will die alongside my sister and my dearest friend. I care not of anything anymore."

"We need to find a certain man to stop this!" Vala shouted.

"Did you hear what I said?" Ikaria screamed. "I don't *care*! Leave! Get away from me!"

Vala glanced down at the Empress's body. A glimmer of indigo magic sparked from her body…then began to glow with her magic.

Ikaria must have noticed, because she stopped and stared in disbelief.

"SISTER!" she called out.

The Empress began to burn brighter and brighter, encased by her power.

"Ayera!" Ikaria said, shaking her sister's body.

But Ayera was dead, yet the remaining magic from her life force was spilling out into the sky.

"You must leave her," Auron said.

"Ikaria, stay back! You might get hurt," Vala warned.

Ikaria's naturally dark eyes met Vala's. "Get out of my sight!" she snapped.

Vala backed away. "As you wish, Sorceress." She turned away, seeing the white light intensify. The sky continued to melt, quicker by the moment. Screams echoed all across time.

Bodies started crashing onto the landing areas, like falling rain.

Auron summoned a weak barrier over them. A body came crashing next to them, splattering blood over his barrier.

Vala cast another spell, but it fizzled out. Her magic just wasn't…working. And her uncle's barrier…it was fading too.

"Uncle…"

He put his hand on her shoulder and began to whisper a prayer.

In the midst of all the chaos, there was something very curious: bright gray light.

Vala's heart skipped a beat.

It was *gray magic*.

"Uncle! Uncle!"

Auron stopped his prayer, quickly turning his head, his eyes going wide. "By the God of Light…"

The gray magic came toward her. It appeared as if it were traveling through dimensions, but locked behind a time wall. The magic—it looked as if it was being excluded from the time compression. Within the gray magic, Vala could make out the outline of a man.

"It's him!" Vala exclaimed as the gray magic became brighter.

"Hurry!" Auron grabbed Ikaria, clutching her in his thick arms. Ikaria screamed, struggled, and slapped Auron every which way, but he ignored her, continuing to move with Vala.

They ran toward the gray magic as Auron cast weak barriers over the group. Vala tried to cast another spell to move through the plane of existence quicker, but she couldn't—time was all wrong.

"You there!" Vala shouted, waving her hands toward the gray light.

"I hate you!" Ikaria yelled as she fought with Auron's mighty grip.

Vala ignored Ikaria as the gray magic came closer. The shadowy man's detail became more clear. As the man neared them, he, too, noticed that he was behind a time wall. Behind the man were other shadowy figures, their details shrouded.

"Now is the time…" a voice called out to the skies. It was the Empress's voice!

Vala spun around, seeing a gleaming stream of indigo magic, bathing the Empress's body entirely with indigo power. The Empress's eyes narrowly opened, filled with glowing indigo magic.

"AYERA!" Ikaria screamed as fought she Auron. Auron held her back.

"My soul awakened for this moment…" Ayera called out, her voice echoing. There was a stream of indigo magic flowing from her body to the barrier of the time wall where the gray man stood.

"SISTER!" Ikaria screamed.

More indigo magic flooded the time barrier. Then a giant burst came from Ayera's body.

The indigo light was so intense that Vala had to shield her eyes. There was a loud, thunderous tear, like fabric being pulled apart.

Quickly opening her eyes, Vala saw a small rip in the time dimension. But the Empress was gone.

"AYERA!" Ikaria screamed.

"She sacrificed herself to create this wrinkle in time," Auron said in awe.

The wrinkle in time created a hole, and now the outline of the man with gray magic could be fully seen, along with the group behind him.

"Come with me," the gray-gifted man spoke to Vala. "You will be safe."

Vala nodded, then held out her hand, and he took it. Loud rumblings surrounded them as the gray light enveloped Vala, Auron, Ikaria, and the group in the time rift.

Ikaria fought wildly. "Let me die here, priest! I hate you…"

In the corner of her eye, Vala saw a few other gifted running toward them from the platform. A young yellow-gifted priest and a thick bald man with a bo-staff.

Auron's face lit up. "Jude!"

Jude and the man with him were running toward the gray light as fast as they could, the world around them melting away into nothingness.

The bridge under Jude's feet started to wobble.

"HURRY!" Vala screamed.

Echoes of Elyathi's and Derek's voices could be heard. Time was fading.

"Everyone to me! NOW!" the gray-gifted man screamed. "Stay in the gray light!" He held out a staff, the orb radiating with gray magic as the folds of time collapsed.

The gray aura grew as bright as the bright white magic, and Elyathi screamed.

"Wait for us!" called out a young boy's voice from inside the time rift. "I have to fight the bad guys!"

Shadows from the other dimension appeared behind the gray-gifted man—shadows of a young boy and a teen girl running toward him.

Then a loud crack roared across the sky as the sky turned pure white.

"It is time…" Elyathi cried out.

Then loud explosions of white light.

"It is done…" Derek's voice answered.

All Vala could see was white light while Ikaria's insults and cries filled her ears.

CHAPTER 84

◆

RED

The elements were violent. Meteors crashing to the earth. Rumblings in the ground. Red storms, hail, ice, rain, snow, slush. The surface being shredded apart like nothing.

Kyle drove furiously through the storms. He tried to use his magic, but it wasn't working like it should. He just needed to get to Geeta, and she could help. He would wait at the camp after she returned from rescuing that girl. With the earth tearing itself apart, Kyle was starting to seriously doubt that Geeta had been successful. But he had to believe it. Because what else was there left for him?

There was a massive flash of red lightning, the earth opening before him. He slammed on his brakes, hydroplaning.

His bike spun uncontrollably, and he nearly flew off. He veered toward the spin, then stopped. His heart pumped wildly, and he nearly shat his pants.

Suddenly, a ghostly figure ran in front of him. His mouth dropped. A fucking ghost. More spirits, images of peoples—from the past and future— were blipping in and out like a low-end broadcast. Buildings, old and new, fading in and out, undecided on which time to appear in.

Holy mother of god…

There was a weird purple magic radiating from a section of the sky, followed by the sound of a loud crack coming from it, as if the atmosphere was torn into two pieces. The strange purple color suddenly dissipated.

Then, Kyle saw something that looked like a bad acid trip. The sky was *melting*. The upper sky was pouring down onto the earth like hot candlewax… There was nothing above in the sky as it melted away. Not black. Not white.

No heaven. No earth…

Elyathi—she had completed the spell.

"FUCK!" Kyle cried out.

The sky warbled and rippled like water. Then, with another loud booming sound, the sky poured down upon itself like a giant waterfall. A dark void sat where the sky once was as the clouds all melted away into oblivion.

More ghostly dimensional bodies passed by him, all doing their own thing in their time.

I have to get the fuck out of here!

In the distance, there was a blast of gray light. It was at the camp. Then, it struck Kyle. Victor had gray magic. It was his magic…

He instantly remembered what Geeta had said: Victor's magic nullified other magics in the area. Victor was the only way to stay safe from this.

Without another thought, Kyle hopped onto his bike, then drove straight ahead toward the camp.

The sky above kept melting, pouring across the land as the two voices continued to echo. The voices were Elyathi's and Derek's. They were chanting the ultimate spell from across the ripple of time.

There was another echo that rumbled with the thundering clouds; this time it was a laugh that echoed across the skies. The dark void above was growing as the earth melted into nothingness.

Kyle screamed. Screamed because he'd been warned by the God of Light. Screamed because he had made the same fucking mistakes in both his lives. Screamed because the love of his life, his soulmate, hated him. Screamed because he was so fucking selfish.

More images blipped in and out around them, but they slowly became more permanent. The land shifted, started to form new masses around them. Mountains rose as the melted sky poured onto the sands below.

White magic suddenly flooded out of the void, pouring onto the shifting earth. Bright white light was all he could see. The magic was too fucking bright.

"VICTOR!" Kyle screamed into the white light. "I'M COMING! WAIT FOR ME!"

There was gray light that superseded the white light. It was straight ahead.

Em…I love you. Always.

Kyle kept driving, headed toward the gray light as time collapsed onto itself.

EPILOGUE

◆

Soft sand cushioned his face and fingertips. The wind against his skin was warm and soothing, like a lover's kiss.

Victor gently opened his eyes to white sand all around him.

Struggling to sit up, Victor noticed an imprint of himself in the sand. Where he had landed, there was gray sand instead of white.

Victor sat up, looking around. Sandy white dunes shone, stretching out as far as the eye could see. The sky was a perfect crystal blue, like on a summer day.

A crystal blue sky…wasn't the sky melting moments ago?

Just beyond the strange desert, Victor saw vivid colors gleaming from a distance—each in their own section of land, all spread out in different directions from where he sat. There were several distinct crystal palaces—each one glowing in their respective colors—that rose in each section of land.

Victor knelt down to inspect the sand, then stopped to look at the grains in his grasp. "No…no…" he said out loud as his stomach felt sick. "This can't be happening…"

He was in Elyathi's new world.

"No…no…" He shook his head in disbelief. Tears formed in his eyes. He had protected those gifted when time collapsed. He had thought doing so would halt Elyathi's spell. But here he was, standing in her new world.

Where were the others? Where was the staff he had been holding moments ago? Glancing around, everything that he knew was gone.

Leaning down as he wiped his tears away, he noticed that his hands were different. Bringing his hands closer to his face, he studied them, turning them back and forth.

What…?

He realized why they were different. They were the hands of his youth—as a young adult. He glanced down at the rest of his body. It, too, looked youthful…

Victor turned and saw a small oasis, as if appearing through his thoughts.

Getting to feet, Victor sprinted to it. It was much closer than he had thought. Or had he wished it? He slid down next to the water and dared to look.

His youthful reflection stared back at him. He wasn't old anymore; he was in his early thirties.

But what made him stop and stare wasn't his youth.

He was now a white-gifted.

ACKNOWLEDGMENTS

I want to start off by saying a huge thank you to all of my readers. *Fragments of the Heart* was a difficult book to write and took a lot longer than expected. For those of you who have waited several years for this book, I am sorry. My life had many unexpected events that directly interfered with this project. Some were physical events; others were matters of the heart. I will say though that if these events hadn't happened, I wouldn't have been able to write certain scenes of *Fragments of the Heart*. I had to live through hardships to write the hardships. Several of you sat on the sidelines and cheered me on during my darkest writing hours. I cannot express how it meant to me getting a fan email or a comment on social media about their love of my novels. It kept me going when the going was rough.

I also want to say thank you to my developmental editor Amy. If it weren't for her, my story wouldn't be what it is today. She went the extra mile, not because I asked her to, but because she believed in my story – and in me.

I also want to extend a big thank you to my line/copy editor Crystal from *Pikko's House*. I also wanted to say thank you to Sarah who was the proofreader on this project. I am humbled that she gave kind words about this project when she wrapped it up, as well as gave valuable input for the prologue of this book.

Thank you to Yam for the amazing art as always.

And lastly, thank you to my husband and my beautiful children. My husband has been my number one fan ever since day one. He has a passion for my story just as much as I do. My children proudly tell all their friends and teachers that 'My mommy writes books.' Their excitement of my writing makes me strive to be the best that I can be.

I hope that *Fragments of Time* will not take as many years to write as Fragments of Heart. I always knew that *Fragments of the Heart* would take the longest to write because of the complexity. It was and hopefully will be (knock on wood) the most challenging novel I have ever and will ever write. For those of you who made it this far, I ask that you continue your journey with me to the end. I am already in the midst of writing *Fragments of Time*, and you won't be disappointed. Until then, we will mourn the loss of some of our favorite characters, and hope and pray that some serious payback will be dealt in the final novel. Until we meet again!

ABOUT THE AUTHOR

Beth Hodgson has always had a love of reading epic fantasy books since she was young. She started dreaming of *The Spectrum of Magic* world and characters back in 1997. During that time, she wrote mini stories and comics about Princess Emerald being experimented on, Ikaria being a failure of a sorceress, and comic relief when it came to Drew and Telly in their lab. It wasn't until 2016 when she sat down and started writing her story into a full-fledged novel, releasing her first book *Fragments of Light* in 2018. Currently, she is writing her fourth book *Fragments of Time*, and occasionally freelances as a beta reader.

For fun, Beth loves to draw, paint, read, do photoshoots, blog, and write fanfiction. When not being creative, Beth hangs out with her husband and three children goofing off and playing games. She also has a major pixel art and vintage computer addition. Her most recent accomplishment was restoring an old 1993 Zeos 486dx2 pc.

For more information about this book series, please visit:
www.thespectrumofmagic.com

To dive into Beth's world, please visit:
www.kaolinite-dreams.com

The Spectrum of Magic

Main Magic

Red = Elemental magic: earth, wind, fire, water/ice. *Emotion: anger*

Orange = Illusion and transmutation magic. *Emotion: joy*

Yellow = Prophecy and protection. *Emotion: love and devotion*

Green = Healing, restoration, life, renewal and revival magic. *Emotion: fear*

Blue = Time and dimensional space magic. *Emotion: sadness*

Violet = Force and control over mind and objects magic. *Emotion: jealousy*

Tint Magic

Light Red (Pink) = One magic only *(earth, wind, fire, or water/ice)*

Light Orange = One magic only *(illusion or transmutation)*

Light Yellow = One magic only *(prophecy or protection)*

Light Green = One magic only *(healing, revive, or rebirth)*

Light Blue = One magic only *(time or dimensions)*

Light Violet = One magic only *(control of the mind or force over objects)*

Dark Side of the Spectrum

Dark Red = Meteor, sun/moon/star magic, gas, metal, foreign elements. *Emotion: wrath*

Dark Orange = Permanent illusions and unnatural body transmutations. *Emotion: ungratefulness*

Dark Yellow = False prophecies and disarming protection. *Emotion: loathing*

Dark Green = Life-drain and death magic. *Emotion: terror*

Dark Blue = Summon magic from other dimensions, compress all time eras into one time. *Emotion: despair/anguish*

Dark Violet = Full possession over mind and body. *Emotion: hatred*

Please note: Magic is like an art. Some gifted are talented at casting magic naturally, others take years of practice to hone their skills.

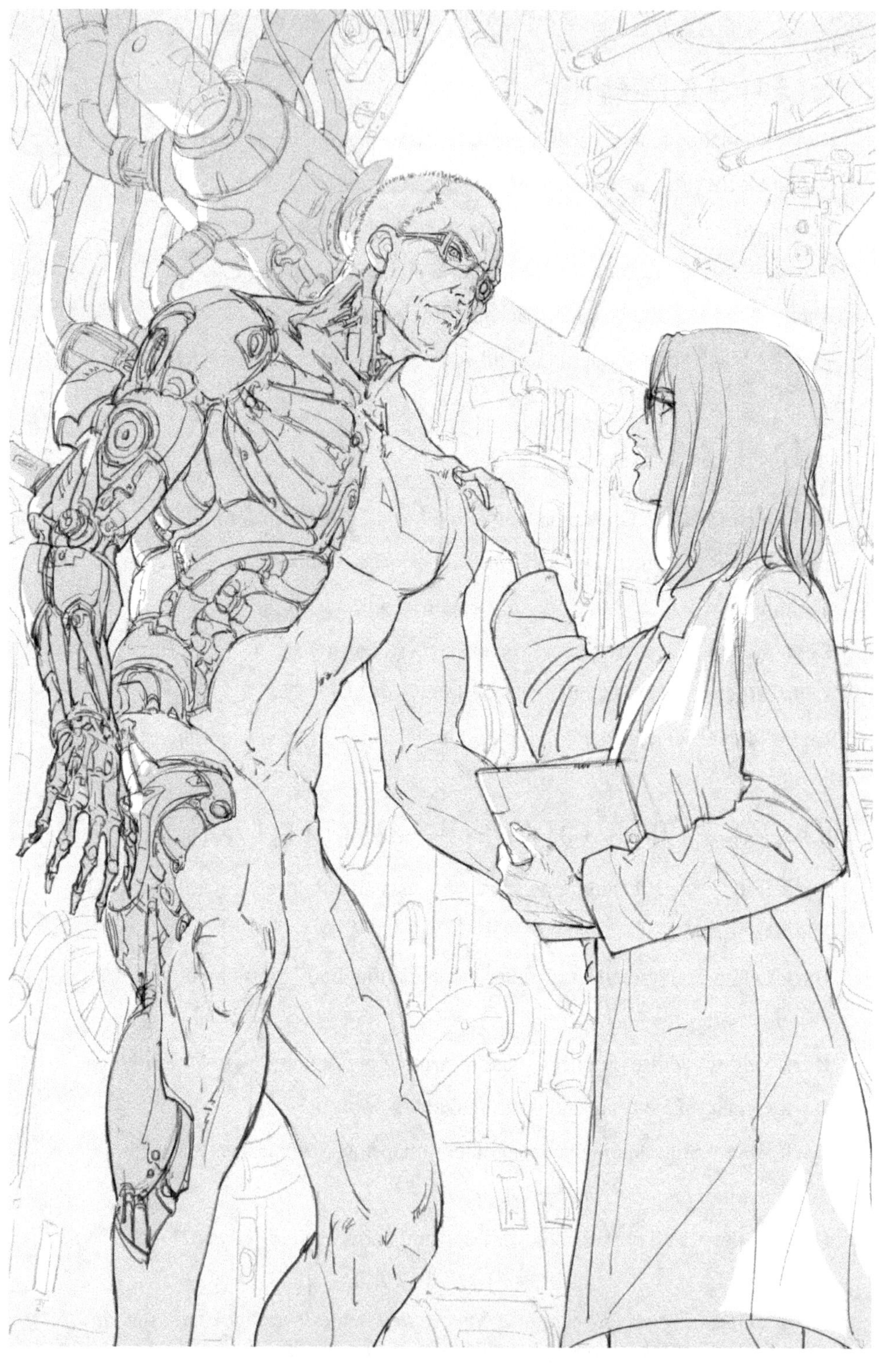

Color Complements

Color complements are opposite magics of the color wheel. When combined together, they can unlock the Spectrum of Magic. At the time of unlocking the Spectrum of Magic, both casters must summon their adjacent colors with their main color. This white magic that comes from completing the Spectrum of Magic is different from holy white magic.

Red + Green = The Spectrum of Magic (white light)
Orange + Blue = The Spectrum of Magic (white light)
Yellow + Violet = The Spectrum of Magic (white light)

No gifted can pair up with their opposite color. Only one person is made for the other. It could be a romantic love pairing, a friendship pairing, or a polar-opposite soul pairing.

Analogous/Adjacent magics

Each gifted magic caster can tap into the two colors next to their main color to some degree. For instance, if the gifted has green magic, they have full capabilities of all green magic powers. They also have the potential to use small amounts of yellow (casting magic shields) and blue magic (dimensional magic.) Some gifted can practice and train to use the full potential of their adjacent magics.

Also, if the gifted uses an analogous magic, it manifests and a combination of the two colors. For example, Emerald's magic is green. If she uses yellow protection magic, her magic power looks greenish-yellow. If she uses blue magic, her magic power looks greenish-blue.

Black Magic/Blood Magic

If a gifted consumes the blood of another color, they absorb that magic, and their magic becomes a shade darker. If the gifted consumes two colors, their magic becomes an even darker shade of their color. If the gifted consumes all six colors of the spectrum, they unlock black magic, and their magic becomes pure black. See note about the power of black magic.

Holy/Unholy Magic

White = Ability to absorb a gifted's magic temporarily and drain a gifted's magic and lifeforce permanently.

Gray = Nullifies all other magics in range of caster.

Black = Power of the gifted's heart's desire, magic of their choosing when black magic is unlocked, gifted's original magic power is increased 100 times their original power.

THE SPECTRUM OF MAGIC

✦

Now Available:

FRAGMENTS OF LIGHT - BOOK 1

FRAGMENTS OF THE MIND - BOOK 2

FRAGMENTS OF THE HEART - BOOK 3

TBA:

FRAGMENTS OF TIME - BOOK 4

Sign up for 'The Spectrum of Magic' newsletters:
www.thespectrumofmagic.com

*If you liked this book, please rate or review it
on Amazon and/or Goodreads.*